Feral Eyes

Book Two

Glen "Rocky" Meyers

© 2023, Glen Meyers

All rights reserved. No part of this book may be reproduced or used in any manner without the prior written permission of the copyright owner, except for the use of brief quotations in a book review. This is a work of fiction. Unless otherwise indicated, all the names, characters, businesses, places, events, and incidents in this book are either the product of the author's imagination or used in a fictitious manner. Any resemblance to actual persons, living or dead, or actual events is purely coincidental. Let me emphasize that the stories in the NIA Series are Fiction based. All names, characters, and incidents portrayed in my novels are fictitious. All make-believe… No identification with actual persons (living or deceased), places, buildings, businesses, or religious institutions is to be alleged. In some of my writing, I may use names of entities, churches, or corporations. These manuscripts are totally fiction based and should be inferred as such. Surely I have fun with my characters, and some of them do too! ☺ . I appreciate your patience in reading this necessary legalese.

ISBN: 979-8-9867067-1-9

Library of Congress Control Number: 2020903428

Printed in the United States of America

Dedicated to my mother,
Barbara Jean Hayes-
thank you, mom!

By Glen "Rocky" Meyers

Feral Eyes: Book One

Feral Eyes: Book Two

Sara

Kam: Book One

Kam: Book Two

Covid 57: Book One

<h1 style="text-align:center">The 'NIA' Series.</h1>

<h2 style="text-align:center">'Feral Eyes 2' is the second of 13 books in the NIA series.</h2>

I printed some Incomplete Manuscripts a couple of years ago to test the market, called ACR's… which stands for Advanced Reader Copies, and I had some Beta readers preview some of the storylines in the NIA Series. In a word, they were 'Awful' and needed editing and punctuation, and many of the plots were discombobulated. I have been working on cleansing these books for publishing since 2019; yes, it's been a journey! Today the fruits of my labor are here to be read and hopefully enjoyed. I will publish Six books at the same time in May of 2023. ☺ .

<h2 style="text-align:center">The First Amendment.</h2>

Freedom of expression is a fundamental human right and a central tenet of an author's work, livelihood, and American Society. The First Amendment protects freedom of speech, the press, and citizens' assembly to protest or march in groups. Freedom of expression is the freedom for us all to express ourselves. It is the right to speak, to be heard, and to participate in artistic, political, and social life. I am a firm and staunch believer in our First Amendment! Using someone's name, image, or life story as part of a novel, book, movie, or other 'expressive' work is protected by the First Amendment.

<u>'A Preface.'</u>

<u>An introduction of how's and whys… with explanations.</u>

<u>'I'm a Felon… and enjoy using Disfluencies in my manuscripts.'</u>

Within most of my manuscripts, I incorporate the use of disfluencies. There are many reasons why I do so. Many purists will find this form of writing unprofessional and of a lower standard… which is fine by me. Some authors have distinctive writing styles, <u>'prose.'</u> In writing, prose refers to any written work that follows a basic grammatical structure. Prose simply means language that follows the Natural Patterns found in everyday speech. It isn't well known that disfluencies pop up in everyday speech or conversations in most languages on our planet. In conversations, it has been approximated that about every 4.6 seconds, a disfluency is used. I try and combine disfluencies to emphasize points or for the reader to slow down and reflect on what was just read. I have fun using disfluencies, and I use them to directly communicate concepts, ideas, and stories to my readers. If you were to really concentrate on a person's speech or a friend's conversation… uhm, or listen to an interview, you might find yourself amazed at how many of these 'placeholder words, filler words you hear. Even some highly esteemed professionals use an abundance of disfluencies.

<u>Please reference this great piece of work regarding disfluencies ('Well, um, you know, you're saying more than you think.) You can find this article in the November/December 2022 'Psychology Today,' magazine.</u>

To paraphrase, some of the substance in this awesome article is that most of us use disfluencies; for example, have you ever been conversing with someone and lost track of where you were going? You pause momentarily and think of your next words… using Ah, Uh, Umh, then pick up where you left off. Disfluencies can be used to emphasize your topic of choice, aligned with appropriate expressions, and you see this at comedy clubs and in everyday conversations. We roll our eyes and pause and use 'Um' ☺ . Disfluencies are common in humorous or even serious discussions. Stop for a minute and truly listen to someone's interview, either on TV or the Internet, Social media sites; you will hear an abundance of Disfluencies. We as a society have become immune to the dozens of common disfluencies many speakers use them for repeating a phrase or revising the sentence structure in midstream. I use disfluencies in my writing for emphasis, and because they're fun for me, I hope they aren't annoying to readers, umh, especially the purists. If so, I apologize, ugh, right up-front. Um, I don't want any of you not to enjoy my books. I do believe that over usage of disfluencies can become a nuisance, Uh. ☹

Okay, umh, so here's the rest of the info that I'll share with you regarding disfluencies. Now I'm not defending my overuse of these words, or maybe I am? In many of my 13-plus written manuscripts, you'll read and see or hear words such as… 'um, uh, ugh, ah, umh, huh, so, uhm, ughhhh, ahhhh, and other variations like… oh, yep, yup, yay, yum, ahoh, lol, lmao, huh, and the list goes on…

The argument can be made; according to some Professors of Psychological Science, disfluencies help listeners and readers concentrate better on the narrative, and the use of a disfluency sometimes tells the audience there is likely new information about to be disseminated. Disfluencies seem to occur at discourse points or are used to indicate a Major plot change of direction. These educated professionals have said that disfluencies 'focus listener's attention' and sometimes allow the listener to analyze what has been said, sort of like a pause for reflection. In testing theories regarding using Disfluencies… when appropriately placed in a narrative, they actually increase a person's attention and memory of what they have heard or read. 😊

Disfluencies have been used to help emphasize the topic being discussed. They are proven to help the listener or reader to remember storylines or points of contention better than most other deliveries of verbiage.

To sum up, highly esteemed intellectuals use disfluencies, from our Presidents right down to street urchins. They have been proven to increase listeners' attention. Please try and catch disfluencies either by yourself or others. You might be surprised at how many of them are used in a single day. Like… Well, heck, that said a lot, lol… Umh, okay. Yup! 😊

How I became an author after my arrest for growing and dispensing Marijuana.

I'm sure you've heard the term 'to make a long story short,' which indicates that the story will likely not be short and concise. Lol. I've penciled over a thousand pages in a book named Sacramento County Jail, a harrowing non-fiction venture. Below is a short passage into what caused my life changes and thus led to my creative writing hobby.

In the year 2012, suddenly, health issues befell… my body and mind. I was beyond listless, with no energy or motivation to do anything felt like a Slug. I was a regular at the gym and in the past was active… this all stopped. I sought out professional help. First things first, I had to donate blood for a wide variety of tests. A sex hormone panel, 'SHBG' amongst other tests, was ordered since I was approaching the age of male menopause. The endocrinologist called me in and informed me that I had several anomalies. One was that I had extremely low… deficient testosterone levels, but what bothered her more was that I'd had the highest Estrogen levels she'd ever seen in a man. In fact, her words were with a smirk, 'Mr. Meyers, welcome to female menopause. Your levels are off the charts.' Thirty-five years of being an endocrinologist, she had never seen these numbers before. After checking with her colleagues, it was decided that I needed another hormone test because there must have been a mistake! My test numbers were impossible to comprehend. Well,… what would you know? Two weeks later, I was called back into her office. This time I didn't witness a smirk from her countenance, nope. She beckoned me to have a seat across from her magnificent mahogany desk. She folded her arms up elbows on the desk, clasped her fingers in a temple, and bent her head down. With her not saying a word, I'd automatically jumped to the conclusion, 'I WAS DEAD,' something terminal. I must be on my way out 😊.

>>>>Please visit <u>'Gembooksrock.com'</u> and finish reading… Yep.

<u>Former Federal Inmate.</u>

I am a former prisoner and felon sequestered by the IRS… Federal Government on Marijuana charges… was imprisoned and locked up in Terminal Island Prison for about Seven years. A short synopsis of the events that led to my writing career can be found on my website 'Gembooksrock.com,' please check out my homepage. You will find some interesting tidbits… along with links to my arrest. 🙁.

Mark Feral… Friday June 21st, 2019.

On another sweltering afternoon in Northern California, heat waves were a common nuisance for most people, but not for me. However, the temperature on the last billboard I passed on I-5 North flashed at 113 degrees. The Rolling Hills Casino had many advertisements on the highway. The previous billboard sign had a cute couple with drinks in their hands, ice cubes glistening, swirling sticks, and a swimming pool in the background.

I left Sacramento at 2:45 pm and planned to make it home by 5 pm or thereabouts. All I could think about was dunking myself in Shasta Lake, living on 7.5 acres less than 1.5 miles from Jones Valley Resort. I was… Then, out of nowhere, I nearly lost traction someone had hit my bumper. I lurched forward, and my entire rear-view mirror was filled with a giant black iron bumper with a winch attached. Then the out-of-control truck hit me again. There was nowhere for me to go on this rural two-lane highway, both lanes ahead filled with semi-trucks, and heck… I was already slowing down from my average cruise control speed of 75 mph when the out-of-control truck attacked me. An air horn blared, hearing… constant honking. Then I was pushed from behind again the truck bounced into my car. I had no recourse but to veer off the highway onto the soft shoulder; gravel sprayed up… the sounds of the tires on the grooves cut out of the road hummed eerily.

A jacked-up 4-wheel drive Ford extended cab pulls by, not so subtly, a finger held out the passenger window, a beer bottle flung by the driver that bounced off my hood and cracked, uh, Busted my windshield. The couple was apparently wasted, drunk looked to be in their early 30s, perhaps five years my junior, not kids! The black and silver-streaked truck was brand new with paper tags in the back tinted window, a 2019 model.

My soothing music morphed suddenly toxic; I switched genres from cool Jazz to Horrorcore and raged the volume to the max. I hadn't any options, no license plate to track the truck, as my Chevy Impala spun out into a 360° spin… gravel-dirt, dust, facing south, towards oncoming vehicles, the motor still running.

'Stop,' take a deep breath; it's essential for you to understand that I'm not a panic-stricken type of human, no stress. Even now, my blood pressure flashes a calm 135/75, according to my Apple wristwatch.

Sure, I was angry and pissed off, although other concerns took precedence. Needing to get back on the freeway was first and foremost before a CHP spotted me. Now that would elevate my BP for sure, no doubt.

By the time I was back heading North, the rude drunk-ass couple was a blur sinking on the other side of the rolling hills. At that moment, I hadn't resolved how I would deal with the violators as the first glimpse of Mount Shasta came into view. Aah, I always had a good feeling that was magical for me. Looking North, snow glistened on its peaks, even on the longest day of the year, June 21st, a Friday.

Having not-so-precious cargo in the now most likely dented trunk was of optimal significance to me; the human was heavily sedated, 'Stop' I know how that sounds but give me a chance to defend myself.

First, though, I needed to exact retribution on that couple, pardon me… I was their Karma. Call it like it is. Uh, it was their bad luck that I quickly gained on the truck, which I found pinned behind two Walmart tractor-trailers. Staying back, cognizant of real-time video by the 'Big Brothers' cameras, all overpasses and many lamp posts were armed with stationary spies.

I passed several signs showing CHP airplanes monitoring I-5… my non-descript white Impala had legal tags that were not of any connection to yours truly. I nearly relaxed; this couple would cause a slight delay, but hey, I couldn't sleep if I allowed them to tread on my ego.

Even though it was like a furnace blasting dry heat up from the black pavement, my windows were down I hadn't turned on my supercharged air conditioning system.

Leaning down with my right hand, pulling a case from under the passenger seat, opening it with a smile seeing my cobalt blue pistol attaching the matching-colored modified sound suppressor to the barrel of one of my many toys, silencer snuggled tight, and my 9mm Glock was ready for action.

My visor was pulled down to block the sun; this was only the secondary reason, the reflection of my handsome features back at me in the mirror the primary reason; gosh. I was gorgeous with bedroom smiling brownish hazel-flecked pupils, winked with a grin, although they were contacts. I owned contacts of every shade. I'm tanned, just shaved my head face displayed a Fu-Manchu type mustache soul patch kind and bronze skin in color, grinning dimples blasting out, blew a kiss to yours truly… Yum!

Some humans would consider me Narcissistic, nah, but I'm undoubtedly an irresistible lady killer Sshhh, don't say that. Ooops, my plump, pouty upper lip needed a smear of lip gloss. I could see in the mirror the start of a chiseled lean-muscled male body and my trapezius or trap muscles bulging… neck of a Pitbull, one of my nicknames. Enough, oh, I could go on and on, but I need to stay focused. No time to masturbate physically or mentally… Nope!

The drunk Ford truck squirms between the Big Rigs, almost hitting the back of a 40ft trailer, then turns off at Woodson Bridge. I follow not-so-close behind signs to Chico, direction East. The drunk couple nearly crashed into five Harleys heading West. The bikes had to take evasive measures or be flattened by the grill of the massive Ford; bottles tossed out from both windows again as they rolled down the road. Obviously, they had forgotten about me, but that was okay and fine by me. Soon all memories of their short lives would expire. A smirk shines back at me from the rear-view mirror, drop 'dead' gorgeous Yep!

I followed them into Woodson Bridge Park the River was full of partygoers, and the weekend was upon us. And I have to admit the cool flowing Sacramento River had its allure. Unfortunately, being a disciplined individual with determination, typically not spontaneous, I wouldn't dunk myself in the water.

Yuh, see if the damn truck had a license plate, I could, at a later time, take my revenge, except I hadn't any way of reconnecting with the hoodlums, looking through my spider-cracked windshield ugh-pissed me off, angrily keeping the Ford in view but I'm always in control. Really, folks, this wasn't me. With adequate surveillance and reconnaissance, I usually plan and enjoy the kill. Believe me. I'm aware that this is precisely how some serial killers are caught... can't let my temper get the best of me... spur of the moment stupidity.

I'm far from ignorant, a psychopath beyond genius levels, IQ 173, um, No dummy! With the last adjustments, my dark sunglasses and auburn wig in place, I drive by the entrance of the Park... Head bowed down, no grins for these cameras, of course. I had a pocket cam filming all for enjoyment later on. I'd sip a cool one and watch this replay from my comfy couch at home. Hopefully, this necessary detour didn't take too much time. Otherwise, the body in the truck would awaken and start kicking, making noise. Wrapped in chains, shackles, yes, had the body secure, although in my vast experience about trunk occupants, umh, when or if they come back to life, invariably the banging noises start, the super glue keeps their lips closed, thank goodness for that.

Slowly at five mph, I wound around picnic benches of groups of guessing Chico State students, not a hard guess because they were wearing shirts and blazers depicting the University. The black and silver truck was parked up on a grassy mound.

Driving by them, I watched an older group of about nine greet one another like long-lost friends. Some had lifejackets on, a boat, and Sea-Doo's in the distance parked at the shore. I stopped the car at a block building bathrooms and showers and was cognizant that the park was regularly driven and checked by the local Sheriffs or Rangers.

Paid stickers were to be seen on nearly all vehicles, yet I drove right past the unoccupied shack and made sure to button up my light gray shirt, all tattoos hidden. Cigar lit, music buds in my ears it would seem to all, not the case though enhanced hearing aids turned down low, for music blasted from each campsite.

Oh, I almost forgot I opted out of the 9mm pistol; instead, I carried a new 'Toy' recently bought via the Dark Web using my 'Tor' browser with one of my Bitcoin accounts had it in the palm of my right hand easily concealing a 3-shot Dart Gun. The darts were dipped in a killer potion, um, Poison that I'd bought from the same site on the Dark Web... 'no fool' testing it on wild animals, Squirrels. It was toxic, potent, and deadly; this would be my first test on humans! ☺ .

Timing is everything in life, the luck of the draw; think about it if I had lingered another minute at the gas station before entering Highway I-5 North, I would never have seen that truck. Fate was inclusively garnered by the ticking of time as is... and should be. The beer bottle-throwing couple walked just ahead of me, merrily holding hands, staggering slightly, and heading towards one of the bathroom buildings.

Ahh, no challenge, too effortless... good timing for me, uh, not for them. I closed in on them as they followed the concrete path easy as 1-2-3. I fired the darts into their glutes, um, ample butt cheeks. Reaching backward, they tumbled over as I nonchalantly veered off the walkway. Yes! Felt like shouting with glee. Naw, I would have liked to hang out and go for a swim, but alas, I had other work to finish.

I checked my B.P. I was gladly calm and collected 123/73 heartbeat 81, flexing my ripped biceps and rolling my shoulders, opening the Chevy door. Screams not of joy could be heard as I casually drove out of the fun park. Glancing up with a long stare, a familiar image winks... winking back, I wiggle my cute, pert nose.

Finally, after this short detour, I-5 North again... lost 27 minutes as Emergency vehicles speed by... going in the opposite direction, heck, even a helicopter. Needing a temporary reprieve break from 'present tense,' I select a song by 'Shaman's Harvest' 'Dangerous' volume raging singing along... sure! 'Got no regrets, and that makes me Dangerous.'

I relaxed, secure mind drifting up the highway. Life was good today, and I took Hwy 299 turn off East, Belle Vista

Town, Bear Mountain Road, my final destination. I wondered, did I have time for a drink at Dry Creek Saloon? After some contemplation nixed that idea.

I couldn't risk it even though I had filled Hypodermic needles with one injection. My trunk prisoner would still be in blissful sleep; instead, 17 minutes later. The automatic steel gates opened as I drove into my solitary compound. Happy at the greeting by my pets, five Canines, three Pitbulls, and two Chow's 'Home Sweet Home!' It was 5:55 pm on the longest day of the year still had time for some water recreation. I just clicked the automatic rolling doors to one of my steel framed barns, drove inside, parked close enough to the other coffins, and in less than 5 minutes. I'd secured the person in his very own air-vented coffin, umh, the culprit locked inside.

With a cursory look into the back seat, I saw my gym bag, swimming suit, and miscellaneous stuff ready to roll... out the gates in no time. I parked less than three minutes from my home, Jone's Valley Resort walking down the dock to the store... on all sides of me, the tempting and refreshing water of Lake Shasta was calling my name. Regular workers nodded Hi's, hello's, and greetings.

I stepped onto my 55-foot houseboat fun; yay, 'Warren Hills' Jazz played on the surround sound speakers, and the song 'Tamara' played. I pulled out into open water and went Northwest towards Silverthorn Resort, the Restaurant bar, lounge, and dance floor; why not? The lake was just about my favorite place on this earth, wakeboarding boats reverberating Hip-Hop from their racked speakers, passing me by. I clicked up the volume on my super surround sound system, which had cost me nearly 15,000 dollars... that covered all 55 feet and more, lol.

Was I a man with a superego sort of a rhetorical question, indeed. I was, uh, wouldn't have it any other way? Just before the inlet to 'Silverthorn,' I slipped into a cove and pushed an anchor release switch. A splash now, heaven enveloped my entire epidermis, and dived deep. The deeper I swam, the colder the water. Fifteen minutes later, barely breathing above normal levels, I climbed the ladder, dropped the winch, and

jumped on my race bike with a Bombardier Sea Doo vest on…
wind on my bald head.

I jetted off, standing up and topping out at 77mph, a
daredevil Adrenalin Junkie, spraying water and fishtailing. I
turned too hard to the left and was propelled into the air,
skipping across the waves fkn fun! The Sea-Doo was slowly
circling me, bouncing off the ripples as I jolted back up onto
the Sea-Doo in one motion with ease. Check the side view
mirrors; wow, I was a 'Hunk Wet & Wild Yep!'

'Woman eater' time to pick up a vixen on the dance floor,
if not willingly, then daddy's little helper a dose of persuasion
in her drink. Then she and I would engage in a bout of jousting
lovin in my main suite on the water. Beckoning me always was
my mirrored ceiling and walls; gosh could peek up and see
myself from all angles. With cameras hidden, my glorious
King-sized bed floated in harmony with my heartbeat!

I tie off to the dock. My mind is traveling in so many
directions. Am I being responsible and staying on point? For
*so many long months, I was covered by my own shell. A recluse on
my 7.5 acres, hiding away like the proverbial hermit. Using online
apps for everything or anything I needed, food, groceries deliveries
for sex, it was easier than doing simple addition, escort services,
dating services, pick your whore out, the flavor of the day, less than
45 minutes away if you wanted?*

*My gate's buzzer would go off using my highest-definition
camera's view. I'd order a girl up-bam, she'd be at the gate, tell her
to turn around and zoom in to make sure she wasn't an imposter,
the girl or girls I'd picked out from their profiles, sometimes they'd
have Photo-Shopped pictures. Other times, they weren't even the
same girl on the site, lol. There were so many to choose from, but
my favs are TNA Board… Adult Look or Craig's list before the
Fed's shut them down.*

*With a finger tap, an order was placed supplying semi-deviate
sexual persuasions; any desire had its price. How much time I
wanted the sex slaves for was up to me. I was temporarily pushing
this out of my mind. Lust, the desire of my physical self-lingered.
Since I'd absconded from Parole, I'd captured or kidnapped several
runaways, cuties who'd hit me from all angles. I trained them in
the arts of masochistic, sadistic pleasures and pains, my favorite*

perversion for gratification, inflicting both mental and physical pain upon my subservient prey. Oh, just thinking about them, blood rushes to my loins, an adjustment is necessary, and sadism equals Fun!

This afternoon, I decided to check out the meat market up the stairs at the lounge, so I tethered off my home on the water and started the long walk up the dock. The Silverthorn Restaurant was up a significant incline. I passed by the gathering of boats on the launch dropping into the lake. Smiles of all, families, partygoers, the anticipation of escaping the day-to-day doldrums, I speculated.

Dusk was still a ways off, but the music could be heard well before I climbed the stairs to the restaurant lounge area, aware that breaking from norms was caustic to my health. No, I wasn't a regular by no means, but I had taken some sluts to my houseboat from this place; I didn't need to drug them; they nearly dragged me outta here.

In my prison cell, many nights as the fog would blanket the prison yard, I'd lay there with resolve to plan my future. Others at the prison would 'party' all the varieties of drugs, and alcohol was even available. It was a business the lowly paid C.O.'s correctional officers couldn't pass up on like 1000% mark-ups on a bottle of Crown Royal or an ounce of white China heroin.

My #1 numeral Uno rule is never shit in my backyard. Thus far, despite urges, cravings, aches, repine for hunger and yearnings, I'd restrained myself; the last thing I needed was to draw attention. I was on the FBI's most wanted list, so if I didn't score, which was unlikely… the worst-case scenario, I'd drive back to my cave. In privacy, I'd replay my homemade movies in HD, slip the cock ring on with lubrication, and masturbate masturbation was sometimes better anyways less subterfuge.

A visit to the Silverthorn Lounge.

Stepping through the doors, I saw the familiar guy and girl tending the bar and strolled up; before I got to a stool, a placement with a menu of tonight's specials was resting on the counter along with a vodka-club soda. Ahh, so much for the low profile. Was I not adhering to my #1 rule? I never abused this area's humans, killed, kidnapped, or hurt any of them. Thinking back to only hours before when I allowed my temper to get the best of me, double slaying at the park, not too smart, No!

Yet that was a different county miles away, but too close to my domicile. I can't let my guard down; I've read many stories about mass murderers, and almost always, it was complacency, egotistical self, and pompous satisfaction that led to the downfall of many of the arch-villains, serial killers, one Mickey Mouse mistake then Wham!

His mantra, the all-encompassing promise, oath, and vow to commit suicide if capture was imminent, was always on the fridge as a magnet. No fear of death equals peace, a transition into another dimension... another existence.

Lol, with that being said, I wasn't in a hurry to experience that kind of enlightenment. For certain, I wouldn't be taken back to San Quentin alive! Surveying the patrons, masses were multiplying from different areas vacationing from Hawaii to Mexico, and San Diego, the beaches and bars, no dress codes bikinis, hot shorts, halter tops, legs bear with flip-flops. Treasures right in front of you for a quick or long appraisal. Evaluations, decisions, oh so many choices, like a candy store, for the odds were always in my favor handsome, ripped, defined muscled body, golden tongue, oozing with pheromones, confidence.

I figured, at minimum, 55% of the women here wanted just what I willingly offered. Better yet, my houseboat sat idle. Life was a game; play the odds and know the rules of engagement. Coy, shy, sometimes better than brash and bold, intuition aligned with proper analyzation... isolate your prey, then conquer and stabilize the situation with subtle manipulations, never be over-anxious but flow carefree. The key was the selection process; for example, an overcrowded table of five girls sat five feet from the dance floor, three of whom were asked to dance the song was a lounge favorite 'Brick House,' Artist, 'The Commodores.'

The gender mix was about even the girls barely clad with short skirts covering their bathing suit bottoms... The Brick House song had been playing for about 25 seconds, and already three guys were rebuffed by girls at a table seven feet in front of me.

Females were in charge until the proper suitor stepped forward. I could see her face light up, expressions changing as he approached. Yes, she took his hand and started gyrating. The dynamics emphatically resounded in the XX hormones court of favor until after impairment, drugs, alcohol, and powerful antidotes that usually were accompanied by porous inhibitions like Nitroglycerin exploded, apprehension was waved the male now in command. Time to take advantage of dysfunctional behavior, but this was a game. Last week in San Diego, I used one of my award-winning strategies, simple mathematics. In an area with three to five popular bars in the proximity of the Pacific Ocean, heck, you could see the ocean waves splashing on shore from the windows. Prime location for picking up the female persuasion. Just cruise in for a drink and watch for the 'look,' then hook em up and go.

At times I'd sit at a bar with an open laptop or iPad and work the financial markets overseas, stock market trading, or read a book. This act of nonchalance within the bar scene is unnatural but effective.

I was already dashed with smell-good cologne, showered, spiffed up, and shining. Sober or a few glasses of wine, wait till approximately 10:30 or 11 pm. Enough time for the 'pumps to be primed' sweet, pungent, tasty girls or stinky with sweat longing for engorgement. What did it matter... shower them up and down? I enter each establishment with one solitary purpose, scan the likely candidates, look for the sultry moist sexual desire in the glassy eyes, inhibitions gone. Absolutely no need to buy them a drink; that's way too 'old school' the new breed of a woman was supposedly, to a fault, independent; chivalry was indeed dead.

I made it an exercise in discipline; objectively shrewd, I would peruse each lounge and then circle back to the finest juiciest USDA-fortified piece of meat. It never failed... bluntness was a sharp sword.

I simply joined the table or bar stool uninvited. Depending on the vibe... eyes, I introduced myself cordially and requested their moniker, or like last weekend, a dark-haired beauty that seemed to need some nurturing eyes had been sobbing, poor thing! Perhaps 15 years, my Jr. I pulled her hands towards me with a sympathetic grimace morphing into dimples. I said, 'Hey, why don't we get out of here? Come with me!...' 'I know, not clever, umh, but to the point-heck, why not?'

A friend yanked on her other arm, and the equation stiffened; the variable of a GF who was looking out for a friend, odd's shifted. "Nicole, where are you going?" "Nicole and I are going to get something to eat... you want to tag along?" I said to her bodyguard, who was less desirable to me, who I thought would have to wait till closing time to get laid. Wrong, moving past my peripheral vision was a horsey-headed guy, butt ugly... a toothpick of a man looking right at us. A Horse's wag, and he appears before us. He asks Nicole's friend, "what's your name?" she was looking at the thin dude, "oh, I'm Cathy and yours?" "Hi, I'm Steven" "why don't you join Cathy, Steven?" I exclaimed as I stood, pulling out a chair for him. 'Not a freakin matchmaker, just a subjective adlib.'

Lustfully I sat back down, eyes mingled, grasping my gorgeous black magic woman. Her natural brown skin glistened as she swayed a bit inebriated, just as I liked to devour them. Yum, Triple Yum! off Nicole and I went leaving Steve and Cathy at a table, another conquest within my grasp.

That event was fresh in my mind from last weekend; oh, what fun, we'd made love and sex for hours overlooking the crashing waves. Now I was on the hunt once again as the Commodores Song Brickhouse was about two-thirds finished, cozy Silverthorn Resort, my waiting houseboat, docked and tethered, let's do this... Yes!

Nursing my first drink at the bar long enough, I swallowed it down... A glance and the bartender was fixing me another. I ordered a batch of hot Chicken wings. Then I got up to make my move, unorthodox for a male, not a female; stereotypes be dammed some would think I was gay, others would gap mouths open, but no doubt I would draw attention; advantage me. I had entered dancing contests in the past 'pre-prison,' winning many victories. Yeah, 1st place finishes winner in freestyle dancing competitions. Not wasting a moment, I didn't bother with asking a girl to dance. Nope, that was part of the ploy!

On the floor dancing solo, in my own space, dancing to Brickhouse, smiling confidently as others gawked. Oh yeah, eyes were upon me when the song was over; I casually sauntered confidently, knowing my dancing moves still lingered provocatively, scintillatingly slowly regaining my stool... done that!

Of course, I didn't meet the stares pretending not to notice as the cutie bartender measured me up, "where'd you learn to dance like that?..." "Aah, it comes naturally. I move with the music," then added. "You know it's a fact that you can learn what kind of lover you got by their moves on the dance floor; dancing is like having sex visibly with clothes on!" Wink, she grins, 'Yup!' giggles. "I've heard that too umh, sure wouldn't want a 'lump on a log'... would you?"

Standing at the edge of the bar, impatient servers yelping for pitchers of beer moved her away. She was a possibility later, much later, maybe! Never failed like covered wagons... being encircled by Indians, the squaws came a running, as per usual psychology at its best, my confidant, nonchalant disposition took eminence. I acted the opposite of the macho hound dogs, which were bar hounds. I acted like I didn't give a shit about the females, not ever even holding eye contact for three seconds, a strategy that had its effect. This unnerving disregard for traditionally accepted behaviors, secure, dominant Alpha male, left the full-on perception that exuded my every pore. I feigned self-sufficiency and didn't need the female to dance, buy drinks, or flirt. I played no games, yet I was the mastermind of this strategic game.

"Excuse me," said a petite blonde, "is anyone sitting here?" I almost felt like joking. Yeah, can't you see my hot invisible GF? No, I shook my head no and sipped my drink; in the next 15 minutes, I had three girls ask me to dance, two of whom no one would kick out of the bed. Also, drinks were bought for me, lol what a fkn stud gigolo, Yah!

The tables were turned; I was the meat that was sought after! Like sharks sniffing blood & guts, the girls vied for position, and competition demanded boldness!

I left my phone on mute with vibration mode enacted. It had been humming, and I scanned the bar, lounge, and game room with the typical pool tables, foosball, Ice hockey, and dart boards.

I'd guess that maybe 35% of the crowd had their phones in their hands. The percentage went up at the tables surrounding the dance floor. The D.J. was finishing up, and a local band had their groupies set up.

'Wthell,' my vibrating phone was relentless, so I said excuse me to the current Redhead that had ogled me. "Be right back, don't go anywhere" "I'll be right here," she replied. Down the stairs into the men's restroom, empty the bladder time and check the 'Tracfone' (untraceable), better than the old toss-away burner phones of the past, with more options. $15.00 per month, I had nine stashed away. I had five texts from the oldest of my bros, Joe, and several from Tank, pretending to be reading them as the first guy walked in.

No question, the other two were on the outside of the door. This dude was the larger of the three who were giving me 'stink eyes' ever since I danced by myself… One of them had purposely stuck his leg out to trip me as I swung a hot-to-trot brunette across the floor.

It was a small bathroom to start with. As the 'Tripper' stepped inside, I had watched the three of them follow me down the stairs, looking forward to this confrontation almost as much as the sex I'd have later.

"Hey, fkn Romeo, that Redhead is mine. I've bought her like three drinks and been dancing with her. She belongs to me," says the big dude. "I'm warning you; you need to get the hell outta here, old man before I stuff your bald-ass head in the toilet."

The other guys had joined him in the crowded bathroom. The smaller one finally grew some balls, "Yeah, and I'll flush the fkn toilet scum-bag," stepping backward against the three urinals, giving me more space.

I flashed a smirk, then said, "So you bought the girl three drinks, so now you own her, is that it?" Grinning, teeth bared, I added, "for your information, she bought me a drink too. Maybe it came from you… Thanks!" "You fkn wise ass" he lunges towards me with his huge right hand, throwing a 'haymaker.' At that precise time, I ducked, then jumped up, grabbed him by the shoulder, my left knee aimed for his liver bulls-eye crack air left him like a popping balloon, reeling on the tile floor was he.

Simultaneously I spun around and squared off with the other guys. They promptly skidded sideways and out the door. I opened the door cautiously, but no one was around, so I double-stepped up the stairs, past others going up and some the other way.

In the redhead's left hand, her phone in her other was a compact mirror; she saw me and shot me a seductive smile, slipping the compact into her purse. Making my way through bumping and pushing patrons, the place was packed; what the heck was her name? Oh, that's right, Becky… "what took you so long 'Mark?" I froze by the stool, for I never gave her my name, noticing my confused look, "oh, when I ordered us another drink, I asked Stella if she knew you. She said you were kind of a semi-regular customer, and your name was Mark, hope I wasn't being too presumptuous?" "Nah, that's fine, Becky."

'From the corner of my eye' came three men. One was the doorman, a bouncer who, a month back, had been on my houseboat a small after-the-bar closed party, the sweet night a fun foursome. Both of the girls were delicious and yummy from Las Vegas, I think… His name was Richard; standing next to him were the two guys that were friends of 'Liver boy,' the guy I disabled with the liver shot.

Rich seemed annoyed as the band started to play. He leaned in with a 'wink' "Excuse me, sir, did you get in a fight, beat somebody up in the bathroom?" "He did. I told you I witnessed it," said the wimp. I put my hands out, showing my knuckles. "Not I; you must be mistaken." "Bullshit, kick his freakin ass out of here, do your job, and call the police!" 'Rich' alligator quickly spun on them, "No, it's you two that needs to leave here. Pick up your friend and get outta here before I call the Sheriff's department… now Go!"

"So, what was all that about Mark?" asked Becky, the luscious redhead. I was caught staring at myself in the mirror over the bar. "Ahh, had a short run-in with the big lug with the red bandana." She let out a whiff of air, "oh, that guy, couldn't get rid of him. I broke a Cardinal rule of mine never accept a drink from a guy. Evidently, he saw I was drinking a 'Bay breeze,' then I had two of them, and next thing you know, he hovered over me like a Vulture drooling on a rotting carcass." 'Whoa,' I chuckled. "I like your description Beck" "Yeah, then he asked me to dance, felt obligated, didn't want to appear stuck up, not a bad-looking guy. My friends enjoyed his look, just not my type."

"Becky, this is what I find hard to understand; why didn't you either turn down the drink and thank him or accept the beverage and say thanks but no to his request to dance!" Smiling, she retorted, "uuhhh, right to the point, huh?…" "Yeah, yuh look around. There's got to be 55 girls and about the same number of guys." "So, Mark, what's your point ah…?" "Beck, let's take the average and use simple math so 55 girls, including you, 15 of you females, are here to have a few drinks hang out with friends, dance, and have fun. The faithful 15, let's call them, who have significant others and are bonded in an ongoing relationship." She gives me a sly, lopsided gleam, a twinkle of her green eyes, and a dimple popped out with sexy raised eyebrows. "So, you're a professor of sociology of human companionship relationships, huh?"… 'Did I mention I liked this girl!'

"Naw, I'm a professor of the 'pick up artist schemes' principally a self-serving man who thinks and uses stratagems and schemes to get what I want, and that is to take a lovely lady such as yourself to my houseboat. Come on, let's go!"

"Whoa, Boy Wonder!" an explosion of contagious giggles "are you for real, Mark?" With her back-peddling momentum on my side, after all, she could just walk away; I followed up with, "Yes, what you see is what you're going to get, no games from me. My mind, personality, and body are a package deal, Becky!" "Your either the biggest egotist I've ever met or...." I interrupted her; "Is there anything wrong with being forthright, candid, honest? Surely I'm confident. Is there a difference between being a megalomaniac and a man with integrity?"

We were leaning in towards one another; the music was way too loud; she clinked her glass against mine, "I'm a psychology major at UCLA. You're beyond the most interesting guy I've met. It's been like 25 minutes since we met?" She snickered then, "can we back up? I'm still waiting on your mathematical equation, so 15 of us females are faithful, kind of low odds out of 55."

I liked her more, needed to keep my objectivity, and just wanted to fk her was all dammit... she asked for it, so being a fantastic soldier, I 'soldiered on.'

Get this I was wearing some cargo shorts, a Tommy Bahamas shirt, brown sandals, toes covered, and as was my M.O. modus operandi sunglasses all the time, even at night, like the song, Yeah. Taking my left hand, I slid my glasses down on my adorable nose. Then I swiveled my wrist around my Apple Watch, B.P. 113, over 73 heartbeats resting 77 pulses time was 7:55 pm. The Sun, like me, was in rest mode, dropping below the tree line.

"Beck, plain and simple, cut to the chase that is, bluntly, concisely, of the 40 girls left, 25 of them for various reasons are undesirable for me umh, don't energize my curiosity. Not my type, either, a BMI, body mass index, thing. Or just not my cup of tea uhm, the girl doesn't turn me on. There is a certain look that I'm attractive to... my taste, meaning my pheromones, testosterone, don't gel. There's someone for everyone, but I'm selective!"

"Geez, you're a piece of work, dude. Wow, all right, ok, so now you're left with 15 females-where. Am I in your calculations?" "Well, since I'm still chatting with you, you're one of the fortunate 15!"

We both laugh so hard that tears form and fall. "Oh, god, Fortunate 15, I'm so blessed and honored," more laughter. "You know laughter is the fastest way into someone's heart…." "Oh no, mister, don't even try that crap." Her friends wave from her previous table while the band breaks for recess, three guys and two girls. I said, "Yuh wanna get back to your table?" A quizzical look unfolded, examining, internalizing a sense of right and wrong. Becky's divine alarm system disabled, and the truth revealed I had her by the 'short hairs' unless she was shaved bald. Lol. I liked a long, narrow landing strip with a hairy arrow pointing at the swollen clitoris, in any case. Will see, I hope, "Wait, I believe you just told me I was one of the 'Fortunate 15,' she cackled."

"All right, I'll play along 'Beck,' so let's, assume, despite the 25 ladies I'm not interested in, that leaves the 'fortunate 15,' why are they here drinking? partying-dancing?…" "Why don't you tell me?" she smirked. I winked and tossed in a shoulder roll, "I betcha, uh, we can guess if you're honest with yourself? Where I'm going with this scenario?" she shrugged.

I soldiered on. "Umh, just like the guys standing against the walls, they're all here for sex -to get laid, find that special person… why else? It's not even 8 o'clock. Give it another three hours, and judgments are hampered… inhibitions dropped. Don't you know alcohol spreads the legs… it's easy."

She guffaws, "Oh, it's so easy, huh? So, let's pretend it's 11 pm. How would you approach the more inhibited girls you know compared to the ones you assess to be overly lubricated-loosened up, ready to get 'laid in your houseboat.' So what would be your seductive line, come on." she cracked a colossal smirk. I smiled, grinned said, "damn, I like you, Becky. Let's get out of here?"

She paused! Reticent thus, I said, "Okay, let's pretend it's 11 pm, and I want to take a luscious piece of ass to my king-sized bed on the water." I scanned the nearby tables, "see that beauty with the yellow headband, the redhead with the orange halter top, or the blonde with the petite Lil boobs."

I went on describing several more of the bar patrons of the female persuasion, judging endearing attributes. She was all in now focused and enamored with my assertiveness, um, assessments, appraisals. "Now Becky, keep in mind that the timing isn't right, but I'd meander over to each girl and say hey there, why don't we, you join me on my houseboat for some drinks in the hot tub!..." "You're kidding me." She gave me a lopsided smirk. "No way like that, blunt to the point, and that works for you?" "Oh, for sure," I said. "It's only a meat market; I play the odds. At least three of the 15 will come with me with 'no holds barred.'" "Mark, that's your hypothesis, assumption, umh, discombobulated theory at best let's complete the experiment with proper due diligence, shall we?" My dimples exploding out, grinning, I replied, "so theoretically, we need to wait another three hours till the girls are dripping with… the pumps are primed, you know!"

Becky put her well-manicured nails and palm on mine, "all right, Mark, I get it, but even now, you should be able to prove your theory, right? Oh, come on, we know you will have lower results, I get that, but you should still 'score' if your logic is correct!"

I had been eye-flirting all along with another vixen, a strategy I often used but kept secret. The girlfriends of the girl, yeah, working them with shrewd flirtatious nuances, these so-called friends didn't know it, but they were competing, almost like jealous, like why her and not Me! They enviously try to capture my attention. Maybe it was a contest to them; I don't know nor care. Hence, I really wanted Beck in my bed, so I used the come-on-line. "Hey, there 'Becky' why don't you join me on my houseboat for some drinks and some hot tubbing?" She only winked at me and said, <u>"okay, that's a practice run; go get 'em, Tiger!"</u>

I'm not a man who doesn't take a challenge seriously, rollin my shoulders and giving Beck the look of 'your loss girl!

I walked with purpose a beeline to her table. A black beauty sat erect, obviously one of <u>Beck's 'friends'</u> sadly or happily in my case 'girls were like this learning in high school there was this innate inner competition, suppose its instinctual um natural tendencies, females want what their GF'S have, sad but over the years there isn't a doubt in my salacious mind. I don't bother in small talk, no names, I say, 'Hey,' I lean in conspiratorially a sexy whisper, "Yuh, want to join me on my houseboat for some drinks and a splash in the hot tub?"

Her dark eyes explored mine as she pushed her chair back, picking up a green-clad key to one of the cabins here at the Silverthorn Resort. The Ebony bomber turned to view Becky with intrigue, furrowed brows a glimpse of a smile said to her friends at the table, keeping Becky's stare. "I'll see you, girls, later…." She took my hand as we strutted right down the stairs. From the corner of my eye was Becky, mouth covered by her right hand, standing gesticulating with the other like, Stop! 'Too late,' smiling to myself. Yuh, snooze, you lose bye… bye now! ☺ .

-3-

San Quentin, Prison.

Five hours Southwest, at the prison 'San Quentin' stood 'Tank' he could swear that he could see the cold, moldy bricks sweat. Damp, humid mustiness systemically infiltrated his being. He resembled an 'Area 51' alien with grey skin and pale, dead eyes had to get the hell out of here before he was a Relic, a damn shadow.

On his illegal cell phone… a tan man looked at him, opposite… contrary to his warped beliefs. Alive was he, full of vigor and optimism for the future. Tank stared at him, lost and depressed, mused here in this prison; he had little hope.

"Tank, you got to believe at the next Parole board meeting, you're going to be released. Listen, it's a done deal, bud!" "Joe, how many times have I heard those words?" "I'm not you, Joe, nor am I, Mark… I'm not wearing Rose colored Sunglasses."

The signal was a triple flush; a Correctional Officer ah Guard was making his or her rounds. "Gotta go…" punches end, and the 'Skype' connection' went blank. Tank was lucky to be one of the inmates at San Quentin to own a cell phone. It always boils down to money. A $15 phone costs anywhere between $300.00 to upwards of $500.00, which helped supplement the low-paying occupation of being a correctional officer living in Marin County next to one of the most beautiful areas on the planet. Cost of living through the roof, easy to make deals with the willing guards. Taking five short steps, he fell back on his bunk; the TV was tuned to 'CNN' for the fifth time like on a visible loop.

Attorney Pat Hale had been abducted and kidnapped right from the parking garage behind his law office in Sacramento. Tank's smile had been reduced as he saw the close circuit replay a husky, fluid-moving man who quickly pressed a 'stun baton' with a shocking jolt of 50,000 Volts to Pat's hand that he suddenly put out for defensive measure, his Neuromuscular system, shocked. The Attorney dropped like a rock.

He spasmodically twisted like a beheaded serpent, all that could be seen of the assailant was dark black clothing a balaclava covered his face. A dull white van with a sliding door opened in went the lawyer, and in the split moment, the last picture from the garage showed the driver still clad now in a skullcap. He slid a card in at the parking garage gates and drove out.

The Feds had accessed all the cameras in front of the Sacramento County Jail and Federal Building in total, like 13 different views of the same kidnapping movie.

The van passed the cameras at the Holiday Inn and then shot into the underground parking slabs next to the entrance of 'Tourist Ville <u>Old Sacramento</u>.' There, a handy, dandy-blocking device was used!

The van was found empty later without a clue left for forensics… detectives were perplexed as to why the assailant hadn't used the 'blocking device' from the beginning, which was until veteran agent 'Rico Captor' clarified; since 2017, there had been a fail-safe system in place at the Federal building and county jail if the cameras were shut down a silent alarm sounded. US marshals went into fever mode with all the FBI Agents on alert. This was an inside job, for how would the assailants know that this fail-safe system was en vogue?

Tank's left hand was cramping up as he recognized the smug countenance of Rico. His middle finger was shaking "we're going to kill you, you fkn bastard!" Muttering under his breath, looking at the bars across his tiny window in his concrete cell.

He calms himself meditatively, with peaceful resolve mulling over how it had all gone astray, wrong, a childhood memory from when he was 13 years old. His gut-inner voice was saying no… He should have trusted his conscience's warning signs. If only he could have stepped back in time and changed that first wrong from there like a toboggan on a snow drift decline… no brakes, warnings of oncoming dangers or consequences, sped down the embankment of hell out of control.

Almighty God knows I was a gracious kid… set up for greatness inheritance from grandparents who owned acres and acres of valuable land and the 'Nut Tree Resort' in Vacaville. My best friend BF, Mark Feral, and I orchestrated the 'Dog napping' of 'Pinky the poodle mascot' for a $5000 reward.

He went along with the plot, even though now, in retrospect, he felt good ole buddy Mark manipulated him; hell, he had nothing to lose, but in the end, truthfully, he despised the spoiled rotten dog. If not for Mark's baby sister Wendi Feral they would have been successful. She was a freak, and still is… dammit months after 'Pinky' the nasty Poodle was returned to the Nut Tree, his Aunt and the Vacaville police had sniffed out the trail.

Mark and he were implicated, not being a novice to the tricks and intimidations manipulations of the 'Juvenile Hall' system. Social workers would attack the children with ulterior motives. I'd kept my mouth shut… Tank shutters rolling over on his prison mattress, oh so uncomfortable.

In Juvenile Hall, a nice black policewoman had broken him with the false trust she, her words still could be found in his memory banks decades past. Tank <u>"Sin… warps perception. It's important to follow your heart and clear your conscience so God and goodness can permeate and transform your soul."</u>

Yeah, kinda heavy shit for sure he'd spent some time on the ten commandments but chose the ones that related to him, which made the most significant impact or didn't! His realizations (religious zealots >equals hypocrites), hiding their immoral impurities behind a man-written, contrived series of books, so-called Bibles. Blinking his left eye open with a squint, King James Bible sat on a shelf. Was he a hypocrite himself? Lol!

Before his afternoon nap, he'd meet his gang in the prison yard, Pump some iron work out for a couple of hours; stomach-flexed body beautiful only if his face were as admirable! He could use a suntan for sure, Lol.

Wendi Feral's gorgeous face flashed before his pupils. The reason he had been incarcerated was the Feline with now five lives left. Mark, Joe, and he had tried four times to eliminate the snake-eyed beauty. Hopefully, she didn't have nine lives, and last he knew, she was in a mental hospital: yep! NIA Napa Insane Asylum. Although he was aware that the Vixen... Wendi was far from nuts. She was a nemesis, the genesis of their problems, causing strife for her brother and them, highlighted with a saintly aura, some would even say! A formidable arch-enemy indeed!

<u>JOE SABLE.</u>

At another retreat in Northern California, Joe reclined on his deluxe lounge chair, the automatic actuating awning fixed above him. If he leaned out, he could view the heavens lit up, stars of the Universe and beyond. He'd be frustrated if he didn't know how his lifelong Bro planned out his actions.

A Friday night, most likely, his pal Mark was out cavorting with the female persuasion by now rollicking about in or on his houseboat with an emphasis in the 'Sex' Mode.

Mark's sport was catching 'Tag and Release,' girls he was making up for the times he was locked up, calls and texts left unanswered, Twitter, Instagram, Snapchat, and even Facebook.

Mark became 'Low Tech' when he was on the prowl well, except for his five hidden camera angles of his sexual conquests and exploitations. Not that the willing and not-so-willing participants were not left satisfied, lol... it was exhilarating and fun. His cameras had built-in motion detectors. You can bet filming was ongoing whenever there was action on the houseboat or at his cabin.

At times good ole bro Mark Feral would let him watch the videos of their scared faces of apprehension as he strapped them down, then orgasms and blissful delight ensued, sex toys, their blushing cheeks cum again, he'd whisper, oh what fun that boy has… thought Joe.

Joe's motorhome had three pop-outs on the driver's side and two others on the passenger side; attached to the back was his super trailer. He felt secure in his magnificent diesel pusher motorhome, a $575,000 machine that was his form of ecstasy. Every human had vices, and this was his; the door flew open a lusciously built woman, ahh young girl of 19 years old, grinned.

Joe slugged down the rest of his Scotch, holding his empty glass up. She tauntingly struts down the steps, provocatively taking his drink. Aah, I didn't believe in self-denial, saying no to temptation. His Lil slut… escort sex slave, knew precisely what he wanted and needed. She would satiate his every desire or 'die' trying… Yeah, that's for sure!

Suddenly his phone chirped. Joe snatches it up; *a picture lights up on his phone screen A goddess, black beauty. 'Oh, how yummy' was the caption from his BF, Mark, who was up to his nasty self; an urge enlarged him, he called out, come here whipped out his unfurling cock, she bent and engorged, 'Life was good' as he sipped his cocktail.*

He whispers to her, "so you will have vitamin-induced juices as an appetizer, then we'll move into the main course, babe!" 'oh yeah.' ☺.

-4-

NIA.

***

Wendi.

'I'm 'Wendi Feral,' the blessed Seer-cursed depending on one's perspective. Please listen to me; I am a woman… hear me roar. Whom the heck was I fooling, dormant-flat on my back, a Zombie in a vegetative state, A coma hooked to machines clinging to a life that I wanted to dismiss? Pull the damn plugs.

I heard the latest gifted doctor Scientist speaking to my parents, Ed and Barbara. Today was day 255 of my incarceration within NIA > Napa Insane Asylum.

She sounded young, wish I could see Doctor Hawkins, that is; then I heard a familiar sound that I associate with pulling drapes. No choice. I'd nearly become desensitized to the dressing change; my sponge bath pans were clacking I felt hands tugging on me from both sides. The insidious process begins again, and I want to disobey, kick my legs out, leave me alone, and get away from me. Alas, there wasn't any rebellion, for my conscience repeatedly warned me. It was undoubtedly a concerted effort by nurses, doctors, and physical therapists who helped me stretch and rub out the impending bedsores. All were there to help me. Unfortunately… silence was all I spoke.

I can hear the hushed mumbling of my parents, Dr. Hawkins, with others, must be at least five people in my room with a TV program belting out the terrible news. 'Good morning America'… it was like I was at a busy intersection without traffic lights, a recipe for human disaster; noise and words intervened.

The TV in my room sounded an alarm… a name I'd known well… memory recall worked fine… I yelled and screamed in silent fright, be quiet, shut up, my ears worked fine, even more acute than ever. The name was Pat Hale, the second attorney to have been abducted from his Sacramento Law Office only 15 days prior a public defender. John Manson was kidnapped.

I knew those names, not the individuals but was stifled… memory recalls not engaging, ignoring the distress signals trying to zone in on my loving, nurturing parents. Unexpectedly I was filled with a sense of optimism and promise. "Listen, I don't want to get your hopes up, but Wendi is improving by leaps and bounds." Are you kidding me? I was pissed off that the doctor was feeding that BS to my parents, but I kept my mouth shut, for that was all I could do… listen!

"Categorically, yes, she is in a persistent vegetative state, as most coma patients are. Wendi is not dead inside or, as society labels these living beings, not a vegetable nor brain dead. Sure, she can't move or talk." Said a voice I'd never met… Dr. Hawkins.

"I've watched her twitch her face; she sweats, her eyelids flutter, legs and arms fingers even move at times." "Yes, Mrs. Feral, this is all common, synapses nerves firing; with your permission, I'd like to perform some additional tests on your daughter?" Dad said, "well, of course, anything that would help," mom said, "Not so fast; what exactly are you proposing, nothing invasive?" I loved my mother always such a calculating and analyzing soul.

'Daddy just wanted me back if a damn lobotomy promised success. He'd sign the release forms, not Mama!' Dr. Hawkins voyaged on slowly. As I was rolled onto my side, my back wasn't as numb, stinging feeling… unlike I'd felt before, evolving some things were happening below my epidermis.

Oh, I was over the oppressive guilt and embarrassment of being 'spread eagle' Vagina wiped, butt cleaned didn't care if the nurses were male or female anymore.

I'm lying to myself, I care, but as my bottom lip quivered, shaking incomprehensibly, I couldn't cry, sob, shed a tear, no emotions. Wiped, washed, and dried off like a baby girl infant.

Back hitchhiking again on the conversation regarding what I had in store for me, contrasting sounds, a catchy tune, commercial… turn the TV off, please.

"Here at Napa's Neurological treatment center outpatient ward disability ward, we've begun an innovative new technique of trying to communicate with some of the patients. Now that Wendi is off the intrusive feeding tube, she is a candidate. I'd personally like, with your permission, of course, to conduct an experiment. I would need at least one of you present!"

Mom and dad exclaimed simultaneously, 'we'll be here!' Sadly, hearing their anxious, suffering, desperate terror-filled words hurt me deep inside, punctuated by my mother's wail, 'oh my God, I want my baby girl back.'

My lips were frozen, framed by a silent scream as my rigid, fragile body lay dormant beside the warmth emanating from my parents. The Doctor continued to inform my parents and, unbeknownst to her... me of the many studies that are now being performed worldwide. Scientists and Neurologists are researching newly innovative EEG brain scans that can now analyze and decipher variances and identify signs of communication in patients with similar cranial injuries like your daughter. Mom's intonations and voice perked up like at Christmas time when I was a little girl. "So how would we actually recognize any form or type of this new way to communicate with coma victims? Tell me if she can't move, I mean...."

"Ms. Feral, many patients, including Wendi, I suspect are fully integrated. Let me explain that patients are locked into a loop of memories, data, worries, uncertainties, a network of imaginations and thoughts enclosed with MRI scans and brain scans. We can capture the neurons passing impulses and synapses firing to different parts of her brain. I will try to explain to both of you when we have her set up for this experiment, okay?"

"But let me leave you with this example in layman's terms. The different parts of the human brain light up when accessed. In Wendi's brain scan, we can see this process in real-time by synapses firing neurons and light flashes. When she is spoken to, and let's say you were to say out loud, Wendi, this is your mother, 'I love you!'

'Suddenly Wendi's brain lights up like an NFL stadium... memories reacting to the stimuli, providing her brain is functioning she hears, understands alive within her Amygdala flashes neurons from her Cerebral cortex across from the hippocampus!”

“Mr. & Ms. Feral think of it like this different parts of her brain become energized. We can then follow the synapses generated by her thought process via her brainwave’s reactions to the words she hears, proving she is engaged and alive inside.” I am sure Wendi is alive, striving to regain her conscious self!” “Oh, that would be terrific. Can we schedule her this week?” Asks my mother.

“I will run this by Doctor Honcho and put a rush on it for you, okay, remember? I don’t want to have you too optimistic if the experiment doesn’t show her responding to your words. It doesn’t mean she doesn’t hear you. Let’s hope and pray again to oversimplify this new test… it will show if her brain generates responses to your verbal stimuli. It has been proven we can realistically discern between a ‘Yes and a No’ answer most times with our patients.”

“Please, again, don’t get your hopes up uhm, cognitively… some can’t grasp the concept process of communication; there are limitations!” “I don’t care, let’s do it… when can we begin?” “Yes, put a rush on it now!” declared my father.

“Please excuse me; let me make a call to Doctor Honcho right now then… why wait,” said Doctor Hawkins. A few minutes later, the Hawkins doctor reenters. I heard her say next Tuesday morning at 11:15 am, “I’ll meet you here until then, Mr. and Ms. Feral. Have a good day. As I said, don’t get your hopes too high!” “Thank you, Doctor; please call me Ed and Wendi’s mom Barbara. Oh wow, we are excited. Thank you for rushing this along!” said dad.

Well afterward, the warmth of the sponge bath felt better, re-dressed in my no doubt stylish hospital, gown-looking forward to trying to let all… Mom and Dad know I was alive inside. Please don’t give up on me! I was eternally grateful, seeking to let my parents and all know not to give up on me. I am coming back strong.

I feel my mother on my right side and my father on the left. “I just don’t get it, Barb. In the first 90 days or so, Wendi was doing great even started an exercise program and was in counseling on her way back to being herself, then she had that fall from the steps, and…" "Ed, she's regressed, to where she began fighting the head trauma you realize they couldn't get all the bullet fragments that were in her skull…." "I don't get it, Barb; with the finest doctors on the planet, they can't bring our Wendi from her fugue… oh well damnit anyways, let's get some lunch!"

<u>I remember Sunshine and me speaking; don't you recall the fall from the steps? I drift back again to where my first memories began, constantly living in Reverse!</u>

'Okay, thinking back on what I remembered of my life in HD color, not so vivid, my first memory came at around 18 months old it was foggy then my memories went into overdrive from 3 years old on. The first memory that was emblazoned on my mind started with a hairy beast, lol Rocco, the Gorilla San Francisco zoo, saving my life.

Solid memories were available up to about 12 years old, then blank for the next nine years until I was 21 years old. I have a partner, Sandi, my BF, and she is a beautiful albino girl with pink eyes uhm, our business 'Feral Feedback' was a fantastic and growing success. Since the day that Rocco, my gorilla, breathed life back into my drowned-dead body, I could telepathically communicate with animals.

By 2007 'Feral Feedback' had signed various contracts with the FBI to use our trained animals, like our specially trained Canine dogs. I flew to Tennessee in 2007 with our dogs and birds 'Hoot' my Owl 'Red' my Hawk; and 'Blackie' our Raven. Left Sandi in Vancouver, Washington, where our business is located, to ensure our company continued the success we'd built at Feral Feedback.

I helped save a precious little girl 'Maddi' from a serial killer; next, my memories found us, Sandi, and I, in Northern Florida, The Ocala National Forest. I just wanted to wake up again, no stop, no more merry-go-rounds. I want off this roller coaster vibrations, buzz. I was being again drawn away '<u>my closed eyelids closed once more!</u>'

Where was I? it was pitch dark… no breeze, help me! 😫 .

28

Joe.

The alarm clock was hissing, ruining his contentment, ughhhh, sleep rest that he'd need, all the expectations leveraged upon his head, turning to whatever her real name was.

One scoop of brown sugar with a splash of half-and-half creamer. As he nudged her, a derisive moan came back.

He mulled over an urge, glancing at the naked female, and whispered in a hushed utterance, "you can finish fulfilling the rest of my desires after coffee." Her response was less than motivating as she unfolded herself from the pillow sandwich.

Joe's head was humming with sharp streaks of pain coinciding with his heartbeat Dewar's Scotch had him dehydrated, lips tongue parched. Pulling a warm water bottle from the headboard, I swigged it down!

The young Lil whore that he chose was a repeat offender, as he liked to say; in the last month, she'd occupied his motorhome three times. Now and again, many of the escorts would invariably get used to the arrangement and become comfortable with his lifestyle.

They then would try to align their personal goals of the future with his... most, in his estimates, had 'fallen and couldn't get up' drug users who couldn't extract themselves out of their intoxicated abyss of heroin, crack cocaine, and or mixtures of pills ah just plain ass junkies that had limited perspectives of time.

When young, they were desirable and sought after; alas, this was short-lived, for their lifestyle tore them back; a thirty-five-year-old looked 55 years old. It's a hard life, for sure. With that being said, they better save monies. For the most part, their employment a decade gone by was limited. Joe had witnessed some of the older sex workers ignoring all the distress signals until one day. The phone doesn't ring, and no more tweets or texts, no more sex work, worn out and used up… dried-up faces that appeared like ghosts lived in past mirrors.

Rode hard and put away wet and wrinkled, always within a step or stumble from being replaced, their best pictures were of years… earlier mugshots.

For these Sex workers, it was always about competition, a vicious cycle paralleled in many occupations, like professional athletes, starting NFL running back, then you're on the bench older, used worn-out second string third string, oops out to pasture you go.

The non-injured younger, stronger, more robust, agile, and flexible, aah, replaced!

"There you go, Joe, just like you want it" He takes the mug from her, slides the sheets back points like a compass; being obedient isn't always easy for her, he knows; her warm mouth promises early-morning pleasure as he eases back and rolls his shoulders sipping the perfect coffee, Yep!

Trudy, or Samantha, I referred to her as 'Sam,' was lost in addiction. She played her part 'to a Tee' excellent actress, the Private Investigator, was first on my expiration list, and then I'd eliminate her… all this whore was is a valuable cog. Sam didn't have much time on this planet, and I might as well take advantage of her while I can! Both the P.I. and Sammy were as good as not breathing. Unbeknownst to either of them, this was their last day on this earth in this dimension, at least! Lol.

Aah, as Joe toweled off after a long steamy shower, unlike typical Motorhomes, which had small shower enclosures, his was deluxe blessed indeed. 'Trudy,' her stage name, the 19-year-old escort whose real name was 'Samantha Timmons,' was to meet him at the agreed upon location. With a well-placed bullet, she would not be providing any more monies for her 'Pimp, drug dealer.' 'Trudy' had been busted, arrested five times for prostitution and three times for shoplifting. She was not a bad girl, really. Sadly, most of her family were wealthy politicians living in the Sacramento area.

Surveillance and reconnaissance were all but complete… escape routes were practiced daily; strategy challenged his wisdom. We all

The Feral's moved to Vacaville, a couple of hours away this
hampered their friendship; they'd talk regularly on the phone,
and Mark's parents would drop him off when they brought
Wendi to the San Francisco Zoo to visit that gorilla, Rocco.

Joe met Tank while visiting the Feral's several months after
the Pinky the poodle fiasco. Then, Joe had his first caustic,
negative encounter with Mark's little sister Wendi.

Joe ruminated back to when she'd crossed the line… Tank,
Mark, and I were robbing houses, stealing valuables, jewelry
cash. We'd watch as the man would leave for work, then learn
the schedules of the lady of the house, using glass cutters after
jumping fences into the backyards… we would copy TV
shows. The criminals would wear gloves so did we; we'd gone
to Radio Shack and bought walkie-talkies.

It was way cool like super-duper secret agents even had
masks. Not yet 15 years old were we, but we, even at that age,
were a force to be reckoned with. Things were going great, and
I'd take the booty back to Redwood City and sell all our stolen
goodies to one of my friend's brothers who was part owner of
a pawnshop off El Camino Real Blvd in Redwood City; yep,
the good ole days indeed.

From robbing houses to office buildings, we graduated.
Mark, Tank, and I were the Three Amigos B/E's… breaking
and entering. We broke into the schools and cafeterias, stole
candy food, and wrote on the blackboards, not in our
handwriting, of course. It was so freaking fun once at a liquor
store downtown Vacaville. We purposely set off the alarm at
the back entrance. We started tripping the alarm right after the

store closed. Tank, Mark, and I had grocery carts lined up. Too young to have a driver's license, we laughed hard as our plan unfolded.

Watching for the 3rd time, the manager opens the liquor store with Vacaville Police by his side; a false alarm, again, right?... way wrong!

By 1:55 am the police nor the manager was bothered by the alarm ringing. The manager just turned them off and would deal with the nuisance in the morning, just like Mark had predicted the manager would take it up with the alarm company in the morning Lol.

What a haul we broke the glass cabinets holding the most expensive wines, booze, and cases of beer. Oh my lord, all three carts were filled to the brim then the fun began. We were trying to get back to Mark's house into the garage without being seen. We had finally made it at 3:15 am pay dirt, then the real work of climbing a ladder into the attic to stash the alcohol. The cashbox and register had a total of $1,550 too! We were like rich for sure, then the man door in the garage inside Mark's house popped open, and we were still loading our bounty into the attic. I was on the damn ladder.

Oh, shit, on the threshold of the door stood 9-year-old Wendi in her 'My Little Pony,' pajamas, "What are you all doing, Mark? I saw you from my window; what did you do now?"

We hovered by the last cart, trying to hide the contents. Mark said, "Wendi, go back to bed. I'm warning you, sister, you say one word to mom and dad, I will kill Tara and the two pussycats, I promise, you got it?" Watching her puffy eyes water, she clutched a Cabbage Patch doll and walked away. We looked at each other, then went back to work.

Sunday afternoon, my parents picked me up on the way back from Lake Tahoe, where they often went to gamble and attend plays... Shakespearean enthusiasts.

Well, everything was all right until my next visit with Tank and Mark. If I only could see the future, ugh, mistakes and miscalculations. Wendi, with her best friend 'Lynn,' had formed a group of girls to search for lost animals, 'Pet Detectives,' they called themselves.

Initially, this wasn't a problem for us, but what we learned became a major issue for us. We thought at the time what luck that Lynn's parents owned a thriving jewelry store in town, which could be our largest haul. We would steal all the jewelry... Yes.

We walked by her family's jewelry store and thought this was how we would become rich; greed took over, and we developed a plan. Mark befriended 10-year-old Lynn flirting and acting as if he was interested in her... being 15 years old. She was in 'crush mode' despite Wendi's warnings and pleadings to stay away from her brother 'he was a bad boy!'

Okay, we planned to rob Lynn's house; first, her mother wears expensive diamonds, tennis bracelets, and earrings, thousands of dollars for sure. This would be our biggest coup until we robbed the jewelry store!

We rode our bikes over to Lynn's house... Wendi didn't like me and hated Tank barely tolerated her brother, Mark, out of fear, for sure.

Lynn's home was luxury at its finest, a 3-story mansion... pool even had a tennis court all fenced with lush hedges, and a kennel in the backyard for breeding the AKC pampered German Shepherds imported straight from Germany!

After weeks of planning and casing the home, the night finally came. Mark had cleverly found out what the alarm code was... to shut it down. He even kissed Lynn on the lips and umh, would hold her hand when Wendi wasn't around. We even played games like hide and seek, and we all played Monopoly in Lynn's Deluxe Tree Fort a few times.

The timing was good. My parents dropped me off on another trip to Lake Tahoe. Lynn's parents planned a 3-day getaway... tickets to Dallas to see the San Francisco 49ers play their archrivals, the Dallas Cowboys; Lynn was all excited, and so were we! Lynn's grandma, who would be drunk by like 7 pm, was going to babysit... Yay... Perfect!

Mark laced some steaks we got from Albertson's with Rat poison to shut the German Shepherds up, who were let out of the kennels to run free while the parents were away.

It took a couple of hours till the poison worked; it was already dark out when we entered Lynn's house and punched in the alarm code… perfect the drugged dogs were quiet.

Grandma was snoring on the couch when the pesky Heinz 57 terrier came yapping down the hall, trying to nip at our heels. A swift kick by Mark, then he shut the door on the yapper. Mistake number one we should have cut the Terrier's throat. The German Shepherds were dead, our plan was going great, we made it out stealthy, and all went great! We were lucky that Lynn's room was on the 3rd floor, and her parent's Master bedroom was on the 2nd floor. Wendi was spending the night at Lynn's house. They never heard a thing and stayed asleep excellent and fun, incredibly excited that our plan worked without a hitch. We were geniuses, for sure.

I still remember the visit to the Pawnshop. Omg, my pawn shop connection, the owner was looking through an eyepiece and nearly shit his pants, diamonds galore, and a pile of gold chains. We were rich, and he gave me $15,000! The plan was for me to cut school and take a Greyhound bus from Redwood City to Vacaville the very next day…Yay!

-6-

***

<u>Wendi, back in her present state of being… dormant.</u>

Strangely hard to comprehend unless you've been there, time stands still for Coma patients. Nothing ever changes, no differences, like a constant, and yet there are so many varying degrees of being in a vegetative state. MRIs, Cat scans, EEGs… a relentless circuit of testing well, at least the results were somewhat optimistic. Some of the tests proved that my brain was actively sending signals. Ugh wasn't brain-dead.

This gave hope to my family and friends, and unbeknownst to others, hope for the cognizant self-uhm me, also energizing the medical staff, or as I referred to them, the spectators... nurses that merely gawked at me or changed my clothes not much changed. My life was as dormant as my body, like in a catatonic trance; this was the outside layer of me.

Not paralleling within me, though, I was raging inside, shouting loudly, imagining myself screaming out, wanting to tear down the metaphorical walls that held me! Today was a huge day for my parents and me, cutting-edge innovative brain tests Dr. Hawkins mom, dad, and David, yeah.

I was once again a 'test dummy,' another attempt to communicate with me! Off the respirator, uhm, feeding tube, no question I was improving; how could I show them that I was 'alive'? Yes, 'Alive' inside.

Frustration beamed into my head felt chained down, shackled... lucky for my indwelling Spirit that fought my negativity, being relentlessly optimistic, sovereign, and virtuous, my spirit a driving force in constant pursuit of accountability. Reasons why I was like comatose, conflicts unresolved always festering, although even with my guiding spirit, I couldn't stop feeling sorry for myself.

I suppose asking oneself, uh, 'Why Me' are or is human nature; for many, life was filled with despair, pain, and suffering. It's an imperfect world; promptly, congruence was restored. I lied to myself for harmony was a pleasing balance, symmetry of internal calmness. Not I... a refusal to compromise my morals and beliefs, I fell backward into past replays of what was my life preying to be brought to the current me!

In 1995, I was ten years old.

Not a waste of my resting time, nope, finally, my brother Mark was the centerpiece of the next segment, my life's film; crawling past Mark's vacant room down the hallway, little Tara, our family dog 'Dachshund's' nails clicking clacking on the hardwood floor, I kept pace. <u>I tried to obey 'Sunshine,' my invisible guidance counselor, inner being an imaginary friend. It was her fault that I was the 10-year-old traitor to my family.</u>

My mother was wailing, sobbing… my father was doing his best to console her, with his own demons tethered. My ear upon their bedroom door, 'how could she do this to her brother, Ed?'

'I haven't any answers, Barb, why didn't she come and talk with us first? Our lives will never be the same here in Vacaville five police cars, neighbors standing in clusters pointing at our house, geez, furthermore, the newspaper and local news. Wendi was wrong this time, Barb. We should have kept this in the family 'in house' ugh, now we're like the plague around our neighborhood. We know that all of this will make the Vacaville newspaper and maybe even the damn TV local news shit we move from Redwood City to get away from the limelight, and now we're again on the dinner table being devoured.'

'Babe honey, our names were not mentioned, Mark being a Juvenile and all,' dad replied, 'Barb, word by mouth; it will not be long till the whole damn town will cast us as evil now.

Wavering, suspicious eyes on all of us, remember Wendi's best friend Lynn's parents are city council dignitaries; Hell, there's a poster of Mr. Wright, her dad running for Mayor.'

Pervasive silence as I could hear my own breath at their door. "It's not her fault, Ed; how could she have known?" My mom went from being angry with me to defending me. My dad said, "She knew; she's no dummy. Our daughter is precocious and wise beyond her ten years. Of course, I'm sure she hadn't any idea of the ramifications of her actions. She loves her brother." Then my mom let out a derisive cackle, "if that is true, Ed, her love is a one-way road. Mark hates her. He screamed from the police car that he'd get even with her if it were the last thing he ever did… revenge would be his, wasn't that his words Ed?"

Honey, he's only 15 years old" I hear another scathing cackle from under their bedroom door. My mother says, "it's been five days now, and more charges are filed against him with every hour, it seems. The damn Vacaville Police are emptying all their unsolved crimes. Look, they will not release him from Juvenile Hall. He's in jail; oh my Lord, our son is in jail! I cannot understand this. If Wendi would have kept her damn trap shut, damn her!" I heard dad say, 'it's not her fault,' but didn't hear another word, for tears drowned me out like a flood. I was a deplorable lousy girl to my family. It was all my fault, ugh, because of me. My brother was in Juvenile Hall. My best friend Lynn wasn't allowed to mutter my name… the kids at school were so mean, shoved me down to the ground, and kicked me, knocking my books out of my arms. The names they called me, ugh, horrible cuss words.

I didn't have one friend even the teachers scowled at me; the principal locked me in a room after the school nurse cleaned up my scraped, bloody knees, and I was pushed to the ground constantly. The last shove by a bully caused my head to hit the playground asphalt hurt, ugh, bleeding, my teeth biting my bottom lip. Oh, how I hurt the mashing of my nose into the blacktop on the playground ouch, a bloody mess.

I was alone. No one showed up at my clubhouse, not one friend, for our weekly pet detective meeting. Lynn's kennel of dog's German Shepherds breathed no more… Mark's poison had killed the sire 'stud dog' and three females.

Lucky that a few of the puppies survived, never to be the same, 'Pixey' the Lil terrier, was still in the animal hospital with internal injuries, broken ribs from where Mark had kicked her while walking down the hall in Lynn's house. There I was, lying with my head under the covers. I couldn't stop crying. Tara's whiptail twitching… in her eyes told me she loved me. Our cats, Maling and Tinkerbell, cuddled alongside purring like turbines. They were proud of me.

I was sort of a heroine; at least, that's what my invisible soulmate Sunshine kept intimating.

Looking back at the harbinger of ill will, Sunshine was wrong… come on, let's face the truth, if I'd kept my damn mouth shut, ughhhh… it's all my fault. It was Monday night that the police came knocking, surrounding our house search warrant was served to my dad. He had just gotten home from his job in San Francisco. Mark saw the cops standing at our door and went out a back window and over our back fence. He was later caught down by the creek with his friend and now codefendant 'Tank' in a tree fort.

They were counting money, planning to run away to meet up with Joe in Redwood City. They were going to Reno, Nevada, a plan never enacted.

My parents and I watched the police detectives become enraged finding Mark's hidden cache of tools for burglary, B/E's suction cups, glass cutting instruments, three walkie-talkies, police scanners, binoculars, brass knuckles, and several switchblade knives, nun chucks, no guns thankfully.

Then all hell broke loose I could hear the excited yowls, muffled but discernible, up in the attic above the garage, bottles of alcohol tagged with stickers from the liquor store robbery. From there, it only got worse, with what was found in a notebook… were the intended plans to rob the 'Wrights' my former BFF Lynn, their family jewelry store. A small chest of costume jewelry was dropped down to waiting hands on the ladder from the attic, along with masks, gloves, and hoodies. I was guilty, demonized, and hated by my classmates wrong, but it felt right in some odd way. What would you do if you were me? Given these circumstances, please help me understand what other options did I have.

'Sunshine,' my alter ego, grabbed control and stepped up to the plate with her strength and conviction, and Wendi went on vacation. The faucet was wrenched off. I got up, aah, Sunshine did.

The first thing we did was take a well-deserved shower first one in over five days. Out in the kitchen, I ate something. A big bowl of fruit loops, my parents were still in solitude. Out the door, I went rolling on my stingray bike, visiting my only friends, who turned out to be non-humans, animals, and reptiles. I pedaled fast as I could to the vacant lot where my former best friends and I would hang out… Cindy and Lynn.

Our make-shift tree fort deep in the brush by the creek, blankets, books, and a transistor radio, food… umh, not much real food, more snacks like chips and cookies, a jar of chunky peanut butter and crackers.

Oh yeah, candy, of course, from Halloween, I was set up. No Ants had invaded my, umh, our treasures. I rolled up my backpack, head down, pulled the cover-up, listening to KFRC AM radio the top 40 countdown!

'Sunshine,' my alter ego did her best to control my mood swings and thoughts; despite her wanted intrusion, I kept returning to the caustic mistake, a breakdown of stupidity.

Unfortunately, to some, probably most thought that I knew what my brother and his friends were up to since I spent the night with Lynn while her grandmother drunkenly slept. We played and went to bed late, and some people believed I was the inside conspirator, ensuring Lynn didn't hear my brother and Tank, and Joe robbing her parents.

Early the following day, her dad and mom returned from Dallas; they had a blast at the 49er game, umh, a bunch of fun. Monday at 7:25 am all changed for the Wright family, Lynn, and me.

Oh my God, a horrible wake-up. Lynn was bawling her eyes out... her German Shepherds were dead in the backyard, the house was robbed, and little 'Pixey' was bleeding from her snout, barely breathing, it was chaos. The police, man, oh man, hell broke loose. I cried so damn hard.

My parents were friends with the 'Wrights,' and dad and mom drove to Lynn's house ahh mansion. Before my parents even entered the driveway of Lynn's home. Bad vibes slammed me... one of their outdoor kitty cats who lived in the spacious front yard gave me a scowl-ish yowl as the 'Tomcat' cornered me before I'd made the first step down the porch. The Tomcat had admonished me like I was used up kitty-litter. Through his cycs, I saw my brothcr... No!

Mark and his friends Tank and Joe had, oh no, no, no, killed the dogs, suddenly from behind me, down the steps nearly falling, was Lynn snot-boogers, her hair glued to her face, sad wild eyes, we like hugged for days, her whimpering on my shoulder, I dared not say a word of the Tomcat's accusations.

The police were everywhere. A van sat parked by the front gate animal rescue, the Wright's personal Veterinarians in a white van, although there was no need for cages or dog catchers. Bodies of the German Shepherds were loaded on little gurneys past me into the waiting van for autopsies.

I followed Lynn and saw a kind lady veterinarian whom I recognized she'd helped Tara, my dog. Passing us on a small rolling cart was the little terrier 'Pixie' crying, whimpering in agony; she spoke to me, her eyes replaying what my brother had done. I then screamed aloud, 'no, not Mark! My brother didn't do this, please no!' That's when dad grabbed me, turned me around, shook me, faced me, kneeling, taking me by my shoulder down the stairs, "ssshh, what are you saying, Wendi?"

The police stopped what they were doing a detective walked up. Oops…

'Sunshine,' my imaginary friend yanked me back to the plywood floor of my… our tree fort. She told me to stop! Nothing positive could come from replaying the events at Lynn's home.

Blinking back a mixture of emotions, we decided that I would run away from home. Looking around at the games and stuff that sadly belonged to Mark, Tank, and my ex-friends Lynn and Cindy, woefully thinking back in time, was doing no good, but how could I forget what had happened if I only had kept my damn mouth closed!

The good times and memories blasted two the forefront, remembering how my friends and I worked as a team building this fort way up like 35 feet in the air in a huge well-developed Oak Tree. No one would find me here. I jumped out on the rope swing, not feelin' tired after all. It wasn't long till I was joined by Squirrels, Chipmunks, and varieties of birds in every color, my true friends for sure; yep! An hour or so passed by, and I became tired. I fell into a slumber. Finally, I could sleep for the first time in five days without caustic nightmares.

Juvenile hall jail, like a prison, was the home for my brother Mark and his friends Tank and Joe for nearly three years until each turned 18 years old, all my fault. Gosh, I felt so guilty. Not a day passed without a remorseful thought; our family dynamics were altered forever, not to the positive. I must admit that, at times, I didn't feel any regret… why? For I thought that Mark and his friends might learn a lesson and come out changed for the good. My parents visited him religiously…

unhappy times and days when they did so. I was never invited to go with them to visit. Although I tried several times, even seeing him once, Mark hated my Guts. He never ever returned my, like, 27 letters. I sent him pictures that I bet he tossed into the toilet.

-7-

(Present time)

Rico Captor.

Tanya and Rico weathered another tense meeting via video conference; he thought it better to call it a lecture by a superior. He leans back in his chair, eyes closed. A hardy sigh leaves his mouth and lungs… his chest heaves.

Sacramento's Federal Courthouse, his location Rico had moved up the ladder super spacious office. He was a much-decorated celebrity ultra-agent 'Rico Captor' with awards of distinction and accolades bestowed upon him. A man's man on display, notoriety honor soaked the walls, medals, even trophies from the FBI games of competition all this, and he sat now in a cesspool pressure cooker, the tension kept mounting, no relief in sight.

The comparisons and similarities to pro athletes were his favorite analogy. You're only as good as your last game swiveled around his gaze, looking down on the city of Sacramento.

This was his final destination; he decided he'd retire here a while back, yet he was still considered innovative, matching the young breed of Agents physically; age was only a number. This was proven time and time again as his physical performance continued to improve, aligning with his renowned intellect, guile, sly cunning, and intuition in his meteoric rise… There's no question the catalyst was Wendi… without her, his life surely would have been different.

'Thank God for 'Wendi Feral,' his recurring mantra,' well because of her unique talents, he was one of very few who hadn't any doubts about her paranormal abilities, surely the rumors about Wendi could fill 13 blogs and websites around the world's social media had sensationalized exaggerated Wendi's achievements.

The mixtures of outright fabrications about every age of Wendi's life, from birth to life-saving efforts at the San Francisco Zoo, where Rocco the gorilla brought her back to life. Poor little girl, well before she was five years old, was scrutinized under a microscope.

The stories multiplied like a 'rash' measles, a virus. The start or inception of her problem began with Detective Judy Girth. Who catapulted her career like a supersonic rocket.

She was now the Police Chief of Redwood City, all thanks to Wendi!

Wendi's family escaped to Vacaville, California, where anomalies kept piling up regarding her paranormal gifts. Luckily most laughed at the thought of a human being, uh, having the ability to talk, aah, communicate with all forms of animals. The majority of humans called it total bullshit-like witches, ghosts, goblins, and aliens.

A recent survey of believers in Wendi's superpower worldwide put a smile on his face, 87% versus 13% non-believers. Overwhelmingly, people didn't believe that Wendi had a gift… Yup! Rico reminisced back some 11 years on his initial get-together with the young 21-year-old Wendi Feral. She had already made a name for herself at her Feral Feedback business based in Vancouver, Washington.

Rewinding back 11 years, how their relationship had started with a tense search for a Killer of children, he sat in his cubical. It was a rainy day. He was scanning websites for Canine instructors and animal trainers, even though the Feds had their training centers, cadaver dogs, bomb sniffers, etc.

Rave reviews were the norm bestowed upon Feral Feedback, testimonies from the Lions Club for the blind who were sold seeing eye dogs, some of the accolades that were heaped upon Wendi were worthy of 'comic book' cartoons, so Rico said why not give her a test run.

He was stifled and thoroughly frustrated. He had memorized the FBI profiler's reports about the serial killer, in Tennessee, child murderer kidnapper for like 25 months. He had searched and chased leads and had the best Canine units the FBI could provide… yet lost the trail in the same area by the banks of the Tellico River. The trail went dry, pun intended, at the river's shoreline; of course, they had canvassed the river via helicopter umpteenth times, nothing to show for all the hours and manpower.

After reading about Feral Feedback's achievements with various species of trained animals, he pleaded with his superior Director, Ms. Tanya Firm, for a subcontract and permission to use 'Feral Feedback' Rico was rebuffed several times cuz most considered the start-up business as nonsense Hocus Pocus. Nope! Wendi miraculously saved little Maddi from the kidnapper.

Then there were the missing hikers who were lost and then found near the Rogue River in Oregon, found and saved by Wendi Feral with her animal's guidance. The extensive resume included a capsized fishing trawler off the coast of Alaska and search parties with the US Coast Guard scanning the oceans. It was no laughing matter, but behind the scenes, most were howling at the literal desperation of the owner of the fishing trawler that called San Francisco it's home… docked at Fisherman's Wharf.

Scoma's was a fine seafood restaurant on Fisherman's Wharf. The owner hired 'Feral Feedback' to help aid in finding survivors of the tragic accident. His lead fishing trawler was fishing for Halibut at the time of the accident. Lost at sea were the entire crew missing nine men, including Captain Mike McCutchen. The angry white caps… waves on the ocean were averaging double digits in height. A tumultuously vicious storm had toppled the boat. Right behind that storm was another one forecasted in less than 35 hours, 'Feral Feedback' was hired, and Wendi and her partner Sandi traveled out into the Alaskan waters, bringing three trained Dolphins!

The Coast Guard and search teams laughed openly at the start-up's hiring. All that changed in less than five hours; the laughter ceased tears, and emotions of family members sobbing uncontrollably. Seven of the nine men were saved, floating on debris, clinging to life, hyperthermia had set in, but the men were alive and saved; it was the case of who stood laughing last that mattered!

<u>Sacramento kidnappings.</u>

Wash. D.C. on line 5, sir, Rico hesitated then punched the speakerphone, "Agent Captor, we've allocated another 15 US marshals to work with you on this ongoing crisis; we need answers. I expect updates regularly" 'yes, ma'am,' he said. Click. Wow, that was rude; what did they think? Was he a magician, Rabbit out of the hat? Valid threats against AUSAs and Federal Judges with two local attorneys kidnapped and abducted right here. He mused their offices less than five blocks from where his eyes stared out the window.

So far, not a word, no demands for ransom on John Manson or Pat Hale. They just disappeared without a trace!

He takes a swallow of an hour's cold coffee; all hell has broken out in the State Capital in the last five weeks. With a team of Agents trying to connect the dots in mutual cases, there must be a link between the two abducted attorneys.

One is a Federal Public Defender, the other a well-known former Federal Prosecutor who switched sides and opened an office across from the Sacramento county jail. John Manson was the public defender who had a pile of complaints leveled against him by his clients.

Rico had three full-time Agents scrutinizing Mr. Manson's disgruntled client base!

The two abducted lawyers couldn't be more different opposite polar wise, 'J.M.' John Manson would visit the Sacramento County Jail in shorts and a T-shirt, 'P.H.' Pat Hale would wear a Gucci deluxe tailored suit he the GQ who wanted to emulate the 'Richard Gere' look, the suave and sophisticated persona.

Rico sat reviewing the reports gathered by his staff; on the kidnaped attorneys, the guy Pat was working on his third marriage, the others ending in divorce. 'J.M.' had a steady partner now, a gay man… with quirks that led him to be a conniving, evil, mean-spirited man, someone who could never be trusted, always playing the middle ground. Looking for Brownie points, many defendants were confused at times. Was he on the other side colluding with the prosecutor?

Well, according to many of his clients, he was a sinister fellow, wearing two hats catering to the prosecutor's whims for his selfish aspirations, which led to his dream of working as a Federal Prosecutor.

Rico had interviewed their individual secretaries, the attorneys never communicated, ran in different circles, zero, no links, no cases. Their cell phone records were scrutinized, proving they never spoke, so were the kidnappings… Random crimes? Nope.

A vibration as Rico felt for his cell seeing the 707 prefix would let it go to voicemail, listen to the message later, and then it dawned on him that maybe it was Napa. Punched send; "Mr. Captor, it's Barbara Feral. I wanted to….." "is Wendi all right" blurts Rico.

"Oh yes, she is improving. I know you're a busy man, but her latest Neurologist, Dr. Hawkins, wants to conduct an experiment on her." He felt excitement via his phone speaker, and hope shouted into his ear. "We're going to try and communicate with her!"

"How-aah, I mean, I just saw her a couple of weeks ago, Barbara, and she…." "Listen, Rico; she's off the feeding tubes and respirator Wendi's coming back to us… tomorrow afternoon at 5 pm. We're going to meet the doctor, David, Ed and me. I know how fond she is of you, just wanted to…." "Say no more. I will meet you at NIA. I'll be there at 4:30 pm, wouldn't miss it for the world… yes good news, thanks, see yah then." "Thanks, Rico, goodbye."

Private Investigator Robert... KTM 1290.

Joe eased down the back gate of the motorcycle trailer attached to his motorhome; he'd left his Harley at Mark Feral's property near Lake Shasta in Redding, California.

He looked inside at identical street bikes, 'KTM 1290s' charcoal colored. He stepped inside, unstrapping and rolling a motorcycle down the ramp, already dressed in all-black light gray leather matching the pull-down smoke dark helmet, not a shred of skin exposed, his look androgynous.

The exact semblance, a guise that Samantha was last seen wearing. Besides being a sex toy, Sam was a skilled, daring rider; Joe smiled, not in a cowgirl position, did he mean lol. She used to race motocross starting at the age of 7 years old.

'Robert,' the private investigator who worked cases for the scandalous now coffin-laden evil attorney John Manson, had met Samantha once before North of Sacramento on I-5 at a Chili's restaurant. She was riding the identical bike he had now idling, warming up.

Staring up into the sky, early nightfall, stern with resolve revenge, a brilliant plan only the week before 'Sam' had met the P.I. in the same parking lot on the same bike dressed as he was.

He watched the P.O.S from a distance; before he got out of his dark blue SUV, she rode up to his window, parked, then they both walked into 'Chili's' the plan, the strategy was to hire this imbecile to follow her husband whom Sam suspected was cheating on her, all fiction.

Sam played it up as Joe listened from the other side of the shopping center, whimpering with the necessary tears. The blockhead P.I. tried to calm her down, then, being the ruthless cold-hearted asshole he was, brazenly asked her out on the following Friday night. This guy was a piece of work, despite the jerk having five kids and being married. Whew, a jackass. He 'Robert' said he would take her case at a decent discount reaching out over the table to squeeze Sammy's tiny hand.

Joe didn't worry that the P.I. was the same wimp that worked for Attorney, Manson, knowing that eventually, the connection would lead the Feds to make a list of likewise clients, possible vengeful dark Angels such as he saw himself.

Tonight was the Monday night the P.I. was to meet Sammy at the same location with a contract to be signed. Sam told him she would bring a check or cash for the first down payment toward his fees. He had intimated he was sure they could come to a better understanding of some sort of reduction of his fee with a smirking gleam.

For her part, she left him with a cock sucking pose and a wink! Before Joe pulled the clutch in and clicked down his left boot to shift the gears, he checked the sound suppressor on his 357 magnum and screwed it tightly… unique custom design. His adrenaline excreted a Feral smell giveth from every pore. Muttering under his breath, "you fkn bastard, I've waited years… dreamed of this evening.

This P.I. had tormented his life and mind so many… too many times, always on the other side of thick glass visiting him at Sacramento county jail; the vile man had even set him up to be beaten up by another one of John Manson's clients.

Joe could and would relish this evening for the rest of his life, no matter how long that would be! 'PBMF' (payback is a mfker!)… Yup!

The time of the meeting was 7:45 pm; she was supposed to meet with the weak-assed ugly Private Investigator Robert. Joe's hired prostitute, Sam, had done her job setting ole Robert up to help him finally get his revenge. But instead of her, it was Joe dressed as her. 'Sam' couldn't be left alive, for she knew too much she was already drugged and disabled in his master suite, doors locked of the motorhome. He'd have to take care of her after finishing the P.I. off. He'd left her alive in case the P.I. didn't show up. He might need her on a follow-up meeting to cage the P.O.S. (piece of shit) again.

Dammit, he said to himself… had to take another 'leak' coffee, and Red Bull's charging through his system, bladder kidneys, too young for prostate issues, right?

At precisely 7:15 pm, Joe sat on his bike watching the blue flashing tracking dot on his Tablets screen heading his way, the GPS device that Sam had placed on the scum bags undercarriage. The P.I. was on his way, just passing Golden 1 Center south, Yes!

One habit that Robert, the P.I., had was that he liked to park his new SUV in the open, away from other vehicles. A distinct advantage for Joe because this guy wasn't being abducted like the two other attorneys. No, this one was going to die tonight.

Joe had remembered at the 3-ring circus kangaroo court set up orchestrated by his three-faced attorney John Manson, an enemy in a cheap suit, wolves disguised as empathetic souls, in the pews sat the P.I. across from the AUSA Prosecutor the practiced semantics, an act that was redundant as the Gavel slammed down, Joe was sentenced to Federal prison for legal marijuana duh sad, but true.

Worse though, the state of California had sentenced him to an additional three years to run consecutively, 'piggybacking,' so when he completed the Federal term, off to San Quentin chained and shackled.

Lucky it turned out to be, uh, no, wasn't a bad thing at all, for it was there in the prison yard that he was reunited with his best friends Mark Feral and Tank Shaw.

'Why wait to exact revenge Joe?' asked Mark. I said, 'well, I've decided that I would get even with all of them if or when I was given a terminal deadline like death was eminent for I fought Malignant Melanoma Cancer, caused by the Sacramento County Jails prescription medications, my vow, oath covenant to myself… I would get even. My list consisted of just seven others who had harmed me in this life, evil culprits I had allowed to get close enough to me to hurt me. The P.I. would be the first kill of many to come… vengeance and retribution will be mine. We already had the two attorneys under wraps. Oh, pleasure would be ours. They would die horrific deaths designed for their phobias, mentally, physically, and spiritually broken. He'd enjoy breaking them down, the best kind of revenge. Yes!

Mark and Tank had lists of people that would also be extinguished. This was a fun time to be alive. I was fortunate to have such trustworthy and ruthlessly loyal brothers for my compadres. Finally, I got lucky in this life. I had won an 'all in' poker game between us three at San Quentin. In the winning pot was a list of our most hated tormentors, the scourge of humanity. Each of our nemesis was aligned. The winner of the pot would get their list of miscreants vanquished first… I won!

The seven insidious unethical, nefariously evil humans would go to the top of the list. On all 3 of our lists, near the very top of the most wanted dead list apex, the zenith was none other than Mark's sister 'Wendi Feral.'

A failed attempt to end her life, then another actually three shots in all, now under guard by US Marshals at NIA… Napa Insane Asylum. Aah being politically correct, now The Napa Hospital for specialized treatments, substance abuse rehabilitation, um, recoveries.

Wendi Feral was the 'Anti-Christ' from our teenage days. She snitched and informed the police of what she knew about our crimes ughhhh, she rolled over on us. She was the Rat that had us locked into juvenile hall for over three years until we were adults, umh, 18 years old.

She had cost us our freedom, chances to work legal jobs, make money have material things, relationships, girlfriends, sex, marriage, children… love. Had estranged us from our families, Wendi was on our minds constantly; she essentially ended our childhood and ruined our lives forever… neither of us three would rest till she was buried in the ground!

-9-

<u>Mark Feral… at Silverthorn's dock on his Houseboat.</u>

The bronze bomber whom I'd picked up from the dance floor with her best friend Becky watching was delectably delicious; I mean genuinely Yummy. What a goddess tasty, savory from all angles, my Jacuzzi jets blasting tirelessly, a cleansing douche of all usable orifices. Being scandalously me, I tried to visit them all. The hot tub was blowing steam bubbles… cocktails, and music, another piece of my type of heaven. Yay! Five hours of blissful synergetic integration, ahh, exploration with a smidgeon of exploitation.

Our bodies melded, marathonish, sexual loving, um, zero inhibitions that neither of us ever wanted to cease experiencing. We were in synch… actually, I liked this ebony-skinned, loving girl who could and should be a 'Keeper!' if I didn't believe in Catch and Release. 😊 *.*

Having tethered my houseboat back at the docks at Jones Valley Resort, I pulled out her card 'what was her name again?' 'Chloe' yes, she was worth a return voyage.

I laughed out loud as I stretched out my sore legs, a combination of my Sea-Doo riding crash on the lake prior to me heading to the dance floor and the flexible sexual positions we'd engaged in. The ladder, umh, the last exercise, was punishingly satisfying.

The look on Becky's face as she eyes glued to us as I strolled out of the lounge with one of her best friends, was utterly priceless. Oh, my first climax was a direct result!

What was even better was watching the shadows on the dock as 'Chloe' and I, arm over arm, walked down the pier; Becky followed us. I still wanted that woman, 'sometimes if you play too hard to get yuh don't get got'… Lol!

In a game of calculations, the hunter may find a more accessible source, prey, but you're left with unneeded lubrication and a swollen clit. That was where Becky's flight ended up the next night. The ladies were going to school down in LA, at UCLA. Their childhood homes were in Redding, California. All graduated from a local high school renowned for its academics, 'U-Prep Highschool.' Man, what I'd give to be sitting next to Chloe and Becky on that flight South; it had to be hella awkward!

Driving back to my cabin, the sun already in blast mode, I pulled my visor down, pushing my fob button, the gates open, rolling into my compound. The dogs greet me with enthusiasm… quick pats and pets, then I duck into the garage up the stairs, hitting the switch on my espresso machine.

I peeled off my clothes and stepped into the shower. I analyzed what I needed to accomplish today, 'Saturday.' For Monday was a day of reckoning. Ensure the animals are fed and check on the two lawyers living in closed coffins in one of my outbuildings.

In preparation for the US Stock Markets opening on Monday, cyber currency trades entered at the open, been making a small fortune on Bitcoin trades…$$$!

'Tank' was being paroled from San Quentin… Joe was going to deal with the P.I. and his 'lucky' whore 'Sam,' but the thought that most exhilarated me was… it was the end of the road finality for my sinister evil bitch sister Wendi who would cease to breathe her last breath on Monday Yup!

Mark's down payment of 25,000 insured the deadly poisonous needle; a Nurse named Danny Spike, appropriately… lol, would inject ole Sis with a hypodermic shot at the Napa hospital. The nurse was eager for the second and last installment of 25,000 when his job was completed; little did the poor dude know that's when he'd cease to breathe.

I must say, um, admit it saddens me that I couldn't be there. I'd so much like to mash her face flat with a sledgehammer first, but oh well. Sister dear and my pathetic parents deserve what they reaped!

<u>-10-</u>

<u>The Nurses at their apartment.</u>

Danny, what's up with you, boy? Or rather, what's not up with you? What's on your mind?

You're somewhere else, has my our-loving already grown old. Danny didn't bother with a retort as his flaccid member fizzled out and shrank back into its thick black mane. After a long spell of silence, a long-lasting pause, he got off the bed they were inside their apartment.

"Nah, I love you, man just have a lot of burdens and demands and various circumstances that negatively affect my bodily functions. Let's have another go at it after my bath!"

"All right, I'll make breakfast; it's a glorious Sunday already. Why don't we rollerblade at Golden Gate Park this afternoon, Danny!"

He turns to him, "yes, um, why not? Hey Peter, I'll yell for you. Can you run a razor over my back again? The hair is prickly," "sure, honey!"

Pete waits till he hears the shower initiate 'harboring toxic memories of past relationships, a weight that never left his scarred heart. He had troubles in his young life. He'd been cheated on like five times in other caustic relationships, and he was only 31 years old.'

Danny had proposed to him five months back, and they had been in a relationship of three years going strong. He was steadfastly committed to Dan but far from naïve. The hardships of life in his tattered fallen world were overwhelming. Both of them had met on the job, nurses at Napa, NIA.

Peter's intuition sucked his stomach in, the painful hurt emotion of deception and betrayal, so now he would break their confidence, step across the proverbial line, and investigate his Fiancé BF. Pete was at a 'crossroads. He entered the intersection' attached in love but again not naïve he inputs his boyfriend's password, iPad logged on. The first search was Danny's debit bank statements. Was he spending money on another love interest?

Pete fell back on the couch, left hand covering his lips 'Wthell' where the hell did $25,000 come from? Peter was incensed, seething; Danny had changed in the last five weeks. Dan had been acting weird. Unfamiliar territory indeed. Damn, where the hell did that money come from?

Danny had put a locking number password sequence on his phone, simple numbers, their birthdays backward, please, he thought Dan yah got to be cleverer than that! Then he sees the text which rattles in his head 'tomorrow, satisfy your contract for the last installment.'

'What the Hell did that mean?' No one just hands you 25K, and it was cash dumbshit Danny had deposited a Red flag to the IRS.

His heart cries out with sorrowful discomfort. The horror of finding him cheating had relented swiftly now. Fear took him down another path direction... confusion reigned.

Pete quickly shuts down the iPad as he hears the pitter-patter of footsteps watching Dan enter the hall, then meander about in their bedroom.

Pete had spent the next few minutes searching spots where they would hide monies or some recreational drugs; under the coffee table taped to the underneath, he found pay dirt. Only two initials W.F. a sticker in red ink, a clear fluid inside the hypodermic needle with the date of Monday, the 24th of June, written on the wrapper, only nine days away. Omg, with a convoluted discombobulated loss of reality, he thinks ponders that there is no such thing as genuine love, trust, or integrity in our lives.

Yeah, we really never know what another person is thinking planning as unpleasant a perspective that was, it's best not to wear blinders. We're alone on this earth; we enter and leave the same way. Alone! It's all B.S. fake; superficial loving words we allow to penetrate our bleak circumstantial existence, ah hope gives us unrealistic comfort. The Sun is shining from above, words were spoken, the vows upon the altar, sanctified, its semantics acts of the manipulating scoundrels that leave you with Lip service. Yuh, no, you're told precisely what you want to hear... always the same bullshit.

Peter brutally had been down the aisle twice before marrying his handsome spouse, consecrating love. He fell hard no-pun, 'In Love' with all that he was, a romantic fool like the song by the 'Doobie Brothers' 'What a fool Believes' Sad!

Hey, like his last ex-hubby had said when caught in bed with his boss ('Peter; Babe, honestly when I told you God wouldn't just bring us together to tear us apart and I love you more today than yesterday, more than anyone or anything I really meant that when I said that Peter?'), this was humanities truth superficial sacrilegious bullshit, ahhhh I meant it when I said it but times have changed nothing lasts forever... huh?

So somberly, with a measure of disconsolation, Pete had figured out the only clear reason for the money and the hypodermic needle, their patient. <u>It had to be 'Wendi Feral' W.F.</u>

<u>Wendi was in a coma under a 24/7 guard, watched over by US Marshals who were always beside the entrance to her room. Never was she left unguarded.</u>

Peter pondered about the decision he'd made after another restless night… he'd slipped a note to one of the Marshals a few days previously. The man himself met him at NIA, and a secret meeting was agreed upon where he betrayed his fiancé lover Danny. Marshal Evans gave a sample of the fluid in the needle to Rico. The Agent in charge… the test had been returned round trip in less than 7 hours. Agent 'Rico Captor' had told him the clear fluid was akin to battery acid. After being injected into Wendi's veins, the solution would burn excruciatingly painfully through Wendi's veins, slowly bursting her heart! Now only a saline solution was in the presumed killer needle, replacing the poison his mate, fiancé, a paid assassin murderer, ugh, with regrets like his mommy had said. 'Echoes reverberating like a superball in his brain Petey, you sure could pick 'em!'

'Yum, that's my salaciously-delicious man,' grinning at me, says Danny as he snatches up a piece of bacon, 'Peter, I love you' Peter plays the game with tainted toxic undertones and says, 'I love you too, Danny' ugh two can play this game he thinks… Sad!

<u>Back in Joe's Motorhome.</u>

Samantha, weak and unsteady, groggily tried to shift her body weight out of the middle of the king-sized bed.

Blurring eyes burning, blinking to focus, the red flashing light showed 7:55 pm; the damn bastard had injected her, that's right, a fuzzy recollection. She was set up after some doggy action. He shot his load, then shot another load out of a needle in her ass cheek.

Little did this guy realize 'Trudy' Samantha had built up a tolerance to barbiturates, hypnotic sedatives, uuhhh opiates of all kinds. She was a junkie, ugh, Veteran drug user. A shot that would knock out the average human only temporarily held her in the subconscious world.'

Joe was a mercilessly harsh and cruel man, not like she was devoid of character flaws, but she knew from the beginning that the situation couldn't end favorably. She'd been paid to set up the P.I. Robert, a heathen of unmeasurable latitudes. This seemed always to be the case. Once Sam became fond of a man, she'd allow gullibility to run rampant, fooling herself that it was a mutual feeling, like who could fall in love with a whore or, for that matter, trust one.

In the end, she was discarded like garbage. Perhaps this would always be her life... frowning into the ceiling mirrors. Her 25-year-old face peered back at her looking 41 years old... wow.

Samantha hopped up to check on her escape taking wobbly steps to the motorhome's door locked deadbolt keyed close. Finding a window that a regular-sized person could never fit through in a pop-out, she crawled out of the motorhome onto the ground with her purse and a set of keys she'd taken from a drawer, holding a Red Bull. Still, under the influence of the narcotics that Joe had injected into her, normal humans would be comatose, not moving with the drugs Joe had injected into her body. Sam knew she was lucky, but now she was vehemently enraged, seething with anger, and Sammy wasn't a person to take lightly. She was a protagonist who had learned in her short life either fight or... be eaten ah cannibalized, and she wasn't on the menu 2nite, Nope!

His miscalculation would bite his ass, wondering what the prick was up to. She'd find out if it <u>killed her</u> she let down the trailer gate only one bike remained inside. Yeah, he was on the other identical KTM 2019 model, knowing just where he was. Ugh!

Sam quickly put on her biker attire, heart beating fast, perspiration soaking her skin. She was on the opposite trajectory… Than what this devious prick thought, adrenalin rushing shoved the barbiturates from her epidermis. Sammy knew exactly where she was heading, going to crash the freakin Bastards plan! ☹ .

<u>Joe waited anxiously, feeling a sense of euphoria a dream cum true.</u>

Joe sat on his KTM 2019 under an awning with the restaurant Chili's in the foreground. The GPS tracker showed the P.I. was stopped like seven miles away. Why?
The meeting was called for 7:45 pm, and it was now 7:57 pm… what the fk! Using Sam's Tracfone, he texts, 'Hey are you coming?' three minutes later, 'yes, in a traffic jam, some fool hit a bus. Be there as soon as possible, Samantha; I can't wait to see you, sweetie.'
'Samantha, sweetie, huh, he mused. Yes, he'd miss that young bitch, yep… she was a fun one!'

Sammy shifts her crotch rocket KTM down into 5th gear as her exit is but 1/4 mile up the highway. Joe was old enough to be her father, although she was super fond of him, unlike many of her other stinky 'Johns'… Tricks. She'd told him she was barely 19 years old. It seems men wanted the younger girls the most… huh?

Sadly, he was a deceitful liar like all men. Now she's been missing for five days, and nights her pimp would beat her silly when he got his hands on her… what a fricken disaster. She'd fallen under Joe's web of lies like he'd take care of her, right sure thing, dude.

She was such a lousy judge of character; her mother's words were ringing in her head, always finding the worst crowd this continued to be her. Sure, she'd heard it 1000 times growing up; she was a good kid, 'good shit,' her dad would say, 'but Samantha, you better lose your demons, or I will disown your ass.' Why regress into remembrances, reasons for her to prostitute herself, why regret the past mistakes? She was the prototypical, stereotypical weak-minded person who should have never tried 'Smack or heroin' once addicted. She had to support her heroin habit, the same ole story heard and told by many of the drug-addicted whores she hung around with, humiliating truths.

Same old same old, then tattooed Joe told her he'd save her, like many other clients, 'Johns' had said over the years he had her favorite drugs seemed to be wealthy and paid her well, all she had to do was help him set up this guy Private Investigator named, Robert.

Replaying Joe's words laughing, he'd said it was just going to be a payback, nothing more; no one was going to get hurt. Yeah, sure, dude, you're a liar, Joe!

'Samantha Timmons,' she said to herself, you've been played-used again, as she parks out of view behind a delivery truck… she was supposed to meet the P.I. tonight.

Kickstand down… takes her backpack off and rummages through the stuff till she finds the camera he'd given her to use to follow him, take pictures and track the P.I.

He gave her a Canon camera with EF 100-600 f/4 zoom lenses with an easy attachment lens for night vision. It had to be worth like $5000 easily; she was going to keep the camera to pawn later, already decided, done deal.

The fool-ass P.I. was an easy target, just like Joe told her Sam scans the shopping center with Chili's in the foreground. Oops, there he was as she spins the 'zoom,' the asshole was dressed like her. His lean body was 5 inches taller, though, but not much of a difference at night while he sat on the bike.

She clicks off a quick seven pictures and checks her wristwatch, man. The dude was 'way late' 8:05 pm… with the camera in hand. She ventures across the parking lot, looking for Robert's blue SUV.

How many times has she said it? she needs to find the strength to escape this life firmly fixated on the man via a camera lens and needs to avoid the tendency to trust men now in trouble again, always immersed in chaos, was she an adrenalin junkie also or just doomed? Fk!

She watches Joe lift his black smoke visor through the camera's lens, leaving his helmet on, he slips a Camel non-filter cigarette to his thin lips; she'd joked with him nicotine would kill him, he'd say 'nope' he'd die young most likely in a gun battle!

Clicks away on the Canon muses. Well, if not for your nicotine habit, I wouldn't have your face-framed pictures ready to print and download.

He takes a long drag … exhales; he is not a handsome man GQ look but a ruggedly macho, good-looking, confident guy with sharp features and piercing bluish eyes bright to a haze of paleness. His body was taut, not five pounds of excess weight. Why did I like this guy so much, geez? He'd paid her $500.00 for each meeting with the P.I. to lure him in and more money for following and taking pictures of his family and his mistress.

Robert the P.I. was vulture ugly. I mean nauseatingly, so when she looked at him, her nipples shrank… repulsive was a kind adjective for his appearance.

Joe had told her the story of how the guy betrayed him, and all she was supposed to do was allow him to seduce her… giggled. Sheesh, that would be easy, him married with a horde of kids.

The plan was for Joe to take pictures with the camera she now held, then print them out and send them to his unlucky, trusting wife, who was entirely in the dark, no doubt.

Gosh, I wonder how this will affect the poor children, anyways Joe was going to bombard all social media and even post pictures of Robert screwing me at a hotel on their… the wife's Facebook homepage. He'd laugh then say, 'payback is a mfker,' which was one of his favorite sayings.

Tonight was to be the evening that I'd let the guy P.I. take me to Motel 6, adjoining rooms, as Joe would pop through the man-door I'd leave unlocked, and he'd take the compromising pictures. But now she realized that was never his plan, 'Never' as she watched the blue Caddy Escalade SUV slink into the parking lot, always parking away from other vehicles.

Joe flicks the cigarette away, coughs takes a short breath, checks the bulge with the silencer attached, and pats the weapon with a grinning smirk, exhilaration exuded 357 mag.

He slips down the face shield as his resting heart rate only increases slightly. This was finally going to happen all these years, months, days, and miserable nights of a torturous serpentine hell, tossing and spinning, turning on his hard mattress in San Quentin. He was going to get even with this asshole, finally.

Life's agony behind the stone walls, bars, and cells that filled him with anguish, the hate-filled P.I. hadn't any idea that the last time he raged, screaming at him through the thick glass of the visiting room at Sacramento County Jail would come back to haunt him Kill him, what were his last words? How could I forget them *('I bet that you would kick my ass if you could get through this glass?')* His ugly distorted fat face was correct.

His Fate was settled… at that very millisecond in time, I'd vowed to get even with him. He was on my list for retribution; dreamingly, I fantasized imagining each of my tormentors, demise… tonight was merely his turn.

My partner, bro Mark had already sequestered two others on my list smiling, the attorneys who awaited physical and mental agony not to die too fast, elongated misery, like they put me through… he was in charge now. Joe would decide when it was time to end their pain and his ecstasy umh, all good things must come to an end, lol.

Left foot clicks the KTM 1290 into gear. Joe slowly glides towards the P.I. flashing the bike's lights. The raunchy P.I. was once again behind glass, this time tinted and being lowered open like… magic, yup!

Slides the motorcycle close to the driver's window as the smiling ghoul's teeth showed… Joe deliberately kicks both his feet off the bike, straddling the bike, left hand removed the gun in his right hand and slowly lifts the smoke visor; 'You fuck Hey there!' he sees ole Robert suddenly recognize his face, which was grinning hugely the guy opened his mouth to scream as Joe fired three shells point blank into the P.I.'s now mangled countenance, brain matter sprayed with other body fluids over the leather interior.

On video mode, Sammy couldn't comprehend what she was filming. No way, Joe murdered the dude. Oh, fk me then; like a Hawk with a 7th sense, his helmet turned swiveled, looking directly at her. For a split-second, a stall he stalled, frozen in shock.

Oh, shit, wtf? As he sees her tuck the camera away, his double they'd been riding around Sacramento even made a trip to Tahoe the damn girl could ride; how was she here?

Ugh, he reaches back in his leather pouch to retrieve the warm pistol, then sees a Sheriff's car turning into the lot. He watches her awestruck stunning skill, the KTM on one freaking wheel like a stunt rider. Ain't no way he was catching that girl. Sammy realizes her bad mistake instantly. Oh no, she drops the bike down, now on two wheels. As the lights and siren simultaneously sputter forth, the chase was on. Could he have scripted a worse ending?

Joe began to sweat, knowing she was the missing cog. She knew way too much and had been staying with him in his motorhome at the KOA for five days.

Damn, thinking back at the camera that she had focused upon him revealing all, why would she continue to 'run' from the Sheriff? Why, when she had all the proof she needed and besides that, she was an eyewitness? Sam obviously knew I conned her falsely into collaborating with me for monies. Hell, she has the pictures. She knows the story of the P.I. damn, why try and to escape the cops? She's got me nailed on murder! He didn't get it; why didn't she just stop the bike safely and pull it to the side of the road? She would then be considered a heroine or hero.

Joe kept pace from afar nine minutes into the chase. He watched as three cop cars joined in, thinking, where were the helicopters at? It's only a matter of time. A mixture of convoluted analysis spun past his brain; could he make it back to the motorhome in time? Umh, Nah, not worth the risk! Sammy was even more confused than Joe, illogically assessing the situation from a tainted perspective.

had issued a violation against her, she'd absconded, busted again for solicitation for prostitution five counts… now conspiracy to commit murder… actual murder life in prison.

Sammy wasn't thinking clearly, only reacting. Having the camera in her side-saddle takes the parallel side road next to the I-5 Hwy, a paved 2-lane road. The motor wounding out howling hits 6th gear at 85 mph, then sways, straddling into a turn at 105 mph. This bike could scream! While her vocal cords were doing just that.

-11-

<u>Tank Shaw, inside of San Quentin.</u>

Earlier in the day, the fog had already lost its skirmish with the winning nuclear reactor in the sky over Marin county.

For some unknown reason, the prison's constant rotting aroma, the redolence of staleness, and the musty scent that felt like you couldn't wash it off had morphed. The ambiance around me seemed to be disinfected, umh, a fresher fragrance of possible euphoria… as the guard escorted him to the same room he'd been in several times before.

In the same room his bro Mark and Joe were enlightened within, the Kangaroo laden, Weasel-based board members, you know the types… glasses either high up on the ridge of their nose cartilage or hanging low condescendingly as they stared at the stench-burdened inmate.

The Parole board, what a farce, superficial pre-orchestrated jargon typically a preposterous waste of oxygen-preordained terminology ending with the inmate being interviewed who at the end stand's with bowed head before the executioners… with the hope of an altered future, perhaps a 3rd chance at life. Nah, like a premenopausal woman of 47 years old ain't no recourse no fight to be had menopause didn't cease 'pause' Nope!

This was life behind the San Quentin façade, the inmate population like a mantra we all could repeat the words as the

Parole board exits the razor-wired gates. <u>'Yuh got nothing coming'</u> and 'see yah in another five years' like duh!

Tank's apathy and mental attitude weren't from any form of a manifestation or embodiment, not a spiritual perception of nascent overtones. He need not propagate or disseminate um... broadcast a single phrase as he inconspicuously sat boldly upright in an uncomfortable chair facing his prompt and punctual freedom... The disposition of enlightenment was a foregone conclusion. He'd be a free man in less than five weeks. Yep!

Money is the vice of the human majority, moral depravity, and corruption of habitual offenders. Yet some Parole Officers were struck with this same trait; a select few of the board was not unlike the criminal masses within the prison systems, and bribery was effective.

<u>The FBI on Watch.</u>

Agent Lori Parks sat side-by-side with Agents Avery 'tech wizard' and Baker watching the proceedings via close circuit cameras. Lori tapped the table with her pen, "ok, guys, the target will be released. We need him to lead us to his Rabbit hole... lair, den.

We cannot lose sight of where he travels and need to know whom he communicates with. It's all on us; he is the 'key.' Rico Captor will hang us up by our toes if he escapes us. Is that clear?"

Agent Avery asks, "so how do we inject the micro-chip into this 'Tank' guy's skin, Lori?"

Agent Tom Baker lifts his left palm up. "Well, all inmates have to be medically cleared before they're released," he chuckles, "so why don't we get you 'Bill' inside the...." "Oh no, Tom, I see where you're going with this. No way" "umh, hold on, guys, am I missing something?"

Lori sees Tom's wry smirk; Tom releases a smug sideways glance swinging his dimples at the both of them, "So I wonder what is on the list of the procedures that an inmate is mandated to have ah I know they will undergo a physical before being paroled what it actually entails let's get a list of exactly what tests they give the inmate, surely there is a standard procedure,

STD's, etc. Maybe we can have the chip injected under his skin at that time?"

"Tom, that's brilliant," Lori spins on Agent Bill Avery, "no nope…I know what you're thinking. Not going to do it, Lori. If anything, let's have the doctor place the micro-chip into 'Tank's' arm or glutes." She nods. "Okay, please get me the standard release procedures at San Quentin, and I can see if there is a way to stealthily inject him, like maybe a Tuberculosis test," said lead agent Lori Parks.

She adds, "I must say a dermal tracker just under his skin would be optimal, much better than us following him from a distance or placing a GPS chip on his vehicle.

At this juncture, we haven't a clue as to how he will travel from 'Quentin,' let me run this past, Rico."

"The Tank guy in his 30s probably hasn't had many physicals, although I read that every inmate gets a total go over physically when admitted into prison."

"Yeah, Avery, you're the tech agent making the big bucks. You ought to play doctor and inject Tank." Lori holds both palms up, stop sign, "we'll see; maybe Rico has a Fed Doctor who can help us out; let's get out of this prison."

The three agents drove to the prison to visualize the Parole hearing from a 2-way window because they'd received a tip that the fix was in and Tank would be released shortly on Parole. Agent Lori Parks was again reading a report on her iPad that 'Mark Feral' had left his calling card again at the Woodson Bridge Park off Hwy 70 near Chico, or thereabouts!

<u>Wendi.</u>

****

<u>Wendi and Rico once again.</u>

I felt tired. I know how the heck could that be as I lay flat on my back, unmoving, not burning any calories, uh, zero exercises. Yet, I felt like yawning… let me plead guilty to being emotionally exhausted, uhm, speaking only for myself because that's all any of us humans can genuinely do. I am plumb, worn out.

I don't know, but I have been around plenty of manipulative, controlling individuals that will have you doing their bidding as if it's something you wanted to do all along… Oh my god, what am I thinking? Geez, this isn't even relevant. Where did that nonsense come from? No, what did I want to analyze? Am I competent to trust my analytical reasoning? Confused, discombobulated to the max, Sick! 😖 .

I should be energized, for today is a big, humongous day for me; Dr. Hawkins will be here with mom and dad, David, my husband's voice, and maybe… even my delicious male friend Agent Rico Captor. I'm still flummoxed over my missing absolute best and dearest friend in the world, Sandi. Finally, thankfully I'm off life support machines hope does permeate my bloodstream, and oxygen like a Hi-Fi fidelity sound is carried to all the non-working extremities engaged in physical and mental combat with a spiritual battle waged every waking minute. Many times not sure if I am awake, definitely not in the eyes of society. Today is for optimism, not a defeatist attitude, yet afraid and anxious apprehension engulfs me… amid today's crucial procedures. I was going to be tested to see if I was cogent inside my docile body… an attempt to communicate with me via MRI brain scans. Wouldn't anyone of you feel trepidation and be worried and weary?

Yes, back to what I said earlier, I'm tired and frustrated with not knowing what I even look like all the time. I feel faint-hearted, not on the precipice of giving up panicky perchance, because it seems apparent there's no solution in sight, no hope for victory heck, I cannot even blink an eye or wag a finger. Success would be for me just to see again. That would be a great start.

It must be about 7:15 am on Monday because, like clockwork, one of the US Marshals let in a trustee, a maintenance guy who, long ago, received a waiver from Director Firm and Agent Rico Captor… none other than the Infamous 'Mr. Jax Foul' Yep!

In living HD color, not to me. He's my friend, albeit on a precariously brittle limb. At the start of our relationship, his love for his animals, primarily Scooby and his other Chows, helped solidify our bond. In their first years in NIA, he was scrutinized at every turn under strict eyes of supervision. Still, like everything in our lives, routines, and habits, the drab monotony germinates a form of complacency. No worries, uniformity now; Jax tells me the guards don't even pat him down nor check his tool bag or box.

Jax is a complicated man who was arrested and committed to this mental institution, NIA Napa Insane Asylum, because of the help of yours truly… me, and the FBI.

It's way too irksome, tiresome a long story to explain or understand how Jax was able to roam about the grounds of this prison and medical center. Suffice it to say he was a significant asset to the FBI military hero Army Ranger, this lent some leniency, and after a while, Jax became a Trustee working inside of NIA.

He was convicted of kidnapping children and then exonerated, proven to suffer from too many mental disorders to count. I can't even pretend to remember a 3rd of them. He didn't have to manipulate or fake his insanity plea. Nope suffered from significant bouts of PTSD. He was tortured in the desert of Iraq for 23 nights and days, with five bullet holes, vicious, brutal scars from his ears to his throat, and testicles smashed in a vice-grip and cut off. Jax has been through hell for the USA and still resides within. At least he receives all the necessary medication, hormones, and replacement injections.

As he always did, Jax had a song lined up for me to listen to! I feel him thank the powers to be as he carefully and delicately pushes his earbuds into my ears.

The song today? he says, "Wendi, this is a special song for you, an easy selection, yah know" as he whispers a little closer, I feel him lean on my gurney, 'I love yuh, Wendi.'

"Please listen to every word 'Paradise' is the song's name, and artist 'Coldplay' it's for you!"

I wanted to say thanks and hug him. It was a fantastic song then, as if he read my mind, pushed replay, and I was in 'paradise' once again lost, serenely in music.

Like the movie 'Groundhog Day,' his soliloquy monologue is as if only speaking to himself this time though his words were different, the pace, cadence, and urgency of his words, intonations of the rise and fall of the pitch in his voice. Shocking words energized me like a chanting impudent, impertinent teenager not accustomed to his deluge of spontaneous vigilance and him being so hyper. Jax's voice wasn't the calm delivery I'd become accustomed to... His following statement overwhelmed my being "Wendi, I'm going to get you out of here. You're in grave perilous danger." Of course, I didn't show a care in my world, only listened as he explained a bizarre scheme, which I could only try to paraphrase and assimilate within my dormant body... and suddenly, my wired mind and brain alert. Emboldening Jax was what was told to him by another inmate gangster who belonged to the Sinaloa Cartel.

There had been a bounty on her head... or call it a reward for her safe capture, delivery was now five million in cyber currency to whoever could hand her over.

If I could call bullshit or even laugh, the following words were proof of Jax's infirmity "The Feds arrested an imposter, a look-alike double El Chapo was not in the U.S. government's custody nope! El Chapo was living the 'high life' with a dozen plastic surgical operations, he didn't need tunnels to escape into, and out of he had a harem of young ladies, lived right in the open in Mexico City, and owned a restaurant downtown.

The mega Mafia leader now relaxed, kicking his pudgy toes in the warm sand while he endured massages and still had a reward out on the criminal newswires for me. They were still coming for me?

Wendi Feral, the animal seer, would be delivered unharmed preposterous, huh? Then Jax pinched my hand. Wow, the poor man was in a desperate delusional state, needing stronger medication!

Then Jax went even more animated, exalted with the divine supernatural intensity... he explained to my ear lobe that this entire complex 'NIA' isn't what it appears, nope it's a recruiting and training institution, a facility for the largest Militia on American soil.

Jax was a nut, lunatic, and scary to be him for sure! Lucky for me, I needn't acknowledge him and never changed my expression, comatose. He soldiered on 'Attorney Terrance Hallinan' is the CEO here 'Wendi, you're the prized catch. Can you imagine the missions they will send you on with me? Once you regain consciousness and intellectual cognizance, you will be working. Wendi, ugh, your counterpart alter-ego Sunshine and I have been actively...' "Excuse me, Mr. Foul Jax, your time is up," said the U.S. Marshal. I feel his lips touch my forehead, then a whisper I'll be coming for you, Wendi, don't you worry!

Whoa, now I thought without any options, I lay still on the outside inside the human machine I was, raging on overdrive, or auto drive please, I thought I'd say keep Jax Foul away from me. Help!

Rico Captor.

The sleeping pills had lost the battle, even enhanced with a triple shot of whiskey.

Rico sat with his back against the wall in the shower, mixed emotions, wrongs, decisions maybe, uncertainty weighed down with moral dilemmas. He thought back to when he was at the Betty Ford Foundation fighting his addiction to pain medication, now again taking sleeping pills... he had to stop and Get a Grip.

Wendi was preoccupied, and so was her immediate family. He was the only person privy, aware of what was going to occur, orchestrated with precision. Hopefully, that is... asking his conscious repeatedly... was this fair to Wendi's family?

He lets the water go cold, oblivious to the temperature change, lost in thought. Was he being fair and forthright... absolutely not! This was going to be complicated. Wendi's family trusted him. Should he keep them in the dark? Was he being honest with her mother, father, and husband? Integrity-based hum... That answer would definitely be NO! Resoundingly so.

Rico's strategy was necessary for the sake of a natural reaction by Wendi's family to sell the act to curious onlookers without qualms, a believable show of emotions. The details were passed to him by Peter, the head nurse on the floor Wendi was housed on. Uh, without question, Mark Feral would scrutinize the male Nurse Spike, his paid assassin, and also check out the killer's pocket camera, which would be vividly recording all. Nurse Danny Spike would be allowed to inject the hypodermic needle into Wendi's body, expecting her untimely death. This was exactly what her brother would witness, hear the authentic suffering. Dr. Hawkins was the lead actor in the final episode filmed for Mark Feral's pleasure and closure to his sister's life.

Rico suddenly stands, turning the faucets off. I'm going to kill that bastard. This has gone way past being personal, 'no more jail for you, you evil 'son of a bitch,'… no wrong Mark was the son of the devil!'

Peter and Danny at their apartment.

A rare nervous breakfast indeed, Peter's heart and mind convoluted with feelings of tension, he foresaw turbulent times ahead.

Danny was calmly filling his dish with cheesy scrambled eggs, crisp bacon, and Blackberry jam on a thick piece of raisin toast silence wasn't their way. Instead, they were usually animated and filled with energy like enthused lovers and soulmates.

The table was always a time for sharing ideas, dreams, plans for the future, and what they would do together on their days off.

Today was Sunday, and an ominous dark cloud hovered over the breakfast table, the air of discomfort and upcoming hardships impossible to reconcile.

Peter said to himself, hey, it wasn't too late to give back the $25,000. In fact, Danny didn't have to stick the needle into 'Wendi Feral' at all. It wasn't too late to turn around.

With that thought emphasized, Peter ushered in a wave of strength-courage and rational wisdom. He tries to communicate with his fiancé, "hey babe, our love is steadfast. We can get through anything and everything in this world and destroy anything holding us back that's in our path. No obstacles are too large or cumbersome for us to scale or maneuver around." His partner puts down his mug of Black tea, brows raised.

"What are you talking about, Petey? Why the riddles? What obstacles? you're acting so weird, dude." "Dan, don't try to turn my words around. It's not me acting so different and strange; what's wrong with you? It's like you're a different person."

"Pete is all of this because I couldn't get a hard-on with you this morning, really, please!...." "Stop it, this isn't about our sex life, which is fab like we have said many times, sex cure's nothing in a relationship... bliss, satiated for an hour or 3 in a 24-hour period. What about the rest of the hours of the day?" "Fk spit it out, Pete, man, just say what you mean. Listen, guy, ahh... hey, I'm just preoccupied, is all."

He raises his fingers to his forehead, rubbing; Pete wiggles his engagement ring, a gem, a solitaire diamond. Pete frowns, staring wistfully at Dan "life isn't easy. We're not promised a trouble-free life or happiness. We will face adversities, but holding hands, Dan, we can dissolve all doubts, fears will dwindle, and we'll find a sense of peace as our Love grows." "Geez, pal, now you're a freaking poet; what's going on with you?"

"Dan, as long as our principles remain true and integrity based...." "What the fk, dude? I'm not fkn marrying a preacher if I wanted to go to church, I'd go today; you've become a poet nope... don't like this side of you, Petey!"

He slides the chair back abruptly. "I'm going out for a run; the Raspberry toast was good, by the way!" "you asshole, it was Blackberry Jam," yelled Pete. "Where'd you get the money for my ring and the box seats last week at Oracle park when we watched the Giants play the Dodgers? That must have cost a fortune?"

Pete gets up and follows him into the bedroom, watching Dan as he ties his running shoes in an agitated hurry, "what... why are you following me like a sick puppy?"

"We'll be married in less than five weeks, talk to me, Danny, please. What's going on? You know, I've been thinking we should combine our accounts jointly...." Like a whirlwind, Danny spins past him down the hall with a backpack. Pete follows quickly, and then Dan shoves Petey right over their loveseat.

With horror and confusion, Pete pulls himself up onto his hands and knees as the front door reverberates, slammed shut!

In a fetal position holding, squeezing a throw pillow between his legs, sobbing, phone in his hand mommy, mom "Pete, what's wrong? What's happening? Are you all right?" He shakes his head and stares at the phone. In the midst of all his difficulties, his mother asks, "are you all right" 'like duh' 'Mom' he screams, "do I sound just fine and dandy, huh? That's the problem with us… you don't even know me." Click, Crying even harder, he ignores his mother's frantic rings back and crawls over to the tub, his image of snot dripping and his red-streaked eyes, affirmation of a weak man.

The safest place for him was death. He twisted off the ring, suicide of which in his 31 years he attempted two other times, both failed. Lost betrayed love-marriages… fear of acceptance as a teenager, this time would be different the third time will be the charm… true-that.

-12-

<u>Mark at his cabin in Shasta County.</u>

Checking the pre-opening of the Stock Market with his large monitors tuned in to CNBC, his bank of computers-powered up trading platforms, Trade Station algorithms graphs and charts interactively flashing across the screens stock market open at 6:30 am on the West Coast, of course, 9:30 am New York time, it was 5:55 am. I was still breaking down moving averages… Stochastics, Bollinger bands, technical analysis with the alignment of fundamental research, all the competition of the 'free market.' Such was the inherent joke, for I was aware of the indirect manipulations and not-so-subtle insider trading. Oh, how I could go on for hours about the inner nuances and intricate complexities of illegal tips that led to millions of dollars of profit; as always in this life, it is not what we know, it's whom we know, Yeah!

Mark hears a helicopter flying low, way too low at tree level. Something was wrong. He shot out of the rolling chair and rushed through a sliding glass door onto the wraparound deck.

Then a high-pitched alarm from the gate's cameras, he had motion detector cameras attached to tree limbs. He rushes to his office, panicking a bit, peering out the window as if the sun was just now trying to take control of the morning.

Really it felt or seemed I was under siege, attack... then another chopper in the air, and oh shit... at my gate was a Sheriff Deputy. A fleet of vehicles was out on Dry Creek road up at the entrance of my property.

I pushed the intercom switch... peering at the perimeter cameras, I said... "morning, what's going on?" "Sorry to bother you, sir, this early, but there is a fire raging up over Backbone Mountain. We're going to have to have all residents in the Jones Valley area evacuated." Mark frowns in the agony of disbelief, shaking his noggin... Why me?

"I'm sorry, sir...." "Seriously, are you kidding me, Officer?" I responded somewhat rhetorically as Firetrucks and Cal Fire drove by on my screens; before waiting for his reply, I said, "ok, all right!" He responded, " unfortunately, sir, the wind currents are blowing in this direction southwest." "Thanks; I'll be packing a few supplies. Load my animals up and leave immediately."

I started packing up for a temporary leave of absence fires in Northern California were the norm, not the exception. Every year we had our assortments of raging firestorms.

Unlike earthquakes that hadn't any warnings, at least a forest fire was similar to a hurricane which you could watch for days predicting the destruction the fire would cause. Mother Nature's wind currents were in total control... fire could destroy everything in its path.

Dammit, what the hell was I going to do with the two attorneys in closed caskets, uh, coffins? By now, they'd be super ripe excrement stinking feces and urine heck. Did I forget to feed them? Aah, oh well, too bad now faced with a debilitating quandary, I could have a stream of CDF Firefighting teams on my property.

On the positive, most of my buildings couldn't burn all steel fabrication. Being a fugitive from justice, the paranoia systemically is inbred within, reeking from my pores, thoughts of conspiracies analyzing all too much... stay calm, Mark!

My mind tries to wrap around this as if I needed assurance that this wasn't a tactical Swat team strategy or a proper plan to disarm me, mentally and physically driving out the gate in a hurry to flee a fictional fire. Nope, smoke filled my nostrils.

I'm compromised; my mind aligned with analysis allows a concession that leads to the fact that this wasn't a game, ugh, realizing now that the sun's rise was also battling the haze, thick soot smoke, a real fire!

I clicked in a couple of planned trades for the opening bell and then dressed for a typical morning. I walk about my home domicile, 'naked as a jaybird,' and always wondered where that saying came from, left it at wondering. Jumping, taking three stairs at a time, I opened my floor-to-ceiling safe vault and started loading weapons inside with all my valuables. I had three such safes on the property, 5'x9' tall in the ground.

I had another two that were undetectable, all hard rubber, no steel for metal detectors, couldn't find them underground. You can't be too careful. The surround sound was blasting off warnings throughout the house.

The updating scanners spouted off updates from the fire officials Law-Enforcement... by the time I loaded in my cats, my five dogs caged in a trailer, visibility was barely 50ft in the clear. Fast like, I went to one of my metal buildings... the automatic roll-up door engaged, then rushed to my super-duty cargo van and opened it to load necessities. Next, I jumped onto my forklift and maneuvered the coffins inside with deft ease, with black tarps covering them.

Quickly put the additional weapons into the vault attached to the concrete slab, 'fire-proof guaranteed,' thinking we might just test that theory out.

In less than 35 minutes, I drove over the cattle guard and through my gates and saw helmeted men and women standing directing what little traffic there was, primarily firefighters and a few box trucks that had hauled inmate crews and guards to battle the flames.

There were vehicles strung along the pavement and trucks parked on the narrow road. The scattered residents were stressed out trying to gather their precious belongings. It was chaotic at worse. Needless to say, the street I lived on… 'Dry Creek Road' was busy.

Living in Northern California, fires were part of life. Then I saw her, ah yeah, I'm sick, gosh I must confess being locked up in Quentin for so long, I lusted for all attractive women, kind of disarming as a green-eyed goddess slipped her helmet inside my passenger window. Her reddish auburn hair was breaking loose about her shoulders… um, Yum!

Women in uniform definitely a turn-on, she said in an all-business tone, matter factually, 'make a right and take Bear Mountain Road out. Dry Creek Road is closed out towards Highway 299.'

I said, "hey, this isn't the place for you. Why don't you hop in? Let's get some breakfast!"

A cheek-popping toothful grin, "must say your original but try to keep it in your pants, Mr." She laughed, "I'm newly married!"

I nodded and pushed the window button to go back up and left her these words under my breath, albeit 'I'll try back in five years then' snickered and cackled marriage equals boredom and monotony to settle for one piece of ass, everlasting punishment, hell.

The traffic was now bumper-to-bumper well could have guessed a Turtle's crawl toward the I-5 freeway. This gave me time to reflect on this eventful Monday.

The insider trades on the cyber currency's market are in place… bitcoins valuations might drop up to 15% in about an hour. China, one of the largest markets in Bitcoins, would announce new restrictions in trading all cyber currencies; yes, volatility, my friend.

The ascension to nearly $20,000 for a single Bitcoin from under $5500 in mere months, whoa definite money maker put in a market sell limit order for "17,500, then after the 'fill' I 'shorted' another large lot taking advantage of the precipitous steep drop a 'Bit' complicated pun intended for non-experienced financial market technicians,

I chuckled at my funny, twisted self.

Nice now that trading can be done on my iPhone, all real-time trading in the market.

Finally, on Hwy I-5, I turned southbound, parked in the now-closed K-Mart parking lot, and would get breakfast at my favorite place, BBD… Black Bear diner.

Didn't give a damn about the human cargo in coffins in the back of my van, uh if they were alive or dead, that was Joe's game, 'all for one and one for all' since childhood Tank, Joe, and I have been like the three amigos.

We would die for one another. We made pacts to take revenge against the humans that wrecked our lives, a poker match that Joe had won.

His winning hand resulted in his list of enemies being the first to be vanquished.

Joe's vengeance, retaliation for what had been inflicted upon him, the P.I. would feel for a millisecond his wrath, Joe's coffin-bound attorneys would see good old Joe later tonight!

This would undoubtedly appease him to reduce and eliminate the number of scumbags in this world. I had a shortlist for extinction, one of which was a unanimous choice, sister 'Wendi Feral.' She was also on the top of Tank's and Joe's most hated death wishes.

Later today, I looked forward to hearing that she was erased from the list. My other two were the annoying agent 'Rico Captor' and the Director of FBI for Northern California Tanya Firm.'

Sitting at the diner reflecting, today's life was a touch precarious, but the rainbow and sunshine beyond the smoke hampered the silver lining that was breaking through. It was going to be a glorious day indeed as I spy my favorite 'sexy, drop-dead gorgeous server' Yum.

I sat in my fav booth, and she approached, "hey, there you are… are you escaping the fire?" her blonde hair swirled around. The place was packed with CDF firefighters checking blonde out as she bent over to pick up a fallen menu… obviously a bottle blonde proof in the pudding, most likely protruding from her G-string, guessed a light brown runway strip. Lord knows I wanted to Jet down on that landing strip.

"Yah want your regular Mark?" "Sure, but for dessert" "I don't have time to flirt today, stud. I am slammed in the weeds," she said with a wink and a lipped subtle air kiss, "but come in when it's not so freakin crazy, k?" I exposed my left dimple divot revealing delight in our ongoing pleasurable fluidity Amorously with serious intent on my part. I would nail this bitch sooner rather than later as her tight rump swayed and wiggled away with an astonishing hypnotic blend prick tease! I thought back to dancing the other night at the Silverthorn Resort, the fun of the chase, then the conquest. Becky, damn, I wanted that girl hotter than molten lava, but she played herself right out of my bed, yep, although the black beauty was a fun, great pinch hitter! Delish! Wonder how many times good ole' Becky had flicked her engorged clit thinking of me lol… yuh think! ☺ .

Invasion shit daydream done, gone as a uniformed dude says, "sir, do you mind if we join you?" three firefighters stood by my booth. I spied a seat at the counter, waved my hand over the table, 'have it,' and jogged over to the last seat in the restaurant line of would-be eaters at the door, hell it was like they were giving away free food. Well, of course, the firefighters CDF were being given a discount, I assumed.

Jax at NIA.

Jax had been given a reduced sentence because of the positive publicity for his fight against the child porn industry and his illness related to his two tours of duty for the US military. He was psychologically delusional with severe PTSD symptoms. He was indeed a very sick man, not a defendant that was malingering. After the physical torture he'd endured during war… went mainstream, including pictures of his deformities and missing appendages, his Testicles crushed in a vice and plucked off, no one could argue that Jax deserved a break. The overwhelming consensus of the world's Dictators,

Monarchs, Oligarchs, Presidents, and even the Queen of England had stood up and voiced praise for Jax and his plight and protested his 15-year sentence locked incarcerated in NIA, Napa Insane Asylum.

Jax Foul's name was synonymous with the word 'Hero.' Even world-renowned authors clamored for his attention, undoubtedly a New York Times Bestseller with all his notoriety. All that was needed was for the novel to be published.

Much of the time he spent in Napa was of his own accord, being a free man years before, meaning that he could leave at any time with a simple application for release.

This, in and by itself, proved what others had mumbled under their noses for a while. Many of the staff Psychologists thought Jax was surely insane, albeit probably not criminally insane. They came to the same conclusion why would he remain in NIA unless he was mentally challenged? Lucky for him, seven years into his sentence back in Federal Court, Sacramento… President Obama had pardoned him.

Jax was given complete exoneration and acquittal with only one mandate that he remains in treatment programs… aftercare counseling. A renowned Forensic Psychologist and head of the Psych ward was to supervise his future recovery. Her name was Dr. Liz Honcho.

It was a mixed bag, like always, uhm, human nature. Many of the world's citizens were outraged by Jax's lenient sentence. Hell, he was guilty of kidnapping 18 children saving the 18th and 19th child… guilty. No question never denied his culpability.

Jax was in a war with the Cuban mafia, who ordered the kidnappings of the children; in retaliation, Jax went on a killing spree attacking this organization's predators, eliminating this faction's soldiers in the double digits. Some or most of the spectators at Jax's final sentencing couldn't restrain their tears and emotions. Not a dry eye could be found in the courtroom. Even the constantly stoic Honorable Judge Cynthia M. Moore had wet eyelids. The Federal Judge had several times adjourned the preceding to blow her nose. Adjudication and passing judgment were difficult, for the world was at her feet scrutinizing her every word. It was a spectacle; news reporters packed shoulder to shoulder sensationalized social media went beyond 'viral' an inadequate term for the millions tuned into Jax's trial.

'In the End' it all boiled down to these words... the phrase "Before I sentence you, Mr. Jax Foul, do you have anything to say to this court?" Jax stood up before he muttered a word a boy of 6 years old in the front row alongside his mother jumped up on his left. A tiny blind girl of 7 years old reached out and held the boy's hand, Juan Ortiz Ramos and Leah Ruiz.

The last kidnapped children that Jax had saved from pedophile hell and the porno industry, thousands of predators were arrested across the globe because of Jax's efforts. Juan called or referred to him as uhm, like his father. The heart-wrenching stories by Leah and Juan were just the beginning. His advocates, like a merciless onslaught, pleaded for mercy. This segment of the Federal hearing was the longest in memory. Speaking on his behalf was 'Wendi Feral,' Agent Rico Captor, and Director FBI Tanya Firm; his list of advocates was awe-inspiring-indeed. The line-up of people who wanted to be heard was mind-boggling, and a selection process had to be placed en vogue. There wasn't enough time for all to give their testimonials.

As is often the case, there was plenty to take the other side of the story, coin, and cast negative vibes... words and aspersions against Jax Fouls persona. Many parents who lost their children because of his participation and actions while working for the Cuban Mafia were beyond angry and frustrated.

After 13 days, the judge had to put an end to Jax's endorsements and public support.

Even the caustic prosecutor, who was righteously out for blood and guts, relented at times she was the type who would have made a torturous executioner in a proud skirt AUSA Ms. Beckweck conceded if not verbally but physically at times was red-faced, her makeup twisted down from her eyes a soft Kleenex nearby.

Jax was one of many notorious, infamous characters calling NIA home... to Napa Insane Asylum, yet unlike many inmates, he hadn't many or any limitations. He was a free man and had been for years. With his freedom to roam the Napa hospital grounds, he spent time working as the lead maintenance man and felt relatively happy as he drove in and out the gates of concertina razor wire.

Now without being scrutinized, given leeway, and freedom to move about, this had upset some of the Correctional Officers whom themselves dealt with more scrutiny inspection than Jax.

At various times Jax would drift off in his delusional compartmentalized world, elucidating… expostulating about the insidious mob to whoever would listen to his ranting behavior.

The Russian Mafia and the Sinaloa Cartel… El Chapo, most rolled their eyes. The exception was Dr. Liz Honcho and the Warden of the Napa prison 'Ms. Ursula Anders' amongst VIPs later mentioned.

Jax, a war hero Army Ranger, worked out like a maniac like he was… for three hours a day, choosing different body parts, from powerlifting to aerobic anaerobic combinations of body weight exercises. There wasn't a person, guard, no one that came within 15 percent of the shape that Jax was in. Other inmates were the closest match. Jax was in training for his next deadly assignment. He would command the next mission as always; he was like the General for NIA!

-13-

<u>Samantha is running from Law Enforcement in Sacramento.</u>

Sammy, on the KTM 1290, was now riding in complete darkness. The sun had long set into the Pacific Ocean.

The police sirens were now a distant echo; the only lights were the stars above reflecting off of a full moon. She was straddling the motorcycle on a plowed path in a farmer's field. Rice was planted, and soon, where she was positioned, the land would be flooded by water for the rice to grow to fruition. Sam was a dirt racer moto crosser first and foremost; even on street tires, she took to the dirt. Mud clots bounced and spun off the tires, off-pavement happily. She flicked off the lights, a toggle switch that Joe had installed on both KTM's; in the darkness, she'd quickly lost the Sheriff and Police cars.

Lucky that a chopper wasn't close enough at the beginning of the pursuit, although now there were two of them flood lights flowing beaming down. Sam felt she was hidden well enough under an overpass just south of the Sacramento airport on the other side of a rest area. What could she do? Better, what did she need to do? Pacing next to the bike, thinking to check, the time is now 10:15 pm. That bastard Joe… if that even were his real name!

Pulling the camera out of the backpack and watching the LCD screen, the scene unfolds again before Sammy's eyes, the stunning clarity of the gruesome murder of Robert the P.I. proof in her little hands 'what do I do now?'

Joe finally decides to creep back to the 'KOA' campground to his motorhome, grabbing any evidence that could be held against him, Mark, or Tank.

His task was to clean up all before the authorities arrived, plumb ass certain that 'Trudy, Samantha Timmons' would either be caught, not likely, or would call the cops herself she had the damn camera pointed at him. How did she even wake up? Why ask why or how… common people wasted time on what ifs, whys, when, whatever it was… It was the reality get on with it. Just as he again dwells on his miscalculation, uhm, mistake, I should have given her a more potent dose of tranquilizers! Like, duh, really? The first thing he does is turn on the scanner, then next takes a massive swig of tequila; never a man to panic, a veteran under pressure started to pack up then muttered three words, slowing his movements. 'I've lost her' although he had confiscated her Galaxy Android and the Trac phone burner before drugging her, he thought into oblivion…Wrong, she must have been immune to the barbiturates.

The scanner was still going off; what he heard were the frustrations from the search party. So, she got away! He thinks maybe I should check in with Mark but thought better of that, umh, like, please, I couldn't handle a simple plan and didn't want to lose Mark's respect. He had enough on his plate with Tank being released earlier this afternoon. Heck checking his phone, uh, not a text, tweet, or call from 'Feral,' which can mean either all is fine. He's shacked up with another woman. Or, in chaos, opted for the former, then his burner ironically started to purr and vibrate the screen showed a 916-area code unknown.

<u>Sammy calls from a payphone.</u>

"You fkn bastard ugh, liar you used me, but I got your ass uh got it all on film just finished watching it you drugged me I...." "Hold on, Trudy.' 'I'm not Trudy, you asshole. You know my real name is Samantha. No more bullshit, you fkn liar; I was the next to die.* You kept me alive just in case the P.I. didn't show up and needed me to bring him in for you again. What were you going to do....?" "Shut up, where are you calling from?" pausing, her breathing begins to normalize... "Hello, you there?"

"Yeah, I figured I'd call you first before calling the cops to give you a chance to explain yourself, Joe!" "That's nice, thank you, let's not talk on the phone, can I meet you? I..." "Not gonna happen, Joe, your Tracfone is secure enough to talk on, no need to meet don't want what happened to the P.I. ..." "stop not on the phone 'Sammie' please baby doll. I promise I was never going to hurt you; we need a face-to-face..." "hold on," as the reverberations of rotors and helicopter blades echoed in his ear.

(Joe was working feverishly tracking her phone signal had to be a payphone because he had her phones) "listen to me, Joe; I want $50,000 in cash delivered by umh 3 hours or ..." "Sam, are you nuts? I don't have access to that kind of money. It's almost 11 pm, be reasonable." "Oh no, Joe, a couple of the CHPs just pulled into the rest area lights are flashing flood lights, oh shit!"

"Don't hang up. Stay on the phone, Samantha" she turns into the phone booth, her back towards the door; a loud crack as a door slammed, then other police cars slid into the parking lot.

The rest area was lit up; she had parked the KTM 1290 on the outside perimeter in the dirt. She had stripped off her leathers, driving attire, helmet, and backpack. All her riding paraphernalia was about 100 yards away near the bike, camouflaged by high grass and several Birch Trees. Nothing she wore resembled riding gear. Sam was wearing loose-fitting jeans and a matching blue blouse, her hair brushed out and flowing down her shoulders, knowing fair well the police were looking for a man and a motorcycle.

Suddenly all went into reverse mode, doors banged and crashed shut with louder thuds. Then seconds after, came shrieking noises violently, the sirens blaring into the night's air.

Sounds of squealing tires, smells of rubber burning, Sammy had heard a code over one of their radios, a '187' murder… ugh, a homicide!

She frowns… transforming into a sad face; the P.I. Robert was discovered! Still holding the pay phone, she heard Joe's scanner dictate codes and static, '187' in Chili's parking, lot… then his yowling shout, "Sam, hey, hello you there?" Click! Sam hung up.

Sam had to decide whether to ride the bike to the bus depot or the Sacramento Airport and lock the camera into a safety box. She only grabs the helmet and rides in civilian clothes, packing her leathers into the backpack heading North on I-5, exits at the airport stops at United Airlines.

Meanwhile, Joe has his 3rd cup of coffee sitting outside the motorhome under an awning. Several hours had passed he had the scanners on low and followed the reports of the police, knowing that Sam was still out there, not arrested.

A few more hours had passed. Joe rubbed his face, sighed, and leaned forward as he heard the familiar hum of his other motorcycle, she parks, and he watched her as she kicked down the stand.

Then she just struts right past him and flings the screen door open, no words spoken.

Sam then returns with a sugar-free Red Bull, lays back on the other lounge chair, and merely sighs, saying, "it's been one hell of a night, Joe" "you don't have to say that again," he replies.

<u>Mark back at the diner.</u>

Mark Feral switched his mind and told the sexy server to put his breakfast in a to-go bag. The crowd multiplied, reminding him of the prisons he'd been vanquished inside. Prisons where the constant norm involved 'human Lines' for everything laundry food at the chow halls, pill lines, commissary to buy your necessary items, mail, cardio machines, and weights at the steel piles. There were lines to shower or even flex out a 'biological function.' Lines uh remembering an incident in his last days in San Quentin; having lastly engaged in a brutal fist fight because someone Disrespected him cutting in front of him in line at the shower stalls... no lines were not for him.

He was watching all the impatient, angry souls hungry, looking him up and down as if he were lucky to have been through the ordering food process. His bag was hot in his hands, he strolled past them across the K-mart parking lot, then kept on walking. Mark smirked, seeing a T-ball game in progress... mulling back to when he was a young boy playing T-ball. The game was going on at the school ballpark, perfect some entertainment while he relaxed eating this scrumptious breakfast. Mark found a vacant area on the bleachers, sat, and eagerly consumed the delicious meal while listening to the parents scream at the children. The poor umpire was taking a verbal onslaught, complaints... he stifled all out numb, oblivious to the obnoxiousness surrounding him.

Tempers flared from both sides of the bleachers, pervasively adults using 'foul' obscene language as if the five and 6-year-old boys and girls were in a life-or-death struggle... ugh that was no fun.

A mother screams, 'swing the bat level, Tommy hit the fkn ball, dammit, it's on a 'Tee' for God's sake!' Keeping my mouth shut, sitting on the 5th row of the 13-rowed bleacher, I wanted to step forward and say something to the angry, yelling father.

He belligerently gave hell to all indiscriminately. I wanted to spill the remaining warm coffee on him, grab my blow dart gun or taser him.

Tell him to shut his fat lips; aah, too much risk. I was already in the top 15 most wanted by my buddies at the FBI Bureau. Damn, add in the fact that in the trailer behind my van, I had two live bodies of Joe's tormentor's attorneys inside closed coffins with drilled-out holes to let them barely breathe.

I took the least aggressive path, tossed the empty food bags into a steel drummed garbage container, and slipped out my iPad to check on the ongoing stock market and the fire out by my home by Shasta Lake.

I must state irrevocably that my ascension up the list of most wanted was bothersome and unwarranted. I was paroled from San Quentin (money talks, bullshit walks.) 'I walked out a free man just didn't show up to see my probation officer and absconded.'

'So what? No other crimes have been attributed and officially pinned on me. Of course, some detectives had alleged that I had committed many more offenses, but at the end of the day, I am guilty of absconding.'

They had outfitted me with three years of parole, so at the worst, if I'm captured, I do three more years minus good time; lol could do that standing on my head.

The truth is, it's all because of my sister Wendi and Rico Captor alongside Tanya Firm, who railroaded me because of subjective circumstantial evidence, ugh suspicion that I was the cause of little Ms. Wendi being in a coma, no proof, none whatsoever assumptions at best. To come thoroughly 'clean,' I suppose my connection with the Montana Militia isn't helping my cause! I'm not admitting to any other crimes, innocent of 95% of what the Feds were trying to pin on me. I used to repeat these words like a mantra 'if not for bad luck, I'd have no luck at all,' but as I've aged and wised down or up, life's fate can be self-driven if aligned with timing, in many cases like says the axiom… 'we can make our own luck.'

The stock market trades were rewarding; it was only 9:25 am, and I reaped more capital in two hours trading bitcoins than most could hope to make in a month… grinned confidently. I must concede that this trade was possibly illegal, just a bit, you know, like Insider trading.

Now I awaited the China news of restricting Cyber Currencies already prepared with a filled 'short' position in the market. Oh, I had some additional good news the fire was moving away east towards Burney Falls and the tiny town of Fall River. My path back to my home was all but clear. The burden of the coffins weighed heavy on me needed to eliminate this stress immediately. Here I was, risking my freedom because of a poker game that Joe had won; enough was enough. It was time to snuff out the attorneys. Ah, so much for Joe's revenge and his list of paybacks. Here I was, stuck in the K-mart lot with them covered in the back of my trailer.

His torturous plans for the evil dynamic duo of lawyers will not be. I will finish them off... sorry, Joe. This is an unnecessary liability and detrimental experience that I no longer want to take part in. This was a busy day, indeed full of optimism; later today, I should have confirmation of my little sister's untimely death; aah, poor baby girl!

Tank was being released this afternoon from San Quentin. It's going to be a fun day. Joe will have taken care of the P.I. later tonight, along with the cutie pie Sammy.

Oh, so many people dreaded Mondays, not me driving back. Traffic cleared within 45 minutes, and I was back at my large retreat in Jones Valley, the kitty cats back inside the air conditioning, my five dogs happily fighting with each other playfully.

Heck, within 15 minutes, I had my wakeboarding boat. A 29-footer hooked to the back of my truck. The most time-consuming and complex task was taking my forklift and carefully lifting the bastard coffins up into the boat; I surely didn't want to damage the upholstery.

Finally, with a tarp over them, I drove out of the gates and headed for Shasta Lake, supposing the fire had run off many boaters hell, the resort was empty, and not an employee within sight. I dropped the Malibu Wakesetter into the water in under 15 minutes... I had the boat tied off to my houseboat, and off I went. The thick smoke of the fires remained, hanging over the water, affecting visibility. It appeared to be a cloudy and overcast foggy day, yet the Sun was in full-blast mode elsewhere. Finally, I found the deep serene water in the main channel. Yes, I throw on my Captain's cap. Coasting over the small crest of waves behind the wheel of my houseboat, life is glorious, and after I dump the attorneys overboard, it will be much better indeed!

Hey, it wasn't even 12:15 pm, a feeling that I literally never have, uh, feeling a tinge of apprehension, um, alien-like unchartered waters, as I motor on underneath the train tracks with a freight train heading north on the I-5 bridge above me.

I putt past the largest, finest resort on Shasta Lake 'Bridge Bay Resort' my destination is near the Shasta Dam, deeper waters, and better places to sink the coffins at. Then once again, the hairs on the nape of my neck tingle… sting. What's up, bad vibes, premonition, unnatural abnormal feelings of regret. Yes, I've been diagnosed by several Psychologists as being a psychopath sociopath and a narcissist with total disregard for anyone's human rights. If push came to shove… I was the only one that mattered on this planet. I have zero feelings of empathy for anyone, um, nonexistent, so what? I don't give a shit!

With that being said, Joe and Tank are my loyal partners. We have a bond, but I'm the shot-caller, the leader, and I have always been since we were young boys.

It's not essential, you see. I do understand how much Joe was looking forward to inflicting agonizing torment on both 'Pat and John. The attorneys not at law anymore who were despicable Vultures,' but I just don't give a Rats ass honestly about anyone. Let me try to rephrase that I hate all living things, one might argue, 'well, Mark, you have animals, dogs, and cats' yeah, well, that's another story, for sure.

I couldn't even begin to count the animals that I've mutilated and cut their eyeballs out while they were still alive, wild, and domesticated when I was a child… which brings me to the point of clarity.

Ughhhh, by now, I've lost most of you; hell, I'm having a difficult time following my discombobulated mind myself, but if any of you are paying attention to me? Aah, by the way, I have a tendency to speak aloud. I like to hear my voice and words, which help me analyze the subject matter that bothered me, perhaps like a 3rd persons evaluation.

Swiftly to the point, why do I have five dogs and two cats on my property? Wouldn't the urge to kill... be too much for me? Why save them from the fire? First and foremost, that was a childhood thing, just curiosity. I grew out of dismembering animals way before I was 11 years old... really, the reasons I stopped this fun are not crucial in the grand theme of things.

I kept the animals safe for selfish motives, as embarrassing as this sounds, simply for financial benefits and to help secure my freedom. Yeah, I'm merely a caretaker. The animals are a necessary evil; I am the babysitter, not the owner, nope, not I.

Indeed, I'm the protagonist leader King... with Joe and Tank below me in the hierarchy, but the 'puppet master' if you will? Is in control, owns all the toys, the home I live in, uhm, everything, even this Fkn houseboat, isn't mine.

A puppet on a string that would be me! What truly is worthy of life's happiest moments for me is nearly as blissful as an orgasm, genuine exuberance, the climax ahhhh epitome of this existence is to watch the lights go out in all living things, their eyes go still. Yes!

Of all animals I hunt, people, yes, people are the easiest prey and most enjoyable. A close second is a sexual conquest chasing women, the art of domination, a combination of both is akin to my epiphany a caged scintillating female beauty, naked chained my slave for days S&M, pain is fun for all. The final orgasm for her as my thumbs close off the esophagus, strangling her as life leaves her body, the finality last breaths as she 'squeezes my cock to her death.' I know a little 'TMI' (too much information.) Sorry, I'll be back having a raging 'hard-on' um-yum, I must relieve the tension, excuse me!

Back whoa, that didn't take long must've been all the pre-talk, uh, like foreplay a tease, lol.

The 'puppet master' has forbidden any of my fatalistic jubilations... unless preapproved, of course, Lol. Hey, fine with me because I ain't got shit, no monies, really stock market trades are in her accounts. I have nothing yet, well, at least materialistic things. I'm promised a share of the profits and will abide by all the rules of the group that's in charge… enough for now.

Relax, I say no worries, I have a plan to aah better shut up 'she' might hear me! 😊 . It's tough being a misogynist, having a female in charge of my current situation pulling the strings, but patience is a virtue. <u>Soon, I will end up on top</u>. This I must believe optimistically, not euphemistically!

<u>-14-</u>

<u>**Rico and Wendi.**</u>

Rico finished the video conference call with a selected number of his Agents; he was in charge, referred to as a Senior Agent. Which caused him to sort of chortle, then he openly relented and laughed. For he was barely in his 40s, in his mind… age was and always will be only a number that means little to him, although many of his Agents were older than him.

Well, that is, after you turn 30 years old, or was it 21 years old, your mind wastes too much time away over such silliness; age is but a chronological measurement. The biological clock matters the most as he finishes washing his hands. The mirror catches the true essence of the wear and tear of the five previous months, how fast he fell from the penthouse to the basement of um… celebrity hero, accolades galore, medals plaques, a decorated FBI Agent, with mandatory visits to the White House.

Rico was given his choice of destinations and decided Northern California would be his final resting place. Retirement and where he'd finally rest his head, he loved the area it felt like home, a natural decision being born in San Francisco.

A name was made for him; he didn't discount that in life, it's timing and luck sometimes, the latter luck of the draw meeting Wendi Feral. She was the motivating reason that he separated from the rest of the pack and ascended from being the typical field agent starting from the first case that he hired her to assist. He pushed his superiors for a subcontract for her company, 'Feral Feedback' his life was changed in Tennessee, as is said. The rest was history!

Since then, 13 notable investigations have been solved, concluded because of the extraordinary young lady who lay comatose in a hospital bed, his failure to protect her ate at him. He couldn't deny that this bond went well beyond a working relationship… friends, temporary lovers, heck, no doubt he loved her!

<u>Wendi.</u>

***

I was plumb, worn out, bruised, and sore 'how?... I'd like to understand!' What happened to my body? As far as I could tell, I did the same thing every single minute uhm, lying on the same gurney in the same room inside an outpatient hospital. My parents, Ed, Barbara, and husband I've never met 'David' had made their way back down to the Napa area from the Vancouver, Portland area. I felt a tinge, a glimmer of hope for today was a 'big day' Rico would be here too, Dr. Honcho and Dr. Hawkins. It was my day to shine and prove I was alive inside… today, I would communicate. Yay!

"Wendi, listen to me please, girl, don't get your hopes up. I'm here with you and have been all of your life to protect you. It's always just been you and I!" 'Yes, Sunshine' as I acknowledge the obvious reality that without my stronger self, without my second friend, trusted soulmate alter ego, I'd been dust, dead many times she was selfless, the protagonist yet always played 3rd fiddle in the background of my compartmentalized mind. We had mutual respect for one another and unconditional love with a grace that sustained us. The first to arrive in my room was my father and mother… Jax had left not long before.

"Hey, honey, we're here, Wendi, we love you," my mom's voice as a heavy hand finds my arm with whiskers on my cheek, daddy.

"This is an exciting day for all of us," as she brushed back my bangs, touching my forehead <u>'ouch'</u> I said to myself. It was awesome. I could feel everything, but why was my forehead bruised badly? How couldn't my mother notice?

"Hey, Ed, what is this? hit the nurse's button now…." "What's going on?" my mother yelled. "I demand to know how our daughter got this bruise and scrape on her head. Where is Dr. Hawkins at?" Then my dad harps in, "We will sue this hospital for everything it's worth. We're getting her out of here. I told you that she'd be better back home!" "You stay with her, Ed. I'm filing a complaint and finding someone in charge around here."

"Babe, she's on 24/7 video. Whatever happened to our daughter will all be on the cameras," said my dad.

So, this was new news. There was a camera in my room… instantly, I felt uneasy, like thinking about my daily sponge baths, changing my clothes, and diapers. Did they close the curtain?

I know stupid of me, inherently I'm an insecure bashful, shy girl, unlike the confident other side of me, 'Sunshine,' who'd be just as thrilled living in a commune naked!

Rico.

Rico enjoyed the drive winding down roads, up and over rolling hills, beauty as far as one's eyes could view, wineries, stocks of every variety, bushes filled with hanging fruit, grapes. Never would this drive be boring, thought Rico. Did he bite off more than he could chew uh swallow? 'Director Tanya Firm,' his friend, had given him all the latitude he'd ever wanted, unlike her much more controlling sister Sandra, who was back in Washington DC. Rico knew the sharp triple-edged sword it could slice and dice him into smithereens.

There was no passing the ole buck, his decisions his ass; it was his plan, his strategy, his Baby, this pre-planned act regarding the faked death of Wendi.

For the umpteenth time, shit couldn't run uphill. He had to shut down his mind and reopen it, subtracting emotions. Okay, as he crossed the yellow lines swerving, 'think damnit Rico, heck am I spread too thin' … this new case that has taken the media by storm now into a frenzy and him into pressure cooker mode. 'No clues other than the playing cards a 3 of spades left at the scene of the first abduction clever with an artistic flavor meticulously planned with painstaking details the knockout gas, through the vents coinciding with the air conditioning van parking in front of the law office. This was as brazen as a person or group could be... Hell, directly across from a minimum of 35 Law Enforcement Officers, Correctional Officers, and my U.S. Marshall's office at the Sacramento County Jail.

From the minute the frequency alarms were disrupted by a blocking device, the assailants moved with prudent speed but not in a hurry. Nope, controlled movement. It took the two men less than five minutes using a heavy 'dolly' to move a large used box with what anyone would think was an Air conditioning unit.

Not the human being that was out cold and shackled. Inside the box, they went up then down the elevator, both of the predators dressed in non-discrete white overalls hats matching smooth as ex-lax, some would say. The kidnappers locked the office door and closed all the shades. Attorney John Manson's five employees were knocked out fast asleep.

Brazenly they wheeled Manson out, loaded him ever so casually into a van, and drove away, leaving a 3 of spades tucked sideways in the cleavage of his head secretaries breasts.

Printed in bold black magic marker were these words '(*FEAR ME CUZ I'M CUMIN 4 U)*' all in Capital letters.

Rico was anxious; being stuck behind three semi-trucks with crates of grapes this didn't help his disposition. He was barely rolling at 25 mph, drifting in and out of daymares.

He checked his dash clock, still with plenty of time to spare to visit Wendi; hopefully, this plan would work the way it was supposed to without a single hitch. Wendi would be safe from her brother Mark and the rest of the wood-be assailants, who either wanted her dead or to kidnap her to take advantage of her paranormal skills.

He then relents and allows his mind to drift back to the Sacramento kidnappings. This was just over 49 hours ago; another card, the third, was delivered with the exact phrase as the ones left at Pat Hales and John Manson's abductions...

both attorneys. Oddly, this event had nothing. I mean absolutely no connections to the legal world.

A young couple was murdered by the Sacramento River at Woodson Bridge Park, poison darts… found under a small rock near the dead bodies was the 7 of spades 'Fear Me Cuz I'm Cumin 4 U' thus far, the killer had left playing cards a 3,5, and 7 of spades at the kidnapping sites and lastly at the kill site, uh no demands nothing no other clues.

This confirms the connection. Now we have a homicide investigation with two bodies sitting in freezers at a morgue. The card player was not a kidnapper anymore. Nah, a confirmed murderer!

The beginning of a serial killer on the loose in Northern California. With a sigh glanced at the visor mirror geez, I could surely use Lil 'Wendi Feral's' insight. I felt kind of lost without her company. Their friendship had evolved… he grinned, remembering their loving sessions, oh, such happy smiles. She was dynamite in bed. Because of her, he climbed the ranks and garnered advancement through the ranks of the FBI. This day he would save Wendi's life; the scene and acts were in place; up over the next horizon, he sees the infamous Napa Hospitals Castle façade on the other side of the tree line.

Wendi Feral.

***

A sense of hostility and antipathy filled my inner being. Perhaps it was because my sensory perceptions were further enhanced by being in a catatonic state of being.

A domineering female's raspy voice sounds off intonations like the vocals of Joan Jett's music. I'd heard this voice many times before but couldn't recall when and where.

"Ms. Feral, I can assure you I will get to the bottom of this. We, umh, I will watch the videos. I'm sure it was only an accident; maybe your daughter rolled over and fell out of bed. It's not so unusual that patients in comas flinch or…." Mom said, "Please, Dr. Honcho, don't patronize us with your condescending tone and

words. Wendi is bruised. I want to know why or how this happened."

"Yeah, we want to see the video ourselves," yelped my dad 'Yes!' "Maybe during her dressing change, she rolled off...." "<u>Maybe</u> it isn't going to work for us; we're filing a complaint. I want to speak to Warden Ursula Anders at once," declared my Mom. "Listen, I'm the head of the medical department. I can handle this," says Forensic Psychologist Doctor Liz Honcho. "We'll just see about that" then I feel the sleeve of my hospital gown move up. "Oh my God, look at this, Ed, she's black and blue like fingers imprinted on her arm."

"Umm, aah... probably when she was lifted back onto the gurney; I'll be back as soon...." "Oh no, you don't," barked my father.

Next, I hear another man's voice, 'what's all the ruckus about in here?' I haven't an alternative but to listen as U.S. Marshall Evans and Dr. Honcho, with my parents, communicated. My bodyguard's statements seemed heartfelt with empathy, even apologetic.

He said, "Nurse Renee was attempting a dressing change by herself; normally, she had other nurses helping her. She did not lift the railing on the gurney up. Ms. Feral fell off the bed. I heard her scream out I rushed in. I could see under the curtains that Wendi was lying on the tile. Blame me for the bruises on her arms. I grabbed her and lifted her back off the floor onto the gurney. I'm so sorry!"

Silence, no one spoke for an eternity. Gosh, I wish I could see out of my eyes... futile useless insignificant was I... flustered and emotionally distraught. My fragile mother holding my hand and crying fretfully was just too much for me to absorb. My dad shouted, "Look, Barb, Wendi is crying... oh my lord!" More silence as dad kissed my bruised forehead, holding my other hand, and mom dabbed at my tears.

<u>Rico Captor.</u>

Unbeknownst to him, this life he'd chosen from the on-set was an evolving self-sacrifice, living and breathing in every investigation. As if possessed, he often allowed resentment to boil over, at times, no wife, no children alone.

Rico saw the signs, then the first razor wire fences. Napa, NIA was near; he thinks of why he strived so hard to thwart the world's evils, at least his small piece or slice of it.

Rico didn't find it difficult to reconcile how his life had evolved. Heck, time flew sadly by… sure, he was umh albeit unsatisfied, humbling his ego resolutely instilling a measure of undaunting strength, setting an example of how he should live. Wendi had altered his existence from the first FBI case they'd worked on together; never was he the same! None other than her majesty the goddess, a selfless human being, her name 'Wendi Feral' he knew she would bring his first genuine smile since the last time he stood before her, there was only one Wendi! Admitting, yes, he was In Love!

<u>Danny and Petey.</u>

A knock on the door, then the doorbell chime. Peter puts down the Oxycodone prescription bottle and tries to wipe his face 'could it be Danny coming back?' Why wouldn't he use his keys?' He looked through the peephole, and the woman across the way waved at him to open up. Nicki shouts, "open up, Petey, I see you looking at me through the peephole…" he does so.

"I'm not trying to be nosy," as she takes him in her arms for a warm hug. "Oh, you poor baby boy, I heard the fight. Are you all right?"

Peter stares into her deep brown eyes, her dark hair pulled back into a bun, and one side of her face is made up. It looked like she was just starting to apply her mascara. She looked sort of clownish with body piercings on both sides of her nostrils, eyebrows, lips, ears, and a post in her left cheek. As she spoke, her tongue flopped out a silver stud. They hug again, he was on the other side of this embrace less than a week back. Her partner… ugh, girlfriend, walked out on her.

That night was caustic, and loud screaming brought the police. The girls had returned home and began arguing. They'd fought after leaving an all-night 'rave party' which raged out of control. Peter went over after the screaming had subsided and Aimee had slammed the door. He'd held Nicki tightly, rubbing her head, soothing her as best as he could.

Tonight, it was his turn for reciprocation as he fell into her arms and sobbed. She'd held his head to her bosom, rubbing the back of his neck, and spies the open bottle of pills sitting next to a liter of vodka. Re-positions his skull, for he was mashing her nipple ring. She led him over to the well-worn couch as they sprawled out, he was now laying his head on her lap.

Nicki thinks about what this must look like as she looks out into the hall with the door wide open, a lesbian consoling a gay man smirking… oh yeah!

She liked Petey… he was no threat. They got along better than her, and Aimee, if he only had a different package, decides to change the focus with warranted concern. "Have you seen the guys in the suits in the parking lot walking through our apartment building?" He turns his head upwards "no, I haven't" "well, looks like the 'pigs' police are after someone here!" He shivers and shakes with remorse knowing exactly why the Feds were here at the apartment complex. They were keeping an eye on Danny, his fault!

"Why are you twitching and shaking? Are you cold or getting sick?" She reaches over to pull a quilt over him "hey yeah, ain't no one worth taking your life for, boy, I'd done that or tried a few times. The last time cost me about 11 days in the hospital. My stomach was pumped internal organs were damaged forever. Heck, a respirator took care of my breathing, but it was not worth it. Petey, what was worse was the fkn mental therapy three months of in-house treatment."

"Suicide dying, Petey hell that was freaking stupid yah don't want any of that boy think about this there's almost 4 billion cocks a wagging out there, all shapes and sizes colors plenty to choose from if Danny doesn't work out pick another one out!"

"Nicki, it's not about 'dick,' it's about love feelings, our bond, we're soulmates, it's...." "Lol, that's what Aimee has told me many times. Then I caught her down on this woman's gash."

"Cock for you has to be easy to get... you're a cutey-pie; it's simply a fact Petey gay men are notoriously unfaithful philanderers. Ugh, I suppose that goes both or three ways, huh-all humans are... ohhh, how long did you date him? Were you friends before sex?" "Fk girl, that ain't none of your business!"

Petey pushes himself up while sitting side by side reaches out... and takes her hand. "Actually, we had sex in the first hour we met kinda sick, huh? Well, Danny had gotten into a fight with his man at the Palomino bar downtown." Pete muses wow, now we're in a fight, an argument... "So, how do you know Danny isn't doing the same thing?" Nicki tries to retract her words geez. I'm supposed to be helping here. Perhaps I should just grab the fkn vodka bottle, hold his mouth open, and pour it down his throat with the pills.

The conversation pauses, and he says, "We've been together for three years now, going to get married." Gasping, "no, we are not doomed to fail," his voice sinks. She wraps her arms around him. "Yuh know we're like best friends. We take turns comforting each other and sharing our feelings, hurts, pains, and joys. I enjoy your companionship... dinners and talks just us for now were best friends Petey!" Grinning "almost the same three years that Aimee and I have struggled. It's been the same with you and Danny. We've lived next to each other. We have a special bond, and please don't do anything to harm yourself, do you promise?" Nicki stares at him and then barks, "something feels wrong here.... what's really going on?" Peter stares at his friend, wanting to tell her what is happening.

"Petey, you're hiding something from me; we can talk about anything, boy." She then let her words flow; "You really want a 'howl?' I woke up the other night, and you were in my dreams up in me inside me freakin weird see we can talk about anything nothing is taboo."

"I've never had a man before, but you know what? If I were to try one on for size, it would be you, Petey." She grasped his head and pulled him in for a quick peck!

Timing is everything they smile; leaning back, he said, "okay, I need your help, Nicki; I have caused a serious problem with…." Neither of them had noticed the large, buffed out, and enraged woman not smiling standing on the door's threshold… Aimee. ☹. No!

-15-

Rico.

Rico had parked now, making his way through the cumbersome security protocols before giving up his cell phone and briefcase to go through the X-Ray scanner stops in the lobby of the NAPA institution. On the 5th ring, his boss, Tanya, answered. She was his friend; also, they were fond of one another, with Loyalty being their bond.

"Huge day for you and us today," she said. "Yes, it surely is. I've got everything in place. The nurse Mr. Dan Spike is scheduled to work at 1 pm. He is under 24/7 surveillance oddly, didn't go back to his apartment last night, and slept in Sonoma at a hotel and not alone." "Rico, I know you… you're feeling horrible about not letting Wendi's parents in on what's happening, but…." "Yeah, and don't forget her husband Tanya, who…." "But we did decide we wanted to sell this act, have an authentic scene as if Dan's hypodermic needle's injection had murdered Wendi, right?"

"True, but I am betraying her family, including Wendi. I suppose uuhhh, what if her dad has a heart attack or something goes wrong?" "Rico, with responsibility comes consequences life is about taking risks and demonstrating faith with the conviction that our objectives outweigh lost temporary emotions. Furthermore, we've sat hours upon end analyzing…." "I realize all of this; if I weren't so close to her family, uh Wendi, it would be 'cut and dry,' Tanya."

"Dan Spikes will lead us to the person or persons that no doubt is behind this 'hit.' Mark Feral is our best guess; we're fortunate to have the informant, Peter. Without him, Wendi most certainly would have met her demise. Let's be positive, Rico. Remember the Golden Egg after the dirty deed is documented; Danny is going to Golden Gate Park to pick up the last $25,000 installment... we'll be there!" Tanya clears her throat and sips some bottled water.

"Rico, you see, we've come full circle. If Mark thinks he's failed to kill his sister, another attempt will be forthcoming. We might not be as lucky to have another Pete as an informant!" "Dammit, Tanya, you're speaking to the choir. Those were my exact words to you!" "So be it. Good luck Agent Captor" she cackles. He retorts, "Have a grand day, Director Firm" click. He contemplates easy for Tanya to say, sitting comfy on the sidelines, then recall's the grilling under the microscope she absorbed at the Pentagon after she was released from her hospital bed. She defended his actions and her own at the massacre in Plant City, Florida, where Jax was apprehended. Tanya was always on the same page with him and stood behind all mutual decisions, just like her sister Sandra's genetics were in play.

Still uncomfortable with the deception planned, even more so as the only other participant in this 'act' scheme was Physician Dr. Hawkins, who was under contract by the Government. A Forensic Psychologist she had, according to the plan, moved up the testing of Wendi to 10:25 am, brain scans MRI, EEG (electroencephalogram), an innovative experiment... to communicate with Wendi.

Barbara & Ed Feral, paced by Wendi's gurney nervously waiting on Doctor Hawkins; David was off in La-la land staring at his phone screen when I walked into the hospital room. Following me was Dr. Hawkins. After salutations, she spoke, "the purpose of today's experiments is to prove that Wendi is not brain dead, that inside her skin, she's cognizant, listening alive, with the question that should be answered today, um, can we communicate with her? With new scientific and medical innovations came strategic experiments, causing families and loved ones to have anxieties running rampant after 257 nights and days of dormancy, comatose, vegetable-like. I hope to have a clear answer either way."

There was a vibrant feeling this day, laden with pure optimism. Wendi was already achieving impressive improvements from being kept alive via machines previously, now breathing without the assistance of devices. Wendi's tears were exposed. Her skin color had changed, and her heart rate; blood pressure had elevated. These changes happened when her mom or even I spoke to her. This was proof of her being able to understand us or at least being able to recognize our voices.

I stepped back out of the room to check with my Marshals and again, for the umpteenth time, said aloud, 'I want Wendy back, please!'

Moments later, I took the elevator up and saw the whole family minus the evil Mark Feral and her business partner and best friend, whom I'm also fond of… again where is Sandi? We gathered around her gurney in a spacious operating room; computers and screens were hooked to Wendi. The air is crisp, tingling like a scent of umh ambiance of hope, anticipation unconditional devotion surrounds and engulfs the entire room, and 'Wendi Feral.'

Even Dr. Hawkins had a twinkle of expectations; guard duty at the door was Marshall Evans. We listened as the parameters were described to us, explaining what we could expect. The overwhelming mantra was that we could not get our hopes up. 'Duh, too late for that, yah think!' Dr. Hawkins continues to say I'm not going to use technical terms nor spend or waste time educating you about how the human brain reacts to words. She takes a telescopic pointer out, touching a 45-inch screen.

"Wendi's entire brain will be scanned; I will ask Wendi a standard set of questions which, if she is cognizant, she'll understand we should see her responses in various areas of her brain which 'will' light up on the screen, flashing signals are you all with me?" she pauses for a split second. "Okay, before I get started, do any of you have any questions?" Barbara Feral speaks out, "I want to speak with her. Will each of us have a chance to try and communicate with Wendi?"

Dr. Hawkins sighed. "In tests similar to the ones I will be conducting today only, the Doctors communicated with the patient... we will be following their protocols without varying." She holds up her hand, stopping the oncoming rebuttals mouths open, "I want to remind you these tests have been studied from all over the world. Better results were always achieved when a non-family member Doctor spoke with the patient first non-emotionally." She emphasizes the importance of stability in one voice, not to confuse or overwhelm the comatose patient.

<u>Wendi.</u>

****

'Look, Sista,' this is your chance to shine, our big day, time to show our loved ones we're alive inside. Don't look back, girl, it's now or never 'Enough Sunshine.' I said to her no pressure. Huh! My eyes lids were closed, my BP was about average, 125/77 heart rate was 83 bpm. I was fully aware that David, Rico, and dad and mom were by my side still lost to me was where my BFF Sandi was at. 'Wendi, concentrate, girl. I'm with you like I've always been whenever devastation, controversy, disputes, or clashing dissension invaded your brain. I was there always faithful to your salvation....' 'Sunshine, I love you, but you're putting it on kind of thick we're one and the same, right?' 'Pay attention, Wendi, our Pow Wow is over' Sunshine sank back into 'our' minds.

Doctor Hawkins checks the monitors, "Okay, all the tests have been uploaded. We can visualize them on this screen; now, on the left will be the tests conducted previously. The real-time EEG scan of her brain will be on the right side of the screen," she points to a 3-foot monitor on the wall across from my gurney as the rest of the wires are attached to my head. Surely they have shaved my head in spots. Not sure no idea if I'm even bald.

"The EEG brain scan will be the first to come up," said Dr. Hawkins "then we will view the MRI." "Okay, now, I want you to focus on the screen. When I activate the scan, you will see

Wendi's brain in real-time." I hear my mother gasp, 'oh my God, look at this part that's lit up and blinking.' "Please, Ms. Feral Barbara, sshhh."

I think the nerve of this doctor that's my mom. Then I listen to mumbo jumbo technical jargon that Dr. Hawkins had previously said she wouldn't invoke like the ole adages used, like one of my favorites, 'to make a long story short' nope! After someone says, 'to make a long story short, be aware you're in for a Long story!

Or 'to the point' suffice it to say Dr. Hawkins with telescopic pointer 'this is Wendi's Cerebral Cortex 'sensory-motor functions' front Cerebrum, Hypothalamus and Amygdala where her 'emotional feelings originate.' Gray matter, you're seeing neuron synapses synaptic neuron impulses are passing, firing one neuron to another. Ugh, something like that I'd heard uh made zero sense… if I could speak, I would have said to get to the point.

"My goal, our goal is to establish a simple set of questions that I will pose to Wendi yes and no, easily answerable with only one word. Her vitals, heart rate, and blood pressure are being monitored, so without further ado, ah delay, let's get started," collective sighs could be heard. *Yeah, 'Just do it!' belched Sunshine!*

"Hi Wendi," she gently tugs on my fingers, "I'm Dr. Hawkins, your Forensic Psychologist, Neurologist. I'm here with your family to conduct an experiment." (*Like, duh, get on with it now, I'm so impatient, damn.*) Silence, then Doctor Hawkins soldiered on… "We need to set parameters up. With that being said, I've been studying your history. You were a champion swimmer and 100-meter freestyle champ; your breaststroke and butterfly were mere seconds off some past Olympic records. So if I ask you a question, and you want to answer, 'Yes,' I want you to pretend in your mind that you're in a swimming pool on the last lap of an intense race. Wendi, you're giving it your all… stretching, kicking, using all of your energy to reach up and touch the pool's edge… winner." My mother gasped 'yes Wendi was a…' "sshh, once again Wendi,

YES, means you're swimming in a race!" I feel a hand on my thigh, mom.

"Now for your answer to be 'NO,' what I want you to think about is this, most of your young life, you have participated in yoga, even being a Yoga instructor and teaching forms of meditation; if your answer is a resounding 'no,' you're in 'downward dog' position, silent relaxed nearing a calmness, tranquility based."

'Okay, sista, this should be easy for us, mutters Sunshine. I concur with swimming and yoga, a few of my favorite activities.'

I lay there as dormant as a tree yet was in full-on anticipation mode, ready to scream, jump towards the edge of the pool, and race down my favorite lane, #5, to win; Yay!

Conversely, if it were a resounding no, I'd find myself on a mat in peace, stretching my legs out and trying to relax.

'Silence can't be seen, only felt' then Dr. Hawkins voice, a different tone like a half whisper near my left side ear, "Wendi Feral, are you listening to me?" 'I jumped from the ledge of the pool' "Oh, my Lord look," shouts my mother. A Christmas light show flashed brilliantly. They watch my neurons fire my brain, sending electrical signals impulses from one section of my brain to the next, flickers of light displayed on the screen.

Dr. Hawkins raises her eyebrows, "please refrain from speaking for now," she then points to the parts of my brain in full-go mode. My heart rate jumps to 101, and my BP to 149/91. That's just one question, a yes. I'm here and listening and excited in my skin!

"Wendi, are you an only child, no brothers or sisters?" An easy answer for me, I have a brother who hates me. Mark Feral 'No!' Dr. Hawkins watches with the others as my brain images transform, flashing inside me. Another side part of my brain is now intermittently glowing, erratic unsteady, and blinking slowly (Yoga.) BP drops off the cliff to a quick 115/71 heart rate at 75 in seconds. I'm relaxed. Then suddenly, my imagination took over, and my eyelids opened… At first turtle slow, like a rusty garage door stuck in motion pulling an anchor from the ocean bottom by hand. But unfortunately, that didn't happen!

Although, I was thrilled and exhilarated by the questions and answered each one eagerly with enthusiasm, either racing in the pool or inhaling and exhaling with the purpose of relaxing. The experiment continued for another 45 minutes until I finally wore the plumb out, curtains closed down, yoga, rest relaxation, and finally, for real.

I was alive, proof in the pudding, ruggedly handsome Rico, and my husband, my mom, and dad were permitted a question each I gave a yes or no.

What was decided was that I had a case of 'abnormal memory loss' amnesia. Due to head trauma, I couldn't remember why I was in the hospital or how I was injured, nothing about the last quarter of my life. I didn't want to hurt David's feelings, so I even faked a yes. Dr. Hawkins was not fooled, though, as he asked his question. 'Do you remember our marriage, umh wedding oh, how much I love you, Wendi?' A two-part question, I believe the truth was I didn't know the guy… it was Rico I yearned to hold, wanting him to love me!

I didn't know David, although he seemed kind and acted as if he cared about me, um, loved me; sadly, my mind was blank when it came to him or us.

At 1:15 pm, I was rolled back into my room, Dr. Hawkins, Rico, David, and my parents by my side. I was beyond exhausted yet so happy, just like they were. Dr. Hawkins said, "Wendi needs to rest for a while; I'm going to ask you all to leave!" Dad said, "well, heck, it's time to celebrate. Let's go to lunch, everyone… I'm buying," then his whiskers touched my left cheek "I love you, my dear daughter, to the moon and back, sweet dreams. We will be back by dinner; it's party time."

Goodbye, hugs, kisses, xxx, oooo's gleefully mirthful voices exit into the hallway. The door closed with an enormous effort, I cracked my left eyelash open, and I could barely see Rico's shadow hovering over me.

Dr. Hawkins, on the other side, both faces contorted and twisted unnaturally, left no doubts they were not in a party mood, quite the opposite, a foul mood indeed!

He speaks to me; his deep resonating tone always mesmerizes me. I think I loved him, maybe always have! Rico somberly spoke, "Wendi, I can see your eyelashes fluttering. We now know you're cognizant and are listening to what is being said. I must inform you of this uuhhh; unfortunately, I have some alarming news, a dire situation, to reveal to you. Wendi, my dear, you are safe, so don't worry. I'm going to be here for you." He takes up my left palm and squeezes it.

"Most likely, within the next 75 minutes or so, an attempt on your life will be made. A male nurse will inject a hypodermic needle into your body. Don't worry; with the help of an informant, we've exchanged the toxic poison with saline. You're safe, Wendi… girl, you trust me, right?" Dr. Hawkins adds, "Wendi, I have your body connected to my monitors. Can you dive into the pool if you comprehend what Rico is telling you?'"

I tried concentrating as hard as possible but couldn't even flick one of my eyelashes; my motor functions were not accessible. I was plumb-worn out from the 45-minute plus experiment; damn, why didn't Rico start with this dilemma? "Wendi can you hear me?" asks Rico. "Her heart rate has gone up from 73 beats… BP is now 157/101. She is listening and understands," states Dr. Hawkins.

"Rico, it's a process that could be long-term; she may not open her eyes again for some time, not like a light switch where the juice is just turned on… we must be patient."

"Yes, Doc…" "Wendi, please pay attention. It's now 1:55 pm. The sinister nurse starts checking his patients at 2 pm. He has been paid to end your life and has already pocketed $25,000. The same amount will be paid to him after the deed is carried out."

Rico paused, inhaling a large breath "this is precisely what he must believe, that you die from the poison. We cannot make any mistakes… let me try to answer questions I'm aware you would ask me; no, your parents are not privy to this information and haven't been informed, for we need natural reactions. I know it's very cruel but necessary. We need real emotions to show from your family. Besides me, Dr. Hawkins and Director Tanya Firm are the only people aware of this situation. Oh, Wendi, I almost forgot the informant. Peter is also a nurse who works with you here. He will know that we're play-acting your murder. We need authentic reactions, and even the U.S. Marshals haven't a clue.

This is what will happen, Dan; the nurse will enter your room to do his standard check on you, and he will block himself away from the camera's view. At the same time, he adds the toxic formula to your I.V. Dan will leave. For all intents and purposes, it will appear that you have a heart attack." Rico raises my left hand, and I feel him kiss my palm with a gentle squeeze.

"Danny understands that even with a thorough process by our Pathologist, the standard testing of your organs and blood, these stealth-like chemicals will not show up during an autopsy. The natural cause of your death will show a typical heart attack. The poison chosen by the Assassin is slow working and would have caused you excruciating pain for approximately 25 minutes before you succumb to death, right Doc?" "Yes, Rico, obviously whoever paid for this execution wanted her to suffer significant agonizing pain until her heart stopped beating. We have rigged your B.P. machine to go bonkers or to sound alarms. That's when I'll roll you into the awaiting surgical room. I will pronounce you dead before other medical staff arrive and get involved."

Rico interjects, "I will be by your side the entire time, and so will Marshall Kara; yes, Wendi, I have brought you another Marshal whom I trust thoroughly. Also, sweetie, no one will examine you. We will have you under guard." Doctor Hawkins whispers, "I'm not leaving your side, Wendi!"

Rico continued, "I know how you think, so this is what will happen after your orchestrated heart attack. "We will then follow the would-be assassin to his preplanned pick up of the final payment and then arrest all involved like you probably have guessed. It's no doubt your brother that's behind this. I'm sorry, sweetie, he is still on the lamb, absconded from Probation. We have added Mark to the FBI's top 10 most wanted list." A short pause then… "Wendi, don't worry about your parents and David. I will meet them off-site and bring them up to speed. The important issue here is that Nurse Dan Spike must believe he murdered you. Wait, there's another person involved in this pre-fabrication, Nurse Spike's fiancé, who, as I've just told you, is our informant, a fellow nurse.

Peter who has been the head nurse for you the last 90 days. We will also detain him as a witness. He is fully cooperating and will be locked up in an interview room. I haven't yet decided what to do with him."

Rico leans in and kisses her on the forehead… then gently whispers in her right ear, "I love you, Wendi, umh, Tuffy!" His words echoed and rebounded, again and again, warmth in my spirit. "Stop girl, aah, ain't that's so fkn sweet sista you're married uh, someone wants us dead geez forget about Rico.' 'Sunshine, I do believe there's a hint of jealousy, umh…' 'no, not jealousy, ugh, reality girl, we can bet it's your fkn loser psychopath brother Mark who's behind this attempted assassination. You know he put you, uhm, us here!' 'Sunshine, if you can remember how or what happened to me, please let me know now!'

Seventeen minutes later, 'Ssshh sista, look who just walked into the room' through squinted eyelashes. It's him, heck it's barely after 2 pm. The killer nurse is now moving the drapes to cover the cameras.

-16-

<u>Nicki and Peter.</u>

Aimee had enough of watching the two of them as she entered the open apartment door, "What do we have here? Look at you two, oh fk so touching, a faggot and a dyke kissing so sweet."

"Aimee, Aimee, I can explain," cries out Nicki. Peter and Nicki are instantly on their feet, blushing, trying to distance themselves from each other. "Danny and Peter had a big fight. I just…" "Save it for someone who gives a shit. I want your slut ass out of my apartment today… before I get back from work. If not, I'll throw all your measly stuff into the hall or off the balcony. Why don't you move in here with your new gay boyfriend" "Aimee, it's not like that, please!" Nicki stepped in front of Aimee "please, lover-girl." Before Peter could move, Aimee was on top of Nicki,

Blurred vision coincided with a throbbing cranium… concussion, most likely, as he succumbed to the migraine's poundings. His head felt warped out of whack golf ball-sized hematoma bleeding, and he found himself in the bathtub.

Sunday afternoon vodka bottle empty, not sure that he'd even drank any of it or was he in a vodka bath… coldness clutched his skin and soul, his body in goosebumps, uh, chills.

Wrapped a towel around himself, he wandered into the kitchen with a cell phone in his hand thinks of his sequence of calls Danny, his mother, and then Nicki, in that order. No one answered, nor did either of the three call him back, heck not even a text; sadly, Peter stared glumly into a mirror. This life isn't worth it! ☹ .

<u>Nurse Danny at NIA in Wendi's room.</u>

He tugs on the curtain ever so slightly, positioning himself close enough to her, blocking the camera angles. Danny was on his rounds checking his patients per the norm. In total, he was assigned to 13 patients on the third-floor wing. Many would never wake up nor ever move again. All were in stages of unconsciousness, um, comas.

Some were Inmates from the prison across the way; even if they could move being chained shackled to their gurney, it wouldn't be far. Dan suspected many of the prisoners diagnosed as delusional with mental disorders were here only for experimentation, but he couldn't prove it. Dan thought of them as a waste of resources, air… if he wouldn't get busted, he'd do the humane thing and end their pathetic existence.

Danny stared goon style, licked his upper lip, and said 'not you, my dear Wendi, your famous a celebrity, even notorious

the 'animals seer' he snickered the globe, National Enquirer…
Star, the Tabloids all over Social Media. What the public would
buy and believe is insanity, and yet there had to be a reason a
U.S. Marshal stood next to the exit door,' and your ass was
worth 50 K to extinguish 'undoubtedly, you're a freakin Rat,
snitch, bitch. I despise weak-ass Rats who snitch to save their
own skin.' He takes her I.V. attachment and slides the cylinder
into place from the hypodermic needle, gently methodically
pushing the plunger as the poison enters her vein. 'Good
riddance to you, Wendi Feral!'

I heard my name, something about Rat but couldn't see
the evil countenance of the nurse named Dan Spike. He hadn't
a sliver of compassion for me. Noxious fumes of hate exited
from his cpidcrmis. I did my part, 'not trying to bc funny, nah'
I laid there comatose, not an act, but I was excellent at it.

Sadly, in this reality, I wondered if it would've been a good
thing for me to have died today, shockingly I fell into a
snoozing slumber instead of a wake-up call seeing a partially
shaded view through eyelashes on my left side that flickered
Nurse Danny had left my room or tomb as I preferred this
gurney to be referred as a Tomb!

*'Closing my closed eyes,' 'I was in a field on a gloriously
overcast day Pacific Northwest just galloped past my business sign
'Feral Feedback' riding my pure white stallion 'Sunshine' in a jeep
with zebra stripes sat my best friend forever the albino one of a
kind Sandi waving with a phone in her hand and a grimace across
her cheeks.'*

All of a sudden, buzzers rang, sirens and alarms, and the
gurney was jerked. I jolted awake from a dream state, umh, not
wanting any part of this world, uhm. Please leave me alone. I
tried to tell my subconscious… I beg you, whoever you are,
leave me alone.

Despite being aware of what was happening didn't change
my disposition. Several times I'd heard Rico with Dr. Hawkins
speak in a panic. I listened to the familiar voice of U.S. Marshal
Evans, who said, 'I got Wendi.' Rico replied, 'no, Evans, you
stay by her room. I'm taking Wendi,' Doctor Hawkins shouts,
'come on Rico, this way to the operating room, hurry up!' like

a whirlwind blowing past me, a tunnel door swung open shut voices hummed mutterings. Heck, I was torn up and exhausted from the 'show and tell' only hours ago 'swimming' communicating no exaggeration. I mean to say I am bruised and sore. My muscles ache like I just finished five rounds of fighting in the UFC cage and ran the Boston Marathon all in a day! For my part, I tried to quiver or flinch, flick my lashes or brows, and act like I was in severe pain from the poison. But I was frozen. Ugh, I was dead, right... a hard act to follow, not! Didn't need an audition or second take.

I couldn't differentiate how much time had passed. I probably fell asleep and shook awake. I was moving downward, a shift in my equilibrium if I had any. Oh, it was an elevator ride. Only Dr. Hawkins and Rico were by my side. "Hey girl, I'm right here; we did it... good job, Wendi. I'm going to take you to a secure jail cell. You'll be safe, I promise."

I must not have heard him correctly. I'm heading to a 'jail cell' good job; dichotomy, oxymoron, and paradox help me differentiate. I'm confused! ☹.

'Whatever doesn't matter anymore,' belched out Sunshine 'suck it up, sista, it is what it is!'

<u>Mark planning to discard the lawyers.</u>

A thick fog blanketed me in a matter of minutes, not fog but smoke. It sat layered over the lake. I wondered if the fire had shifted again, the wind was blowing towards my houseboat, and Mother Nature's wind power had changed directions. I was driving in slow motion at 15 mph, music in the air towing the wakeboard boat, scary if I was one of those pipsqueaks who were frightened of the unseen and unknown; one thing was for sure, this was the perfect opportunity to dump the attorneys in the lake. Their not-so-cozy coffins were on board with me; visibility was like zilch.

Often I thought I could live out here on this houseboat, fish for food, everything at my disposal stores, restaurants, bars, gas stations, women flauntingly unclad easy pickings. Just take ownership of a 'finger island,' a Cove with a white sand beach, the houseboat set up a permanent camp, all the toys Quads to ride over the islands Sea-Doo's, a boat, and women. Yes! Life could be grand, toss the phone in the lake, no social media oh, what a fleeting thought of nonreality.

Choking on my saliva as it sounded like a fkn helicopter was landing on my roof! Sheriff boats directly in my path out of the haze lights, then over the Salsa music, "stop your vessel now." Under the Captain's wheel, dashboard, and now in my left hand was a Sig Sauer P-220 fully loaded, one of my favorite pistols.

I tossed a windbreaker over my shoulders to cover the gun's bulge, umh, despite it being a bit warm out. The stench of burnt rubber and fire enveloped me as I stepped out of the enclosure, slipping the houseboat into neutral.

Why the fk can't the cops leave me alone shit in my right hand, I had a packet wrapped in plastic, zip-loc all legal paperwork registration, title license, insurance, the whole kitten caboodle... enchilada. I was an upstanding, outstanding member of this society, no doubts!

I took five steps and leaned over the railing to see three Sheriff boats, two officers on each, doing my best to restrain my giddiness. A frivolously numbing sensation engulfed me trying to keep my facial expression from busting out a goofy fatuous grin Cuz of the text I had just read... 'Done! My sister Wendi was finally dead. Yay.' ☺ .

Party time, I reached up, tugged my Captain hat down tighter, and saw a sweet-looking officer had to be a cadet. Young, curved out, curvaceous, yum, I'd like to get in.

I pushed my sunglasses up, my handsome nose exposed... in the foreground, the smokey lake. I could barely see the humongous bucket being yanked out of the water. I could hear the RPMs wounding down as the chopper hovered, then lifted the bucket back up; almost at once, a different helicopter in the distance repeated this maneuver, dropping another bucket. They were filling the buckets full of water to drop on the out-of-control forest fire.

"Excuse me, sir. We have a fire blazing behind the dam; you're going to have to head back towards Bridge Bay Resort, sorry!" I nodded, then acquiescently raised my right hand in a salute checking out the luscious hips and ass. So horny, dammit. So many fish in the lake, but I can't pull that one in! I think she smiled at me. Yeah, she did!

I'm a man of beliefs, aah omen's warning signs of future occurrences, auspicious phenomena of a foreboding nature. I was out here on Shasta Lake for one purpose, to sink the coffins today… no worries, it's Party Time.

'Time to celebrate,' I sighed dreamily… if only exciting news or information could produce a wet orgasm. Wendi was finally dead. Jesus, life was good and getting better. I needed to peek in on my passengers in the coffins. I wouldn't want them to expire prematurely, I howled… Yeah!

-17-

FBI, Tank Shaw… finally leaving Prison.

Tank stares up and looks out towards his long-anticipated walk to freedom proudly. He held his head high, finally out of San Quentin, as he ambled down the steps strangely. He was neither happy nor sad.

Not a soul stood in the parking lot before him, no family to greet him, no loved one's nope Tank was by now conditioned to accept the fact that he was alone in this world content with a mixed convoluted truth. Uber should be there at any moment. He strolled by the makeshift buildings on the outside of the archaic dungeon and walked past the rolls of razor wire that he always looked through in the prison yard. The walls seemed to be rotting from the inside out.

He slowly strolled along like in a time warp, encompassing years of remembrances, thinking of his fellow inmates and their most treasured times, the tiny cottage playgrounds, swings, and conjugal visits for the lucky prisoner and his family.

Tank couldn't reconcile his abandonment and unresolved guilt. His mind was filled with self-defense mechanisms using phony remedies to soothe his conscience. This compelling truth, however, engulfed him. He was exiting this dank prison, the loyalty and stability of lifelong friends, brothers in arms Mark Feral and Joe Sable, who made this possible they were his only soul mates.

He left San Quentin with nothing. Tank kept zero stuff and gave all the assets he'd accumulated away... radios, TV, clothes, books, commissary foods, and workout equipment to fellow inmates. He left with no pictures or cards, only the clothes on his back sent in by an anonymous donor, 'Mark Feral.' Oh, yeah, he'd worn brand-new Wolverine Boots out of prison. Physically, he was checked out and given a clean slate. Hell, the state even paid for several inoculation shots.

In his front pocket was his Social Security Card and his California Driver's License that would expire in three months, along with a debit card with his name on it worth $9000.

The Uber driver pulled up; it was a female pulling down her sunglasses a tad and introducing herself, "Hi, my name is Megan. Where too?"

Tank gawks down at her, thinking this gal Megan comes to San Quentin to pick him up alone. Geez, times have changed; wow, this girl seemed so confident and unafraid. He tells her, 'Take me to Redwood City to El Camino Blvd... Rubio Auto Sales, please!' Megan nodded, not a word exhaled, music played on low. He recognized the Artist 'Brian Culbertson' ...'The journey,' the song's name. He released a shallow smirk. Yeah, the journey was in go mode as he deafly checked to see if the Feds were on his ass yet!

What Tank didn't know could hurt him. The Feds weren't on his ass, but we're lodged deep inside. One of the three inoculation shots held an injectable tracking chip.

Agents Bill Avery and Tom Baker were in separate vehicles, with lead Agent Lori Parks in a mobile unit. "He's leaving Rubio Auto Sales now, driving out of the lot in a Chevy Malibu 2007 model heading south on Highway 101," says Baker. "Okay, give him plenty of room. The tracking chip has a range of 25 miles. Let's not spook him. Tank, as we've discussed, was penniless. The nine-grand had to be deposited by either his partners, Joe or Mark. With any luck, he will lead us right to them."

"We had a trace on the $9,000.00 which has led to a channel of fictitious alleys to the cloud, nowhere, last we tracked it to the Dark Web no chance in finding the sender.

He has to check in with his Probation Officer parole agent, so we can assume he's on his way to San Jose." They watch as Tank stops by an ATM, withdraws $300, and cruises down the 'Bloody Bayshore,' Hwy 101 South. He then pulls into Walmart to buy a couple of burner Trac phones, secure lines with cash, some snacks, and a bottle of Gatorade, fully aware that he had to be under scrutiny. With this day in mind, he'd walked the prison yard with Joe and Mark. This was a foregone conclusion that the Feds would track him with the belief hoping he'd lead them to Joe and Mark... Duh.

Soon the three of us will be reunited, but first, he was to lead the FBI in the opposite direction, lay low, see his parole officer, and even look for a job lol. Thus far, everything was according to pre-plans. Both attorneys captured the P.I. has met his demise, and the evil archangel Wendi Feral would breathe no more. She was the main reason that his life had unwound.

Tank remembers his teachers and coaches had told him through High School about all his potential; throw in the fact his family had money, and it was a no-brainer he would be successful in anything he endeavored to do... Wrong.

Whew, shaking his head slightly, the year being 2019, you'd think the cops would have figured out that the sunglasses, suits... Crown Victoria in the parking lot of Walmart would set off incongruous alarms to all. Still, no, there was a man on his phone leaning on the hood. I'm being followed, no doubt.

Tank checks the air above him. Nada... he had kept an Eagle-eyed lock on the car he'd bought, then it 'dawned' on him if that were a cop, ugh, no if's when he was in Walmart, they stuck a GPS chip magnet under his car. His partial smile flashed that his plan still was engaged. Let's all go together, follow me, and see how slick you are. Lol, as Tank slips his Malibu into drive.

<u>Wendi, Rico.</u>

Director Tanya Firm sat in her spacious office. From her perspective, all was going well… sipping hot ginger tea, she frowned at herself and corrected her last thought; it seemed that, at least on a few fronts, all was going according to the plans she and Rico had spent hours detailing, at least how they wanted the attempted murder of Wendi to unfold, on another front locating Mark Feral was of top prominence.

Tank was under surveillance now, just leaving his parole office in San Jose. He was the key to their success, an assumption based on facts. Tank would eventually lead them to fugitives Mark Feral and Joe Sable' who had both absconded. Neither of them has been seen since their parole from San Quentin.

Tanya had it all on her partitioned screens. Wendi was under the special care of Dr. Hawkins, who had signed a contract subcontracted for both the FBI and CIA five years ago, happy to be back in the USA after her last project, the interrogation of war criminals in war-torn Syria.

Special Agents were assigned to Wendi, who was resting comatose-bound but alive because of Rico and her intervention. She rubs her forehead then places a thumb and forefinger between her lips and chin, pushing her chin… inwards, pondering the following sequence of events that were already in motion release to the mass media Social media the death of 'Wendi Feral' of natural causes a heart attack.

She checks the time 3:15 pm Monday Rico, at that very moment, was meeting with Barbara and Ed Feral with her husband, David. The three of them would've been informed of the plot to murder Wendi; she wondered how the family would react. Would they be able to face the camera… investigative reporter's scrutiny and sell the fact that Wendi was dead?

Nurse Dan Spike was still working the floors at the Napa Hospital, albeit with a swagger. He was followed from the apartment he shared with our informant Peter a fellow nurse and fiancé.

Sunday, Dan had met a man at the Palomino bar who we later discovered was his ex-boyfriend. They left for a motel room Sunday night. She sips her tea and ruminates; Dan will be off work at 9 pm. He was the crucial and pivotal piece of the Chess game, the key instrument that would lead them to Wendi's brother Mark everyone hoped, uh, but could it be that damn easy, huh?

Shakin her head again, there wasn't any evidence that Mark Feral was the protagonist behind the murder plot. Wendi has other enemies, mainly the Sinaloa Cartel and Cuban Mafia, an outstanding reward for her capture and delivery to Mexico City 17-million-dollar bounty on her pretty head, <u>but she had to be alive-for delivery, so this plot had to be orchestrated and must have originated from her brother no questions about that.</u>

The intercom buzzed 'Yes' 'Ms. Firm line 5 urgent' Tanya doesn't rush. A veteran taps the phone and listens, "we have a problem here, ma'am. The subject has been called into work the night shift; guess there was a no-show at the hospital!"

She bites her inside lip. Always something isn't it, she thinks, calls down to the jail cell he'd been sequestered within "well, how is he holding up?" not so good, ma'am um…." "Let me speak with him." He mutters, "hello…." "Peter, you're under protective custody. It's your day off; you're not due back at NIA till Tuesday afternoon. By then, we hope to have Mr. Spike in custody."

She listens to him whimper, whispering, "we were going to be married… omg, what have I done if I could take it all back" Petey broke into tears. Tanya, as cold and brutal as she could be at times, unleashed a barrage of reality-based verbiage; 'suck it up dude' pun intended, she wily grinned, changing her tone to an aggressive intonation "we have video of Dan dancing and cavorting with his ex-boyfriend Eddy they ended up at a hotel get over it he isn't worth the tears… now put the Agent back on the phone." "Agent Amarillo, they will have to find someone else to work the night shift. Petey is going nowhere till we have Mr. Spikes in custody." "Yes, Director Firm, I understand,"… click!

For the 3rd time, she reads her twin sister's tweet, 'Sandra Firm' who was stationed in Washington D.C. 'Tanya reliable info puts Mark Feral in your neck of the woods ugh, Northern California… be careful sister!'

She'd called Sandra they had concluded that there had to be a connection, none as of yet though the 'serial killer' um, was it too early for that given moniker, for to date only two deaths could be attributed to him the couple at the Sacramento river park, both attorneys could still be alive. At each site left was a playing card with the words 'FEAR ME CUZ I'M CUMIN 4 U! The numbers 3,5 and a 7 of spades. Tanya pulled open a middle drawer, staring at intercepted mail meant for Rico. In a plastic Ziploc bag was a playing card that was a 9 of spades. She ominously read again, 'Fear me Cuz I'm cuming 4 Rico.' This particular card was kept private. It was mailed to the FBI's main office in Sacramento.

<u>Sammy and Joe.</u>

Despite Joe's three jugs of nitro coffee and Sammy's 16 ounces of Sugar-free Red Bull, they rested back in lounge chairs as a mellow breeze blew by; it was a tolerable, even pleasant 69° at 3:25 am slumbering dormant bodies that were numb, desperately in need of recharging their human machines. Both could be asleep in the motorhome, but they hadn't even spoken since Sammy had returned from the police chase and Joe's murder of the P.I.

They could be found in their subconscious worlds, him reliving personal trauma most self-inflicted, searching his mind for positives. She, Samantha blazes, trespasses into his dreams a horizontal bar suspended by two parallel ropes, a circus tent above crowds of onlookers. They were flying through the air 35 feet from the ground on a trapeze gymnastic apparatus. 'Sammy was free flying towards him. Her arms reached out, and her eyes were boring into his frantically Aglow, below no cushioned landing, only hard dirt. Trusting him as she flung her arms up and out... the crowd, uhm, audience entranced... collectively holding their oxygen, gasping... children screamed. Sailing up in the gravity-laden atmosphere, Joe stretched his arms out, grasping at air. His fingers were trying to reach out to grab her to save her from imminent peril, immediate death. All he could do was reach for her with <u>Alligator arms</u> as she tumbled to the earth. Then amazingly, in the last second before impact, suddenly Joe became a superhero 'Elastic Man' his hands and arms stretched out and swung her right up on the moving trapeze, roars of jubilation all around.

He wasn't aware of the perspiration that soaked his clothes. He wasn't a man susceptible to trickery. Was his mind playing games? What was the meaning of this dream?

Always in tune with his inner spiritual guide, his internal security system, he can't get tied up with a female no 'In the End' (a title of a song he enjoyed), it was only he that mattered then next in descending order was Mark and Tank, the music of 'Linkin Park' continued to reverberate in his head.

Swiftly Joe floated off again on another magic carpet ride… He and Sammy were on a sailboat sipping colorful drinks, resting their bones in bubbles, jets a warm tub, not a landmass insight they embrace, planning to vacation on the island of 'Seychelles' floating in the southern hemisphere crystal blue water with Dolphins swimming alongside their magnificent Sailboat… Ahh, sublime Bliss!

Sammy, lamentably lost in past reciprocal redundancies, flying low amongst the clouds in another dimension, it was about trepidations of the earlier skeletons comingling with the present, past, and future events. In minutes she went from childhood to adulthood, eyelids closed a range spectrum of light from a prism, her mother and father, her upper-class family politicians, attorneys, stockbrokers tossing a few doctors into the mix, a Professor at UCLA she literally had life by the 'lips' down by her groin… what happened? Was it way too late? Oh my Lord, who was she? Please, as her heart begins to race, navigating away from the negativity of her reality. Who has the wheel? Please drive her subconscious to a happier destination now!

Like nuclear fusion, she's 13 years old in a renowned Catholic School for girls. In front of her was the Priest. He was preaching beside her. Fifteen other girls sat prim and proper in likewise attire in a large classroom with three nuns in attendance.

She listened attentively, albeit preoccupied, still feeling his slimy claws on her, inside her, sick to her tummy with fear looking, staring in disbelief as the priest morphed snout jutted out Werewolf veins popped. On a large screen, a nun was standing with a long wooden broom handle pointing, levitating in defiance of the gravitational pull.

The words and numbers are in super large fonts (Matthew 7:15-23.) Twisted, convoluted interpretations scolded her nightmare as drool dripped from the Wolf onto the Bible.

Sound waves drummed and echoed, resonating. She tried to plug her ears with tiny fingers and turn her face away, but it was not possible for a steel chord was drilled into her chin, metal straps bound to her blonde hair with cutting screws. She was caged in a human mold, bolted upright as the wolf slid his slick tongue across his canines. Reverberating in Lil Sammy's head were these words.

'These Wolves are false teachers and prophets who appear to be genuine spiritual guides but are quite the opposite full of schemes, evil, selfish intentions to advance their own agenda. They look and sound authentic and forthright, but it was the ole adage Wolves in sheep's clothing indeed.'

On the outside, they look like ordinary humans, but inside, internally, they are evil entities consumed with lust and greed, immorally masked by clothing and the pages of scriptures. None of this is apparent. They are stealth-like covert, especially subserviently correct when conversing with their preys... parents portraying a perfect persona aura of falsehoods. Their smiles turned upside down to ghoulish greedy frowns invisible because they preach a good gospel in the most compelling charismatic manner. The adults are manipulated easily for the power of righteousness enlightenment is the path they yearn to follow. But if cognizant wise of the world's ways, <u>Reread Matthew 7:15-23</u> not a naïve 13-year-old child's preponderances, to understand the Evils on this Planet, Sammy's incontinence felt.

Gradually, worn down and manipulated, some Sheep of the congregation seem to blend inaccuracy with facts, and at some point, people seem to forget that Truth mixed selfishly with egregious errors purposely hailed for ulterior motives is no longer truth morphing into deception, betrayal, lies of Omission equals absolute Truth! Sammy's ghastly nightmare laying on the lounge chair under an awning of the motorhome only morphed horrifically into hideous collateral damage that she'd been exposed to as a child.

The Wolf has her alone again. His long sharp tongue is pressed into her navel untethered. He was thirsty and drooling froth. She was frozen, frightened into a stupor, swinging in a birdcage covered by a circus tent. The demonic Wolf morphs into a Vulture swooping through prisms, its talons razor sharp exposed, beady eyes glowing Red, snatches her up airborne, flailing mid-air, then a wooden handle rope trapeze!

Unable to recognize and differentiate the dream world from the earth Plane, Joe's blood-red eyes and protruding sharp beak… he the face of the Vulture.

Without harmony, Sammy and Joe… were abruptly awakened!… a lightning-quick life-or-death reality. Joe still kept his sound-suppressed 357 Magnum pistol under the pad of his lounge chair. Simultaneously 'speed of lightning' Cold steel was placed against Joe's left temple. Another man pounds the barrel of his weapon into Sam's chest.

Sam's Pimp says, 'get the fk up. We're going in the motorhome now; I'll shoot you in the fkn head if you blink!'

"Sam, you fkn whore" the voice of her controlling pimp resonated inches from her ear "let's go." Joe fires his gun through the pillow into the other intruder's intestines as Sammy, with deceptive agility, surprises her pimp with a knife stabbing his shoulder; Joe is already in motion as the assailant begins to fall.

The following bullet entered the pimp's throat and then exited. No words were spoken as Joe quickly opened a latch as little Sammy was pulling the loose limbs of her deceased pimp towards him. Joe opened the blue tarp, and in less than five minutes, both bodies were covered.

Joe had parked the motorhome in the back '40' of the KOA Campground, but still, campers on the left and right had turned their lights on, even though the sound of the gun was squelched having a sound-suppressor attached and reduced even more with the pillow… neighbors were up.

Joe checked the time. It was 4:20 am; he quickly grabbed her and started to swing her around as curious eyes reached them. They

It took less than 25 minutes to pack up and load the two men's bodies. Retracting the awning and the five sliders of the magnificent diesel pusher motorhome, they rolled right out the gates and onto I-5 north. No music, no words… in their own thoughts. She said one sentence, but he didn't respond in kind. "Joe, I'm not 19 years old. I'm 25 years old just wanted to set the record straight."

She watched the monitor, the aerodynamic coal-black motorcycle trailer attached followed behind, and backup cameras showed the moon still alight as they drove over I-5 on Highway 505, then 35 minutes later on Highway 80 heading towards San Francisco. Sammy, hungry and thirsty for caffeine, went to the back and had fresh coffee brewed and was mixing a bowl… Its contents included peppers, onions, tomatoes, a smidgen of garlic and butter, and whisking eggs with a dash of milk, ham, and Swiss cheese sliced into Lil chunks. Tasty omelet sandwiches were on the menu as she hummed silently to herself.

Joe only nodded with a slight smile or was it a grimace she couldn't figure, then he said 'thanks,' and he chomped down on the toasted sourdough breakfast sandwich sipping on fresh coffee while they veered towards signs that read Napa Highway 36, Sonoma.

It was Tuesday early morning. The Sun had arisen as Joe pulled the motorhome into a rest area; she stepped out with a cigarette in her slender fingers.

Moments later, he had a Camel lit and puffing, then said, out of the Blue, "We gotta quit smoking. It hampers our cardio breathing, endurance." Her skin tingles. Wait… did he just mutter that inclusive word 'we?' She decided to follow up, "Okay, if you do, I can too!"

Joe then used the pronoun 'we' once again "We have a task to complete this morning." Watching him now retrieve a burner phone powered it up, she couldn't see the small LCD screen which read 'success it is go mode.' Joe then took her by the hand "you shower first; do you have any dark clothing?" "No, I left some of it by the rest area when the cops were chasing me" Joe nodded. "Okay, we will stop at a store."

Inside the shower, she stood confused. He never asked for the camera umh or film of the murder of the P.I. she had irrefutable evidence of his face shown in 'high-definition color.' Not a word did he utter, odd.

The camera was in a locker in the United Airlines wing at Sacramento Airport.

She toweled off, thinking, what the heck were they going to do with the pimp and his brother's body? How long did it take for them to start stinking and rotting? Sammy steps out and sees Joe's reflection in a mirror, his back to her in the spare bedroom. She faked a cough, making sure not to scare or startle him. He didn't flinch, so she meandered forward.

Feeling her presence over his shoulder, he said, "this is a McMillan 50 Caliber sniper rifle, my favorite for the type of job we're going to complete." She watched as he spread out a package wrapped in felt cloth… pieces of a sophisticated weapon made for destruction on a fold-out table.

On the table nearest them sat an open laptop with a flashing dot on a map close to Napa. It was a hotel, but the blinking dot wasn't moving. It was stationary. "Samantha, here is our objective this morning" as he taps the screen, an effeminate man is exposed, a video. I might need you to draw him out. Let's get you some better clothes; they left the rest area, yet she was far from rested.

-18-

Director of the FBI, Tanya Firm, and Rico Captor.

Rico had listened to Tanya the night before describing the murder of the Private Investigator. His face and head had been blown to fragments, ugh, smithereens. Once again, a playing card, the Jack of spades, was pinned to the windshield wiper with the replicated serial killer's written phrase.

Her tone was foreboding. Between the words and inflections, something obscure ominously lingered. He kept asking her, "what else is that all? What are you not telling me? Tanya!"

He had known Tanya 'inside and out,' but she only provided him with the words, "we will discuss it in person, Rico."

The playing cards confirmed the connection between the two attorneys and a private investigator, all based in Sacramento. He was confident they would uncover motives for the slaying and kidnappings shortly.

Up before sunrise, his team of Agents had watched nurse Dan Spike meet up with the same man he'd been with on Sunday and Monday night. They hadn't left their hotel room, ordered room service all the information gleaned from the informant Petey had come to fruition. Pete didn't exaggerate, only spoke sadly on the verge of tears when informing them of Danny's mindset, how he had changed like the wind in a storm.

Pete was invaluable. He had snooped and found the details on Danny's phone of how and when the final installment for the killing of Wendi was to be paid. It was going to be at Golden Gate Park in San Francisco… Danny was getting the last half of the contract to kill Wendi 25,000 dollars today.

The park was massive, about 1.583 sq. miles, with way too many places to hide. Rico was confident Mark was behind the ordered slaying of Wendi. It was possible that Mark could be the person who was going to pay Dan, most likely not, though, unless in disguise. One way or another, they would be there, follow and capture all culpable parties he was pumped up. The FBI team waited patiently for Rico's orders. Soon the would-be assassin would awake and leave the hotel to pick up the $25,000 final installment for the dirty deed.

<u>FBI: Peter was distraught and sequestered.</u>

There wasn't a way to prevent the hurt and despair or heartache; drugs and alcohol were only temporary solutions, depressants that left you lower in self-esteem and self-worth once

Next thing Pete knew, he was invaded by the FBIs three Agents stood in his living room, escorting him out to something like protective custody. He'd tried to remember what the difference was but had never been locked up in jail. He was locked inside a motel room. It felt to him more like how prison would feel. He was told he wasn't allowed to use his phone or to communicate with anyone and was hitched to a macho man Agent, with straight disdain towards him. At least, this was his gut feeling.

The only positive was that he had seen a Doctor received 15 stitches, and was given pain medication, he slept all night. His shift was covered at the Napa Hospital. It was Tuesday morning. Remorse leached into his skin as he sat up in the strange bed. His mind and heart were in tatters. What had he done?

<u>Agent Kelsey Marie and Rico Captor.</u>

Rico sat hunched over in a corner booth at a Denny's restaurant nine blocks from the hotel where Dan and his ex-boyfriend were at. On his laptop, he was typing out the start of his daily scheduled paperwork. He was unlike the many other Agents that had stopped typing into their devices using voice recognition apps; for some reason, the words were all wrong when he tried this new lazier way, taking even more time to fix the mistakes.

Although he watched others speaking into their phones and mobile devices for him, sitting in a public place that wasn't a feasible alternative even if it was, Rico was from the old school mentality of 'use it or lose it,' typing mathematics memory working his brain kept him sharp. He allowed himself to drift off as he took the last bite of his Grand-Slam breakfast and gulped the coffee.

A couple of months back, a helicopter landed him and Agent Kelsey Marie (he smiled, a young cutie). She'd grown up in the tech world, intelligent, innovative, and intuitive, an 'up and comer' she sat beside him in the Land Rover near the small town of Elko, Nevada. They were 25 miles from a stealth runway landing strip in the middle of the high desert where an antigovernment faction had another drop of illegal weapons. The Montana faction 'SOJ,' the acronym meaning 'State of Jefferson, ' the militia was led by Jaybird and his followers, which had grown like wildfire.

Kelsey started rifling through her carry-on bag and then purse… like crazed in a panic, ransacking her belongings in obvious search mode. I asked her after a bit, 'what's wrong, Kelsey?' 'Oh, damn, it's my parent's 25th anniversary and my husband's 30th birthday today!' I drove the Land Rover over some rough terrain, saying nothing, uncertain how this could cause her to stress out. I suppose I was more amused than anything else. 'I left my phone on the chopper, damnit, she whined.' The savior that I was I slipped out my phone and handed it to her; yep! She looked at it, then raised her cleft chin. 'What am I going to do with this? Thanks for the thought, though!' 'We're stopping at the next rest area for a meeting. Call your parents and husband from there.'

I was never going to forget Kelsey's look… blank, blushing, and blanched. 'I don't have their phone numbers, Rico. I can't call.' It was my turn to express verbally, uttering words like, umh, what-flabbergasted shocked, I said to her, 'what, you can't be serious?' Kelsey seemed to feel embarrassed and fidgeted with my phone, 'I never memorized their phone numbers. I imputed them into speed dial numbers just pushing one number for years or used my voice commands like verbalizing 'call mom.' I'm lost; I think I remember some of my husband's numbers.' I rolled my shoulders and eyes with a bizarre expression on my face. Kelsey already had her iPad out, going to Google their names. Hopefully, their numbers would come up, 'Kelsey, you're a brilliant young lady, but if you don't use it, you will eventually lose it!' said I. She mumbled. 'Heck, I guess I can email them or Facebook,' she murmured off…

So, chalk up another win for old school memories; back in the day, people had memorized phone numbers, but now not so.

A text flashed across my screen, breaking me out of the revelry… 'movement at the hotel.' Danny and his boyfriend Derek were packing up; Danny's VW Rabbit was tagged with a GPS chip. Out the door, I went. One certainty was that we wouldn't lose Nurse Spike my lead Agent of the three on the ground was Agent Kelsey Marie; we kept our distance in different vehicles. I parked at a Walgreens drugstore, knowing that 'Dan' would be traveling to San Francisco Golden Gate Park. At our disposal was a helicopter and several CHPs no way for him to avoid or lose us.

<u>Samantha went shopping with Joe.</u>

Sammy and Joe were stumbling out of Macy's with shopping bags in 3 of 4 hands, clothes, perfumes, and miscellaneous for Sam. Joe couldn't pass up the fragrance aisle as he loaded up in excess of $500 worth of cologne. They had parked the motorhome trailer behind Walgreens. They had already lowered the ramp and taken the KTM's for a ride. Finally, his target was up and moving. The phone Danny carried was being traced. Joe thought as he walked with her by his side. Almost a fatal mistake, his fault, stupid arrogance. The pimp had traced Sammy's phone to the KOA Campground easy as 1-2-3; nowadays, even Facebook would alert users. 'Oh, by the way, you visited this place or that place a week ago, and social media tracked you… humans were on the maps, and there was nowhere to hide if you engaged with technology.'

Joe believed in off-the-grid living but used high-tech when it was to his advantage. In the corner of his mind, he had to figure out a place to drop the pimp and his brother's corpses.

Sammy felt bewildered, a tiny tinge of anxiety, for indeed, they had barely spoken to each other… strange nuance. She'd listened to Joe speak with a guy named Mark. They were debating, Joe had preferred a close-up kill shot like the P.I., but Mark, whom I'd never met, wanted a sniper shot to finish the job. It was not a personal 'hit.' The main problem was, where can you hide a gigantic motorhome with a trailer? Joe seemed steadfast and deliberate in his motions.

According to Joe, looking through the scope attached to the McMillen 50 Caliber, the target was 255 yards off a relatively simple shot for Joe, an elite marksman trainer for one of the more prominent Militias in Idaho. We watched as the two men made their way into the hotel lobby, watching the tracking beacon on the laptop screen. The target had stopped moving for now, seven minutes. Joe orders, "Sam, take the bike back out of the trailer, and don't waste any time, find out what's going on with the target, and be quick about it. Here is a mini helmet radio."

Joe didn't have a clear shot when the guys entered the lobby. The goal was to shoot him dead in or by his VW Rabbit.

Sammy did precisely as she was told. She dressed in her new clothes, leaving her long blonde hair to flutter about in the wind out of the helmet, cruised the hotel's parking lot once through no sign of 'Danny' staring at the picture that Joe had given to her, decided to make a final pass, into the helmet mic radio "I'm going to go inside, wait something is wrong." "Whatcha mean? Something is wrong, girl?" "hold on!" Sammy was a veteran of the streets… instinct-intuition based learned to develop a 7th type of sense and had been arrested a total of 15 times, but none in the last three years though she was still finishing off another probation term non-violent charges of such petty theft, shoplifting stealing a purse, vagrancy, stolen checks, prostitution… yup all of that.

By now, she could smell the police; the stench overwhelmed her. An incongruently dressed woman sat in a white Volvo in a neat business suit, a man in a Dodge truck on the other side of the lot. She kicked the gearshift down and slowly puttered by the Volvo glanced in and saw a woman wearing a skirt with a briefcase on the passenger seat. A screen flashed on the center console. Oh, shit, a police scanner and radio with a fricken pair of binoculars on her lap. "I'm on my way back," relayed Sammy.

Kelsey hits the radio mic, "Rico, it's probably nothing but a woman with blonde hair on a crotch rocket just rode by closer than I'd liked" "where is she?" "Lost her out of my line of sight," the Agent in the truck adds. "She just passed by and out of the parking lot. I got her tag!" "all right, call it in; never can be too careful!"

Sam drives the motorcycle up the ramp into the trailer as Joe closes and locks it up. "There is a police presence like a Sting. I've seen too many drug busts at raunchy motels. I'm telling you, Joe, it might not be the 'target' that they're interested in, but ..." "Okay, I trust your judgment. We will only observe; we got the guy or at least his phone's whereabouts." "They must be eating at the café...." Several moments later, she's watching through binoculars, and Joe is zooming in with his scope "hell, and I got a shot." Sammy holds her hand up and says, "look at the guy at 5 o'clock. He's got a shoulder holster, classic law-enforcement officer." Joe stood down, and then her intuition was confirmed as the caravan left the parking lot.

'Give them some space,' says Rico watching Danny stop at a bar or lounge parking lot and lean over and kiss Derek goodbye. Now Derek drives off in his vehicle while Danny holds a phone up in his palm.

Joe had Danny's phone number, for he was the person who was supposed to pay the last installment of $25,000 to him at <u>Golden Gate Park. He texts Danny 'GGP' at 1 pm.</u> Seconds later, 'K' pops up on his phone. We're heading to Golden Gate Park, girl; make a fresh pot of coffee, please!

'The tags came back clean. Sir, the bike was registered to 'Ben Abbott' out of Fairfield, okay,' said Rico on the radio. He checks

the time. It is 9:45 am, and his main phone startles him recognizing the number "uhm, Morning, Tanya" *"Good morning. Just a couple of updates Marshall Evans turned in his retirement papers. He's quitting Rico, I think; well, hell, I know he's been Wendi's bodyguard the entire time she's been at Napa. I realize we couldn't divulge the orchestrated fake murder plot with him because we wanted natural reactions, nothing that Nurse Spike could catch on to. I think he blames himself, though, and that's why he wants to retire." "You're most likely correct, Tanya. I'll have a meeting with him after we play this out. You said a couple of updates, didn't you?" "Yeah, it might be nothing, but we've discussed last night's homicide of the P.I. a frequency blocker was used after reviewing all police records around the city. Ironically, there was an ongoing chase of a motorcycle that involved the Sacramento Sheriff's Department and CHP. Get this, Rico, it began in the same parking lot, 'Chili's' that the P.I. was found shot!"*

Pause, "well didn't they catch the rider? Why the chase?" "That's just it; the guy whipped out an elongated wheelie, showing off on a crotch rocket a kid goofing off. We're guessing, umh, he got away!" "It would be a stretch to try and connect the dots!" "Gotta be unrelated, but a motorcycle rider did see to ride super close to one of our Agents just now. I'll forward you the info and keep you in the loop, Tanya," click.

-19-

NIA Concerns.

By Tuesday morning, the floodgates were obliterated. Chaos reigned from the NIA investors… on down to the Sinaloa Cartel. The word that Wendi Feral had died was headline news on CNN, and Fox News… broadcasts around the world. Social media went full-on Bonkers storylines 'Jax Foul,' her involvement with saving the children from the Cuban Mafia. She was like a folk hero. Most didn't buy into the fantasy world of a person being able to communicate with animals. The tabloids sensationalized and exploited Wendi's life. Most people were nonbelievers, witches, goblins, and superheroes, then Wendi.

On a highly secure conference call were CEO Terrence Hallinan, Warden Ursula Anders, and the head of the Medical Department at NIA, Doctor Liz Honcho… Terrence shouted, "how the hell could you allow this to happen right under your noses here? We have one of the most secure prisons in North America, and you let the Fkn Feds inside. Who the hell is this, Doctor Hawkins? what were….." Liz hurls herself into the fray. "Now listen here, Ursula and I had everything under control. No one, not even the Marshals, were involved. This plot involved that bastard Rico Captor and that Doctor I'm ….." "Excuse me, says the Warden. We've found her. She's in the SHU secure housing unit under FBI guard as far as I see it…." "You both listen to me. I don't give a flying fk what you think we have. It's a catastrophe spinning out of control. We have a planned mission for next week. Wendi is a crucial piece of our team uuhhh; actually, without her, we will flounder." Paused takes a swig of scotch. Terrance gazes out of his penthouse overlooking the beautiful city of San Francisco.

"Ladies, we have a problem," he lowers his voice to almost a whisper. "Calmer heads will prevail, so let us all take deep breaths and start over. One of our highest-level moles… FBI informant gave us reliable evidence that a 'hit' on Wendi was paid for by Wendi's brother Mark. At least that's what has been assumed a nurse under our employment at NIA was the assassin, and yesterday was to be the kill."

He takes another sip. "Rico brought in outside personnel to make the hit look authentic and to ensure there weren't any leaks from other sources. Otherwise, Marshal Evans and Burke and Marshal Rand would have notified us…." "we've paid them well enough to guard Wendi hell five times what the FBI pays them," says Liz. "Well, in a way, we are fortunate that Rico got wind of the 'hit,' or we truly could have lost Wendi for good!" exclaims Warden Anders. "Yes, very true, but where do we go from here? How do we take back control of Wendi? Aah, damnit, must go. I will meet you both at 7 am at the Calico Winery. The red line is flashing. I have to attend a video conference" click.

<u>Joe and Mark.</u>

"I know these phones are secure and untraceable, Joe, but call me paranoid. I don't enjoy talking on them. Right now, the feds could be pointing one of their listening cones spheres right at the motorhome can tape and hear every word we speak." "Whoa, Mark, why would they use them? We're not under scrutiny or suspicion. We must discuss what's happening here if we can't talk face-to-face. This is the only alternative that we have; we got terrible news." "Okay, bro, where are you at?" "Driving north, just passing the city limits sign for Petaluma on Highway 101, the rabbit is five cars up ahead." "Fk it; I was gonna tell you to text me everything, but let's throw caution to the wind, bro. I'm sitting on the lake, so it's your ass if they're eavesdropping," he laughs. "Funny boy Mark, you won't be laughing long 'nursey poo Danny' has a tail. Think it's a Federal one, an Agent in a truck ahead of him, another a few cars up behind him in a Volvo, get this, there's also a bird in the sky still funny?"

"What the fk why huh this doesn't make any sense uhm he did his job Wendi is dead it's all over the wires um internet. We have to analyze this what reasons…." "Bro, should I pull off? It's way too risky to continue with our closing theme, and you know what I'm saying?" "Joe, even with my disguise, he could pick me out of a lineup. Remember, I had to have a one-on-one with the faggot to lure him in, reel him in, and couldn't just drop the coins off; we need him out of the equation. Let me call you back?" "Well, I'm going to fall back. I have him on the screen. Call me soon, brother!" click.

Wendi and Jax Foul.

Jax Foul was a complicated individual, a war hero Army Ranger 23 days and nights under the middle East's desert sky-shackled, chained, tormented physically & mentally deformed, doomed. He lived his life in everlasting punishment until a six-year-old blind girl and a five-year-old boy, both exceptional precocious children whom he had kidnapped into his life, had altered his mindset... The children were terrific, with loads of compassion, love, empathy, and forgiveness for him. Despite him being a 'kidnapper,' their bond had transformed him, melting his animus for society.

In just five weeks, Juan and Leah would visit him, now 16 and 15 years old, in high school. Among many disorders, Jax suffered from PTSD; he attended group therapy sessions and regularly visited the psych ward doctors. He'd kept a medical regimen, including prescriptions. Unlike other patients, inmates... Jax could and did leave the steel razor irons of the gates at NIA whenever he wanted, which surprisingly wasn't often.

He was allowed to go shopping for groceries or even to see a movie. Jax had free reign and had taken on the role of the head of the maintenance department at NIA, a paycheck he didn't really need. He was pleasantly compensated for his leadership in the Missions he'd completed for Terrance and the NIA organization.

But he always laid his head down inside the prison. It was his home, unlike many of the tormented who'd been terminally sentenced and incarcerated, the isolated suffering within themselves due to internal & external alienation; he was at NIA because he wanted to be!

Jax had learned empathy and compassion; kindheartedness was on his mind for most of the humans he encountered unless it was Work! When Jax heard about Wendi's death, he absolutely refused to listen to or believe the heart attack story. He had only visited her hours before on the same Monday morning. She was on the road to recovery

Wendi, that is 'Sunshine,' her counterpart alter-ego. She was in NIA's Psychiatric treatment center because she was deemed schizophrenic and still in protective custody. Wendi was in control of her mind and completely sane. This Jax was sure of. Jax had thought of Wendi as lucky at times, for she had but two personalities, a split mind Schitzo. He felt like a multitude of voices were inside his own head, and unlike her, he didn't have control of a single one. Having shuffled past the nurse's station and witnessing the distraught emotions and tears, what struck him was the quietude of the people he'd known, like zombies in a morgue or humanoids... the staff was on auto-drive, and blank stares abound. Jax pondered the situation as it unfolded. He was working with eyes wide open, changing out air conditioner filters on the 3rd floor that Wendi's room used to be on.

He felt compassion for a few people, most he looked on with intense hatred, and for some of the others, he had a form of indifference ah ambivalence. He gaged the solemn reaction via close-circuited cameras. The video recordings he'd watched many times seemed fake and orchestrated. Agent Rico Captor, alongside a new doctor pushing a gurney that held Wendi, falsehoods, and lousy acting because Rico would have been torn up and out, Jax knew Rico loved her, as she did him ain't no way she had died... Nope!

When chaos hit, he had raced to Wendi's floor just in time to catch the end of the act; he'd crept along, staying back, watching the elevator open and close. The elevator stalled, stopping on a floor below in the basement, staying open at the floor where they conducted autopsies, ugh, where they took the dead. Nope, not only autopsies, but it was the floor for solitary confinement Wendi lived. But why this elaborate playacting? What was really going on here? Where's the logic? He reaches into his tool pouch, take's out a bottle of prescription pills, and chews one of them up. He sits back in a cubby hole by the water cooler inside his head, the throbbing pain and temporal suffering, uh, an infinitesimal irritation compared to the horrendous Train churning-turning echoing migraines that inhabited his skull daily.

<u>Why Wendi was injured?</u>

<u>Jax and Wendi were on another NIA mission. One Week before! Wendi's orchestrated death, how she became bruised and battered.</u>

Marshal Evans with Marshal Burke, who was driving the van. It had been a long flight to Washington, D.C. the language preferred was Russian, which they spoke fluently.

The pre-conference plan at the embassy was as tense as Jax could remember. He'd been on so many missions, campaigns military operations truly had lost count now in his 40s in the best shape of his life. His workouts were legendary.

President Trump had become nearly synonymous with the Russian investigations, staff firings, and conspiracies were poured out like salt on French fries. Washington, D.C., was encapsulated yet unable to digest the Russian involvement in Trump's rise to power. Was it all smoke and mirrors? Clever diversionary tactics by anti-Trump haters, the Democrats, none of that mattered a hoot to Jax. His heart monitor, along with Wendi's <u>'Sunshine,'</u> was rhythmically shown on a portable screen with blood pressure flashing.

Doctor Liz Honcho sat by; there was a narrow window with the shades drawn closed. They had to conclude this NIA operation quickly for Barbara and Ed Feral… Wendi's parents were due back down from Vancouver, Washington, in merely three days. Wendi had to be resting in her induced coma at Napa when her parents and husband, or for that matter if the pesky Agent Rico Captor, visited. Regrettably, Wendi was injured during the last operation. No broken bones, but had some soft tissue scrapes and bruises. Wendi was a main cog in many of these missions, but not all for sure. Sometimes Wendi wasn't needed, but in this operation, it was her and him dressed in light armor with all the sophisticated technology available in 2019… they lacked nothing.

Jax had known what Wendi had gone through… they were subjected to treatment programs to regain their footing, and

NIA needed Sunshine, not Wendi, for these operations; Sunshine was cut and dry, a mean-spirited force to be reckoned with. Jax's torturous past will always linger... PTST, his brain was trampled, manipulated, and intoxicated with designer drugs and psychotropic remedies. Ah, and concoctions that, at times, had him so high that he thought he could fly!

Grounded, with self-control, focused on limits, his aim was as if it always had been. Pure omnipotent awareness would enable him to protect the Saint, his hero, the good 'Wendi.' It was an onerous grueling task solely his own.

Jax cared far less for her alter-ego 'Sunshine' her invisible childhood companion and domineering personality 'Sunshine' who had wrested control through drugs that initiated the manifestation, and gravity was in charge and did the rest. Would the real Wendi ever appear or live again? Sadly he shook his head. Jax knew, for all intents and purposes, he was not traveling on these Missions with Wendi. Nope, his partner was 'Sunshine.'

A Russian Diplomats young daughter was abducted... an inside job right under the thumbs of the security forces at the Russian embassy. She an innocent five-year-old only saving grace was that they also captured her mother. The diplomat was engaged in releasing harmful proprietary information of exclusive information uh facts, dealings, and contracts with Trump's clan, family, and friends. It is like the old adage 'loose lips sink ships,' and Trump's Yacht was far from sinking. Sure, it had a few holes, but nothing. A little sandpaper and putty couldn't cork.

Not a Single word of this extraction is found in the media. The 'trouble' wasn't easily comprehended. Trouble being (father, husband Diplomat) wasn't going to waver and undauntingly refused to capitulate. Instead of surrendering, the man went on the offensive and didn't budge or knuckle under. The threats were taken seriously; in a vault was unmitigated proof of a $355 million investment into a parcel in South Florida on a golf course. Putin's regime was inherently connected to all... although was it merely hearsay?

The caustic dilemma reached boiling points as the mercenary kidnappers, believed to be from the CIA, threatened to start amputating the little girl's fingers and toes, umh, stalemate!

'Sherlock Holmes' had nothing on 'Sunshine,' for he couldn't communicate with animals. Sunshine is deviously corrupt; we'd entered the triple ironed spiked gates of the Embassy 55 acres right outside of downtown D.C. the perimeter was crowded with Russia's elite special forces dogs moved about untethered verbal commands adhered to. Marshal Burke parked the van. The side door spun open on its hinges as Marshal Evan reached for Sunshine's hand.

I followed her out; you would have had to been there to believe it 'each dog was paraded up as Wendi kneeled to pet their furry foreheads' a meeting of the minds, not a word nor syllable spoken, then, at last, a Russian Wolfhound barked with a 'purring growl.' Wendi regained her feet and walked to the open van. Pulled out the snacks we had started to munch on. It was already 1:25 pm, no lunch, so I supposed she was hungry like I was. Uh, I've learned never to underestimate Sunshine because that wasn't the case at all.

She reaches in, grabs a small bag of potato chips, and then starts crunching them up. The bag pops as she walks away on the edge of the pavement, where it met the flawlessly manicured green grass. Pouring in a pile, the chips fell, then stepped away. Where did the birds come from?

Before 15 seconds had passed, five pigeons were chewing, clawing for a position, and devouring the chips as fast as their beaks would chomp. Then a well-placed boot stopped the voracious activity that's when the birds noticed her stare, now birds eyes wide, beaks likewise.

Bird brains intertwined as the Russian guards amusingly peered out beside the Marshals, Dr. Liz Honcho, and me. It seemed surreal while, from a branch far away, a chirping songbird landed right on Wendi's palm, a baby Robin. The birds just stood, their heads twisting back and forth. Hunger was alleviated; she put her forefinger on the Robin. Its tiny head wobbled. Wendi aah Sunshine then regained her footing and walked back to the van leaving the other birds in a feeding frenzy crunching potato chips. All but one bird dined.

With the Robin in her left hand, Doctor Liz Honcho started to approach her; then a right hand was thrown up, stop, opening tearing a bag of roasted salted sunflower seeds de-shelled pouring into her right hand the bird ate, ever so slowly. "Jax, can you pull up the pictures of the females who work here at the Embassy?" I did, then she and I flicked from photo to photo on the laptop till the Robin hopped into the air a few inches. Then abruptly flew out of the van, we waited for we'd been over similar scenes in the past as a group. 'Fanny,' the Robin left frustrated. Wendi explains, "we all look the same to her, people that is... she went in search of one of her friends, a Crow that was perched on the window seal. The Crow had started the gossip rumor of the abduction and supposedly had a 'birds-eye view' one of the Pigeons claimed to hear muffled cries as a large Black Lincoln Navigator drove through the exit gates. A woman with Raven black hair pulled into a bun was driving. That's the same description that 'Fanny' had told Wendi that the Crow saw, so we wait. None of the pictures matched the woman with her hair in a bun."

Didn't have to wait long till 'Charlie,' a disheveled greying Crow, arrived closed-beaked. The wise old bird started obviously negotiating with Wendi; he explicitly made demands for a piece of wheat bread, fresh to the dismay of Dr. Honcho. Wendi unpeeled her sandwich and placed the mayonnaise bread on her knee, and Charlie didn't mind the mustard either as he tore into his favorite food.

We patiently watched as he gulped down an entire slice and hopped over to the next piece... nope. Wendi held it up; apparently, it was time for Charlie to sing, um, after a moment. Wendi angrily scowled, shaking her head in disgust, and tossed the other slice out of the van. With disdain, she said... "Bird brains, ugh, this birds playing games," smiled, then declared, "I need to interview 'Jack' right now." Of course, the three of us stare at her with, I suppose, an exasperated look like, who the hell was Jack? She declared that the Crow said the family dog had been in the same room as the kidnappers, had a better look, and would be a much better eyewitness. 'Jack' was a five-year-old little Jack Russell Terrier!

It seemed to take forever to get through security. Finally, the puppy dogs sadly pronounced eyes were front and center, and the family pet 'Jack' bowed anxiously before us. His muzzle perked up when their eyes met, and he became a motormouth in a flash and a shake. Jack had picked out 'Natasha,' the child's nanny caretaker umh, malefactor, offender, and culprit. She drove the mother and daughter out of the basement garage in the specially designed undercarriage of the SUV. Jack had ridden the elevator down the five floors and saw it all through puppy dog eyes. He chose three of the culpable bodyguards on the laptop, and he growled, barked, then lunged at the 11x17 picture of the soon-to-be-arrested Natasha!

Jax absorbed all in contemplation, thinking about his tours of duty in the Middle East, how Wendi A.K.A. Sunshine could have saved thousands of lives literally interviewing Camels, cats, dogs, rodents, and birds, she made his 'detailed job' so much easier with Russian assistance and the loyal diplomat's protectors it was so straightforward.

I mean, think about it mother and child had been held for five days and nights, the viable threat of delivering the child's pinky finger in hours if her father 'Diplomat' didn't cease his campaign to take down Trump and Putin.

It was per usual for the three bodyguards and Natasha, who was doing her best at playacting as if in downright turmoil because of the kidnappings. They were all onsite coincidentally and were arrested in less than 15 minutes. Out of the four collaborations, ugh, tied, and chained accomplices, I chose the weakest of them to torture. This wasn't the female nanny. She was kryptonite. Her unwavering resolve aligned with what only came with unadulterated love and commitment to whom she loved is what only mattered to this woman. Natasha was staunchly determined.

It turned out that Natasha's parents and siblings were captured back in Russia. If she weren't compliant and complicit, their abductors would kill them all; her younger brother's head was delivered to her grandmothers the day before she agreed to conspire with the gangster's plans. Under extreme duress, she decided to aid in the plot uuhhh kidnappings. In less than 45 minutes, the nanny had taken us to a once lucrative amusement park popular in the 70s… long since closed. The park was fenced off with chain-link fencing at a height of 11 feet. Strangely there was a guy in a golf cart that manned the rolling gate. Still, this was as far as the nanny had gone in transferring mother-daughter into a van.

This is where my expertise came into effect; the problem was that the 75-acre dilapidated rusted park had too many buildings that could hold the little girl; time was wasting not much time till the pinky would be amputated. I had access to HHTI heat sensor scopes, Military satellites, and thermal imaging nothing showed up on the screen. How could that be? With the most advanced technology, I couldn't find a single human except the Golf cart guard.

Marshal Evans and Marshal Burke were part of our NIA team along with Doctor Liz Honcho. I stood in front of the open van… Hoping the three of them listened. I was in charge, uhm, and I could tell they didn't like following my instructions, at times, showed a smidgeon of contempt outwardly. They constantly complained to Terrance Hallinan, CEO of NIA, asking him how he could place a man like me in command. Oh well, anyways, that was a few missions back. Now they didn't argue as much; for the most part, they jumped when I barked. Okay, let me lay out the logistical quandaries. We had surveillance on the entire complex. The park's circumference was open pavement, with a large parking lot of past use. The gatekeeper could see me from 300 yards out before my approach, cameras on fence posts. Surely I could use a tech-blocking device, but to what means? We couldn't locate the prisoners; option number one was to disable the gate man somehow and then press him… to convince him to tell me where his accomplices were, along with mother and daughter.

Shit, how did we miss it? Yep, another golf cart came into view. This cart was obviously used for a sentry. How many other carts were there? The golf cart pulled up to the gate. A slender woman with a ball cap, ugh, Yankees, bounced out of it. Immediately I saw an unnatural bulge by her left breast unless she had a tumor about ready to burst. It was a shoulder holster, a gun. A game of tag as the first cart took to patrolling the inside perimeter.

Our superiors were trying to stall and not give in to the demands of the kidnappers, then an about-face suddenly the staunch, steadfast father, Diplomat, was in the backtrack mode acceding acquiescent ready to come to the table. To negotiate for his family's safe return, all of this truly put forth enormous pressure on our team. The rumor that the C.I.A. was behind this operation... stratagem had just been substantiated.

Wendi sat alongside Liz as the Marshalls played with their phones wandering around the van. We were in front of another industrial complex, the hustle and bustle, trucks coming and going. Wendi gently pulled her earbuds from her ears, listening to a select music blend that sounded like reggae kinda upbeat music as if that mattered. "I'm not sitting here any longer, Jax. I'm taking control of the situation." With her left hand, she opened her small suitcase, "please turn around. I'm going to change into some civilian clothes," non-plussed Liz, and I did so.

She removed all the body armor, now capris and a pinkish rose-colored blouse finished with a make-up touchup. "I'll be right back." Marshal Evans cautiously would heed her directive to stay a decent distance in the rears. I watch Wendi head right to a 7-Eleven convenience store she entered... moments later, bag in hand as she left. We only watched her, um let me explain in my many ways of thinking we all have different personalities, 'Yah-see;' Wendy was like a sole proprietor worked alone. Her mind was an independent wheel in motion at a whim; she flowed, most often not a pre-planned scheme. She was the foremost intuitive pinch-hitter using creativity at a whim, spontaneously winging it. Gosh, I love that little lady, all 5'1" short and 131 pounds.

She strutted from past the Lowe's store to store, and then we nearly lost her in Petco. Can you understand, um, imagine being her... with all the animals like, duh, talking for days, right? She reappeared, and on a leash was a grayish silver racing dog, skin and bone a Greyhound.

I grinned. Yes, ole Wendi, um, Sunshine had a plan and confidently strutted towards us.

Strolling up like not a care in the world, we gather around as if she was the Puppet Master. With a smirk, "this is Slim," which coincidentally was my nickname. She rolled her eyes at me with knowledge. "Slim will break ranks. I will be walking him on a leash. He will break away from me." Pausing as if she was winging it herself, "um, guessing he will be able to sniff around the inside perimeter. The security guards will give chase maybe, of course, I will be frantically putting it on hard and heavy my doggy gosh got away-oh please catch him. I will implore the guards to help me!"

Our heads swivel about facial acceptance, wily beguiling, fascinated stares. Why didn't we think of this? "Okay, Slim, you know the plan, right?" He barked three times, and eyes met 'sure, yes,' she said to him. Out came a bowl. 'I need some water.' Out of the grocery sack came some deluxe dog food and another bowl, food that I bet could be sold at a Chinese restaurant... yum!

Off walked Slim and Sunshine, her hair in a ponytail, a hidden radio, her phone, and one bag. The shopping center at the closest point to the front gate, where the guards patrolled, was about a city block away. We set up behind some thick Oleander bushes, and then Slim broke loose.

Wendi, on the script, screamed and jogged after him; she calculated adequately for the chained gate had barely enough of an opening for Slim to slide through; few dog breeds were as quick, fast, and thin as Greyhounds.

The guard of male persuasion lumbered out of the golf cart as it shuddered with relief he was massive, not in a healthy way, with imperfect extra girth. He raised both arms turning towards Wendi, who grabbed the steel links shaking the fence. "My dog, get my dog. Let me inside now! My dog is getting away!"

He wobbled his head at Slim, who was partway across the lot, nose to the ground on a mission, then looked appraisingly at Wendi. No doubt he enjoyed her look as he slid a triple chin and a cavernous dimple towards her; "stay here, Ms., I'll get him," on the radio as he stumbled back into the scared golf cart.

Soon enough, the slender woman guard was in the hunt, both Golf carts trying to corral 'Slim.' Try as she could, there wasn't enough room for Wendi to squeeze through the chained gate.

Slim was having fun dodging the futile attempts of catching him systematically, going from one building to the next, having previously been given clothing of mother and daughter, so Slim had reference points of smell.

Binoculars in hand, Jax watched and accidentally let loose a chuckle… six eyes of disdain greeted his momentary lapse of judgment. He thought, what the hell is up their assholes? It was him, him alone, that would risk life and limb to save the prisoners. His partner Wendi was out there performing her best to further this operation. His iPad bleeped, glancing at the profile that popped up of the unhealthy guard. Ain't no way it could be the same dude. Wendi's purse Cam… had taken sharp HD pics of both guards. Omg, I muttered, thinking are you kidding me? No way, but 'facial recognition' nowadays is nearly infallible.

They were both CIA; the woman guard had a long successful resume, uhm, same as the guy who had put on serious weight, upwards of 125 pounds being barely 6 foot, had to weigh 375 pounds… impressive that Facial Recognition worked with his face… it had to have been expanded by three times. The guy was ex-military, a marksman. Jax further researched the overweight Agent, thinking about how he could still be employed.

Then another click and Walla, there it was, uh, uncle and father big wigs with the same acronyms, way up the food chain in the CIA. Wendi's radio mic clipped to her bra sounds off, with the male guard close enough to be heard, "Jane shit, we've been chasing the damn dog for 15 minutes, ugh, we gotta handle this…" "I'll open the gate. You get the owner Hugo uhm, let's make this quick!" "Sure, that's a great idea, Jane. I will grab the owner; the dog will come to her."

Jax watched as the gate was unlocked, a scowl on the woman's face looking down upon the diminutive Wendi with purposely intended intimidation. "Come on, get in the cart. Let's go get your dog," he says. The female hangs at the gate as the two go on dog patrol. "Hey, sir, thanks a lot for helping me get my dog. His name is Slim; I'm so sorry for the trouble. It looked like your girlfriend was pissed off at me, though!" "Aah ummah, my name is 'Hugo,' and she ain't my girlfriend. Ugh, she's into women." "Oh well, I guess I was wrong just thought a handsome fella like yourself would be irresistible to any woman."

This time Jax wasn't the only one of the four listening to laugh. Liz says, "oh, that Wendi, what a bullshit artist." Evans adds, 'A charmer for sure,' Burke mutters, 'The guy's eating it up!' I couldn't help myself saying, 'ain't the only thing the guy eats, lol!'

Wendi watched his face reach near blush mode. 'So what's your name?' before she could answer, Slim darted in the opposite direction. She grabs the roll bar and tries to stand, shouting, 'Slim, come here, boy! Slim.' 'Oh fk,' Hugo growls and swiftly turns to her "sorry, your dog just crawled into the old auditorium through that small gap at...." "Well, stop, Hugo, let me out!" His whole demeanor had changed. Evil lurked, loomed, teeth clenched, "No, I don't have the keys and no way you could fit through that opening." Spinning the golf cart around, "you're going to have to wait outside the gate for your damn dog. I'm done with this... a waste of time. Yuh better train your mutt, damnit!"

Back the way they had gone, "Hugo, please, can I wait by those trees? It's a hot afternoon. I promise not to cause any trouble!" Just then, Slim powers out in 3rd gear. Over Hugo's radio, the female guard yells, 'We're not fking dog catchers, not our problem; we need to get back to work' His retort, 'I'm dropping her over by the fence by the Oak Trees till the dog comes out. She replies, 'shit, it's always something I'm calling the boss.'

"Hugo, hope you're not going to get in any trouble," as he parks. "Stay over there and call your stupid dog. You have 15 minutes if your dog doesn't come to you... you're outta here; that's how it is, you understand?" Hugo wipes his brow with an undersized kerchief. Wendi is precisely where she wants to be as she walks between three ginormous trees.

She opens the bag of stuff she'd bought at the store. A handful of raw walnuts are thrown to the leaves, and then some Pine-nuts were spread out underneath the Oak Tree. In less than three minutes, the inhabitants were out feasting squirrels, chipmunks, and even a wayward Skunk. The rodents didn't mind the smelly mammal devouring the treats too. The rodents were grabbing some nuts and then going to stash them… hiding some for later; once again, Wendi is kneeling, shaking the remainder of the nuts for her audience to see.

Earlier, Slim had signaled her that he had tracked the mother and daughter's scent into the auditorium, then lost the trail down a hallway. Their scent had just disappeared into thin air.

Try as he could, there weren't hints or a whiff of them. His olfactory organs were peaked and charged up, yet slim was confused. It was like a spray bottle was filled with their scent, thick aroma leeches out of the torn carpet and pads below, then nothing as if someone had capped off the spray bottle.

Having sent Slim over towards the gate, perhaps 75 yards off, to tease Hugo while the woman circled the inside perimeter again in her cart. Wendi leaned in, finding the eyes of some of the animal's telepathy. 'I need your help. Have you seen a little girl and mother flashing their pictures from her phone?' The animals all started speaking at the same time till Papa, the elder Skunk, took charge.

'Yes, I saw them,' a chipmunk interrupts and says, 'about five days ago.' Papa whipped his tail up. The rodents squeamishly turned silent, 'quiet!' Papa wouldn't be interrupted again.

'Five large men in suits took them into the building over there. I haven't seen them since… Oh, by the way, the two humans in the carts will be replaced at dark by two more. They will bring a bunch of food and drinks. One of them goes with the stuff into the same building, and then he comes back out after a while.'

Papa whirls around, frightened almost, then says, 'we don't go in those buildings. The River Rats and rat packs live there. We don't mess with them, do we?' As he asks the others, they all nod. I reach into the bag and, being of the 'Girl Scout Motto, Be Prepared,' pulled out a huge, wrapped chunk of pepper jack cheese. 'Get me a meeting with the head Rat! will you help me, please?' 😊

-21-

Catherine, Natasha, Adam, the tortured… Torturer 😦.

Like a piece of driftwood floating upon a slow-moving stream, again shipwrecked, his 9-year-old eyes weeping without moisture, his father plaintively trying to express his innocence. His mom is on a gurney, bloody and unconscious dad is with handcuffs on as he watches him being loaded into the back of a police car.

It always seemed to start and end the same way because of his father's addictions to alcohol and drugs. Adam could never do anything right… this night was the same as last night, every night! He floated aimlessly, abandoned, shoved into the prevailing attitudes of the norm of modern society, no shallow water, just a waterfall, a cliff over the edge of a brutal disaster, never would be hugged by mom again. Adam lived this nightmare redundantly and hauntingly on repeat. Poor little boy Adam grew up nastily unable to recycle his childhood, bent and broken… he naturally decided to propagate the same. 😞 *.*

An ambient temperature of 65 degrees, regulated and recirculated air shafts from above all power ran through narrow channels underground 'The bunker' as it was known by a few of his colleagues, his associates within the CIA. Three floors below the surface were one of the most secure 'holding tanks' uhm, prisons or, as some of the visitors were told, 'safe houses' for witness protection. A total of 13 cells all isolated and were soundproofed. The walls and floors were rubberized. Currently, only five were occupied, the most recent of which were the Diplomat's wife, Anastasia, and daughter Catherine.

Adam, at 45 years old, readily admitted he was an evil soul, but that was fine. He'd have it no other way, saw nothing wrong with how he was, smiling most of the time, and enjoyed dishing out agony and torment, enabling him to feel good deep inside. Considered himself an amateur writer, he had carefully finished page 315… an astonishing and impressive accomplishment. His book detailed narratives of how to extract information from prisoners and showed many of his diabolical ways of relating with his captives. Adam had titillating videos and pictures and used physical and mental nuances to manipulate his prey, which most likely would… expire ah, soon-to-be-dead souls. He'd written about his innermost emotions as he would torture the men and women with the goal of not killing them quickly, for his fun would end then, no fun cutting off wilted appendages. He would break them; then the begging would begin, certainly a best seller on the Dark Deep Web soon. There always came a time when he could sense the change in his prisoners. This brought Adam pleasure personified orgasmic teasing, euphoric harmony, and a blissfully satisfying silent paradise. This always culminated in physical and mental masturbation…Yum! ☺ .

In the past, umh, his childhood… some of the useless Psychiatrists whom he had zero use for had written up reports that he was a Sociopath slash Psychopath because of his Father and childhood trauma. He'd made a name as a Special interrogator, umh, torturer in Guantanamo Bay.

Oh, how he enjoyed his life's work, the scintillating stare of vulnerabilities in his victims, in which he'd always Glued their swollen eyes Open, their eyes filled with oppressive fear dreadful to his captives lol. Yet, this heightened his exuberance and brought sexually elevated bliss to his groin. For him, more fear equaled more pleasure. The more direful, mournful their expressions, the increase yep exponentially of his ecstasy. His manuscript detailed everything to a Gnats ass. Probably not the reading for the mainstream, but certainly a must-read for the sadistic closet freaks ah, the wicked, ghoulish, playful minds cloaked from the populace. Adam looked back on his finished pages, fondly reliving fantasies that became realities. He was the ultimate Executioner/Torturer. Adam wanted to pen the final chapter of the torture mutilation of a 5-year-old girl. His job had never included children… spots of pre-cum stained his briefs… oh how excited he was.

Just imagining the look on Anastasia's little angelic face as he snapped the bolt cutters on baby girl Catherine and held up her Lil bleeding pinky finger for her to see, would the kid pass out and go into shock? What would the screaming sound like? The terror on her face, it would be all caught on his cameras? Would she pee all over? Gosh so many questions… inquiring minds wanted to know? 😊 .

He'd like always cauterize the amputated member with the searing heat of a branding iron. Adam felt a touch panicked, for his fun had been put off for hours now. Apparently, the father, a high and mighty Diplomat, was negotiating. His eyes sprung open; gosh, how long had he been drifting?

Whoa, his 12-hour shift was already over half over. He worked from 7 am to 7 pm in charge of the monitors and security below ground. He glances at cell #5. Mother held the crying girl. He zoomed in. Ahh, then a fast movement in his peripheral vision, other monitors flashed um WTHeck a fkn dog raced across the pavement, a woman an intruder. What the hell was going on? He hit his secure radio "Hugo, what the fk are you doing? Why is there a woman…?"

Adam listens and then pans out all the cameras while Hugo is explaining. He zoomed into Wendi, who was feeding some animals; ugh, something felt wrong. "Jane, Hugo, get that woman off our property. To hell with the dog. I want her name… where did she come from? Move it now!"

I was answering the most popular and redundant question of all time asked about how I could talk with animals. It's impossible to communicate with animals, said the Chipmunk. They were all mesmerized as Chip the Munk said, 'ah-oh, trouble coming' in different directions were golf carts. Slim made a beeline in the middle of the carts heading directly towards the animals and me. They dispersed, gone, disappearing underneath the Oaks.

Slim made it to me. I had him back on the leash before the first cart arrived. "You're trespassing," yelped Jane her tone was harsh as she seemed to feel her weapon. Hugo stopped moving and jumped out of his seat much quicker than I thought was possible… agile for an obese man, saying, "I need some identification. Ugh, get your dog in the cart now."

I reached into my small purse and flipped open my wallet, showed him my fake I.D. he clicked a picture of it with his phone, then before I knew it, a close-up of me darn. Out the gate, I went shunned away. The Sun would set in less than 55 minutes as I was debriefed by one of my fun, good friends, Mr. Jax Foul.

The five of us sat at a medium-sized café on a patio having a lite dinner "all right, we've discerned that they're somewhere inside the auditorium, but where, we don't know. The scent vanished. Slim lost them. Slim caught five different scents of humans while he trespassed below the first floor of the auditorium, so at least there are five inside the building and two guards patrolling by the properties fence line; food is delivered twice a day via van at shift change which is soon."

Jax checks his watch and says, "There must be hidden rooms inside that building." Evans pays the tab and adds a 21% tip. We make it back to the van, which was parked stealthily behind 9-foot-high Oleander bushes. Sad as it was, we were consumed by the screens of our phones when a high-pitched octave… the squeaky grinding sound came out from under the open sliding door of our van, a plump 'Fat Rat' with a twitching tail and whiskers that were vibrating in perfect motion matching his wired appendage.

I took a step back and gave the Rat some crawl space, then our eyes clenched, locked. He finally broke the silence. "I thought they were all pulling my leg. You're for real, huh?" "Yes, I am, and I'm in desperate need of your help." "I'm known as Rod, your 'Sunshine Wendi, ' right?" it was a statement as he swiveled his head about and took several more inches forward closer to me. His tiny nose was flicking, nostrils flaring. I reached into my oversized purse, brought out the wrapped pepper jack cheese, and placed it by his feet.

That's when I realized I had misjudged Rod, for he was a 'Ripped Rat' with bulging muscles. Like a Rat on steroids, no natural, he would have been much happier with a nutrient bar. 'Thanks,' he said. It took Jax and me less than 15 minutes to have all the answers we needed, right down to how many rooms there were below ground and where the enemies would most likely be located. Most notably, Rod told us where a lever was that would cut all power to the three floors below.

Informing us which room had the backup generator easily disabled, Jax would employ his favorite night vision goggles. The prison cells were on power locks. They would pop open once all the electricity was cut.

Thanks to Rod, Jax had the cell that held mother and daughter #317. It would soon be attack and recover time… our goal was to save Anastasia and Catherine. Jax thought he'd wait till just after shift change they would be busy consuming food… as he took out the gate guards.

Joe… Sammy, and Mark Feral.

Joe is leaning into the large steering wheel of the enormous motor home, bumper-to-bumper traffic, Novato City limits in five tortuous miles. Sammy positioned at co-pilot checking out her laptop Nurse Danny's VW Rabbit barely in sight Hwy 101 South… Golden Gate Park, the destination for the entourage, the Fed's, we're somehow involved. Chopper and vehicles on either side front and back of his target. Joe nearly pleaded with Mark to drop the kill… no. He was adamantly told it was too dangerous to let the guy be arrested or interrogated. Owing to Mark his life, he would follow through with his orders. Joe allowed an inner smile to break his epidermis's barrier projecting a wry smirk. He couldn't wait to see the torn-back faces of the attorneys in their coffins who had tortured his very soul. First, Joe needed to finish off this Danny guy, and then he smiled… get my ass back up to Shasta County.

She laughs, breaking him from thought as he almost hits the bumper in front of him. "What am I going to do with you? What's so damn funny, Sammy?" "Oh, I was reading the Sacramento Bee how the guy on the motorcycle popped a 55ft wheelie and then lost the police; funny, it's always a man no one would think of a woman riding a bike with such skill!" Joe doesn't reply… rolls his shoulders and ponders his next moves.

Sammy drifts off into her morose mindset, stuck in traffic on Hwy 101 South, sitting abreast of Joe. In a split second, how life could be altered; for the most part, people luckily don't know how fast life can become traumatic. Some people, like trained Seals in mundane routines, enter their workplace only to be shot dead by a disgruntled ex-employee; others freeze catatonically zombified like robots staring down the weapon, unmoving till they face-plant. High schoolers walk into 1st period, and then a fellow student unleashes a barrage of bullets... why? A drunk driver lives while she kills a family of three. A wife or husband drops dead from a massive heart attack. Life sometimes jumped up and took a bite out of you... No warnings, sometimes plain and simple human nature. Sam chews on these scenarios of tragedy over and over again. She often wondered, after dwelling on all the negatives in this world. Humanity was plum filled with greedy and evil people. Why uhm, were there never any fond happy remembrances or hope, for that matter?... Why always did the negative memories seem to outnumber the fun ones, why were they so out of balance... Why ask Why? ☹ .

Nurse Danny suddenly erratically turns off the freeway onto 'Roland Blvd' Joe instantly flicks his blinkers on, using the motorhome's leverage, and shoves his way into the exit lane despite the blaring horns of agitated drivers. Up ahead, the VW Rabbit is already on the overpass lady cop is three vehicles back of him. "What do you think he's doing?" "Maybe a piss break, I don't know, girl. We will stay back and observe."

"Rico, he's heading east on Roland Boulevard...." "No worries, Kelsey, we have solid air support. Let's not spook him unless the plan has changed. He's still heading to San Francisco's Golden Gate Park; agents are waiting and ready." "Sir, aah Rico, I mean he just pulled into the Shell Truckstop probably for fuel, umh maybe a bathroom break." The helicopter rises higher in altitude. Rico pulls off at the same turn-off and parks at a Jack in a Box. All Agents are on hold, in wait mode.

Joe's B.P. elevated; he sought the high ground, parking at the Truckstop. There had to be 15 recreational vehicles, perhaps 35 diesel big rigs. The place was buzzing with humanity in the foreground, an automatic gun was stripping lug nuts off a jacked-up Peterbilt truck, and tire shop mechanics were huffing and puffing. A clear, brilliant day, crisp air, very few clouds, another typically pleasant Marin County morning… almost afternoon.

Joe mulled over this opportunity timing was everything in life, including the luck that's bestowed on oneself, yet most of the time, we must make our own luck! So not pressing the chasm of spontaneity, he anchored the motor home closest to the Truckstop exit, a position that gave him total coverage and dual advantages. In his view now were both Law Enforcement vehicles and the target nurse Dan who had parked at the gas pumps and was nowhere to be seen. Sammy noticed his wayward look. "He went into the store, Joe." "Thanks, now I want you to pay attention. We cannot afford to allow the cops to dictate the ground that we engage on. If you are afraid, you better bail. Uh, I plan to die with a weapon in my hand! Were seriously disadvantaged, outmanned, and outgunned. They even have air support. For whatever reason, the nurse is on their radar. Maybe they suspect him in the murder of Wendi Feral. Not sure we're not here to figure it out, only to eliminate him from the equation."

With a subtle nod, he gazes into her eyes, "this is your chance to extricate yourself from this toxic situation. I will permit you to leave this motorhome. All I ask of you is to take the radio with you and let me know if more police arrive. I have a feeling that Golden Gate Park will be swarming with cops. My only advantage is a surprise. Hey, by the way, destroy the pictures you took of me, okay." "Joe, I'm going nowhere. Your wasting precious time worrying about me like you have said several times; let's stay on point!" With that being said, Joe swiftly moved to the back of the motorhome, which was specially retrofitted, designed walls with 3" drilled-out openings, rings of rugged rubber grommets made for the barrel of the weapon his Macmillan 50 Caliber sniper rifle. He twirled the scope in an experienced perfect sequence. He moved effortlessly, disciplined even with such a narrow channel to navigate. He exuded confidence. Through the scope, he was able to see the female and male cops and had an unobscured clear shot of the VW Rabbit.

Sammy asked, "should you use the frequency blocker? There are cameras everywhere," his muffled answer "no, most likely the chopper is filming us. It would be useless now. Keep your eyes open and scan the entire area; if you see something I should be aware of, Sam, let me know. Otherwise, I need perfect silence, girl." He zooms in, dialing his victim's images into the swiveling lens of the scope, and watches as the nurse steps out of the store doors. Joe ceases to move, barely breathing, closes his eyes, and seeks his inner mind's analytics optic nerve non-flinching keys in his mind with the impetus to be able to evade subsequent confrontations and a shootout. How the heck could he possibly escape in the slowest moving of vehicles? His only advantage was the element of surprise.

Indeed if he had the time, he would have unloaded the KTM motorcycles, which would be a much better exit strategy. Still, if the cards played out correctly, it would take a minimum of 5 to 7 minutes to cordon off or shut down the perimeter of the Shell Truckstop with us about 1/3 mile from reentering highway 101 either North or South. There was a glutton of different vehicles leaving and entering in broad daylight at 11:55 am. Joe patiently observes Danny's nervous demeanor as he slips the pump nozzle into his car. His other hand holds a phone to his left ear. Joe, with the barrel, barely protruding from the grommet, swiftly for the 3rd time, took the three shots in his mind swiveling his head a Marksman who had fired thousands of bullets from the very same kind of weapon in his training seminars up in Idaho, Montana, and the Dakota's. Heart rate up a bit B.P. fluttering, adrenaline flowing depressed the trigger entering troublesome waters a center shot bullseye between the nurse's eyes before the echo stopped reverberating a shot placed directly in the sternum of the bulletproof vest worn by the Police-woman, nonlethal most likely but would suck the breath from her chest, disable her. The 50 Caliber bullet propelled her into the air as she bounced 5ft from her car, unconscious.

The officer standing by his truck tapping his phone had no idea that he was in the scope's crosshairs. Another sternum shot down like an imposing skyscraper. Three shots were fired in less than 5 seconds. Joe pulled the sniper rifle out... the motorhome had been idling, rushed back to the cab, slipped it into drive, and calmly entered the lineup of vehicles leaving the Truckstop. The scanner was on high volume, and nothing was said. Thundering sounds from above as the chopper drops from the sky. Joe swings the motorhome onto 101 South chaos slammed the radio waves, exploding verbiage rampant. Shots fired, screams!

Rico was chewing his last bite of a 'Breakfast Jack' with an iced tea backer when the radio went bonkers. 'Man down shots fired, Shell Truckstop Roland Blvd.' He shouted into the radio, 'Kelsey… Kelsey, come in. Kelsey' nothing. 'Agent Gonzales, yuh got a copy?' nada, multitasking as he pulls out of the lot, iced tea cools his lap spilling, phone on Bluetooth mode cries out to the helicopter pilot at the same time having the Novato Police Department punched into his radio. "Pilot Cahill, what's happening?" "Three shots fired, Sir. It's mass hysteria down there, three men down." "Land the fkn chopper next to… ugh, blocking the exits to Hwy 101. Call in emergency personnel and paramedics; no one is allowed to leave the area." Novato police dispatch was online, stopping all the exits covering the perimeter. "I'm on my way," exhaled Rico.

Calmly traveling South, they listened as the CHP was in the process of shutting down the 101 North towards Petaluma and the Southern route at Lincoln Ave in San Rafael; Joe veered off at the Marinwood exit. In less than 10 minutes, the air was clouded with CHP helicopters, news choppers, Sheriff's department. The area morphed into a military zone. Joe parks the motorhome at a Safeway shopping center. Packs only necessities and all weapons except his pistols went inside a hidden wall. "Let's go for a ride, Sammy. Have you ever been to 'Lucas Valley? It has some fine places to have lunch then Stinson Beach. What a fabulous day we'll have." He leaves the Micro cameras on blast, motion detectors actuated, KTM 1290s offloaded down the ramp, packed up some gear, the trailer closed, and off they Putt down the road.

'What a gorgeous day for a bike ride thought Sammy. I like this guy a whole bunch. I think I've met my purpose in this bleak, tempestuous world. Maybe my soulmate is Joe!' ☺. Yep!

22

Tank and Mark.

Tank takes the elevator down from the 5th floor at the Federal building in San Jose. The Parole lady wasn't so bad, not a 'looker' kinda nerdy, besides the 'U.A.' urine analysis, uhm piss test, it went well. He had an apartment five blocks from the 'Shark Tank' where the San Jose Sharks Hockey team called home his favorite team, an avid sports fan being a homespun boy born in the Bay Area, San Francisco. Proud, no city could claim 6 world championships in the past seven years; he was proud of the Golden State Warriors, who had just beaten the Cleveland Cavaliers for their 3rd Basketball championship... The San Francisco Giants World Series champs in the years of 2010, 2012, and 2014 and the 49ers were up and coming with 5 Super Bowls in their coffers. The San Jose Sharks couldn't get over the hump, damnit. He looked forward to having season tickets to all four teams, but first, he had to take care of the responsibilities and promises he'd made.

Agent Tom Baker with Agent Bill Avery had the tedious task of which they'd complained several times about, manually following a man that had been Chipped. Why not involve rookie Agents? Termed a loose 'tail' of Tank Shaw 'Tail,' the humor had ceased. It was funny for a while because Tank had a GPS tracker inside his left glute. Avery, known as the tech wizard, kept wondering why it was necessary to use human resources. Just have someone track him on a map, um, screen, or monitor. Still, they watched him open his apartment door, vanishing inside. Agent Lori Parks, with another team, was set up in Golden Gate Park at the request of Director Tanya Firm and lead Agent Rico Captor. At around noon on Tuesday, all hell had broken out. Lori was aboard a helicopter with others of her team, heading to Marin County Novato, two Agents shot with Nurse Dan Spike murdered.

Her best friend in the bureau, Agent Kelsey Marie, had sustained broken ribs; two Agents were in the hospital. They would survive thanks to their bulletproof vests and the precise shots of an expert marksman. The one bullet fired nearly split their rib cages, sternums shattered. The chopper Lori was in flew over the long winding parking lot that was highway 101 Canines out, each vehicle being scrutinized. Other Law Enforcement types were busy replaying videos from 45 minutes earlier; Rico greeted Lori with a somber nod, and she went to work detailing the vehicles that had left the truck stop in the seven minutes before it was locked down.

Mark Feral was disgusted with his lack of discipline and proactivity and should have never taken the coffins onboard. I'll tell you what I do for friends even though, like, 99% of humans believe 'one good turn deserves another. Of course, this is wholly untrue. It matters not if you are a person blinded by 'Do onto others as you wish done to you' unadulterated hogwash! Why I had agreed to keep the attorneys alive in their coffins was beyond rational belief. He'd already dealt with the three Sheriff boats, the thick haze of fires out of control to the east and west. I should have just put bullets in Pat Hale and John Manson and sunk them in the lake. It dawned on me, laughing, why waste perfect bullets… Lead on them? Merely tip the coffins overboard done. Not to be… more, CDF helicopters and Sheriff's boats outnumbered the public. The resorts on Shasta lake resembled 'winter season' skeleton crews; most humans were inside, leaving the 111-degree days for air conditioning. I sat, drenched in sweat, the teasing waters of Lake Shasta below. I needed to take a dip, but no, I had other issues to resolve. Ugh!

I'd rather not describe the stench, putrid pale ass skin on Pat as I hosed them down. He was a zombie gone plumb-ass crazy, a man who had a debilitating phobia, claustrophobia. Can you imagine the torture for him to be enclosed in dark blackness, a coffin unable to lift his legs or arms even to itch? Ugh! Pat had already visited insanity now existing within his wild eyes, lips super-glued closed, naked perforated openings drilled out of each coffin kept some oxygen… enough for both John and Pat to exist. John fared better; I must confess to a tiny bit of fun as I zapped him with my 50,000-volt baton. I've read somewhere that humans can go weeks without food, but water must be absorbed within 75 hours, or your body becomes toxic. So, this is what derailed my plans and took my precious time. I shouldn't even be out here on the lake. Instead of chasing women and enjoying my life here, I fking was spraying solvent on their broken, parched lips, feeding them, watering them down chained and shackled on my Wakeboard boat; it took another hour, and I had them back in my steel barn on my property all for a friend... Bro Joe Sable.

This was risky business asking myself what else I could do. 'One hand washes the other, right?' In less than 15 hours, ole Joe had eliminated the P.I. and the nurse right under the piece of a shit dead man's watch... 'Rico Captor's' eyes. The two lawyers were on leashes in a sound-proof building. I sat in cold air, breezing blowing by as I finished my workout, 35 minutes of intense power rows on one of my favorite machines, testosterone raging trying to fight the urge to pull up some of my favorite porn sites or traverse the real-time online dating sites just order me up a whore.

I couldn't place a finger on it, like acid devouring my veins. Something was wrong. 'Helter Skelter,' amok in disorder... if you will. Hence, ergo couldn't possibly think to analyze the heretical truths. I've always been a non-conformist. My sister Wendi Feral is whom I hate. Let's not dwell upon that uh, I need to calm my B.P. down, take a quick rinse, then do 25 laps in my Olympic pool. Seventeen minutes later, I towel off, the music soothing me, wandering now back to the quandary like a boat without oars drifting inside my logical mind. Even as a boy, I couldn't let a subject go without some form of a conclusion logic inspired... Yes, dogmatically stubborn.

No way to deny there weren't any reasons for Rico and the FBI to put Nurse Danny Spike under surveillance. Why, other than the obvious again, let's take it from the top, sources inside NIA confirmed the death of... dear sister. Let me play one of my favorite tools, uhm, the 'Devil's Advocate.' How did the sources confirm this? Only word by mouth for their but inmates, nurse Dan Spike did text that he had accomplished the feat; why were the Feds on the nurse? If they suspected he injected Wendi with the poison, then why not arrest him uhm... wait for just a fricken second? A dim light flicked on, and I logged onto the Dark web. One of my homepages... then entered a select private chat forum Blog knowing the fastest way to get what you want in this greed-laden world was to offer money!

With an eye on my trading accounts in the world's market, the current bitcoin price was $17,555, so I tossed a coin out there on anyone's plate, one coin for detailed satellite images of Golden Gate Park. The time I typed in was between 7 am and 1 pm. Worldwide hackers went to work for me immediately; all I did was let go. A firm believer in multi-tasking, uh, relaxing. No! With a smear of lubrication, one of my adjustable vibrating cock rings in place, leaning back soothingly working its way up my shaft, I joined a porno room POV an orgy ah then clicked for one-on-one action just a deep throat job would suffice timing impeccable as I blasted off oh relief. My Dark web chimed, info awaiting my perusal. Oh, life was grand, wasn't it? Taking a warm cloth, I tenderly cleaned my groin area, still twitching and pulsating with leftover pleasure, flipped off the cock ring, closed down the porn site, and took a long swig of iced tea, a bit melted like me.

With another iPad in my hands, I opened the link from a cyber-hacker with deposit directions where to send the cyber currency bitcoin. I noticed the moniker, I'd worked with him or her before, and I didn't waste time debating, wanting to see a part of the video I'd requested. Oh, my Lord, there she was, that sexy bitch how I wanted to sodomize that blonde, prove to myself that she wasn't a bottle blonde! Uh yeah, Lori honey-bunny, I'd pluck some hair from her... hard-proof enough and bag it for my growing trophy case. Agent Lori Parks was a Hottie, and she was at Golden Gate Park, ahha! I'd been duped, hoodwinked, ain't no question.

I was deceived and cheated. What the fk? An easy basic mathematical equation of one and one equaled three. Somehow they infiltrated his scheme sister Wendi no doubt, was alive and kicking, and my entire system went into shutdown mode. Morose was a happy word in comparison. If they didn't know the plot and circumvented it, there was no chance that the FBI would have cordoned off Golden Gate Park, waiting for the Nurse to be given the last installment for cutting Wendi from this earth plane. You'd think with my hardened heart, deadened, desensitized soul-my conscience would become anesthetized, but not so. Sister must be freakin alive, devoid of permanent satisfaction like a computer keyboard pressing Ctrl-Alt-Delete. I shut down right there in my comfy ergonomic chair. See ya! ☹ .

<u>Joe, Sammy, and Tank.</u>

He stood bare ass naked alone. It had been a long seven years since he was solely independent, with no other humans nearby. He released an exasperated long-winded, exhaled sigh in the narrow full-length mirror. His body's image stunned and shocked him. Where had all the tattoos come from? Furthermore, why the obsession, infatuation, ugh compulsion, ink from his fingers up to his sleeves prison tattoos? Ink coal black covered the skin. Was it a repulsive look?

Contrary to whom he was at times, staring back from the reflection such as now a personal dislike for himself umh a bad seed, distaste of hidden principles long gone inbred into him by his family. Tank was his real name on his birth certificate, 'Tank Lee Shaw' at a young age, he found out that he would be teased, chastised, and have to fight to defend himself. Children were cruel and used his name to tease and ridicule him.

Back to the reflection resembling Tank, not a super tall man 6'1" but a solid 235lbs bulk muscled ripped an enforcer, literally hundreds of scars from punishing altercations would fight at a 'drop of a hat' or just for fun. The mirror revealed almost 37 years of hard work; out loud, he asked, 'was he only a manifestation of a name, 'Tank' labeled and stereotyped, growing into the iconic image, merely a set-up he no question was a Tank, congruent matching the image' what if his name would have been 'Tim'?

Laughing out loud, he recalls meeting this kid whose name was 'Rock,' really. A scrawny, skinny kid, a botched name indeed, man how he would complain through high school to Tank, who would protect him, for he was constantly picked on and beaten up. It was outlandishly bizarre, even screwy a song churned in his mind as he ran the water in the tub, shower his first bath in Seven years, peace, relaxation, and how he loved aloneness humming the song by 'Johnny Cash.' 'Boy named Sue.' Yup!

No, not a pretty boy with girlish good looks yet a ruggedly handsome man of Nordic ancestry, lineage not the all-so prototypical brown or black-haired man, but when he let his hair grow out, it was reddish-blonde matching his bushy eyebrows, long lashes, and mustache, high cheekbones with Ivory white teeth and a dimple from either side able to flash without effort bedroom brownish eyes with a gleam, twinkle of mischief, never had a problem with the ladies especially the wannabe naughty girls.

Found it amusing, though; many times, it wasn't the biker chicks at the bars that were hot and horny for him. Nope, he seemed to attract the prim and proper gentle, polite, respectable looking girls, figured they wanted a 'walk on the wild side' learned at a young age 'never judge a book by its cover.' An interesting caveat was that these women were the best screws. Tonight, he would hit the bar circuit and pick up a girl or three, whatever worked. First, he needed to go shopping; the fridge was vacant and just now working to cool. What the doctor ordered were a fully furnished apartment and shopping for necessities and some 2019 stylish clothing. Strangely another first after the long prison stint took a soapy sponge, squeezed it over his newly shaved, massive bald head laid back, and sighed; life was good now, no doubt getting better as the stench from San Quentin leeches from his body finally after the third soaking his pores were cleansed.

Inside his mind, shadows lurked behind every 'nook and cranny' mused. Was he as evil as others believed, maybe? Tank rinses off under the cool cold shower, thankful that the furnishings included soap, but he needed a toothbrush with some minty paste. He steps over the threshold it hits him... with no towel to dry off. Well, not actual towels like dish towels; instead of getting annoyed, he chuckled he'd drip-dry. Tank thought how stupid he didn't buy other things when he purchased TracFone's at Walmart. He felt a tad bit disappointed in himself... for Tank perhaps was overly anxious. Tank was a renowned thinker, Chess champion, Scrabble finalist, and Bridge player extraordinaire...

competition with best bro Mark Feral was intense. They came to blows often… fun stuff.

Breaking him from his revelry, a secure phone buzzed. It was busy-bee Mark…didn't answer, only pressed, in a text, 'Talk with you later' no conversation from the confines of his apartment or car, only in the wide-open spaces outdoors. He goes down the stairs to his car. 'Let the cops watch. Follow him as he shops.' Tank was also dogmatic, unrelenting, oddly stubborn hardheaded to a fault… analytical, dwelling on subject matter to fruition. Voices returned to the old subject matter twirling inside back at the 'name game' what if he was Henry, Harold, Bart, Walter umh Martin, or Isaiah instead of 'Tank' which brought bearing on all things in his existence independently controlling unforeseen circumstances a divine omnipotence violent storm, ahh he shutters with paranoia. Institutionalized thinking was everyone watching him? He had to rein in his paranoia and suspicions of collusion by society like everyone knew he was a dangerous Felon. At times he felt like a player in a plot had to get a grip on reality before he was swept into unforgiving furious oceans. Uh, what was in a name? Trying to close this train of thought as he walks into the mall, a mall he most likely wouldn't have entered if his name were Herb, given his situation, then thinks how ridiculous that thought was. Laughing at his insanity-laden self, I'm institutionalized… my mind is frenetically chaotic.

<u>Motorcycle ride.</u>

Joe watched her sway, leaning into the sharp hairpin turns as if she was one and the same with the motorcycle, curving through a patch of a forest full of Redwoods… Trees blocking out the bright blue sky yum, the overwhelming aroma he always enjoyed the smell of Eucalyptus trees indigenous to and from Australia. Sammy was alive made him grin easily. He had to face it. He adored this girl and felt aware and full of gusto around her life could, in reality, be pleasurable, even fun. She equaled a buoyant, exuberant effervescence like a little girl, shameless and bold with a mixture of brazenness, yeah, an audacious, sexy female. She might not have 'balls' gladly, but with cockiness had 'brass vagina lips.'

Affectionately, with familiarity & experience before their relationship could propagate with trust with intimacy lol. Whoa, unearthing possible serendipitous synchronicities and offering perspicacious perspectives he'd never known, time ticked sadly. Sammy wasn't long for this world!

Lost in lust, imagining what a real loving relationship with Sammy would be like, her attributes blended with who he was perfectly damnit, mercifully he'd kill her quickly, no need for her to suffer. The authorities had already hunted him. The FBI even had Bounty hunters after him, like his partner Mark. He didn't need murder charges; the cute little ass girl had documented video of his slaying of the P.I. her being present, clicking away on the camera. Let's not forget she also conspired with him, an accomplice to the nurse's demise, and my shooting of the FBI Agents still had the Pimp and his brother rotting in the motorhome… crap!

Mark Feral was a psychopath whom he had known since he was three years old, so for around 33 years, there wasn't any room for a woman, whore, slut… prostitute, nope, he presses the weak-sounding horn, unlike a Harley Davidson, his favorite ride. She looked back over her left shoulder as her full-faced helmet shook in a nod. The Pacific Ocean before them, they found a Café patio taking seats with the picturesque beach in the foreground, having a scrumptious lunch and a couple of glasses of wine. Ahh, no hiding the fact he liked this little bitch way too much, dammit. She peered over her shrimp cocktail, took her glass of wine, and sipped. "I sure would like to have an open helmet for a ride like this one," grinning "how'd you know that was precisely what I was thinking a few moments back, Sam?" She didn't reply as a CHP Officer sat at a table far too close for comfort then another joined him. They didn't have to stretch their ear lobes to hear the sensationalized topic about the search for the sniper on highway 101. The highway was closed down, and the authorities were tracing all the vehicles that left the crime scene Shell Truckstop was locked down, and both CHPs were flipping, sliding fingers across their phone screens.

Cautiously she gaged Joe's countenance as he fidgeted in his comfy seat, at times a good-looking, handsome man, other times a plain Joe. Average in most ways, height and weight discounting the innate fact that there was something peculiar emanating from him, an Aura of animalistic luminousness radiating from his skin. The man was dangerous but passionate, the type of man she had yet to know. It was her occupation to understand the male gender, not a street walker most of her young life but a high echeloned Escort… blending in unambiguously.

Before Joe said another word, three more CHPs invaded the café patio like a freaking convention or something. He mulled over his lousy luck choice for lunch! Wondered while the Sig Sauer 9mm was pressed to his side, fingers rubbing it on the outside of his leather jacket 'calm as the proverbial cucumber' ordered a couple of espressos from the happy-go-lucky server who was a throwback hippy. His eyes squinted above the sunglasses knowing the odds were against him, 5 to 1. Although the ultimate surprise of him yanking out his weapon slightly evened the spread a bit. This was her chance to exit this caustic life and definite incarceration in prison for possibly her life.

At the same time, his thoughts meandered. Sammy's convoluted mind was elsewhere on multiple fronts, thinking about the shooting at the Shell gas station and the highway closed off, why were there five CHPs sitting at the Café? Shouldn't all of them be in hyper-mode? She wondered, as Joe and her locked eyes… how long her pimp and his brother could avoid detection. They had to be ripe by now, rotting in the motor home's spare room, her DNA all over the place, blonde hair in the brush she'd forgotten. Intuition had been her saving grace thus far, tense reverence as both met in the middle… eyes of acknowledgment. Joe was in tune like her on the same exact page… no actually the same sentence, he thought was she curiously pondering, wondering if escape was being measured.

Sammy reached her small hand over and tugged gently on his arm. "Come on, let's check out the shops along the beachfront, Joe." He dropped cash on the 'bill' in a tray on their table hand in hand, and they crossed by the five officers without a glance; Sun was bright, reflecting off the brilliant crystal white sand. They found a bathroom with backpacks in possession, changed into shorts and sandals, toes whipping across the splashing waves strolling along like any other couple of lovers. I spied some huge boulders wet with ocean spray silence was natural for them, comfortable in their skins. They sat dangling feet into the on-rushing waves smiling.

'Joe was musing about his next moves…'at least Sammy was a good companion and intuitive and yummy ah, too bad. He felt like hitting her one more time before killing her. This broke out a grinning smirk from him. "What's yuh smiling about over there, Joe?" He winked, and she ventured out on the metaphorical plank… knowing what he was mulling over and chewing on in his psychopathic mind. "How yuh wanna get it over with, Joe? Points out at the water, drown me, or is the plan to shoot me in the back of the head when I'm not looking the coward's way out?"

For a split instant, he gave it away; mouth opened instantly, composure regained. "What, come on, you can't be serious, girl. Dontcha have me over-a-barrel video pictures implicating yours truly?" "Yes, sure, that is inherently a nonplus fact… in a secure locker at the Sacramento Airport, a combination lock as she taps her temple. It's right here for you to take… maybe some delectable torture is in the cards. Let me ask the obvious why didn't I take the camera to the cops? Why did I return to your murderous soul at the motor home?"

Sam picked up a seashell and placed it to her left ear posing with a confident smirk.

"Maybe I've got a death wish, Joe, don't think it's because I've got some Mickey Mouse probation warrant like duh, Joe, not only would the authorities not give a hoot about that, but I'd also be in line for a reward turning your ass in!" He raises his left palm, fingers to his forehead rubbing slightly inquisitively, examining her curiously. "Okay, I'll bite; why the fk are you still sitting with me, Sammy? What the fk is wrong or right about you?" 😊 .

23

The CEO of NIA, Terrance Hallinan.

Terrance was delayed leaving the city for a 7:25 am meeting at the Calico winery in Napa. It was Tuesday morning, the day after the Wendi debacle. He'd have to reschedule the meeting for good measure. His compatriots informed him to stick close to the opening of the New York stock exchange pre-opening. China and the USA were continuing their threats of tariffs and surcharges as the trade wars with Trump… only escalated. Insider information had been leaked from Mother Russia if played out correctly, hordes of cash to be had. Timing everything, Terrance postured in front of a bank of computers. Trading accounts open, commodities markets, his interest was principally in the oil market. Russia was going to enter the fray; insider trading could net the CEO a clean, not so… 3 million dollars before noon. In the options market, he bought huge calls contracts out 90 days, for he didn't want to buy the 30 or 60-day expiring options, which could possibly alert the SEC of suspicious trading activity. Better to play the market out three months waiting for the announcement that Russia would curtail and reduce shipments of the precious black gold starting this very day… millions of barrels of oil would be kept from the world's oil markets!

He stood up, pacing as the Stock Markets ringing bells were heard. Anticipation held him in place within three hours. Oil shot up from $61.00 a barrel to $83.00. It was pure unadulterated manipulation by the 'big boys' once again grinding and chewing up the minnows and guppy's… supply and demand. Terrance mulled over history's lessons going back further than the Tulip wars, the oldest of games, yet still as profitable percentage-wise, the magnetic deals were electrifying, addictively intoxicating. Terrance, spellbound, smirking while the naysayers who were on the opposite trade had miss-predicted set-up by false information uhm grinning… the buyers of 'Puts' oil short callers betting for Oil barrel price to collapse were destroyed, uh annihilated.

Feeling giddy with a 3.5 million profit in 3 1/2 hours, a cool million an hour, he sat relaxed in the back of his stretched-out limo moving across the Golden Gate Bridge, watching the fog swirl curling up around the edges of the massive structure driving North into Marin County. Terrance was a man who was raised by a long lineage of leaders, and his father had an extraordinary Castle that was next to Trump's retreat in Palm Beach. Terrance Hallinan Sr. was still an intimidating figure, a magnanimous persona no one crossed him. That would be dangerous indeed. Perilous, worse still, if daddy-dearest perceived a rebellion was unfolding even at 77 years old, he remained virulent. With nothing but bad intentions if he was betrayed.

Terrance always showed daddy loving kindness with overtones of obedience. Outraged that the FBI had infiltrated his 'Baby' NIA's outpatient Hospital right underneath their thumbs, Jr. had seen and felt his father's wrath via a video conference. He was prepared to pass the buck he would give as good as he took from Daddy. In essence, there was nothing that he or anyone could do but bring suspicion on NIA if they refused to allow the Feds onto the property. Wendi was the asset they couldn't allow to leave the facility… ahh institution.

Waiting now for his arrival at the mental prison were his disciple's figureheads, his select team Warden Ursula Anders, Assistant Warden Larry Walden, and Doctor Liz Honcho. The limousine slows abruptly, braking a bit faster than was warranted. He jutted and lurched forward, almost spilling his 'Kettle One Bloody Mary' chauffeur bodyguard lowers the glass partition. "Sorry, boss, there's police action ahead: a helicopter on the freeway. It's a parking lot, sir." Terrance slid open his laptop; after checking his phone, he wanted a larger screen to view what the holdup was… um, damnit, he made the wrong choice. Instead of a calm ride in his Limo to Napa, he should have flown… the city of Novato was cordoned off, and he heard the familiar rotors of choppers in the air.

Life was about decisions. He could have opted for his personal helicopter, just above his penthouse, a skyscraper resting on its pad in San Francisco. Social media was buzzing 'YouTube' already had 23 videos. Nothing in today's world is sacred, not anymore. It was all found on the Internet… ugh, back 25 years ago. The FBI could withhold the names of the victims or the assailants not in today's world.

He sucked down the rest of the stiff Vodka drink as his eyes didn't betray him. 'Omg… A man under his umbrella who worked for his precious institution' was all over social media. Dan Spike, Nurse at NIA, was murdered by a sniper and two FBI Agents were airlifted to Marin General Hospital.' 'Are you kidding me?' Front and center NIA was now being censored… bloggers, chat lines, tweets speculations only the day before the infamous heroine herself was found to have died, the one and only 'Wendi Feral' consecutive days of bad press as his father's red nose blinked up on the screen.

"What the fk is wrong with you, boy? You can't get anything right, can you? It looks like your mother and I must cut short our vacation and fly 3,000 miles to handhold you again!" Terrance wasn't in the mood to kowtow and cower, so he mounted a futile pusillanimous attack verbalizing, "Pops, you and mom are always on vacation stay where you're at. I don't need any more stress. I will handle it!" "What" as a finger is pointed up at him from the monitor, "Are you fking drunk driving this early, son? Remember, son, I, fortunately, had the insider information on that oil trade for us. It originated from 'Putin' himself. He doesn't burp without me wiping his face with a napkin; boy, you better get a handle on these issues. NIA's stock is falling off a fkn cliff. If you don't do something, we will lose more than we made on the oil trade."

Terrance gazed at his father, blinking seeing him but didn't… his mental state elsewhere recalling a thesis he'd read about years before 'Disassociation' a known phenomenon referred to constantly by Forensic Psychologist Doctor Liz Honcho. Terrance was a breathing living caricature in which his mental state inhabits two or five worlds simultaneously, sometimes on autopilot like driving home after a long day, drifting, not really listening to the music, nothing lost in your own world before you become aware you had passed your turn-off 15 miles ago. He stared wild-eyed at his Papa, then with a cartoonish pout, he skittered out a minor infraction and closed the laptop. Bye, father dear!

In a caustic stressful meeting at NIA were Dr. Liz Honcho, Warden Ursula Anders, and Assistant Warden Larry Walden, preparing for CEO Terrance Hallinan's arrival!

Watching nervously listening to Liz's pompously self-assertive yowling protestations of innocence Warden Ursula Anders turned menacingly, staring defiantly from her high-heeled perch, stomach, growling, "how could you allow Dr. Hawkins complete control of Wendi? Where was your due diligence? How couldn't you know she was in the back fkn pocket of the Feds and that sinister prick Rico Captor!" Angrily Ursula slammed her empty coffee mug down on the table.

"Beyond the obvious, how could you approve Doctor Hawkins experimental tests on Wendi in the first place, and why were you not present, huh Honcho? Are you not the head of Psychology here at this God-forsaken hell hole of a prison? Now all our heads are in a vise that weasel ass prick Hallinan will be here to ream our anal cavities!"

"Ursula, please refrain from your foul contemptuous language. Let's try and rationalize this issue with the absence of slanderous, insulting verbiage that is naturally your customary way. Ursula, why don't you cease to be an antagonist? You might as well throw fuel on the burning corpse. Your logic is tainted, and I'm done with you constantly undermining any mitigating circumstances. What would you have me or my staff do? Rico and Director Tanya Firm contrived the plot we were not privy to the...." Larry angrily stands up for Ursula, "Shut up, Liz, now you wait just a second. I will not sit here and listen to this crap. You, woman, need to stifle this argument, you...." "Who the fk do you think you are, Larry? Your, my lowly assistant with peanuts for balls, you just sit there and cross your legs." "I'd rather have peanuts hanging than your moldy lips." As he slams the door to the conference room. Liz and Ursula stare off into space... not 55 seconds later, Larry re-enters the room with his phone out in a Hitler salute. "Yah better check out the news; we are front and center once again. The news went Viral. Uh, Nurse Spike was just shot and killed.”

After what has been categorized as human nature natural as a fart, the three of them were deposed, mesmerized just like small children of the latest generation who could view porn at nine years old sad but true, cell phone shocked into silence stupor like frozen in space and time the 55ft by 25ft conference board room, became noiseless.

Dr. Liz Honcho was the first to mutter a response, “terrible negative publicity for us. I bet Terrance is yanking out his plugged hair right about now.” “Oh no, the quantifiable pain we’re all going to feel ah, our stock price has fallen below the 50-day moving average, nearly a 15% drop in share price,” yelps Larry. Liz adds, “I just read where Goldman Sachs gave us an ‘omg’ the infamous dagger ‘downgrade’ announcing a phenomenally bleak prognosis for future earnings. Terrance will be beyond irate!” “Listen, surely we can hover about dwelling on our current dilemma, um situation, but it’s much better to be positively proactive, umh look for the bright side, stop reacting and subjectively to….” Ursula tosses her hand up towards Liz, scowling, “Speak freaking English, you witch, don’t throw out your uneducated bullshit.” Then simultaneously, all three of their phones chimed. Mr. Hallinan was calling for a video conference.

Morgue-like quietude exhumed, depleted exigency neither of them accepted his attempt at communication… outward signs of stress were exhibited beads of perspiration on blushed cheeks and foreheads as Ursula’s legs were bouncing, shaking at around 35mph. Larry’s knees wobbled at a slower, pedestrian pace. ‘All right,’ Liz ambled forth. “Fear can and will cannibalize us freeze us in place we can’t thrive, only be devoured. Let’s look at our tangible defense the three U.S. Marshals we control had no idea of the FBI’s scheme. So in our defense, what are we clairvoyant? How could we be held culpable for this attempted murder of Wendi? I ask you, how could we have known of Nurse Spike’s complicity with Mark Feral? We don’t and cannot control all that occurs within our stone walls. I say no way, hey, the good news is little Ms.

Wendi Feral is alive and kicking, currently held down in 'SHU' solitary confinement under Federal protection, not dead, for she would most certainly be if not for the Fed's interventions all we need to do Ursula is take back control of Ms. Feral… she's downstairs!"

"Ursula's shaking knees slowed to about 15mph as she nibbled on her upper lip, "Your right, Liz. We're fortunate that Wendi is still alive three floors below…." "Yeah," joins in Larry, "we three need to be on the same page when the boss gets here. Hell, he's the one with all the underworld connections. Why wasn't he informed of the Fed sting?"

"They ummah, we have moles spies all through the American legal system." Warden Ursula Anders then taps the table with her knuckles "let's communicate with our CEO, Hallinan. We cannot duck him. I think it's better if we call him back, I don't know about you two, but I'd rather speak to him on video conference than in person." Finally, matching smiles, "let's call him back now on our secure encrypted video conference line," exclaimed Larry.

The screen lights up with a larger-than-life headshot, displaying a frowning sneering countenance that explores the three of them. "Well, well," he rebukes outward, "You finally dare to face the consequences of your actions. Our board of directors are screaming… and the share price of NIA's stock is currently plummeting down 17% below the opening! I'm stuck on Hwy 101… the freeway is a parking lot. The police are searching vehicle by vehicle looks like our employee Nurse Spike was just killed by a sniper, along with two officers shot. Ugh, not a good follow-up to yesterday's fake news about Wendi's demise. Of course, as you three are aware, Wendi lives. Still, the outside world isn't privy to such news… currently, our market cap in the Stock Market is down over a Billion dollars from yesterday, and that's screwed up… we will meet soon. Unfortunately, I didn't commute today in my chopper. See you in person… till then, and I'm counting on you to help mitigate this falling knife later" click.

Wendi was locked in a small snuggery cell inside of NIA.

Yes, Wendi is under guard down in the basement.
I opened my closed eyes to a change of venue; the room was closed off, far from as cozy as my earlier hospital room, with only a few machines connected to me. Now only my heart and blood pressure were being watched. I'm on the road to recovery. It was a hectic few days even for a person like me, who was dormant, vegetable-like in the catatonic stages of a coma. Yet, I had finished successfully communicating with Dr. Hawkins, Rico, mom, and dad, with David all present.

Sadly, I was made aware that one of my nurses would attempt to kill me after my parents and David had left. The afterward visit by Doctor Hawkins and Rico enlightened me of this. We were focused on the future. Strangely, I felt so much better being able to differentiate the gravitational pull of my protector, 'Sunshine' maybe it was all the prescription medicines effects and changes, but now I was on a new regimen provided by Dr. Hawkins.

The gravelly-faced Dr. Honcho, who at times looked menacing, stopped visiting me as often; I felt better without her weighty bedside manner. I had a new set of U.S. Marshalls attending my cell door and new nurses as well. I wished for some fresh air and sunlight, yearning to feel wind blown over my skin.

What had become a quandary of proportional stress was my imaginary friend and special protector, Sunshine, who didn't want to relent and let me take back control of who I am, Wendi; our interactions had nearly become toxic. I had to refer to it as a rebellion by my inner self, 'Sunshine.' She was intolerable and wasn't relenting in her control of my body and mind, another internal conflict by the minute.

"Sunshine, what do you mean when you say don't worry about it? I don't get it?" "Wendi, I've always been there for us since your first major trauma when you were but five years old if you don't trust me, then you can't trust yourself, sista!..." "I'm sorry, I just feel like my body is beaten up; I don't have any memories of how I got all these bruises; my sacrum, umh, butt bone feels like its cracked throbbing all the time besides that my left hip is aching on fire. Tell me, Sunshine, where have you been, and what happened to our body?" I then had second thoughts about reigning down negatives. "Aah, never mind, Sunshine, you're being deceptive, but it's true you have always been like my guardian Angel." Sunshine smiled within us. "Of course, I'm right; when have I ever been wrong or misled you?"

For the fifth time, Jax tried to gain entry into Wendi's cell. The unfriendly Marshal scowled with disapproval. She was a well-built female and wasn't having any of it. "Why don't you just call the Warden or head of Psychology, Dr. Honcho? I'm a friend of Wendi's, and I am on her visiting approved list. I visit with her between three and five days a week. Please call. I need to see her!" "Listen, fella. I only take orders from Agent Captor, so buzz off. I'm sorry I don't mean to be rude; I need this job. I am…" "Okay, call Rico then. Rico Captor is also a friend of mine."

She squinted her eyes then took out a notepad old-school, Jax thought, a real pencil on a little paper pad. Wow. "What's your name again, mister?" "I'm Jax Foul," "oh shit, no way your… that Jax Foul fella. I knew something was familiar with your scarred-up face, and oops, oh sorry, I was…." "No problem, I get that all the time," "I watched your entire trial in Sacramento; I even was in the courtroom a few times. You are a true-blue bonified hero in my book Mr. Foul." "Oh, please call me Jax" "Jax, you sure put a hurtin on those Cuban pedophiles." "I guess there's no harm in your visiting Wendi but let me try and call Agent Rico Captor. Five minutes later, Marshall Kara receives a text 'What is it, Kara? I'm super busy?' texted back, 'Mr. Jax Foul wants to visit Wendi, sir!' 'Well, sure, let him visit her, but not anyone else, and that includes the NIA staff. Is that clear?' 'Yes, Sir, Agent Captor, thanks.'

24

Sunshine 'Wendi' and Jax, near Washington D.C… only seven days before the attempted murder of Wendi by nurse Danny Spike at the NIA hospital.

Rod scurried away with his whiptail, then stopped turning back to me; inspecting my vision, the King river Rat telepathically espoused, 'My Rat pack will be there for you. Remember the backup generator!' as he hastened away. Our NIA team was standing beside our van outside of Wash. DC.

Dr. Honcho's phone alarm went off like clockwork without a thought, a habit, or was it a pattern. Uhm, either way, I'd become accustomed to it. She held out five pills for me to swallow like the obedient patient I was. I grabbed a bottle of water down they went.

Jax then spoke, "We haven't much time till darkness and shift change at the gate. I could use one of you for a diversion; Wendi has already been compromised with her dog, Slim." Both Marshals gave condescending scowls in unison, a look of superiority Evans leads with, "Jax, that's above our paygrade. Neither of us has been offered hazardous pay, and our jobs are to watchdog you and Wendi or Sunshine, whomever she believes she is at the time. Damnit, Jax, don't forget our objective is to return you both to NIA safe and sound. Besides, we're not going to do anything that jeopardizes you or us… that's it, uh remember. Our identities cannot be found out."

"Jax, you're the high and mighty war hero one-man wrecking crew, the notorious Army Ranger, aren't you the one who is the military mastermind, no this is your baby. We're here to assist on the sidelines!" added Marshal Burke. In a calming voice, Dr. Liz Honcho pointed to a white and red 3-foot by 3-foot First Aid kit that hung in the back of the van, "besides being a Forensic Psychologist. I was also a physician with three years of experience in emergency rooms in the city of Chicago years ago, it was a war zone at times. I'm only here for the dual purpose of medicating Wendi, treating her mental disorder, counseling her, and of course, if an emergency occurs. Ugh, or if any of us gets injured, I'm here," Marshals Burke and Evans laugh "no worries, Liz, none of us plans to be shot or injured," declared Evans.

"We have information that besides the two guards at the gate, there are five other CIA agents below ground. That's seven in all, Jax; what do you want me to do to help...." "No, Wendi, I got this just have to figure out my approach. The 11ft chain link fence is electrified with motion detectors and cameras attached if the fence is shaken even by a strong wind, alarms go off, and you can't cut it or climb it; also no way to disable the circuit. The system has a failsafe connection to the underground bunker." "How is it you know all this to be true?" asked Evans. I answered for Jax, "if you had done your due diligence into Jax's history, he had owned several high-tech security companies in the state of Florida."

Anyway, with all that being said, Jax was working, preparing himself for the evening's mission. He finished belting on his mercenary tools and gadgets while pacing to and fro. Jax raised his voice and said, frustrated, "other than driving right up in this van to the gate I...." "Oh no, you don't. You're not taking this van anywhere," yelled Marshal Burke "this is our only mode of transportation, so ..." We were all outside of the van, knowing there wasn't much time before the torturing of the mother and daughter began. I was anxious to seek the help of the Marshals, but none was coming. How could we enter the gated complex other than just aggressively ramming through the front gate?

Becoming annoyed and unrelenting, *'I, Sunshine,'* yelled, "Hey, there is a five-year-old girl and mother underground probably being tormented, and all you three have to say or do is cast negative aspersions at Jax. Your harsh acrimonious adversity-laden words are pathetic. Come on, Jax, I'm going in with you!" "No, no, no, you're much too valuable, Wendi dear. I appreciate your willingness." "No way," adds Evans, with Liz now standing.

Liz yelped, "We're not going to deal with the consequences of you getting your ass hurt which would put us all in a wrapped sling." "I have body armor, am skilled in MMA, primarily Judo, and had passed the brown belt test a decade ago. I can, and I will fight… Liz." I feel his arm slap upon my taut shoulders. "Let's go for a walk," says Jax. "All right, there isn't much time. Do you think we could use the dog again as a diversion…." "No, uh, yes, I guess so, but Jane, the security guard, shouted that if she sees that dog again, she will shoot him." "But they're changing out the guards." "I don't know, Jax, but you're in the opening for a country block; without a vehicle. You'll have to walk right up to the damn gate… just don't see any possibilities." "Correct, they sure picked a perfect refuge for prisoners. The entire perimeter is asphalt with no way to get close without being seen by cameras, sensors, or the security forces."

He squeezed his lips, shook his painted face, his furrowed brows dropped down over squinting eyes, covered his mustache with his thumb and forefinger in a perplexed look… Stalemate.

Meanwhile, five football fields away and three floors below the pavement was lead CIA operative 'Adam' who was itching to perform his barbaric interrogation technics on the little girl, his wrath evident to his colleagues. For the 3rd time, Adam reinserts the picture of the woman with the dog that had violated their operations gate. Boiling over with anxious energy, the portrait wasn't turning up a match, so he tweaked it. He again tried scanning it into the computer system linked miles away at the Quantico complex. Adam never believed or gave credence nor cared much about technological innovations. He had serious reservations regarding facial recognition 'F.R.,' having played around with it himself. It worked when he inputted his own picture!

The picture Hugo, the guard, had taken of the petite blonde with a ponytail proved his point of how worthless F.R. was. Photos with the identity that came back from the Facial Recognition search were 'Wendi Feral' Lol. She was currently in a mental hospital in Napa, California like, 3000 miles away. She was not walking a fricking dog outside of Washington D.C., no way!

He scanned some of the headlines about the Feral woman... guffawing at what ridiculousness people would believe dramatized Bull Shit! Supposedly, according to some of the bizarre news articles, she had an innate ability to communicate with animals. Sensational publicity, wow, and I can walk on the ocean; people were fools, ghost hunters chasing paranormal freaks, what fricken righteous idiots.

Adam decided to run another picture by F.R. the photo on her Identification with the same results; the image returned as the 'animal seer' pinching his boney chin. Some said Adam looked like a skeleton with a thin layer of latex plastic covering bones, milky white chalky skin afraid of the sun and melanoma, malignant cancer, always had bottles of the strongest sunscreen, paranoid with an extremely high IQ for what that was worth.

Adam had admitted long ago that he had a disorder, but it was his. He didn't believe in categorizing or stereotyping it as OBD. Sure, he was an obsessive-compulsive type of individual. Blinked and concentrated, continuing to research and scrutinize the Feral woman's eyes... Adam, for the umpteenth time, was glued to the replay. Wendi Feral, the woman in question with the dog, stood in the trees rodents came out from nowhere. Even a Skunk sat up on its haunches as if speaking. The dog stopped running then, as if it instantly morphed into being re-trained, walked up to her, allowing it to be leashed, acting like it was a show-dog, then heeled at her side.

What the fk could this be? He speaks into the wireless radio system, "Hey Greg, can you come to the operational room." Adam decided that he'd get someone else's opinion, even though he wondered why... was he going nuts? He cackled... Adam had debunked the assertion of his doctors that he was a hypochondriac, something was biting him under his skin again, what was it?

<u>Jax Foul and Wendi Feral planned out their next moves.</u>

Jax was all man-male despite being castrated as a prisoner in Iraq. He was on hormone replacement therapy drugs, and if there ever was a more masculine macho man on the planet. I hadn't met him yet 'no fear' was the word on his T-shirt underneath the armor; of course, my Rico was a close second place, ugh, most likely not. I trusted Jax like I did Rico.

We walked out of hearing range distance from the van's three occupants. I decided to sort of come clean "Jax, only a few human beings are privy, um, aware of how I've evolved into the person you see in front of you. Fortunate to survive the trauma I experienced as a child, nearly drowning at the San Francisco Zoo, where oxygen was breathed back into my lungs… I was saved by the gorilla, Rocco, in which he had bestowed within me an innate 7th sense of telepathically being able to relate with some willing animals. Jax, my young life was altered because of a case I helped solve for Judy, a policewoman. She worked for the Redwood City Police Department; this case changed my life forever. It caused irreparable caustic changes in my personality and mental state. I thought I was going crazy. Somehow I developed an alter ego, not unlike many children, a secret invisible friend playmate… my survival made this essential…" He chortled "oh, now you're coming clean 'Sunshine' yuh really think that this is all enlightening news? Your kinda speaking to the choir I'm the guy with PTSD so many disorders it would take the both of us 15 minutes to realize a fraction of them. Supposedly I'm a raging Schizophrenic. I see right through you, Sunshine." "Aah, you do?" "Yeah, as corny as this may sound, your shyness, coy innocence, the flirty, dainty girly act is just that, an act. Not only that, Wendi, but you've told me all of this before."

"Okay," giggling, 'K enough' we laugh together. I added a derisive snort for good measure; we were smirking. 'Gosh, I liked this dude!' he soldiered on "it's not the case of a good/bad split personality, Sunshine, whom you are right this moment is your default personality uh… when times get tough that is. Your no-nonsense survival mode takes charge. You become forthright a 'She Warrior.' You act and think like a man with the added instincts and intuition of a female. I love your ass, Sunshine." Well, fk what was left for me to say other than "let's do this." So wow, awkward, I'd ventured out on a cracked limb; very weirdly, we embraced then shoved off... at the strange stares of our company.

"We hadn't anytime, so let me run this by you there's a 'murder of Crows.' That's what the English call them. I heard their raspy cawing out screeching in a blatant, aggressive chirping rage, Ravens black as night harvesting a dead cat." "Murder of crows can't say I've ever heard that term, but..." I pointed to a Birch Tree amid 9-foot Oleander Bushes, "there's got to be thirty-five birds in those bushes nests everywhere their smart birds. What if I could talk them into making nuisances of themselves at the gate, dive bomb the guards, cawing kind of like that Hitchcock movie." "Yeah, one of my favs, The Birds," he adds. I nodded, "We can also incorporate Slim again to break... through the opening in the rolling gate, have Marshal Burke drive you up close enough to the entrance while the two gatekeepers are being harassed... you slink inside."

"Wow, brilliant like it much better than firing my sniper rifle and shooting them dead; the problem with that is I'd need to get them close enough together to have clear shots on both of them simultaneously." 'True' I said then added, "they check in with the Commander down in the bunker or basement remember Rod the Rat told us that we know that one operates the gate the other drives the golf cart around the inside perimeter."

"Okay, then I can use the frequency blocker in 15-second increments. That way, an alarm will not sound off from their surveillance system." Watching her stride away with purpose towards the Crows, he pulls out a cylinder tube made of aluminum. Inside were five small darts also, a tiny secure eye dropper with an application pad, 'Novachek' a poison developed during the Cold War, a Russian invention uh concoction, oil base gel that can be smeared on a doorknob or anything for that matter, one of the most deadly poisons ever developed. It systemically is absorbed into a person's epidermis, um, skin by touch. Unlike other poisons that can take days of torturous agony to die.

This poison mixture killed instantly if it entered a living being's blood system. It became a silent, quick extinguisher of life, highly toxic immediate paralysis. The problem with this method of the kill was that he had to get close enough to the victim and have a shot at a body part that didn't have body armor as a protectant cover. Veiled with a cloak of darkness, night had fallen, and lights appeared in the not-so-distant parking lot of the archaic former amusement park. He was pumped up, exhilarated, ready to do what he enjoyed the most in life, attacking aggressively with calculated objectives. He nodded at Marshal Evans... with only one place to go, the extended van with government tags headed straight for the gate. Jax was now truly in go mode!

Just as Evans was driving to drop him 50 yards away 'Wendi' had signaled him via radio that it was now or never 'from the corner of his eye,' Slim the Greyhound darted past the vapors of the Halides shinning down from the fixed streetlights. Full-on convergence in less than 55 seconds. Patience, a virtue, stalled as they circled the outside perimeter in the van, waiting for the delivery of food that was being offloaded at the front gates. This had to be a daily procedure with seven agents and five prisoners within the closed facility; food was a necessity. It appeared to be boxes of pizzas.

What the guards couldn't surmise would be to their disadvantage, for the cold black Crows were just out of view above them, waiting as Wendi had instructed. Beaks were dripping at the sight of the all-meat and cheese pizzas. Jax is in the van still, Evans driving as they watch another woman and man team replace Hugo and Jane in the Golf carts. Taking an SUV and driving away were the former guards. A few moments passed until the prior guards were nearly out of view... perfect timing. That's when all chaos unfolded dive bombers, Kamikaze-style attacks not suicidal though hungry and fierce, cawing loudly in a wave of three controlled assaults with 13 bird teams. It was an onslaught.

The ambush massacre beaks, tearing fleshy faces. Claws ripping at the woman's long dark hair and screams of hysteria from the new replacement guards were ear-shattering talk about a diversion. Now it was time to enter the gate!

Adam and Greg are down inside the basement chamber.

Adam was perplexed, three floors below the surface sitting next to Greg, showing him the facial recognition results of Hugo's pictures. A YouTube video played on another screen with Wendi Feral's exploits from Tennessee to Florida. Both were so enthralled in the bio of Wendi that the ingeniously devised orchestrated attack by the winged warriors went completely unnoticed on the other screens in the main office. The C.I.A. operatives were distracted, fascinated, and hypnotized watching her exploits from Ocala, Florida, dealing with the Sinaloa Cartel to the Cuban Mafia, sex slavery child abductions. The light went on…!

Jax sprinted from the van Evans was driving. The departing guards, Jane and Hugo, were just now turning down a side street out of view. The gate was still unlatched and unchained, with the replacement guards, in the process of loading the Pizza cartons into their Golf carts to deliver to the underground bunker… when Jax burst through, and that's when Jax noticed her. "Hey, what the heck are you doing here?…" "helping," said 'Sunshine.' It seemed to take a lot of time, but in the grand scheme of things, barely a minute or three, Jax didn't have to utilize the poison nor take the lives of the replacement guards now handcuffed, shackled, and muzzled at gunpoint. Wendi helped pile them both in the golf cart. They were bleeding, disoriented wide-eyed… pecked, with beak marks across their necks, faces, and arms… hands trying to fend off the 'ravenous Ravens.'

He snatched up the radios while she drove what was left of the pizza to the familiar grove of trees, mass consumption for the celebratory birds, rodents, and now Papa along with his family… mammals of the Skunk variety.

Jax holding a guard's radio, had no idea what the protocol was for how to communicate with the… hostage takers inside the basement bunker, then didn't have to "Hey Randy, where's dinner? I'm fking starving." Jax muffled his voice. "Pizza open up!..." "ok, right on," said the voice back at him at the door intercom system entrance. Instantly the door automatically popped open; he entered the auditorium, following precisely the information gleaned from 'Rod the leader Rat' with his monocled Nightvision. He saw an entourage of Rats and maybe five scurry onward; he was on their tails. Jax walked past a Red laser beam by a vent grate. Suddenly a hidden wall moved open, and he was the last to enter, still on the tails of his allies. To his amazement, a full-sized elevator was directly in front of him. Preparing for it to open, knowing he had the 'upward hand' ultimate shock. The surprise attack should be the equalizer.

In his left hand was a super powerful Elephant dart tranquilizer gun with 3-inch sharpened steel needled injector projectiles, with instant acting sleep agents that would knock any human out for a minimum of 3 hours. The same darts he'd fired into the injured guards that the Crows had disabled outside in the parking lot with Wendi. In his right hand was an 'M-5 automatic machine gun' either way, with the armor-piercing bullets, he had leverage and the advantage. Jax was oh so calm. This was his solitude mantra, cool as a cucumber; even when the elevator door began to slide open, he was aware that he had to make the decision to kill or disable. Either way, it could happen ultra-quick. He stood in the boxed elevator bending his head downward, trying to evade the camera. His rodent accomplices were patiently scuttling around the doors enclosure. Luckily, there was only one button; he pushed it and felt his stomach… falling.

Jax inhaled a large breath, thinking he'd rather not add to his total of 69 kills. Unbeknownst to him, the Rats had their own orders and goals soon as the steel door had opened 5 inches, they surged out, scrambling lightning-fast, and the elevator door finally was open far enough for him to squeeze out. Jax was confronted after several steps with ungodly yowls inside, screams of shock high pitched, then low grunts stepping to the side and ducking around a corner. Jax swore what he witnessed could have been a hilarious skit from an episode of 'Saturday Night Live' up on the tippy toes was a tall thin man and a slender woman, maybe in their 40s, with matching boots. They were terrified of the Rats, visibly shaken and freaked out.

Blue jeans with wind blazers acronym letters of C.I.A. fear exploding in their eyes seeing him. Quickly he ascertained no body armor fired the dart gun at point-blank range into their upper torsos. They collectively gasped, lunged out towards him holding their weapons, then fell! I had them cuffed before the elevator doors had closed now, simple math down to three Agents. Followed the RAT patrol into a maintenance room and disabled the backup generator just before cutting the power and electricity, a horn sounded raucously blaring, and alarms sounded.

Adam saw the intruder first on the 2nd floor. Greg punched the alarm on another monitor, and two of their crew were down. Lightning fast, they bailed out of the security room, ready for battle, hearts pumping blood to all extremities, and had their body armor buckled on with weapons in their hands. Adam again attempted to communicate with his superiors in the CIA and the prior guards... to no avail. A blocking system was en vogue.

They hadn't run five feet Bam, and total darkness encompassed them. Blind as a Bat... couldn't see their own fingers "oh fk," yelped Adam. "The cells are on auto lock." The cell doors sprung open all five prisoners were free to leave their purgatory, yells, shouting, and chaos surrounding them. Adam took charge and screamed for the guard patrolling the cells. "Tom, where are you?..." "Over here," waving a flashlight.

Greg and Adam were sliding with their backs against a wall as they watched the flashlight beam bouncing off the concrete and heard Tom's gasp.

They had their sidearms out, Glock 9 mm pistols poised in ready mode, blind as both were, now fully aware that the prisoners could escape their cells. Adam conceded he should have left the prisoners chained up after his fun torture sessions. A hoarse Voice in the dark uttered, "hurry before the lights go back on... let's get that freakin bastard Adam and give him some of his own medicine." Hyena hysteria burdened...

ghoulish laughing ensued. The two hobbling prisoners were holding hands in the dark.

Greg's shoulder leaned into Adam… uh, the odds had been reversed, and paranoia had frozen Adam in blackness; "listen, Greg, we shoot to kill." Jax rushed back down the hall right behind the Rats, his night vision glowing greenish as the elevator sprung open again. He almost shot her dead, whispering. "Wendi, oh my God, girl, whatcha doing down here? I told you to stay outside by the Oak Tree, damnit." Next to her was the Greyhound Slim, his paw's nails scratching the floor. She was wearing the same head hear night vision monocle… "Let's get Catherine and her mom Anastasia out of here," she whispered. A door rolled open to sounds of men violently raging, "I'm going to cut you into pieces using your own knives, you fking prick." "Come and get us, says another voice."

Jax and Wendi could clearly see the images of three men, one with weapons crawling towards the two prisoners who were bloody and naked, and another man who couldn't walk was clunked against the open door of his torture chamber. The two prisoners had their backs against each other the wall abutted their shoulders in a defensive stance, unaware that guns were pointed in their direction in the cold dark hallway.

Jax recalled what the military manuals had dictated… wasn't going to work by the book; he had to adlib now. He watches Slim bolting in the opposite direction down the hall.

I murmured into his ear, "Slim will get the girls; let's stay put," he replied, "you stay behind me." He pressed the button on his gadget. It was the time for the frequency blocker, stopping all phones and cameras halting communication again in fifteen-minute intervals. They watched a tenuous situation get closer to imploding. The CIA crawlers were but 9 feet from …

<u>Anastasia and Catherine.</u>

"Mamma, mama mommy, there's a dog." Slim had found them outside their cell hunkered down, shaking like leaf's in the wind, yet there wasn't any… with no direction to go, they nervously held one another. They were sitting on the concrete, Catherine on her mother's lap, being caressed.

Slim gently, with reasonable force, tugged on Catherine's 'My-Lil-Pony' pajamas adding three sharp barks. 'Let's go! 'Mama the doggie wants us to follow her mother felt Slim's twitching tail and, while holding her daughter in her left arm, blindly took Slim's wiry strong tail using it like a leash. With the help of night vision, Jax had located them. Less than 75 seconds later, the elevator door closed. Inside were Wendi, Jax, Anastasia, and Catherine with a wagging-tailed Slim; in the corner perched on his back paws was 'Rod,' the Rat leader King of the rodents.

The sounds of gunfire were heard as the door closed. "Who are you" yelped Anastasia. I said, "we're here to free you and save you.…" "Uh, we're still not out of the woods yet," added Jax. 'How profound were those words' I later mused. Taking the staircase up the five steps to exit the auditorium, my umh, our world flip-flopped. Jax pushed the heavy door open at the landing. I was the caboose in front of us. A night Owl screeched out, warning alarms… danger then repeated, followed by the cawing of the Crows. I was tumbling backward, falling down the stairs reaching for anything to stop the gravity-based trajectory. I was wrong… I wasn't the last in the line and tripped over Slim. Down I went five concrete steps, knocked my head on the railing, and landed on my ass and elbow… rolling and bouncing off both knees. This didn't prevent me from shrieking out. "Stop, Jax, get back danger… be careful. Don't go out there!" ☹ .

<u>Lucky because we made our luck</u>, it took Jane and the heavy-set Hugo too long to realize that Jax was not one of their 'CIA' Operatives, or Jax would have been shot to smithereens. Bullets raged out as they had us in a crossfire Jane on one side

of the exit door, Hugo 25ft on the other. We hovered on the landing; the door had swung open, staying that way. The moon glowed with stars twinkling as Slim blasted past us like a bolt of lightning. Rod, the king Rat, blew by us also. Jax said, "we haven't much time. I'm positive they've called for backup and reinforcements. I'm going out there. You all stay put...!" "Stop, No, Jax," I yelled, "let the animals do what they can, please... give them a few minutes, umh, seconds," more gunfire. Yapping, wounded screams peering out the opening, the Crows were dive bombing from the air-ground support were the Rats. Then, a hushed stench as I watched through my goggles Rollie-Pollie guard Hugo... getting sprayed. A black-white and silver tail held high, and proud Papa let it all out. Flatulence invaded the area, almost toxic 'Skunkticity.' Hugo started screeching out an inhuman holler, rolling like he was on fire mama Skunk, with a few babies, unloaded on Jane. Bullseye squirted right in her eyes she started squealing in agony. I will never forget the convoluted heaving she couldn't breathe fighting for oxygen... oh well, too bad.

Jax didn't wait... he spun on me, scary how fast he moved, snatched me up with a hug, then laid a soppy kiss on my lips. We watched... writhing on the asphalt where Jane and Hugo, who were out of commission. Side by side stood mother and daughter clenched, holding their noses because, oh my Lord, no description. None could give you a clue at how the stench leaked straight past your clothes. We'd have to shower several times, indeed... Rod slinked up to me. His eyes told me what I didn't want to know. Oh no, I went with him, and in a puddle of blood lay 'Slim' who only had enough strength to flick his eyes open 'you're the best, Slim. I love you... you're going to doggy heaven,' I told him as he breathed no more; tears bounced off my chin.

'Oh no,' howled Catherine, 'there's more of them coming through the gate!' She was right. The gate was wide-open, our backup came screeching up, and Marshal Evans, Burke, and Dr. Honcho sped through in our Van. We drove away with one casualty wrapped in a blanket, Slim the Greyhound. We didn't know why Jane and Hugo returned to the fenced facility.

Maybe there was a protocol in place for them to check in with the replacement guards, and because Jax initiated the blocking device, they couldn't; who knows? I didn't give a damn!

Sadly, I didn't hear anything about the others we'd left behind and never was told a single word of what had happened after we drove away with Anastasia and Catherine.

-25-

Sunshine Feral.

Marshal Kara's shift was Monday through Friday from 5 am to 5 pm; I was being watched and protected by a three-person team Rico and Tanya, with complete transparency, left orders that only Doctor Hawkins was allowed inside my locked down cell umh and Jax too! Fortunately, or depending on how you choose to gauge it, my parents and husband David had to fly back to the Vancouver, Portland area. David was a construction manager on a five-story building uhm, I think he was the project manager. Mom and dad had to fly back home because my mother was having surgery for growths formed in the mucous membranes in her colon... polyps, thankfully benign after the biopsy... whew!

Jax would visit with me sometimes two or three times a day... at the beginning of my new drug treatment program. I suffered tremendous withdrawals and counted on Doctor Hawkins to help me. At times after I was given the intravenous medicine, the staff had to strap my limbs down to the gurney for I would scratch the skin plumb off of me. Shaking and drooling, wished and prayed, even begged for death, pleaded with Jax to show mercy... and strangle me! I'd never experienced this form of agony and pain. It was physical and mental horror... <u>'excruciating didn't come close... Merriam-Webster dictionary had to come up with a better word than 'excruciating'... for me!'</u>

The sheets I laid on went from Iceberg frozen to Death Valley sweat. Three to five Registered Nurses were selected

183

personally by Doctor Hawkins, and they would work around the clock, trying futilely to soothe me.

In the first days, I had to be restrained to the gurney… I'd listened to Jax but feebly couldn't mutter a single syllable. 'Sunshine did all the communicating… Jax was the only person she didn't play the catatonic act with, no hiding act! It had been 13 days since doggy Slim had died. I was brutally sore. Jax would slip up my gown to expose my skinned-up knees and apply the soothing salve to the scabs. The bruises had gone from dark black and purple to now a lighter shade of brown. It was my bones that suffered the most from the fall down the stairs. It was now going on seven days and nights without all the Psycho-Tropic medication therapy used by NIA… and Doctor Liz Honcho. Mind control drugs induced me into a mere robot controlled like a puppet allowing Sunshine to remain in power. She was on autopilot, an all-powerful protagonist, the one and the same 'Sunshine, my Savior' she insisted our body was safer with her in charge. Yeah, my alter ego blocked my memory when she was entirely in control, but without Dr. Honcho's chemical mix, I was coming out of my relegated, sad unconscious state.

With the NIA regimen, I was fed 33 pills every 24 hours, so with simple math, my body had to absorb 231 pills a week! Oh, and that didn't count the intravenous solutions. Now I was going through severe withdrawals, dependent on the residual drugs that melted from my fatty tissues throughout my body. I finally could nearly think like me, 'Wendi' the real me realizing now how I'd got the scrapes and bruises my parents had gone berserk over last week; I had amnesia induced by drugs that allowed my alter ego Sunshine to take control of my body and mind! Uh, potent Pharmaceuticals had Zombified me. ☹.

In the first three days of the new medication provided by Dr. Teresa Hawkins, I suffered withdrawals that I wouldn't wish upon my worst enemies. The thousands of pills my liver had to process caused a pinging throbbing sensation. I started trying to speak in spates, unable to formulate simple sentences, my thoughts were discombobulated, and I couldn't focus, lost in the opaque drugged-out abyss… cloud-based. On top of battling the rehabilitation from the poisonous cocktails I had been inhaling from Doctor Honcho and the NIA staff. I'd had another battle ongoing with my pretend savior, who wanted to keep control of my body and mind. I became incensed, enraged… bickering, and arguing angrily with Sunshine, our caustic animus, was felt from inside of us… acrimony increased exponentially. I had always given in, acquiescing to her way of thinking. I decided I wasn't a confrontational entity, easily controlled by my counterpart, uh, Alpha Female's influences and demands, bridled I shut my mouth.

Then the proverbial worm had a change of direction, turning ever so slightly in my favor. Sunshine, by the 5th full day, became disheveled markedly in disarray, like disenchanted couldn't maintain a decent debate without becoming flustered. Her temper was exposed disingenuousness leaked from her cerebral resting spot.

I captured my inner strength, which I integrated and corralled, feeling the incarnate embodiment of my soul returning. I had lost at least 275 days in a drug-induced coma on a live wire. I pounced up from my gurney, so many questions to be answered. Omg, this show of clarity… cognizance was on display for Jax. The battle against Sunshine became a War she didn't want to relent and give up her control. Still, Jax worked hours on end with me. Mentally and physically, we began to work out together, doing Burpees and Jumping Jacks. Jax had the nosey cameras eliminated. We exercised in the SHU solitary housing unit confinement with no windows.

He informed me of the killing of my former nurse Dan Spikes and the ongoing investigation of the shooting of two FBI Agents, adding sadly displayed by his expressions that it was my brother Mark who was suspected in the latest attempt on my life.

I was about to explode with energy and wanted my life back, calmed by Jax. He was my mentor. Rico was planning a visit with Doctor Hawkins on Friday. Today was Wednesday. I shut down Sunshine and re-decompartmentalized her ASS while Jax brought me back up to speed. I had my life back?... uh, no.

<u>NIA... Attorney and CEO Terrance Hallinan scolding his employees.</u>

Terrance was standing at the center of the long conference table... "we've been over this numerous times, your making excuses..." Terrance felt like a Sheepherder from medieval times (pounding the table with his fist.) "Your whining as Wolves plucks Sheep whenever hungry, without retaliation... none. Yuh wanna play the sacrificial Lambs, then so be it. I will have you all replaced; I want answers, not statements of negativity for the circumstances we find ourselves in, no speculations or conjecture, just some fricken refreshing optimism!"

Terrance was in a foul mood. Ursula, Larry, and Dr. Honcho sat wide-eyed. "This is absurd that NIA, a private institution, has been subjugated by the U.S. Government, FBI infiltrating our very walls." "Terrance, you realize we have a contract with the Feds for holding inmates for evaluations, no doubt a very lucrative binding agreement that adds tremendously to our bottom line." "True, Warden, but Ursula, with that being said, that same contract is for bed space, medical food, custody uhm, supervision, and miscellaneous, not for the Feds to commandeer like usurpers our facilities for their own appropriations...."

Doctor Liz Honcho interjects, "I might add that it's been over a week since I've been able to treat Wendi. It's like out of nowhere that Doctor Hawkins has taken over true I added her to our staff. Remember, I was under pressure by Rico, for he threatened to take several of the Federal inmates out of NIA. One of them was Wendi. I'm afraid that without psychotropic medications. We may lose Wendi, AKA 'Sunshine' forever."

"Liz, for Christ's sake, this is our 3rd meeting. Done with all that... kaput, I need answers on how we regain our foothold here, for, like, the 5th fricken time. Damnit... woman, let's stop sensationalizing the problems and reiterating the same crap. Wendi has three new Marshals, three outside Nurses, and Doctor Hawkins. They're occupying one of our cells down in the solitary confinement wing of the hospital. It's too risky to approach any of the Marshals or nurses to bring them under our envelope… plus we haven't the time!" Sneering, Terrance coughs into his palm, staring at them…

"Besides, we didn't have the time to choose the Marshals like before it was a stealth operation signed off by the freaking Attorney General in D.C. We have an approaching date for a mission in Seattle. Our NIA Forces are prepared and have been briefed. We've been hired to stifle the pilfering that's going on in a Russian organization. It's been proven that insiders are stealing large sums of money from the gang's illegal gambling and prostitution rings and even subverted some of their strip clubs and porn shops in the Seattle area…."

"Excuse me," says assistant Warden Larry Walden "why can't we utilize Jax? He's permitted to be alone with Wendi… she trusts him. In every one of her missions, she's had him beside her. They have a unique sort of bond…." Excitedly Liz exclaims, "Yes, why didn't I think about it? I can give Jax her medications. None of you realize the significance of her being weaned off my prescriptions of controlled drugs. She's liable to regress, and we could literally lose 'Sunshine.' It's a fine line we're trying to walk here, and there isn't a book that we can read and learn by it's all experimental our brain washings and manipulating Wendi's mental state will melt away if we don't continue our drug regimen. Basically, all our induced indoctrinations, ugh ideas…." "I get it enough, Doc; other than putting guns to their heads and locking all the Feds into their cells, what do we do? I've even had to curtail our training facility on site."

Ursula sighs. "It boils down to this. Think about how the Feds see this; 'In House,' one of our very own employees tried to assassinate Wendi, Rico, and the FBI naturally feels that our staff cannot be trusted. So he's instilled his protection. It wouldn't surprise me at all that Director Tanya Firm decides to move Wendi from our institution." "What, that's not possible," says Liz. Terrance bows his head. "Yes, that's the worst-case scenario. Remember, Wendi is a self-commit. Her husband admitted her for only 180 days. She's been incarcerated here going on 275 days. They could essentially roll her right out our doors. We wouldn't have any recourse!" Terrance smiled and released a jolly chortle. "Oh, but yes, we do… the worst case could be viewed as the best case for us. They take Wendi from NIA, and we then use one of our select teams and kidnap her back, lock her away deep down in our dungeons. Wendi then becomes a permanent solution, resident our paranormal animal seer till death do we part; yes, that's a possibility!"

They stand in unison while Terrance packs up his briefcase.

"Okay, let's be progressive and take the proverbial 'Bull by the horns,' Dr. Honcho. You get with Jax. Let's get Ms. Feral back on your drugs. Warden, I want you to start dropping subtle hints that it might be better for Wendi to be moved behind the razor wire to our secure prison hospital instead of this outpatient treatment center. Like I've said, worst-case scenario, they might try to take her from us." He sneered, *"the feds don't realize we have spies throughout the government. Ain't no way to hide her without us finding her. Until then, we go ahead on our goals and missions without the use or expertise of the Feral woman, done I'm outta here unless any of you have anything else to add…"* no one spoke up. *Nope, See Ya!*

<u>Wendi and Jax.</u>

Wendi had been moved to the Presidential suite of Jail cells, even had three windows to look out over the Rollin hills filled with various varieties of grapes for as far as she could see, a mini lake ponds park-like setting, even playgrounds for the children who visited the mentally hampered inmates. The only reminder of the solitary confinement cell was a locked steel door, a Marshal on the other side. His arm over her shoulders, both smiling at the vibrant sky colors of life, gardens below filled with blooming trellises and wooded lattice walls helping reinforce the Bougainvillea, which zigzagged climbing through the openings in the framework. Azaleas, Roses of all the colors of a rainbow, Rhododendrons blazing pinks, violets white Peonies of so many persuasions, a profusion of flowers that had Jax and Wendi peering out the windows plainly in Awe!

"I want a book on flowers to know their names. I want to touch and smell them full-on. Omg, they're so glorious, the best-living things on earth, like Heaven in this caustic world!" Jax grins wide, squeezing her tightly. "It will be done, madam," they giggle together; in the background of Wendi's mind 'Sunshine was nearly vomiting flowers fk, kill them all.' With a serious tone, Wendi says, "all right, tell me again, I still am having a hard time understanding all of this, please, Jax, it seems almost laughable, like something seriously out of a complicated novel written by 'Dan Brown' suspense, intrigue, Russian syndicate Mafia, espionage, thrilling but no doubt fiction right!"

He pulled up a chair so they could sit and look out the windows and at one another with barely a turn of the head, with an amused gleam of a matching smile, vibrant life full-on was resonating under the sun's glow. Jax took a pillow from her bed and put it on the seat for her to sit on to raise her up a bit. Wendi slyly knowingly smiled, not having the most extended type of torsos, was about 5'1" tall; Jax couldn't help his feelings of attraction, her eyes greenish flecks of hue's that sparkled seemed to be ever-changing reflecting her moods. Her long blonde hair was pulled up and stuffed into a feminine bun giving form to her slender muscled neck, sexy nape with tiny curls squirreling downward, cute ear lobes ears matching her adorable nose. It appears she had run a brush over the skin of her face, maybe some blush, but no, he decided the all-natural color was back on her skin. She looked alive with vibrancy. This girl didn't need a touch of make-up, a barbie doll. He glances at her chin and eyebrows. His eyes followed the contours of her body, wearing a pink blouse with white and purple petals of Roses fluttering about braless with her petite roundish boobs standing at attention, nipples hardened when they slid across the fabric that kept them concealed. Bright white shorts with a thin black belt just for the ensemble thighs that snuck out. Taut calves and quad muscles popped as she adjusted her feet toes feet like 'Wilma Flintstone' fat pudgy, perfect in sandals, feet toenails pedicured, and dainty feminine hands not painted but a manicured shape. Dammit, even her kneecaps were delicious... Jax was on a new regiment of hormone replacement drugs, uhm, injections which might have to be adjusted as he squirmed in his seat, readjusting his package minus two testicles. He could stare at Wendi for days, admitting that he Loved her in so many diverse ways.

"You know your voice is kindlier to my ears, um, ladylike," he said, wanting to add that her voice seductively mesmerized him but didn't. "Sunshine has a harsher voice, more like Janis Joplin's, raspy throaty, purposeful, straightforward, no, nonsense always in control barking." He grinned broadly, "but I have become attached to her." She smirked, sipping her Cranberry juice. "Wendi, it's nice to have you back," her bruises now fading, the last remnants of scabs that had once been part of... "Jax, why does it seem like I'm under a microscope? You're like measuring me with your stare?..." "Sorry, it's everything, like transformation, your crossed legs movements, everything about you is strange to me, opposite from the person that... was you. I realized that I'd become accustomed to her 271 days and nights, having spent more time with 'Sunshine' than any living person ahhhh, girl... I don't know how to explain it to you properly, Wendi. Ugh, it's like I'm starting over, getting to know who you are once again. Scary and anxious... we had a tight bond!"

She sighs exasperatingly "geez, I'm sure this is difficult for you, but please empathize with my current situation. There were so many questions you could answer for me. I have only flashes of black-and-white memories."

I watched Jax say nothing smirking a dimple that rolled into a mini frown. I was frustrated, stood, moved over to the desk, and took up a notepad and green-inked pen. His eyes seemed to undress me. I could swear he'd been checking me out like awestruck, caught him focused on my ass, or was it just my imagination? I wondered what was going on. Did 'Sunshine' lead him on and flirt her butt off? I'd aah would've known for sure, despite being drugged out of my mind, if Jax and my alter ego had been intimate, I was into Rico. He was my style of man, I dropped the worry for there wasn't a reason to dwell on it, and I jumped to my first question.

"Tell me about '<u>David</u>' to whom I'm married to; what do you know?" even though I heard his hesitant voice struggling with description and other information. I was elsewhere like noise reverberating in my skull, speakers on high volume, thinking about what he'd blurted out days ago. I'd asked him why I was so sore? my body ached; he said I'd fallen down some steps on our last 'mission' 'mission, I asked?' 'You and me. He then elaborated that I, umh, Sunshine, and I have been on seven missions in the last nine months, all of which we succeeded in accomplishing all the goals outlined in our original plans and exceeded all dreamed objectives.' I became a sponge soaking up as much information as I could. I sipped some iced tea while waiting until Jax stopped texting on his phone.

Then he continued to say that, bizarrely, 'NIA' wasn't what people thought it was. Sure, it's a mental hospital and a prison for the criminally insane, nope! On the outside of the concertina, Razor wire, and the guard towers, there are three large airplane hangars and numerous obstacle courses. It is a training facility for mercenaries, a 'cell' of highly sophisticated professional insurgents with decades of military experience.
Still recalling his words, 'Wendi incarcerated here are the 'Who's Who' of the criminally insane masterminds. They are not only the most deviously evil intelligent, and ruthless individuals on earth, but their assortment of criminal skills were second to none, a diverse selection unmatched on earth. 'NIA is a recruitment center controlled by a conglomerate of global militias like Independent Contractors, if you will.'
'Here there is a worldwide nest of the worst of the worst mass killers, serial killers, psychopaths of every flavor, and talents unmatched in humankind; in fact, he said the staff, principally Doctor Liz Honcho had the entire 5th floor for specially trained warriors ugh, inmates, who work out for hours in the all-encompassing auditoriums and gymnasiums. Physically and mentally prepared without distractions from the

outside world, we even have indoor firing ranges too much to describe. Really, it's wholly unbelievable!'

'There are all kinds of classrooms for education and evaluating plans of attack. Every participant is mentally tested on five tests for IQ… MENSA, SATs, ACTs, military variables Science; my favorite testing is for the 'what if's or thinking out of the box set up in calamitous losing propositions. The scenarios are mind-blowing, sort of like contingency maneuvers. Suffice it to say that nowhere from Oxford… Stanford to Harvard, was there any close comparison for collected intellect collectively? The results of the test scores are off the charts. Take any complicated conundrum, word problem, or mathematic calculation with calculus… uhm, methods of computations with commonsense denominators… twisting invented terminology we don't stop until our analytics coalesce. We use physics to analyze current technological quandaries. Our prodigious group of psychopaths are as 'cold as dry ice,' becoming single-minded, shrewdly discerning the dynamic processes necessary and astutely. One absolute advantage of empowering psychopaths is that they never let Emotions get in the way; it is always Cut and Dried!

There is never just one correct answer to a complicated scenario. All variables have to be equated sometimes despite having three seemingly valid conclusions; contingency variations muddy the calculations bringing to the forefront semi-partially unconventional answers; we as a group don't conform to any specific ideology. We settle on a leveraged logical accurate, precise conclusion… analytically, not spontaneously aligned with algorithms that weigh the averages of success, all co-signed by CEO Terrance Hallinan.'

<u>I sat mesmerized… and listened to Jax's rant.</u>

"NIA has teams of trained assassins, 'Sunshine' has become a major Cog, a floater taken to the farthest point of this world where her specific talents were called for. Sunshine was audaciously bold and proactive. No fear in that woman Wendi.

You can now join me on our next mission in Seattle. I look forward to working with you."

Jax had in detail explained Sunshine's last foray in saving the Russian Diplomat's 5-year-old daughter Catherine and her mother Anastasia, where I'd received the scrapes and bruises. It was just Jax and her, with two Marshals and Doctor Honcho. Unlike other missions he intimated, which involved upwards of dozens of inmates.

I asked him, a bit confused, about why the CIA would be involved with kidnapping Russian Diplomat's family members and wasn't Trump and Putin, uh, friends or partners in land purchases in Florida and other forms of investment corruption in politics. His last words were really Wendi; you're a touch naïve... that's all-political jargon nonsense propaganda, the power brokers with their own agendas; next thing you know, you'll be telling me Putin and Trump will be playing 18 holes of Golf in Palm Beach tomorrow, lol.

'NIA' is antigovernment and autonomous, completely independent, a sovereign kingdom self-governing. We are affiliated with mercenaries/militants, and we want chaos among the empirical power mongers... therefore, we merely saved the Russian diplomat's family because 'He' was an essential part of 'our' integral hierarchy. His proof of collusion between Trump's family and the Russians sensationalizing the truths would have caused upheaval throughout all regimes, leaders, and dictators from all over the world. Besides, he portrayed a shit-eating wide-ass grin. The monies weren't bad either!

'Wendi' ahh girl, as he reaches over and hugs her, "I stopped speaking five minutes ago; you, all right? It's like you fell into a trance?" "I'm emotionally and physically beaten up, Jax; I'm suddenly tired. Sorry, it's all too much for me to...." Knocking on the door, I leaped up in three hops and am back in bed. Jax stood over me. The heavy steel door glides open Marshal Kara glares inside in her hands a wide wheelchair, "Let's go, you two Doctor's orders, it's a beautiful day to take a stroll." She helped Jax. I act nonchalantly as I'm loaded into the chair and wheeled out. The nurse that had dressed me earlier came along. If what Jax has told me, and Lord knows I trusted him, I was in a perilous grave dangerous position, for if the Warden or Doctor Honcho and the staff suspected that I was no longer a drugged-out robot not brainwashed 'Sunshine,' we hadn't any idea or clue what their recourse would be. Maybe even eliminate me, which we both doubted; indeed, it was easier when I was pliable Sunshine, under their power.

I couldn't wait to see Rico tomorrow and my parents the following weekend. <u>David</u> was also flying down from Portland. I played the zombie in the wheelchair, even flopping my head back and forth, for the staff not only had cameras everywhere, but they lurked around corners with a team following me like Sloths. Lucky for me, playing the catatonic patient was uncomplicated. Having plenty of rehearsals, I could do the act in my sleep, duh, yep!

<u>-26-</u>

<u>Rico and his FBI Agents.</u>

Rico was speaking with Tanya, "I'm at Marin General Hospital, and we have some great news, ma'am um Tanya, both Agent Gonzales and Kelsey Marie should be released later this week. I'm enacting around-the-clock security for them and will have them at one of our safe houses for a couple of weeks until they recover. We will have them under protective custody until any deemed threat can be neutralized. Of course, as you and I believe, this is an isolated attack, but you never can be too careful." "Rico, have you seen their Doctor yet? Both are fortunate to be still breathing. Their vests saved them, but ultimately if the shooter wanted them dead, they'd be dead." "True, Tanya, the shots fired by the sniper weren't designed to be… kill shots. The sniper knew they wore armor and aimed for sternum shots, although, with 50 caliber shells, it must have felt like being kicked point blank by a double-hoofed Donkey in the chest."

'Mr. Captor, please come to the front desk' "umh, they're calling me. I'll get back to you when I know anything, okay?" "Rico, um, Lori is working with a team of Agents, video at the truck stop previous to the assault, then directly afterward she's… Gotta go, Tanya." Click.

He spots a short-haired woman dressed in baby blue with a pull-over white jacket-coat. With Piercing brown eyes, her hand held out. "I'm Doctor Sanchez, Mr. Captor, um, I presume," shaking hands as he nods, "how are they? Can I see them?" "Yes, Mr. Gonzales fared better than Ms. Marie. I admitted them both for observation. Both were on respirators, unable to breathe in full breaths. They were hyperventilating because the bullet's impact nearly split their ribcages, causing trauma, internal bleeding, and deep bruising. They're sedated. I can't find any reason to prevent them from being released in 72 hours, and I'm confident they will not have any long-lasting effects," she turns to a nurse. "Can you escort this gentleman to room 315?" 'Yes' "Thanks, Doctor," as Rico spins on the heels of the Nurse. Curtains are partially open; he sees his Agents lying across from each other with drapes as a barrier. Agent Gonzales is passed out. Rico sighs, shaking his head, and sees Kelsey's eyelids waver with a flicker. A struggled dimple appears; he places his hand on her shoulder and caresses her auburn hair, happy to see her awake; her cheeks quiver a blush appears for the first time. He looks at the Agent, whom he is fond of, with a paternal view. Kelsey was a natural with a smattering of tiny freckles across her pert nose and upper cheekbones, not a classic beauty nor playboy material plain Jane type unlike many of her gender she'd age into beauty. He liked her, as he knew she was also very fond of him. He had found himself overly protective of her, wanting to help her further her career in the FBI without showing too much favoritism. He remembered the time when she had too much wine at a retirement function several years ago. She was dancing and carrying on enchantingly, um, flirtatiously, had several males chasing her short skirt, alas. Tanya and I drove her back to the hotel we were all staying in. That night again, he'd almost broken weak and allowed her to seduce him, but no way. She was married, and we would have regretted any extracurricular activities. 'Kelsey, the girl, needn't any makeup besides lip-gloss. She could have been on the last page in a calendar for the wholesome….' Suddenly entering the hospital room was a colorfully dressed older lady with two vases in her hands. There were name tags on the vases from the gift shop on the first floor. In each vase was a single white Rose card attached; Rico found a dull aching pain start to throb across his temples; no one should have known which rooms his Agents were in hell, not even the hospital was named in the media… ugh, press.

Kelsey blinked and then closed her ocean blue eyes; he watched the lady put one vase down on the end table by Agent Gonzales. Rico thought again, who could have known that his Agents would be admitted? Tanya maybe, "Excuse me," staring at the lady's name tag from the gift shop, "ah-um Betty," grabbing the vase meant for Kelsey. I opened the card, stepped over to the other vase, and read the same riddle. Betty, is there a record of who sent these flowers?" "umh, yes sir, I'm sure there aah…I can just check with the manager at the gift shop… Toni, I'm only a volunteer runner!" "Thanks, Betty. Have a fine day!"

The words were underlined in Red Ink written in block letters (<u>"Blessed divine intervention, sustaining faith, redeemed sacrificial fate… 'R.C.' requited closure ASAP"</u>)

A chafing ping clogs his esophagus, and Rico felt red hot flashes. He chokes on his saliva and coughs. The signature, uh, initials blared up at him and hushed his rapidly beating heart with fricken clarity. Sweat emanated immediately from his skin, and with forbearance, he purposely inhaled a large breath, then gritted his teeth. Yes, transparency made everything clear as glass. 'R.C.' was himself Rico Captor for years of texts, Tweets, emails, and cards… threats made from Wendi Feral's brother Mark now for over 11 years since his first extended contract with 'Feral Feedback' in Ocala, Florida. The company was co-owned by Sandi and Wendi; this proved that Mark Feral indeed arranged the assassination attempt at NIA on Wendi. He also orchestrated the killing of nurse Dan Spike to silence him. Rico's educated assumption, umh, theory was proven out… for the quote that ended with <u>R.C.</u> was the doing of Wendi's brother. Now there wasn't a doubt.

To him, it became fact-verbatim who the sniper was… he'd assumed the shooter had to have been the fugitive Joe Sable, who was connected and working with co-defendant Mark Feral. Knowing Joe Sable was a renowned Sniper… winning many tournaments in the military… an expert marksman, he was the one assumed to have fired the shots. If he wanted them dead, all he had to do was raise his barrel about 5 to 7 inches higher, and 'Joe' could have torn both Agent's necks out.

Rico went into the hall to use his phone, relaxing more after ending the conversation with Marshal Kara. She'd told him everything was copacetic. Jax was visiting Wendi at that very moment. Only his approved nurses and Doctor Hawkins had been allowed to enter the room. However, there was ongoing strife, for she and the other Marshals had dealt with the angry staff many times, including the Warden and Dr. Honcho's attitudes, who were far from cordial. In fact, let us call them irate! she relayed all to Rico.

<u>FBI Agent Lori Parks… in charge of the investigation of the shooting on Highway 101.</u>

"Nothing as of yet stands out. I'm sitting in front of three screens and have five other Agents doing the same Hwy 101 is still at a standstill. The CHP, Sheriffs, and local police are checking all vehicles, Canine units galore." "Lori, aah, Agent Parks, umh." "Come on, Rico… Lori, all right, no reason to be so formal. Hey, how are Gonzales and Kelsey doing?" "They're going to be fine. I'd like to call it a miracle, but it was definitely calculated shots. What's happening with Mark Feral's buddy Parolee Shaw?" "He's playing it all by the book Rico. We have him on multiple tracking systems. Tank showed up at his Probation Office on time, and he's been a model felon thus far. Last I checked, he went shopping and is hold on, let me check." Lori pulled up her iPad GPS locator, then snickered and said, "His ass is at a 24-Hour Fitness Gym downtown San Jose; I have three agents on shifts despite him being tagged with a chip Agent Avery just sent me a message that Agent Baker had searched his apartment found nothing out of the ordinary all's normal he can't get away Rico!"

"Lori, he is our only link to Feral and Sable. They were inseparable at San Quentin and have been since they were children. I just got cards from Mark Feral, letting me know it was him behind the assassination attempt on our fellow Agents and the murder of the nurse whom he hired to kill his sister Wendi. Have to go. Lori, I need to let Director Firm in on the latest" Click.

<u>Tank is showing off at the gym.</u>

Tank has an audience like always as he was in the midst of his chest routine workout; he just racked 405 pounds on the flat bench refusing a spotter; he needed no one behind him in case he failed to lift the weight off his chest, mind over matter. Only the weak had a helper babysit a lift. If he couldn't push the weight, then he hadn't any business getting under it. Mental and physical empowerment… strength with conviction sitting up after five controlled reps, umh, repetitions, feeling energized, exhilarated, with a natural high from his own body's endorphins.

Tank was always the strongest human in the gym, playing up to his ego with crowd-gathering aggressiveness. Add in his dramatic flair of rumbling growls while lifting; why not? Running through his blood and DNA was the genetics of a showman.

Great Grandfather was known as the 'Gorilla,' a Circus performer and strong man traveling the circuit worldwide. In later life, he became an alcoholic and still performed acts of enormous power which one evening was his literal undoing.

Grandpa was again at one of his local watering holes… taverns, sitting cavorting with the 'ladies of the night' in a bar on the dirt roads of San Francisco when the bartender and other friends egged him on to lift a Horse drawn carriage that had a broken wooden wheel axel, a feat he'd done dozens of times even making the front page of the San Francisco

Chronicle 3 decades prior. Drunken and disorderly staggering out of the saloon's swinging doors, the patrons on the heels of Granddad and people from shops all around stood out and watched Great Granddaddy.

Depending on the luggage, a Horse-drawn Carriage carried an estimated weight on each side of about 700 lbs. He'd heaved and grunted, and up it went. Lifting it wasn't the most difficult of his task, which reports with pictures proved true. He was smiling, showing off, holding the axle up waist-high for an extended time period while the large wheel was attached. Two men fumbled and let the gigantic wheel fall not once but three times in all. It certainly didn't help the situation that it was raining, and the dirt roads were a muddy mess.

Unfortunately, as it turned out, the two trying to attach the large wagon wheel were so inebriated and fumbling about that Granddaddy holding this enormous weight up started to shake... his skin blended redness, wheezed. His blood pressure went through the roof, combined with his alcohol intake; he let out a booming calamitous ear-splitting howl as he regained his hold on the carriage, suddenly dark blood flowed from his ankles and boots, a hernia exploded, and he bled to death from his rectum right there in the street before he died he saw the wheel attached grinning with a smirk of lasting pain.

A crowd of onlookers pretended not to notice as Tank loaded more 45-pound steel plates onto the bar. A total of 10 was resting on his bar, five on each side; then, a tiny two-and-a-half-pound plate was attached with a locking chrome collar.

A gym trainer braved the approach and said to Tank, "geez, man, that's over 500 pounds if you add in those collars. The record here at this gym is 485 lbs." Tank nonchalantly rolled his shoulders as if 'duh,' for he was the one loading the bar. The brawny trainer asked, "you want me to spot you."

"I don't need a spotter. That's why they made this bench like this." (he points to the steal prongs that were welded on the posts that held the massive weight just above the flat bench) "If I miss

the lift, I'll rack it on the 'suicide prongs,' but if you want to stand back out of my peripheral vision that'll be ok."

Tank enjoyed being the lead actor scanning the perhaps 55 members of 24-Hour Fitness in the vicinity, who were mesmerized, and most of the so-called studs acted as if they didn't see him or care. He sat at the end of the bench press, waving his arms, flexing his pectorals, stretching out and rolling his shoulders, wobbling his head on what most wouldn't consider a neck.... his head seemed to be glued to the middle of his shoulders.

He laid back under the weight and then abruptly sat up. Everyone gawked, froze in time, and he could have heard a pin drop if not for the sound system Tank was listening to. Now assured that he had his audience's full attention. He shoved the earbuds in deep, punched a song on... max volume 'George Thorogood and the Destroyers' 'Bad to the Bone!' Bald head, cleanly shaven, rests under the bent bar, grabs the gnarls with his hands, fingers grasped and wrapped like steel coils underneath the bar. He takes three lung-filling pumps of oxygen reflexes pulling himself up, then recoils and, in a swift motion, rips the 500 pounds from its rack, perfect form drops it right across his hardened pecks, nipples, and turns his wrist, cognizant of keeping the weight balanced pushed evenly with an orgasmic, raucous, garish scream racked the weight to a sound of hoots and holler's, some were clapping as he sat back up on the end of the bench as if it wasn't a big deal.

That's when he felt an anomaly, wetness from his underwear briefs strange sensation indeed stood up, grabbed his towel, wrapping it around his waist. The gym trainer walks up. "Can I get your name for the new record?" "Not now. I have to go to the bathroom." "I'll take the weight off the bar for you; that was impressive. Hell, you could bench a lot more than that, I bet!"

Tank didn't respond only thing that changed his path was a person who had caught his eye earlier, a Hispanic beauty who gave him the 'come and get it gleam,' he strained to leave her with a dimple as he rushed to the bathroom and found an open stall blood droplets from his buttocks.

Strange just had his first-ever colonoscopy at San Quentin and was still sore from the probe. No polyps, hemorrhoids dabbed around his sphincter, put a wad of toilet paper inside his anus like a tampon-Kotex combination. The doctor had told him that he might spot some blood, not to be worried. It was a natural reaction to the probe.

Tank's confidence revitalized as he exuded pure cockiness and approached her. "Hey, there, what's your name, girl?" coy smirk 'umh Gloria' she lets go of the handles on the rowing machine to stare up at him. "What you say to us getting out of here for something to eat or drink, Gloria?" She busts up, howling into a cackle, "whoa dude, you move fast. Wow, slow down. I don't even know your name?" "Oh, that's easy. I'm called Tank," she returned a knowing nod mixed with a slight smile. "Should have guessed either that or Rock. You certainly don't look like a Fred type" "Yeah, funny, Gloria, kinda ironic cuz I was only earlier considering what's in a name?" "Tank, why don't we meet in the swimming pool? I still have to finish my workout, including 25 laps in the pool. Then we can slip into the whirlpool together and get to know each other better!" "I'd like that but don't have a swimming suit…." "There's a shop by the entrance. I'm sure they have a suit to fit your fine-ass body."

Yum, oh yeah… that was it. Tank envisioned her tight muscled legs spread open, welcoming his manhood possessing her body aggressively, slamming her into blissful oblivion.

Back in the locker room, he checked his Tracfone text from Mark, 'Hit me. I might need your help sooner than we planned.' Tank found the pool; sex was all he could think about… a taste of a woman hell been inside San Quentin for years; sorry, bro, he muttered, gotta take care of this biological function. He saw the lady that would be naked bouncing all over his apartment soon. Shit, what was her name? Ahoh, that's right, Gloria, she was swimming laps. hopefully, she'd preserve enough energy for their sexual escapades later…Yay. ☺.

Mark Feral is on the prowl.

The familiar sounds of slot machines ringing away a cacophonous, discordant inharmonious blend of Winn River Casino's gaming machines, packed with people hoping to get lucky just like Me. I was on the prowl and had waited until the ladies should be primed with alcohol and drugs. The dance floor was empty, the local band had just taken a break, and body heat had warmed the lounge area. I pushed the double door open to get some fresh night air on the outside deck. The smokers were gathered in groups, and a small river flowed in the foreground.

Slightly angry as I again checked the time on one of the phones, 10:15 pm. Tank hadn't replied to any of my five texts; how could he be so damn irresponsible? Last I'd heard from him. He was heading to a gym in San Jose. Taking solace, at least Joe was on the ball. However, major problems persist. They could use Tank's help at a minimum as a Look Out... for the disposal of the bodies in their motorhome. Soon Joe warned me the bodies of the pimps would stink of rotten corpses and would be a bust. Joe could use Tank's assistance, and hell, he owed us his fricken freedom! Things had gone this side of haywire, Joe should never have wasted the pimp and his brother, but as he explained it, there wasn't anything he could have done differently.

Joe and I were wary and fully mindful that the Feds had their sights fixed on Tank. He was their connection to Joe and me since we had ascended the top 10 most wanted list. Actually, he was the only connection to us. It had always been Joe Sable, Tank Shaw, and me... we were bonded and trustworthy to one another till death do us part. One common denominator hate was mutual for dear sister Wendi, who had snitched us out as young teenagers, and we ended up in Juvenile Hall together. Wendi, who by now had to have way less than the assigned '9 lives of a mangy lioness' she's still alive and kicking a source inside NIA, had relayed the info that she was under guard in solitary confinement.

The frustrations boiled over for me; sure, I kept the two sloppy attorneys breathing for Joe's revenge, but against my better judgment, loose ends were like holes in a rowboat. Too many of them, and invariably, you'd sink, Ugh! Leaning over the rail with a vaporizer in her pouty lips was the night's finest candidate; I cruised up so I could get an overall appraisal of her ass. She was even better looking up close lovely shapely legs, a trim upper torso, doable and wearing pumps, nylons flesh colored up underneath her silver and black mid-skirt tattoos on her sexy calves couldn't make out exactly what the tattoos were of, that would cum later.

Three buttons opened on her short sleeveless black blouse. A frontal view didn't disappoint, lift up bra ahh 'C' cup left tit was the smaller one of the couple… bangles of gold and silver adorned her arms. Her face was clouded in shadow. She turned towards her healthy friend. There were three so far in the group, two of which were not my style. Certainly for 'last call' last standing sure, I already knew I was a shallow, superficial man, so what… sue me! ☺ .Why settle for raw hamburger when you could lick and chew on a filet mignon rare with just enough warm pink meat juicy, umh, delish!

I moved in as the local pop group played the top 40 songs; again, the break was over for them and me. A song they butchered, sung by 'Cardi B, Bodak Yellow,' time to shuffle this party to the dance floor.'

I closed in on my prey like a hungry Wolf, a scent of fresh meat wafting into my nostrils. Finally, I caught a glimpse of the masterpiece, the gorgeous finishing touch of a face that would consume my body; oh no, what happened? She was a beauty queen with missing pieces of mascara running down her face leaving cruel clownish streaks on her supple cleft chin. Crying, ahh she was… ugh, this presented me with a precarious decision. It could be an 'easy as pie' pickup, just play up the emotional shoulder to lean on, or maybe too much work for me. Heck, the girl could be a Drama Queen, which would be mortally hell based because I genuinely didn't give a raging fk what was bothering her! Umh, second thought on that motif, raging fk was precisely what I needed… Lol!

I just wanted her naked body strapped down in leather, take turns, and fun stuff. Why not live a little, huh Disgustingly, a wimpy man appeared and took her into his arms for an extended hug and kiss. Geez, a waste of time. I'd leave the veggie burger to the skinny guy, bit my upper lip damn back on the prowl, hunt heading over to the Blackjack tables, ahh another possible conquest, uhm, counting chips sucking on a straw. Already was primed an elbow holding her head up on the bar, passable from a rear entry I meandered over.

<u>Sammy, Joe in Stinson Beach, Marin County, California.</u>

Sammy let his words float past on the waves of the Pacific Ocean. They were perched on a section of smoothed-out jagged boulders where they could hear and see the relentless sounds of water rushing and hitting the beach… "Answer me, Sammy," said he. "I was just thinking of how the waves had smoothed out these rocks on all sides but had left the tops jagged, alone." "What the hell does that have to do with what we were talking about?" snorts Joe. "Sorry, a change of venue. The subject was all I was attempting…." "Not going to work for me, Sam, so let's recap. You just said or asked how I was going to kill you, for you are sure that is part of my plan." "True, and it isn't?" He waved his hand out, not wanting to concede the facts. Lips pursed tight, and she continued, "then I asked you verbatim how were you going to kill me?" "Okay, I'll bite. Why the fk are you still sitting with me, Sammy? What the fk? If you are certain, that is what the finished product looks like, why not speed off on the bike or say something to the CHPs or whatever?"

"Maybe I'm mistaken here, but I have learned to 'read between the lines' though I understood the male gender far better than my own… my intuition is normally dead on. With you, it's an emotional bond of feelings, cuz, unlike all the others. I really like you, Joe, odd as it is, incongruent as all hell, I trust you, weird huh!" *…<u>She watches his mouth gape open, rubbing the mist of suds</u>*

spraying in his face, "come on, I saw a super cute outfit in a shop window that you'd look terrific wearing." Sammy couldn't resist her subsequent retort, "Cute outfit, huh? I betcha to die for...uh or in!" Interestingly they both howl laughing, ending with his deep chortle, her... an embarrassing snort hand in hand. They walk from the beach.

Lori and Rico.

Without reconciliation, dusk intercedes and intercepts the receding sunshine sunlight diminished, not unlike the moods of the eleven Agents who sat in front of computer screens at the Hilton in a conference room, coffee and tea smoldering. Agent Lori Parks was awaiting Rico, who was on his way. Nothing thus far had turned up.

Everything progressed like a typical night in Marin County, and the Truckstop was jammed with traffic as if nothing had happened only hours before... Hwy 101, North and South flowing, the perpetrator had escaped their web.

The question was how did he escape with dozens of video feeds and satellite images. There was no doubt the sniper was gone, a certainty, but where and how? It took upwards of seven minutes before law enforcement could cordon off the entire area. That means vehicles had entered and left the truck stop after the shooting. The freeways and the Truckstop's cameras were scrutinized. Each truck, trailer, and car was searched. They'd even used handheld scanners that would expose gunpowder and investigated every suspicious source, yet somewhere they had missed something. The Agents were busy going over the evidence technology, CSI forensics in play. The angle or trajectory of the 50 Caliber bullets, where the sniper fired from all being vetted. Rico entered the stuffy conference room, beckoning Lori out without a word.

He takes her right elbow and ushers her out into the hallway "preliminary analysis by our CSI team has the breakdown of where the shots were fired from!" Before they get to the door, it opens with Director Tanya Firm hurrying in with an expectant expression. Her countenance seemed flush with excitement. The hotel suite had a portable 5ft x 3ft cart on castor wheels, with computers on top and a 5ft screen attached to the wall. The room was dark except for the monitor. Rico says, "This is Agent Shelby; she is our specialist in the trajectory orbital projectile curve technology field. The aligned velocity and acceleration point an algorithm that analyzes each component of where the bullets could have been fired from… the dissection from," "Madam Director," Shelby interrupts, "this picture is 5 seconds before the sniper fired his first shot… standing at the gas pump by his V.W. Rabbit is the deceased Nurse Spike."

She clicks on close-up pictures, "here are snapshots of Agent Rodriguez and Agent Kelsey Marie on opposite ends of the parking lot. We separated and eliminated all the noise and ascertained that the expert marksman was able to fire all three bullets in precisely 3.7 seconds. Now we had to take into account elevation/trajectory's impetus angles and momentum…." "Excuse me, Shelby; we don't need a breakdown of your analysis, just the 'meat and potatoes' conclusions, please; time is of the essence. Where did the shots originate from?" A perplexed scowl was conspicuously evident. Shelby's presentation was cut short… her passion reflected in her voice as if she'd been scolded. She flips the screen with her bright red hair pointing at three vehicles that appeared on the screen.

"All right, look at this…there is a U.P.S. truck; next to it was an SUV pulling a tent trailer and a deluxe diesel pusher motorhome with a car trailer attached." Tanya, Rico, and Lori remained glued to the enlarged picture of only the motorhome. Agent Shelby then encircled the back 15 ft. of the R.V. 'There' she explicitly points' "was where the sniper was positioned at." Instantly they left Shelby standing there, and the three of them stalked out of the room. Tanya went one way, Lori and Rico… briskly the other way back to the conference room… collectively instantly, optimism had invigorated them a high! Matching a new burst of adrenalin… the direction of investigation had a clear objective now… locate that Motorhome.

Agent Lori Parks addressed the 11 agents; Rico stepped out with the phone in his hand. The CHP, Sheriff Department, and locals were alerted to be on the lookout 'BOLO for a recreational vehicle black and silver; as of yet, not one discernable picture of a license plate the plates had been obstructed or removed as was the case for the front cab of the RV. The back was blocked by the matching car trailer. The tags on the back were conveniently smeared with mud as if it had been off-road filthy with the purpose of the apparent concealment.

Rico mused to himself, ain't anywhere to hide a 57ft plus RV with a trailer; Cal Trans cameras showed the RV re-enter South on Hwy 101… it wasn't if they would find the RV. It was merely when.

NIA.

Leaning over a balcony were Dr. Honcho and the Warden. They had made their way to the mezzanine overlooking a walkway that soon Jax would appear upon. A nurse and their patient, Wendi Feral, with Jax leading the way down the path, was accompanied by Marshall Kara. They watched Wendi sitting in a wheelchair with a giant straw sombrero.

Serenity would be or could be the description of the day in Napa… birds were singing, humans were maneuvering around happily, colorful air balloons were in the distance, landscapers working, and children playing in the designated visiting area, if not for the ominous fortifications of stone, and guard towers within the cyclone razored steel linked concertina wire fencing… The prison could have been a fairground or a family park, with many ponds and mini lakes surrounded by acres of rolling hills with grapes of the finest manufactured wines.

Of course, like over 325 patients at this Outpatient hospital could be signed out of this facility, the only inmates allowed at the so-called 'Camp Zone' were trustees.

Liz, with a mini pair of binoculars, zoomed into the wheelchair. "Oh shit, I just saw Wendi move her hand; she's out or coming out of the induced coma." Ursula had her phone out, calling Terrence, "this is trouble."

Terrance answered on the third ring, "what is it now, Warden? I'm walking into City Hall and then flying to Seattle for a high-level gathering of compatriots. I'll be incommunicado from now on. Handle it or find another fkn job!..." She disregards his temper tantrum, hearing it all before a dozen times "aah, they got Wendi out this morning in a wheelchair. Liz saw her move her arms. Damn... she might be out of the coma!" "What the fk, are you kidding me? Hold on..." he finds a cubby hole alcove for further privacy. "Okay, so the Feds are letting the 'Cat out of the bag' last week's news that Wendi Feral died will be reversed... media and the newshounds will be on this 'like stink on shit' it will go Viral again all over the Internet, and Social media uhm, really not a bad thing for our stock price, but we don't know if she's still Sunshine or if she remembers any of the missions she has carried out for us. We need to get a bug and an audio device into the cell Wendi is now in. I have to go; text me with updates. As I said, I will be out of range for a few days."

Terrence wasn't psychic, but what he said came to fruition. Only 55 minutes later, a text from assistant Warden Larry Walden scrolls across the bottom of Liz's phone screen. 'We've got vans of Newsies, FOX, NBC, and CNN lined up at the gates, demanding entrance!'

The following day Wendi once again was parked underneath the trellises of Bougainvillea's, the same ones that Wendi and Jax saw from her deluxe cell. A wonderful fountain splashed the water with white and black swans in the nearby pond, 'glorious morning,' said Jax. Wendi nodded her head. "I hope Tanya and Rico have thought this out. I could have played the coma victim or remained dead to the outside world... you know!" "Listen, sweetheart," said Kara, "the rumors were already spreading, umh swirling, your much too high profile. Rico has released a statement that you survived miraculously and are cognizant and out of the coma. He told me to be prepared. An onslaught of reporters would be hunting us. Rico told me to tell you just to smile if we get cornered, only say I have no comment at this time."

"But Marshal," "Please call me Kara" "Kara, I don't understand why didn't Rico say something when he visited." "He must have his reasons," interjects Jax. "Oh, your parents and husband will be here this afternoon," adds Kara. Jax slips his hand in his front pocket, takes out a zip-lock baggie of prescription pills, walks over to a water fountain, and downs a handful in one swallow.

A shot like a laser-sharp pain delves into her forehead temples on fire, her eyes rolled-up whites veiled. Wendi starts to sputter, convulsing, blood-spattered from her neck quaking lurches forward, head wobbling and bobbling back as Wendi lets a high-pitched agonizing scream part her lips. Kara takes charge in a sprint with Jack, the male nurse alongside… already pushed the emergency button on his beeper; Jax led the way into the lobby. Doctor Hawkins greets them, and they all disappear into a locked operating room adjacent to the front desk.

Moving briskly down the hall, the shooter lurked and vanished into a maintenance room.

-28-

<u>Agents Baker and Avery.</u>

"I hate this part of the job, Sitting here twirling my thumbs like a fricken stalker. Yeah, I'm still here, and several people have stared me down… it is pretty obvious what I am. Anyways to hell with it, they've been in the hotel room now going on for over five hours." The sleepy voice on the other end of the line returned a scathing retort, "why did you wake me up, Tom, for this? It's freaking 12:15 am in three hours, I will take over your shift, damnit only bother me if there is an emergency," shouted the groggy Agent Avery. But this didn't shut up, Tom "why didn't he take her back to his apartment? Beyond that, why are we wasting our time following and watching the fking convict get laid? I mean hell, we have a bug stuck up his ass, right he ain't going nowhere, Bill!" "Tom the 'chip' only tells us where he is and has been, not whom he meets with or what he is physically doing." "Damnit, I can tell you what he is physically doing in there with that hot bitch" click.

Agent Baker looks down at his phone, 'that damn peckerhead hung up on me!'

Tank was having a blast... several, actually, had been hammering her from every angle and filled every accessible orifice. She was tight and lusciously yum, yep! Out of the tub for two, we fell intertwined onto the disheveled king-sized bed, yanking her up onto her knees. I grabbed her hips from behind, and she moaned, 'oh fk not again,' my raging, relentless hard-on plunged deep into her enticing crevice; she tried to crawl out, pulling, clenching her hands on the headboard; I was having none of this... lifting her petite bum up. I jack-hammered away, then in a mellow motion, went side to side. She quivered and shuddered, letting out kitty kat yowls. However, I was still a ways from my 5th orgasm, five hours of body surfing, and I couldn't get enough of this Hispanic Vixen. Sweet sweat bubbled up as I flipped her back over rather aggressively onto her back, took her legs, and pinned them above her ears; lucky she was so flexible. It was my time again to ram it seriously home with deep rapid thrusts. 'Stop, stop, ahh!' Then her nails clawed into my back 'please fkn stop, you're hurting me,' she wailed.

There was no way that was going to happen... I was on the verge of a massive volcanic explosion and felt her slapping me, which only enhanced my throbbing ejaculation. She fell back spent as I released her legs and let them fall like a rag doll into place. I was still inside her with a bit of after lovin twitching... friction when she literally kicked me plumb off the bed with both feet.

I tumbled back, fell onto the carpet, and rolled over. "Gloria, what the hell!" she stared at me like a deer in the floodlights. "You're a fking animal sex machine. I've never had a man like you. You're like orgy material. It's been five hours. I'm worn out now. Leave me alone." I plopped back on the bed, climbed up on her, and tried to kiss her with a bit of tongue action; she twisted away "enough, I'm serious. Tank enough is enough. What's wrong with you? Uh, you're a sick man..." she whined. "Gloria, why don't we take a break? Let me get you a drink." "Tank, you're a damn nympho; I'm raw inside and out. I really have to get going" "No, not yet, girl, I'll be gentle. Let me have your bum again. I'll use a ton of lubricant," she giggles "oh no, you don't. Not even my husband goes there. I can't believe I let you." I Raged, "Husband, what, Gloria? You said you were single… sure, I saw the untanned mark on your finger, but you told me you broke up." Tank rolled away from her, feeling instant revulsion, 'with all the women out there, I chose a freakin lying cheater…' he heard her mumbling some defensive nonsense but didn't reply.

"So how would that have changed anything, Tank… come on, guy, huh what? We wouldn't have ended up here, like please, Dude." Looking at her in the mirror over the headboard, I saw my naked body on the end of the bed. "No, I wouldn't be here… there are millions of single ladies in this world, and at least a dozen I could have chosen from at the freakin gym. In my life, I've been betrayed, deceived, and hurt by a woman I had loved who cheated on me. I promised myself never to screw with a married or taken woman ever!"

"Oh, shut the fk up, boy; what? You're the almighty Saint, yah just got out of prison, and it's obvious those are prison tattoos that are all over your body." I then abruptly stood up and started to gather my belongings and clothes. "You're just going to leave, that's it?" "Didn't you just say you had to get going, Gloria, or is that your real name?" She seemed to be in her own little world and muttered, "What am I going to do? He will return from San Diego this morning, raring for sex. I'm ripped raw?" "What are you saying?" As I start to lace up my boots. "My name is Amie. I'm married to a cop he's been competing for the last week at the Police Games down in San Diego." I bailed out the door in disgust, just what I needed, wide awake… uuhhh, a cop's wife. 'Later, Amie!'

<u>Samantha with Joe Sable.</u>

Honestly, it felt like an enormous weight had been lifted off us, dynamics had been altered, Joe and I were more relaxed after our uproar of laughter when he didn't deny that the plan was to 'off me' ugh kill me. Then I said, let's go shopping for an outfit 'to die for, lol' hand in hand, we walked on the uneven sidewalk, not as lovers nor working as an escort but like sort of friends. Nah, conspirators, codefendants, colluded souls with secrets, an aligned purpose, and the aim of not being apprehended.

I'd proven my loyalty at the Café when the CHP officers walked in sitting next to us, not that I didn't consider it. Wouldn't I be a fool to have not let a subtle, fleeting weak moment take me from known harm's way undoubtedly, Yes!

Joe is a merciless psychopathic killer who I believe could dine on dead bodies without a speck or morsel of remorse, uhm… Wait, not to eat or cannibalize them, but I mean, he was almost robotic. His demeanor while killing the pimp and brother tandem was 'matter of fact' like a soldier on a mission. I hadn't any qualms that he'd slit my throat while his tongue was still in French kiss mode inside of my mouth; maybe my parents were right, 'trouble always found me.' I was a bad seed. Why couldn't I be like my siblings? We were not in the 1% of the rich, but we wanted for nothing you'd call us comfortably wealthy. Torn from my revelry, Joe points to an outfit in a quaint clothing shop window "look now, that's fking pretty. It's your style, girl. Come on, let's have you try it on!" the mannequin wore a short skirt ensemble purplish, matching blouse, black belt with sharp Van's black boots… bells rang as we entered the shop.

An aroma swiftly took our senses. Incense wafted, swirling into the fan-blown air the fragrance of a Pine Tree forest. A woman smiled with a full-length flowered dress with peace signs drawn in the middle of each flower set and long dangling earrings. Sterling silver hair and stone-cold blue eyes wearing old school converse high tops that I could barely make out as she fluttered over to the mannequin. "Omg, I just dressed her; this is my first shipment of this clothing line from France. Let me guess size 7," I grinned, 'Yep,' before she could guess my shoe size, umm aah, "I have been told I've got huge Ogre feet size nine men's damn," the shop owner tossed up her palm with just a smirk, "give me a sec."

I must say, in my limited experience, usually men are bored silly with shopping, especially for women's clothes, but Joe was the first guy that followed me into the dressing room, not for sex! But to appraise my look in each outfit, let me tell you we had a fking blast. He said uh, told me like it was… One white dress I'd put on… he stood back with a queer look and instantly busted up laughing into an outrageous howl and said that it looked atrocious on me. He started like gagging, 'fk, you look like a big 'sack of potatoes,' clearing his throat with a harrumph. We were laughing so fking hard I was bawling my eyes out. I told him to get the fk out. Of course, Joe had to have a second opinion that of the owner Sylvia. Who had caught our virus contagiously, she cackled. I was wrong, and she didn't have cold blue eyes; nope, warm pale blue smiling eyes were a better description; being the only customers, we had all her attention.

Then the bells rang out not once but three times more customers were browsing. I kinda was relieved. It was like Sylvia and Joe were ganging up on me. I felt like a Princess… I can't lie. It was way fun. We walked out with two big bags costing $1,155. As the bells sounded off the door closing behind us, we walked back the way we'd come. He said, "let's get a drink before we ride back." 'Only one,' I added. We found a corner table put the shopping bags down… and we removed our backpacks. A blister was forming on the back of my heels; I'd bought sandals a bit too snug. "How the heck do you think we're going to get all my clothes on the crotch rockets?" Joe took his eyes off me as a server approached "looks like someone has had a good, fun day." His elbow pointed to my bags, and I glowingly smirked: "Yes, we'll have a couple of Kettle One Bay Breezes, please, and some of your barbecue honey Chicken wings. They smell great."

We looked at the round table next to us that had a messy-faced older couple gnawing on Chicken bones. We're alone again. I realized I hadn't even thanked him. I stood up, moseyed around the table, hugged him around his shoulders kissed him on the neck. A mixture of a lick-suck-nibble and a pucker "thank you, Joe, you're too sweet. That was the most fun I've ever had shopping before!" "No problem, Sammy. I had a blast also, and so did Sylvia. If she'd worn makeup, it would have smeared all down her face with fun tears… she said we were the best fun!"

Then a severe tone came from his perfect lips "now, do you think I'd spend that kind of money on you and go shopping just to take you out back and put a bullet in your head?" I shivered; good thing our wings with blue cheese dressing and extra sauce, uhm, drinks on a tray were delivered!

Not sure if it's a mood disorder or just part of life's struggles, I constantly drift off, letting my subconscious take me wherever; possibly, it was an accumulation of drugs I'd ingested. But there I was off in another bout of wonderment I go… drifting back in time on another of my ranting tirades. *My parents had drugged me from an early age believing in the medical system. This IMO in my opinion, caused me irreparable damage, which I'm still living with. They did so not to harm me but to help me. Ah, they'd bought into the capitalistic propaganda strewn out by the medical field.*

Doctors worldwide made it a practice to categorize every so-called human anomaly. Every cough or ache had to be named and given new terms for another batch of medicines approved by the FDA for the Pharmaceutical industries aah monies, sadly even at the age of only 25 years old. I'm skeptical of the capitalistic environment that most of us have succumbed to and are part of. We are conditioned habitually brainwashed, trained to believe there is a specific disorder or acronym to describe all maladies enhancing the hypochondriacs, maybe even propagating them a pill for this, a cure for that, oh, you're not one of those nonconforming humans? Lol!

All are manufactured for or manipulated by the medical Professionals. Heck, if you feel sick or not yourself, don't worry. A medical professional will devise an acronym to reflect your disposition, and the busy bee drug companies will fall in line; soon, there will be prescriptions for your supposed ailment! Bipolar disease: Pharmaceutical companies with physicians prescribing their drugs are all about profits, and the Guinea Pigs are in line. No worries, a decade after you ingested their concoctions, the ambulance-chasing attorneys will seek damages for you from the pharmaceutical companies for causing your Stage 4 Cancer.

At 11 years old, my mother and I sat in a doctor's office. Why? Because I was listless unenergetic, unmotivated believed, depressed, and lived via social media, lost in trying to figure out who I was, ugh, that was what was told to me, not correct. But hey, I went along with it because that's what the norm had proliferated and morphed into believing the fix was always different drugs, umh Doctor Feel Goods were building shiny new offices… and stashing monies galore.

I remembered at that visit, only 11 years old, watching this thin woman with rolling suitcases and a shoulder bag with straps. She dropped them in a patient's room across from me, then disappeared, reappearing in minutes, guessed from the parking lot, and came back grasping wrap-around suitcases with many more compartments.

Strangely or fortunately, depending on one's perspective, I didn't need to eavesdrop, for the exchange of words was easily discernible. I was sitting on a white paper table in a paper-thin hospital-like robe. I watched the 'Legal' drug deal unfold across the hall. Gosh, I saw so many colorful packets of pills in all shapes and sizes. The woman dressed in a pantsuit was apparently a legal drug dealer saleswoman for Pharmaceutical medicines. Listening as best as I could, "There's a special bonus if you can prescribe enough prescriptions of this ADHD drug. If you hit a 50-unit benchmark target, we can move you up to 15% net sales your profits will soar." Sadly, I mumbled, 'so will your unwitting patients!'

The saleswoman starts unloading little boxes of pills. A PA notices our door open and closes it while holding my thick chart, sliding it into a slot on the door's exterior! Don't you or wouldn't you know the fine doctor diagnosed me with an extreme case of ADHD, sent mom and me on our way with a sample packet and a 3-month supply of the drug the saleswoman was peddling, business, legal drug dealing!... yup.

A firm believer that the Opiate Crisis was exploited the same way… habits formed by the addictive drugs on unknowing unwitting patients and some drug-addicted people, no doubt. The doctors were given incentives, and the naïve populace, like Sheep, bought into the scheme Oxycodone, Vicodin, and Norco's Hydrocodone for sale. In addition, the addictions Fed the criminal system and law enforcement ugh, violent crimes, junkies, ah, Walla, The War on Drugs… manufactured by the insidious greedy medical faction. In the 1990s, Purdue Pharma promoted OxyContin, which was approved by the Food and Drug Administration…(FDA) triggering the first wave of deaths linked to the use of legal prescription Opioids, Duh folks… it's always been about $$$ money! Then, like a swish of wind, the weak humans went from pills to Fentanyl patches to smoking heroin, then eventually, the ending result of using hypodermic needles, spreading Aids and other diseases. No worries, we have a fix for your addictions… Ironically once you were addicted to their pharmaceuticals, they'd invented a cure… of course, more pills LOL. ☹ .

The way of this world, greed, selfish, gluttonous desires, mixed with the weak masses of lost souls, humans without self-control, discipline swimming with bleeding ulcers in a dangerously warm ocean, large sharp Saw-edged Teeth are clamoring about, encircled by giant Great White Sharks. Wearing white jackets portraying caring doctors, not all but just a few, ruin the recipe.

<u>I bounced from my harangue… back smelling spicey sauce.</u>

Omg, the Chicken wings were delish, and so was my drink as I kept my attention on Joe, who was enjoying himself, at least it seemed.

Oops, instantly, his face went from copacetically satisfied to deranged insanity flashing before me, evilness; I'd seen this look before when he put out his cigarette before blowing the PI's face to smithereens or when he relaxingly ended my employer's life. The next time when he exploded the nurse's head only hours ago.

Joe was indeed a candidate for a secure line connected to a pharmacy. Maybe there was something to be said about the overly diagnosed Bipolar malady; Joe was no longer easy and carefree like in the dressing room with me. Nope! In defense of his reaction, mine might have been worse. Where the hell was a few opiates when I needed them; my BP blew up, and my heart fell off a cliff in perfect or imperfect sequence. Our eyes were locked onto the TVs that sat on shelves at the corner of the café... Oh no! 😞.

On the screen, the prototypical blonde beauty bombshell broadcaster, a lady news reporter, who, with excitement, showed our motorhome drive up and over the overpass with the bike trailer attached. A $25,000 reward was posted, a phone number scrolling across the bottom of the screen, Instagram and Twitter... email accounts even a text contact number. 'IF you've seen this Motorhome, you can be rewarded with 25,000 dollars... call at once!'

The search was on for us... with harsh timing, Joe's backpack started to buzz. I reached down from my stool and picked it up. He snatched it away like a Vulture's claw would a piece of rotten meat! The throwaway phone took away any remnant of serenity as he stumbled out of the bar restaurant. Many of the patrons watching the alerts cross the screen could have cared less. Just another violent incident, desensitized, numb hearing a woman say, "well, at least it's not another school shooting," the guy retorted 'yuh, only one guy was killed.'

I couldn't really blame them for their insensitive reactions. This had become everyday life sensationalized depictions of massacres daily, from famine to executions. Another 3000 humans were bombed to pieces in Yemen, so what... right then, it became a personal thing for me. I was tapping away and sliding my fingers across my iPad when the loud emergency beeps came out loud from the speakers on the TVs, like a weather alert, fire, Earthquake, or hurricane warning. 'We were just given the enhanced pictures of the wanted Fugitives in the motorhome' 'did she just say as in plural fugitives? No!

OmLord, there I was, a bit blurred, perched on the luxurious passenger seat Joe in the captain seat. We were turning onto Hwy 101 South the reality hit me. I hopped up with the urge to pee! True, our faces were distorted, um, blurred, but no doubt it was me. I found a stall. Unlike me, I put no coverage on the toilet seat and tried to squat. But felt dizzy feeling as if my guts spilled out, ugh, diarrhea, wiped again, and saw blood, red dark on the toilet paper 'whew, now what a bleeding ulcer?'

By the time I finished cleaning up, the table was empty. Joe wasn't in sight either were our backpacks. All that remained was a $50 bill under a pepper shaker; my shopping bags were gone, as was he.

'Where are you, Sam?' the text was a wake-up as if any near-average person would have needed one in my position. I simply could walk behind the bar and out through the kitchen doors; this was another chance to alter my destiny, guilty for what exactly? Being complicit in all Joe's murders, ahh, I could always fall back on 'The Stockholm Syndrome,' couldn't I pull that off, huh? I could play the weak female who was dominated and manipulated by the superior male persona, a strategy that had worked for the ages.

Unfortunately, I wasn't the housewife… professional or business owner, nor the ordinary worker; I was a known prostitute slut, whore, and petty thief. I lacked the proper playing cards for the innocent, blind, naïve female, a pretentious display of emotions, distraught frivolous righteous levity gone. My feigning naivete was of no benefit my 'full dress' had been removed. I was a blight, tainted to both genders. Ugh, <u>'The Empress wore clothes!'</u>

Texted back, 'leaving the bathroom, where are you?' 'Get out of there. I'm across the street.'

Destiny called as I stepped off the curb; clarity was picture perfect. It was gloom and doom. The sun had lost the mini battle with the low-lying clouds. A grayness with a cold wind blew the sands from the beach as I followed his shadows towards our motorcycles. He still held my unique wardrobe, remnants of our mini shopping spree. The late afternoon was the time. Surprised we fit all our things in the leather bike bags, he only barked Sammy, stay behind me. I just checked the cameras at the motor home it still hasn't been found. We have work to do!

Mark at Winn-River Casino, Redding, California.

I've lined up a tight Lil piece of ass, arm around her walking back to our stools inside the lounge at Winn River Casino. A provocatively alluring Asian beauty enjoyed several of this race um-yum breed, typically they as a whole, their sufficiently snug, small petite breasts, possibly inherent was their servitude… demurely humble and unassuming appeasing and pleasing their men perfect wives, but ahh not into a long-term relationship Nope!

Most were subserviently intelligent, a delightful race and culture to explore, indeed solicitous and eager lovers expressing attentive care, giving all to satisfy me. I checked my wristwatch 10:35 pm 'Joy' was her name, which I hoped to find appropriate. I should have launched a search party, for I was lost in her beige-brownish eyes. Quick assessment about 27yrs old, weight 115 pounds, 5'3" tall with lusciously dark long hair past her scrumptious waist. Her stare unremitting boldly, she pinched my arm and assertively said, "I like this song, come on, let's dance." She winked at me, and I then had to admit she was the hunter, I the prey. "You know you're all eye candy for the ladies. How'd you learn to move like that on the dance floor?..." "If you like that, you're really going to enjoy my bedside manner." She guffawed, yeah, sure, with a wink grabbing my hand and leading me out to the strobe-lit floor again; I guess she couldn't get enough of my sexy gyrations.

"Mark, you're a confident guy," grinning, I replied assiduously, integrating a matching smirk, and even tossed my tongue over my front white bright teeth for added effect! "You'll see and feel me, Joy!" Three songs later, back at the bar, ordering two more doubles. "Whatcha say we find a quieter place to talk, maybe snuggle?"
She rolled her eyes up then and around. "Mark, I'd like to say your cute, no question that your good looking, nice body,

and all, yes, hella dancer, but I'm not in the least interested in having sex with you!" Shit, I gulped, slurped up excess saliva "why Joy, it was you that initiated contact. Why don't you let your hair down and live a little girl?" While I tugged on her bangs affectionately, she moved away. "As if you didn't notice it, I'm independent and not into getting caged… just like my hair is free-flowing, so am I, and that's the way it will stay, Mark. The reason I'm not interested in furthering our contact is that you're a predator. I've followed your every move since you entered this bar area, a hunter on the prowl scanning all the ladies here. Hey, nothing wrong with that, ah, just not into it personally."

Rather than play coy, being a straight shooter, I said, "Well, if you were eyeballing me, then you must have been interested." "Wrong, I'm not," she shook her gorgeous round head; well, I said, "is this the classic female game of playing hard to get Joy?" "No, I speak the truth, I…" no reply. I was already gone; I'm not the type of guy to waste my time if this bitch doesn't want to get laid. There's plenty of meat hanging out all around me, some giving ogling flirtations, back in search mode as I see another Asian girl raise her eyebrows at Joy, then bob her head back, a weird gesture indeed. I felt suddenly on alert. Something inherently felt wrong, but testosterone-based flipped caution into the Gail force. I approached the luscious girl asked motioned toward Joy. "Do you know her?" still sipping my drink "who" "um, the Asian girl across the bar." She snickers "which one and by the way, we're Laotian." That's when I noticed like seven Laotian girls and a few of their male species of the 75 or so people in the lounge area, and with a quick evaluation, there were at least 15% Laotian. My mind shot back to an article in the Record Searchlight newspaper. I remembered a census report that Laotians were one of the largest minorities in Shasta County.

I realized long ago that I'm a male chauvinist, egomaniac, and unquestionably a misogynist, so what…I proudly represented the word, Misogynist. Someone would have to be labeled as such otherwise, the word Misogynist would never have been contrived. Lol, women are only good for one thing that's to satisfy my craving for sex, not to clean my house and have a miserable whining baby. Nope, women were made to satiate my every desire, umh. As far as cleaning and cooking, I can hire a woman for both tasks. 😊 .

Also, another of my irresistible traits is that I was born stubborn and dogmatically proud Yep, prideful, so being fair to her, wanting to give the cutey-pie another chance, loved her cocky style. I walked back to her. "Joy, you see your twin over there, who seems to be enhanced with a better rack, most likely medically induced boobs. This is your last shot at me and a scintillating evening…." Whew, mistake, she let a vile serpent-like scathing growl out, "You arrogant, pompous asshole get the hell out of my sight." I stood by my stool as she clawed my arm. Her loud barking had others' attention in the lounge as she left me with, "Don't believe in the stereotypes that we're all submissive and ready to worship you from our knees. You couldn't handle what I'd dish out, boy!"

Whoa, a challenge indeed! I Stoically remained next to her. Joy's face went ugly, frowning, her pert nose curled up furiously. She pounded her fist on the bar top, seething, bobbing her head, and sneered eerily. Something felt wicked, terribly wrong, rotten Ugh, tiny hairs stood stinging the nape of my neck. Either she was having a seizure, or I was in trouble!

I scanned my surroundings aah, and from the corner of my eye, I saw a large man in a suit standing by the exit door to the patio then another one joined him. Usually, I'm very tuned into my surroundings, freshly aware, but I had missed the woman by the dance floor with the unusual bulge where a side holster most likely was under her blazer.

The music stopped playing; was it all my imagination? Then Joy seemed to chill out and nodded at me. "Your pocket keeps vibrating, 'Mark,' aren't you going to check it out." I was determined not to panic "it's not important," I said as I stepped away from her. What was happening hum… I had, which is my custom, only indulged in a few alcoholic beverages, no paranoia, right? My appearance was changed by cosmetic surgery; my nose, lips, and eyes even added a cleft to my handsome chin, so I was somewhat secure that the Casino's facial recognition system didn't run a red alert, 'Mark

Feral' number 5 on the FBI's most wanted list, is in the building!

Cameras were everywhere. I pondered what probably happened. Joy earlier was nearly shouting. It would seem to anyone that we were arguing, most likely, the suits were bouncers or casino security. Plain-ass paranoia, the weariness squelched, rolled my shoulders, and proceeded towards Joy's big-boobed twin; on cue, the music started up again, leaning in because all seats were occupied. "Hey there, would you like to dance with me?" Joy stared at me with an expression I couldn't figure out; from afar, a bit of amusement sliced with disgust and a smidgeon of perhaps jealousy. Sucking the last bubbles from her Rumrunner, leaving red lipstick on the straw, "I'd love to dance with you!" Yeah, no prob. I was a hot Dude, for sure!

Song by the late and loved 'Prince' 'Little Red Corvette' we were revved up. I whirled her around, both of us busting out conceited smirks fun; she took my hand as the next tune was strumming forth and walked me back to the bar. Her friends were gone leaving me a seat. I ordered another Rumrunner with a double shot as my phone continued to annoy me. Finally, I relented as the band took a break pulling it out and powering it down. I still felt violated as the bartender brought my drink that I left beside Joy to me. "By the way, my name is Lola. What's your name?" I bypassed the inquiry with one of my own "How do you know Joy?" Before I could answer her question, she popped up, "Please excuse me; I'm in need of the lady's room." Oddly, with a twist, ugh, better than perfect English. A few minutes passed by as I saw a scary group commingle. All were cops or part of the security forces. I wasn't armed like always. Metal detectors prevented me from my toys; sure, I could have brought other weapons, but that wasn't the way I rolled when chasing tail. Although I did have a hard rubber shock stick as I was surrounded by five men and one woman, 'Joy!.' Huh! it turns out no Joy!

<u>Lori and Rico.</u>

'It's the best we'll get, Sir; I've forwarded all the files and video to Agent Avery, our tech wizard. Remember that Wash. D.C. has done all it can with the shots from the Cal Trans Cameras.' 'Thanks' as Rico punched off the speaker on the landline. "Lori, how is it that here we were in 2019, we have the video and still pictures of the R.V. driver and a female passenger and cannot increase the 'dot-pixels' or sharpen the pictures?" "Well, at least we have the pictures. Whom could the woman be? That's what I'm trying to wrap my head around from her outline and the guesswork by trying to break down the blurry pictures of her. By taking her upper torso, we can presume that she's a little over 5 feet tall, body type slender, um too thin with blonde hair!" "Lori, it's the guy that's important. If we can learn his identity, we may have hers. He's the shooter!" Sighs, "Why do you make that conclusion, Rico? You don't believe a woman is incapable of firing those shots?" She leaned in with a smirk; he didn't bother with a reply. "I'm betting he's ex-military, may be trained as a sniper. Have we searched all databases for snipers with felony records? It's gotta be a professional shooter, Lori. I want answers now! We have two Agents in the damn hospital!" "No, shit, Rico! Like, I don't understand that. What's up with your ass tonight?" "Whoa, Lori, that's out of character for you… what's bothering you?"

"Sorry, it's just that I've already enacted a search through our databases for a shooter with your parameters. It was the obvious assumption the shooter was Joc Sable, but we need to prove that's the case, umh, we have to do our jobs…." Rico raises his left palm into the air with a disgruntled glance pinching his nose. Lori spouts off again, "Counting all the ex-military that have joined the anti-government movement 'Militias.' There are now, at last guess, well over 100,000 members or volunteers. I have discovered at least 551 candidates, uh, possibilities. It's like we're breeding them. The Desert Storm War to the present, frustrated, disillusioned ex-military patriots, I suppose…." "Why don't you take the rest of the night off, Lori? Get some rest." "It defies comprehension… The propensity for violence amongst mankind to sin and hate; it's all in the human genome from childhood. We throw tantrums, cry out, hold grudges, and are selfish with envious self-centered desires and petty jealousies; we deserve condemnation!"

"Shush, now you're tired… you sound like your father preaching from his pulpit the wrath of God and such. Go take a hot bath and get some sleep," he hands her the plastic card to her hotel room. "Don't make fun of my Father Rico… he's a good man." "Jeesh, what's wrong? Are you itching for a fight, woman? Do you need a vacation? I'm going to suggest that Tanya puts you on leave. A month should work!" "Oh, great, now you're threatening me, uh, I run around chasing my own tail for the Bureau, being a good employee, my only objective is to punish the wrong doer's." She slaps her forehead "why'd you attack my father knowing he is a Pastor." "Whew, slow down, girl, you're getting out of control, Lori…." She spun around, clicking her heels "you don't get it, Rico!" He snatched her back, grabbing her shoulder.

"No, I guess I don't get it, Lori… I'm off base, right, huh? Lately, your always fricken angry and bitter about something, what's wrong with you, woman, we've known each other…." "Just leave me alone." "No, Lori, come clean; what do you think I'm doing? I have misjudged you. I'd never threaten you… listen, your only hurting yourself and others you care about by holding onto anger and bitterness; resentment is like a thick sludge of mud. It can contaminate your heart, clog your internal body and mind systemically and poison your soul." "Aah, Father Rico, you missed your calling. The next thing you will say is that my only remedy is forgiveness. Lol."

"Come over here" he reaches for her they embrace a long-lasting hug. Oddly afterward, he pushes her back and pecks her forehead. "Now get some rest. I will wake you if anything important comes up!" "Promise?" "Yes! I promise."

She thought she'd felt his body part rising to the occasion, trying to rub him in tight, probably her imagination, well perhaps, she mulled over the pent-up truths, sexually frustrated with unrelenting fantasies of having Rico deep inside her… possessing her. Five years her senior, his smell, maleness magnetism, mannerisms, dimples with a deliciously ample tongue he wagged at her at times of humorous enjoyment, or was this a figment of her imagination closed the door with a last subtle glance back at Rico's posterior.

Hot, Lori made a mental note to buy a new vibrator. The others were worn out; boring, same ole um, maybe change up the porn, do something even if it was wrong. Twenty-five minutes later, standing in the shower rinsing off the bubbly suds from the hot bath… steps out; the steam had dissipated. What was left was a slender no, a healthy, full-figured, curvaceous female body with all the essential curves, breasts of proper proportion, perked up nipples high and proud. Mid-thirties, her body, was only getting better long legs, 5' 9" tall, and a buck 55, uhm, 155 pounds, muscles toned, often called a workout fiend. Muscle outweighed fat 3 to 1 because of its density. She flexed in the mirror. What was there not to like or enjoy about her V-shaped trimmed-up pubic area and light brownish blonde hair? She took her forefingers to spread her lips apart.

Yup, it's enticing and juicy all in there. Then why had it been over three years since she had a man or woman for uuhhh, enough! Ask, and you may achieve receive, with a female purr looking at the door between their hotel rooms WTHeck, why not? Knocking on the mandoor behind it was a man whom she'd dreamed of as her fantasy-based paramour, wearing a slinky robe with nakedness underneath. Lori gambled.

He opens the door phone on his left ear, looks from her slippers to her short-wet brown hair, the robe revealing some tasty cleavage, lets her in with a mixed frown and perplexing expression, and continues speaking to Tanya. "Well, we have discerned that it was Mark Feral who paid for the attempted murder of Wendi, so it would make sense that it was one of his compadres who fired the shots on Nurse Spike, either to shut him up or, heck, not have to pay him the balance of $25,000, that sounds about right to me. Yes, we're on it, Tanya. Get with you when we have something concrete have a good night," click. He exclaims, "well Lori, what's up?" Before he slipped the phone back into its pouch, she'd locked the door. He turned, mouth gaped open, muttered, "we've just got a huge break, Lori." Dropping her robe, it falls slowly to her ankles, leaving erect nipples; the bed just behind her… wiggles her forefinger, "I need some lovin cum over here, Rico!"

Rico quickly strides over in a swift motion, retrieves her fallen robe, takes her around the neck, and kisses her mint-flavored mouth, tongues wagging, then he pulls back with a lipped kiss on the tip of her nose. "So this has been your problem, uhm, mine too. It's time we 'hooked up!" Leans down and nibbles each protruding exploding nipple, "we've got an I.D. Lori, the motor home is registered to Ben Abbott. Let's get on the ball and do some work on this so we can play later." "No, come on, Rico, this isn't fair. Your such a tease," he giggles as he unbuttons his pants. "I'm no tease, you'll see," she leans forward and yanks his pants down to a popping pair of undies. Suddenly, hurried pounding knocks on the door.

"Oh, no," he shouts' "just let it be Rico, ignore the door please," then more impatient banging mixing with the doorbell ringing. "Shit…" he zips up, wanting to hide his bulging erection. "Lori, damnit, get in the bathroom. The last thing we need is a rumor like…." Stepping the seven feet quickly like a juggernaut, he stares one-eyed through the peephole 'oh crap' it's his last sexual conquest staring back at him with haste and seriousness 'oh fk,' he mumbles. "Lori, it's Director Tanya Firm." He whispers, "we'll both be fired." He thinks the latest sexual revolution was called the 'Me Too Movement' sexual harassment. "Oh no, this doesn't look good. Get out of the bathroom and return to your room quickly." He goes to the door and says loudly, 'hold on, Tanya, I'm on the phone.'

Tanya shakes the door handle, yelling 'Rico' impatiently, 'open up…' Instead of running back to her room, Lori panics; he points miming to the shut mandoor to her adjoining room. Shit then watches her wigged out, Lori holding her robe, sprints into the walk-in closet, shaking his head in irritation; damn, thinking, 'shit Lori… why'd you panic?'

Rico takes a deep breath, pulls his phone back out, and pretends to speak to someone as he unlocks the hotel room door nonchalantly. Tanya bolts in and brushes by him. "Have you heard?" she says. Rico declares in the speaker, "I'll get back to you. I have to go," as the phone begins to really ring, he rolls his eyes as he now sees… what Tanya's fixed glare was glued upon, fk, Lori's forgotten, lost slipper… oh crap not good!

-30-

Agent Tom Baker and Bill Avery, and Tank Shaw.

"Hey, Avery, he's on the move didn't seem like he had an agenda, it seemed his only objective was getting laid… wonder what happened? He'd been in a hotel room for over five hours… doesn't look happy." "I'm way busy, Baker. I'm running a filter on some images of the R.V.'s license plate for Rico; I'll bite, in any case. Why do you think Tank isn't happy he's been locked up for years and just got his first woman?" "Umh, it's the way he was walking and throwing his gym bag into the back seat, burned rubber out of the parking lot." "Heck, Baker, maybe he figured out what we did when we ran her plate. He's been screwing a cop's wife; Amie Stroke was a slut!" "Wow, Avery, that's a bit harsh. Remember what we heard from the rumor mill's gossipers? Amie's husband, Steve, has been to a boatload of anger management treatment programs. He was suspended by the San Jose Police Department for physical abuse and spousal assault." "Ugh, maybe that's why he beat her for cheating?" "Nah, there's no reason for physical abuse divorce is the answer, Baker, but I agree there are always two stories to be told, maybe three!" "Oh yeah, forgot to tell you, I'm not going to make the shift change; sorry, Tom, Rico has me busy on this project. I might have had a breakthrough. It looks like my last filter is clearing up the blurred pictures taken from the overpasses cameras gleaned from Cal-Trans.

<u>Tank Shaw is satiated but pissed off at the lying wife of a cop!</u>

Gloria, aww, 'Amie' was fun and quenched some of my pent-up testosterone reserves; sadly, she was dishonest; I'd vowed not to nail another married woman why because I'm a man of integrity, obviously not in the way society sums it up or measures the qualities, definition of the word integrity. When I sought pleasure from a lady, I wanted her to wish the same, not for her to carry black clouds of deceit and baggage into our short romance… uh, betrayal into our hook-up way too many willing beautiful single women out here, hot and Horney.

I read somewhere that there were over three billion 'girls' and counting. All I need is the vengeance of a cop in the same city I have been paroled to! Great fk, though. Just wonderful, my big mouth telling her the truth as she licked and sucked some of my prison tattoos. 'Where did you get these?' Aah, I said, 'Quentin' whew, dumbass, coital bliss as she nibbled on my pecker, no excuses. How long did Mark and Joe want me to be over the radar like I didn't see the Ford Interceptor with the FBI Agent parked across the street from the hotel?

I yanked the Chevy into my garage at the apartment. Time to shower, then I will take a gander at the nine missed texts on my Tracfone. If it took me longer than 15 seconds to figure out that my apartment had been violated and searched, I'd be an idiot. I had bought a small sewing kit; yeah sewing kit took a spool of white thread out and wrapped it at the bottom of both the bathroom and closet doors. Superman, with X-ray vision, would have missed it.

Like Mark, Joe and I didn't assume that part of the Fed's plan was that I'd lead them to my bro's Feral and Joe Sable. I was led to believe by Mark that it was maybe one of the precursors for my parole! Like the FBI was so desperate to apprehend Mark and Joe that they would allow me to be paroled… doubt it, but certainly, it wasn't without merit!

<u>Jax and Wendi at NIA.</u>

"Oh no, she's shot in the neck," shouts Jax… Dr. Hawkins, without panic, calmly states, "help me get her out of the wheelchair and up on the gurney now." Marshal Kara, with Jack, a male nurse assigned to Wendi, he was a no-nonsense individual wiry, muscular, and sinewy, one of three African Americans employed by the doctor. Carefully with ease, she is lifted onto the gurney; Jack is wrapping her arm for the blood pressure machine. At the same time, the doctor was attending to Wendi's wound. Jax hovered next to Kara, who was on her phone ordering the facility to 'lockdown' immediately. "There's a shooter at the back patio exit nearest the nurse's station, lockdown the entire facility nobody moves, is that clear!"

Alarms went off like fog horns from a lighthouse or a Coastguard vessel blaring sirens. Security forces ran with the correction officers all on the move, a practiced strategy enforced, and all inmates were locked down immediately… after a strip search.

Jax heard the doctor mutter, "This is extremely odd blood had seeped out and down her neck, coagulated. There's no wound, just an entry point," reveals Dr. Teresa Hawkins. "Her B.P. is only 101 over 57. Heart rate is 55,' declares Jack. He checks her eyes which are dilated, a weird type of conundrum. No blood loss patient is unconscious, and her B.P. H.R. is extremely low.

Doctor Hawkins has Wendi in one of the emergency rooms, which was private and locked down with Marshal Kara and Jax standing by.

There is clamorous banging noise as the double doors slam open, and five correction officers, Dr. Liz Honcho and Warden Ursula Anders, barge inside. Kara steps in front of the group at the feet of Wendy. "What is going on? What's this… Wendi has been shot?" screams Kara. "Back up, Wendi is under Federal protection. No one is allowed close to her but approved personnel." 'It had to be a gun with a sound suppressor, silencer,' says an officer.

"This is my facility. I don't give a rats ass if you Feds have her under protective custody, ugh some protection, huh, pathetic." Ursula furrowed eyebrows matching her upcurved lips stepped forward as the others with her did the same I want Doctor Honcho to…."

Before anyone noticed, Kara had her Glock forty-five Caliber ACP in her hand… 15 round magazine with three more on her hip belt. Kara was outgunned as the guards pulled on their holsters. Ursula looked to defuse the situation with diplomacy. "Look, Wendi has been a patient here at NIA for almost nine months. We understand an attempt was made on her life. Therefore the need for extra protection was necessary… it was super lucky the FBI caught wind of the assassination attempt and foiled that. I'm extremely distraught and apologetic for it was one of my employees here at NIA, but with that being said, this is my Institution. I am in charge, and I am…."

"We have this all under control, Warden. I appreciate your concern, but if I need your assistance, I'll ask for it now, please leave us to do our job, and you find the shooter since this is your facility, Warden. We have discerned that Wendi was shot with a dart gun. We are now drawing blood to test what was in the dart that was injected into Wendi's body. Right now, Doctor Hawkins has her medical situation stable. It would seem the dart had an injectable hypodermic needle attached. It's been lodged in Ms. Feral's neck."

"Listen, Ursula," Doctor Hawkins added, "she is stable. Her eyes are dilated. She's been tranquilized. Please go, leave us, and find the shooter."

Calmly Dr. Hawkins espouses, "Jack, take five vials of her blood and send them to our FBI lab. We'll discover what's in Wendi's system," he turns "sure thing, Dr. Hawkins,' I've three vials of blood drawn; I will take two more and get them over to our lab."

Ursula had ordered the guards to help with the search for the shooter of the dart gun, but she and Liz didn't budge, "I want to speak with your superiors, either Rico or Tanya.

Marshal Kara, I can assure you this wouldn't have happened if we were in charge of Wendi's care. This isn't an FBI matter anymore! I want to keep this 'in-house.' We cannot afford any more negative publicity… our shareholders are already berserk at the downturn in our stock price over the assassination attempt. This is solely an NIA matter now!"

Kara exclaims, "I'm sure you have Director Firm's phone numbers and email addresses along with Agent Rico Captor, be my guest. Call them if you want. I don't like it here at your mental hospital, and I must say, since when do guards at a prison walk around with loaded guns?" "My officers are not on the high-security floors or the prison grounds with guns; they're kept in a locked safe here on the minimum-security side. Only the gun towers have lethal weapons, although that brings up an interesting question why is it that you Fed's think you can?" Ursula nearly spits, "I'm wasting my time speaking to a lowly Marshal in the food chain. This is not a Federal institution. I will take it up with your superiors, Sayonara!"

<u>Wendi and Jax, 'Sunshine,' was she back in control?</u>

Strange as it may seem, I knew where my bread was buttered. Standing next to Marshal Kara and Dr. Teresa Hawkins, listening to Kara scold the Warden and Dr. Liz Honcho. Jax stood on point, trying to meld and blend into the caustic gathering. My status as a freelancer and trustee able to come and go freely… I wasn't the kind of man to upset the Applecart. My mouth was zipped shut as wretched accusations of transgressions were slung back and forth. I was only observing the power struggle and must say. I sided with Doctor Hawkins and Marshal Kara but remained neutral, for NIA was my home.

I wasn't any fool about to pick up sides. I was only present because my best friend Wendi was lying there 'comafied' again. No one said, hey, Jax, what did you see? So therefore, I remained silent, yet I saw all… the rifle, the shooter ex-military whom I regularly fought with sparred with in NIA's on-site training facility. One of his specialties was the big game tranquilizer dart gun, uhm, rifle…I couldn't quibble with the shot a definite bullseye.

Now compartmentalizing my mind and thoughts, I sought to roll with the punches and wasn't going to point fingers. 'I was loyal to Terrance and NIA,' tenderly rubbing Wendi's left arm, wondering if Sunshine was lurking beneath the skin.

With purity of mind despite all the pharmaceutical drugs running through her veins, I had realized in the last five days how much I had missed her, Wendi. That is not that I wasn't fond of the crass Sunshine, her alter ego; amazingly, I enjoyed both of them as unique and exclusively their own persons. They were total opposites contradictorily from their voices across the board, cadences, rhythms intonations. I'd referred to the raspy voice of Sunshine as a replica of Janis Joplin in a fever pitch. I couldn't hide from myself. I admitted that I loved Wendi. She'd filled my inner ear with mellow mellifluous sweet tones and soothing articulations. Contrasting with my friend Sunshine who was assertively sexy…with her hoarse guttural yowling, both of em unique, no doubt.

Acknowledging even within my discombobulated minds and relative existence, I knew without any doubts that NIA, the powers to be aligned with American politics and the World's syndicates, were odd bedpartners. Who called the punches? I hadn't a clue; with that being disseminated, I wouldn't let Sunshine re-emerge without a fight or struggle, not that I'm a worthy judge of character in the battle over control of Wendi. I'd have to give round number 1 to NIA.

I stood back, peering down at her. It was as if nothing had changed. The body before me was once again in a coma; leaning over her while the shouting and yelling subsided, I kissed her flush cheek. Oh no! I shuddered. Was that a wink? Yes, umh, it was a replica of a Sunshine wink. No questions, Crap! No… ☹ .

31

The Warden and Doctor Liz Honcho with the NIA staff.

Ursula was scowling at Liz tossing her purse on a chair. "I'm glad it's not my balls, uhm, Lips on the line here. Yuh got giant lips, woman." Ursula continued berating her underling, turned a sneerish upturned snarl at Liz, and sat down.

Liz fought back and stated, "tell me, what were your original options?" Shaking her head at Ursula. "you agreed we had to do something, right?" "True, Liz, but now look what's happened. Take responsibility; after all, your concoction was loaded in the injection dart that our sharpshooter shot into her blessed neck, so take the credit due or at least some of it. Sure, I co-signed it because I felt like I hadn't any choice… in my book. You're as culpable as our shooter!"

"Hell, Ursula, you said we had to make an executive decision. Terrance is off the coast of Seattle on a chartered cruise ship in a high-level meeting with do not disturb orders…." "Liz, it was you who recognized Wendi's voice." "I know it was a shock; I'd become accustomed and used to relating with Sunshine's tones ahh accents."

"Listen, let's cut to the point here. The question is, how much did Wendi remember Doctor? You're the woman with 13 years of Forensic education, Psychologist, and all that stuff…." Liz twirled around. "How the hell should, or would I know? There's no tellin I warned Hallinan ole Terrance about the mixtures of the Psychotropic drugs we were injecting into Wendi. Hell, we changed and modified the formulas several times and told him this was a very stark possibility, but now it's a reality. Wendi reappeared, ahh, maybe? I'm sure I heard her voice, Ursula. It was an executive order, and we need to stand together!"

They paused, staring out the windows onto the prison yard then Liz regained her thought process. "I might add I was successful with my mixture of Psychotropic chemicals that, like planned, had weakened Wendi's resolve. The drugs were bent on enhancing her anxiousness and insecurities. Such was the case when Wendi's alter ego, Sunshine, first surfaced. She fell back to her default personality, which always took charge when trauma was present... her alter ego stepped out of the dimensional fugue that was housed inside her cranium. Since she was five years old, her invisible twin had protected her when she was in trouble saving their lives several times. Sunshine had become Wendi's savior."

Ursula spins around "all right, let's see how we must proceed," they walk down a hallway, lost in their own personal turmoil.

The elevator doors opened as they crossed the threshold into Ursula's spacious office. "Liz, we need to stick together when the proverbial shit hits the fan, afraid that impotent ass Larry will break weak and throw us under the bus. He voted like us for the dart to be fired if he doesn't find the courage or man up, he will be lucky to be an assistant manager at Taco Bell. I wasn't enamored with him when the board voted him the assistant warden here; I believed that being the Warden, I should have had a choice, but that wasn't the damn case."

Timing is everything. A knock could be heard the Assistant Warden appeared. Larry Walden, "so now it's done. All we have to wait for is the repercussions of this deplorable act. Ugh, the ramifications of which I want no part of... this is straight up bullshit I...." "Shut the fk up, Larry," admonished Ursula. "Wtf? Were we going to jeopardize the entire operation we've incubated for over 15 years?"

Warden Ursula Anders decides to use diplomacy and reason... "relax, Larry, please... enough inner conflict. It's done now. Come on, let's have a seat and discuss our next moves." She notices the defeatist empty stares of her conspirators "look at the two of you, Larry. Why don't you give back your Villa in Spain, or you Liz your beachfront Castle in Maui, or divulge your secret bank accounts overseas? Freakin focus, don't be divisive. The three of us need to be on the same side, fk. We're on the same team, aren't we?" asked Ursula.

Silence as heads were bowed at her, no arguments forthcoming after her words were spoken. The threesome sat across from one another, elbows on the table. Ursula pressed the intercom 'yes, ma'am,' 'I want some fresh fruit, and some sandwiches and a pot of coffee and iced tea delivered to my office enough for three… aah Kathy, don't disturb us until then, hold all calls.' 'Yes, ma'am Warden.'

Ursula pounds the table… "all right, what is done is done, and we can't go backward, so it's useless to whine over spilled milk. With that said, we must be prepared to be scrutinized by the Feds and Terrance; I want solutions, not negative rhetorical whims. Let's start working together, Liz. Let's start with you." 'Um,' Liz utters-stutters, "you heard the Hawkins doctor was running a blood panel on Wendi, which will invariably show some of the drugs I selected for the dart. Not the new designer drugs, for I think there isn't a test for them yet. I also believe that the cocktail of chemicals will react in her system and be a catalyst to bring forth all the residual remnants of likewise medications she's ingested for almost nine months stored in her fatty cells. I suspect she will be reduced and seduced into another catatonic state of being!"

Larry raises his right hand. "Yes, but that is the true crux of our dilemma who would fire a dart filled with Psychotropic drugs the same shooter could have just as easily fired a slug of a 22 Caliber bullet 'IMHO' in my humble opinion, it all falls into our laps again." "Okay, I can concur, Larry, but why isn't that the true question, um, why would someone…." Liz interrupts, "It depends on what Wendi remembers of the 7 or 9 missions she's completed. If anything, that is, her personalities are partitioned and separated. Sure, there is an ongoing overlap and an inner power struggle, but we give Sunshine the overwhelming advantage with our drugs!"

Larry adds, "still, I can't resolve the 'Pink Elephant in the room' the way that it went down it's…." Knocks are heard, then two staff members enter Ursula's office with refreshments and sustenance… nourishment for brains left with a dichotomy of quandaries, with many ambiguous scenarios to quantify.

The door closes like robots, they pick and choose foods filling paper plates and cups for liquids in an indecisive mood, processing what they can. A depressed state of mind lingered.

32

Joe and Sammy.

Sammy was behind me about three bike lengths. We were winding our way from the Pacific Ocean by Stinson Beach in Marin County, a gorgeous ride, and it was a typically pleasant Marin evening we'd pulled off at several scenic vistas.

No matter how either of us tried not to stress the current situation with the motorhome and the dead brothers inside, it wasn't happening. Frustratingly, my calls to Mark and Tank were left unanswered. Texts, tweets, even my Instagram and Snaps, zero communication. Gladly interrupting my train of thought. Sammy sent me a quick TikTok video while we were overlooking a cliff with the sunset and ocean in the distance. We laughed, releasing some pent-up pressure, realizing we were on our own.

Constantly resurfacing was her true statement, haunting me since our conversation on the sands of the Pacific Ocean, that I was going to end her life, duh. Why was she still following me? It didn't make any sense to me. She could quickly ditch me hell; the girl could ride that bike like the wind! Checking the GPS, the motorhome was only 25 miles away. We were riding East through the quaint town of Fairfax when I saw a coffee shop with outside decks and a patio, so I yanked the 1290 KTM to a stop and parked in the bike zone. Sam did the same.

Seven minutes later, we were sitting with our backs to a 7-foot Redwood fence. The table and chairs were also constructed with Redwood... iced Caramel lattes sat on a table next to us. Of the 11 tables, there were only five occupied. It was 7:47 pm we started hitchhiking on the Wi-Fi. She had her iPad out, and I was staring at my 13-inch laptop screen.

"Okay, Joe, what's the plan? I mean, we cannot just ride up to the RV, right?" "Sam, that's not actually true. I am checking out the five cameras installed on and in the RV; not a single soul has been by it, not approached since we left it there. We will know the instant someone shows up at the motorhome.

The motion-detecting cameras will alert my cell phone with a silent vibration." In unison, they sip their lattes peering around at the other customers chatting at their tables, luckily not paying any heed to them.

"We do have one thing going for us there were several RV's and truck trailers parked on the back '40'of the Walmart shopping center. Also, the Safeway store is open 24 hours." Sammy interjected, "we could use all the luck possible I'm checking the local news so far, and nothing on the motorhome, Joe." We zoned out into our mindsets amalgamated, um, blended in with all the others sipping coffee drinks, and everyone had their devices out. No one was talking, nope, just staring at screens so was this world we lived within.

The couple with matching rings sitting on stools at the nearest table was enthralled with social media... phones out. Next to them were a couple of guys who were lovers, for at times, one would place his hand over the other. They were playing each other on a video game via phones.

After a few more minutes passed, she said again, "Nothing new so far, Joe... wait!" her face lit up, "oh shit, there's like a dozen blogs started, one of which has 517 posts, umh hits. Wow, it seems people have nothing to do with their lives but be online!" He wasn't paying attention on another wavelength; he was going back in a time-lapse from when they left the motorhome. "Check it out, girl; besides a dogwalker, I can't see anyone that took an interest in the RV since I parked it, and all the cameras are clear of obstructions. The place that it's parked under the shade of trees alongside the chain-link fence borders Hwy 101 South heading to San Francisco. I think our luck can hold out. Maybe we should ride over to the motorhome Sammy and drive it out West towards the beach where there's plenty of places to dump the bodies!"

"Ssshh Joe, please, I'm paranoid enough," she leans over closer and whispers, "I got something from a blogger his moniker is 'SFPD*' not good, listen... ('friend works for Caltrans cameras prove the motorhome that is under the microscope a BOLO search for it. get this it didn't cross the Golden Gate Bridge, it's still in Marin County') Joe that was posted 57 minutes ago." "Great more freakin bad news, girl. You better follow his chain of posts." "Oh, crap, 49 minutes ago ('the motorhome didn't reverse directions and head North from Novato on Hwy 101 into Sonoma County it's here in Marin') ('39 minutes ago; just learned the Perp's have been using a blocking device which normally has a range of 55 to 300 feet.') 31 min; ('choppers are in the process of reviewing all video along Hwy 101') reply to SFPD*.'

Another blogger writes, ('Choppers what? Where could they go? You know there's a $35,000 reward for the location of the motorhome. The occupants shot and killed one person and shot two police officers who were in Marin General fk were out in force. I mean, my friends were going to get that reward!') ('$$$Mine$$') 23 minutes ago ('my advice to all of you amateurs is let the police do their job. The couple in the RV are professional killers SFPD*.')

Joe becomes more agitated by the second, "Fanfkntabulous; now we have a bunch of vigilantes out playing bounty hunters. Geez, how life had changed in only a few decades before you had the nosey wannabe cops on the short-wave radios, uhm, CBs. Now all the fkn scanners are Online… sickening!"

"Joe, that's true. All people do now is follow their phone's GPS. They don't even know how to read a map, but you don't plan to aah, umh, I mean, we're not going back to that Red Hot RV, right? That would be insanity!"

"Woman, that's the reason we're sitting in this coffee shop. I know you wish I had a plan of attack, what to do, where to go. Sorry, truth be told… I haven't a clue as to our next move. Help me, ahh us, you're a resourceful gal…" She sourly gurgled "oh damn, I've never been called a gal before like that's an old word for a guy that's only a little older than me. What are you nine years, my senior?" "Ha-ha, ha, I'm glad I could bring out some humor in such a distressful time but let's chew on this-help me… ah, help us. Sam, I believe it's time for me to divulge this to you. I'm on the ten most wanted. Ugh, FBI's list, and yet the worst crime suspected of me are gun-running. Oh, and my affiliation with one of the largest Militias in the USA in Montana, they have no proof of anything I've done. The worst crime they could charge me with is absconding from parole!"

"That doesn't make sense. Why would they put you on the ten most...." "Let me finish. There's a long list of accusations... incriminating circumstances, such as an office building in Boise, Idaho, which was detonated... U know, bombed to smithereens. It was one of those businesses, ugh Anti-N.R.A. anyways my name surfaced snitches without proof, just word by Rats mouths." "Geez, dude, you're like a terrorist. Gosh, I sure know how to pick my friends... lol." She paused and thought, then he exclaimed, "friends, is that what we are?"

"Maybe or maybe not. I guess it depends on your perspective, or am I just a whore to you, Joe?" Shaking my head. This girl was way beyond blunt right to the nitty-gritty or meat of the subject matter, nada subtle with her approach. So, I told her like it was and is, "Yeah, you're a fkn Slut ugh, whore there's no question there, and one hell of a motorcycle rider. I like you, yes, and I'd refer to you as a friend... cuz in my lifetime, I have exactly two friends, Mark, and Tank, whom I've known since childhood."

I reached across and nobly gallantly took her tiny paw up and kissed her palm, then the opposite side of her dainty hand then. I cackled... she squinted, twisting her face towards me like a whiskered feline "what's so funny, huh?"

With a Cheshire cat snarl, I said, "ain't no way I'd be kissing your Ogre's feet. Lord knows yah got some ugly feet for a sexy beautiful woman." Then I couldn't stop from cracking up and chortling some, leaving giggles and hostile stares from the phone-bearing folks nearby.

Her look of shock led to another hilarious bout. We fell out laughing again towards tears. I suppose it was the pent-up stress imposed on our minds and souls, but it felt good to laugh together, kind of a Bonding experience, heck. 'It had been over a decade or more since I expressed such hilarity, a high-spirited connection for sure!'

I was sweating and having fun in the cool evening... me having a bout of boisterousness was unsettling until this point; I never knew I could feel so good from a natural human reaction to laughter which was unnatural for me. I thought I was an obsolete Grinch-like person. Although this was the second time in less than a few hours that this phenomenon happened with her in the dressing room was the first. Wow, we annoyed the trance-like Zombies whom Dot-Pixels transfixed; their glaring eyes cast evil vehemence in our directions, staring at Sammy and me as we separated them from intercourse... 'hey, maybe we did?'

Sammy shoulders me with a quirky smirk and a possible 'blushment' "you know us working gals sometimes have 'tightening operations' yeah, no for a tighter squeeze or snug fit, certainly not 'Virginesque,' but I'll have you know, mister your my first fellow since that very operation. I'd been on retirement for over five weeks well, at least that orifice...."

Matching smiles, I added, "oh damn, that busts out my belief that it was because of how well-endowed I am." This resulted in a devious grin "oh yeah, that too!" she blew me a kiss.

Her iPad beeped with that sound, and our humor and levity seeped away earnestly. I zoomed in "so Sam, back to our debacle, ahh, our earlier conversation, back to the point the Feds have only circumstantial evidence against me. Not a Capital One murder case I have skated thus far, yet I'm guilty as sin. You know, in the RV is irrefutable DNA evidence of not only me but you, my dear, and your dead Pimp and his brother. They swabbed me a couple of years ago in Quentin. It was mandated by the district court and passed into law that all felons be imputed into databases using their DNA uhm, what I'm saying is I'm in that database." She sat erect, showing a worried expression, "and that umh brings me to your pimp and his brother, those killings will lead directly to me." She rubbed her eyes and blinked a sad face.

"Hell, it was self-defense. I bet you a jury would exonerate us. They attacked us, not premeditated hell...." Her words floated off into the abyss. We slugged down our Caramel lattes with a pause, lost in time and space, wishing oddly that we were both different people out and about, in love. Yep, a weak-ass moment of emotions that I'd not known. I soldiered on, leaving all the soppy bullshit. "This is what I'm getting to and why I've stopped so many times on this drive. I'm trying to contact my partners for some reason; both are incognito, not returning any communication."

She looked at me with an expression I had yet seen... despair-riddled. "Joe, it's our Freakin ass's on the line here. Sorry, I don't know your people. But this becomes like for me speaking for me aah self-preservation, I don't know if I'd still be sitting here with you for my Lips are on the line don't take it the wrong way-but like it or not, were tied to the hip! I am a gambling-spirited woman of 25 years who has been down the street a few times and am certain the only reason I'm still breathing is because of the camera in the safe box at the airport with the video of you murdering that Private Investigator, so let's cut to the chase WTHell are we going to do?"

Of course, she was correct. There was no room for a female in our trio, even if she were willing to serve our male desires at a whim. Mark would enter the world of ballistic 'Hate. There wasn't a chance in hell that I could show up on his doorstep with this girl. If you looked up 'Misogynist' in the dictionary, Mark Feral would glare back at you!

"Well, Joe the Cat better not have your tongue; if it were up to me, we'd burn the motorhome to the ground!" then added, "DNA can't survive a fire. I saw that once on that show 'Forensic Files' am I right?" again, her iPad blatantly broke my train of thought, raised my hand motioning to her computer a moment later, she muttered the Blog is on viral all pumped up 7 minutes ago from 'SFPD*' ('I have news, confirmation that the motorhome is either East or West of Hwy 101 the parameters now are locked into this zone from Lincoln Ave in San Rafael to Sausalito City limits.')

With that, I closed my laptop and sucked down the last drops of my sweet drink "let's go. That settles that!" "Settles what?" "With the woodbe internet sleuths, it won't be long till they discover the whereabouts of the RV." I didn't have to waste any more words. We were riding down Miracle mile towards Hwy 101 within seconds.

33

Tanya and Rico.

Holding the damp-warm slipper up inches from my face Tanya, with a distinct undertone of visceral contempt, skewered across her countenance, "where might Cinderella be hiding at Rico?" Quickly I jumped to a defensive stance "it's not what you're thinking, not even close, Tanya." Just then, the single-slippered Lori ducked out of the closet "nah, Tanya, definitely not what it seems like here!" "Then why run and hide in the closet, Lori? Your faces look like you've been caught red-handed in the 'Cookie Jar,' aah." An awkward silence then pervaded the room. I soldiered forward but only stumbled over my own words. "Lori just showered and returned to tell me something she'd thought of, is all." I wasn't clever enough. Tanya stood their hands on her hips rigid, unyielding... "looks to me that we all can figure out what Lori was thinking!" hummed Tanya.

"Now stop, that's so unfair. Sure, this seems awkward, and that's exactly why I tried to hide because of what it looked like, but I merely showered. Look at my hair... it's still wet," she slides her fingers through her hair. "I tossed my robe on slippers and shot back over here." Before Tanya could add to the assault on our integrity, I threw out a mortar shell. "Tanya, I'm willing to take a Federal Lie detector test. I've had no sexual relations with Lori." Tanya mimicked a Stallion Filly tossing her head about, then let loose with a cackle. <u>"Isn't that almost verbatim what President Clinton said? I've had no sexual relations with that woman!"</u>

"Listen, legitimately, you both have signed contracts that there will be no... No, and I repeat, intimacy between FBI Agents. Lori. Have you not heard of an Old Gadget called a phone? Why didn't you just call Rico rather than traipse, um, slink over here in your open robe?"

Lori dropped her chin, noticing her left tit had found fresh air nipple rigid, erect, covered up quickly, blushing dark red, "I'll be going now" "no, you're not, Agent Park. Sit down, both of you... enough!"

Whew, she was pissed off and agitated. The ironic fact was that neither Tanya nor I could ever pass a lie detector test. We had been intimate a dozen times, at a minimum, a tiny or large bit hypocritical; yes, this was all due to jealousy. I surmised, without doubt, I'd hear more from her, ugh, toxic fuming thoughts behind closed doors soon enough. I was not looking forward to that.

Suddenly Tanya morphed into all business mode, grimacing, eyeballing me with one last scowl leaving me with a scrap umh, a morsel of disingenuousness. Her left nostril flickered and then returned to its formal self. She banged her fist on the counter "so thanks to our Agent Avery's proclivity and skill base and his use of filters, he provided us with an identity only minutes ago. The motorhome is registered to a Ben Abbott." Lori and I nod, relieved. "Rico, I'm surprised you don't remember that name, Ben Abbott. It was the name of the registered bike owner of that KTM 1290 that drove past you and Agent Kelsey Marie at the stakeout in the Napa shopping center!"

I felt flush, still recovering from the brutal verbal assault of caustic accusatory sexual implications with Lori. I mumbled, "damnit, that's why the name sounded so freaking familiar," I said, "shit, sorry." Up till that time, I hadn't noticed the manilla folder that she'd brought with her taking the pictures out "the motorcycle rider had blonde hair behind the full-faced helmet. It looked to be pulled up into a bun, but strands of long hair fell onto her feminine neck… it was a small man or a petite woman. No doubts now remain.

'Whoa,' belched Lori, finally recognizing the implications. Tanya paused for a breath, and I believed an inkling of effect, sliding out another 8 X11 photo. "Ben Abbott doesn't exist although he's the proud owner of the magnificent motorhome, with motorcycle trailer attached, oh and not one but 2 KTM 1290 motorcycles." Lori and I flipped past the photos looking back at Tanya.

"The address given to the DMV umh associated with the phony fake license was an estate at a country club in Granite Bay East of Sacramento. Not a single lead and the photos of this Abbott fellow does nothing for us!"

I jumped in with my 3 cents "how can that be? It's impossible in this era. He walked in and bought a $500,000 RV and a trailer, then traveled to another business and bought two Motorcycles wow, really, and used cash, please… there's got to be pictures from those establishments we could then use Facial Recognition, somethings wrong with this picture hell this is 2019 for Heaven's sake!"

"Rico, good points, all true I shot over to your hotel room the second I hung up with Agent Avery, so now I need you and Lori here to get on this immediately, and yes, I concur with your assessment; we should have sufficient evidence. I mean, our technological expertise has been enhanced. It is being refined by the hour, but many people don't realize that with new technology, the criminal element also benefits from additional resources. Such is the specific case here. This Abbott fellow purchased all electronically. We traced the funds to bitcoin accounts… Cyber currency. The trail is dead-ended and ceases to exist. The last known location was the Dark Web. All paperwork Agent Avery told me was carried out legally with computer-generated signatures electronically. The transfer of funds was legit too."

"All right, if that's the case, someone, a human, had to take delivery of the RV trailer and motorcycles as of yet… robots aren't used for those tasks, right." Declares Lori, somewhat befuddled.

"According to Avery, there are approximately 13 companies at last count online that will take care of tasks for a nominal fee; in today's world, it's all about the service industries like Uber, Lyft, Door Dash, Amazon, the list goes on the Perps took advantage of a company called 'What you need.com.' Avery was able to trace the individuals who took possession of the package deal that subcontracted for the Dot Com company. He was told all was left parked at the Sacramento Fair Grounds. Whoever took ownership of the RV disabled the GPS systems and used a signal-blocking device when they picked up the combination RV and trailer." Lori and I had matching expressions with our mouths open.

Tanya frowns and says, "What we can ascertain is that there has never been a Mr. Ben Abbott." Lori and I watched Tanya pull out several more 8X10s photos and corresponding sheets of typed papers then she opened another window on her laptop. We waited for the next slipper umh... shoe to drop.

"This is the site, Chili's Restaurant, the site of the Homicide, the killing of the P.I. up close and personal our Agents have some observations. Our team has concluded that the victim pulled his vehicle up in the parking lot next to the 'Perp,' and the victim rolled his window down to speak to the assailant. The Perp could have been on foot or in another vehicle, uh, or even a motorcycle. The Perp once again used a signal blocker, so we haven't any video, but what we have are these."

I'm handed hard copies of pictures taken by the Sheriff's cams. One shot, in particular, was telling... Tanya enlarged the photo on her laptop screen. Blonde hair waving, spotlights on the back of the motorcycle from the pursuing Sheriff cruiser "how were these pictures taken if the Perp used one of those fandangled devices bought on the Dark Web?"

'Ugh,' Tanya bellows, her furrowed brows dipped "that's the crux for my timely interruption uhm, who knows how far you two would have gotten?" she scowled at us. Lori tightened her robe up "an eyewitness that was taking a break from washing dishes at the Chilis Restaurant saw not one bike, but two bikes. He was outside by the dumpster smoking a cigarette and had an iPod in his ears. The guy is a motorcycle enthusiast, accurately calling the make and models of both bikes. He saw the first motorcycle as it rode off, then he saw directly across the lot a Sheriff's car drive-in. As that motorcycle went... in his words, 'An Frkn awesome wheelie for like 75 yards crazy burning up rubber it was quite a show had to be a professional stunt man,' said he!" Suddenly Lori and Rico caught the gist of what Tanya was laying out.

"We don't have to jump to conclusions. No, the perpetrators have left us confirmations. It's more than a 99% chance that the kidnappings of the lawyers are aligned with the private investigator's homicide. The assailants left the same evidence, ah, playing cards. Cards left at the scenes of the crimes remember the Perp's quip, 'Fear me cuz I'm cumin 4 U' ... it's from the same group of criminals, most likely the same person or organization that also paid Nurse Spike to assassinate Wendi Feral. Sent flowers to her room and the rooms of our Agents that were shot, Agents Kelsey Marie and Rodriguez. The execution killing of the nurse with a headshot from a 50 Caliber McMillian Sniper rifle favored by many militias." Lori interjected, "So I see where this is going. Our number one suspect has to be Mark Feral; his affiliation with the SOJ Militia leads us to conclude that they are also involved. Mark was last identified a couple of weeks ago by one of our informants at a militia function in Spokane, Washington!"

I added, "Well, I remember reading that one of his longest friendships is with fugitive Joe Sable, who has been our leading suspect from the get-go! Joe is a quantified Sharpshooter bestowed the highest medals during his military campaign. He was purported to be a marksman, a champion shooter at military contests. It's gotta be Joe Sable." Fumbling on my own words. Tanya sighed and rolled her eyes like a teacher; Lori and I were kindergarteners.

"Agent Bill Avery is currently trying to enhance the Caltrans Pics of the male driving the RV. He, at this time, can't discount the driver being Joe Sable; between us, it was Joe who was the shooter at the Truckstop. The question remains who is the woman not only in the passenger seat with the blonde hair but we can now assume on the KTM in the Napa parking lot, also at Chili's doing the trick riding wheelie!" barked Tanya.

I blurted out, "Not many women can ride like that, and I'm not being a male chauvinist. It takes years of riding to gain the confidence and experience to do what she did, so we should check with all the local riding organizations, Motocross, all Street Racing groups, and bike clubs. I'd bet the woman had ridden or rode motorcycles since she was young; we don't know how old she is. Still, it's worth a shot to research all the Motocross events in Northern California, mainly scrutinizing the Sacramento area." "Not a bad idea, Rico you and Lori have a lot to do, Lori; get dressed and meet Rico and me in my suite," yelps Tanya. "Oh, I almost forgot the first rider who killed the P.I. had the blocking device… which was lucky for us. The device only has a range of 300ft. We have a video of the female rider, for she was about 350 feet from where the Private Investigator was shot and killed. CSI measured the wheelie; it was 57 yards long!"

Lori threw in her 11 cents as she headed for the mandoor between our rooms. "Yeah, but it might not be a woman; the rider wore a full-face helmet."

Lori's statement went unheeded, as if Tanya had some pent-up bad will towards her lol… it's possible that this was my imagination ☺. A smidgen of what I'd been thinking when Lori 'came onto me' dropping her robe, her nipples standing erect still flashed by my… "Rico, are you with us" "yes, sorry, Tanya, just analyzing" she popped up a map of Marin County with highlighted areas. "The RV has to be between these sectors; here's an aerial view of the last area that the RV was pictured at. It's more like an industrial area, warehouses, storage facilities, office buildings, and the Executive Airport of San Rafael." She pointed to airplane hangars, motioning to the other side of the map, "this is a residential area to the left along with some farming properties with barns and outbuildings that the Perps could hide the RV within. I have allocated a massive number of Agents on the ground with accompanying local Law Enforcement Officers who are going to search this entire area."

Tanya looked up at us. "I'm not sure if you're aware there's a reward for the location of the RV, and the local populace is out in numbers; the RV didn't cross the Golden Gate, nor did it backtrack and enter into Sonoma County. It's only a matter of time till we find it. Therefore I want you, Lori, to get dressed. We are working tonight…." "But I've been at it for 19 straight hours" "sorry, you're going to be at it till we find that RV. Do I have to remind you that we have two of our fellow Agents in the hospital on respirators, Lori? Lucky to be alive. Who knows, by God's grace, it could have been you two being shot. Drive out to the Executive airport and take charge out there."

"Rico, you're coming with me in the mobile command unit. You've got 15 minutes. I'll meet you both in the lobby!"

Tanya needn't slam the door, but I supposed she couldn't help it showing her disdain-perhaps it was only her adrenalin or maybe emphasis that I was in for a tongue lashing in the closed confines of the mini-RV mobile unit, not lookin forward to being interrogated this evening. Lori made her way to her feet. "Well, hell, that didn't go as I planned fk umh, excuse the language." I replied, 'yes, fk,' and opened the mandoor as she brushed by me, her robe fluttering behind her slippers. She flipped around 50 feet inside, staring at me, which gave me the alternative to say something smooth, "Lori, let's put it in the category of a Raincheck" disappearing into her hotel room, she left me with a wink and a smile!

<u>-34-</u>

<u>Agents Tom Baker and Bill Avery with surveillance on Tank Shaw.</u>

Okay, I'd been a good boy and followed through with the directions and plans previously demanded… wait, not mandated but required. Still, when Mark, Joe, and I were in prison on the yard at San Quentin, we'd made plans. I did everything according to plan, including buying the used car. I made it to my first appointment at the Parole office and shopped for my rented apartment, setting up a home base. At the same time, the eager Feds watched my every move. I took a break from their agenda for personal satisfaction. My time… went to the gym taking advantage of a hot and willing aah… let me rephrase that, she took advantage of me. But hey, it was a fun five hours while it lasted. I mused sadly that we couldn't hook up again. I liked her taste, but instantly shit soured everything went sideways; she being married ruined the whole experience, uh, sort of.

The slut was married. Damn, the red numbers blared back at me at 3:17 am, tired but not exhausted as I should have been with the great sex workout, but the flashing phone proved to be an irresistible annoyance. Knowing I'd regret it even so… I'd have to listen to the voicemails and read the texts; this would be my undoing for the rest of the evening. Having completely ignored the phone and my partners. I felt compelled to flick on the screen, entering my passcode.

Knowing farewell, only two people had my number before I opened the texts, I checked the legit phone that the parole officer had. As per usual, after leaving prison with a substance abuse issue, she'd left a message that I'd had a U.A. uh pee test tomorrow, no shit, I mean later this morning.

Then I did something I could never have done before Quentin's last stint. I shut down into a meditative state, being deliberate, slowing my breathing, and calming my inner noise. I waited, not touching the Tracfone, patience with resolve, a discipline developed in my lonely cell. I could still smell the damp rot of the block walls, humming a song by the Great Late 'Johnny Cash' 'San Quentin.'

I Fell sound asleep, woke in just under five hours, showered, had coffee was a touch dchydrated, pounded a couple of bottles of water, and was off to the courthouse for the piss test geez. The shower did feel amazing. I must say it was like another life as I walked untethered without guard towers, ominously watching my every step. It went well, 'piss and go' walking back out to the courthouse, back to my car powering on my Tracfone, a total of 11 messages, with the last being the 911 kind. Most were benign, the 'where are you varieties?' 'what's going on?' The most recent messages and calls got more concerning, stressed with anxiousness in their voices. The last few began with 'Call Me!' then the last one shrank my lungs, sucking in a huge gulp of air; I reread it.

'Tank change of Venue plans. I need your help. Call/text me immediately, Mark… I'll have the phone on my side while I'm out chasing tail… TTYL (talk to you later), Bro ☹ .'

Joe added another trauma-laden text, 'serious issue needs your help brother call or text me right away. I checked the time, and it was nine hours ago. Strange that neither Mark nor Joe had sent another text since the night before, thinking that there was a 911 help needed text from Mark… what happened? I'm not a panic dude, but I was a touch unraveled!

I couldn't help worrying and became a tad bit apprehensive. Instead of driving back to my apartment, I found a park and sent texts back to my partners sitting on a bench. I waited, keeping my attention up and surveying all people that were nearby. Where were the Feds? And beyond that thought, why hadn't Joe or Mark sent back a text, now going on 11 hours, should I go back to my apartment? Was there a serious problem? Am I being paranoid? I'd left the probation department less than 75 minutes ago. Hell, they'd sequestered me if the Feds suspected my connection with Joe or Mark was ongoing.

<u>Tank decides to do something he'd enjoyed before being incarcerated… rollerblading.</u>

I returned to my car, grabbed a pair of rollerblades I'd bought the day before putting my music earbuds in, and flipped my phone onto 'Spotify,' tuning in the Bluetooth option was all new to me; wow, technology had gone crazy indeed scary almost. I took my ball cap in my left hand and flipped it backward. I wore green shorts and a matching green and black T-back muscle shirt. I hit the asphalt a little off balance. It had been years since I'd rollerbladed, but it was like riding a bike for me. I had spent hours upon hours roller-skating and skateboarding before being arrested… it's great cardio.

The hardest trick was avoiding the traffic of bike riders, walkers, runners, and skateboarders; children presented another obstacle to be wary of. The playgrounds were full of life, children of all ages in the sand going down slides and swinging, um, fun stuff. This was a life I hadn't known or visited for the last seven years or so. Exhilaratingly I inhaled a large breath, nearly releasing a smile. Still, the gnawing reality of precariousness kept me from thoroughly enjoying myself

250

completely… chewing at me was what was going on with Mark and Joe?

In my ears, I heard a mix of music. It wasn't Heavy metal or Hip-Hop, Pop… Nah. The genre, for me, was Jazz this morning. The Sun was just warming the San Jose hillsides the sweet music of 'Brian Culbertson' streamed into my head. 'The Journey' played.

There wasn't a way of hiding from my inner being, umh, spirit, although I tried with much contemplation. I wasn't 40 years old yet, but what was bothering me oddly, uhm, was what had happened to my life in the past two decades plus.

I'd spent thousands of hours ruminating on my past choices; prison does that, I've been told, and I'm living proof, I suppose. Perplexed with clarity Lol, I was undeniably confused. Why hadn't I contacted the bros earlier, or why didn't I pay attention to the flashing Tracfone? I definitely ignored it.

I'm sure it was business as per usual with them. They would harp… declare that I owed them… for if not for them, I'd still be behind the molding block walls of Quentin. Surely that's correct, and I mused that I'd still be locked up if not for their connections with the parole board!

What they forgot was that I would never have been in prison in the 3rd place if not for my association with them! Nope, damn, I nearly fell down, hitting the pavement, barely missing a massive pothole. I stopped reiterating to self it had been years since rollerblading, duh. Was that a form of rhetorical blundering? My dreams were vivid and inspirationally driven. I did want a 'Plain-Jane' faithful, loving wife, the grey picket fence children, even bogging myself down working a 9 to 5 job. Lord knew I would be happy with that; it still wasn't too late, right?

Did I want to repeat replicate my societal indifferences and remain on the peripheral side of 'evil vs. good' perceived dilemmas of inner conflict erupted from my bones and soul nerve endings standing on edge! I found another vacant park bench. Like the Holy Spirit was my guide, a family of five was cavorting and laughing, playing nearby oh so much fun, the natural beauty of love and peace. Never had I known that life it was alien to me!

A mother was swinging a baby boy as the father was racing their daughter to see who could swing up into the air the farthest, umh, highest the sounds calmed me.

Yes, even the sharp shrills of exuberance, festive fun, ah dare I say frolicsome, yep kinda like that word describing the children who seemed to haven't a care, just having a carefree fun time. I'd pulled the AirPods from my ears, taken a big breath, and listened to what life could be like, delightful squeals of families enjoying themselves. I missed out on this kind of existence.

I closed my eyes sadly; I never left my haunted life sick, clenched guts, and nauseated feelings overwhelmed me, traveling back to where my mind drove on autopilot. The 'Highway to Hell' 'AC-DC' song… mimicry burdened me and powered down my phone's ringer, but it was too late. Before my vision, my eyes were on the Quentin Prison yard. In my hidden left hand was a razor-sharp shank-steel sharpened knife-the date was only five weeks past.

Various gangs control prisons. Most had affiliates they could count on in an emergency. I was the proactive leader, the protagonist for the prison slang, 'Car' uh gang named the 'Woods' white pride. Being the 'shot-caller' went with my intellect, and it didn't hurt my prospects that I was also the strongest in the group, but with my status came responsibilities, and trouble always presented itself when least expected.

An Islamic guy in the chow hall disrespected me. Therefore this called for a quick rebuke and concise retribution. I watched the guards inhabiting the gun towers walking on top of the walls and looking down with lethal weapons within reach; this didn't bother me, and I had no fear of dying. The quandary facing me did I stab perforate his liver? How ludicrous would that be with me being five weeks to the door or gates, uhm freedom, either going home and back to the streets or locked in the hole of solitary confinement? It's not like I'd not spent months on end in the 'SHU' solitary confinement unit. Do I cut his freakin heart out ughhhh not a hard decision for most!

Indeed if not killed, I'd have to recalculate an added sentence of at least five years more; conversely, if I backed down, I'd face my entire faction, who would gang up and end my existence anyways. This was prison life, like animals 'eat or be eaten.'

Okay, so I soldiered onwards a purpose of annihilation, a kill or be killed mentality. The Islamic guy caught my approach, obviously on guard; we stepped into a circle around the dip and pullup bars in the weightlifting area. His weapon was an iron bar with sharp welded grooves bent on tearing my skin and breaking bones.

I had a shank in my left hand and a block of wood for a shield; a crowd of inmates gathered around for the show, then shots rang out rubber bullets, tear gas. Later it was proven that a prison Rat snitch had informed the Warden of the upcoming melee fast as I could, I tossed my shank likewise, and my adversary did the same with the bar.

<u>It took a woman to alter Tank's existence and his future.</u>

Suddenly I was brought current happily… my disposition was altered in a split second. I had company on the park bench; sitting next to me was a woman who seemed to be watching the children play in the sand. I checked her out; she had a natural look, no pizazz makeup, a plain enough looking woman, maybe 35ish, with black and pinkish silver Rollerblades of her own double laced. At a brief survey, no wedding band ring, I quickly surmised, and no stain of one either. Lol, of course, with her dark skin, I had to study her ring finger for indentations… of where it would have been none.

Which precisely meant nothing. She was sipping water from her pink fluid container, me being the obnoxious type of man with a propensity for boldness. Some would say I was outspoken, and others gregarious. I am discounting those stereotypes. I just was me, and I said what I felt… A confident entity that understood years back, if you didn't speak up, nothing would ever happen if yuh sat like a lump on a log you'd only mold.

I offered up uh or supplied the opening line, "Isn't it a bit early to be drinking that stuff?" no smile, grin, or even acknowledgment. I recognized that I'd missed a mini set of earphones in her braids. She peered over at me, "sorry, I saw your lips moving but couldn't hear you." Tapping on her music player, 'awkward umh.' With nothing to lose, I repeated my dumb words without hesitation, and she replied, "Yes, I wish I had some cranberry juice to go with the Vodka!" I'm startled, which wasn't easy; she gaged my expression and snickered like touché.

It was her turn to be blatantly audacious, blurting out loudly, "man do you think you have enough tattoos?" my turn, "all the ink on my skin tells a story. Each tattoo has its own reality living on my epidermis, reasons for their being!" Then she let loose a shining white smile; I'd always thought black people had that advantage. Their teeth always seemed brighter against their pigmentation of... "that being the case, you'd have plenty of stories to tell... my name is Whitney yours?" "Tank" "not really, come on, what's your name? not your description," as she once again chortles.

"Really, it's Tank" "okay then, Tank come on, let's get some exercise and go for a roll," she was up in an instant. We were off just like that.... that's when I noticed the guy who was out of place. It was blatantly apparent... seeing a 'fish out of water' the FBI Agent dressed in a suit whew 'sharp as a tac' truly incongruent like a 'blight of incontinence' really dude, 'get with the program' Duh, we bladed by.

I hadn't been able to assess and rate her body. Sure, call me 'shallow' for some reason it was important to me; maybe it was the ways of society, actresses, magazines-billboards the way a woman should look to be desirable, Yep. Superficial, stereotypically shallow can't dwell on this topic and could take me hours to not come to any conclusions. Suffice it to say I'm shallow, so kill me. Whoa, she had long muscled legs that went deceptively into a pair of silver biker shorts matching knee pads dressed like a Victoria's Secret Model. I'm not going to comment on my first thoughts regarding her sway-backed rear-end ahh; I guessed she was just a tad under six ft. tall and had one of those figures with ample boobs that I'd enjoyed with my very first G.F. girlfriend. A swayback beauty that could enable a more comfortable 69er position, a simpler delight, umh yum, there I go, mind in the sewer pondering ah dwelling on sex again. What a curse we men have been left with, not fair Testosterone!

What about her head? Ah, I mean, what's in it? Intellect, what's her personality like? Would we hit it off, uh, what the hell would we have in common? Stop assessing what it would feel to make passionate love to her like a freakin animal Tank, thinkin what pundits would argue the most important asset that a female um mate should have is compatibility!

Silver and Pink with dark Blue were her colors. The stretchy top matched in sync with the frilly socks, elbow pads, and a sports bra that was having a devil of a time keeping the pair of mammary glands at Bay... Let the Hounds out, willya!' ☺ .

Long bouncing Afro braids with strands of Blue and Silver beads adorned her luscious head, no helmet with dark, sensual eyes behind an oversized pair of sunglasses fingernails painted a light reflecting Silver shined from where I bladed on her right side. Whitney had punctured openings on her plush ear lobes for five earrings, but at this time, only one dangled a silverish pearl.

Pouty lips with a gloss of Pink, umh, yum, am I forgetting anything? Oh, her other facial features were perfectly aligned, congruently with her toned muscular bod. She could have been a gymnastics enthusiast or even an instructor. I had to zip back, traffic pushing me into single file behind her, revealing a most titillating 'thigh gap' Yeah!

Of course, I followed closely, mesmerized by her ass down the asphalt paths blindly at times, for I was lost in uhm on her glorious glutes, each luscious cheek moved independently to purposely annoy me with the need to throw her aggressively, brutally down in the bushes. Grab her from behind, rip the Spandex off 'Doggy Style' no gotta relax, hell, I had five hours of sex, not 13 hours earlier.

Following her as she rolled up to a refreshment stand with half a dozen fixed tables, benches, a mini food court, confections a small line in front of the vegetarian deli called 'Veggys' this is where her fine ass posterior was deposited. Stopped, as did I… just within grasp of those buttocks!

Whitney said, "Tank, I only had a small breakfast. I'm going to buy some Veggy rolls. Can you go over to the juice bar and get us some drinks, please? I'll take care of the rolls, umh; you do like Veggy rolls, right?" I shook my head affirmatively "what kind of drink would you like?" smiling exclaimed, "something with cranberry in it, of course" showing me a brand-new asset to appraise curvy dimples!

This is where it must have shown or become clear that I had been incarcerated, uh, locked up for a long time, for I was almost obnoxiously bold and forthright. Not in the least did I even try to be cool, suave, um, debonair, nah, not a twitch of eloquence. We were enjoying our Veggy rolls; she sat across from me at a round small wobbly table. Like a gruff train's horn blowing in and out of a tunnel, "this is yummy Whitney, and so are you. I've never been with or dated a black lady before," shit. I let my words reverberate, listening back onto my statement couldn't take it back, damn. Ah, nor understand how or why I'd blurted that out ah crap. She only stared at me as I consequently stuffed a large bite of the Veggy roll into my big mouth.

Whitney didn't flinch; she only sucked on the red and white straw, provocatively took a napkin, and wiped just under her pert bottom lip, where I noticed a silver stud post, she had a damn tongue ring too! "Tank, which means we already have a few things in common besides being Rollerbladers and enjoying working out. I've never bedded a white man before." Giggling, then she moseyed on, "but by the look of you, there's more black on your skin than white uuhhh, at least from what I can see anyways, we're not dating, come on, slow down there, dude! Please, I only met you like 25 minutes ago. Your acting like a starving Wolf… Tank, just the size of you is scary, should I be wary of you now?"

I took my straw and sucked ferociously, restrain was needed. I stalled and slowed down, trying to regain my composure. Floated away into my mind as long as she allowed, we ate in silence. I was a convicted felon, and the only money I had was from my partners Mark and Joe, no job… without a future. How could I even get a job with the record that I had? Maybe a nominal trivial minimum wage job, indeed not a real money-making job, was out there for me no way. This subject matter hovered systemically at the edge of all my thoughts felt like I was on a U-turn maze, locked in and stereotyped. Ain't no way out of a life of crime of constantly living with a dark thundercloud layered above my head had no chance of a true-loving relationship. I was an outsider… outlaw. My cards had already been dealt and marked, all coming from the bottom of the deck!

"What are you thinking? Tank, you have been quiet, not like the person I've known for, let's say, 31 minutes." What did I have to lose? a firm decision to try and live my life with Integrity and honesty, I forged onward… "okay, what is troubling me was that I feel trapped like in that movie did you ever see 'Ground Hog day?' I'm living it!"

'Yes,' giggling, "I actually have that movie on a CD."

"I'm like the leading character in the movie stuck in a pattern of hopelessness. If I allowed myself to feel sorry for who or what I've become, it could devastate me, lead me to morose disillusionment straight down a shaft to a hellish depressive fugue."

Her perplexed scowl of unnaturalness, eyes wide, "why is that? Do you really think it's too late to alter your destiny, Tank?"

Leaning back, bringing my left hand to my chin in retrospect, I felt a baby twinge of rushing emotions fighting to the surface of my pupils Wthell was happening to me? I purposely bit my finger. "Whew… Whitney, look at me, all the ink I'm labeled uh tarnished pigeonholed. It's all my doing. Tell me why are you still sitting next to me. You must realize that I'm a predator. All I want is to penetrate you, not make love as much as pound you into blissful oblivion sex, uh, there I said it!"

I had her backpedaling, so I continued my leveraged momentum. "I'm an untypical shallow horny man who envisions you as an object, a piece of meat-not a Veggy snack!"

To my utter and ultimate delight, she laughed hilariously, "Aah, not a Veggy snack, huh? Let me address the former Tank… before your outbreak. The coloration pigmentation of your skin certainly is excessive. My body is black all over. Evidently, you got your tats in prison?" She reached across the small table and took up my right arm "this is why I stopped at the bench you were sitting at alone, watching the families swinging merrily. I saw 'Ephesians 5:6-17' one of my all-time favorite Bible verses, on your forearm. Life is just a series of decisions, some of which can seem small and inconsequential… while others could permanently change the course of your destiny. Um, life to me is sort of like making choices, major and minor decisions; life equals the sum of those choices. We're inside a labyrinth, um, maze. Most times, it's never too late to change your direction; Tank!"

Suddenly just as fast as she appeared at the bench, she stood up, looking at her phone that she'd pulled from a fanny pack around those voluptuous hips "gotta go, it was splendid, umh nice to have met you, Tank." "Wait, no, please, for Christ's sake, I'm having a real conversation with you. Don't you want to know why I had inked this Bible verse pointing at my right forearm proverb aligned with… I'm not finished. Let me see you again, Whitney. Can we meet? Ugh, a get-together for dinner. Promise no ulterior motives, uhm, listen, full clarity and transparency. I was just released from San Quentin last week!" I bowed my head in assuagement, knowing farewell there wasn't any mollification or mitigating my last words like Seeya!

Whitney stalled, rubbed the palm of her right hand across her forehead all the way down to her cleft chin, keeping direct non-wavering eye contact, opened her mouth, says, "look, I have to be at work in less than 35-minutes, so I have to go sorry good luck Tank!"

I didn't remember standing up. Next thing you know, I held her hand without pressure "where do you work?" "a clothing boutique on 3rd Ave and El Camino Real Blvd." "What's the name of it?" Whitney smiles, dominating the distance in inches between us. "I really have to go now!" "Let me have your phone number, please," as if honestly begging by this point, umh, guess I was... Her pert lips parted, releasing a sigh and an undecipherable mumble; I heard somethin to the effect. "I hope I'm not going to regret this?" Reaching into her wallet "here's my card. Text me your full name, Tank I will Google you; we can go from there... now I really have to Roll!" She slides her hand from my grasp, rollerblading away with a fluttering look, and waves back her braids... gone.

Wow, I felt like I'd climbed Mt. Everest and done something great, soothing my seething mind, now neutralized. I dropped our remains into a waste basket, pulled out my iPhone, and texted her my full name, Tank Shaw. That was it, probably the last of that girl... brief laconic, precise, and concise. I'll see if this leads anywhere. I yank out the Tracfone, reading a text, 'Wtf is wrong with you, Tank? I needed you in Marin County like yesterday. Call me immediately,' ordered my friend Joe... 'so what could I do?... I called Joe!'

-35-

<u>Sammy and Joe at a hotel in San Rafael.</u>

I was just drying off from a warm shower and had some unfulfilling sex, um, awful if I wanted to admit it, barely able to sustain a half a hard-on, although Samantha worked 'hard-aah soft' at it in the end. I guess I got what I needed a stress release climax, unsure about her... as if I really cared. Backtracking, "hey girl," she followed me out of the shower, "did you get off?" "no, Joe, but it's all right. I'm preoccupied like you and paranoid ugh, the guy who checked us in last night spent too much time staring at us!"

I reflectively looked at the sweating pistol by the sink and stepped from the light steam. Motel 6 was where we were not 13 miles from the RV... music pervaded the room. <u>'Who let the dogs out,' a tune recorded by 'Baha Men'</u> alerted me... being my phone's ringer. I yelled abrasively, 'finally, their calling.' I dropped my *towel in seven strides and had the Tracfone on my ear. "Wtf is wrong with you, Tank? AWOL, you're lucky to be out, dude. This is the way you thank Mark and me. We're not playing games. Haven't you been paying attention to the media, TV, and news online, dude?"*

No retort, nothing, but I heard him breathing, or was it him? Hell, I just jumped down his throat, uhm could be... 'hello ahh hello, Tank, you there?' "Yeah, Joe, it's... um-me, what?" "I need you to get over to Marin County like now." I inhaled some much-needed oxygen, tried to calm down, and continued; the last thing I wanted was for Tank to get all worked up. Despite the perilous hell Sammy and I were buried under, not speaking with Tank since he got out of San Quentin, I needed to reverse my methodology. Take a softer approach, for momma taught me yuh get more with sugar than vinegar!'

"Hey, it's nice to hear your voice, bro... sorry for yelling, just stressed out, uh, shit hitting the fan is all. Are you at the apartment in San Jose?" "No, the Feds have been all over me. They just searched the apartment and have been on my ass constantly, shadows of stupidity, blatantly obvious. Like just par for the course, we figured Joe they'd be tailing me like we suspected they haven't let us down, just did a piss test at the courthouse this morning and went to the park for some exercise, with Agent Dufus watching me oh, and about last night I'm sorry bro I was getting laid, nearly an all-nighter. I haven't had phones on nor perused online news, nothing, just was into self-satisfaction! Hell, you've been there before as well as Mark... so relax, I'm back in the fold!"

"I am happy for you, Tank. You're correct. I have been in your shoes. Once I breathed freedom, getting laid was high up on my list. No worries, one thing you'll figure out sooner than later is that it's a lot more stressful out here on the streets. No, you don't have to be wary of someone stabbing you; it's more like mental stress... monies, how we're going to survive in this real world, the nuances of dealing with people of all varieties, at least in prison, all was handed to us... food, clothing, you know...." "Joe, let's cut to the chase. What do you need of me, from me, and how is Mark doing?" I didn't bother in saying I hadn't heard from Mark, yes, unless he was on Lake Shasta on his houseboat at a cove with no signal... something felt wrong.

"All right, when are you supposed to see your Parole agent again?" A rumbling sound drowned my words out. "I didn't hear you, Joe. I'm outside by a main road, trucks everywhere, and there's a Truckstop across the street." "What a coincidence; go online, get familiar with the Shell Truckstop in Novato, then take down this number. I'll text it to you, oh, most likely. The Feds are tracking your car, so be aware of that. The contact name at the 'chop shop' is Van. Van will hook you up... of course, try not to be followed. Most likely, they have a GPS chip on your car. Try to..." 'Oh no,' shouts Sammy from behind Joe; he quickly spins around, pointing a 357 magnum in her direction. She ducks then breathes again, "don't scare me, woman... shit!"

"Super bad news Joe from that blogger 'SFPD*'" "what did they find the RV?" she spun around and showed me her laptop, which had the picture of our RV on the screen undisturbed. Hearing a garbled sound damn left Tank on hold, picked the phone back up, "call Van. He will give you clean transportation, then make it over the Golden Gate, then call me!" click.

"I'm telling you, this guy SFPD* doesn't sleep has been posting on his blog all night. He's driving around hunting the RV hell; they've increased reward money to $55,000."

"Sammy, could you make us some more coffee, please?" 'Sure,' I flipped on my iPad, checking if Mark's connections with a group of Cyberhackers who worked on the Dark Web could be of use to see if they had any information on the current dilemma we were engrossed within. I had thrown out a few bitcoins for a tease a few hours back. Bing-ding some paid-for information was a click away... "geez, get a load of this girl, ugh, Sam, it isn't a 'He' actually SFPD* is a 33-year-old female whose husband is a 49-year-old detective in the San Francisco police department."

He's giving her Real-time, credible information. They're after the cash reward, no doubt!"

She only nods, handing me a hot cup of coffee, then reapproaches me holding up her laptop, clicking and highlighting a section of the fast-moving blog messages 'there working section by section hunting for the damn RV' despair was obviously felt by both of us.

I continued scanning down the pages sent to me, 'Law Enforcement has yet to be able to sharpen the pictures of the couple in the RV. This was about 77 minutes ago. Now the blog participants numbered more than 11,000 logged in and growing exponentially. Another post by our nemesis SFPD* 3 minutes prior (a suspected link to the homicide in Sacramento 'Bolo' search initiated for 2 KTM 1290 motorcycles black in color, possibly a blonde woman rider.) I clicked on the link. Oh crap, there was a police cam video of Sammy riding through the Chili's shopping center doing an impressive wheelie in and out of the lot. This was only moments after I had shot the P.I. dead. The piece of shit got what was coming. I clicked on another highlighted title then an interview popped up of a busboy from Chili's 'yeah, both bikes were the same' this jolted me to my feet.

"Geezus Sam, our bikes are…" she stood up nervously and opened the curtains looking back at me 'Joe' pointing, "there are our bikes under the shade tree if the searchers start checking out; hotels were sitting ducks here!" Strangely eerily, I felt like we were part of a Horror film watching the screen in a movie theater… the audience all knew the outcome of the poor scared girl hiding behind a cabinet, as Freddy snuck up on her to decapitate her lovely blonde head.

Approximately 25 minutes later, we were ready to get the heck outta the hotel; one last scan of the hotels parking lot sent shivers up and down our spines, and trouble-like premonitions came to viral life a Marin County Sheriff was on a direct line towards our motorcycles, we quickly exited stage left with our belongings wrapped around our shoulders, the only difference was now Sammy had holstered my other weapon a Sig Sauer

9 mm fully automatic.

Down the steps out across the street, timing is everything in life. My mantra, we were blessed, must be doing God's bidding, lol, for a Marin Transit bus stopped not 35 feet away at the designated bus bench sign. As nonchalant as was humanly possible, hearts beating in unison 'rapidly,' I paid. We found the back of the bus, and our destination was downtown San Rafael.

-36-

<u>Agents Baker and Avery.</u>

"Avery, I've been saying this all along. This is a waste of time and manpower. He can't escape us with the chip in his glute, so why am I following his Impala?" "Baker, come on, please, how many times have you and I discussed this? I'm not the boss, contact Lori or Rico, but I'm in their camp, sure the chip shows us where he's at but not what he's doing or whom he's meeting with. Call me back if anything changes. I am super busy here breaking down pictures and video trying to enhance all the distorted pictures of the perps in the motorhome." click.

Baker shook his head with feelings of being taken for granted and neglected. This job of following a chipped man was for a lowly police cadet or a 1st year Agent at best, not a person with his credentials relegated to following a criminal that anyone could see move about on a tracking screen Tank Shaw was going nowhere, without our knowledge.

Agent Tom Baker's home life had evaporated three years back; his wife had complained for years about him not being married to her, but to his job, complaining and bitching were a constant annoyance. That progressed into threats that he'd not taken seriously, one evening tired as hell after doing another all-nighter for the FBI, the house was empty, the kids were gone, and all that was left was his stuff, not even a note.

Divorce was initiated; it had been a hellish three years; visitation with his three children was without reward... all they wanted to do after being dropped off at his house was go back to their mommy.

Perhaps he's miscalculated his life. He wasn't valuable like his partner, Bill Avery.

The 'goody2 shoed tech wizard.' Tom was the low man on the totem pole even though he graduated from the academy a few years before his team. Lori Parks did have about three months of seniority on him, he didn't have anything against the other team members... Kelsey Marie had the sex appeal he'd liked her. She was in the hospital with Agent Rodriguez, a good man.

He checked out his bleeding sore cuticles, resorted to biting and tearing at his fingernails, hiding them from others because of embarrassment, and wondered if it showed that he was overly anxious or insecure and undisciplined. Staring into the rear-view mirror, he mused now that he wouldn't have minded being in the hospital like Kelsey having been shot, at least, I'd have some sympathy. There'd be some people who cared who'd empathize with my situation. At least being shot, I'd had some value; uh, what am I thinking? Tom said aloud, 'I need some action, that's what I need,' not put out to pasture with this worthless task of following a loser, umh, I'm sick.

It was getting warm in downtown San Jose, staring out at the concrete and asphalt jungle, the pavement insolating and insulating the heat that emanated from the sun. There were buildings as far as he could see. Tom rolled up the window in his police interceptor cruiser and flipped on the air-conditioning. He yawned at the same time and glanced at his wristwatch. Agent Roble was due to replace him in just under three hours in the reconnaissance of Tank, a useless waste of resources.

He scanned the ongoing updates of the investigation in San Rafael on his phone. That was where he wanted to be involved in the search for the perpetrators that drove the RV, the manhunt that he should be the Lead dog on. Word around his world of Agents, his reputation tainted unfairly from his past aggressive arrests, rumors ratcheted up bullshit that he was to 'Gung-Ho' a loose cannon. Screw it all stemmed from him standing up for himself, quarreling with the FBI review board, remembering sitting across the counter in Sacramento at the Fed building trying to push away, squelching the supervisor's scathing attacks on him. Not even Rico stood up for him.

Yes, his attitude had drastically nose-dived after the divorce; that was when the first written complaints started showing up on his desk; other Agents he'd worked with had said all he was about was spewing negativity. One even called him garrulously rude, annoyingly talkative like a Chatty Cathy motormouth, refusing to work with me.

He rips a hangnail out of his thumb and snatches up the mini set of binoculars. Finally, Tank was leaving Whitney's Boutique. It had been like 45 minutes since he'd entered the woman's clothing store. Strangely he didn't leave with a shopping bag, and then he saw her step out under the awning, a beautiful black lady, ahh yeah, the rollerblader Tank had been with at the café in the park. Checking his log, he only had 95 minutes to go and off work. These 12-hour shifts were killing him.

Trailing Tanks Impala again, Tom almost chuckles. The dude would have to be an imbecile not to know he wasn't being tailed. Staying about five blocks behind, the Impala enters an industrial area with welding shops, auto body repairs, heavy equipment, and mechanic shops warehouses everywhere. Baker parked behind a cyclone steel fence and watched Tank walk from the street, stepping over a curb looking for work; employment was Agent Tom Bakers' educated guess. Having scrutinized his work history and the files from the Probation Department Tank was a certified Tig, Mig, and Arc welder. The itch struck him again. Feeling bored opening the car door, he thought about calling the ex-wife and maybe being allowed to speak to his children, phone to his ear, optimism of hearing familiar voices. <u>'That was the last thing he could recall, Nada; Agent Lori Parks stood over him, badgering him, 'where was he? What's going on?' 'You're in the hospital, Tom!'</u>

Tom clenched his teeth, grabbed the rail of the gurney gulped some oxygen "hospital, what, how, why did I have a heart attack? What happened?" Shaking his frazzled hair with unnecessary vigor, rolling his eyes. "You took a tranquilizer dart in your back and have been knocked out for over seven hours!" Agent Parks turned to another Agent delegating to her, "get his full report online with a hard copy on Director Firm's desk and C.C. Agent Rico Captor, I want this accomplished in the next hour." 'Yes, Ma'am.'

Lori says, "you take care, I'll check back…" "but wait, Lori, stop," he begged… she was gone.

Tom still couldn't focus, had blurred vision and a massive headache, and was dehydrated, laid back, closing his eyes, then noises of people by his gurney. He could only listen to the two Agents he didn't know; the more he'd learned of how he was found on the pavement with his phone clutched in his left hand. The greater degree of embarrassment a video in the cruiser relayed all real-time to the department until it was disabled, a homeless woman obviously disguised a fkn set-up. Baker was stripped entirely naked, laying on his back with not a stitch of clothing, not even his freakin socks. His wallet, watch, and weapons were stolen, along with his computer and his bulletproof vest. Worst yet, everything in the car, including the brand-new Ford Police Interceptor, was missing, gone, stolen, the GPS tracker thrown in a dumpster a mile away from his nude body.

The pair of Agents were snickering; one stated, 'that fkn would never happen to me.' The other laughed, 'sshhh.' Despite the cool, regulated temperature in the hospital room, Tom was sweating profusely. The sheets already felt clammy, vowing to himself that he'd shoot Tank dead between his eyes the first chance he got.

Joe, Sammy, with Tank on the way.

I was finally approaching the World-famous Golden Gate Bridge in a used Caddy Escalade, mulled over what intensely took precedence over my conscious state, not the conversations with Joe. But ruminated, contemplating my reactions to and with Whitney, specifically the internal feelings guided by an abnormal attraction such as love at first sight, realizing how nonsensical that was. Strangely it wasn't just a sexual thing. She seemed to be able to relate to him. Tank felt different around her, even though he'd spent barely over an hour with the lady at the park, but hey, they did have a fun conversation at her store. Tank grinned wide ahh, hell… okay, kind of like teenage days, I had a severe crush on Whitney. It had to be because of his institutionalized mental state from incarceration.

I knew I had to eliminate her from the ongoing equation, yet my mind kept drifting back to her. Uh damnit, stay focused… I bit my lip.

Being on a mission now for Joe and Mark, I had to compartmentalize my objectives categorically, step by step, and deny myself the pleasure centers in my amygdala, uhm, brain. I was comprehending my given circumstances and knowing farewell. Whitney was only a distraction; I didn't have a chance in hell of being with her in a long-lasting relationship. One of my most underappreciated attributes was how I could zone in and out of my mind. A supernatural competence to fully manifest my being within a current event, uh, situation, I become one and the same cogitatively like drawn into a meditational trance. This was how I lived in my cell in prison, always working with my inner being… spirit.

I had an instinctive notion of intuition unique like I had a Guardian Angel influencing me. I started laughing out loud at this revelry; gosh, I am not sane. I live in my own world of Grandiosity.

I slammed the brakes down, and whoa went from 67 mph to zero within seconds. The car on my ass swerved sideways to avoid my back bumper, tearing me away from reflection. Traffic sucked; I'd dreamed of buying and flying one of those Ultralights fly over the masses of humanity in my own mini chopper.

I was now in a better mood, thinking of how I had lost the FBI guy, going in reverse about 2 hours before, my face smiling. Everything went smoothly. Escorted into a warehouse, a Chop Shop that was owned by a man named 'Van' stolen vehicles, cutting into pieces, parts rebuilding and redistributing the Vin-numbers, re-sale of clean papered cars and trucks, a well-oiled business.

I was quickly strip-searched at the shop to ensure I wasn't hiding a bug or listening device before being introduced to Van, who had been in contact with Joe via text... in less than 15 minutes. They had me in the Escalade, and the rolling steel doors re-tracked. I was on my way. No bugs or GPS on the Caddy. Having inquired about the Agent that followed me into the industrial complex, Van only cackled. Ugh, he will live... No worries.

For an odd reason, Whitney was trespassing on my thoughts; I had to remain focused because if I let my mind drift... not be engaged in the task at hand it could become dangerous for me. Ugh, the idea of her threatened to dislodge or thwart the tunnel vision that was essential for me to be able to overcome any upcoming obstacles. I needed to remain vigilant... had to maintain a locked jaw mantra.

Squeezing my eyelids tight, blinking with a roll of my shoulders, umh, if it were meant to be, then it would cum to fruition, shoving the dinner date with Whitney aside for the following evening 'Focus,' I repeated aloud, Concentrate Tank!

Back to the task at hand... The plan was to meet at <u>San Rafael Joes, Restaurant</u> on 4th Street... yup, apropos to pick up one of my lifelong pals and best friends, 'Joe!' ironic indeed.

"How long, Joe, do we have to wait here? The server is giving us the evil eye. He wants to turn the table over. We're like camping here." Taking money from his pocket. Joe peeked above his phone screen and waved, gesturing for service. I watched Joe hand him a twenty-dollar bill 'could we have a refill of our iced tea, please sorry, we're taking up your table, but we're waiting on a friend,' the server grinned, snatching the money up. 'No problem, man BRB, 'be right back,' Joe peered over at me. "Sammy, problem solved."

Meanwhile, I went back to work on the iPad expecting the proverbial shit to be flung from the fan at any moment, and it wasn't if they would find the RV; no, it was only a matter of time before they did. SFPD* was still at it… again posting on her blog. She must have Meth or speed or incredibly strong Java to keep at it for so long.

A group of bloggers continued the orchestrated sector-by-sector search, using citizens in airplanes and ultralights. The investigation, including all details, had gone into the viral mode, unfortunately for us.

My nose was itching, so I reached into my small purse and yanked out a compact mirror, shocked at first glance that I'd messed up as I stared at my face. I was like shocked sideways, forgetting my metamorphosis… coal black hair so dark it seemed alien to me. That wasn't the alarming image, only part of it. I still had blonde eyebrows fk forgot to dye them… stupid. I'm going to have to head to the bathroom to use some dark mascara to match the Raven hair. It wasn't natural for me; I was like bleached out to white and needed a tan… ahh, to hell with it.

Leaving Joe with a short explanation, his features included a fake mustache hair of darkened brown. Why hadn't he noticed that I'd dyed my hair earlier before leaving the hotel in a tizzy and forgetting to dye my blonde eyebrows? How incongruent was a woman with dark brunette hair and blonde eyebrows, umh, lashes? Well, I guess not so in this society, as

I see a woman with pink hair across the dining room and another with fluorescent green.

But being a sensitive prostitute, I realized sort of a dichotomy or one of those types of words. Joe not noticing or saying anything about my mistaken dye job spoke volumes, increasing my already fragile existence umh insecurity was dashing within rampantly. He didn't notice because he cared zilch, ugh, zero about me.

I was like a living liability to Joe, better off dead, yep, pushing my already destined bad luck "hey Joe, I heard you talking with your friends who's on the way to pick 'You' up… yuh never mentioned me never said to him that you, aah that there were two of us, why?"

"Sammy fkn relax. It's way better not to complicate things. Tank is a cut-and-dry type of individual who wouldn't want to get into a lengthy monologue about you, and he's all business. Sweet stuff, geez, calm down. It's all going to be okay!"

"Easy for you to say I'm the odd girl out when they find the Motorhome, my life ain't worth a dime-my DNA is…." "Sam, that's the first task on my agenda," as he shifted his sunglasses underneath the brim of his fedora. "Look at me, Joe, what do you see that's not right?" he paused from his phone's screen-smiling and said, "I see a few more worry lines, babe… you're still hot as fire even with your Raven black hair."

"My eyebrows, asshole look at them, will ya? Are you fkn blind or don't give a Rats ass about me, uhm, or possibly both." "Chill, keep it down. People are staring in our direction; calm down, of course, I see your brows, umh I only didn't want you to stress or panic is why I didn't say anything, girl!"

"Fk Joe, your good dude, but not good enough. That was a horrible attempt to clean it up. Nice adlib, actually, you suck, your such a Con man liar; what's the real plan for me? Should I get up and leave this table now, leave town right the fk now?" Yeah, I was angry and not afraid of the Serial Killer who sat perplexed, locked into my pupils.

His arms opened broad palms up on our table, to my utter surprise. "I got an extra 5 C-notes you can have, $500.00 that should help you get on your way back to Sac-town!" I watched him peel the crisp greenbacks from his wallet and placed them on the table within my grasp. "You go girl and Good luck. I'd say stay in touch, but I don't think that's a good idea."

I placed my hands over the money, swooped it up, pushed my chair out, and sauntered away. His eyes never diverted steady Blue as the Caribbean Sea, sturdy and serene, like a mountain lake. The host held the front doors open; I stepped down and out of the Restaurant onto the sidewalk of 4th street, which was bustling like always. People were out in force, everyone going somewhere, not me. As I looked into the restaurant's large windows from the sidewalk, an urge to take off running squelched. Joe couldn't see me, nor did it seem he even cared if I left, never to see him again.

I was seriously weighted down backpack stuffed satchel, a suitcase with rollers that had once been attached to the motorcycle. My oversized purse had to weigh 25 pounds; what stopped me from Zipping away? Slapping my rosy cheeks was the caustic truth; holding me back was the DNA in the RV. Sure, I could explain to the cops and tell them that I have proof on camera that Joe killed the P.I. and murdered my Pimp and his brother-um, what could I do? Joe had kidnapped me, drugged me, and raped me!

Wrong, they have me in the parking lot of Chili's on the bike, possibly having proof that I was an accomplice and conspirator in the Chili's killing.

He had to admit to himself... nope wasn't surprised that Sammy would 'take the money and run. She was like a polliwog out of water. He shook his head negatively, ruminating almost with an ache in his heart, damnit, he had to admit it. He'd become rather fond of the Whore, umh kind of a stigmatizing word Whore, but wasn't that who Sammy was, uhm, a prostitute? Nevertheless, he enjoyed her companionship. Well, she wouldn't get far. The GPS chip was lodged in a seam in her leather jacket. Lol!

Standing across the street, kitty-cornered with a vantage point to watch the front door of where I'd just left a guy who was Massive, not in height so much but in width, tattoos marking his skin all over his arms, up his neck, sunglasses a seriously mean looking Alpha Male the man had a charisma about him. Confidence exuded his entire persona, and he was a dominating omnipotent sort of fella. She watched him swing open the solid wooden Restaurant doors with ease. This had to be Joe's contact.

I waited, deciding which was the best alternative for me, go it alone or reenter San Rafael Joes Restaurant. Not a choice, really; I did the latter. Walking back into the lobby, the big guy was standing alone in a corner, staring into the dining room. I followed his eyes, and I didn't see Joe either; then Joe strutted out of the bathroom hallway. The big man brushed by me in a hurry. I waited heck and had to pee, so I hit the lady's room… my phone vibrated, and I saw the screen. It was a text from Joe. 'I see you, Sam; he's here. Join us, please.' That was it, I thought. I might as well meet this Tank guy that I'd heard so much about then a second text flashes, 'hey Sammy, second thought, please watch the front door and make sure Tank wasn't followed.' I texted back, 'Sure thing.' I dropped back outside to become a part of the pedestrian crown back on 4th street. I reworked my eyebrows and did as Joe had asked.

-38-

<u>Agent Rico Captor and Director Tanya Firm.</u>

'Take the Central exit,' San Rafael, she orders; her tone hasn't changed much and still has nasty edges to it. I flinch whenever Lori's voice comes over the radio because Tanya's adverse reaction is unhidden.

A hesitation as the cab of the mobile unit heats up, wondering how it really works in this hectic life of good and evil, all describing adjectives used with varying degrees of attainment of which word corresponds best to the individual's inner conscious. There are no parameters or guidelines to adhere to. How is it that Tanya is jealous we only had a brief form of a relationship such as I had with her twin sister Sandra back in Wash. D.C. Uh, why can't it be like a 'Booty call' service call for human releases of emotions with comfort just a physical release to sort of 'Clean out the Pipes!' Am

I shallow, or just a real person without hidden agendas? Whatever will be will be… so be it. ☺.

I was driving on 4th street, turning left onto a one-way road that was on 3rd street. The 35-foot RV FBI mobile unit handled surprisingly well. Tanya looked over at him, thinking he must be looking for somewhere to park, not easy on these busy streets.

"Tanya, we need to keep the Agents way out of view; you saw what happened to Agent Baker. Still, I don't understand why you had Tank Shaw tailed. He has a GPS Chip embedded in his glute with a range of about 50 miles or so, right?" She flipped her hair around, adding a disgruntled expression. "I've explained my reasoning. Let's not go backward now that we have seven Agents on the ground in downtown San Rafael with locals as backups."

Back in regress, as I mused, mistakes, duh; it's true having sex with your boss can only complicate things for a while blissful fun maybe, personal trauma can result… evolve if the boss becomes possessive and controlling like I'm a proprietary piece of Italian Sausage!

The ambiance was stifling. A question is still on the tip of my tongue, should I just spit it out and confront her immaturity, suspicions, and jealousy? Never have I been a man to shy away from conflict, a protagonist, a macho man taking on adversity head-on. Hell, I could repeat what I'd said, 'nothing happened between Lori and me.' But what if she asks, 'if I didn't show up when I did, you both would have been in compromising positions. Face it… she was hot to trot out to fk you, Rico.' Then I'd reply it takes two to party, uhm, Tango, right?

Is a person guilty for thinking or fantasizing about what it would be like to have sex or make love to another human? What am I guilty of… for imaginative wondering lusting with pent-up desires and unfulfilled fantasy of seeing a luscious woman that gives me a 'head rush' to visualize or envision? Wondering how it would feel to have her legs wrapped around me as we grinded together in loving motion.

On the other edge of the coin, is it wrong to have been in a sexual relationship for years and want to spice it up a touch a bit, kind of like foreplay we watch a selective Porn show either together or apart, bringing a new form of arousal um lustful expedience to the love scene. Um, that's what bothered me the most about Tanya. She was an avid porn watcher; she'd get all hot and bothered and jump my bones. Some people were so insecure that they didn't want their lovers to watch others having sex, for they'd immaturely thought that they weren't as desirable as the porn actors. That's what she said to me when she played one of her favorite porn scenes. So with that being thought of, why the hell is she jealous of Lori? Huh, it doesn't make a lick of sense. Tanya was an advocate… watching porn to heighten the sexual desire for loving your mate. Is this aligned with cheating, like many sheltered or shallow humans believe, with mates hiding like roaches watching these perverted videos? The jury is out for me. I must divulge that it was fun for us to take in a romantic love scene together in 'sexual loving lust.'

I guess we're all guilty for what we think or imagine, like a superior being is taking notes on our demented thoughts. Ahh, Soap in the mouth bad Boy I … "Yikes, Rico, whoa man, you nearly ran that lady off the road. What's wrong with you? Where the hell are you at? Get with it. You haven't said nary one word" shouted Tanya.

"Rico, fast, find a damn parking spot. He's on foot; Tank is walking down 4th street now." She was working on her phone, the iPad on her lap, and the radio coordinating the Agents on the ground. I found a parking space large enough to parallel park the monster 35 ft mobile unit, then peered over at the Dot that represented Tank flashing, slowly moving on a 3-dimensional map of the downtown San Rafael area detailing the current names of the shops accurately with addresses applied.

Agent Avery was in his cubby hole with five screens running in a swivel captain's chair that took up most of the walkway in the rears of the mobile unit 'check this out,' he yelled towards Tanya and me. "These are all the cameras that I've been able to access or Hi-Jack on 3rd and 4th street…

there he was, Tank Shaw." We watched his deliberate pace strutting purposefully. Our Agents managed loose surveillance. This time our agents are not getting within a block of him. We'd been compromised with Agent Tom Baker still in the hospital.

Lately, I have been feeling odd, not like myself in so many ways, not yet 45 years old, feeling weird, overanxious, not panic-stricken, almost anxiety-based nervousness. Too young for 'Manapause?' Was it a lack of secreting Testosterone? Chewing on the inside of my mouth, ominous feelings of preoccupied tumultuousness like a tempest wailing far out at sea, then invariably turning directions like an edge on a dime heading for shore. I was in a rowboat in a devastating storm in its wake, concentration, and my focus was elsewhere. Lost at sea was I … a step behind where I'd typically be… past tense. Circumstantial evidence has hung many enslaved people tortured many innocent civilians, and people convicted and sent to death row because of word by mouth the witness with ulterior motives. I felt, without corroboration, that the Sniper in the RV we have yet to find was none other than Joe Sable, although we'd not had substantiated proof. Whom I wanted to get my hands on was this Joe's lifelong pal Mark Feral.

Agent Avery had tried every techno gadget he was aware of. All the tricks in the trade scoured the tech manuals written and unwritten on the Dark Web. But the blurred photos of the motorhome driver couldn't be confirmed to be that of Joe. The RV and KTM motorcycles were registered to a phony name, Ben Abbott, a similar female rider assumed, or a smallish male was seen at the P.I. slaying and a Napa shopping center and no doubt a blonde alongside the driver of the RV. So maybe we should be on the lookout for a petite blonde as well? Facts that we did have; Mark had put a hit on Wendi Feral. It would make sense that his partner and bro killed Nurse Spike for advantageous dual objectives… point one, to silence him and, secondly, not have to pay him the final installment of $25,000. It all made sense. Of course, Mark's most hated nemesis, his sister Wendi was supposed to be killed by the nurse. What I believed was not substantiated had no valid proof, hypothetical speculation. We did have circumstantial evidence thus far. Screaming in my very inner core was the reality that now the 3rd amigo Tank had reentered the fray in Marin County. If my assumptions that have influenced my boss Tanya to get on board are accurate, Tank will meet Mark Feral or Joe Sable this afternoon!

With that being Masterminded out, the net we used had to be untethered loose fitting, unrestrictive we were only to observe, leery because with a bout of 'premature ejaculation,' all could be spent, lost until later regained, the tail trail cold. We were confident that Tank couldn't escape us with the glute chip beneath his epidermis, but our objectives were to capture two of the most notorious scheming killers, who were regular stays on the FBI's 10 most wanted list!

Rico felt it was useless to fight his heart's strings. It was like chasing my tail, a sick convoluted soul I surrender again dwelling in my mind, another struggle I couldn't avoid. It's the beautiful, intelligent, and witty girl of my dreams that I've harbored. Our melded hearts only once conjoined, yet he remained tethered to her spirit. <u>His so-called Soul Mate, 'Wendi Feral,'</u> had to conclude he loved her to death. She is my dream wife and destined lover. Hopefully, we will ride into the sunset. Yeah, a definite age difference, but age didn't matter. I told myself she's like a decade plus my junior. He was happy she was safe for now at 'NIA' geez, pinching my skin, I need to focus.

I reached into the mini fridge and grabbed a tall boy 'sugar-free Red Bull' maybe this will help?

<u>Joe and Tank, with sidekick Sammy… watching the entrance to the restaurant.</u>

I'm standing under an overhang watching from across the street for anyone suspicious who could be tailing Tank. Nothing out of the ordinary; I scanned the crowds earlier, staying on point, not wanting to draw any attention to me. Dusk was on its way… time was 4:55 pm, another mild Marin

County day, 77 degrees. Pushed send on a text 'everything looks fine' seconds later, Joe texts back 'Good.'

'Oh, Fk' a too fast inhalation, nearly choking on oxygen and my saliva, wait… what/ where? I'd spied that same white and black vehicle-nah, oh shit yeah, on video replays from the Shell Truckstop. It's the same one, uh-oohhh, it is the FBI tactical mobile unit that just slinked down an alley. Screw the texts I phoned straight through. He answers before 1/3 of a ring reverberates 'What?' "Just saw the FBI mobile unit" click, he was gone. From down and across the street, I watched Joe with his gear step out on the sidewalk… seeing me. He rolled his shoulders for me to follow… off I went.

Later I found out that Tank had argued with my assertion and said point blank to Joe that he wasn't followed, ain't no way! The Escalade was scanned thoroughly and wanded for GPS trackers. I am clean, no chance of being tailed, Joe… even so, Joe had said, 'better safe than sorry' and bolted out the restaurant's side door.

Tank, remained inside the establishment until Joe disappeared, then ventured out, trying not to stress; hell, he was freed from San Quentin on Parole. Tank's heart was racing, denying him any semblance of normalcy, instantly sweating from Joe's reactions. I had to come to grips with the fact that it had been years since I felt like this and was 101% positive I didn't like this feeling again, like Deja-vu. Shoot, if I was guilty of anything, it was being with Joe and ex-felon; I found the parking garage and finally popped the doors of the Caddy. No one around but a mother with three kids, five slots down. Joe was being paranoid, although if I were in his shoes, I'd be the same. I put down the business card he'd given me on the center console. Written on it were a Code and the directions to the motorhome just before he scampered out the door. I was on a mission, and the sooner it was completed, the sooner I could get back to San Jose my date with Whitney tomorrow night was all I looked forward to.

I punched in the GPS coordinates on the card and took Hwy 101 North not a single vehicle was following me. I made a triple flip-flop, then passed the onramp three times, settled back, and stuck the cruise control on at 63 mph rear and side view mirrors clear of cops.

I'd spent perhaps five minutes with Joe when his phone had jangled, and then he spat out the final details handing me the card. He looked ravaged and worn down and out, cold blackish brown hair dyed, a beard with a fake mustache that couldn't hide his anxiety…he'd aged. On the side of the table where I sat was a 1/2 glass of iced tea on its way to melting, and on the rim was lipstick… hum!

We almost always worked alone. When I asked him about the lipstick on the glass of iced tea, he said it wasn't important… shrugged his shoulders, and changed the subject.

He had a way about him; I met him before we were barely teenagers some 25 years ago. The guy was a cold-blooded killer, no conscious indifferent sociopath who never had a girl for long, whores and prostitutes were his thing, a business transaction. The females he chose meant nothing to him. He neither liked them nor disliked them like Mark. They were always on the same page like a mantra… on this earth, women were made to produce pleasure… sex, uhm, subservient enslaved people doing their bidding.

I noticed a subtle change in Joe's disposition over the years. He had become more like Mark, not a hateful misogynist, just a man to use women like a commodity providing a service, not into the torture, mayhem, and the S&M lifestyle of our leader!

<u>Tanya and Rico in San Rafael tracking Tank.</u>

"Hey, Rico, what are you doing… why are we leaving?" Agent Avery answers from the back of the mobile unit. "While you were in the laboratory, Tanya… Mr. Tank Shaw had returned to his vehicle and is now driving towards the freeway, ma'am." "Cut the ma'am crap. How many times must I say that to you call me 'Tanya' Okay, ur, Southern upbringing is admirable, but…." "Ahh, we watched him go inside a Restaurant, then his movement stopped like he sat down or stood at the bar for uh hold on umh, he was in the restaurant for 5 min and 27 seconds, then he started

to move again on the tracking charts went right out the back door,"
said Avery.

"I have an Agent on her way to see if the Restaurant owner will
allow her to view the store's video. Meanwhile, Lori is behind Tank
by about a 1/2 mile. Our other colleagues are in loose pursuit. The
chopper is back up also," declares Rico.

Sam and Joe blended in with the other pedestrians, cruising down the sidewalk.

Joe and I made it up 5th street heading West where the rolling hills began again, he wasn't in a rush, not a panic-driven man, although I was drenched in sweat and wished I could strip to my underwear, and yet it couldn't be warmer than 75 degrees. I was hot under the hood stressing out over being locked up in prison for the rest of my natural or unnatural Life. Talkative Joe said nothing, just being slightly facetious with his few spoken phrases. He held up his arm ah hand in a stop sign mime pantomime. Of course, I obeyed instantly in my trained subservient ways; I looked to the side. We were at a bus stop counting us. Perhaps another seven waited on the bus nearby.

Joe was on the phone when a sliding door racked open in an extended Brown Chevy van out of nowhere. The driver had a matching Fedora with sunglasses, a look of grey with silver facial hair well groomed. He gestured to Joe. Saying zilch until we piled in and he put the van in gear, speaking over his shoulder, "I was told to pick up one guy, not a woman. What gives?" Uh 'another misogynist, I assumed; never jump to conclusions I'd learned a while later.'

"She is with me. I take full responsibility for her involvement." That was all Joe said as we made our way West, happy I had a bench seat to rest my rump on. Less than 35 minutes passed by, then, under the headlights, I saw a long-running black rod iron fence with spikes on the very top. We stopped at a likewise gate which opened by remote control.

The driver pulled into an extra-large garage in a husky voice, "this is one of our safe houses. Make yourselves comfortable; a meeting is called for at 8:45 pm. Then he, umh, 'she' stripped off the oversized overalls and hat off. Then she stripped off the sideburns and beard. Underneath her attire was motorcycle garb. She gave us a fleeting sarcastic smirk, whipped her right leg over a Harley Sportster 3-wheeler Trike, revved the motor, and drove out the same way she'd driven us in.

-39-

Mark and Joy at Winn-River Casino.

Resetting my predicament in my partially inebriated mind in reality, not so buzzed, I had only nursed three drinks in total. Lola was taking an inordinate amount of time in the lady's room. Whoever designed the bar and lounge area at this Casino had done a disservice to the bladders of the patrons uhm. Customers, the damn bathrooms were out of sight across the gambling tables, and the cacophonous unrelenting slot machines blowing out every octave and note you could imagine loudly obnoxious. Moments later it occurred to me, wow, most likely it wasn't an accident. The restrooms were so far off, probably designed impeccably, for, of course, the urge might grasp an inebriated soul to gamble after they relieve their pinging biological function!

I pretended not to envision what was blatantly wrong with the current situation around me. Yeah, I was surrounded by a security force. These bouncers looked like cops and were at the forefront of Joy, the Asian-Laotian beauty. That's when I recognized the tell-tale tiny wires snaking in and out of shirts and blouses into left ears; these were Police or, worse yet, the Feds.

The music restarted a true oldie again, but goody depending on your perspective, 'I shot the Sheriff' by 'Eric Clapton.' Sitting sideways on a stool, the crowd wasn't thinning out; as the clock ticked past 11 pm, even more partygoers were amassed.

I nonchalantly took the double shot of 'Meyers Rum' and poured it on top of Lola's drink, a Rum Runner not to spike it, only to help her loosen up a smidgen, a natural move by me, one which I'd completed uncountable times. Lola, where are you, honey? I think I see her from across the lounge. Nope, it was Joy beelining towards me with an effeminate strut. Alongside the petite frame of Joy were three humongous giants that looked seven feet tall, one of them with a Python-sized pony-stallion tail hanging down the back of his neck nearly to his waistline.

Let me remind myself again that I'm not one to be a panicky-nervous individual, no fear-stricken type of fella. It didn't hurt that I had my 15-inch shock stick made of hard rubber in my left hand on the other side of my leather vest, concealed but now firmly in my grasp. I didn't want to get caught with it, so I slinked it out slickly and pushed it under a table. A strain of the three… F's moving about in my brain like molasses, and everything slowed down, all movement happening at a snail's pace. I was in the… on-guard mode, analyzing intuition, 'Freeze, Flight or Fight' our human brains can never be matched by 'AI' computers and technology self-preservation strangely the human's strongest inherent instinct, certainly omnipotent omnipresent and omniscient with a singular caveat incomprehensibly aah indelibly I had zero fear of death… for dying was as natural as being birthed.

But never underestimate the Fight to survive against all odds. Relentless hate motivates me, not love. I allowed a cackle to leave my succulent lips. A simple equation flashed like math cards in 5th grade. If these Bozos knew I was # 5 on the FBI's most wanted list, the man none other than Mr. Mark Feral… Grandmaster blackish of belts, an innovator of Taekwondo, uh, if they had an inkling of whom I was, a Swat team would back up the Law Enforcement officers. Yeah, they'd be an Army of attackers to either capture me or kill yours truly.

Calm and collected, I released my grip from my drink and coolly displayed a wry, amused smirk. Joy missed nothing or missed everything, not sure. That depends on... "Mark, would you please accompany me? Let's not cause a scene." We looked around, and others were intrigued by whatever blew their dresses up. Most were still within their own personal agendas. Lola appeared from the corner of my eye. I proceeded to walk towards her with the Rum-Runner drink in my right hand. She took it from me and handed it to a giant guy.

I pondered, saying to the 3-some, 'hey, I didn't buy lard ass that drink' but only remained silent' several officers were in the rears. My newfound entourage didn't leave, and they stayed glued close. I followed the bums of Joy and Lola into a medium-sized conference room.

A giant who had held the door ajar opened his hippopotamus lips. "Sir, please stop right there...." I ceased to move while Joy spun on me. "We're special Agents for 'Indian Affairs' I'm Joy Silva. This is Lola Kim" she didn't bother introducing the real Indians nor the others in the room. They remained anonymous.' "Can you provide us with some identification, please, Mark?" "Sure, but first, humor me; why have you chosen me to pick on?" I slowly reached into my vest pocket and handed my fake-real I.D. to her Mark Blake; joy tapped the information into a Tablet and stepped away. Lola took charge 'Mr. Blake' would you mind if one of these gentlemen searches you, and would you be so kind as to submit to a body scan through our walk-through X-Ray unit?'

This was when I ceased to be compliant. "No, am I being arrested for something... you don't have the right to harass me. I am finished cooperating. I'm calling my attorney and leaving." I reached into my pocket and clutched my phone from the side of me. A male voice said, 'put that away' Joy added, "please, Mr. Blake give us just 5 minutes of your time. Then if all checks out, you can be back on the dance floor hooking up. No doubt the Casino will give you a $500.00 voucher for your inconvenience."

With certainty, I didn't want to cause a scene and be scrutinized by the authentic Feds hell, 5 minutes I could afford, and then I'd get the heck outta here never to return. 'Please have a seat' while the two women pull out chairs around a little table. I had time to count the group. There were nine of them in all that was excluding the three of them with badges that were now visibly exposed... Casino security.

Lola taps on her iPad and declares, "a Caucasian man who fits your description has been working the I-5 corridor, specifically our Indian Casinos from San Diego to Portland, Oregon. Rollin Hills Casino in Corning had a female abducted only three weeks ago. In all, there have been 13 victims with only one common denominator. All victims were of Asian descent. I will not go into particulars other than to say we are teamed up with a separate task force with the FBI who." She checks her timepiece "will be joining us in approx. Fifty-five minutes." I hoped my expression wasn't transparent, the fluttering of my heart or showing any nervous twitches; I maintained calmness while going 101 mph inside my skin the FBI was toxic for me, and even with my ample disguises and plastic surgeries, I still had to be wary.

Yes, full alert now, these Indians, Asians, and, ugh, wannabes wearing security uniforms had my fully erect and wired attention. The last thing I needed was the FBIs scrutinization of my property, financial accounts, and 'IRS' reiterating inside my skull a smidgeon of paranoia, even though my facial changes and plastic surgeries were splendid... if a trained surgeon ran their magnifier over my skin, there were little, tiny, microscopic white scars.

I needed to be gone before the Feds arrived, so I dropped the forcefield deciding to put on a display of Feral no, Blake charm. First, to warm into my academy award performance, I gasped loudly, which had the effect of some men reaching into their oversized jackets. Joy and Lola lunged backward, tipping their chairs on two legs. I repeated what was just told me, like, "omg, 13 ladies kidnapped. Have they been found? Geez, sure, you can search me? I have absolutely nothing to hide... I'll help you any way I can!"

The room's ambiance altered, 'Thank you,' said Joy as she clicked on a mouse; this is when I noticed a large screen behind her light up in sequence. The lights were dimmed pictures of the gruesome predator showed in high definition. He didn't resemble me much. The evil guy seemed to be aware of the cameras and was in disguise. Every shade of hair makeup and fake mustaches, sideburns, beards, umh facial hair he'd used, the dude was impressive. Almost in awe was I. He could have been a makeup artist for the Mission Impossible TV episodes. I chortled, leaving a remnant of a cackle for effect "that's not even a close resemblance of me, Joy… R-U-kidding me?"

Joy glanced at Lola, then said, 'his I.D. came back crystal clear-clean,' she turned to me "your incorrect, Mr. Blake" she zoomed in on the vile creature's epidermis, specifically his facial features. Impressive… the guy was talented from picture to picture. His nose was altered, with fake beauty marks, fattened cheeks, different teeth caps, earrings, and eyebrows. The dude was remarkable. Joy said, "your ears are a match," as she pulled up three other pictures, stupefied with overtones of exasperation, I raised my voice a bit "yeah, got to be joking," come on, my ears are not like that freaks." "Please pull your hair back. Let's take some pictures of your ears." Joy meowed while Lola stared closely at my ears. I then shook my head onerously and spouted out, "you know what, this suddenly smells of straight-up harassment my ears, huh please!"

I'd say it's hard to distinguish a blush on these Asian women, but they were heated up; a man to their side said to me, 'this perp only goes after Asian girls, and that is the real reason you've been scrutinized, ever since you entered the lounge, you had only approached….' "Okay," I interrupted, taking the offensive with some back peddling, "all right, where's my disguise." 'I tugged on my nose, opened my mouth, rubbed my head…' Lola seemed to ignore my words "thus far, the victims have all been released within a week. The longest abduction has been 13 days. The women endured ugh sustained suffering at this predator's hands." Joy leans over me with a picture of the victim's bruises "she was chained and shackled. Look at her; she'd suffered the longest tenure of torture."

“I'm not saying it isn't traumatic, Joy. I'm sorry, I'm not that kind of man look. Before I walked up to you, I was hitting on a lovely stuck-up Hispanic gal, check it out, then a redhead,” and I rambled on, “don't forget the bottle blonde that I danced with we were gyrating on the floor to the beat.” Joy nodded at Lola; I was on a roll…

“It's untrue that I was only flirting with Asians; I'm being picked on here because, Joy, you don't like my macho misogynistic ways. This is plain ole harassment!”

Some of the men began to slouch; both women had reserved countenances, so using a Chess analogy, I decided to move my King castled with my Queen in attack mode. Soon I'd have them in Check, ultimately Checkmate. Cognizant that I had to speed up this game for I didn't want to see the Feds, time was ticking away, and the real FBI were on the way. I couldn't fake or plastic surgery my ass out of a DNA test!

Unwavering, Joy “the victims were drugged” she pressed play the video and began to play once again. We watched the predator help the Vic's empathetically maneuver out of the Casinos. Many of them were walking sideways, with him holding them up and steady. I said, “back up the video” we watched how the predator had slickly slipped a powder into the lady's drinks, a combination of Ecstasy and Rohypnol; Rohypnol is the infamous date rape drug. 'I made a mental note. I'd have to be a little more careful next time!'

Of course, they had watched the videos dozens of times, no surprises there, but I played my card anyways 'asking' “where was my powdered drug? If I was the guilty tormentor?”

Timing, as had been redundantly stated, is everything in life as the door glides open a melted concoction in a pitcher with a test tube visible the Rum Runner, “this drink is clean,” says a white lab-coated Indian-looking female who was kinda hot. I wouldn't throw her out of bed, geez, I thought. Get a grip, Mark. This is a dire situation, and all you can think about is sex, get your mind out of the gutter! I stood looking around and mumbled, 'see, you got the wrong guy.'

The monitor on the wall still played the sex offender escorting women out but then went blank. I added my 11 cents; obviously, I knew but still asked, "with all your cameras and surveillance, where's the guy's car at, huh? Why didn't you track that?" Joy, in retreat, said, "the perp uses a signal blocker once he gets out in the parking lots knowing that he couldn't do so inside of the Casino. The entire establishment would be locked down if our cameras went dormant or froze inside. But outside, for various reasons… we didn't have any such fail-safe system. The perpetrator always waited till he was about 300 feet away, then he'd actuate the blocking device, which wouldn't affect the Casino's normal activities."

My next move was diagonally moving my Bishop… Check, "I said; come on, search me, put me through your X-Ray machine time is wasting. I'm sorry for all the Victims, but now to a lesser degree, I'm being victimized by all of you; ugh, enough of this!" An older gentleman with a gold blazer pounced forward with a black and gold card in his palm, a voucher for me.

"Please forgive us for our intrusion and insults. There will be no need to search you, sir; we're sorry. I want to express our deepest sympathies." Joy and Lola also stood, hands extended, apologizing 'CheckMate' pushing my advantage like I've been known to do humorously. "So I suppose neither of you ladies would like to have a late-night dinner with me?" This brought about laughter from the guys 'you're a regular 'Don Juan-Romeo' type,' said the giant security man… Joy nodded her cute round face "happy hunting, Mr. Blake." I grinned and exited stage right.

I was done kaput, exhausted toast, I headed to the exit with two security guys beside me, over my shoulder, I told them, 'this ruined my night, seeya' 'yeah,' came a retort 'well, at least you're leaving with 'house money $500, said the other hulk chuckling 'you're leaving a winner, not like most that exit our Casino.' I meandered away, muttering, replaying their words, 'yes, I was leaving a winner for far more than a measly 500 bucks.'

I couldn't have ignored the noise of three slamming doors, five rows over… under the lamp posts, a group of well-dressed individuals stood. A Crown Vic Ford, uh, the FBI was on site… 'timing is everything' Yes!

<u>What a relief to be driving in the country again on Drycreek road.</u>

Happy to freely get on Hwy 5 and head to my abode, arriving at my iron gate just after 12:15 am. The Carr fire was still burning in the Redding area. The greetings from my dogs while clicking the gate shut, relief engulfed me. Omg, I'm… home sweet home.

I laid down in a hammock on my porch, staring out at the smokey sky with glimmers of stars breaking through, rested for several hours, then, like a beacon calling my soul, I jumped on a Quad and rode out the gate and up the hill to Jones Valley Resort, parked and walked the dock to my Houseboat finding the waters of Shasta Lake soothing… fell asleep.

Lake Shasta's draw on my spirit brought me systemically back to my belief being a transcendentalist knowingly asserting the primacy of my inner being spiritually over the material and empirically tainted observers of false Gods. Wow, that was quite heavy, off base, I suppose, as I rolled over and swatted a mosquito back to reality, the bloodsucking life I was devouring, umh, or was it cannibalizing me? Heck, I was slacking on commitments. I needed to feed the coffined hostages Pat and John… attorneys would be ripe if they were alive, spray them off, feed the dogs, then check out my Tracfone, where I'm sure there were messages from Joe and Tank.

My mundane tasks were completed. It was almost 11 am, burner phone in my palm missed 17 correspondences hell hadn't spoken to either Joe or Tank since Joe dropped the fkn nurse; last I knew, there was a search for Joe and our RV. At least, that was the last I saw on TV and online. Time to catch up, with a triple expresso, I went to work.

By noon I'd caught up to speed with the precarious situations that Joe and Tank were involved in; I gave Joe one more day to get up here to Shasta. Time had passed for his revenge on the lawyers. I wasn't going to keep them alive much longer, on the other hand. I was enthused to see Tank again. I stripped off my clothes… aah; I wish I never had to wear clothes a nudist at heart and stepped into the hot tub.

-40-

Jax, Wendi and Marshal Kara.

The dayshift had once again started… another 12 hours of monotony. For the 3rd time, Marshal Kara had put in for a transfer. She hated, uh, despised the staff at NIA, hell, the job sucked. Living offsite in a hotel where the other two Marshals stayed was past getting old, fast food, garbage, and lost motivation to even workout. She felt she was drifting into the doldrums and relentlessly pessimistic. It wasn't her job detail that bothered her. Kara truly adored Wendi Feral and had become very fond of the idiosyncratically diverse and odd man named Jax Foul.

Kara was embroiled in an internal investigation that hung over her like a death wish, for she was on duty when a tranquilizer dart was shot into Wendi's neck. Hell, why didn't the powers to be… uh, realize that NIA was dangerous for Wendi, primarily 'Rico Captor' who was in charge. Geez, only days after the damn nurse uuhhh the assassination attempt on her life, Kara had asked, 'why not move Wendi out of NIA to a safe house.' Freakin frustrating all requests went unheeded, for some reason unbeknownst to her, all her inquiries fell upon deaf ears. Kara dwelled backward in time, not 49 hours ago. A glorious sunny day, Jax, Wendi, and she was full of life, smiles, and laughter, a beautiful day in Napa. In a split second, all changed. She felt like a failure, disgraced, ignominiously humiliated by the rumors, small talk, chatter colleagues talking behind her back, even the two Marshals who were on the same detail looked down their bird beak noses at her, for she'd failed to keep Wendi safe!

Kara knew there would be no relief till Rico returned with Director Firm from a high-level investigation down in the San Rafael area. The manhunt is currently taking all FBI resources they had been relocated to that area, so she was ordered to 'hold down the fort.' Pacing back and forth outside Wendi's cell door in a daze, Doctor Hawkins had just left Wendi. Kara asked her how the patient was doing. The doctor's answer was demoralizing, like a thud with unintended gloomy dispersions. She demurely shook her head "not a change to the positive; I'm afraid the best we can do is keep her stable. It's as if she has been set back, regressed deep in the folds of her mind, again lost in her subconscious state, ugh, a vegetable-like coma. Kara, I'm waiting for the blood analysis; then, I will be better able to diagnose a possible treatment program."

NIA had proactively added a guard posted at the wing entrance down the hall. Wendi's prison cell resembled more a hospital room adorned with machines beeping curtains blocking out the Sun's rays, covering two large windows, and a big screen TV. Jax had said while closing the drapes that we don't want to let the 'Sunshine' in with a grimace; it took me several moments, then I got the double meaning 'Sunshine in like Wendi's alter ego!'

<u>Wendi & Sunshine Feral.</u>

****

'I wasn't up to the fight. It was futile to debate with Sunshine. Of course, she was correct. Per usual, my guardian Angel was only with me to protect me… us.' It was as if I had taken one step forward and seven steps backward; I was full of vigor and vinegar, ready for the world's conflicts, and couldn't wait to see mom, dad, and David again, umh, aah, still piecing that one together. Indeed only one person increased my heart rate, and his name is Rico; Jax came in a distant 2nd place.

How can I describe my feelings or this shrouded conundrum of being me? I suppose the best way was head-on… last night, my parents, with David, flew down from the Portland Airport. Only days before, I had been excited and animated. Our conversations on speakerphone were fun and exuberating. I couldn't wait to see their faces. We giggled and laughed till we were near tears like in old times. Our phone conversation lasted for over 57 minutes. Although when David entered the fray, umh, my parent's living room up in Vancouver, Washington, there was a touch of awkwardness and silence that prevailed. Oddly when I mentioned my partner and best friend, Sandi, the most beautiful Albino on this planet, David got quiet… Sandi was in charge of our business, 'Feral Feedback.' At our company… we train our animals for tasks to help the authorities with cadaver dogs, blind seer dogs for the Lyons Club, bomb-sniffing canines, and drug sniffers. We even had a division of Dolphins. It was like the three of them were hiding something from me about Sandi. It felt strange and worst, yet I couldn't get Sandi on the phone. Where was she? Sandi was not answering her phone, and when I called the Feral Feedback office, I was told she was on site and to leave a message on her voicemail. Rubio Animl would most often take my calls; he was our new Vice President of operations. Why were David and my parents always stifling any of my inquiries and quickly changing the subject of where Sandi was at?

Mom told me I couldn't wait to hug and kiss you but shied away from any details about Sandi. I felt her recoil via phone. My father took the helm and said, 'certain subject matter is better discussed in person,' so being side-swiped, I let the glancing blow slip by.

I was in a familiar position on my back again, as was the case for many months. After a short reprieve of euphoria, now again… no motor skills, and my eyes closed. Lost in a confused state of mind, drug-induced fugue, ugh, like I couldn't even mutter a single syllable.

Marshal Kara accompanied my parents and David into my room later that afternoon. My mother hovered over me, tears cascading down her cheeks daddy was raging mad, yelling, and screaming at Kara, "how could you allow Wendi to have been attacked again? Where was Rico at?" he scoffed. "FBI, what use were all of you? I'm going to take my daughter out of here and back to our home!" Then it became chaotic. My parents, alongside David, demanded my release at once. I listened but couldn't acknowledge them, knowing that my tenure here at NIA was up long ago. The 180 days and nights had passed by. My husband had signed the admittance forms and um contract, and the date had expired. They wanted to take me home today.

Unfortunately, what no one except Sunshine knew or observed was, 'I wanted to go with them now' noiselessly, muffled silence shrieked out at them, groveling on my metaphoric knees, pleading, get me the hell out of here, Please!' Shouting and howling until I was hoarse, knees bleeding, yet not a soul heard a syllable nor a word from my closed lips… eyes, not a singular movement could I find. Zombified again, drugged into oblivion. ☹ .

Sunshine heard it all with blinders on and a quaint shallow dimple quivering below the surface of my left cheek in control now, like turning a dark, curtained enclosed cell into a sealed vault. Sunshine compartmentalized all for us and flipped the switch. I no longer existed, but in the peripheral dimension, I could only penetrate her world after recharging my batteries. Ugh, energy depleted. Left bedeviled in a dimensional space in time, shivers of hallucinations floating, flying around me like a horde of African killer bees drugs that were shot into my internal glands inhabited my body which, like melting icebergs, took me farther out to sea, the gateway back closed, rolled down. Sunshine was now in complete control of our destiny. I was once again subservient. Uh, last silent words permeated our schizophrenic cranium. 'I, Wendi Feral, whispered, 'welcome, Sunshine Feral… Seeya.'

<u>Sunshine Feral!</u>

Sunshine wasn't a happy camper even with regaining control, thinking to herself, and speaking about us and to me in our shared cranium… 'I'll tell yah that bitch drives me fkn crazy batty,' kept saying, 'step back from the ledge my friend' a verse from one of my favorite songs, the artist 'Third Blind Eye' song I was singing is called 'Jumper' how appropriate!

Wendi had morphed into being a whiney-sniveling nuisance, a major distraction and annoyance I had zero misconceptions about; if she were allowed to take back dominance of us, we'd end up a useless fkn housewife watching soap operas for entertainment, pregnant and barefoot. A subhuman species, a slave to a man who would relegate us to substandard stereotypes, ain't no way we're going down that muddy path toward the abyss of swampland! R U Kidding me? Nope!

I'm 'Sunshine Feral,' dominant, disciplined, and proactive, a leader as masculine as any woman on this planet, born without testicles but not a docile prissy pussy type, no. I'm ready for action. I finally succeeded in shutting down the cowardly weak-ass Wendi. She will never arise again. This is my life. My destiny awaits… <u>'Wendi is Dead forever!'</u>

Oh, my, looky here, my dearest bestest, a most precious person alive just entered the room 'Jax,' I loved this man might be scarred, from missing toes to missing fingers. Some would call him ugly, but not me. He was by far more handsome than Wendi's laden downed heartthrob fantasy guy, her dreamboat paramour Rico. This guy was a male manly a fkn stud, um, my stud! His rough hands are on my forehead then I feel his lips upon each cheek. He whispers words that must be misconstrued wrong in so many ways. He says, "I love you Wendi" in my left ear-surely he intended to say Sunshine, aah no doubts.

Jax's smell was intoxicating. I willed my eyes open and then heard my sexy raspy voice say, 'hey stud, how about a smooch… kiss on the lips? His face blinked as a bright flood light blinded him… me, 'My-my Sunshine, there you are' perplexed, I said, 'well, Hellyeah mister, the one and only kiss me, you foolish sexy devil!'

He bent down, and yum, my arms reached up and yanked his head down for a Frenchy, then I, we heard the locks on my entrance door being keyed. I fell back into my self-induced coma state of not being. Jax resumed the façade as his fingers gently massaged my face and rubbed my eyelids closed, then a forefinger across my moist lips.

In walked a black male nurse named Frank, whom I suspected had dual purposes, for he moved 'BlackPantherish' he checked the monitors, wiped a cool damp cloth over my forehead, then changed out the bag hanging from a stainless-steel rack that was connected to the I.V. in my left arm. Strangely neither Frank nor Valerie muttered a word to me. Uhm, all business. I was familiar with Jack, and he was like my other guard nurse. I had six nurses now, three females and three males. They were doing 8-hour shifts. Unfortunately, I couldn't see their eyes; mine were shut. When Frank's voice reverberated deeply, 'any changes, Jax?' 'Nope, same ole same Frank' then the door closes, and Jax pinches my wrist.

I perked up 'hey, you know what? I was just reliving?' he replied, 'not a clue' 'that mission we were on a couple of months ago in Seattle, you and I in the utility closet together!'

Jax shyly smiled 'that was a major success, Sunshine; you were unstoppable and simply amazing. Without you and your innate ability to communicate with animals, we could never have pulled that one off. Your 7th sense and paranormal insights are one of a kind, and your presence blesses me!' 'Yeah, I was… wasn't I fabulous?' Downtown Seattle, we were at a board meeting between investment bankers Wallstreet and Goldman Sachs big wigs of all flavors dealing with an IPO. The topic is the initial public offering of an Americanized Russian company. New innovative technology that Amazon and Microsoft were drooling over… it became an aggressive battle with vicious and spiteful bids, and a takeover war ensued. I could recall every detail!'

'Yes, woman, literal billions of dollars were on the line that evening… we were quite the team in sync per our norm.'

41

<u>Jax later at the training center adjacent to NIA.</u>

Standing despite plenty of seats unoccupied in a pavilion on the outside of the Prisons concertina razor wire that surrounded NIA, the pavilion was enclosed within an airplane hangar. One of three such enormous buildings in the foreground… inside were mats, gymnastic equipment ropes for climbing and pulling, and a deluxe obstacle course. Also inside the hangar was an Olympic swimming pool, rock climbing walls, and five separate cages for combat sports and training-sparring and fighting, reserved for the finest Warriors that NIA could recruit. All were physical specimens to be wary of.

Most of them were considered mentally insane or, if not… with far too many psychological disorders to be allowed outside the facility or on the streets of society. The majority were ex-military with acute syndromes PTSD, the prevalent disorder of choice. Some were adjudicated, determined to be a danger to humankind, and sentenced to 'life' the worse of, the worse. Insanity was in vogue; serial killers and psychopaths from all the reaches of this world were incarcerated here at NIA, the new mecca for these Hannibal Lector types, umh, specified criminals.

<u>Inside another of the airplane hangar buildings was the</u>

<u>Hierarchy of NIA.</u>

Terrance Hallinan, the CEO and the board of directors at NIA, had moved mountains to now be ordained the number one institution for the mentally ill, with many outpatient buildings and hiring the most talented professionals in the medical field. Neurological testing was a constant with the added experimentations on many inmates who would never see the light of day within the prison's dungeon basements.

NIA was known for an array of innovative procedures involving stem cell research and had some Neurological breakthroughs to help people who had spinal injuries and brain trauma. NIA had several articles written up in premier and mainstream medical journals attesting to a few miracle cures for forms of paralysis and had opened a clinic for fire victims.

With all of this notoriety came a medical staff second to none, on the other side of this Public Relations Spiel, NIA had collected world-renowned Psychologists NIA had the monies and notoriety for feeding its insatiable desire for Psychopaths. Like a boneyard, they were locked up to die at least, that belief was propagated for... public opinion. Yet not close to actuality nor reality, trained masterminds, killers of diverse skill sets who didn't have anything to lose, gains were to be had by all participants in NIA's militia housed on the 640-plus acres in Napa, California.

Jax was not only a spectator but was in charge of all the personnel that made up the specialized teams of fighters. He was akin to being the 5 Star General, viewing a highly competitive jousting match... that the participants had made it to the Medal rounds. The competition was ongoing, a 25-man-women tournament using the round-robin formula system. Jax's subordinates, uhm soldiers, were aggressively testing their agility skills, hand-eye coordination, and combat with light armor and dulled-tipped swords. It was more for fun, an exhibition for the leaders of NIA. However, some participants fought with wicked intentions of harming their foes. The elevator opened, and Terrance and his cohorts walked out; they were the controlling characters at NIA.

Jax was enjoying himself, cheerfully watching as... he beckoned the group to sit down on the other side of the bleachers nearest the competition. Still, out of the camera's view, all listening devices were also squelched.

CEO Terrance Hallinan with Warden Ursula Anders and head of the medical department Doctor Liz Honcho with Assistant Warden Larry Walden sat at a long table in a heated disagreement... argument. Terrance had just arrived back from an impromptu excursion, a large gathering off the coast of Seattle.

Terrance had weighed his approach to how he would bring his team together and, coalesce, had to strive to keep everyone on the same page. There wasn't any illusion that the FBI was on site inside their facility, evisceration, guillotine-like proactively something needed to be done. This was the mantra on the cruise ship out in international waters near Seattle. He had flown directly to Napa after boarding his personal Leer Jet at the executive airport outside of Federal Way, Washington.

Terrance used his innate tunnel vision, absolutely nothing he allowed to enter his thought waves... but the vitriolic debacle, an inevitable cataclysmic calamity, that was on the horizon. He learned that the only reason the FBI Director Tanya Firm and her sidekick Rico Captor hadn't shown up with force at NIA was from a leak of information from a placed informant that had made her way up the hierarchy within the CIA. The caustic information was disseminated to Terrance on the cruise ship he'd boarded on a deep inlet in the Puget Sound in Northwestern Washington. The FBI was concentrating on the attempted killing of FBI Agents in Marin County, but when that investigation cooled, NIA would be the next target of the Fed's wrath. Terrance's syndicate, with Worldwide overtones, had spies in high-level positions throughout the USA. NSA, CIA, you name an acronym, and NIA had a finger on the entry key... inside these Government entities. The other reason that the FBI wasn't on NIA's doorstep was what they termed 'domesticated insurgencies.... The SOJ militia.'

The Government had scheduled a mandatory meeting of the minds in Boise, Idaho, with the head of NSA and the U.S. Attorney General with all the prime characters from various organizations, a so-called emergency. Many would travel from Wash. D.C., so there was a lull. Terrance and his cronies felt lucky that NIA took a back seat, for the Government was more interested in the militant fanatics. Rumors about the growing militia were consistently substantiated... '5 tons of C-4 plastic explosives' were hijacked from a secret installation in Utah. This had earmarks of the SOJ militia... <u>'State of Jefferson.'</u>

So, the shit hadn't hit the fan as of yet, and NIA was on the back burner for now, even with the attack on FBI Agents and the murder of the Nurse who tried to eliminate Wendi, all of which directly led to his institution, NIA would be under siege soon enough. He worried that the Federal Government would investigate his operation because of not only the attempted killing of Wendi by the Nurse who worked at NIA, but now she was shot inside the minimum-security outpatient hospital's grounds with a freakin dart gun.

Terrance had an upset stomach. Gurgling with unwanted flatulence, he stepped from the auditorium, waddling to the nearest toilet. His sphincter couldn't hold out much longer. He moans with a longish groan, and neither would NIA last long knowing that the prison was prominently on the FBI's radar. His staff and security had to arrest the shooter of Wendi.

He finishes his biological releases, reenters the arena, and beelines toward his three employees.

The jousting semi-final match just finished, as he finds his seat, "all right, this is between us four individuals only; our dialogue and conversations about this toxic situation are not to be embellished negatively. I want positive affirmations only. Is that clear? Solutions only… there's no reason to rehash what's happened. I will remind you that none of you had permission to make any decisions without my input. Now that you did, we need to alleviate and reduce the results of your miscalculations. Call it… damage control."

"Wait for just a second, Terrance; you were unavailable for three full days and nights. I sent Tweets, emails, Snaps, texts, and even used Instagram, even as archaic as it is today, I even called you and left you a voice mail." "Yes, Ursula, I was 35 miles West of Seattle like I had informed you on the Pacific Ocean with our comrades. You all were aware of the mandatory gathering!" His fist hits the tabletop…

"No fricken excuses, what you enacted was beyond stupid, why couldn't you wait three days… erstwhile you contemptuously had one of our sharpshooters fire a dart into the neck of our most prized asset Wendi Feral…." Liz entered the fray. "Terrance, this wasn't a decision we took lightly. Larry and Ursula, and I weighed out all options we...." "Liz, you weighed out all options on a broken scale. I..." "Please, Terrance let me finish; our entire operation here at our establishment NIA was in jeopardy due to my chemical concoctions, being circumvented after the attempt on Wendi's life by Our Nurse Spike! Wendi's alter ego, Sunshine, was losing control, and Wendi was reemerging! As all of us know, Sunshine's control of Wendi is essential. Okay, once, the clandestine, covert assassination attempt by one of our own nurses and staff members failed... this brought more scrutiny, empowering the FBI and, uhm, the Fed's gathered steam taking impetus with momentum; they controlled Wendi/Sunshine. Listen, Terrance, the Feds were naturally paranoid, knowing they could no longer trust our staff. They brought in new Marshals... and nurses, another Physician assistant, and mealy moused Doctor Hawkins took charge of our patient... Wendi."

Larry felt invigorated, finding the strength boosted by Liz, who had taken some control of the debate. "Not only was Wendi's voice heard speaking cognitively to Jax, but one of our guards saw her ambulating along and smiling, coming back to life as Wendi. The longer she was off our Psychotropic drugs and on whatever new medical protocols that Dr. Hawkins had her on... It became apparent that we were witnessing the disappearance of Sunshine. Uhm, it was the distinct voice of Wendi that we heard on recordings. Terrance, even her mannerisms were different. Visibly Wendi had evicted Sunshine....." Spinning around, he took up his iPad. "Look, not seven hours after you left for Seattle, everything was going to hell in a handbasket Terrance. I was able with techies to zoom into this dialogue between Jax and Wendi." Ursula and Liz displayed stunned expressions. 'What,' asked Ursula.

"Here, you all can listen to this for the first time. I've played it back a dozen times. Let me preface this video Marshal Kara and Jax, with Wendi in her wheelchair, were at the Camellia garden area overlooking the pond. Lucky that the video showed that Kara was too far away to hear the proprietary information that was spoken between them...." 'Enough,' yelled a thoroughly annoyed Terrance, 'play the damn video!' Larry slumps back as six depraved soulless eyes lasered into his pupils.

Overwhelmed, he hit play… the first words heard were from Jax. "I thought I'd lost you haven't heard your sweet, cute voice in almost nine months. Oh, I'm so happy to have you back, Wendi. This is awesome!" "Jax, thank you, but I'm far from feeling myself lingering haphazard visions and experiences; Sunshine has run rampant over my mind and body, exploited me, and can't help from being discombobulated. Umh, fact from fiction is hard to discern; imagination on top of dreams, the variance between reality from fiction is like a super thin line. I search my mind for normalcy, for clarifications, some form of elucidation, asking why all these bruises, cuts, and scrapes are on my body!"

Wendi took a long sip of her Apple juice and chewed on a Fig bar cookie. *"Jax, tell me something. What is NIA? What happens here, Jax? I have a feeling it's something way sinister?" "Ahh Wendi, that's a long subject for another time, sweetie, but first and foremost, it's a prison for the mentally insane and a mental hospital. It's so vital, in my opinion, that you blot out, uh obliterate, umh, wipe out this train of thought for your wellbeing. Suffice it to say, even discussing this subject could be toxic look at me, girl. I love you, Wendi, and I implore you to eradicate anything to do with this extemporaneous nonsense from your mind. Please stop thinking of anything about NIA for both of our sakes… please!"*

Larry taps pause, gyrating at each gapped mouth, saying, "so, as we can see, Jax is solid. He is truly on our team and a true asset that didn't break our confidence with regard to Sunshine's missions. He evaded her questions very cleverly, I must say." Before any of them replied and muttered a word, Larry played the closure.

The video/audio starts back up. Wendi is seen speaking, *"Jax, sorry, but I've got a sneaky premonition that what we see, umh, we don't really see… there is something sinister here. Ugh, I'm not describing the birds, trees, Swans, ponds, and all the grapes in the vineyards. The beauty is choreographed like a set in a Hollywood studio. Look at the happy children and family members visiting the inmates on the surface veneer is congruent enough,*

"Timing is everything," mumbles Larry. 'Screams shouts the dart lodged near Wendi's carotid artery. She quakes forth then backward unconscious.'

'That's it' Larry pounds the table with both palms. No one stirred or moved like a paused screen, lost in their own warped minds. 'Silence was golden' seconds clicked past finally with a seldom heard intonation by Terrance, his tenure voice… concessions conceded. His arrogant disapproval uhm reprimands of condemnation halted after hearing the exchange of dialogue, and he no longer had the wherewithal to censure the group nor reprimand or denounce the action taken by his subordinates. Instead, he took the higher road, glad that he'd chosen them to be part of his nucleus. Terrance said, the obvious periscoping his head around, taking in Jax, the jousting cages, and the small audience of combatants. "Of course, we will have to eliminate and kill Wendi if Sunshine loses her dominant position within their shared skull. We cannot allow Wendi to return. You did the right thing ordering the medicated dart!" He raises his fist outwards and rotates 'fist bumps' engaged; solemn obedience understood.

"Now that I fully comprehend the urgency of why the dart, let's see if there is a way to put out the oncoming blitz, mitigate the blazing, raging fire to come?"

Terrance then sighed and exclaimed, "Sorry, poor choice of a metaphor. Just saw the latest report on the 'Carr fire' it burned over 49,000 acres, and two firefighters have lost their lives just north in Shasta County. I uuhhh, lost a 35-acre ranch up there." He pauses.

"All right, let us place our feet in the Fed's shoes, guys. They will conclude the obvious that the attack on Wendi was an inside job, the tranquilizer dart filled with our drugs of choice. Why wouldn't the perp shoot Wendi to kill her? Why drug her?" "Even more precariously disheartening is why anyone would want to drug her? It does inherently fall straight back into our laps; this is a maximum-security facility. What will the FBI decide to do? How do we buffer NIA from an internal, um, external investigation? We realize we can't allow this singular transgression to dissolve, ugh, destroy what we've accomplished in the last 15-plus years!"

Ursula sighs then yawns "yes, but I've not slept nary a wink since the dart incident and cannot think of an excuse or a way out. Tell me, don't any of you believe we have to give up a fall guy and let the Feds arrest a shooter? Although that raises more concerns, I'm flummoxed here!"

"Were exposed to the hilt," adds Larry. "True, and the blood tests will come back proving that the injected drugs were the same that I'd previously prescribed, albeit more concentrated. My head will be on their platter," Liz declares.

Abruptly Terrance jolted up from his seat "look, put your fkn thinking caps on; none of you are leaving NIA this evening. We will reconvene in the 7th-floor boardroom at 9:45 pm; ahh, don't be late; we need a plan of attack… a direction!"

They solemnly stand and leave purposely in separate directions, each bearing weight, knowing that it was incumbent on each to display or show the value they bring to the table-also to validate their positions and the monies they were being paid. This was akin to a 911 emergency alarm.

Liz thought she'd overheard Terrance speaking to Jax on the closed-circuit radio system -communicating to him that all training exercises must cease and all inmates must be returned to their cells. NIA was going on 'lockdown.' Liz surmised that if the FBI overran the institution with search warrants, totally infiltrating the Prison and all adjoining businesses associated with the enterprise, we'd be in detrimental jeopardy and scrutiny. NIA was, uh, a public entity, a growing enterprise trading on the Stock market at a brisk pace to become a conglomerate.

The goal was to appear transparent, above board, and prepare for the worst everything would be up to snuff at the prison facility within hours. However, there wasn't a way to conceal the three large hangars on the training facilities grounds. Terrance would fall back on the fictional permits filed with the county's building department that plainly documented the buildings were essentially training centers for the correction officers. The NIA staff a plausible untruth that the County building inspectors had bought hook, line, and sinker, so he would call for the staff and officers guards to populate the hangars to substantiate this falsehood.

Liz decides to break from the current dilemma to change her focus, clear her mind and come back later to revisit the conundrum. She sought out Nurse Renae whom she had an ongoing competition over the years, and they'd kept the records. Reconciling the wins versus the losses, Liz was up 517 wins to 511 in their intense 'Scrabble' contests. Both with a dictionary in hand, they sat across from each other for a 3-game run, then a 4th. Liz had been blitzed and lost all four games… shit couldn't concentrate, didn't make any excuses, and just exited her tail between her thighs, leaving a cackling Renae to put the game up.

Liz retreated to her office, turned all electronics off, refused to answer a page Doctor Honcho to the 3rd floor Psych Department, flipped off the lights, reclined in her ergonomic comfy chair, and meditated and analyzed what she could do to alleviate the upcoming siege by the Feds.

Assistant Warden Larry Walden undressed, exchanging his restrictive business suit, tie, and cuff links for shorts and a T-shirt. He slipped off his 'old school' black wing-tip shoes throwing on a pair of Nike high-tops… tennis shoes inside a locker room reserved for the 'who's who' the elitist personnel at NIA. It had been too long since he had gone for a run. Today was as good as any other to run 5 miles and then try one of the obstacle courses to help clear his mind. Pump some re-invigorating adrenalin into his veins, new blood oxygenating a fresh supply to his dormant brain. He needed to supply an innovative idea and solve the dilemma they faced.

Warden Ursula Anders stood at attention in front of her 'wet bar' overseeing over $5,000 in delectable spirits, wines booze; in her left palm was a cocktail glass iced and filled to the brim with some remarkable vintage 50-year-old Crown

Royal muses staring at the drink before her wonders if it was the equivalent of a 100.00 dollar shot. Alcohol was where she'd visited then lingered when stressed out in a panic. She chased a buzz, fully aware of what the wrath of Terrance could evolve into couldn't afford to get soused. She loosened up some having under four hours until the mandatory meeting; she'd be okay, certainly. What could be wrong with five drinks, or so her best thinking happened when she was on the verge of inebriation like booze undid the tethers of society's rules and regulations. Get a little buzz, then mull over the quandary she and NIA were embroiled within.

Attorney and CEO of NIA Terrance Hallinan had jetted, no choppered away, would be a better description, having a resting helicopter pilot waiting and at his disposal, he'd flown back to his skyscraper on the skyline of San Francisco. His Penthouse overlooked Alcatraz and Fisherman's Wharf. On a clear day or evening, he could see the Golden Gate clearly to his West and the Bay Bridge into Oakland to his East.

He was scheduled to return to Napa for the conference with his underlings in just a tad over four hours. He'd landed on the roof of his Law Firm that had his name emblazoned on four sides, a reputable, respected man in Bay Area politics. San Francisco had been home to generations of his family... their genetics were based in the old country of Prussia, known as a German state on the southeast coast of the Baltic Sea. Terrance was known as a problem solver, a nickname he neither disliked nor enjoyed. His moniker was 'Tsar of Northern California.' He was the head of the snake of the so-called American Militia, even with this prestige from as far away as Moscow and Berlin. The world's power brokers who had deep investments in NIA were beyond livid... learning of the troubles at NIA. At the onset, they financed the operation and takeover of the institution years ago. They then doubled down and recently the group of investors bought millions of additional insider shares in the last several months.

Terrance had a dry throat, and his tongue was parched no matter how much he hydrated with his deluxe bottled water brand for the last six hours he'd rehashed his current conundrum, conference calls with notable leaders he'd communicate with all on a first-name basis. None of which had practical solutions or valuable answers nada nothing tenable defensible or sustainable, so he decided to do what was natural to him when under a pressure cooker about to blow!

Awaiting a knock on his suite's thick wooden door, he slid his hand over to the button. He pushed it down, opening the door after confirming who stood in his entryway via one of his monitors uhm, his favorite secretary pranced in 'Delish!'

He sighed heavily with a twinkle in his eyes… everyone had their ways of mitigating stress. His was as natural as a caveman. 'Sex' was what he demanded, his necessary stress relief 'AU-Natural' cleared his mind, and all his pipes a long-lasting bout of 'Fellatio' in his jacuzzi and sauna room… nothing better to reenergize his brain!

2 1/2 hours later, Terrance stepped out of his helicopter and entered NIA's main building. He felt oh so relaxed, and recharged endorphins had kicked in. It had been months since he'd endured a workout like that one… yummy.

Now back in his office at NIA way ahead of his ordered conference gathering, he was stuck ruminating over the last several hours at his penthouse in S.F., where he videotaped the sexy, satisfying interlude knowing he'd revisit it later. Enjoyed replaying them in the mirrors, laying back in Awe at her perfected movements, finally letting her engulf her prize, uhm, have the juicy surprise her reward for slurping engulfing his phallus 55 minutes of straight blissful scintillating restraint like a hot-balloon detonated terminated. He was feeling and looking like a masculine stud in the mirrors. Invigorated now with fighting aggression 'ballsy,' he got dressed after a cool shower. He left his office for the chopper promising his favorite secretary that he'd take care of her sexual frustrations once he'd returned. She howled at him for his selfishness, and he listened attentively to her harsh rebuttal … then she yelled, snapping at his back! 'Don't bother; I'll handle it myself, Terrance. It will be more satisfying anyways!'

Larry made a mental note, a promise that he'd make time to run and do calisthenics from now on at least three times a week. The obstacle courses were terrific. Felt better than he had in months, a definite challenge. He was minutes off his best times no way that in the next few days, he wouldn't be sore. It would be a good kind of pain. Gosh, he'd let himself go! With his new mindset, a restart to being fit and disciplined enough with his sedentary lifestyle, he steps into the boardroom.

Someone had ordered refreshments trays of snacks and drinks from the staff's dining cafeteria… it was 9:35 pm the others would be arriving soon.

Ursula watched the elevator door close, then saw several carts being pushed down the hall towards the conference room. Her stomach growled; that's what she'd forgotten to do 'Eat' feeling no pain, just empty pinging in her tummy food would suck up some of the acid left from the alcohol. She had a pleasant buzz not overly noticeable as she chased the food trays being early, and maybe she could satiate her hunger before all the seriousness began.

Dr. Honcho dried off from a short shower pants suit on with a smattering of makeup couldn't remember the last time she was able to allow her subconscious to go dormant… and cleared her mind thoroughly. Meditation helped the revitalization; sufficiently rested in an introspective state, she'd had a breakthrough.

The grinning smirk was in place, recalling her 3rd attempt to push all peripheral thoughts from her brain, vanquishing impending doom to meditate pensively, washing away the subterfuge. She cleansed the sullen voice that echoed with a melancholy tune that melded, becoming benign and soothing. Awakened with enlightenment, earnestly beguiled answers flowed… rewards from her inner self. Liz felt as if she was gifted, discounted her self-medicating and the tablet of 'Ecstasy' a euphoric hallucinogenic drug akin to a form of intoxication related to Amphetamines, raring like a purring beast anxious to get to the meeting now in gung-ho mode!

Terrance's mood had shifted, fleeting at best paralleling sexual releases once done finished. Nothing had changed. You were still in a caustic relationship. The toxic situation had gone nowhere, just a temporary glitch reprieve Ctrl-Alt-Del. Terrance grinned. Why did he look at the glass half empty when in a negative mood? Terrance was back to being himself. His disposition was rebellious, filled with defiance as he opened the double doors to see his subordinates seated already, drinks and food in view. He grabbed a glass, filled it with some ice, and mixed in Orange juice with a splash of Cranberry juice, then took his seat at the dominant vacant place at the end of the table in silence.

Eager eyes loaded with optimism and anticipation zoned toward him. Eagle-like were his eyes staring unwaveringly back. "Okay, we all know why we're here. Let's get to it" coincidently, before he concluded the opening statement, one of his phones had chirped. He angrily powered it down, "turn off all your phones and electronics unless you're going to use them for this meeting. We will not be leaving this office until we...." The desk landline phone squealed for attention. He belligerently stuck his paw out and snatched it out of its cradle. Rotating his eyes, he glowed disdainfully and stabbed the flashing # 5 button.

"I told you not to bother me all calls on hold what. Is it that you didn't understand Molly?..." "Sorry rrh-aah I'm sorry sir, got a call a moment ago from a guard at the front gates if you want to see, it's on-screen number 15 there's three black SUV's that are waiting to enter NIA sir it's the FBI, and they want to be allowed inside a umh Agent 'Lucie Link' sir."

Astonishing was how fast droplets of sweat formed above his brow, "tell the guards to keep them out. I'm on my way. I'll handle this personally," Terrance stormed out of the conference room, leaving these words for them to chew on "don't leave this room if you want to remain employed; I better have answers to this dilemma when I return!"

42

Tank and the Motorhome.

It made zero sense, no matter from what perspective you analyzed the situation. He'd gone over it umpteen times, changed vehicles in San Jose, the snooping Agent disabled by Mark's people at the mechanic shop. Damn, I was beyond cautious; not a remote possibility of being followed, yet this was the case. According to his bro Joe, he had failed to lose the tails and was tracked to the restaurant in San Rafael. Tank decided to take a radical approach… driving the Cadillac Escalade. He veered off highway 101 and took evasive action, moved quickly from the fast lane three lanes, and exited on the Marinwood exit, following the GPS coordinates that were provided to him by Joe. This was where the motorhome was hidden.

Tank looked around and drove west into a residential area. It was an affluent neighborhood perfect for figuring out if someone was on his tail. It was a maze, although he was always glued to the rearview mirror. I'd drive around until I was certain no one was on my tail. My contention was of no value to Joe; I hadn't seen the guy for like 27 months in San Quentin. He was the same obstinate soul; way too late for him to change. Joe took my words and spat back at me. I told him, 'after joining him at the restaurant, uh, not five minutes went by' when he received the call from the girl Sammy. He told me I'd been followed, and I replied that's impossible, flipping it back on him and said… it was he that was being tracked, not I.

He'd explained that an ongoing, seriously unrelenting search for the RV had turned up evidence that placed parameters of where it could be hidden. The online hype was crazy. The pictures of his woman Sammy in the passenger seat, the man-woman hunt was closing in on the motorhome. The impetus for the civilian posse was the reward that kept growing.

I was given a task to complete-being in debt to both Joe and Mark, a feeling I despised and never liked owing anyone, an independent soul but alas, even with the clear truth, I was being manipulated… used here. I was a couple of hours North of San Jose, damnit. Joe could have handled this issue himself; um, why me?

I was on the verge of, ah-don't know if this is the correct word, 'epiphany' most of me wanted an everyday existence poor, broke, destitute, or whatever, but free to make my own decisions. 'Maybe a real family, children, a wife, faithful Love, so what if we struggled? We'd have each other Right' looming larger than life was the Ebony beauty, the date with Whitney tomorrow night. Yay, maybe she could be my, uhm… female Saint.

I decided to park the Caddy in a cul-de-sac pointing the front end toward a quick exit. I got out acting as if I needed to check the engine, which probably looked odd, for the Escalade was nearly new and was in terrific shape, at least on the exterior. I waited for my supposed tails, of which none appeared seven minutes later; I was back behind the wheel mission to be completed.

Agent Lori Parks.

Barking with a high-pitched octave was Agent Lori Parks, who was orchestrating the surveillance of Tank 'telling the pilot of a chopper to stay way back remain over Hwy 101 let's not spook him this time okay?'

Inside the mobile unit, the radio is linked to the proper agents. "Tanya, did you copy that?" Rico asked, watching her close the bathroom door and approach the co-captain seat. She nodded "we just passed the Marinwood exit and will pull a U-turn at the next overpass!" Tanya yelped out, "this mobile unit is like a white Elephant, like we're leading a parade with all the FBI Emblems and adornments. It's fricken ridiculous." She spewed into the mic, 'we're going to have to stay out of the mix, or Tank will pick us off in a split second. I want everyone to give Tank room… I repeat, don't engage.'

Rico couldn't help but be amused as he turned to her "this Mobile Unit was never intended to be a chase vehicle. You know it's only supposed to be a command center, a mobile base to coordinate our forces." Director Tanya Firm rolled her eyes into a wrinkled 'Frowl' (frown and growl) combination. Rico bit his tongue, never been on the wrong side of Tanya's ire, wrath like a spoiled brat. She was still pissed off, with Lori and her lost slipper nearly naked in his hotel room…so what!

"Rico, don't state the obvious, all right I'm in no mood for your embellishments like duh, were not going to follow this perp Tank into Marinwood, but we can backtrack and get as close to his position as possible," pointing to the moving interactive map on the screen. "Tanya, why don't you just spit out what's eating at you… this has gone on long enough!"

Joe and Sammy.

We were sitting together on a low boy sofa, large comfy cushions, her iPad zinging my laptop flashing updates inside the Safehouse like inoculated nonfunctional, waiting for a meeting at 8:45 pm in a tense holding pattern. Partner Mark Feral is AWOL, probably chasing Leg. I had my own 15 inches to the left. Hitherto hadn't any urges or inkling no desire to engage Sammy sexually, knowing full well she was a whore, slut easily useable with a hint she'd be on her knees. Although inwardly, a passivity groped my loins, an initial sense that my testicles were shrinking might be a better state of mind to forego sex entirely, feeling at the moment that I could, for whatever reason, commiserate or relate with Eunuchs.

The main concern was, what would I do with this gorgeous 25-year-old, hum? Mark would not condone her involvement or existence. She knew too much. I felt paralyzed. I could hear his words 'no women,' no use for the weaker gender. Remove the problem immediately and eliminate her before she destroys all that we have worked for Joe!

I believed this girl, Sammy, could genuinely be an asset… then I dropped the desperation that was my life's circumstances, my pride and attitude of self-sufficiency, and my inner power akin to a mountain of strength and conviction. The presence of my willpower, 3rd to none, enabled my life to have a purpose and a design of hope for the future. I was in control of my own life, not a clone or enslaved person to Mark's whims! A prideful person, and I have to admit it. I adored this girl. It felt like she was a perfect counterpart, a Yin-Yang thing.

I realized that I'd lied to myself. I was stressed out, and fear of going back to prison for the rest of my life was taking a chunk out of me. It always seemed to be bad news at my doorstep, heck I hadn't a doorstep, no home, just living like a hobo from place to place. Doing Marks bidding 'danger… my heart burns, warning blasts starboard, felt like crying out loud audibly, with urgency, my B.P. had to be skyrocketing and a sudden urge to pee; was it cancer prostate? Maybe that's the reason why I remained flaccid and limp, not like me. I'm sick inside. That's it. God's wrath, no God geez, getting fricken weak never had I ever been morally accountable for my conduct, always in pursuit of my form of self-righteousness. I was standing in front of the toilet with Joe Jr. in hand, pushing and squeezing my bladder to release the urine, only a damn dribble with pain, a burning sensation. Oh no, that bitch gave me an 'STD' disease, that's it!

Then finally, I breathed in a long, exasperating breath as a stream began to grow 'nope, I wore condoms, and Sammy had that tightening operation and had been thoroughly checked out, clean of any STD, so what gives? As I sprayed off my hands and wiped my handsome face. The mirror didn't lie; I appeared tired and worn out. Still, a good-looking hunk wasting away; ugh!

Stepping back out to the living room, dizzy and lightheaded, I was coming down with an illness; Sam came into view, and I felt barfing, nauseated ominous forlorn sorrow grasped my innards. Oh, now wait a fkn millisecond, um, no damn way, oh shit, mournfully, the verdict was in. A Terminal diagnosis detailed self-diagnosed hopelessly <u>'In Love with Sammy. Samantha Timmons'</u> fear struck me, taking my breath away. I'd never felt like this before. Gosh, I'm Infected, ugh, sick to my stomach!

What was I going to do now? The last time I felt this way was a puppy love thing in high school. I resisted touching her but let my thigh rub upon hers as she grinned up at me. Yep, I was terminally afflicted, agonizingly bedeviled, cursed. Oh, No… I was a Sick Bastard!

<u>Rico and Tank.</u>

The sun dipped below the tree line as I waited in the borrowed Escalade, a 'Nos' energy drink nearly empty I'd made three passes of the motorhome. At first, it was hard to see it because there were semi-trucks with 40-foot trailers everywhere and other recreational vehicles parked, like resting dinosaurs. The shopping center's parking lot was an ideal stop for easy access to Hwy 101 North or South. Worker bees and owner-operators were resting in their sleepers, remembering a long time ago. It was a dream of mine to make a living with my co-pilot being the freedom of the road.

Hesitated, I realized that I'd been far better off if I had followed that dream rather than being a darn puppet on a leash, a follower. Where had that gotten me, ugh? Prisons were plumb stocked with lost humans, controlled, manipulated fools, people who were sold a bill of goods for a better way of life. Yeah, like 'soldier Ants ah worker Bees the Queen or in my case King Mark, dictated his own personal agendas' wow. I crushed the can and tossed it to the passenger floorboard in no time like the present enough self-flagellations. I needed all my available senses about me.

If I didn't stay focused, I could end my life in Quentin. The question posed, why was I endangering myself? Like a foot soldier, I took out the business card that Joe gave me at the restaurant, still recalling his facial expressions and words, 'Tank, you're out of Quentin because of Mark and I, do us proud we're a team for life do this job and get back to San Jose. We will be in touch, bro; soon after that, the three of us will have steaks… a barbeque on Lake Shasta on Mark's houseboat!' Reflecting back, his words rang true perhaps from his perspective, my trip North could have been obviated by his following due diligence and simple protocols. I carefully eased the door closed and yanked my beanie down over my bald-head sunglasses at night as one of my favorite songs strolled across the shopping center parking lot.

The words kept humming between my ears. 'Tank, you're out of Quentin because of Mark and me, but wasn't I originally incarcerated in San Quentin because of my affiliation and friendship with Mark and Joe? Ugh… like, duh!

Agent Lori Parks.

Lori whispers into the mic. 'I've got a visual; he just left his vehicle on the other side of a 24-hour Safeway store,' the chopper pilot adds with brimming enthusiasm. 'I can clearly see the RV now. It's under some trees, covered up pretty good back by the fence that borders the freeway!' using the premier military version of night vision made their jobs so much easier.

Rico turns to Tanya without words spoken. She takes charge from the mobile unit that was a mere five blocks West of the RV parked in a residential area "all right, take the chopper up… Lori, keep an eye on him." "Yes, ma'am Tanya, but why? Not take him now, heck, ma'am, we have a 7-man team just around the corner. We now have the RV location, so why wait? Let us arrest him; even if we can't pin anything definitive on Tank, remember he's out of his district. Ugh, he's out of his jurisdiction. His probation allows him to be in San Mateo County; if he leaves the county, he is supposed to alert his probation officer. He's ours now; should I make the call?"

Tanya spins around with a glare at Rico, clicks off the transmission with vehemence, and shouts toward Rico. "Hey Cinderella, um, 'missing slipper,' Lori will always be just an Agent with no advancement. The woman plainly… can't think out of the box," wagging a gruesome wry grin.

Rico only nods and takes up the radio. "Lori, this confirms all of our suspicions. Tank will lead us to Mark and Joe. We just saw him meeting with Joe, who evidently told him where the motorhome was; otherwise, he'd not have known. Joe has been confirmed to be the driver of the motorhome. He was the marksman who shot and killed the nurse and shot our Agents. Lori, also, we can assume Joe set up the attempted assassination of Wendi ordered by his partner Mark Feral. If we capture Tank, as you have suggested, it takes us nowhere closer to Joe and Mark. The embedded tracking chip will eventually lead us to his co-defendants, so we only observe and track him for now!"

Tanya bows her head and then says into the radio, "check out the app I just forwarded to you from San Rafael Joes Restaurant." Lori does so, and in seconds Joe Sable blows up the screen. Fedora, blackish hair sunglasses with a woman by his side using the same hair dye in her hair. "Agent Avery is running a Facial Recognition program to see if we can come up with the female's identity as we speak. We can substantiate ah confirm that two of the ten most wanted on our FBI list… Mark Feral and Joe Sable are involved, and if we play our cards correctly, don't overreact. Let Tank lead us to them. We will Kill three birds with one stone!" Tanya declares confidently "oh Lori, we have roadblocks from Novato to Sausalito by the local police and the CHP that all now have copies of Joe's picture and the unknown female, so relax and do as I say!" ☹ .

Tank Shaw does the deed.

I hear the rotors looking skyward, but the helicopter seems to be ascending, not interested in me, with regret already manifesting. I increased my pace by the generated refrigerator trailers and dormant diesels. I was ominously dwelling on fragmented and muddled thoughts. I will pass the 'point of no return' all because of loyalty, commitment, and a debt I can't possibly pay off to Joe and Mark.

Stopped an odd disconcerted intuitive emotion stimulated my awareness like a thousand eyes were upon me. My guardian Angel warning me near panic-stricken, calmly took out a cigar cutter then lit it up, peering around, knowing full well the motorhome, which sat perhaps 55 yards away, was the Hottest and most sought-after RV on Earth at that very moment in time.

Nothing seemed peculiar or out of whack, um, out of the ordinary as I listened via an earbud to the local police scanner, leaning against a large Eucalyptus Tree. I had my phone's screen up and was checking all current news, irked indignantly. 'I tossed caution into the slight breeze.' Glumly I meandered closer to the RV and felt an odd zinging in my nervous system like I'd entered a trap. The tiny hairs were bristling uncontented suddenly. I was standing next to the key code at the slide-out on the passenger side. The mini-LCD screen blinked… Sequentially a chronological clock ticked away. I couldn't make a mistake with the timer. I concentrated while tapping in the code that Joe gave me, 7-11-57-12-21-57. I tapped in 7:57, seven minutes, and 57 seconds, all according to the card I held, then placed it into my dry ass mouth and chewed on it, walking away at a brisker pace. I took a warm bottle of water out, chewed, and swallowed the paper card with the instructions on it, clicked the door open on the Escalade, and drove out of the parking lot.

The fuming stench the closer I got to the RV still mortified my nostrils death was within that motorhome. Bewildered in less than three minutes, I was entering Hwy 101, heading South to get back over the Golden Gate and my home for now, San Jose. Mused for all the crimes I've committed, I'd never killed anyone; that was where I crossed the line, indeed. Some of the altercations and fights in Prison nearly ended that way, 'but that was self-defense….'

Lori takes up the microphone. "Tank Shaw just approached the RV, stood next to it for a minute, then walked away. He didn't even check out the motorcycle trailer heck wonder if we were compromised. He's now merging onto the South onramp of 101 freeway. I think we should secure the RV. I'll stay on him, Tanya, ma'am."

Lori's monologue apparently repulsed Tanya. Rico put it off to her being jealous. The more she acted like this, the more he unabashedly looked forward to penetrating Lori hell, I might as well indulge if I'm already guilty of philandering, remembering he was single and unattached, but the way Tanya acted as if they were married… or something? Her sad wicked hidden expression flustered him this wasn't who he was.

"Lori, the RV isn't going to grow wings and fly away. He didn't even enter it," utters Tanya.

Precisely then time stood frozen Rico's bewildered, dazed stare locked into Tanya's… no oh fk, she opened her mouth wide to yell, Screamed into her radio… from five blocks away it sounded like a Nuclear Bomb… Volcanic explosion eruption, several after blasts, banging and shrill alarms of vehicles going off… Sounds reverberated over the ground and airwaves.

It sounded like a Sonic Boom, and damn, I was nearly a mile away. The plastic explosives C-4… He'd carried out his last payback to Mark and Joe. The RV was far enough away from anyone to hopefully not kill or hurt or maim anyone. That would be horrendously awful, please, Tank mumbled 'no collateral damage' his imagination ran roughshod. Could one of the truckers have been walking a dog near uuhhh, pushing this from my mind hell, no one was out and about. All the trucks were like sleeping fossils. Besides, there was plenty of distance between the RV and the nearest truck; maybe the debris hit the trailers or cabs, definitely blowing out some windows… whatever it's done now.

Taking out the Tracfone, texting 'Done that, later good luck' like 75 seconds later, 'great, we will be in touch! ☺' I powered it down. If I made good time, I could be driving my car, the Impala, back to my apartment before midnight. Tomorrow I get to be with Whitney, aah, a grin, a smile broke loose. There's something about that girl, kinda like the movie 'Something about Mary,' Lol.

The devastation shocked everyone, sirens took the night's air, and Tanya dry-heaved wretchedly. Rico was already driving the mobile unit to the shopping center. Paramedics and ambulances were on the way; the area was cordoned off with bright yellowish tape. Who was to guess there wouldn't be another blast? Enraged, he watched a couple bleeding from head wounds being wrapped up. Windshields had been blown to smithereens thus far, and there were no human casualties, only cuts, abrasions, and fractures.

An unlucky trucker fractured his hip and leg when he fell from his Kenworth Conventional driver's side door trying to escape, fires burning smoke filling the evening's air. The pilot had said the mushroom-type cloud went at least six miles high, and a deep crater was now part of the asphalt. The moon was blocked out, and visibility was hampered; floodlights were called for this calamity. Rico sighed and watched Tanya apply ruby red lipstick to her dried lips.

-43-

Joe and Sammy are at the safe house.

The fully furnished safe house had almost anything that a person would need. The large Victorian home was divided into three living quarters, three kitchens, and bathrooms. Sammy and I were in the kitchen making sandwiches when we heard someone enter from the garage door, umh, mandoor. We had our weapons in our hands at once. A knocking sound, then verbiage broke the suspense. 'I'll be in the Livingroom; we need to talk,' said a man's voice.'

We left the sandwiches unmade and walked out to see an elderly couple perched at the end of high-back chairs around the dining table "aah, Mr. Joe Sable and Ms. Samantha Timmons, this is my lovely umh better half Rhonda, and I'm Lester, this is our abode, home umh one of them that is… That we keep for our organization. We are here to inform you that the meeting has been canceled until tomorrow morning."
Lester waved his arm "come along." Sammy clutched my hand while Rhonda took up the older gents' arm, and we went out the patio door and up a flight of stairs. Oh crap… I didn't realize I was like starving to death till the wafting scent hit my nostrils. The smell was eating me alive. My eyes didn't leave the closed pots, pans, and bowls; how long had Lester and Rhonda been cooking up a storm? They were either in their

late 80s or early 90s, but their eyes still twinkled with life; the old gentleman smiled with glistening teeth.

He waved his sun-damaged hands. "Oh, Rhonda has made us one of my favorite delicacies pot roast, mashed potatoes, and…" 'shush up, Lester' came the freaking cutest voice ever 'Blackberry pie for dessert' she winked. Sammy had helped to set the table with cloth napkins Sterling Silverware and four dinner plates, 'fine ass China bowls,' like we were dining at a fancy restaurant.

I had to ask, "how long have you been here working on dinner, Rhonda?" "Umh, for some time, you youngsters were busy, Lester, and I didn't want to disturb you. We thought you could use a home-cooked meal. I shut the door loudly to let you know you had some company; I hope we're not too presumptuous." Sammy smiled and grasped the little lady with a slight embrace "oh, this was such a wonderful surprise; we thank you both."

Suddenly it hit me as I rotated about, realizing why Sam's roving Deer like expression was so skeptical. It happened at the point when Lester had used Sammy's full name. Not even the FBI knew this, and if being honest with myself, not even I remembered it when I was doing my due diligence choosing a prostitute from the hordes of whores online; I'd written it down, then forgot it. It was my way to research who the prostitute was, checking out her real name… bypassing her stage name. Although I did like Sammy's OnlyFans fictitious name 'AmberStrokes,' I used due thoroughness… especially since I needed a girl to set up the private investigator. Hey, I was going to subtract her anyways.

Slowly I swayed my cranium awkwardly forward. She caught my drift, and the elder couple remained seated, "I have a question, if you don't mind," asked Sammy, their necks stretched, tightening some of the excess skin at attention; "how is it that you know my full name?" Rhonda gleamed at her husband with a 'Cat who devoured the Canary look' "well, missy," she demurred. "I'm clairvoyant, of course," as she let loose a cute-ish cutey pie snicker, slowly raising Sammy's phone.

"Samantha, you left your phone in the van that delivered you here, I touched the screen, and your name popped up in the main menu." Sammy started to laugh we joined in. I guffawed "of course; my scatter-brained girlfriend had lost her phone." Sammy giggled again, shyly embarrassed, smiling wide, twirling her fingers in a curlicue motion with her left hand inside her dyed Raven hair.

Samantha blushed like a punch: "did he just call me his girlfriend?" We pulled the chairs out simultaneously to sit, then Samantha noticed what was missing, something to drink with dinner pantomimed the hand-to-mouth motion. I went with her to the kitchen; she snagged a pitcher of ice water and four glasses, and I spied a bottle of Caymus Cabernet Sauvignon, my absolute favorite wine yum, obviously someone else's also. Because there were another three bottles of the same in the wine rack. Snatching four wine glasses, I made my way behind Sam, who spun around to say as the ice cubes clunked into the glass pitcher, 'aren't they the most adorable couple in this world!'

I replied, 'make no mistake, they're not here; by accident, we left the swinging half doors between the kitchen and dining area to see the couple holding hands.

A few moments later, we shoveled the delectable foods onto our plates; Rhonda was last to lean over, finished heaping her special aromatic meal into her bowl, and then uncovering a basket with homemade cornbread with real corn, ah not from a box.

Not a peep left our lips while the delicious food entered ohmy did I enjoy the succulent juices and sipping delectable wine. Strangely, a weird sensation fell over me. It did seem like I'd been there before, a natural empirical maternal 'Déjà Vu lingering perhaps from my childhood, at the onset of our 3rd helping. Lester spoke, "one of our better friends owns San Rafael Joe's, he informed me that the FBI was only minutes behind your friend and you when you guys left the restaurant. At first, he was reluctant to turn over the closed-circuit videotapes of your meeting. Although rather than running afoul of the authorities, uhm, he relented before the Feds had the time to gather the proper Warrants."

Lester takes another sip of the vino and wipes his chin, "let's assume, with the newest technologies and Facial Recognition software, they will have both of your names soon enough." Daintily, Rhonda dabs her lips and adds, selecting her words carefully, "were certain that your partner who met you at the table in our friend's establishment was being scrutinized ah, followed by the Feds. Lester and I concluded that if you and Samantha were under surveillance, they'd already have you in custody for capital murder!"

I choked on a Carrot whew, Rhonda was so 'unassuming a matter of fact, I was sort of non-plussed. She could have been speaking about a grandchild instead of referring to 'Capital Murder' um casually with a nonchalant delivery and continued her pressing stare. Nothing seemed could unnerve this lady. Here she sat with Joe and me eating her meal like we were family… dining with killers! Rhonda droned on speaking; I listened, mesmerized at her doldruming undulations and casual delivery. Her voice stayed the course like a hypnotist or a mother reading a bedtime story to a great-grandchild, maybe a nursery rhyme.

I caught back up with her soliloquy, "we've been assured that you both were not followed, but my sister-in-law's daughter, whom the Marin County Sheriff Department employs, informed us that Mr. Tank Shaw was on their Radar out of prison on parole previously and was out of his jurisdiction a man who was known to be armed and extremely dangerous" she snickers.

Joe Sable.

Only speaking for myself, seeing Sam's slack jaw, I wasn't the 'Lone Ranger' filled with tumultuous concern, gulped down some water washing down the carrots and meat, intending to join the mellow fray when Lester retook the helm.

He placed his wrinkled, discolored, and withered palm flat on the deep dark Mahogany tabletop. His wife inserted a phone, 'Sam's phone.' "I want you to take this phone, submerge it, and destroy it at once, Ms. Timmons. Take whatever valuable information off of it. The FBI, no doubt, will figure out who you are. We cannot risk our organization, safe houses, or freedom; please do away with this phone now."

Sammy sprung to her feet "all I need on that phone is in my head!" We hadn't noticed spontaneously that Rhonda had pushed the Pitcher of water towards Sam, then interrupted with a motion and asked, "is it a secret? If so, I apologize and am sorry to divulge this, but missy, you have an 'Eidetic memory.' You can remember nearly anything that matters to you or what you want to focus on in exquisite detail. What you've heard or read, anything that interests you and you concentrate on. You're like a waking walking, breathing recording able to reconstruct even the remotest shelved memories of your past."

I watched, taken aback, as Sam's furrowed brows quivered, matching blinking retracting eyelids. I hadn't a clue as to how long my mouth was agog, but I felt my throat was peeling. I said, "are you kidding me? Is this some type of joke? Ronda, huh" before the 'huh' had left my parched lips plunk was the sound of Sam's deposed phone in the residual water of the pitcher. The eldest lioness most certainly had a grasp on Sam's tonsils, interestingly for me. Instead of denying Rhonda's crazy statements, she only said to the matriarch, 'please continue, Ms. Rhonda Grace.'

Now it was my turn to show external shock "how'd she know the name of this kind woman?"

Rhonda acquiesced and continued her monologue; "despite you growing up, raised within a very wealthy and affluent environment, you rebelled not unlike many of the privileged offspring of iconic families. Your genetics are second to none intellectually based doctors, professors, scientists, entrepreneurs, and financial gurus, with the lowly conniving politicians at the forefront of notoriety. Samantha, you became an outcast, not of your accord it was due to circumstances out of your control; overwhelmingly, my heart goes out to you, your caustic and traumatic molestations by a clergyman, a minister at your parent's church, you poor thing."

Sammy's bowed head told me all was true "you poor child, you weren't believed, and you ran away, relied on the lust of others, sold your body and mind, became a prostitute and a call girl ala escort. Samantha, with an IQ of 171, is just 25 years old. Your birthday is 7/25/94. You were born weighing 7 pounds 11 ounces your….” “Stop, wait! Instantly, a torrential downfall cascaded down her makeup-less cheeks. ‘No.’ Sammy was around the table in a ‘flat jack’ millisecond, embracing Rhonda. OmLord crying, huffing to take an inhalation, “were the same you and I” she gushed. ☺ .

The older woman merely gave an acquiescent passive expression, “yes, child, I am also Eidetic.” Lester trying his best to lighten the moment, said, “Yep, she’s hell to argue with. I can never win; she brings up the past 60 years together as if it were yesterday… forget it, given up. We haven’t argued in, I mean, a real slam bam barn-burner disagreement in nearly five decades.” Rhonda piped in “not true honey ‘looking at her wristwatch’ it’s been 49 years, five months, umh 151 days, 5 hours, and 17 minutes or thereabouts it was about your failing to clean out the cat’s box you do remember our three cats don’t you Maling, Tinkerbell, and Slinky?”
‘See!’ Lester’s amused expression with raised hands brought down the tension in the room, and we joined in… even I did so with limited humor.

After the awkwardness, we’d finished the delicious wine, and Sam and I started to clear off the table while Lester took a call out on the back deck. Sam had a soapy sponge in her hand. I rinsed and loaded the dishwasher. “Why didn’t you tell me about your talent or gift, ah IQ?” Staring up at me with a shade of green flecks, memorizing my pupils, “didn’t seem important is all Joe. How does it change things? Not an iota, right!” I was about to answer with a suitable comeback, aah response, ‘when through the swinging gate separating the kitchen from the…’ “Mission completed, Son!” as the older man held up his fist for a bump “good job, Joe the RV is no more, totally disintegrated left in small pieces, lucky no citizens were killed a few with minor injuries is all. Come into the living room, the news helicopters are hovering over the scene on live TV. It’s one of the things that in our long lifetime has changed. Real-time drama car chases, abductions O.J. in his Bronco, sensationalized life, and death all embellished online… drama live." The four of us stood amazed at the horrific crater and the devastation with strewn debris everywhere. The motorhome blown into pieces in the parking lot on a high def 75-inch flat-screen we watched impervious to the ramifications of the video, our lives, Sam, and mine, forever intermingled Bonny and Clyde like. Well, maybe not that flamboyantly notorious, but we were well on our way… not wanting our lives to end in carnage like theirs… nope! 😵 .

The second bottle of Caymus wine went down faster, uhm easier, I'd shared the text from Tank '(Done that later, good luck)' it wasn't 25 minutes later, 9:05 pm, that my handsome mug appeared on the screen damn. The following picture we saw was a full-on facial shot of my gorgeous accomplice with the caption, 'Do you know this face, woman? If so, call this number now for a reward!'

Not so suddenly, Lester and Rhonda stood, "we must retire, getting past our bedtime. We have so much to do and analyze for tomorrow. See you both after 5 am. Sleep well."

Hand in hand, they stood before us, still, weirdly, we obligingly hugged them; I'm not a hugger type of fellow don't like to touch strangers though it felt almost routine, umh traditional, normal wouldn't make a habit of it but quite cool I guess… wow.

It occurred to me as I saw my girl sitting on the couch later, cross-legged, a pillow below her boobs, that we didn't know who our benefactors were. Talk about 'going all in,' a gambling poker term, the elder 'Graces' took philanthropy to another cloud level. They would spend their remaining nights in Federal Prison if known collusion with us were revealed. I wondered how Sam knew their last names.

44

Mark Feral is on the hunt for some Joy!

Despite three triple shots of expresso, I phased out at 3:07 am feelings of anxiousness and hyperactivity were overwhelmingly insidious… I'd lost hours. It felt like an interrogation at the Winn River Casino. Nope, call it like it was, they'd thought I was the predator. Well, at least Joy did. I'd remember the brutal treatment at the Casino for the rest of my existence and refer to it as the 'Asian Fiasco.' Joy and her undercover partner Lola read me the Riot Act. Anw, uuhhh, I escaped 'by the skin of my teeth.' My question was… did I break clean? Will there be repercussions after the Feds check out my pictures and the closed-circuit video of their investigation?

Since I was paroled from Quentin, I fought against an unwinnable force, that of technology advances… indeed far from naïve, knowing that an integral way for me to remain free from the authorities was to be a step or three ahead of them. By shutting down my phones and computers for over 72 hours, this was the extent of my mini-revolution. Often by doing so going offline, I'd actually hurt my advancements toward goals that I was intent on achieving. Still, it was a necessary evil, sometimes just turning off the world.

My eyes were on fire, burning. I laid down spread Eagle on my quilted king-sized bed and missed 11 forms of correspondence. Lol Social Media at its worse, how irresponsible was I? Just barely doing enough to sustain my way of living, my excuse was the failed attempt at finally terminating, ending Wendi's reign of terror in my life, a sister that had cost me years in Prison along with my compadres 'Teflon Don' had nothing on her.

I was dwelling on the recent past, hoping to learn from it ah not repeat negativities. After my bro had orchestrated the killing by finding a likely candidate, ala the loser nurse Spike stepped to the forefront. I hired the loser to finalize her last breath; what did I do, ahem, rather than 'staying on point' working out strategies with Joe and the newly released, um, freed Tank. Of course, like a male whore I went out looking for, chasing self-satisfaction, uhm, women, sex conquer and control. This was how I dealt with disappointments, or celebrations didn't drink myself into oblivion, drug out, no chased skirts. This was all my red-blooded American maleness engorged in. I had needs, so what I dealt with my selfish demands? What else were females good for anyways, huh Lol? Their bodies were made for attachments. Albeit temporary, they meshed interlocking to perfection. What a Joy, aah, Joy, forget that name!

Blurry-eyed scanned Instagram, Facebook... messengers, Snaps, and Tweets. The list goes on and on, like infinity. I had a dozen plus texts and even dinosaur-like emails that were beyond obsolete from... Joe and Tank.

I caught up with what I'd missed, kept in the loop by Joe, decisions that I should have been part of like the C-4, detonations of our ugh, my Motorhome, our motorcycles confiscated, the list continued it was a Freakin losing proposition monies blown up... gone my Ass was on the line for every copper penny! 😫 .

On one of my monitors, I watched the video of Joe and an unidentified female with captions inducing the public to call in to receive a reward, money the root of all good. Who was this woman? She was pictured stunt riding on one of our motorcycles when the Private Investigator was liquidated. The Feds had found bunches of pictures, uh, photos of Joe and her at a clothing dress shop near Stinson Beach. They were freakin grinning like Newlyweds, what was up with her and Joe? Didn't he understand women were nothing but trouble? Man's undoing, Adam & Eve like, ugh, use them... leave them.

The final message on my VPN 'virtual personal network' was from Jaybirds militia, my partner; it was like a final nail in the night's coffin sent at 2:57 am 'SOJ' (State of Jefferson) had sent an urgent Tweet asking for me to attend an impromptu meeting in Boise, Idaho. The majority of my funding came from this group, the 'SOJ,' which was the most powerful militia in the USA that originated in Northern California and has since relocated up and around Montana, Utah, Nevada, and Idaho. We had several chapters in Oregon as well for the expansion continued like growing, replicating, and multiplying franchises, inclusive of humans that were sick and tired of Governmental restraints and control.

Apparently, Joe had called an operative in Marin County and sought refuge at one of the SOJ's safe houses. The woman was also at the retreat, not going to work, so Joe had to drop the whore, and eliminate the woman.

Awake, not fully functional with not three hours of rest, the time was 6:19 am couldn't shake the corroding, pungent smell of my dream state's putrid remnants. No, let's call it Vile ugliness engulfing me like muddy quicksand, glaring at me was my Sister's Animal eyes. Wendi haunted me, laughing at me and chastising me like when she was a child. I hate her, but there she was, tunnel vision filling her smirking face. I'm strapped down in what appeared to be old 'Sparky' San Quentin's electric chair, pulling on the restraints, biting on the bit, fighting. At the same time, I watch Wendi cackle with a chortle, miming her right hand towards my red sweating face, her right thumb up and forefinger pointed at me a gun. She simultaneously fires her thumb blows a kiss, and slams down the switch to the Electric Chair as my eyes glow with fire… burnt-fried eyeballs.

Next, it was like I was riding a mop, not a broom. I then found myself looking through a 2-way mirror Joe Sable sat with Tank Shaw and the mystery woman. They had knives and forks, cutting succulent pieces of what appeared or looked like prime rib. Sipping on red wine, right across sitting comfortably next to Rico Captor and Director Tanya Firm, they likewise were gorging greedily. Wolfing down a 5-star meal, Wendi's left-hand slams down the lever again, and my eyes spark out… shooting out from the sockets. I was a crispy skeleton.

Would it end, or did I have to slice my own throat? In front of me was a small bowl of grits, plain looking enough, but there was movement, ugh, maggots. I'm chained, shackled, and cuffed on a smallish stool. Sitting to my immediate left was a round-faced woman dressed in an outfit better described as a party dress with frilly flowers split in the low back top like a dancer's exotic frock. Oh, fk, it was Joy the Laotian from the Casino.

I viciously slapped my right cheek, knocking some sense back into my reality, shaking with fatigue, slipped into the shower, and... Jeesh, I have to regain my composure; hell, someone dropped some LSD acid in my water?

Instead of standing erect in the shower, I sat on a custom bench and let the water circulate through my body until the hot water heaters tank lost the battle. Cold water flushed me out. Time to take charge of my life; that's when I heard the helicopter's\ horns, sirens, and my buzzer at the gate was going off. 'They' were here!

The fatigue was temporary, subsiding as fast as an archers arrow, my endorphin glands kicking in, peering at the high-definition monitors at the front gate. It looked like a shot of gloom and doom, a Transylvania-like Vampire 'B' horror movie... where the cemetery is dreary and covered in a layer of fog... with Wolves, of course, howling ferociously.

Stacked on my narrow road at my gate were police cars. The haze once again showed thick grey smoke, and visibility was hampered. Was there another fire nearby? Was I being sought after by the powers to be for punishment? Tell me, were my sins against humanity uh totally undeserved? I have been treated like a stepchild since I was born.

I once again pushed the intercom 'what's going on?' 'sorry, sir, but you must be evacuated rrh again at once. The fire has switched directions. The wind is blowing this way. Your property is in its direct path!' But I started futilely trying to defend my position because my home was built from steel studs. All exterior walls were wrapped with wire lath and then thick layers of stucco. The roof was made of synthetic fiberboard with Spanish tile, with nothing to burn... in fact, my argument could also include proof from the horrific Oakland, California fire years ago.

That raging fire had burned down every wooden home in its path, except three dwellings built with steel and concrete that survived; they didn't and couldn't burn up, such as mine, built by the same 'General Contractors, Meyers Family Steel' although the walls were smudged with soot. Also, the raging fire had caused some of the interior belongings to melt because of the heat, but the frame withstood the fire.

I realized this would be a useless debate as I heard the Fire Chief say again over my speakers, "we need you and your family and pets out within 15 minutes, please." Well, here I go again, besides being alarmed… jumbled self-preservation kicked in unabashed contradictions. What do I do with the two barely living attorneys 'Pat and John.' The quick decision as I took my 9 mm. Glock silencer attached down to the steel barn and put bullets in their heads enough. Sorry for my bro Joe who wanted to torture them to death for fun.

I think there's such a thing as eminent domain; I will have to check, in any case. Even so, I'm dismayed that these firefighters umh police could take over my property and use it as a mini command base. Anxiety stricken wasn't my nature, but lately, I'd have to argue that I'm stressing. I bounce back to a long time ago when I was being analyzed by several Forensic Psychologists like a plural, which diagnosed me umh ugh, how to soften this diagnosis? Nope, damnit, it wasn't true. I am a good person deep inside. They labeled me a predator, a fkn Psychopath with many elongated words on their reports and charts, most with three syllables or more that started with letters such as 'non or un' non-regretful, unapologetic, unremorseful, unashamed Sociopath. Yuh kinda get my point, I'm sure… like screw all of you, uh, to hell with them and everyone. Indeed they were correct about me being an anti-social sociopath heck, take up join hands with me, and I'll lead you to blissful purgatory. That's where all of you are heading anyways… yeah!

I haven't a conscious nope, no fear of repercussions, nada repentance, a viper indifferent to all humankind. If I had a poisonous bomb or a repellant, I'd blow them all away at my gate. How dare they trample on my earth! I know I am on one of my tangents outraged and anal, but this is part of me, uhm, is me!

Eleven minutes later, I am met at my gate parking alongside the Fire Marshal… sitting in my driver's seat, warming up the diesel with a 27-foot trailer behind me. "Sir, I'm going to need you to leave your gate open just in case we need to fight the fire from the perimeter of your land. Thank you, we will also need access to your pond for our water cannons." I guess that was an order, right? The Chief continues, "the closest evacuation center is at Shasta College" he sighs with grey-blue eyes matching the soot that was layered on his upper cheekbones and fire hat. "What about looting and criminals breaking into my house?" I asked, I know, yeah, 'calling the kettle black, yup.' "We will do our best to keep a handle on that, sir."

I left my gate secured by the firefighters, loaded my dogs and cats again into a trailer, and followed an escort car down Dry Creek road and out of the area.

Yes, I'm in one of my standard philosophic moods. Sometimes I drift like in the doldrums. A project of fiction overlaps facts based on our real-world non-fiction, which is the case today. I make lite of these fires, although I can't deny they are devastating to anything in their paths. Killing and destroying all in their ways, but I only care about myself and what I might lose. Is that so bad? Aren't you all just like me?... Liars! ☺ . Yep!

I turned right on Bear Creek Road and made my way to East 299 Hwy having a plan constantly in place. I had a cabin outside of 'Hat Creek,' a super small town or spot in the road. It was a beautiful little five acres and perfect to hide out for a while.

I could check my home and outbuildings from there. My security system had a backup battery system and Solar energy inverter powered up in case electricity was lost. I was flummoxed and pissed off. Just thinking about this imposition irked the shit out of me. Then shoveling more crap on my already negative disposition... ugh, I'm ticked off at the orders given to me... to travel North to Boise, Idaho, for a high-level conference. This was relayed to me by Jaybird. Our Militia, the S.O.J. or 'State of Jefferson,' was the foremost liberator for America's Constitutional rights.

I wouldn't be free out of Quentin if not for Jaybird and the Militia; I just was agitated, for the last thing I wanted to do was attend this impromptu, unscheduled meeting, but alas, the likeminded soldiers of these Sovereign organizations and militias were my only allies.

I reminded myself as I made my way to Hat Creek to try and opt out of this meeting and, at the least, send Joe in my place. Even though the orders were explicit, it was a mandatory commitment that I couldn't shirk.

Fires in Northern California had displaced over 45,000 people. The traffic was heavy, edgy bumper-to-bumper chaos, families packing whatever they could from their homes; plugged into my cigarette lighter orifice was one of my computers and an iPad. Which sat attached to Velcro on the center console. I was delighted and thrilled to see the flashing dot tracking my luscious prey; she was only 15.5 miles away. I was almost in the small town of Shingletown coincidence or fate? Naturally, I sided with fate. I had to hit the brakes abruptly for this fool on a motorcycle crowded in only left a 5ft gap; the asshole was rude and obnoxious still… I didn't allow that to detract from what stimulated my imagination.

A bit of reminiscing brought the reality to fruition 'after being escorted out of the Winn River Casino only the night before, watching the three FBI Agents arriving before me leaving, taking the one-way road out of the parking lot. Recollecting what Joy had said to Lola, zooming in with my sonar ears, 'we're staying at the hotel here at the Casino; you know the Mary Lake Subdivision has been evacuated. The Fire in Igo is closing in on the Whiskey Town lake area.' 'Lucky to find a place to stay at all,' whined Joy. 'Hey, do you know where the nearest 24-hour grocery store is by chance? I need to load up on some basics.' 'Check at the front desk,' said Lola.

With that conversation in mind, I parked my Dodge truck on Railway Avenue and jogged back to the Casino with a pair of binoculars hoping that Lil Ms. Joy didn't park in the back lot. Luck with timing was solidly on my side, destiny, um entrenched, predestined actions later to avail you, truly my ecstatic raptures. The cute Laotian with an adorable wiggle, petite and amorous, nearly my erotic centerpiece, I'd hoped. I watched her pop the door on a Lil green Ford Focus. I bailed then at triple speed, was only five cars behind her; she pulled into a 7/11 store and then vanished inside.

My plan smooth as silk and as easy as pie-alamode, I strolled up and placed a magnetized chip GPS on the other side of the plastic hard rubber bumper... done that, yup.

The powers to be that governed my existence proved not to be stingy and pitiless unsympathetic to my disposition of desired destiny aligned with my self-centered own being proof there was a devil. Because Joy had just parked her Ford at a home, aah, somewhere in Shingletown near exactly where I found myself stuck in fire traffic... she'd be mine now, all fkn mine.

Joy's cold-hearted attack on me, her insinuations, accusations of blame heaped upon me, even her display of castigating disdainful eyes, confident that I was the man who abducted the other Asians. I was the person who kidnapped them from other Casino's held them for days. If they supplied scintillatingly enjoyable sensations, I'd keep them longer than a week, then once worn-out, tortured relentlessly Yum and Done. Knowing the games of disclosure, meaning the authorities tried to keep subtle nuances of felonies secret from the public, for one reason there were so many freaks that claimed they were the violators, what ole Joy and Lola didn't divulge was what the predator also did to his victims, lol. I'd pierce body parts from noses, nipples, and belly buttons to the hiding clitoris. Yeah, I'm an artist, including body paint. I was a modern 'Leonardo da Vinci,' their mesmerizing portraits forever etched into memory chips.

Well, of course, exculpating evidence exonerated me of those atrocious wicked, appalling deeds. It soon would-be time to bring Joy to her knees, I'd be her salvation. How long would she exhort righteousness earnestly? There would be no justice, mercy, or forgiveness. She needed to be fully extricated, circumcised, and punished for her sins... Yep-Yum soon mealtime! ☺ .

45

Jax Foul and Sunshine Feral.

I could not fathom much that could be as dreary as laying docile-dormant flat on your back for days, weeks, or God forbid months, heck, not even close to my favorite sleeping, umh, resting position. I enjoy when conscious... pillows lodged between my thighs and legs, comfy in a fetal-type wrap. Tedious dullness and boredom enveloped all of me. As bizarre as this sounds, I was tired of laying here faking this Coma, raring to go and become the actual manifestation of me. Let 'Sunshine' be free. Jax and I together off-site out of this mental hospital NIA, as long as I stayed on the prescription medications prescribed by Dr. Honcho, there wasn't a chance for interruptions by my wimpy 'worse half' Wendi... A fine line exists, all gaged by perceptions. If I sprung up and demanded real clothes shed this thin hospital gown, all the humans that believe my image to be Wendi would be wrong. No one could see what constitutes the person behind this epidermis. From her so-called husband David to Rico and Tanya, even my Jax has been cursed, um, mesmerized by the other me, the girly female me, not to misunderstand that I'm not 101% XX Chromosomes Naw! Hormones prove this out. It's all about one's mindset. Not ever going to be a typical woman atypical; I'd like to think of myself as exceptionally extraordinary.

Sometimes I believe I'm more Man than Woman... ahh mindful of being able to broaden my horizons by interweaving the various roles orchestrated and played out by both genders. I perceive this as a definite advantage for me. I'm able to use my female stratagem and allure to ensnare or deceive males with the body and look of a petite blonde woman, sexy with matching assets I can scheme guilefully to conquer, manipulate, ah and take dominant control... deceptively. I reverse the male's inherent desired inertia; I'm not the prey. Quite the opposite, for I know how to use my subtle sexiness. The simple-minded men who are known for chasing women wanting only one thing, sexual conquests... what superficial fools. I can play that game for sure, and many more ☺

A mirror in my soul, being Sunshine, would reflect a sly-cunning, subtly wily girl who can be the best of both genders. Maybe I'm a 'tri-sexual,' I think, perhaps… confused?

Nurse Frank gently wipes a cool, wet cloth over my forehead "Jax, if there's any change with her, please push the emergency button. I'll be back to check on her in three hrs. Dr. Hawkins will be back on site in about seven hours, and you still have the beeper, right?" "Yes, Frank, when I leave her bedside, I will leave it with Marshal Kara."

I hear the door latched shut, whispering, "Jax honey, please get me out of this death bed. I'm becoming one with this fkn gurney!" "Sunshine, this topic has been addressed too many times. There would be horrendous consequences if you came out of the coma a different person or your alter-ego." "Not wanting to argue with you, Jax, but I can fake being Wendi to the hilt, fool everyone, even you, pal!"

"Sunshine, every mannerism expression, including your vocabulary, rational… the way you think and speak is quite the opposite of the selfless love and compassion that all the people that know Wendi are familiar with. If you blurt out proof that your back out of the schizophrenic fugue…." "Hold up, Jax, wait for a fkn second" he then puts a finger over, um, between my lips and says, "you couldn't fool your mother for a split second. Your father would take a bit longer; Rico would figure it out soon after that!" Being stubborn-pigheaded, I soldiered on, "you have an apartment offsite. Why can't we live together and be committed to each other, as subcontractors for NIA get paid for the missions and operations they want to utilize us on?" Jax shook his chin "remember, if your family discovers your back in charge of Wendi's shell, they will have you shipped elsewhere for further medical attention. We still don't know how they will react to you being shot with the dart here at NIA. We're on a precarious slope." He slouches down in a chair beside my gurney.

"Sunshine, certainly I sympathize with your desperate conditions, yet it's not terminal… now I have a 55-page um report file to examine about our next assignment and specific tasks which only you can perform, South of the border a warlord gangster cartel boss has infiltrated and hi-jacked the last shipment of Heroin from China, which if not circumvented could cause an all-out war."

I burst out, howling "oh no, for real? I thought you wouldn't engage in drug deals. Jax, the humanitarian saver of children. Yah no, your…." "Ssshh, Kara will hear you, girl, and besides, I haven't fully decided to join the team on this operation. The Procurator-General and Hallinan briefed me on why I was a necessary cog in the mission. The cartel soldiers are guilty of murdering women and children. It boils down to what is the lesser of evil. The true reason I was approached lies on your gurney… You, uh, you're needed, and I am connected to you. Our affinity for each other and the facts prove our dynamics. In total, we've worked alongside one another on nine missions, impeccably finished with unblemished records for accuracy and the goals desired achieved. We go together like peanut butter and jelly… milk, and cookies… if you will!"

"Such banalities, so cliché Jax. I've been musing over the past and don't like the conclusions; where's my money at? Am I a slave? Where's the justice in all of this? Check out our last operation; what saving the Diplomats wife and child, huh… how much were you paid and me? Hum. Maybe we go together not like 'PB&J' but 'Chemotherapy & hair growth!' I'm never going to risk my life for nothing again. I owe NIA nada I…." "Sun, stop. I geez, it's not always about money, it's about…" "sure, Jax, yah got plenty. I almost forgot offshore accounts. Yeah, your rich enough, right set for life after NIA is over, retire, and ride off into the sunset. Yeah!" Jax couldn't deny his fat cryptocurrency accounts or his offshore investments. Sunshine was correct, she'd not received a darn penny, but he had to soldier on…and reign her in. Jax made a firm decision to speak with Terrance and advocate for a slice of the pie for Wendi/Sunshine, it was only right.

"I don't like the direction we're going here" "well, boy, get used to it ain't no way 'Ms. Goodie 2 shoes' is coming back. Wendi is dead forever now. I will not allow her back in charge of my vessel, which, if I dare say, is drop-dead gorgeous; ahh, like that line, I want no less than a million dollars cash for any operation in the future. Oh, in the rears back pay of, let's say, umh. Ugh, 5 million dollars will do and is surely owed to me for the last nine operations. If I don't see proof of this deposit in my offshore account, I will not offer up a bowel movement for any of you. Tell good ole Terrance to put that in his pipe and torch it!"

"Ahh, I forgot how crude and obnoxious you can be; you're really…" "no, I'm a realist tending to believe in capitalism. I perform a task, a service, and risk my tush… life and limb for others to coup billions of dollars, like a trained monkey. No more… don't mess with me, boy." "I'm not your boy or anyone's. Stop with your sarcastic, argumentative attitudes. I will see if I can exclude you from any upcoming operations… now I'm gone. You behave, Sunshine!"

I had to smirk; I was getting under his skin like he was done with me literally before I found that I could not only read and communicate with animals, reptiles, mammals, gophers, or feathered friends, or even a freakin fish. Now I read Jax's mind. 'Yes, it's me. I'm the freak show herself, the animal seer!' "You know something, Sunshine; this is our very first argument.…" "Naw, don't think so, just a reality check, no disrespect meant, why don't you take a day or three break… and ponder all that I've said, relay this conversation to the boss ahh Terrance Hallinan and the so-called board, let them know I am done being used, it's been long enough I'm no fkn, Guppy! Umh, I'm sure you know how damn fond I am of you… I love you, boy!" Jax frowned, stepped to the door, and sneered back at me.

"If it makes you happy, hand me the file. I'll stick it under my pillow and peruse it later, and oh, you didn't answer me. What does this mission have to do with my skill base? Why am I needed on this operation?" Jax spins around. "Very well, Sunshine, the ruthless cartel mafioso has a kinship-like adoration for Hogs trained hogs warthogs that will attack humans on her call and is said to have a few of these pets roam freely in her villas. Pigs are far more dangerous and useable than dogs or, for that matter, any other animals that can be domesticated. With nearly foot-long tusks, the videos of them slaying enemies in cages and pits have been sold all over the globe. The hogs are bloodthirsty, fervently with great ardor-passionately devouring her enemies, then they cannibalize all body parts, not leaving a trace of bone marrow or zero DNA!"

"Did you say she?" "Yes, the mafioso is female and likes to enjoy releasing her prisoners in an auditorium pen or in her specially constructed replica of one of ancient Rome's Cathedral's uh Gladiator pits. She lets one captive out at a time, even arms them with a sword: she's seen laughing on video, saying it's all fair play, right? They have a weapon to defend themselves if they make it out alive she exonerates them and lets them go. As of yet, no one has walked away from the Hogs. Her videos have been banned across social media sites; Sunshine, it's not the Hogs, however. This vixen has a pet pig that travels everywhere with her and goes on a damn leash! I'm sure you can pick the piggy brain for information Sunshine…."

With a noteworthy smirl… 'smirk-smile,' I chimed in, "I have to say it all sounds engorgingly intriguing. You know, Pigs have a higher IQ than Canines challenging Apes and monkeys on the smartness table. Ssshh, don't let Rocco or Koko hear that." I grinned at my reference to Rocco, the Silver Back Gorilla who saved my drowning life at the San Francisco Zoo, and his son Koko who had learned over 200 spoken words via sign language. Rocco was born in captivity on 7/4/71 and was still viable on 6/21/19 at the ripe gorilla age of 47. My gorilla savior, who not only saved my life but instilled this gift or curse that now inhabits my very soul, uhm, the inherent reason I was a paranormal seer of animals! I planned on making one more trip to the San Francisco Zoo to visit my favorite animal of all time 'Rocco.'

I looked up at Jax, who stood unmoving like entranced "give me a kiss… as ridiculous as this will sound, I'm exhausted and need to rest!" He leaned over me, and I grabbed his head, pulled him in, took his left hand, and placed it on my erect boob. He didn't yank away a good sign, indeed. "I'll be back, Sun" he backed away as soon as I closed my veils… eyelids. Nighty-nite.

In a soundproof anti-bugged room with each board member's body scanned, this was to be a 55-billion-dollar deal. Details all in privacy secrets that, if known, speculators could reap a cool billion dollars in a day. The SEC (security exchange commission) was all over any IPOs. All information gleaned had to be vetted meticulously, played out, and orchestrated symphony-like. The Options market in the Stock market was the easiest way to profit from insider information.

So why was I invited or brought on this mission? Well, the CEO went nowhere without her 'Macaw Parrots' bought and nourished straight from Brazil. The aptly named creatures of feathers, 'Ozzy and Harriet,' the wise birds, had fantastic memory retention. Jax and I were in a utility closet, dressed attired in baggy, less-than-flattering Janitorial clothes. I had the near-impossible task of getting the Macaws alone for a debriefing. Mind you, this was no easy endeavor, uhm task, for like has been beaten into my head, 'Timing was everything in life' so we waited then it became 'go time' I got alone time with the Parrots, and oh they were blabbermouths, Yeah!

-46-

Terrance Hallinan trying to waylay FBI Agent Lucy Link.

The elevator opens, and he hurries out. Terrance bypasses the walk-through body scans as he scuttles out to the lobby. Dual confluences caused some foot traffic at the exit of NIA. Visiting hours were just ending, and a new shift change of guards that were coming and going… so there was a line of civilians exiting. Terrance was furious… sweating, and irritated that the FBI would show up in force without an announcement. What was he supposed to do, hum, give them 'Carte Blanche' free reign? Terrance moaned outwardly, 'ahh, I will be allowing zero latitudes. This is my fricken establishment… NIA would not be violated by the FBI.'

Jumping into a waiting Golfcart and driving towards the entrance gates, then slowly bringing his foot off the accelerator pedal, his brain in a quandary, working at 'hyper-speed-warp speed' he had to handle this situation cleverly uhm, 'kid-gloves.' Terrance slowed down his thought process wanting to advance into the political arena locally. Already had a few feathers in his ball cap… having been celebrated and honored just weeks before <u>'Award Ceremonies Attorney of the Year.'</u> Now a record five times nearly an unblemished record in Circuit and Federal courts, Terrance was the 'Cat's Meow.' A superstar lawyer renowned in the Bay Area, with him owning the largest law firm in San Francisco and a skyscraper with his name etched upon it, he thought if he didn't have pull, then no one in this world did!

He radioed the guards at the gates to open up, noticing three SUVs parked at an overfill area usually utilized for when they held special events at NIA, driving the Golfcart up with confidence, now with a calm disposition, relaxingly for that was the demeanor that he must project.

A robust redhead in a Grey pants suit was pacing, holding a phone to her ear, obviously hadn't heard the electric cart approach. She tossed her hand up, pointing, then walked briskly striding towards him. He was already moving to meet her. "I presume your Agent Lucy Link. I'm Terrance Hallinan, the CEO of NIA. What can I do for …" "Mr. Hallinan, why are we being halted, stopped from entering this, uh, your facility? I'll remind you that at this very moment, you are holding 11 Federal prisoners, umh, inmates, for assessment purposes. I will make sure that you never…." "Please refer to me as Terrance. Yes, you're correct; we are grateful for your business to provide the FBI with the finest service and top-notch evaluations. I might add we even have been known to fudge the results of our examinations for your…." "Terrance, I'm not here with a team of Forensic specialists to waste your time or ours. A serious crime has been committed inside your institution. A patient in Federal custody was…." "Hold on a second; we have our own Forensic teams going over the crime scene. We don't need you to contaminate…." "Pardon me, Mr. Hallinan, but Ms. Wendi Feral was shot by a tranquilizer dart gun inside your facility. This by itself is enough grounds for us to enter ughhhh, that gives us plenty of reason to investigate…."

"Lucy, we have everything under control; please show me the precedent or mandates from your FBI that gives you the right to overrule my authority and our in-house investigation of the unfortunate situation; we are on top of it with video cameras and vantage points that have…." "Terrance, we find this curious that Wendi had an attempt from one of your employees to assassinate her not a week ago, and now she is shot after barely being cognizant a week afterward by another of your staff. Who else would have had a sophisticated weapon? Frankly, your establishment isn't safe, I don't know what is going on, but I will tell you I plan to find out; now open the gates and let us in to do our job, or you will be sorry!"

Her phone buzzes and lights up the falling dusk. The sun disappeared long ago now the parking lot light posts were aglow. Terrance thought looking at Lucy walk in a damn circle away from him… he needed to calm down this situation. Staring blankly at her phone screen, Lucy says, "I've got to take this. It's Director Tanya Firm, ahh mister, and you don't want to find yourself on the wrong side of Tanya. She will close down this Prison!"

Terrance strolls away, musing that this isn't going well, not good. How could he circumvent this situation from spiraling out of control should he make some important calls of his own? 'No reasons to panic or to jump to conclusions… although NIA could afford to lose the Federal inmates, subsidization monies… doing so would hurt shareholders and the bottom-line net profit for we charged absorbent fees to interrogate, ahh, I mean to evaluate the Federal prisoners, with overbearing credence directed by the powermongers inside the Federal machine to dictate who was cognizant or sane to stand trial.

Many of the prominent defendants try their minds on the insanity plea; if the Feds were to pull out of the contract, our investors would go berserk for each inmate, NIA profits upwards of $79,000 for the three-week stay, and assessment of our professional staff I must....' I see Lucy barking and trotting once again in my direction.

"Mr. Hallinan, Director Firm, would like to speak with you," she hands over her phone 'hello' "let's bypass pleasantries, Terrance. We know each other, and I don't deal with bullshit well; I suggest you let my team in to investigate this latest attack on Ms. Feral...." "Tanya, please, we've always had a great rapport; I want to keep this in-house...." "Terrance, do you have the shooter in custody? Why was she shot with a dart? For what purpose? How bizarre is that? Uh, kind of ridiculous there's got to be ulterior motives; tell me, when was the last time you heard of someone shot with a tranquilizer gun? Terrance, she could have easily been murdered, and whom the Hell had access to a weapon on the prison grounds other than your staff? Give me one verifiable answer now since you've handled this investigation in-house. What do you have to say... to report? Rico will be there in the morning. I wouldn't want to be in your shoes; answer me, Terrance!"

He didn't want to engage with Tanya anymore and handed off the phone to Agent Lucie Link. Terrance strolled a few feet away, taking his radio from his hip.

Again Lucy invaded his space; he watched her cheeks grow large, face like a Puff adder snake; uh; she sucked in a big inhale, wiping her brow. Lucy held her phone up, the speaker blasting on... "Oh, Terrance, I will be doing you one better if you don't cooperate with me... us. I will do my best to let the media in on a few of NIA's egregious errors regarding your special outpatient Wendi Feral. Whom I might remind you is there in your Neurological hospital of her own free will. My defecating press releases should sufficiently sink your stock price in the toilet...Lol, Surely"

Terrance sighed, sucking in an overpowering breath of oxygen, nearly choking, rationalized at how he could maneuver around Tanya and Lucie's verbal assaults, "umh, aah," he stuttered, knowing fair well that it was his Warden Ursula Anders, who ordered the dart to be fired and that there truly wasn't an ongoing investigation in-house at all. The last thing he could handle at this time was the media to get wind of this latest incident they'd be clawing at the gates, heck already NIA was being pummeled worldwide by conspiratorial theorists with a sniper now identified to be Joe Sable killing one of his nurses who'd attempted to kill Wendi. The negative press continued precipitously like a storm front of an arriving Hurricane; NIA's stock price was in a steep decline, the downward momentum gaining hell, and the price per share had dropped way below the 50-day moving avg. Now was in Bear market territory. Hedge fund owners Mutual funds and ETFs were screaming blood-thirsty like NIA was on the precipice of a cliff kneeling on Banana peels!

FBI, Lucy Link's phone buzzed again; after a moment, the phone was back in Terrance's paw. "Terrance, did the Cat get your tongue? Ahh, you there? Hello, did you hang up on me?..." "Oh yeah, ah, sorry, Tanya, what I meant to say was I need this to remain in-house, no leaks to the public. NIA's footing in the stock market is already precarious enough; we're already facing Hurricane Gale forces..." "I wish I could commiserate with you, dude, but I could care less if your stock price drops off the cliff into the toilet. Maybe I should flush it myself or 'short or buy puts' of some of your shares, lol. What I will do for you is speak to Agent Link and make sure that everything still is confidential in-house. As you've said a dozen times... now we will need all camera feeds and complete cooperation from your staff. You understand this, Terrance, any games, and I...."

Terrance was still peeved at her referencing him as Dude. Total disrespect but muttered a subtle "certainly, Tanya." "Okay, then we have an understanding. Let me speak to Agent Lucy Link!"

He turned away and took up his radio, speaking with his head of security Walter Hale "listen, Walter, as we've previously discussed, the FBI is here. I want you to cooperate fully with them, excluding the explicit photos of the shooter!" "Yes, sir, I gotcha. I won't let you down, sir."

A few minutes later, the cocky Agent Link brazenly struts up as if she'd grown massive balls. He mitigates her aggressive approach "go ahead through the gates. My head of security, Mr. Walter Hale, will meet you in the lobby. If you need anything else, take my card. I told Walter to give you one of our radios for communication. Unfortunately, I am late for a meeting. Good luck, Lucy." She smugly smirks and says nothing but turns to her underlings, who at once jump to attention.

Terrance closed the door 17 minutes later with a gentle thud; Ursula, Liz, and Larry displayed at him wide-eyed questioning countenances in which he merely said, "the Feds are now onsite, full-scale investigation with that being said, if they discover…?" "How do we stem the bleeding" interrupts a panicked Ursula. Terrance calmly says, "let's brainwave all ideas. I don't care how ludicrous nothing at this point is inconsequential, Liz. Will you please start!" "Ok, to state the obvious, why would anyone fire a dart into Wendi, especially with the drug concoction I put together, ugh, chemical mixtures that synergistically interact specifically with…." "Liz spit it out. No need for your intellectual jargon to the point!" Liz shakes her head condescendingly. "Yes, well, I went to our lab and filled our largest beakers with the same drug cocktail that the dart had injected into Wendi. Next, I had Walter take the enhanced darts to our weapons room. He exchanged several darts with that formula, reloaded the dart-firing weapons, and followed Ursula's order to shoot Wendi. Therefore the Feds will find the exact formula in other darts in our weapons room."

He grins and smiles with a long-lasting smirl for the first time since his secretaries fellatio's finish "that's my girl fabulous idea," Liz feeling smug, added, "so when Doctor Hawkins's blood panel comes back tomorrow, it will match some of the darts that are in several of our rifles… this way the

Feds can't conclude that the drugs that were injected into Wendi were specifically made for her and purposely done so. Therefore the same concoction the shooter used was in many chambers of the dart rifles. This covers our butts. Suffice it to say, there goes that part of the equation, umh, of us being complicit or conspiratorial. Remember, our security manuals read that non-lethal dart rifles are to be used against uprisings, melee brawls, or riots." Liz grins, "Excellent, Liz, well done," yelps Terrance.

Ursula gulped iced tea and decided to piggyback this idea ugh, concept because she hadn't a clue, only was jonesing for her next drink sobriety was hell, dry mouth tongue glued, she started like slow crawl to espouse some verbiage with a smidgeon of a slur then momentum took hold "Fantastic sure, but the FBI is going to zone in on why was Wendi singled out and most assuredly who fired the dart." Their eyes were upon her now, "we need to find us a scapegoat, Pigeon, to bear the blame. Someone who had the capacity and combination to our locked weapons arsenal, conjoining that with a grudge or pent-up hatred for Wendi Feral, if we can provide the Feds with the culprit quickly and concisely, it will stop them in their tracks and halt further investigating and get them the hell out of NIA this will solve all of the whys, how's, and who's!"

"Brilliant, I mean brilliant, yes, Ursula, this or that will send Agent Link packing back on out the gates." Ursula glowed majestically from both his accolades and the alcoholic juices flowing through her blood. Seized by cottonmouth saliva-less, she started sucking on a straw of water. Ursula watched the others, chatting it up animatedly. She slyly reached into her side pocket for the airplane-sized plastic bottle of Vodka, then thought better of it, shaking, jonesing with withdrawals, needing another shot.

Fresh from his 5-mile run and obstacle course, Larry felt he was 'clicking on all cylinders,' and he shouldn't be the A.W. assistant warden. Nope stared at the three who sat before him bullshit. He pondered the drunken, floozy, adamantly wood-be Warden Ursula was promoted over him because he was Gay, ah… homosexual, so what? This is 2019, for freakin sake.

Terrance was homophobic, but Larry had decided long ago that he'd persevere... his time was coming. Surely Ursula would falter if Cirrhosis didn't devour her liver first, his multiple fantasies of poisoning her bottles of booze on hold temporarily.

Larry grins within and shouts out. "I've got the quintessential, paradigmatic classic fall-guy scapegoat we've got Correctional Officer, Mr. Billy Goad. The dude has filed multiple grievances on the preferential treatment of Wendi. He took up a dislike for her instantly. He's only 11 months from retirement, a pliable individual whom I believe at the last illegal run of our staff's credit scores showed poor Billy was insolvent divorced taken to the cleaners by his Ex!" Larry looked at Ursula guilefully "a drunken man who when he's not working is drinking his sorrows goodbye, we could offer him a lucrative deal. I betcha that he'd jump on it!"

Terrance replied with less enthusiasm than Larry would have liked, "the problem is can we trust Mr. Goad alcoholics are notoriously untrustworthy. I mean, Larry, don't get me wrong, it's an excellent alternative, a perfect solution, except for him being an alcoholic and being locked up and interrogated for days. He will be going through detox in which he'd sell his own Mother for a shot of Whiskey!" They pause all in their own corners, nose's up against the wall "let's look at his employee profile Liz. Will you scan it for us over to the main screen? While she's doing so, I want to address an ongoing dilemma that we face. As you are aware, I was up in the Seattle area high-level conference, and we at NIA were awarded a contract that will heft or boost our bonuses this year by up to 15% more. Sunshine Feral is an integral part of why we were given this opportunity... without her, a rival mercenary unit from the East coast would have landed the latest contract on the Diplomat dilemma."

Terrance leans forward, scanning their expressions, "Wendi was a self-admit. Her husband had signed her in for the standard 180-day commitment hold, which passed almost three months ago. What's the chance we could get hubby David to re-admit her before Rico and the FBI ultimately take her from us? Inevitably this will most likely be their final conclusion and solution. After all, who could blame them for the latest development? It doesn't look good for us, so if you want that 15% bonus, you better help... come up with some viable answers!"

Liz pipes in, not bothering with Terrance's embellishments nor concerns. "Larry might be on to something here. Billy Goad has had several appointments with our Psych department. He's a touch unstable the divorce has torn him up mentally, and adding in his substance abuse, the poor guy is deteriorating at a brisk pace. He's currently mixing alcohol with Prozac, which has him tittering on a 'see-saw' he has a surefire reason documented in his own words. Heck, his written complaints attacking Wendi Feral should be the icing on the proverbial Cake!" Larry hops into the fray "yeah, as of yesterday, he's filed seven complaints against her!" he throws up his arms. <u>"Wait, that's it... after he confesses to the attack on Wendi, you can throw him over the edge of the cliff with a chemical cocktail that he will be lucky even to be able to recall his own name!"</u>

Terrance claps three times with exuberance "well, Hell-yeah," the others had 'shit-eating cat chewing up the Canary' expressions. Ursula checks her iPad. "Billy is on floor #5 working right now at our super max wing. Do you want me to bring him over to us?" "yes and no," barked Terrance. "I cannot be involved in this negotiation or deal, nor do I want either you, Liz or you, Ursula. This is going to be Larry's baby." Leveling his forefinger at Larry, "your to do all the negotiations; keep me abreast of all the logistics. How much money will be needed to ply our Mr. Billy Goad into taking the fall? Oh, Larry, we will need to include Walter in this, so let's have both of them meet you in your office in 25 minutes. Walter is working with the annoying Agent Link. He can act unwittingly and lead ole Lucy to our conclusions; this is a perfect ending for their investigation, great Idea Larry."

Larry begrudgingly nods, feeling a bit underwhelmed and undervalued. Was he only the fkn sacrificial lamb uh faggot...

because of his sexual orientation. He thought he was being ostracized. Glumly, he stood, then Terrance caught the vibes. "Larry, I have full confidence in your abilities to handle this precarious situation to manipulate Billy into our scheme... this will be a major feather in your cap; get it done. Keep all the inline speakers, and video's on. I will monitor and listen to your interactions. Get it done!"

They all fidget at once as the door is opened, and in walks, Jax Foul "so what brings all of you together tonight? It's obvious your up to no good and probably involves Wendi. The Feds are cordoning off areas and have Walter running around like a chicken who has lost his head or is it a cat chasing its own tail." Jax closes the door staring at his conspirators "what's going on with the Feds? Hey, just an FYI, Marshal Kara has intimated that Wendi will be moved soon from NIA. Worst yet, Rico is on his way, so no bullshit, tell me, Terrance!" Nobody moved in sync... all eyes were on Terrance now, who furrowed his forehead relentlessly, twisted his head rolling his shoulders. "All right, I suppose our decisions impact you, and we all want to be on the same page. This is what has been decided!"

With the help of the others, Terrance laid out the entire plan of attack concerning the implication of guard Billy Goad. Jax, as was his nature, doesn't interrupt. Merely showed annoying expressions easily analyzed as unfavorable discharging hums at the same time wobbling his skull while frowning. Still, he kept his trap shut until Larry finished up with the closing summary.

Jax watched the group finally give him their undivided attention looking for kudos and 'thatta boys' to applaud their ingenuity and resourcefulness; he appropriately howled with undaunting ridicule, "really, that's the plan." Jax busts up, laughing and hacking hilariously... "You gotta be kidding me, right? I'm blown away by your outright belief that the Feds are like Mayberry RFD, a bunch of incompetent fools. You're underestimating this traumatic event. Your ingenious plan has too many moving parts your counting on variables with unknown values. These assumptions are unreasonable in theory; hypothetically, your best scenario could come to the fruition that you've all agreed on and wished for. Although if you thought out of the box like Generals on a battlefield um dealing with war, death, and mayhem, you'd all be beheaded with only one miscalculation… we all go up in flames, kaput it's absurd and preposterous and candidly scares me to death that I am part of this 'Thinktank' which aptly should be renamed Dumb-tank!"

While he had them back peddling, he said, "let's not paraphrase your brain thrusts. Let me take from your mission impossible and tweak it a smidgeon. You see, the more we count on humans for reactions or motivations to do what we want, the sooner we all belong locked in this insane asylum. We cannot count on Billy Goad. I don't think we will be able to leverage him with money. He is a loose cog cannon drunkard he will be locked into an interrogation room, folks; he'll be out of our control. No way we can allow this. The Feds will have us all by our genitals."

Terrance tosses up his palms. "I'm listening to you. Go ahead."

"This is how you should proceed. First, go and get some of the darts that Liz had fixed with the drugs and put them in Billy's locker along with the fired dart rifle; inside the locker, put some copies of his complaints and grievances against Wendi. This will be enough to set him up for the fall. Have you checked to see if he worked on the day Wendi was shot?"

Liz somberly said, "umh, let me check." Terrance backpedals, "true, Jax, you have made a few logical points. I had a lot going on and relied on these three to devise a plan. Still, I'm willing to listen to any contingencies…" "yes, he worked," shouted Liz "great, all right, I will get one of our special techs over to the security office and have her splice in his person, uhm Billy's body at the appropriate spot that Billy would have fired on Wendi. The FBI will scrutinize our cameras and video." Jax took his boot and kicked the table, "Why did you shoot Wendi? This was done without my knowledge; I have a bone to pick with all of you who made that decision. I realize, Terrance, you were in Seattle, but this fricken stupidity in less than a week…" "forget it for now, Jax. Let's stay on point; the FBI is on site." "Ok, Terrance, I will have our techie place Billy at the crime scene. He will have all the evidence in his locker; he will have not only motive to shoot Wendi but access. The only question is, if Billy hated Wendi so much, why not shoot her with a live round?"

Silence meandered, then Jax continued spinning on, "Liz, is it true that Billy had missed appointments with your Psych department?" Liz nodded forward, "okay, he made it to one meeting. Liz, I want you to write up a report of a meeting postdating that in the system. I will have another computer geek-tech time clock that inputs the underlying synopsis in your report and will say Billy could be delusional and dangerous. You're calling for him to be suspended and to seek the mandatory treatment he verbally assaulted Wendi, saying someone should shoot a dart up her ass! Rather offhand and jokingly, that's why you didn't take his flagrant threat seriously!"

Liz nodded, "uhm, okay, I can do that, it makes sense, Jax. What if they want to see the video or audio of the session with Billy?" "Good question Liz. Your to say that NIA's policy and the Correctional Officers Union strictly prohibits that. I believe that's the case unless a representative is there to defend their Union member!"

Larry shakes his head. "I don't think it will get to that. I like your plan. It covers all bases, and there aren't any moving parts like you said," he also mutters to himself with an inward smile... it alleviates his being used as the patsy to make the illegal deal with Billy. Jax finishes with, "then you will have Billy ingest a mixture that will permanently leave him in La-La land."

Terrance regains composure and says, "well, it's settled. Does anyone else have a comment or anything to add? I feel much better, Jax. Thanks for your input. I don't know why I didn't include your knowledge of troubleshooting these tumultuous quandaries, but from now on, you're my first invite."

Out the door they went until Terrance, waiting in the hallway, put his arm out toward Ursula, who tried to pass him in the hall. "Hey Ursula, can I have a word with you privately?"

She spun around on her heels like she'd been shot, thinking, what does this bastard want now? Fuming from the inside mulls over some past lectures. She'd barely withstood and handled Terrance… years back, the misogynistic prick, yet she exuded faith with a blend of cockiness and apathy. She'd dealt with adversity… discrimination stereotypically against females all her career. It was an uphill obstacle course. It was no easy task to gain the leverage to be awarded the position of Warden. She'd accomplished her lifelong goal of ascension as she tailed Terrance to one of her offices.

"Ursula, please have a seat" "no, I'd rather stand. I have to use the restroom, so if this is going to be a long discussion, I better…" "no, listen, I appreciate your input and valuable contributions here at NIA. However, your value to the board of directors and me is diminished by your predilection and inclinations to drown yourself in booze. I'm putting you on notice… warning if I believe you've been drinking during your work schedule. I…." Ursula accidentally literally spits. "Nah, aah maybe um, you listen to me. I'm not your hourly employee; I am on salary always on the job. This week alone, it's been 55 hours and counting if I want a totty, I don't see any reason that I shouldn't… aah if I'm cognizant and…."

Terrance reaches in his pocket "here, blow in this," a breathalyzer is shoved in her face. She pauses and then attacks, "what's worse, Terrance, you getting blowjobs from our staff or me sipping a few cocktails? I'm sure you have been following the upheavals, uh, politicians and CEOs like your very self. Hell, actors and actresses are all being charged with sexual harassment accusations. Even if you're not guilty, you're tarnished for life, but your gorgeous, handpicked secretaries all know you're guilty like the last swallow, umh gulp! In the public's eye, you're still guilty as sin once the charges are lodged. How many untouchables have fallen out of favor, fired, resigned, or taken leave? It's an ongoing saga. Last week: they nailed Bill Cosby…." "Wait for a fkn second, Ursula, are you threatening me with disclosure… if you cross me, woman, I can guarantee that not even CSI will find a molecule of your DNA in the 'Hogs Shit' now get the fk out of here… I'm warning you to slow the alcohol down!"

With her sweaty palm, she closes the door behind her, gripping with her other hand the tiny bottle. Perhaps I should slow the fk down. No, fk the prick. Her whole body shivered with ice-cold sweat. She instantly reverses her direction, knowing how Terrance's mind calculates. She doesn't want to be on the wrong side of this empirically evil Godless man who was an exterminator uhm. What had she lost her mind shit before she lost her head? She better try to make amends damn my foolish inebriated mouth. Talk about shoving my shoe into my big mouth, ah… I better suck it up. She figured she'd race over to his office for reparations and reopened her Suites door immediately seeing him. He hadn't moved, displaying a seriously sinister scowl. Tapping on his phone, he looks up. "I thought we were done," a statement like history. "No, we're not, Terrance, your absolutely correct!" "How so?" he puts down the phone. She spies her last name Anders on the small LCD screen.

"I am drinking way too much and need to stop. I have let the pressure overwhelm me. Give me the breathalyzer," she blows 1.5. He checks it with a Frowl. She soldiers on before his admonishment, "I'm so sorry 'TH' his acronyms she'd used back when their relationship was much closer. "Do you want me to enter a sobriety program, a treatment center like Betty Ford? I value you and our friendship and the position you've entrusted me with, you have bestowed so much faith, and I've gone sideways. I …" Finally, she'd broken through. Whew, this one was close; she tried her utmost to shed a tear, nope desert dry tear-ducts, then saw the look of sufficient familiarity, ah, acquiescence. "Okay, Ursula, I accept your gracious apology. Please take this tester with you and try and stay below intoxication levels. Slow down, please I need your intelligent, intuitive mind fully functional!" "Yes, I will slow down as of tonight; thanks, TH!" Whoa! ☹ .

Tank Shaw and Whitney in San Jose.

Finally, I crossed the San Mateo County line with a long-lasting sigh. The traffic wasn't so bad. It felt weird driving, having been out of prison less than a week; it felt strange how memory recall took over, which always happened in the past when on long and medium road trips. It would be a time for me to contemplate, almost like being in a meditative state. I guess it's a form of auto-pilot because I hadn't remembered much after leaving San Francisco. Other than I was sure that no one was following me, I was confident of this. I wasn't complacent, just in a weird mindset.

I listened to the aftermath… taking a measure of relief that no innocent bystanders were hurt badly other than abrasions, bruises, and a few broken bones from the RV blast. I'd long since turned off the police scanner and wasn't proud of my part in activating the C-4 explosives. I curiously wondered why Joe hadn't set up the Semtex plastic explosives to be actuated via a phone. With a keyed code, he could have blown the darn motorhome up, and I wouldn't have been needed. Ugh,… oh well, it was done.

One thing about spending most of your life incarcerated; you find yourself constantly reentering the razor wire.

Constantly finding solace sitting in my 5 X 9 cell, almost an unknown type of security, umh, safety had thought and mulled over these types of days, doing Mark and Joe's bidding, I had a feeling that had been confirmed many times in the past… I was in third place in this hierarchy last. What would I do or say when Mark and Joe wanted me to join them once again? With so much time on my hands, I'd decided this wasn't the life I'd envisioned. Hidden inside of me was a fervor, a ticking chronological timepiece, an energetic anxious, and unrelenting desire to search out my true destiny to take out a chisel and shape my actual image. Whittled away would be my selfish pride, negative traits, and attitudes, for, without them, I'd be a Master Sculptor. Sure, I could ruminate, whine about my past adversities, and get lost like many blaming the past for what they are today… sold out individuals, lazy and exiled within their minds.

Life is filled with hardships. Make excuses for why I had nothing to show for almost 40 years on this earth plane, no outstanding achievements, victories, or heroic accomplishments. All my family members and friends have written me off as a loser. Sadly, I didn't receive one visit in the years incarcerated in San Quentin. No one cared, aah, except Mark and Joe.

Come to think about it, did they give a Rats ass about me? Was I nothing but a cog, a vise to be actuated and used… like a leftover rotting in the refrigerator? Was it all a façade-fiction? Could I still manage with a sharpened chisel to chip away carefully all my impurities? Can I create a masterpiece and sculpt all the imperfections off? The chisel will hurt, for I will have to strip off all my layers, manifesting into a thin-skinned lonely soul looking for direction; I needed to leave Mark and Joe by the wayside. The question would work its way out could I sustain and persevere from this evening forward, falling back to my analogies or metaphors, leaving me to be an unfinished block of Marble, a slab of stone without form or direction? Was this all grandiosity like make a wish Fairytales? How would I support myself? Who would hire someone that was inked from toe to head, with a criminal record on Parole?

I shoved the brake pedal down hard as another fool cut me off on El Camino Real Ave. it was lucky that I could hear her bass-thumping speakers before I saw her. That brought my attention forward. Like on a switchback road, I turned on my iPod and selected a tune by 'Stanly Turrentine,' 'Troubles of the world,' one of my favorite songs. I glanced at the flashing lights and heard the blaring siren… cringed, encroaching fast in my rearview mirror. It was almost 11:55 pm asking myself whether it was a natural reaction to 'cringe' or was it my basic instinctual criminal way of thinking because I was predisposed because of my guilty conscience. Yep, the criminal mind at work with the notorious guilty-conscious syndrome, lol. Did ordinary law-abiding folks within our society exhibit this same weary feeling?

I must ask Whitney that question as the cop pulls over the female partygoers bouncing to the rattling Bass Rap song five cars in front of me.

COSB (change of subject back) was it a possibility that the shaping tool…a chisel, could chip off all blemishes and scars throughout my lifetime of afflictions, leaving me strengthened and purified, or could I somehow jump into a huge filter and through the process of Osmosis become purified…lol. One can dream, or one can be proactive, not be a dreamer or talker, and just take the first step forward and just do it!

<u>The Obese Psychologist. Or if you prefer the pleasantly plump Psychologist?</u>

This world is plumb-filled with talkers or bullshitters… do as I say, not what I do. 'Hypocrites of the highest order' on every corner. These ruminations reminded me of the prison psychologist I was forced to meet with several times… mandatory sessions that I had to get by before my release on Parole. She was a 450-pound slug-toad, frog-like person; her jowls hung and shook her Walrus blue-grey eyes, which were but slivers, it seemed. Mind you, I haven't got anything against heavy-set individuals unless you were this psychologist, that is. I couldn't imagine the effort needed just to move her obese arms, breathing hampered as if it was her last oxygen intake. The cold ass room had to be maybe 63 degrees still… she was sweating like a Hog lining up for the slaughter, and I felt sorry for her fat oversized feet… a waste of humanity. I'd just left a 3-hour workout and finished up with a 35-minute hotly contested handball match.

I was forced to sit across from her glaring stare, and I flexed my forearms, feeling good, not paying her much attention, just there to jump through the hoops. I was cut up, with ripped muscles, crisp hot lines sculpted and defined. She started preaching to me, told me I'd amount to nothing, a perennial loser convict. What she concentrated on was boring into my head, telling me that I lacked discipline. Yep! Oh, Discipline, like, please. I was downtrodden already in a sinking trajectory and couldn't change the outcome of my destruction… <u>According to her, I wasn't goal-oriented, a lifelong loser with a capital 'L'… looking over my records. She chastised me and disavowed any positive attributes I possessed. It was the proto-typical hate-fest.</u>

Well, hell, I couldn't very well just sit there like a lump on the stool. A straight shooter I fired back freestanding, disconnected from how I should have reacted… suddenly was drawn into interaction with her game of words and articulations. I'd known better than to bark back; other inmates just sat mute and took her tongue-lashing. If you countered her, it would inevitably do more harm than good. Like a self-inflicted cutter for pain blurted out a definite mistake… "You're the one to be talking about discipline, uh, determination. Look at you, or can you fit that frame in a mirror? You're a heart attack rattling in your fat chest cavity. Do you have a clue at how hard it is for your poor overworked heart to pump blood to all your obese extremities?" On a roll unabashed, I continued like running diarrhea out of a spluttering spicket, "why don't you push yourself away from the table you're Fat and disgusting slob-like, here your preaching to me about discipline really huh. How could you ever think anyone could take your advice seriously by the looks of your disfigurement, Doc? You're the epitome of an oxymoron, a total contradiction. Aah, let's cut the shit. You're a gluttonous hypocrite!"

Instantly Zapped like a bug-killer, the room heated up infernal like 'the foot in the mouth syndrome' small room was confidingly stifling. It was a stare-off. I watched as a drip of unwashed perspiration fell from her three-haired chin. Our enclosed space fugue-like slipped into coffin silence. From Hades swiftly manifesting into the North Pole of maybe a lonely bomb shelter morgue-ish, the Doctor's creased face blotched, wrinkled like a Shar Pei for just a split second, I sought coverage she might explode! Her displeasure spewed from her vocal cords an aggrieved raspy delivery of malcontented verbiage, which will forever stay with me. Taking out a handkerchief and wiping her substantial brow.

"Tank Shaw, you're a wretched evil-doer criminal, a viper who feeds on humanity like a leech. You hurt and destroy the lives of decent people. You're a miserable Cretin, a sadistic living predator who would be better off executed. Tank, you're the devil incarnate, a cursed abomination Anti-Christ, I've read about your pathetic life... Yeah, I may be fat, obese, but I will waddle my fat ass out of this prison; you, my Thug. 'Cackling like a clucking Hen' "I will ensure that your never paroled. You're ugly, a 'Bête Noire' sickening, disgusting person who should have been aborted on the delivery table. Oh, I feel so sorry for your poor parents. Look at you. Is there a square inch of your skin that isn't covered by prison tattoos? Really you're destined to die in this prison; now get the fk out of here!"

Wow, did I just blow it? The fat slug really got worked up, and what was that 'Bête Noire' crap term? She then slammed down my files as the cellulite lumpiness wobbled and pushed the button for the waiting guard to exit, who was trying to hide his hysterical eavesdropping laughter. The last I saw of her was her planet-sized buttocks rubbing together, leaving a deposit between them that was wet, grimy, and Grand Canyon-ess!

Well, that wasn't entirely true; about three months later, when I was on the approved list for Parole, I saw her in a violet pants suit. She spied me through the concertina wire, raised her right arm up, palm facing her like see me; she'd lost 55 pounds if she'd lost a single one. She grinned, and I pointed my thumb up, approving her new her!

Unfortunately for her, the next week, she dropped dead of a massive coronary embolism... a heart attack in the very room she'd interviewed me.

<u>FBI Agent Lori Parks.</u>

From a helicopter not so high in the night's air was Agent Lori Parks. On the roads below her were several Agents, Avery being the one in charge on the ground, Who said in her ear, "it's like another day in the 'Park' for the guy ah Tank left the Escalade in a parking lot then got into his Impala drove to his apartment entered then the lights just went dark." "Okay, Avery, put a chip on the Escalade." "Aah, already done that." "Good, we'll follow that lead. I see no relevance in you hanging out and watching his apartment get some rest. If he moves, the GPS body chip will alert us. Thus far, it seems he's already asleep! I'm going to call Rico. Good night thanks." "Sure thing Lori. Good night, and thanks for the night off. I certainly can use it!"

Rico feels the vibration… taps his phone on "hey there, Lori, umh, yes, I'm still here with the aftermath of the R.V. detonations. It's going to be a long evening." "Has she mellowed out yet? It was an awkward situation indeed, all over one missing slipper. Our mistake was me trying to hide. We'd done nothing wrong." "Lori, you're on speaker phone," "fk great" "no, Lori, I haven't mellowed out yet and for the foreseeable future will not; you will feel the impact of my internal investigation," Rico interjects, intervening since it was his stupidity to hit the speaker button. "Tanya, please give it a rest. It was an innocent misunderstanding!" Tanya shut the door of the mobile unit harshly and stomped away in a huff.

Director Tanya Firm trudged off, wondering if she was acting like a teenage high school girl, a jealous girlfriend. Rico wasn't her boyfriend, but they'd enjoyed each other's company and occasionally shared bodies inside and out. I need to admit it; stop being so damn childish. I want Rico all to myself. Life is so tricky; the lines have been changed no gender-based rights or wrongs; we're liberated in a sense. Why not speak my mind assertively and tell him how I feel towards him so what if he shrugs me back off? It's fear of rejection, painful heart-wrenching pride you never know unless… her radio interrupts. 'Director Firm, could you please come to the flashing amber lights? We've found something that you must see now,' said a Forensic Medical Examiner, Ms. Ame Toady.

Meanwhile, at a fever pitch of enragement, Lori was spewing over, "you asshole, how could you have me on speaker phone with Tanya right there? What are you, plain-ass dumb Rico fk? It's like you're conspiring to mess up my entire career what I can't …" "Lori, sorry, she just opened the damn door on the mobile unit and was standing at the steps both my hands were busy working out details on my laptop shit relax will yuh!" "Fine, it's not like your ass is on the line, huh? Let's cut back to the real reason for my call.

"No question we could arrest him for going out of bounds leaving his county without notifying his parole agent, even better for associating with a felon Joe Sable. Couldn't we make the case that he was the instigator or the individual who exploded the RV? Rico?" "Sure, could… I guess woman, uhm Lori, but we have zero proof, just speculation. Remember, Lori, Tank never entered the motorhome. Besides that, with the latest thermal imaging proof, heat sensors and scans proved that he hadn't a weapon inside the Cadillac Escalade. Positively no C-4 explosives which have been figured out were used in the destruction of…" "okay, Rico. Surely we could lock the guy up on a horde of circumstantial evidence he'd not see the light of day. The connection is there. He visited the RV. Less than seven minutes later, it blew up!" "That would negate the value of the GPS chip in his glute. He's going nowhere without us on his ass. Eventually, he will lead us to Mark Feral and Joe Sable, currently, as of this second, #3 and #7 on our FBI most wanted list. Lori, we can take him at any time. He doesn't know it, but his probation officer will be making an unannounced visit to his apartment in about nine hours.…" Over his radio, they hear a familiar harking, "Rico, I need you over here at the motorhome ASAP…

"Gotta go Lori…" "of course you do," she clicks end.

Gulping down the rest of the cold coffee, checking the time near 1 am would make more money by the hour. This contractual salary agreement was for the birds. The night's darkness glowed under the 1,000-watt halides ah, flood lights, helping our vision the most was that the black/grey smoke had dissipated. Still, some remaining firemen… people with fire trucks watched over the smoldering heaps of leftovers of what was a $550,000 motorhome with a trailer… Rico clearly saw Tanya. Her hands were on her hips, and he recognized the pleasingly chubby body type that had become the M.E. of record Ame Toady's cute face and disposition seven months pregnant, a fun, happy woman.

They were standing in a group of smocked-booted-up, wrapped CSI types staring at something on a tray. They were peering downward; Rico stepped in close. Ame nodded at him "evening Rico, aah, Mr. Captor." "Rico will suffice; we've known each other long enough to be on a first-name basis, don't you think, Ms. Toady? She matches his smile… pretty teeth. "Ame will suffice." "That's enough," says Tanya a bit loud, then she adds, "sorry it's been some very long nights," with a scowl.

Ame disregards all and gets back on point "this is a femur bone. Human remains are strewn all over the parking lot 33 yards over there is what's left of a partial skull, and unless the deceased had two sets of upper jaws, we have ourselves at least two bodies here. Of course, we are only getting started."

"Great, just wonderful; I will pull up all missing persons in Northern California at once. It's now a homicide, or should I say multiple; I'd better get on this," shouts Rico. Ame twists away. "I better get back to work; please excuse me." Leaving Tanya with a disgruntled expression, for she could now envision being stuck on a conference call with Wash. D.C. for hours, explaining how they'd had no one in custody. Ridiculous, no doubt… with all the person-hours and resources used, surely they'd gripe about the massive expenditures that this investigation has warranted thus far. She pouted; there was zero to show but mayhem with two Agents still in the hospital, now throw in the caveat, at a minimum, two more dead bodies.

Rico downs another energy drink, hoping for a 3rd wind, exhausted and needing tape to keep his eyelids from closing. At 2:57 am, a tip came in that lit him up. It originated and was disseminated by three separate sources, which garnered his attention, not just another anonymous waste of time. The fact that multiple sources confirmed the same information somewhat validated the tips, even though each tipster was out to reap some of the reward offered. A timestamp of the tip would determine the winner if the information were correct.

Mass media came through again; the tips were about the woman that they'd tried Facial Recognition on and failed, the same woman who was pictured in the RV and riding the motorcycle. A shop owner in Stinson Beach and A server at a restaurant in San Rafael confirmed her identity as none other than the daughter of a City Councilman in Sacramento. A family of notable affluence, Ms. Samantha Timmons had dyed her hair cold black. Still, there's no doubt it's her, now matching Joe Sable's APB-BOLO. She was now on blast, and the radar of Law Enforcement, an accomplice, now wanted for murder in the double homicide inside the motorhome. Samantha was also a fugitive from the law in Sacramento for absconding… on her probation. She'd have additional charges filed against her for killing the nurse and the shooting of FBI agents at the Shell gas station.

<u>Joe and Sam, with the elder couple.</u>

We'd only known the older couple, the 'Graces,' for a matter of hours, but as they left Joe and me, it felt as if we or I had lost someone close to me. Speaking for myself, our conversations flowed smoothly. Well, of course, the wine lubricated our tongues and lubed us up. I was beaten up more mentally than physically when Joe asked, "how'd yah know their last names, Sam?" I might have blushed, maybe, "I peeked out of the van and memorized the street and address of this house, then Googled it… Walla, the last taxes paid were by Lester and Rhonda Grace!" He slapped me on my shoulder "sneaky Lil devil, aren't you? What's this about you having all these special gifts, eidetic memories, and stuff, you never…." "Oh, nonsense Joe I just let Rhonda go on a roll. Don't you like the Graces?" 'Nice diversion, he bit into it like …' "Yes, they are a sweet couple and super nice and accommodating, top class in my book." We kissed good night and fell swiftly into subconscious states.

I awoke reinvigorated, with a dull throbbing headache smelling the aroma of freshly brewed beans. The fluorescent light of lit numbers on the bedside clock flashed at 5:17 am felt a touch or three under the weather with too much vino. I felt like my eyes were glued shut, a mucus buildup holding them partially closed. Ouch, carefully not to wake the slumbering mass of man snoring near my back. I un-snuggled from his cozy cuddle, rolled to my knees on the plush carpet, gently closed the bathroom door, and ran some cool water on a dry washcloth three times over my face and neck, then snuck out of the bedroom with the scent of coffee my magnetic beckoning call. Before I reached the kitchen door threshold, I heard Rhonda's voice: "no, Lester, I think I heard the water running in their bedroom. Let's give them a few more minutes."

Stepping in, seeing their fresh, vivacious countenances, she smirked and shook her head "looks like bedhead is up." Lester snickers "here honey, we've brewed a special blend of beans from Jamaica mixed with some Expresso. Take a mug into Joe, then some quick showers. We have a special umh important day planned," says Rhonda. She slyly winked at me with a shake like no mimed "sorry, Sam; the Feds now have your name!"

I froze with the corrosive news, knowing it was but a matter of time. Still hearing it confirmed one of my worst nightmares my well-heeled family would be disheveled and on the public radar. I was now a fugitive, feeling shivers up my spine. Yeah, I was scared. Fear overwhelmed me instantly. Instead of taking the hot cup from their hands, they paused, without muttering a syllable, reached out, and I touched both of them. Lester on his boney shoulder and Rhonda at the small of her back, they, in turn, embraced me like I so much needed. Omg felt like a missing child.

Where were the hugs and love from my parents growing up? Why did they birth me? Was it a status thing or an expected occurrence? Neither seemed to have time to be parents. I was a burden. Why punish me? I didn't ask to be brought into this convoluted, messed-up world.

Memories flooded into my heart the first visuals as a baby girl being placed on a pedestal with a bunch of people over at the mansion, a showpiece... here look at our precious beautiful, cute daughter; isn't she perfect? Oh, BTW, she is so precocious 'chips off the ole block.' I was a praiseworthy symbol handed off to the Nanny from there out to pasture, off to schools for the finest education money could buy, minus love and affection.

Parents to enthralled, encumbered, embroiled in their own existences. Career-oriented aspirations to run for public office, Governor/Congress. I learned how prim-proper and perfect I was to be like a robot girl at a young age. Too bad mother and father couldn't have just ordered me from Amazon sealed and delivered. I've never outlived my childhood. I'd cry myself to sleep from being a burden aligned with a heaviness of staggering guilt for breathing.

"Sammy honey, are you all right? Your shaking like a leaf; don't you worry, we've got your back!" declares Rhonda. I snapped out of my pensive melancholy ruminations. Who was I to complain? I grew up with the proverbial silver & gold fork and spoon. I think I might have been a happier child on food stamps, a mother who coddled me, a father who took me swinging and playing at the park, and a mom and dad who spent quality time with me with transparent adoration. I needed kindness and pampering, being held tight by a father who tossed me in the air catching me, of course, and putting me on his back and shoulders galloping around like a horsey instead of being abandoned, left alone. My <u>father was a Butler mother was a Nanny.</u>

Lester stopped me as I grasped the two mugs of coffee "wait here, let us add a bit of the 'hair of the dog" he poured a heaping of Baileys Irish Crème alcohol into the cups. "Sweetie, why don't you run some water over you… get Joe up and rolling? We will start a scrumptious breakfast. I hope you like bacon, scrambled cheese eggs, fresh biscuits & Rhonda's homemade gravy." I nodded to Rhonda with a half-hearted twisting smile.

Entering the dark-draped bedroom, I noticed Joe sprawled out as if swimming in search of my body sideways… me his pacifier. I tapped on him, holding a whiff of the coffee liqueur under his nostrils. He released a subtle groan-moan and pounced up with fervor a demonic glare at me. I'd learned over time of being with Joe that it was like he had PTSD sometimes. He awoke ready to fight; I gave him space until he'd realized where he was… thought it was a prison thing, although he and I never discussed it.

Joe's Daymare.

Little did I know Joe was amidst a trauma-induced daymare instead of being stabbed in prison, this time Joe's dream >… 'Running hard sprinting, was I chasing someone or being pursued? Hearing the hounds and hooves from the rears surrounding me, I concluded it was the latter caught and thrown to the rocky ground, wrists tied behind my back, cowboys and cowgirls grouped about… they tied me up.

I sat leaning forward on an Appaloosa horse, a large one indeed. My ass was firmly snugged tight strapped in the saddle (wait, Wtf? I can't ride a horse. Never learned what the hell was happening?) I started to scream and yell-holler with all my might. Wake up, get me out of here, off this wild beast. That's when I noticed a way too swollen limb that stretched out from this Orange Tree. The Oranges were the size of basketballs, punctured and dripping crimson Red, no doubt blood-body fluids couldn't look away tried to close my closed eyelids. But like X-ray vision zoomed into the basketballs, omg no oh-shit faces of the dead, uh, murdered, um, tortured, killed at the hands of yours truly.

The Orange tree was buckling under the weight of the basketballs, and the balls were reduced in circumference; the higher they were hanging, the smaller they were. Tinier limbs-branches all the way up to the top of the tree held these figurines. Humans I'd done wrong were of Softball size, and at the top of this monstrosity were colored Ping-Pong balls, all secreting a Reddish liquid fluid that simulated blood. I recognized the 5-year-old kid next door that I hit in the head with a claw hammer at the creek behind Mark and my house in Redwood City.

Resembling a giant Christmas Tree with ornaments of gore. At the very peak was something moving… I zoomed in uh, and it appeared to be something alive. A ghoulish horned creature that made all the other hanging masses seem minuscule-tiny. Ugh, Red

& Yellow eyes that protruded uhm mushroomed out, swelling from a hideous, grotesque nightmarish mutant ghoulish melting face. The head was bobbing up and down, spewing foam from its Red blood teeth, and was hilariously riotously howling like a Wolf. Mark Feral's face flashed off and on in the eyes of the monster. He stared right through me hedonistically. At that precise instant, he was the Judge executioner, a tightening about my neck. Oh crap, I was having a tough time inhaling a breath.

I tried to communicate with Mark, reason with the Devil he'd manifested into, then a mirror-like in the Cinderella Fairy Fable floated to the forefront uh surface. I saw my face distorted, purplish, an oversized noose around my neck chatter from the other saddled riders yelling… whooping it up!

A woman's screeching scream, <u>'Hang him already'</u> oh no, it was Wendi Feral hooting and hollering. I was going to be hung, swinging headless from the Orange Tree. Mark's scowlish frowlish devious expression told me there was no way out. Suddenly, music started to play out of nowhere, drowning out Mark's howling. The sound got louder and seemed to be amplified, concert style. I recognized it at once.

My all-time favorite song from a Cowboy movie Ohyeah there I sat, noose tight around my throat-hands bound behind my back, the limb swayed above me… the music hit its crescendo 'Old Texas Orchestra' played 'The Good Bad and the Ugly' a Clint Eastwood Classic.

Bizarrely I'm focused, although a pile of sweat was pouring off of me; I nearly accepted my demise, my fate, unreal like in the distance a dust plume, dirt flying, blowing up in the crisp blue cloudless sky. Uh, the noise, a motor, the engine. It's a KTM motorcycle 1290. The rider clad in Black… stops abruptly. Her face shield drops she swiftly slings a rifle up and out. Sammy fires the weapon um, the noose shreds… then the Appaloosa takes off like a 'Bat Outta Hell' wind blows my hair whipping it around as I lean down, holding the galloping horse with my thighs into the night.

'Joe… Joe, Joe, honey, wake up. You're having a dightmare, please, babe.' He was shaking his hands around his throat, sweating profusely. I shook him again and again, felt bad slapping him. Boom, he flashed, wavering. It was as if the yoke had been torn away. He looked up at me, eyes glistening with relief. He engulfed me in his legs and arms and held me as I reciprocated a feeling never before realized. '<u>I Loved this man!</u>'

We washed each other's backs and behinds in the shower. The soothing warm water cleansed us, toweled off together, and dressed without speaking at 6:57 am. We sat across from our elder friends and spooned and forked a scrumptious meal, too busy chewing to converse… that would be later.

Satiated tummy's filled, dishes in the washer, sitting in the sunroom watching updates on the looped news reports, the starving bloggers 'Samantha Timmons & Joe Sable' were visually plastered over all screens and monitors. The reward to anyone who could produce our whereabouts was tripled. I was now undauntingly an Outlaw attached forever to the villainous gang, iniquitous and detestable militia associated with Joe, Mark, and our hosts. They were officers in the (State of Jefferson Sovereign Nation) Militia.

Holding hands, Joe and I, like our bond had intensified, somehow fertilized during his nocturnal nightmares. Hours passed, and Rhonda was calmly following her husband's monologue. They had determined we must leave at once for Boise, Idaho, on the private militia Jet we were to attend a secret high-level meeting with the S.O.J.

The same van that had brought us to the Victorian home was going to take us to the Mill Valley Executive Airport, a small exclusive runway used by the 1% of the wealthy, which I assumed included the couple before us. A ringing noise… the monitor switched, and we saw the Van approaching the gate.

A 4-way hug ensued "will we see you again?" I asked, "not likely," replied Rhonda. Lester chimed in, "oh, don't be so morose, wifey. Ah, yes, we will see each other again at a New Year's bash down in San Diego will make sure you are both on the invite list. It will be at our friend's place on Coronado Island, a magnificent castle."

Joe giggled "now that's what I'm talking about, Yes!" We hear more ringing tones and see another identical van come down the secluded road. Rhonda tossed back her head… "no, worries, that's our cleaners. Since the Feds now have your identity, the personal phone you carried and destroyed will be pinged and traced." "Wait, but I never used it from here. It was powered down!" "No worries, sweetie, only a precautionary measure; never can be too careful. We've learned this over the years. It soothes our paranoid… old minds; long ago, we'd decided to have one of our lifetime mandates include the wise ole statement <u>Better safe than Sorry.</u>"

Before our departure, Lester handed a briefcase to Joe, which looked to be heavily weighted, "please give this to Jaybird for me. Keep it safe, Joe," he answered 'will do' we stepped into the back of the van to see the couples upside down smiles waving good-byes. Something ominously stung me, pinging inside my tummy apprehension took the narrative, but I held onto Joe 35 minutes later, we were in the air Marin County far to the South, safe, I suppose, for now.

I couldn't help the nausea and queasiness, not wholly unwarranted because the altitude affected me also, but it was partially because I felt horrible, uhm, I had to admit I'd harmed my parents and family. They ended up being correct. Yeah, proof I was indeed the rotten blight, plague miscreant that they all believed I was the blackest of black sheep; sadly, it all came to roost.

Across social media were my mug shots of aliases, arrests for prostitution, petty theft check fraud, and so on, onwards now wanted for an accessory accomplice to Capital Murder. My picture and name were splattered all over the local news. They'd had a conclusive match of my DNA found on a can of Red Bull that was blown 125 feet from where the RV exploded. Another link discovered, uh, adding in at least two victims once the Forensics were completed, the proverbial nails would be punched, sledgehammered into my coffin. The names of my pimp and his brother would further implicate me. Both had past arrests like dozens and had to be in the DNA databases. It was only a matter of time till all this evidence hit the Internet, soon enough in print in the Sacramento Bee.

Good luck to my father in his quest to be voted Governor of California. My family would be exiled, persecuted laughing stocks, no invites to the Gala, and dropped from the upper echelon to the gutter!

Joe kept repeating, saying to me, humming the song, don't worry, be happy, Sammy; his voice sucked, but hey, he was trying to cheer me up. 'Don't worry be Happy' is a great song by 'Bobby McFerrin' I shivered despite being relatively warm in the airplane, happy no… don't believe that will ever be me, for sure.

What I needed was a total complete facial reconstruction… plastic surgeries change my profile, or I'd be burnt toast, but yeah, don't worry, be happy! Feeling Joe's head resting on my shoulder while asleep, a light snore emitting from him. How the hell could this dude be sleeping?

I mumbled a prayer, even though not a religious person, changed up and repeated several times, 'help me, please get out of this trouble,' hoping that my inner-being that had misguided me thus far in my short life would finally guide me from imminent harm aah where was my guardian Angel… Lost like me, huh? ☹ .

-48-

<u>Mark Feral on the Trail of his wannabe 'JOY.'</u> ☺ .

Wouldn't you know I was in bum fk Egypt running my diesel with the idiot light glowing back at me low on fuel? Who was the idiot I thought should have filled up long ago, recalling the last devastating fire that caused evacuations? It was last year, and I'd plumb run out of diesel, leaving in a panic when this fool of a neighbor just down the road wanted to mow his patch of dirt in 113-degree heat. His riding mower blades slapped against a rock, which caused sparks to fly. Walla, a deadly fire started ravaging my neighborhood. I got lucky the wind wasn't swirling in my direction. Ahh, that guy ended up in a prison cell, locked up for stupidity!

Searching the limited resources in the tiny town of Shingletown for fuel, I was immediately aware that I had failed at the Boy Scout Motto 'be prepared.' Better yet, I was going to have to get prepared to sit in a 3-block long line at one of the few gas stations; oh well, perhaps I will learn this time.

Sitting there without patience, watching the GPS chip I'd stashed under the bumper of the little Asian beauty Joy's car she'd just parked down an unmarked road off of 'Pinegrove Trail.' Shingletown was a beautiful area surrounded by forests, mostly Pine Trees, country living at its best serene and picturesque with many hidden retreats hunting cabins, and fishing lodges, some of the best fishing anywhere. The area was a haven if you wanted to live off the grid, be left alone, or hide out. I had my own deluxe cabin up the road, a 19-minute ride close to a famous fishing spot in the one-horse town called 'Hat Creek.'

Nobody likes criticism, least of all me, especially when it's unsolicited... and delivered with snarls accompanied by harsh words. Shit, it seemed trouble always found me, ah analyzing um, considering how I should react to the disrespectful people five vehicles in front of me in the lengthy line for fuel. Where a group of bearded men, most likely 'Red Necks on Meth.' I'm not...um, un-politically wrong and all, I just call it as I see it, no bias or prejudice, they had broken the line. They took advantage of some women in a Volkswagen bus, hippy-type females they'd cut into the line.

Now it wouldn't be all that bad if it were just one pickup truck uhoh, no, it was two a '70s Ford and a Chevy about the same vintage. You 'all might know the look... shotguns-rifles on racks in the back window of their cabs worst yet it became clear that they were friendly with the hippy wannabes from a previous era... yep there I go again with wrongly deposed stereotypes but see, I don't give a hoot!

Now a ruckus had started up, and some men in front of me, behind them in line, started honking at the bequest of their ladies who were yelling out of their windows. One was brazen enough to jump out of the driver's side of his SUV and verbally confront them. Those are not good odds. One against five... hands flew up in angry gestures. At the same time, a few of the gluttonous hayseeds waddled towards the SUV one with a

Louisville slugger bat in his paws. Unfortunately, as is the case, I think I mentioned I have a 'mental' in the plural sense uh disorders; underneath the passenger side seat was a 30-clip 'M5 Automatic machine gun' with an added three fully loaded clips in reserve.

The last thing I needed was attention drawn to me, especially of the negative strain 'But' my gut male macho testosterone somehow bothered me, egging me on and out of my Dodge; something told me if I didn't intervene, I would be diminished ego deflated, maleness castrated a lessor man. Like a sieve leaked pride being disrespected. I would die in the prison yard if an inmate cut into the line in front of me, stabbing a shank to the hilt in an out of the guy's neck... been there and done that.

A Forest Ranger was parked at the multi-purpose service station store combo deli with miscellaneous hardware available. On the other side of the large lot was a Sheriff Deputy Nah, just a vacant cruiser. I got back in the Dodge to pull up another car length considering or trying to reject a confrontation. 'But' I wasn't made that way, not a ball-less Eunuch trying to avoid the visor mirror to see my image transforming from macho to feminine critiques valid under scrutiny in times of aggression; females had it easy. Passivity was a calculated plus. Women are typically tolerant and non-confrontational ughhhh, then proving my assumption incorrect, another two women surprised me. They'd hopped out of a Jeep next to my front bumper, lumbering out grasping the row bars, and they started screaming at the guys. The woodsmen gave them no heed with the typical onslaught of degradation of words, 'get your dyke ass's out of my face.' 'You sloppy lesbians better high-tail it back to your Jeep if yah no what's good fer u! The other tossed his beer can, adding yeah, I will shove this Bat so far up...' the woman stopped and stared back at me... my left leg outta my truck.

The toothless group hovered around, hacking and cackling... one more glance at my side mirror. I'd become a stunted man, nope. I reached into the open case on the floorboard and put on a hat equipped with added steel and slammed my truck door.

I passed on the opportunity for spiritual growth, umh, maturity. Maybe I'll sit on my rump in a few decades and just be a vegetable-like spectator. I walked up to the beer-drinking hoodlums who had the two girls surrounded and were chastising them brutally. I noticed immediately that the guys were near my age, not youngsters Naw in their 30s. My back and the left side were blocking the Deputy's and the Ranger's vehicles' views even though neither was anywhere to be seen. Luckily, I mused, ah, now what momentum grasped me.

In my left hand was an old school notepad with a pen; inside my leather jacket was now a holstered 9 mm, Glock. On my belt, in plain view, was a Radio and a fake badge when I was 13 yards off walking deliberately slow so the morons, uh, imbeciles, could read my newly fit hat… acronym DEA.

I was stepping to the side to pretend I needed a better view of the trucks that had nosed their way into the line of vehicles patiently waiting for fuel. 'Hey man, what do you think you're doing?' said the 6'7" lard ass leader of this raunchy crew. Paying zero attention other than purposely unclipping my radio off my hip… exposing my weapon in a holster, that's when the idiots or the smartest one said, 'hey man, the dude is DEA!' Wouldn't you know it, the two women who were not what the rednecks had discerned them to be… stood shoulder-to-shoulder with me. Their significant others joined us. Two slender men had piled out of another pickup truck.

I spoke rather abrasively in my powered-off radio, 'we have a disturbance here,' then mumbled the rest, turning my head and pushing in an earbud as if listening, then pantomiming with a pen to write down their mud-stained license plate. "Hold up, mister; we ain't lookin' for no problem, man!" I said, rather smugly, "then either do the right thing and move to the back of the line or show me your licenses. I'll have a backup here in less than 10 minutes otherwise!"

In less than 15 seconds, the five guys were driving their trucks away, strangely not to the back of the longer line but out of the parking lot and onto Hwy 40. Perhaps they had more to hide from the DEA than a few six-packs of brew. Strangers of all varieties suddenly were my friends out of vehicles thanking me, hero-like. I shrugged and said, 'these ladies are the real heroes.' I quickly returned to the cab of my truck, taking the necessary time to meet my reflection in the visor mirror again. Looking back at me, I heard the statement, 'you macho King stud you!' Yep, there was a wise crinkled, sparkle gleam in my twinkling eyes. No doubt I was a man's-man and a genius to boot!

As was my nature, I bounced from topic to subject, a cursory umh sporadic non-encompassing thorough, and comprehensive analysis meandering on the outskirts of my mind. I didn't allow hurt or anger to derail my ultimate goals, um, desires. When there was a reason to engage a subject matter with tunnel vision acuity, I could do so also reproofing decisions. I concluded that no criticism could be used against me for my DEA act.

Like short flicks screenplays, the 39 min wait for the fuel went by without any more hazards. 'I had sat in my Dodge traveling hundreds of miles metaphorically.' I'd covered such topics as Joe heading to Boise, Idaho, in my place and how Tank had come through with the after-blow of detonating the RV. Then I bounced back to the reasons I was in the town of Shingletown, that being 'Joy,' who tried to arrest me and send me back to prison for the rest of my life. Luckily, they couldn't figure out who I was... also cogitated over the fact that I got out of the Casino before the Feds arrived. She would pay... that Laotian beauty is within my grasp. The plan was to snatch her ass up, bound her, and take her to my cabin to teach her some fun lessons. I could envision her nude chained body like her namesake; we're going to have some pure unadulterated 'JOY'... Yeah!

Joy... um-yum, with several pulsations, the bulge of my manhood had expanded, then at once retracted wild how my mind reflects my cock shrunken smaller like a dip in iceberg Coldwater. The freakin Attorneys could spell trouble, my gates open for the firefighters fidgeting in my front seat... there it was on my iPad's screen, Solar Energy is still functional and maintained at the property, and the batteries are 77% full. My cameras showed five fire trucks C.D.F. lined up, and all colored a limelight mucus green; there was an ongoing meeting at my property, lucky for Solar energy because all electricity in the area was cut off.

I panned my cameras out to the steel barns, specifically, the one where the lawyers were stiff in their coffins. The FBI had linked Joe Sable and me to their abduction, which became a no-brainer, dubbed a serial predator with the playing cards left at acts of violence. Like that wasn't my plan out of the gate. Rather stupid in retrospect; that's the problem with hindsight, huh? I grinned at the phrase I'd made up. It was brilliant <u>'Fear Me Cuz I'm Cumin 4 U'</u> in black marker written on each playing card.

Now with addition, we must add another three dead to our growing list the pimp and his brother and that useless Nurse who failed at the elimination of Sister dear! A conversation with Joe before he boarded the jet to attend the militia's mandatory conference did nothing to ally our alliance with the prostitute Sammy who was now part of our gang. Our dialogue sort of went like this… 'Who the fk why the fk? Damn, dude, we need a whore like a hole in our heads… Shit, man Joe, don't let your no brains 'Lil head' do the thinking. Sex was as old as Adam & Eve, with almost '4 billion holes' out there in this world, with a minimum of 1 Billion doable. With a touch of training, Heck Joe, if a girl had the physical attributes that enticed you and were submissive and eager to learn.' 'Mark, it's always the same bullshit with you. We're not the same, dude, just maybe I do want a lady and…' Laughing large 'what huh a lady are you fkn mad dude get a grip Sammy ain't no lady… Listen, time out, let's backup. I realize we have different values inherently uh in our way of thinking. Ok, women are a necessity, Joe, I get it, bro, but what's needed is the girl's willingness aligned with eager hunger to satiate and satisfy us. If they have the energy and imagination, desire, and the other necessary female attributes, girls were temporary … use em-leave-em,' 'Geez, stop it, Mark! I'm not discussing this anymore.…'

Fk didn't Joe ever listen… its 'catch-and-release? Use them, then discard them simply… never keep them around long enough to get attached. They were good for one thing, our satisfaction! ☺ .

This Sammy was now accompanying Joe to Boise, Idaho, in my place. I told him to keep her in a hotel during the militia meetings. Switching gears to another issue, I'd broached the topic of when to bring Tank back into the fold. Great job on the RV, but Joe had told me there was proof that Tank was tailed and led the FBI to the restaurant they were meeting in! Once we dialed Tank into how to safeguard himself and eliminate the sniffing Feds, we'd get together again. It was going to be fabulous to have us three back together. It had been too long since we walked the yard at San Quentin together.

Joe has placed our crew against the Ape ball and royally screwed us. We will be cruelly reamed for having to destroy the RV and motorcycle trailer and losing the KTMs confiscated by the police so far, a $557,000 loss for our boss. Oh man, she will be Irate. I told myself I was the protagonist leader in charge, but it was her funding... money, along with the SOJ... that kept us afloat. Heck, she owned my property.

Ahh, finally at the pumps, then a grocery stop for perishables that my deluxe cabin didn't have on the shelves, although being fully stocked, didn't have perishables for clear reasons. Hell, it had been five months ago when I was last there. Back heading East, fully loaded with supplies and fuel, the final leg of my forced journey insidiously who enveloped the cab was Wendi, my adorable sister wrong. Still in massive traffic on a country road with other humans involved in the mandatory forced exodus, slogging along, all leaving their domiciles in despair, wondering if their homes would make it... this year from being burned to the ground... an unprovoked reality.

He Pondered his memories of when it all went tragically wrong. Sister was fine as dynamite until she almost drowned at the San Francisco Zoo, saved by Rocco, the fkn Gorilla whom I despised. Things were fine at home until the Amazon woman Sheriff Judy Girth got her tentacles into my baby sister at three years old. Then at five years old, the brutal rapist-murderer that sisters visualizations via a damn pet kitty cat of the dead victim Tabby. Wendi saw it all from the Cat's eyes. She helped bring justice to many of the 13-plus or so murdered, raped, and mutilated victims. Yeah, you'd had to have been there way wild. Joe lived across the street from me. We were inseparable as children and played in the creek behind our houses, killing animals.

We were like nine years old, and then it happened my Arch enemy was Hatched uh born, manifested in the hospital. I witnessed the metamorphosis I saw it happen. Our parents were so damn naïve about the thing inside of Wendi fighting like a slithering serpent reptile-vile ass creature. A snake peered from my sister's refracted glare. 'Sunshine' evolved from Wendi's inner spirit. She'd split personalities. Wendi needed Sunshine to survive. Thusly, she morphed into the absurd, an unruly Psychotic state of being defined cryptically, uuhhh, a person with schizophrenia. It was Wendi and Sunshine. Our lives would be altered forever for the worse.

I've read and heard the words spoken many times 'love at first sight.' That wasn't the case. Call it the truth 'Hate at first sight.' Whoever was inside Wendi hated me, yet I was the only person to see or understand that 5-year-old Wendi wasn't Wendi... no longer, nope, a much older soul evil, devil possessed inhabited my sister's shell body & spirit. The arch enemy that would eventually be known as 'Sunshine' was an anomaly, for she wasn't the least like a shine of the sun. Her apt name should have been 'Cloudburst.' She came from the depths of Hades dribbling from her smoldered lips an inner core of molten lava; Sunshine was Hell personified! She was out to get me, so my little sister's saga began.

Sweet loving, adorable sister Wendi. I was kind of bonded with her and even liked her, but being a psychopath, love was definitely out of the realm of emotions that I was capable of... If I could take a scalpel blade, razor, and eviscerate cut out the cloudburst that was Sunshine, I would have done this in a 'flat jack' second.

A couple of years passed frivolously while enduring my tainted childhood. I never will forget... Sunshine had grimaced furiously at me from Wendi's eyes. My poor sister but seven years old me, like 12. She was seething and said these harsh words spitting in my face. Her villainous rapscallion verbiage is forever etched upon my psyche ("I will see to it that you, Mark, will be locked up in prison for your whole pitiful life, never to see the light of day, not to see the sparkle of freedom" or giggling horrifically the 'Sunshine!') then she left the visiting room at the Vacaville Juvenile Hall where we had our last interaction she'd snitched me out for the Liquor store robbery and killing of the dogs.

'The bitch still lived' breaking me from this daze of past negativity was the hidden lane dirt path to my hideaway cabin. Luckily it was isolated like many places in the forested woods, and this 25 acres was major league secluded. My closest neighbors were 35 acres away through a thick Pine and Oak Trees grove!

Making the last switch-back turn, I swiftly had to shove down on my brake pedal. The trailer slid sideways behind me in the reddish sand... a large Oak Tree had fallen across the trail. My criminal mind instantly went viral... Was this a setup scanning 360 degrees around me like the buzzers sounding on the Enterprise spaceship on Star Trek high alert- put up the shields? Off to the left was a path with branches covering it from the massive fallen Oak, an alternative route albeit stealthily hidden almost. My tree hadn't naturally died in a storm. 'Naw, it was chain-sawed down' major trouble!'

My delusional mind warps out, mulling over a fab movie, the 'Chainsaw Massacre,' a 'B' grade movie, increasing my anxiousness, leering at the downed 55-year-old Oak. Perhaps I will take the chainsaw and do a reenactment on the culprit. Obviously, not the authorities; otherwise, I'd be on my knees with weapons at my head helicopter above. Don't you forget I made it into the top 5 of the FBI's most wanted list... Lol!

I'd back the Dodge up and took the less traveled trail that circles around one of my ponds and motocross track the last of the dust clears, having my window down, enjoying the fresh Pine smells, parked on the other side of the pond my cabin about 5 acres West. Before I could step out of the truck, a short-barreled shotgun was jammed into my left shoulder. Hearing the double-clicking chirp sound popularized in those same 'B' movies, of course, you'd probably guess who held the shotgun. Uh, it was the 6'7" Redneck… who the hell else would it be, right?

"Get the fk outta the truck 'copper' just twitch any fast movement, and your DNA will be found with but toothpicks; where's your backup now, DEA prick." He howls, showing three teeth. "Take that gun out of your holster slowly," then from the other side, a matching look, toothless except for the Bunny Rabbit front teeth, a sibling possibly, his 30/30 Caliber rifle directed at my right side. I wasn't in an enviable spot. How could I let these… "Are you fkn deaf, man? Take the gun out and slide it over to my brother." Wow, ownership, what a dummy… Instantly I realized this wasn't funny, and by the way, who was I making fun of in my mind? They'd had the upper hand; I was the dummy now! Uh, aww, Shit ☹.

-49-

Ms. Harris Tank's Parole Officer is on high alert in San Jose, California.

A hotly contested conversation was ongoing…. "I'm sorry, Ms. Harris, it is a need-to-know basis." "Let me make this clear from my perspective Agent Lori Parks. I work for the U.S. Probation Department, not the FBI, and if Mr. Tank Shaw is a flight risk, as you have implied, then I haven't the slightest clue as to how he made Parole. Although I will keep a yoke ah tight leash on him after our conversation, I will consider him as a dangerous offender!" Lori sighs "fine, damnit, it's apparent there's no middle ground with you, Ms. Harris; I thought I would try and use common sense and inform you that Tank is under an ongoing investigation that's rather volatile ah unpredictable…." "I can appreciate that, Agent, but might I add that my responsibilities are, first & foremost, to follow proper protocol within the guidelines provided by the U.S. Probation Dept. which aligns with the safety of the public. If he commits a serious crime, it's my head under the guillotine, my department which will fall into scrutiny. Therefore I must stress to you, Agent, that I will be kept in the loop." Lori frowns and replies, "Tell you what, I will let the big wigs cheeses fight this one out. It's futile dealing with someone as 'pigheaded as you' click...

Lori hits speed dial and gets Rico's voicemail, then punches Director Firms number with a groan. Meanwhile, Ms. Harris is at Tanks door with a U.S. Marshal at 8:05 am, knocking rapidly. Tank rolls over 'what's the racket?' Crap, did I even sleep... so damn tired listening to the constant banging on his apartment door? He makes his way out of bed and tosses on some shorts and a T-Back muscle shirt to open the door ugh, staring out through the peephole. Damnit, it's that nosey bitch P.O.

Slides the door open to the catch of the useless chain. "Mr. Shaw, I need you to let us in uhm, we need to conduct a site check and search your apartment. Also, I'm going to need you to supply a urine sample."

How I reacted could alter the fundamental dynamics of this already caustic relationship forced upon me by the Feds. Interestingly enough, usually, I'd have a state-certified probation officer paroled from State Prison Quentin but having previously been a Federal Inmate, both restrictive entities were regulating me. Duh, something was wrong with this... believe me, momma hadn't raised a fool... in fact, momma didn't raise me at all. I opened the door wide.

"Come on in, and good morning to you. I'm going to start up some coffee. Would you like some?" This... I asked with a furrowed brow. She was the typical busting balls type of woman given authority over men, condescendingly brutal. I was a perfect candidate for her verbal abuse without recourse. While watching her, I couldn't help but fantasize about throwing a harness on her back, pushing her to her knees without lube shoving it in her anal cavity like in that infamous movie with 'Burt Reynolds,' 'Deliverance.' I contagiously laughed accidentally out loud, oops. "What's so funny, Mr. Shaw?" "Oh, just a daydream is all..." "well, humor me about what?" putting my foot in my mouth kinda, I wish I could just tell her it's none of her darn business. I stepped back 10 yards and punted uhm, finding myself on a bridge behind me. It was crumbling, and then suddenly, in front of me, it started swaying just before I said what I was really thinking, like 'remember the Pig in the movie Deliverance' her phone buzzed… Whew! She said, 'hold that thought' and walked out the front door of my apartment.

Donated some piss for the Marshal and watched CNBC and the local news as he worked his way through my place searching for contraband or whatever. By the time my 3rd cup of coffee was inhaled, which sufficiently lubricated my necessary biological dump waiting impatiently till the bathroom was searched and excused myself… locking the door.

I finished dressing, and still, Ms. Harris was nowhere to be seen. I glanced out the kitchen window, seeing her pacing to and fro, holding her phone, looking somewhat agitated at best. Thinking maybe she was getting her ass reamed verbally! Turned and said to the decent Marshal, "hey, I have to get going on finding a job. What's going on here?" he shrugged "your guess is as good as mine, dude. I'm just doing my job here!"

Then her face appeared. Her demeanor was way off kilter, disheveled, even deranged, as if she'd been ridden hard and put away soaking wet on a type of rotisserie grill. In pain, she handed me a business card "be in my office next Tuesday, Mr. Shaw 9 am." "I hope to have a job by then," added I. She nodded, then walked out of my apartment with a different attitude and disposition than when she had entered, as if she'd just received news on her call that a family member had terminal cancer!

In reality, Tank was way off base. Ms. Harris was fuming. She rolled her shoulders in disgust, harshly reprimanded by her boss for merely standing her ground. Performing her job, the orders from above are plain and clear to the point. Leave Tank alone, give him leniency, umh, rope enough to hang himself, and lead them!

'Lead them where?' she'd inquired 'it's a need-to-know basis, and frankly, you needn't know!'

What a catch-22. He was her participant. Undoubtedly, what he did reflected her somewhat. She'd be the scapegoat, and her name would be trashed in the local paper and by the media. It had happened before, and in dealing with Felons, it would happen again. She slammed the Gov. car door driving on auto-drive back to the office.

Driving in traffic 'deluded in phantasmagorical visions flashed forward, and the headlines exploded off the front page' 'Tank Shaw went on a murderous rage killing five people while robbing a bank in downtown San Jose. His probation officer Ms. Harriet Harris failed to answer our calls!' Stressed out at a stop light, she yanked out her vaporizer from a hidden sleeve in her seat cover needed just one puff of Indica. Blessedly marijuana is legal... Ohyeah! ☺.

Strange indeed, as I tried to reckon, mulling over the hour and 35-minute invasion of my privacy in which my car wasn't searched. It had my Tracfone attached with a magnet under the frame. Luckily, I suppose they didn't go all out and tow my car in for an extensive search. I was driving towards Whitney's dress shop and stopping in the alley on the other side and checking out texts from Mark and Joc that left me with gloominess. Messages of urgency my blood pressure up again. What now? I'd just done their bidding and finished blowing up the motorhome. Now they wanted me in bum-fk Idaho, Boise, for a meeting. They wanted me to call and make arrangements like it wasn't my 'Life' it felt like being on a dead-end road back to prison... although this time, it would be for the rest of my life. Hell, they didn't fricken own me. The P.O. had only just left. Damnit, it was time for me to start living for me!

Whitney was all he could think about a dinner date in less than three hours. His bros were demanding that he abscond, go on the lamb, violate his probation, and leave the Bay Area without permission which wouldn't make the Hawk Ms. Harris's day.

No use avoiding the inevitable tried to call Mark nope, then Joe, but no answer from either, so he texted both. Ugh, call me! Dizzy with anticipation and anxiously driven with unmitigated excessive adrenalin, I found the gym a workout was the remedy for blowing out some excess energy.

My day had started off abrasively; why expect it to get any better? 'Murphy's Law' at its best was right. With my gym bag thrown over my shoulder, I paid for the daily charge for a workout at the front desk and made my way to the locker room. A quick change of clothes, then my intentions, the anticipation of hitting the weight pile. It was a 3-level or-story gym. I hyped out, psyching myself out to pump some iron, gritting my teeth, and smiling. 'Sweet,' I was powered up on an energy drink, 'Monster' feeling like busting out some steam beast like uh… not to be!

Walking down the steps towards the bench press, incline, and decline equipment, I was pumped to rock & roll then I caught the vibes of a woman I'd known for one night. Ugh, her scowling distasteful glare disheveled me. It was the cheating cop's wife pumping the stationary bike she the first and only conquest after getting out of prison. I'd hammered her for like five hours and noticed two changes in her… One, she was now wearing a 'wedding ring'… Two, her cop hubby was peddling alongside her.

Sick, instantly stomach dry, heaved as quietly as I could, making a beeline out of the club-now what? It turned out I didn't have to wait very long ahh, don't turn your back on trouble being a predator. I never failed in being cognizant of my surroundings. I'd watched the San Jose cop hop off the bike next to the whore who was pointing at me, yapping. Saw him stalking me from an ample distance as I'd left the gym, walking through the parking lot, a reflection in a panel van's windows. I had in my left hand the fob to automatically open my car. Also, on my left shoulder was my gym bag. What was in my right hand was of most importance my '3 xxx' heavy-duty weightlifting belt with a thick stainless-steel buckle flapping.

"I've been looking for you, Punk!" before I could turn around, a vicious, nasty-intentioned punch, the cop leveraged all his momentum with a right uppercut to my kidneys. I spun both feet to the left with my body, following the tinted window… showing

The ear-piercing sirens and tires were getting closer, and then a Crown Victoria skidded to a halt, the Fed mobile brakes leaving rubber, the same Agent watching me rollerblade with Whitney, the guy had a two-handed grip on a pistol directed at my noggin.

"On your knees now face down, hands behind your back; now asshole." he screamed, "one false move, and you're going to need a colonoscopy bag!"

Ugh, I was in a familiar position behind steel mesh grate cuffs behind my back, looking no longer at freedom… date tonight with Whitney no, to the County Jail, then inevitably back to Quentin… bye Bye now! Even though it was a case of self-defense that wouldn't matter a hoot, the FBI Agent and the police officer would join at the hip in cahoots collusion, umh, no doubts there. It was a hot morning approaching a more sizzling afternoon. Nice, the A.C. was left on motor running while I watched the circus of officers. My Impala had all four doors open, the hood and trunk in search mode. My only worry was that they would find the Tracfone. Other than that, no prob.

The cop gawked at me through the glass, having recovered with remnants of the belts impression welted um embedded in and on the skin around his neck; his deceitful slut stood in the distance in her slinky spandex outfit, a smug face with a tinge of gotcha prick look … Yep.

My wrists were in intense pain. The steel cuffs bore into my skin, my arms didn't bend correctly could barely put my arms together behind my back on my own. Currently forced there; ugh, circulation was cut off, numbness with excruciating waves of shooting nerve endings and pain came flashing through my skull.

What was wrong with this picture? It was the whore who seduced a willing me, uh, and she was at a minimum 55 % in the wrong and 101% guilty for hiding the fact that she was an Adulterer.

But here I was, and there she was, sucking on a straw of a fruit drink. Where was Karma?

Karma, really feeling my left wrist where the skin was peeled back... a feeling of wetness, uhm, blood. The Agent opened the door before he had the chance to bark at me. I said, "yuh think you could transfer these cuffs to the front of me? I'm losing feeling in my hands. They're going numb!"

He beckoned me forward and silently changed them around, now my hands sitting bloody on my lap. He closed the door saying, "your P.O. is on her way!" Being an advocate for me, no one else was, lol. I believed it worth the effort of defending myself as a form of self-preservation; I wanted to, at minimum, be able to speak my mind even though my opinion mattered not.

I told the Agent, "why don't you all go and watch the camera's video of the parking lot to see what happened." But also, with a dose of reality, I was resigned with the knowledge base that I was less than a human in all their eyes, a guilty ex-con-having zero rights whatsoever. Ahoh, the glum face of Ms. Harris showed up from the other side of the glass window. Painted fingernails matching her full-on red pants suit staring in my direction were the three of them, minus the Vixen cheating snake.

The gauge on the dashboard was down to $1/8^{th}$ of a tank. Soon there would be no A.C., and then I muttered to myself gosh, Tank, such a trivial thought. Next, I watch the estranged in-need of counseling couple holding fkn hands and driving off together, whoa, sickening!

A few other San Jose police cars came and went by, all slowing down to look at the captive after an eternity, it seemed... the Agent and Harris came back, cuffs now off, standing before them. "It's your lucky day, Mr. Shaw. The 24-hr. fitness video shows that you merely defended yourself. You're free to go. With a slight guffaw, the Agent says, "better be more careful as to whom you sleep with. No charges will be filed. This never happened," musing to myself, " Yeah, buddy, tell that to my bloody wrists!

Finally, at 1:41 pm, I drove away from the gym oddly. I wasn't followed but easily assumed that Agent Avery had already stuck a chip in my engine compartment or trunk, heck, he had plenty of time and the opportunity to do so. I drove directly to Whitney's dress shop.

On the way, I phoned her cell and the dress shop, leaving voice mails, then texted her nothing back in the 21-minute drive, being proactive like a mini stalker a few hours before our planned dinner, parked, checked my look in the mirror. Grinning, giving me confidence, I smiled, then winked and made a sexy expression. Yeah, I looked good. I slipped down the sidewalk amongst the tourists and worker bees. After a couple of steps. I froze, reading a sign attached to the dress shop door 'Closed due to family emergency.'

My stomach clenched tight. I took the phone out and dialed, pushing her number in again. When the recording came on, I said, 'hello, this is Tank. I'm at your shop. Please call me when you get this; I'm sorry hope everything is all right with your family.'

Phone in hand might as well check in with Mark aah, still no answer, but Joe picked up on the first ring "hey, there you are. Tank… Mark has been trying to get a hold of you. Listen, I need you to catch the next flight up here. I'm in Boise, Idaho, major happenings up here, conference all the hierarchy of the S.O.J. will be here." I frowned, nose curled up, snarling, "I can't do it, Joe; I'm having problems with my P.O., amongst other issues," a slight pause. "Listen, I'm not asking, and neither is Mark. You better do what's right, Tank… I'm telling you to get your fkn ass up here. It's mandatory, dude. I ain't the boss, but this is where our bread is buttered at!" I firmly stated, "I'm due at the P.O.'s early next Tuesday morning. She showed up at my door fricken woke me up this morning. I get caught out of the area, and then I violate my Parole, which wasn't part of the plan. Mark was explicit I was to do the straight and narrow game, remember brother?" "Listen to me… things change, brother. I'll call you back this time. Keep your phone close; we'll do a 3-way call with Mark… have to go now, Tank…" click.

-50-

Tanya and Rico.

Rico jutted awake spasmodically, umh, and he saw Tanya sound asleep; sitting back, her unladylike pose must have lingered ah been a tinge back to her pre-teen childhood days. Legs sprawled wide open; mouth gapped unclenched with a touch of saliva… drool needed a bib. With scarcely the energy to chuckle, I re-closed my lids. I could certainly relate with the often sometimes overused term 'red-eye' for mine were in the burning mode.

We'd left the horrific RV scene after M.E. Ame Toady had secured the site… via helicopter to a waiting airplane in Vallejo, California. Tanya received a call from her superior in Wash. D.C., the U.S. Attorney General. For all intents and purposes, he was consumed by the infiltration of dangerous anti-Government factions. Spies had weaved their way into such entities as Homeland Security, CIA, NSA, and FBI, a major calamity that could only get worse if we didn't get a handle on it.

Countermeasures were taken with our specially trained Ops slowly infiltrating the most potent Militias. They'd move up the ranks of corrupt groups and bent on overthrowing, ruining our ways of a Democratic existence, undermining moral values with a tainted faith and allegiance to Utopian visionaries. Usurpers who manipulated the weakening masses of human societies. The disillusioned, fractured, and dislocated individual followers, the majority of which, the largest percentage, were ex-military.

Before nodding out the first time I watched a 33-minute clip on YouTube, I must admit the way the speakers and advocates, umh, the leaders of the movement, mixed in truths with falsehoods uhm, they were impressive. Each of their movements was in synch, contagiously addicting... throwing in the Aire of confidence like a charismatic evangelist. They were charmingly captivating. An infectious enigmatic mystification, their zeal, and passion fully grasped me like the others in attendance. I even became enthralled and worked up with the repeated lines of fervor spoken about a utopian world of copacetic perfectibility. Including proposed changes in laws, the Government reverting to the initial constitution, and changing social conditions for practicalities and improvements, yet as impractical as all of this sounded, these idealists had their own agenda. Such is how humanity evolved. It always was the charismatic larger-than-life individuals with magnetic personalities mesmerizingly hypnotic, eloquent, with undaunted enthusiasm. These professional evangelical speakers could easily control the masses cult-like... Ala Jim Jones of the Peoples Temple.

What separated these splintered organizations is influential politically connected persons in our Government and the use of the Internet and social media. The World wide web brought an audience to these subversive groups none more prominent or prolific than the now # 1 enemy of our USA 'State of Jefferson' the S.O.J. was packed solid with military experts and professionals, with status members such as Generals, Admirals including was the uninhibited fact that an estimated 45 % of these covert members were Ex-Veterans.

Thus far in the last seven years, we have lost five moles, ugh, informants, their bodies never found. Here we were, Tanya and I, on a flight to Boise, Idaho, on a tip from our most prominent and prestigious 'Rat' umh informant. We would be there for their annual gathering. The rumor was that two of the most feared wanted felons in America, Mark Feral and Joe Sable, would be in attendance!

On the ground already was our team of Agents, including Agent Tom Baker, who had recovered from the assault in San Jose following Tank, found naked & delusional drugs affecting him no longer. We also had Agents Kelsey Marie and Rodriguez, who had fully recovered from the 50 Caliber sniper bullets fired by Joe Sable. In total, we had 17 Agents on the ground in Boise. Tanya decided to leave Agent Lori Parks and Avery to monitor Tank Shaw, the culprit who could have detonated the RV with the Semtex plastic explosives where human remains were discovered. The anomaly with the suspicion regarding Tank's involvement clearly he was carrying nothing to the RV and that the explosion went off over 7 minutes after he'd left.

Sammy argues with Joe about her exclusion.

"So what? I'm just going to sit here with my hands in my pockets, Joe, while you take off to wherever. Leave me here in this stinking hotel? Ugh, I don't think so, Joe!" "Shut up, Sam. I'm not fkn around here. This is beyond serious shit; you stay in this hotel and use the pool, gym, and facilities. Relax, but most importantly, educate yourself on all the sites I've written down for you. It's time for you to be an educated girl on what I'm about and our movement. Girl going to need you to get caught up to speed on our Sovereign Kingdom. I still…." "Joe, I didn't fly all the way to Bumfkn, Idaho, to sit in a hotel. This is a beautiful area, and I want to explore it. Tell ya what, I'm taking the fake I.D. that Lester and Rhonda supplied and renting a Harley Davidson to explore Coeur d'Alene going to ride on a road trip around the lake, which is supposed to be paradise. That's me, dude. Yuh better get used to it or kill me; I'm not your high-class whore no more; I'm free of all that crap. Hell might find a nice and secluded cabin for us to buy… move away and escape in!"

Joe fought back the notion of rebuking the 'high-class whore' part of her annoying statement for that was bullshit uuhhh, "No, you're not Sam; your face has been plastered all over the media. Have you lost your freakin mind? Forgotten in 2019 with a click or a tap, your face's dot-pixels glow on all the phone's screens in the USA. Stay the fk inside, and that's an order you…" He pauses as the red-faced stare-off continued, not going to subside "okay, Sammy, I promise you will get out there and have some fun when I get back!" He grabbed the briefcase Lester and Rhonda had entrusted him with… to hand it over to Jaybird.

I failed to say with pain and despair in my loins and mind... that Mark had ordered aah, wanted Sammy eliminated at once. This was of utmost importance to me, for I wouldn't co-sign his orders. Ain't no way I wanted to lose Sammy. For many unselfish reasons, such uhm... cuz she had actual value. She was an asset with an eidetic memory. Sammy had proven her loyalty by not running off when having had a multitude of opportunities. Besides all of that, I'd become fond of her... way too much! I presumed Sammy went to the bathroom to cool off; I couldn't help the uneasiness like destined chaos; something smelled awful to me wrong, ugh, Mark had often disappeared for hours. Often for days in pursuit of females, his obsessive form of fun, knowing he was ordered to attend this conference, he should already be here. Maybe he was on a flight?

Last I saw, his neck of the woods, the County was on fire with evacuations ordered... like seven dead burned up, sad that maybe there was a smidgen of truth from the environmentalists that Earth's Ozone umh the warming of the planet. Who really cares, right? Pass the buck and leave it to the next generation to deal with, we'll be dead and buried long before our ruinous existence kills the planet. Wasn't that the way it always was? Pass the buck, ugh, problems down the line good luck to human existence, Sure!

Rico and Tanya in Boise, Idaho.

"So, Tanya, what is the plan? I reviewed your notes and..." "Rico, we first get showers and can meet in the lobby in, let's say, 55 minutes" "fine with me,"... click. Well, by the time I'd removed myself from the soothing privacy of the warmth and solitude of the shower, the knife twisted in deeper... my disposition and demeanor were already crawling on a thin line the Instagram sent by Marshal Kara that I'd almost as if a 3rd person read five times. I faced the steamed mirror with no use in hiding it. I was in Love with Wendi Feral; I've read that stress or pressure makes Diamonds... I slouched like made of silly putty.

No way to hide the emotions. What the heck was wrong with me? If people that knew me could see the macho Rico Captor here and now. Tears watered down and trickled off of my cheeks from my closed eyelids. Was it leftover water from the shower that I toweled off? Perhaps I was deliriously exhausted. Yeah, no, no use kidding myself. My bond with Wendi was not mere infatuation; I loved the girl, and the lovemaking at the cabin in the Trinity mountains still plays on my mind as I jerk slowly in fantasy. Certain in my heart that I would always be less without her in my life… than we would be together, she was a missing piece, um, cog-part of me. ☹.

Damnit, another attack on Wendi's life at NIA, she was stable shot with a dart, and Doctor Hawkins was on site. How the hell? Why? A multitude of variables went up in hazy smoke. I needed to get back to Napa. I still recalled the ridiculous and frustrating interaction with the bossy Tanya. She told me with zero latitudes that I was not flying back to Napa to aid in the current investigation that Agent Link had control of.

I called Agent Lucy Link and directed her to take a team of our best Forensic CSI types to increase the Marshals at and around Wendi's room to get to the bottom middle and top of the corrosive situation at NIA.

I lost my composure a few times, shouting and yelling. Still, in Lucy's favor, she was patient and understanding and full-on relentless in her investigation, 'get inside of NIA' I told her I would be flying in the next day despite Tanya's orders.

I Futilely tried in vain to get CEO Terrance Hallinan online and ended up Tweeting him I had to have answers. My mind spun out as if on hallucination drugs… discombobulated. All the recent memories colliding, Lori caught nearly naked in my room by Tanya, the RV, Joe sniper shot Nurse dead. Mark and Joe were working with Tank, uhm, the serial killings, uh, kidnappings of the attorneys in Northern California. Currently, the murderous duo is in Idaho. I wish I could be in two places simultaneously, alas, hands tied. I got Doctor Hawkins on the line she took me from morbidity to slight relief before I pushed end… on our conversation my BP had reduced by 25%, yet nothing was going to stop me from flying back to NIA the next day to see Wendi and if I had to try and close down NIA… Ahh, cackled as that could ever happen. No, I didn't have the clout for that. First thing, I needed to get her out of the

Neurological Hospital to one of our safe houses. NIA had become toxic as if it weren't lethally noxious all along.

Tanya met me in the hallway as I opened my door like she was eavesdropping, lol. I yelped. "Don't you have enough agents here in Idaho, hell you got half the police force at your beckoning call. I need to get back to Napa..." Tanya, for her part, remained stubbornly adamant, looking around at the others comingling outside their rooms and whispering, leaning into my left ear, "Stay focused; this isn't the time to lose your perspectives. You need optimal use of all your reasoning faculties; otherwise, you will be liable to erroneous miscalculations that could cost you or one of our team their lives," lectures Tanya. Now leaning on the open door of my room. "Rico, we did receive a mini break; we were able to trace Samantha Timmons's phone by using a method of triangularization from towers pinging off from her closest locations she'd been in the Fairfax hills of Marin County before the phone was destroyed. We have it nailed down to only five properties!" "Well, that's fantabulous, Tanya, but where is she now?" 😧 .

-51-

<u>Tank and Whitney.</u>

My phone rang... I finally heard the voice I'd been wishing to hear, not the content that was expressed, "Whitney, I'm so happy to hear your voice. I..." "Tank, I'm not going to make dinner, not now and maybe never with you; let me go I...." "Whoa, girl, what's going on?..." "I have to go, sorry..." "hey, wait a sec. can I help..." "Unless you can rent us a large U-Haul truck, no!" in the background, I can barely discern a man's tone. "Whit, come on, help me with this heavy chest." "Ahh, who's that?" "umh, it's one of my bros. We're packing supplies into his pickup truck...." "For what?" "Tank, our parent's property and home have been burnt to the ground.

They're living in a shelter in Mendocino County outside of Lakeport! ugh it's so traumatic I'm going crazy with emotions I gotta go I...." "Omg, Whitney, I'm so sorry; how can I help? This is awful, so what...." "I closed the dress shop and am trying to compile as much medical stuff, bottled water dry goods to take up to the fire area to help the burned-out fallen victims of the fire have to get mom and daddy out of there so..." 'Whit' using her brother's abbreviation "let me see if I can help out... please answer my next call" click.

Not having many resources, I chuckled none except for the ones Mark had loaned me. I let the Internet do the walking checking on U-Hauls throughout Northern Cali, but none to be had. The businesses were inundated with demand; likewise, it was the same with the other rental companies. Human tragedy had warranted the necessity and need for boxed trucks, and the fires were blazing at last count in triple digits out of control. There weren't enough firefighters to fight the blazes. California was literally on fire; hotels, motels, and rental cars were impossible to get. All booked up and out; unfortunately, the un-American vultures came out to roost and devour the handicapped and heart-struck casualties. Unreal many even raised prices for everything, including a bottle of H2O.

I drove my Impala back to the 'cut shop' and didn't have the contact number to call because the number I'd called to borrow the Cadillac was passe, disconnected, likely a burner phone. One thing was for sure in my way of thinking; this business had its shit together. Having just a name with an address parked in the same spot as I did when I switched out my car for the borrowed Escalade for my trip up to Marin.

"What the fk are you doing back here, guy?" asked an angry Hispanic dude with a mean-looking mustache and soul patch... his tattoo's covered his bald head. I think I'd met my match. He might have more ink than me. The guy was one big tattoo, and '3 tear drops dropped from below his right eye almost matched the '4' below his left. The 357 Mag. In his hand with bad intentions, no worries. I wasn't prepared to be the one to even up the 'tear-drops'

that denoted kills. His name was Jose, but he went by the nickname 'Bandit.' I calmly explained my intrusion as others of his group formed around. He listened till I paused, then, in Spanish, started to speak with his amigo's um compadres. I didn't let on that I understood every syllable. Pointing at me, breaking away from his monologue...

"How the fk do you not know if you were followed again, man? You gringo's are like nothin' but trouble!" I raised both palms and said, "no way I'm clean" honestly, I didn't know if I was, but this wasn't the time to be forthright uh candid, so I rolled with the look of disdain ludicrously like bulletproof confidence exuding from fake pores.

He then sent one of his homeys out to search for a tail and had another check out the cameras. It seemed that I'd made a mistake, hopefully not my last if so, so be it. No fear was my theme. No turning back.

Bandit spun away slightly, but the gun remained poised, constantly pointing at my groin area ('Este Cabron quiere ir a las Ombres en Mendocino y Jugar la parte de El Bien samaritano y octal un toque con Caja grande') Tank. Bandit had used my name as a good sign, right? "what's in it for you, man? Why you need a truck, hombre... drugs, huh, you driving drugs? What are you moving, Wetto?"

What he said in Spanish clenched my following statement ('this fool wants to go up to the fire in Mendocino and play good Samaritan needs a large box truck!') "A girlfriend's parents have been evacuated; home burned down. I want to go and help them and other victims. Just because I'm all inked up doesn't mean I'm a cold-ass bastard Bandit!"

In less than 11 minutes, I was driving a 35-foot Mercedes diesel cab-over truck with less than 45,000 miles on the odometer on my way to Whitney's house... Yay! ☺ .

Jax and Sunshine at NIA.

"Jax, what? Your off base. You don't think I have feelings, sure... yeah, I'm a control freak who dominates the weaker side of our dual existence. Wendi is along for the ride. She should enjoy

the scenery. My intentions were never to undermine her. I didn't become me. It never made me, oh crap. What I'm trying to convey is that I'm manifested from Wendi's mind, came into being as a savior of sorts, secret friend-protector, another side dimension of her, brought strength and conviction born or extracted from 5-year-old Wendi herself." "Sunshine, come on please, let it go…."

"Jax, please, you haven't heard it all, not by a long shot… It was I who witnessed the brutal rape and murder and the torture through the Cat 'Tabby's' eyes. She couldn't handle it, so I stepped forward to help out Wendi, or she'd been lost in her fragmented mind. Sunshine is my moniker without my guidance, humility, and humbleness. Wendi would by now be a vegetable, most likely on so many prescriptions that she wouldn't recognize her own, uhm 'our' reflection in a mirror!"

"I've heard most all of this before, Sunshine, from Wendi's perspective, and yes, I empathize with your position, but it's Wendi's body-shell that you've taken control of and…" "Stop, Jax, the holier than thou all mighty bullshit check this out ultimately I 'put out the fires' dealt with the trauma that she couldn't withstand or handle and reconcile I would drift back behind the scenes. Uh was compartmentalized from her outside life, shunned behind a veil-shroud a wall of obscurity, yet shrewdly cunningly, I learned wily and artful ways to enable me to grow and live within our dual body and personalities from five years old through puberty and adolescence. I was a constant partner, an invisible twin. Each time I was needed, I performed like a freakin trained 'Seal' for Wendi." He nodded.

"It was gloriously enticing being out in the 'limelight' it was beyond Joyful I was alive, Jax, think about it. You should be able to relate… you've been in prison. That was my existence locked away, only to be given freedom when poor pathetic Wendi couldn't handle adversities uh pressures. <u>'Oh, Sunshine, thanks again. Now go back to the shadows!' Bam back shrinking behind the veil I went yuh see once I'd regained normalcy in her life. Obedient slave-like taken for granted at the onset of this way of living, I 'was' happy. Without a second thought, I'd relinquish, capitulate and</u>

submit to Wendi's yearning, beckoning demands. I was like an emergency Paramedic constantly on 24-hour call!" 😥 .

"Yes, you are to be revered and applauded, Sunshine; nevertheless, you must realize it's Wendi's shell that your stealing. If not for her, you wouldn't be here...." "On the other hand, if not for me, she wouldn't be here either. How's it fair whenever a situation becomes precariously dangerous? I jumped to the foreground, always optimistic and thankful and showing full-on gratitude, helping us traverse all obstacles and demonstrating loyalty. Because in true reality, my persona was initiated inaugurated for survival purposes of innocence and the innocent ignorance of the child within us. I'd up to now succeeded in saving her, ugh us I'm frankly tired of taking the proactive precedent and leading us from danger!"

Jax felt like he should be the conductor leading the orchestra... symphony like redundant knew exactly where Sunshine was going. Not wanting to be rude, but this had been played out dozens of times, and he was sick of her justification. If not for the damn dart shot into her neck Sunshine would have been history. Even though he was lost in his own thoughts, she picked up right where her long soliloquy had stopped. "Ugh, since my inception after Rocco saved Wendi the Gorilla at the Zoo, which enabled her the gift 'curse' to communicate with animals animal seer, our lives became a jumbled mess, stress-related working with the police as a child of three years old on. That horrid Judy Girth, the Redwood City cop, then Agent Rico, Captor of the FBI. I was called on by Wendi to the rescue, not counting 155 times to date, sometimes for no other reason than a boyfriend breaking up with her. Held her hand and heart always there for her in times of distress, although just as fast as I was called in with the calvary, I'd quickly then be disposed and relegated to the shadows marginalized like spare parts or three-day leftovers!" Jax rolled his shoulders about to open his mouth; she tossed up a paw and gushed some more.

"Frequently, I lingered longer than she wanted but was eventually shut down. I'm not trying to justify my existence within this body, which has always been me. Pain and suffering brought me out of the shadows, abused, used given zero forms of pleasure ahh fk Sunshine the 'Fail safe option' let me…." "Please, I've heard this so many times. Let it go; you're a figment of Wendi's mind, Sunshine; yes, necessary. We all have many personalities and are different people inside; nevertheless, it's time to let go, please!"

"Hear me out only a few more points, Jax 'look at me laying on this gurney' living in a capsule contemplating the past and looking forward to the future for the first time, which was never a possibility. It was always Wendi's future. I was carried around for the ride. Am I a bad person? Naw, can't cum to grips with that? My heart is filled with Love, grace, mercy, and compassion for Lil Ms. Wendi. It's now time for me to 'shine,' pun intended." She cackled loudly, taking a sip of iced tea in a straw, not losing place as she motormouthed onward. "The more often I was called upon to take charge of our life, umh, the more I became jealous, envious, and enamored, wanting to have my own life unshared. Selfishly wanted to be me, I'd decided no more would I just shrink back to the murky solitude of a sickening voyeur. I wanted to feel my form of sexual pleasures with unsatiable desires and a matching appetite, uh yum, kinky, even perverted. I just wanted to play some fantasies out… wasn't into the Boring Lil Missionary Wendi. No, some good ole S&M bondage pain with delicious desserts. I gave her my service for decades, provided the shoulder to cry on, commiserated with uhm cared for her. After so many experiences umh tastes of what this human life has to offer, I was able to seize possession not with force. I might remind you, Jax, I didn't plan the prescription drug cocktail. It was NIA, principally Doctor Liz Honcho, which helped me… Yep."

Jax realized that before the dart shot had injected Wendi, he'd come to grips and knew now he loved the girl in a different way than how he enjoyed Sunshine. Wendi was a precious girl who hadn't any hidden ulterior motives for what you saw you received from that little lady. Yes, she is a lady, unlike her other crass and domineering side. He wanted to see Wendi smile, and her sense of humor was one of a kind. It was just ugh…

Jax sighed hugely, knowing that however it all turned out, he was on thin ice and didn't want to take up sides and alienate Sunshine. If so, she could shut down into hibernation. Sad truth be told, the next mission that he'd been requested to lead would need Wendi's ability or paranormal talents to succeed. Without her help, it might take longer to carry out NIA's goals in a prompt manner. Jax was still confident he could do so without this new tyrant that Sunshine had morphed into. Listening now again, the woman never shut up, still rambling on…

"Jax, are you listening to me? Um, I'm pouring out my heart; you're spacing out, dude?"

"Ugh, yes, of course, go on…." "Sure, there has been inner turmoil with Wendi in the time that I was off the drug regimen. She and I would grapple verbally and argue and spar. I learned a valuable lesson when Doctor Hawkins had altered the psychotropic mixtures and changed up the formulas. I found out Wendi was selfish. Wendi was strong enough to forge forward like empowered. She booted me back to non-existence. This was now a War, A battle for supremacy, dominance for my survival, and my sovereignty. Never will I cave in again. I will keep her locked in the world that was once mine to troll around within Wendi Feral is Dead for all intents and purposes, seeya! Wouldn't want to be Yuh!"

I watched Jax looking somewhat disgruntled like he was not happy with my statements nor with me… what was going on? He was my BF. Had he forgotten that we'd had sex and loving once not that long ago? Was he having second thoughts, umh, can't get all worked up with conspiracies like a teenage girl? He loved me, just dealing with life's pressures. Now gotta think as I whispered under my breath, wanting to scream out the words. <u>*I'm alive. Long live the Queen 'Sunshine Feral!'*</u>

Alrighty now, with all that being said, I was losing the verbal skirmish with my bestest friend in this shallow world, Jax, ugh. I had to plan my escape from NIA if my man Jax Foul would not help me. Oh well, I will do so alone. I must keep umh… be aware and cognitive to never run out of the drug cocktail that Dr. Honcho has formulated for me to keep Wendi behind the drapes. Uhm, I need a year's supply to start with. First, I need to get my grubby paws on the lab reports and results of the blood tests that the Fed Doctor Hawkins had taken after the dart injected the drugs that are necessary to lock Wendi away forever!

'Oh crap,' I went comatose. The door suddenly opened. Marshal Kara walked up, her large hand on my forehead, and rubbed my hair back, then whispered, 'I'm sorry to have let you down. It will not happen again, Wendi. I promise you that as long as I am near, no one will hurt you again.' She leans down and gently kisses my rosy cheek… door closes.

<u>**Sunshine fondly recalls a Mission from the past in Seattle.**</u>

Finally, my conscious state of giving way, in my favorite dimensional world of dreams, fantasies, subconscious reliving of past events… fun stuff. Standing next to Jax in Seattle dressed like janitors, the power player's I.P.O. initial public offering, our mission was to learn all that was disseminated in the secure, soundproof conference room. The Parrots, ugh, Macaw's names were Ozzy and Harriet. The only way to succeed was for me to question the birds, and our quandary was trying to figure out how to get alone time with the Macaws.

Besides this wayward calculation, who knew if the Parrots were even paying attention to their owners or the proceedings? I instinctively knew Parrots were a curious bird species; I told Jax to get me close to them, and he said, "Sun, as I see it, we have one chance." From behind us, a pervasive moaning growl came from a pile of canvas by a ladder, the real Janitor whom we had to, unfortunately, disable. "Sun, hand me the hypodermic needle from the case he's already coming out," I offered up "hey Jax, why don't we use the Russian killer poison nerve agent 'Novichok?' That way we don't have to worry cuz he will never wake up again!" "No, we only use that vile in case of emergencies. Just give me the needle again, and I will give him a double dose of sleeping tranquilizer."

This mission was supposed to be simple, 'easy as pie.' It didn't include many weapons, just the poisonous nerve agent. The security firm that was hired to protect and secure this high-level meeting had three top Agents that had retired from the CIA. No cost was measured, monies mattered, not all that was important was to ensure there would be no leaks, um, espionage. They took their jobs seriously. The seven-man and four-woman team had taken control of the top 5 floors of the 23-story building in downtown Seattle. The security force was hell-bent on forming a higher level of scrutiny on the floors they'd controlled. Everything was wired for sound and video, sort of Penagonish. The elevators and stairways at each hallway corridor were set up with sophisticated motion detectors that were efficient in discerning any movement and detected guns, steel, metal, or oddities and scanned all bodies for thick masses. Thus even our latest innovative plastic rubber pistols would set off alarms besides those security measures. They'd enacted a unique fail-safe system that also hampered us. If we used our blocking signal device to shut down all frequencies after 15 seconds, a backup system would be employed then an audio alarm would sound.

On each floor were security officers, not the Walmart, K-mart variety, umh shopping center stereotypical types, which were so out of shape, living a sedentary lifestyle out of cardio shape. They were incapable of sprinting 50 yards without huffing and puffing from their knees and heart attacks… matching ah aligning with their fast-food diets. No, these women and men were ex-military. Even the ladies could, without much sweat, do 11 hanging pull-ups. Jax and I were outmanned, outgunned, and in over our heads. This deal was deep into the Billions of dollars. We were even at an added disadvantage because we weren't as tech-savvy as the team against us.

At each entrance into select offices and even the freakin cafeteria, they used 'retina recognition' with an additional pad for a fingerprint check. Jax nor I wanted to amputate the janitor's left hand nor extract one of his eyeballs; if it boiled down to it, the thin scalpels would do the trick. What we did have on our side was that the spoiled Macaws were unique pets of the CEO, and as strange as it was, she was known to have some weird superstitions. One

"Sunshine, the double doors just opened there filing out. Let's get prepared for action!" I reached into a pouch and took out the miniature frequency blocker, which we could only set in less than 15-second blasts, or alarms would loudly wail. Jax had figured out that at full sprint speeds running as fast as we could, the Aviary room with the Macaws was about 11 seconds down the hall, but that wasn't the problem. It was the time it took to access the room. The problem is, how do we get inside without alarms blaring? It was most likely locked all of this in less than 15 seconds, nearly an impossible task.

From the janitorial room, Jax and I stood peering out the cracked door watching the people exit the secure conference. The last person to leave was Ms. Salvia, a native of India. She was a well-known ally of Russia's Putin and was suspected of courting Trump's clan members. Neither of which we, uh, NIA, considered friendly to our cause. Earbuds stuffed in our ears, we listened and watched, anxiety rising as they scattered to the elevators-several of the 19 participants went towards the stairway with heavy briefcases in hand.

"Where is she at?" I asked impatiently in a whisper. Then a woman popped out of the cargo elevator dressed in a colorful outfit like Hawaiian flowers, tropics with birds nesting on branches between the buds… she pushed a cart.

We hear her words, "Ms. Salvia, will Ozzy and Harriet be accompanying you on the chopper this afternoon to Portland?" "Wtf did she just say, Jax? Oh man, now what are we going to do? We…" "ssshh Sun," then we heard the key words, "yes, they will be joining us." The next thing we saw was a large hanging birdcage hanging from a steel loop. The cage was covered in blackish silk and attached to a mobile cart.

Standing there stunned, watching the bird handler and Ms. Salvia with three others take the elevator to the roof to no doubt a waiting helicopter. Jax didn't frown. In fact, his expression remained near neutral, 'as if another day in the park.' I was frustrated, unnerved, and perplexed that he merely shrugged his shoulders like no biggie that we were thwarted, our plans foiled. I felt the oxygen leave my lungs. His mantra was to be continued… 'We would never risk ourselves when the odds weren't in our favor.'

Jax spoke on a secure radio, 'need airlift check with air traffic controller… company chopper leaving the building to the destination of somewhere in the Portland, Oregon region track it keep me abreast we need immediate transfer to their location ETA 9 minutes to ground floor.'

"Jax, what about the knocked-out janitor" "don't worry about him. He will wake up without any memory except for coming to work. The drugs should disable him for another 17 hours here. Help me lean him up." "what about the injection points?" "Sun, unless they check the follicles in his thick hair, we're fine, and there's no reason for that. He'll wake up thinking he was napping on the job. The last thing he's going to do is report himself. Let's get going, girl. We have a date in Portland. Our goal is incomplete!"

"How can you be so fkn calm, boy?" "Girl, if I had to count how many operations across the Middle Eastern deserts that didn't go according to the well laid out plans of superiors, I'd not achieve any of the set forth goals heck, they'd all be still incomplete. In order to succeed in much that we aspire to accomplish, we must align contingency plans. It's a moving equation… now move out!"

I pushed the blocking devices button, and we made a fast beeline to the first exit door… down the stairs we went. Not… retina nor fingerprint actuated. Only the use of a computer chip card slid into the slot down the stairs, and we tumbled faster than the incline was meant to traverse. I realized chivalry wasn't dead as he opened the door of a waiting Hummer; speaking of a Hummer, that's exactly what I'd like to perform gulp down Mr. Hot Jax Foul. Alas, that would have to be postponed… Lol! ☺ .

We were driven to a waiting helicopter while I listened to him say, "Sun, we must always be prepared for the unknown or unexpected to be able to think on our feet, deviate with contingencies from original courses uhm adlib, adapt masterfully and skillfully never allow oneself to become flustered. Our vast human brains kicked in when survival was in doubt and alternative proficiency with improvisation. Thinking out of the box, if not, it could be Adios!" I laughed out loud 'aah, adios huh!' he then took me in his right arm, pulled my head to his muscled shoulder, held me tight mumbled in my left ear, with a slight nibble of the lobe, "I adore you, my-lady." Aah, I melted further into him. Oh, how I wanted this man to hold and devour me whole as I would him. Lust filled with passion and constantly restrained was not a good thing, although time was on my side. Life is about timing. As the chopper landed and we were whisked away to another impromptu meeting.

The birds and Ms. Salvia's group had landed 19 minutes prior in an open lot by the Columbia River, the 3rd largest river in America behind the Mississippi and the Ohio river. I could be wrong might have missed that test question: Umh, quiz in geography class. Nevertheless, their entourage traveled towards Camas, Washington, to a restaurant called 'Beaches' for dinner.

I overheard this tidbit of news regarding their dinner plans while Jax was on the radio, and sarcastically I said to my wannabe paramour, "now what, Mr. Adlib?" He gave me a smirk with a mini roll of his shoulders simultaneously mixed with a wink and wrinkled nose, "Sun, we have patience, girl. Our job is to get some alone time with the Parrots. Who knows if the bird handler and birds are not right now sitting in A.C. in a vehicle? We'll have a report coming in soon. I assure you that both of us are like 'Pit Bull' Dogs chasing bones. Once we get our jaws on them, we aren't going to let loose till we get to the Marrow! If we don't succeed by chance, then, oh well, back to NIA, no worries, this isn't a make or break do or die situation, for hell's sake. This is all for our greedy boss Terrance and his cronies!" "Why Jax, I don't..." Sun, they want to know the inner nuances of the IPO for they want to piggyback and make a bundle of money playing the arbitrage game in the stock market." What's arbitrage?" "Uhm, it means taking advantage of price differences across markets to back a buck, buy it low overseas, sell high in New York."

-52-

The FBI and NIA.

A.W. Larry Walden sat at the end of the black Walnut table. His audience was singular in the present tense guard Billy Goad. The other onlookers were Terrance & Liz, and Ursula, who viewed the interrogation from the CEO's office... two-way mirror.

Agent Lucie Link and her Forensic CSI team followed the breadcrumbs right to Billy's locker, where the rifle and darts were planted, along with copies of complaints and grievance forms against Wendi. His motive was apparent hatred and envious jealousy for how Wendi was placed on a pedestal and treated like royalty. Before the Feds could arrest Billy, he was brought into a borrowed room at NIA for questioning, as it turned out. Billy Goad was bewildered and totally flustered, a damn disconcerted mess. The anti-depressant drugs were working doing their job, his grandiose disposition peaking as the drugs in his system kept flowing; nothing could alter his euphoric fantasy world.

The divorce and alcohol had markedly left him skeletal-like... he would be pliably gullible, easily susceptible to the Fed's tact of interrogation. It would be an effortless endeavor. At times, Billy was overenthusiastic eager to please, and not argue against the facts of being the conspirator that he wasn't... lol.

Terrance and his flunkies worried that he'd blurt out something harmful about NIA under scrutiny by the FBI's investigator Lucie and her team. Still, before Lucie made her way upstairs to arrest him, they'd become confident he was the quintessential fall guy. The pressure on the poor dude was overwhelming. He was facing foreclosure on his home; alcohol had destroyed and ruined his once flourishing marriage/divorce, loss of his children, and just a lost soul. No worries, ole Billy would be lost now forever, seeya Billy-boy. Add in the fact that he'd just inhaled some freakin weird ass drugs. Oh man, the dude was on some severe dosage of untested psychotropic chemicals mixed with the appropriate LSD... Lol, that would eventually put his mind and body out to pasture, umh, misery! <u>Billy Goad was 'Gonzo the Gerbil!'</u> ☺ .

Billy seemed genuinely confused at times. Would he hold up long enough to satisfy Agent Link? What would he say when she asked him, "why'd you shoot Wendi?" Billy's peers considered him a country bumpkin hick aah yokel from Fort Smith, Arkansas generations of backwoodsmen. Due to the long-term effects of drinking Moonshine that was shipped illegally past state lines by his relatives back in Arkansas uhm, another Federal felony. No question Billy had mental deficiencies, and a dearth of inadequacy pounded into his skull... the perfect Sapp!

Terrance would try to mitigate the harm of the latest disaster at NIA by watching Agent Link, who was on video, coming up the elevator with three other Agents. The arrest of Billy was a foregone conclusion. He would advocate that Doctor Liz Honcho should remain his Doctor, continuing the daily injections of anti-depressants he'd remain inside of NIA, a prison holding cell under observation. True, he shot the dart into Wendi, who now was under protective custody by Marshals. Billy had lost his mind. He was insane; what better place to cage him than a Mental Institution Lmao... funny, thought Terrance.

Agent Lucie Link was relaxed, breathing calmly. Billy Goad was quite the opposite, pacing back and forth in the 7 X 11 interrogation room, then in the next second, he'd be leaning his elbows on the table, head in his palms. For the last four hours, the relentless barbs were fired "why Billy, what was your motive? I understand you felt Ms. Feral received special treatment, but...."

Doctor Teresa Hawkins.

Far away on the other grounds of NIA, where Wendi was resting ugh, Sunshine, currently in charge, Doctor Hawkins, was sitting studying charts confounded um, before the evening was up, she would be in a tsunami of inconsistencies. Facts bearing out a definite conundrum, from the blood tests of Wendi and the dart that she'd yanked from Wendi's neck, all were rushed to an outside laboratory, and then the results were returned to her temporary office at NIA... not Good!

Oddly, the formula inside the dart was the same drug regimen that Doctor Honcho had prescribed Wendi, albeit a much stronger concentration with time-release mechanisms. The darts were supposed to be used to squelch uprisings at the prison. Non-violent measures were usually taken before the guards unlatched the mortal rounds.

But the other darts she'd tested were filled with Horse tranquilizers strong enough to drop an Elephant, not the concoction of Super Psychotropic Drugs that were shot into Wendi! An odd problematic quandary.

woman, yah better shower up," she smirked, "yuh mister your ripe yourself!" All were smiling as the night ended with exasperated sighs, relief palpable... done that! They knew that Billy Goad would be essentially brain-dead by morning... drug-induced. ☺

<u>Boise, Idaho, and Rico Captor's escape.</u>

"Rico, I have had all three darts analyzed by our Forensic lab. The exact formula that was shot into Wendi was found in every dart found in Mr. Goad's locker. All others in their arsenal room had sleeping agents that were consistent with something akin to a Horse tranquilizer." "Motive Lucy is weak. Why would Billy, who is like three years from retirement, risk his future? I don't get it, Lucy?" "I'm telling you, Rico, he is not mentally stable. We ran a check on him, uhm; he's insolvent in debt up past his ears-went through the grinder of an acrimonious losing divorce with his children taken until he can get psychological assessments and counseling. I think he just lost his mind, warped, broken, and off to insanity land... the guy is on the precipice of a nervous breakdown. He lashed out at Wendi, maybe a substitute for his ex-wife." Lucy pauses, clearing her throat and staring at the photos.

Lucy once again was taking a look at her picture... "the ex-Ms. Goad has a close resemblance to Wendi. They could be sisters. Well, at the least, Billy's ex could pass for an older sister uh, umh. Psychologist Liz Honcho said maybe Billy associated Wendi with..." "shit Lucy isn't that a stretch?" "I've sent you the video recording of the entire interrogation along with Mr. Goad's credit history and employee records. He is currently under Doctor Honcho's care and sedated, so it would seem this is an isolated attack on Wendi. No conspiratorial theories apply. The guy is delusional and disgruntled...." "I have just one other question or, wait, a combination of things that bother me about this theory, Lucy... Billy is a 'Stage 5 alcoholic.' He was shaking, you said, like a tree branch in a tornado. How was he able to fire a dart rifle and shoot Wendi from 59 yards out, hitting her precisely? Uh, exactly on her neck, which according to the pictures and video, there was about five inches of skin, showing… he's not a marksman. In fact, didn't you say you checked his records? He was near the bottom of the last shooting competition held only five months ago?" Rico shook his head, swallowing hard.

"Lucy, I'm sorry, it's just that I have serious reservations about the unlikely hood he could make that shot, and you, yourself, said he only fired once… The man would need the rifle to be leveraged in a vise-grip to fire that shot. As you said, he shakes like a leaf. Where is the inhouse video showing this Billy Goad with the rifle?" Lucy checks her phone for the time… pauses, tired at her max, exhaustion levels had her running at a low ebb "there was some sort of glitch with the camera that was pointed in Billy's direction or from where he had to fire the weapon to make the shot." "Okay, Lucy, were Billy's fingerprints on the rifle?" "I sent it to our lab, and I'll have that answer tomorrow morning. Let me add that I've been over this several times with Walter Hale, head of security here, Rico, and…" Rico grimaced "ah, I know Walter pretty well. Ironically he won that shooting competition and was bragging to me, saying why not hire him? He'd make a grand FBI Agent! I'll deal with him. It doesn't seem right that all the other cameras were functioning except the one that would prove Billy fired the dart I…." "Rico, I will concede that I can't figure out how he made the shot in his condition; pure luck possibly, but why would he admit and claim he fired the dart? You're right about Billy, uhm correct, it was an incredible shot, a show of expertise to hit her on the first shot 59 yards off in the wind… all I can say is Billy got lucky!" "Lucy, I don't believe in luck. We make our luck, sometimes fate isn't in our control, but lucky shot, nope, don't like it."

"Boss, I'm exhausted. Let's mull this over tomorrow when you arrive. I will have more information to go over with you umh the only good news is that Wendi will recover once the darts drugs wear off. If it's all right, sir, can we close this discussion and get to our hotels? Truly I see nothing changing before we meet…" "thanks, Lucy, yes, pull on out, thank our team for me. I will be there to meet you, aah, in about 12 hours," click.

Idaho was front and center on an end table, a color map; thinks hell Tanya has plenty of support here. Agents up the 'ying-yang' I'm not needed even though the informants have said that Joe Sable and Mark Feral will attend the S.O.J. Militia's conference on seven sprawling square miles of property a Ranch with airplane-sized hangars next to the landing strips.

-53-

Mark Feral was attacked and kidnapped at his Hat Creek cabin.

Ambivalent & dazed watching the 6'7" lard ass who was screaming, 'how did I know?' while the splatter of chewing tobacco was spewing out of his stained teeth. What was left of them? He prods me to my right side the passenger door is opened. I am surrounded by the armed brothers who were evidently unstable at best.

I haven't a clue how it works for other humans, so speaking for the only person I can... Me I see myself in times of trauma and stress, everything around me 'stands still' frozen in place like slow motion. In the milliseconds that the two clodhoppers posed weapons pointing at point-blank range, I flashed to past anecdotes... primed forward.

Flashing before my open pupils were the five jury trials for assault & battery instances where my bare hands nearly killed other men. When the jury returned, it was major league stressful Yup. Then I leap to another life-changing event… in a motorcycle accident on I-95 going to Miami heck 101mph. I was sideswiped by a slower car, and there I was, freewheeling down the freeway, bouncing and tumbling off the highway's asphalt, and ending up in the medium. Or at Mt. Shasta, a mundane incident snowboarding just before I was last arrested, hauling ass down the mountain then air-born, boarding right into a class of novice beginners in a snowboarding class, oh maybe 15 children. I had no alternative as I snowboarded through the beginner's ranks to snatch up a little boy going around 50 mph. The boy started screaming as well as he should have been. I held him tight a bend, turning up ahead on the slope. I was close to the ski lodge. The kid was howling, crying as if he already knew he could read my mind… yup see, I had no brakes. I didn't have a clue how to stop or even slow down. My snowboarding experience was for the thrill of it. I would crash or fall when I got off the ski chair lift, then point the nose of my board downhill with no goggles or padding; some would consider me a maniac.

My ears hummed, my eyes watered, the speed of the decline increased, then I would crash many times because of the velocity I was traveling. I'd skip in the air bouncing off the hardened snow. This was my fun and one of the main reasons I enjoyed snowboarding; each crash brought out the sought-after adrenalin rush. Tumbling catapulting over the snow, air crushed from my lungs exhilarated a thrill seeker with fatalistic aspirations, invariably I would always end up in a heap smashed, clashing wham laying there barely conscious. I'd check each appendage for the ability to move. Was I paralyzed this time? Nope! I wanted to go fast enough downhill to feel some fear, just a little… lol ☺ .

Back to the 9-year-old boy I'd snatched up from the ski school that I held in my arms with tears flowing and trees & boulders of rock directly in front of us. There wasn't a possibility that I would make the next turn at the speed we were going. Ugh, seriously, the inertia gravity torque had magnetized our downward trajectory. I did the decent thing before thunderously crashing with all my strength. I tossed the frightened shrieking child air born. I didn't get to see his no-doubt cataclysmic landing. I had to worry about yours truly! It wasn't my fault the kid was in a snowboarding class. The instructors were the guilty parties, not me. They shouldn't be out on a black diamond run. They should have conducted the class on a bunny hill for beginners.

What happened next was understandable while I searched for my lost snowboard after regaining consciousness. I tried to hide in my torn black and silver riding gear in the bright white snow. A gathering was beginning to congregate by the fragmented Lil boy-ski patrol out-snowmobile with a sled attached ambulance. Oh, shit, loudspeakers blare out from poles and trees and the ski lodge. The search for me was on. Can you believe it?

I was thinking as I chomped down on a broken molar, migraine-bruised body needing a triple shot at the lounge. Not to happen… cameras, video of my grievous act of trying to save the boy. No one saw the corrosive incident from my perspective, nope, not One. Strangely I thought I'd soon be sitting on a sled being pulled to a snow cabin jail for interrogation; uh can you believe the travesty of it all?

I explained to the five ski patrollers, 'hey, I either picked the boy up, or I would have hit him. Aah ran him over at like 55 mph. It was a split decision! I told them it all happened in 'slow motion, and time stood still,' my argument fell on deaf earmuffs now pictures of me were posted online, social media attacked yours truly, someone made a poster of the kid and me, it was kinda sick. I was forever banned from going snowboarding at Mount Shasta Ski Park lifetime ban! B.S! 😫 .

Suddenly I regained some sphere of consciousness… back to where I was being attacked on my cabin's frontage road. The large hayseed was displeased, irked at my catatonic state. The last I saw was a flash of brilliant white sparks-light, not the blissful heaven based envisioned tunnel we enter on our exit supposedly from this life-plane. Nope, the gun barrel splayed open my skull.

I haven't a hint as to how long I was deposed unfocused. An old song was discordantly playing on a loop, 'Led Zeppelin' 'Dazed and Confused.' I could hear voices, yet the articulations were alien-like. I want to remind you that I'm not the type of man to complain, uh, bellyache, umh, or dwell on semantics or garbled sounds of communications. It seemed I was alive-violated with a gashed scalp, hands and feet were bound, and something akin to a noose was around my throat. Not an enviable position for the macho protagonist that I am.

<u>Chagrined</u> and annoyed, leveraged between the subconscious and this reality, I got stuck absurdly without any relevance to my current dilemma ah situation. The word chagrinned caused me to stumble. I was analyzing the syllable, 'cha-Grin,' a repulsed mistake ('mental uneasiness caused by failure ugh, disappointment'), nothing to grin about unless you were a ghoul or masochist. Didn't chagrin mean, like, um, mortified or humiliated? But I'm Mark Feral and all-powerful, aren't I?

Then I stumbled on the reason it occurred to me, umh dismayed, perturbed I was in the thralls of an indignant concussion. Led Zeppelin further mortified my disposition with a new rendition of the song 'Stairway to Hell' click, bye-bye now, I'm gone terror-stricken passed out unconscious, Nah not in terror not yet 'I'll seeya!' umh maybe?

-54-

<u>Whitney and Tank are heading to her parents' fire-riddled area in Mendocino County, California.</u>

The first leg of the road trip up to the town of Lakeport, Mendocino County, was melancholy Whitney was full-on glum. Conversations withered, unfinished, disjointed, awkward, even clumsy; what did I expect? I had only just met the black beauty with intelligent, exploring, glowing pupils. Rollerblading how many sentences we had exchanged, only a few.

We were heading North taking Hwy 505 to Highway 5, not too far from Vacaville and the Nut Tree Restaurant and amusement park of old gardens of a pastime… no time for reminiscing. But I

In my side view mirrors, the Jeep Comanche was always there, Whitney's older brother 'Tony' and little sister 'Miranda.' I was a white man inked black. It was clear that I was disliked out of the gate if you believed in first impressions!

Unapologetic, unabashed familiar territory, not an introverted guy, neither extroverted nor insecure or overly domineering. I was what the renowned author 'Malcolm Gladwell,' termed 'Ambivert' the best of both personality traits.

The 35-foot Mercedes diesel box truck was plumb-packed from floorboards to the ceiling. I had spent nearly all the cash that 'Mark and Joe' had allotted me when I got out of San Quentin $4,575.71 spent, uhm, actually donated to Whitney's cause, from first aid kits, medical supplies, tons of cases of water to the roof, dry goods, and even pet food. We stacked the tents for the homeless folks. Ah, victims that were burned out of their homes. We even had tarps donated by Costco in San Jose. In total, we'd had a load of necessities valued at close to $75,000, although of possibly more value to some of the victims was clothing. We even stopped at the Salvation Army and Goodwill stores and gathered used clothing of all sizes.

Have to come clean at the onset, I was petrified, baffled, dumbstruck, or better, dumbfounded. I couldn't reconcile what I was doing. *Actually, 'Wtf was I doing? I wasn't nor ever will be a philanthropic kind of human being. I always have believed giving starts at home... give to Me!'* Nope, everything revolved around just me. What was in it for me, having always been a self-serving, selfish criminal at heart and mind... maybe not anymore?

The highway signs took me from revelry 'Clearlake Hwy 20' Williams. Other signs with yummy foods glaring off of billboards advertised the glorious Granzella's Restaurant. A planned must-stop for anyone traveling North or South on I-5. "Hey Whit, that's our stop" she was already on her cell to her brother, then "Tank, I can't wrap myself around my emotions." As several tears trickled down her ebony cheeks. "Feelings of gratitude for what you have done for my family and me," however, finding and showing irritation toward me, she soldiered on... "why are you doing this? I barely even know your name, this is crazy. What Is your last name? I don't and can't try and pretend to understand I...." Downshifting the diesel nearing the parking lot of Granzella's, I lost it totally. Bursting out in a huge howling laugh, she alarmed and jumped, shocked like scared, leaning into her door.

"Whitney," I said in between hard-to-find breaths, "there's no halo over my skull haven't a freakin clue as to why I'm doing this. I felt compelled to help you with no strings attached. I don't even expect a kiss from you. That's what has me in such an uproar, quandary laughing contagiously yuh see, 'never in my life did I care about anyone but me.' I was a 'sole survivor' weirdly; this is like an OBE... out-of-body experience for me."

Staring unblinking, gawking with furrowed cute brows, Whitney goes to open her blazingly white teeth. I cut her off. "I've stimulated something inside of me that I didn't know existed, Whit. I don't know, but I'm rolling with it, comfortable with my decision; uhm, it just feels right. No reason to 3rd guess or overanalyze my decisions. Let's roll with it like a gambling term. 'I'm all in' with you, Whit!" Whitney gave me a warm full-faced smile "Mr. Tank, there's more to you than met my eyes. I'm delighted to have made your acquaintance!" I grinned sideways and hit the parking brake... "shall we?"

From that point, I wasn't the white-tattooed stranger anymore to Miranda, Tony, and the gorgeous Whitney. No, I was elated and respected, which elevated me. Being with them felt right, uhm, black or white didn't matter; I felt overwhelmed with true acceptance unlike ever before!

<u>FBI Agent Lori Parks.</u>

Reading the last text was Agent Lori Parks; disgruntled would be the best description of her in the visors mirror. The GPS tracking software app was flashing on a winding hilly road. A blue dot was moving along at 57mph, only 17 miles ahead of her moving vehicle.

Agent Bill Avery was five miles closer on crooked winding Hwy 20 on the way to Clearlake. She hasn't an inkling of where the final destination would be. They would stay behind Tank's Mercedes box truck… running the plate. It had come back to a rental agency all legal. There wasn't a chance of losing him unless the GPS chip somehow became dislodged.

They'd watched from a sufficient distance Tank at the 'cut-shop' then Costco. Nothing was adding up. Nada made sense as to what he was up to. Avery had repeated, 'what the hell was he doing… it's gotta be illegal!' They followed him via the tracking chip to a body and fender shop, then to a yard that rented secondhand vehicles. That's where he got the Mercedes box truck.

What hovered over Lori's head was the certainty that she was being punished and relegated to a menial task that a first-year cadet should be assigned with. This was a 'payback' by good ole Tanya for catching her in that compromising position with one slipper nude but for a slinky robe in Rico's hotel room. If he had the choice, obviously, he does, why would he want to engage intimately with Tanya, who is many years his senior, when she was available? Lori mused, pushing a lock of hair from her forehead. I'm much better lookin, desirable, fresh, and willing.

Frustrations and gloominess matched the sudden change in what was a brilliant cloudless afternoon with typically another three hours plus of blueness now nothing as she drove over the rolling hills in blackness A.C. running. Smoke engulfed the landscape, a 9 to 1 ratio of vehicles going in the opposite direction, leaving the ravaged county of Mendocino.

Rico's last Instagram crushed her further, dropping her pessimistically into wretched despair. Joe Sable and Mark

Feral were to attend a meeting in Boise. She had been an integral cog in that investigation and deserved to be up in Idaho. But here she was following an ex-con doing what bizarrely amounts to a good Samaritan act of kindness. Boredom floats in, depressing the brakes aggressively… traffic jams to a stop!

<u>Sammy and Joe in Idaho…uhm, does that Rhyme?</u> 😊.

"Sammy, Wtf are you doing, girl? I told you to stay put!" I flashed him the obstinate stare of defiance that was one of my classic looks, a rebelliousness that had always defined my personality…Yep! I was a 25-year-old woman in a 'high schoolers' pout!

Joe had just stepped out of the bathroom; he saw that I had some of my stuff and a backpack loaded all by the exit door of our hotel. A map of Idaho sprawled out on our messy bed, and a highlighter in my grasp.

"Don't you get it, girl? Ur supposed to be genius material instead…" "no, Joe, I'm not just going to sit in this stuffy hotel room…." "There's a reward posted for you, pictures of you splattered across social media sites, so…" "Why can't I go with you… shit? Haven't I proved and shown enough loyalty fk here I am in a world of trouble…." "Listen, I'm already running late; gotta go, Sam, you better stay put, don't leave this hotel!" So teenager-like, immaturely, I knocked the lamp over, bellicosely stormed off, slamming the bathroom door with a locking motion.

I retained the map's grasp; he was pounding on the flimsy bathroom door, "Sam, stop this. Come on out of there now. We don't have time for this shit!" I put my cute, pert nose to the door's hinges. I replied, "well damnit, I really wanted to cruise on a rental Harley around Coeur d'Alene's lakes, but it's too far North, so I think I will ride South onto Hwy 84… putt around Arrowrock Reservoir. Get something to eat with a totty or three at or near Anderson Ranch Dam, don't worry, honey, I'll take plenty of pictures for you with my handy-dandy Mickey Mouse Tracfone!"

He said nothing, "Joe did you hear me?" well, no, of course, he didn't. The room was empty; Joe had left without me! I sat on the edge of the bed. Weird thoughts entered my mind the bed, sex… heck, did Joe even desire me? The mirror on the wall reflected the new look, Raven's hair with the looks and body to stop traffic on a busy street. 'Yep, I'm Hot!... Freakin, a dream babe! But 'not to Trot!'

A formidable weight attached itself to me. Still, I rushed out of the room with my stuff. It had become relatively clear to me that I was acting so immaturely like a damn teenager in puppy-fricken love. I was 'All In' smitten with Joe, a chunk of my heart missing without him. So what would any lovesick child do? umh, I followed him. I wasn't going to lose him. Joe sat in the back of a nondescript dark blue SUV on his way to the three-night and day conference at the S.O.J.'s main compound.

<u>Joe Sable was being chauffeured to the SOJ compound.</u>

Joe felt unhinged disgusted, and angry over a few reasons, one of which was Sam's attitude and inability to rationalize the danger of her going on a joy ride. He now could surmise and comprehend Mark's rule never to get attached to a female, emphatically with certainty this feeling of despair… he understood was the precise point of not having a woman. No emotional ties. Gosh, he hated the anxious muddled feeling of his queasy stomach… damn, he must be coming down with a virus and getting sick.

Then his blackish heart stopped aching, and rhythmic contractions immediately left him with bloodshot eyes. Then he'd read another text from Mark 'you know our rules. Sammy should have been eliminated days ago; since you failed to follow our said-forth protocols, I'm handling it for you! No, Joe, I will not be attending the conference. I've been given a pass due to the 'Carr Fire…' good luck Bro, Mark!'
Joe was in a group of five men and two women on their way to the sprawling ranch, where he would stay until the meetings

were finished. But he still had to do something to save Sammy, evident that Mark had leveraged a contract on his girl's head, looking once again at his toxic text, 'since you failed to follow the rules, I'm handling it for you.' The quick paraphrase's meaning had him sweating profusely.

I leaned forward and declared, "I left something important back at the hotel. I need to get a ride back there now!" "I'm sorry, Mr. Sable, sir, that's not possible now... we can always send someone to retrieve whatever it is you've forgotten. Joe sees the first of the five gates automatically open, and a 500-yard driveway starts. He is a prisoner again. Joe wasn't a first-timer at these gatherings and knew all wireless hook-ups were blocked. It would be like the 1970s living with only landlines or radios for communication and no way out. Armed sentries... almost dry-heaved at every turn, barfed some acid up from his throat, his stomach somersaulted, then re-swallowed the acid fk!

Rico... Wendi and NIA.

Rico touched down in Napa, and part of him felt he wasn't doing the right thing. His obligation to Tanya and the operation to capture or kill Mark and Joe lingered on his mind, although only hesitantly, his heart won out as was per usual. It's not like Tanya didn't have a formidable force under her direction in Idaho. Notably, she'd assured him she had it under control. Go and take care of the NIA debacle and secure Wendi Feral.

No person was aware of his ulterior motivations nor the truth behind the impetus that energized his actions, in-fact his restrained harbored heartstrings were tied in knots.

He was sitting back, waiting for the doors to open and the pilot to give the all-clear notice. *Rico drifts back to a conversation he had decades ago with his philandering father. He could see his face as he was given advice. 'Dad was on his 3rd Whiskey Sour,' telling him to sit down. Rico had just been dumped by his high school sweetheart; 'Listen, son, look at all the crowds of humans. In America, from Miami to NYC. to L.A. bumper to bumper traffic*

Rico smirked; damn, that was now going on three decades
ago. I suppose dad meant well; it was his delivery that was
faulted… flustered that it was a little lady in a coma that drove
his spirit. Her smile lit thousands of synapses, and nervous
impulses, neuron to neuron, pumped his circulatory system to
its outer extremities. He loved Wendi and always would.

-55-

**<u>Whitney and Tank are traversing the rolling hills toward a
wild Forest Fire only 37% contained.</u>**

*The landscape was something out of a Nuclear Holocaust; the
fire's destruction was devastating. Not a tree, bush, or light pole
stood. Homes with burnt-out vehicles on rims, wiped out, nothing
living, and they were still 15 miles to the epicenter. They drove
slowly, guided by a Fire Marshal's truck, towards Lakeport, where
Whitney's parents lived.*

*It appallingly could inspire a horror film, but nauseating
reality would place the movie in a non-fiction movie set. It was a
mind-blowing catastrophe from the stench and looks of the
weathered people. I wasn't prepared for this… I was numb. Just
trying to catch a full breath of oxygen was difficult.*

What I witnessed was sadly necessary to bring the plight of
these hurting people to the forefront of the world's populace.
The production crews of TV vans reporters, like eager beagles,
umh… ah, Vultures landed on the victims and sensationalized
the misfortunes of the local citizens. The mass media thrived
upon them like gluttonous vampires. We were parked on Hwy

20, watching the updates on a laptop. The smoke, filled air was stifling, burning our eyes. People seemed to be using their phones, taking still shots and videos of the annihilation caused by fire. It looked like a slew of category '5' hurricanes and a smattering of Tornados had hit the area, followed by a Tsunami. Starkly, I retracted and remembered watching a show on the Discovery channel where earthquakes and tumultuous weather systems like planet earth revolted against mankind… imploding, taking vengeance upon its abusers.

Whitney and I watched the headlines crossing the screen about Shasta's Counties Carr Fire, where now eight people had lost their lives burned, not recognizable. Not with us any longer sorrow-laden relatives being interviewed. Nothing that I'd ever watched brought my five senses in collusion collectively like this smell and stench, with the taste of soot and ashes. It was as if the sky was falling, dropping black leaflets and dark snowflakes from the clouds.

My skin crawled, pores filled, no way of blocking out the greyness, bleak darkness black death. We passed families stricken down and hovering together in circles of despair, visually in disbelief, Zombies slowly seeing what was no longer there. Rummaging through their homes for pictures, anything salvable. Tears flowed, incapacitating many; I'm a tough dude… man, Ugh. "Tank, we're seven miles from the church my parents should be at," I only said somberly. "Whitney, I pray they're all right, and so is the rest of your family!" That's when I noticed the drips from her cleft chin… crying silently.

We were far apart in the truck's cab, moving at a turtles pace. I so wanted to reach out to her, while the vibration on my leg finally ceased, another text from either Joe or Mark, who else had that number. It was the secure line of the Tracfone. Fire Trucks and Cal-Fire vehicles were stopping all drivers; we pulled into a line and parked, dozens of concerned and panicked people surrounding us.

While Whitney spoke to her brother, I took the opportunity to refresh the phone screen and read old past texts that I had ignored while driving. One of which rang out like clashing cymbals thunderously reddened my ear lobes. From Joe, 'Tank, it's imperative that you communicate with Mark… he is AWOL. I have sent you a tracking app. GPS of his phone's whereabouts it appears he's somewhere outside of Shingletown ah, Hat Creek area. Our rule of sending a text out at least every 24 hours has been broken.' The following text three hours later 'Tank, Wtf are you doing? I just followed this map, and Google Earthed Mark's position via the Dark Web. Look at this satellite photo of our cabin. There are two other older trucks and a Volkswagen bus parked on the property. Something is fkn wrong. Get your ass over there now. Text me when you get their thanks, bro. I got my own problems up here in Idaho Tank... don't let us down!'

Tank then scrolled further down to the last text, 'I will be deposed for like three days, Tank, all three of us were ordered here for this mandatory get-together. I hope there aren't any repercussions for you and Mark not being here. I want to speak with Mark and you... get with me Later!'

Silence permeated and invaded the cab. I was preoccupied elsewhere, ugh, how could I be in two places simultaneously? Whitney was on her cell. We'd just passed another checkpoint diesel generators powered up rows of lights on moving stands. Power was down no electricity for many square miles.

The 'Church of Christ' was all by its lonesome up on a knoll, a parking lot that was lit with generators surrounded it... chaos enveloped the asphalt. Humanities last stand, overflowing with pain and filled with suffering. It looked from where we drove up; the church was the first destination of those who had lost everything except themselves.

I saw tents of every shape and form, even a circus tent of enormous measurements, it wasn't even 5:05 pm, and flashlights and floodlights were the only modes anyone could see by... well, besides our headlights. I shut down the truck and felt my lungs ache like I'd smoked a carton of Camel cigarettes in the last 45 seconds. Camels that had killed my Grand Dad years ago.

Whitney snatched up my elbow "come on, Tank... Tony, and Miranda are waiting for us; my parents haven't their cell phones. They were lost in the fire, and even if they hadn't lost them, there are no cell towers up and running... no service. The fire moved in on them without warning!" Tony stepped up "just spoke with Uncle Joshua there, packed inside the church on the 3rd floor!" "Let's find them," shouts Miranda. I felt like saying it but kept my mouth shut. Aah was going to say, 'well, hell, folks, your relatives are black. It shouldn't be so difficult to spot them. I'd seen nothing but white folks on the way... thought better of saying it!

<u>Mark was a captive at his cabin.</u>

Darkness prevailed, or did it? I was working diligently, or was I? My mind was swirling couldn't focus, recalling the butt of the gun hitting my skull. My fingers were raw... wrists ached. I had to be at my cabin; the whys, like an acid trip, left me queasy. I couldn't, as hard as I tried to, um, remain focused. No, it was like tunnel vision into blackness swirling in a cesspool of crap, and my mind fluttered like synonymous with leaves in a dust devil. Umh, or was it as it appeared that confusion reigned that I was disoriented and concussed? Ugh, loud snores aligned with the raspy sounds of a person wheezing. I could hear, so my captors hadn't blocked my ears. I tried to open my blindfolded vision, then a positive vibe, a loose finger. No, uh, yes, with a bit of work, I had one of my hands free, I felt stickiness... There was no doubt that fluid was leaking from my body. Like a slug, my movement was akin to molasses spilled from a top shelf. A jar tipped over in 45-degree air. The real question was, did I move? Was I moving? I slung my blindfold off, uhm, no, peeled it back like glued to my head-dried, wet cranial fluids from where my splayed skull remained to pulsate-no question, a massive concussion from the barrel of the gun.

The first reflection passed from my optic nerves to what was left of brain matter, counting forward then backward five men and two women 7 or 8 assailants. No one was moving the sound of sleep, flashing visions commingled blended. Recognizing my cabin, a breeze blew up the curtains over the wooden table in the kitchen.

I worked feverishly, sweat mixing with blood, body fluids able to lift off the noose around my neck. Feet untied, that's when a pubic hair took precedence; I hacked, choking a coarse prickly hair that was caught in my esophagus. Ugh fk. I was plumb-ass nude. The bastards had stripped me out… my rings, my watch, and my gold chain were gone. ☹ .

Now I was freaking out… wouldn't you? Crawling under the illumination of candles towards a pile of clothing, it seemed wasn't mine. In my hand was a pink & black thong G-string, spun around to see a mound that sat up high Orangeness bronze a Sideways Smile with pouty lips; uh, it was a damn Vagina of a spread-Eagle woman. Unfocused vision tuned in. I must have been in a porno show exhibition for piles of clothes; ugh, no one in the cabin that I could see had a stitch of clothing on. I stumbled over a pink and white hat, 'OnlyFans.' Oh crap, yuh gotta be kidding me…? Nope, not joking, um kidding Mark!

I swiveled around, knocking into a tripod. A large video camera was locked on the pad. I dare not take a gander. Now aligning the shocking visual aid, the sticky gummy pubic region was mine; I must have participated, but how was that possible?

On my knees, I continued towards the cabin door and saw a basket I'd used on my last visit to my cabin to pick Blackberries for one of my famous smoothies.

In that basket on a chair was all my hardware… Tracfone, fake badge, gold chain, watch. Yeah, I got all my stuff, quietly dressed with my truck keys in hand. No one stirred, supposed satiated, worn out. Should I grab the 9-inch switchblade and silently cut their throats before making my exit? I thought better of that; the time was 2:15 am as I gently closed the cabin door. I walked past the older 70's trucks and a 60's hippy van.

<u>Mark escapes his cabin in search of some Joy.</u>

I stopped when I saw my trailer unhitched then I heard the whimpering in a pen attached to my cabin, my whining dogs. I wondered where the Cats were, then didn't. In my vehicle, they lay curled up on the dashboard. I had unfinished business. I spun around, doing a 360-degree turn. A last glance at my cabin that I would return to and slowly kill all the trespassing occupants might keep the scintillating redhead alive for some indulgences of my own desires; she was a definite throbber for my groin region, although she'd have to wait.

My head was on fire, a migraine from Hell amplifying the pain I felt throughout my body. Steadfast in my mind of where my path would lead, I had already tapped into the GPS unit; the chip on Joy's automobile had stopped moving, which was the direction I was driving. She was only 17 miles away; I flipped the fog lights on. No fog, but smoke, bloodshot eyes, and head ringing from one dirt road to the next 'Joy' now was only nine miles off, Yep!

If I played my cards right, I could take out Joy umh, capture her, then make it back to my cabin and finish the night's work of revenge on all who humiliated me.

Some prison psychiatrists wrote reports stereotyping me as a narcissistic and deranged sociopath, so wrong were their descriptive grandiosities. Sneering, I morphed into my imagination, always envisioning my objectives fondly, cinematically in HD color.

I slowed my approach to where Joy was located, grinning in the dark, favoring my avant-garde films on my memory disks. Duplicated and sent to the 'Cloud' with attentive, cautious circumspection, not a trace of my obscene videos led back to yours truly.

If suspected of such atrocities, my first line of defense would be, why would a hot handsome, debonair man like I ever kidnap women when I could pick them out of the bar scene like flies on shit? Uh, yuh can't rape the willing? Lol.

Also, adding an addendum, why the heck would I drug the girls? No need, they fell on my bed already partially undressed, thoroughly wet between the lips lusting for me lubed, ready to 'Rock' no, uhm, what the FBI... Casino police, um alleged of me... Ugh, I must admit that what Lola and Joy accused me of was partially true. Yes, I was the guilty party. I kidnapped all the missing Asians, so Wtf?

It was their first reaction that made my blood boil with ecstasy; their first reality, with my three cameras... zoomed onto their round Asian faces, and bam, their eyelids closed. Aah, never did I wake their naked-bounded slumber... patience was an intellectual virtue. The thrill turn on ah was the various cinematic vantage points um-yum when the captive's brown eyes flick open, sometimes one at a time. Bliss complete on exhilaration; I could masturbate watching the lady victim cum to grips at what was gripping her. Panic, shock OmLord what fkn fun, the cameras pan in and then out. Of course, I'm not in view. I watch with Jerkens lotion in motion. Yup!

My captive then sees herself as perfect twins staring back at her. It's her in the mirrors on the ceiling and walls, yum, only her. The stirrups are not so tight. I'm the Gynecologist of their dreams or daymares, attired with a mask and smock (of course, if they accidentally saw my gorgeous face, I'd have to cut their Carotid artery purposely) lol! I would always be dressed in clinical white uniforms... Doctor Mark Feral kind of like the reverberating sound of my name associated with the Doctor moniker. Sometimes I miss the woman's eye flickering but playing the scene back in slow-mo. I never miss a thing, the soulless females of Asian descent, much more than a doctor am I. I'm an extraordinary Artist, an expert in body piercings and body painting.

I suppose I could be referred to as a humane imprisoner by my captive beauties who are dead to the world, knocked out. Better that they don't squirm or wiggle as I carefully add chrome studs to their eyebrows, nose, belly rings, and studs for their nipples. With fantastic skill, I pierce tongues and rub their female genitalia softly, enlarging the clitoris before that favorite piercing. I, of course, add in a proper manicuring. Oh, what fun 'Doctor Feral the supreme Surgeon!'

Some people would consider me perverted or label me a psychopath or whatever, but what the public doesn't understand well, most of them don't. The fact is, uhm that fiction is far more reality-based than non-fiction. Throughout American history, there have been far worst deviates than I... take Jeffrey Dahmer, serial killer extraordinaire who would eat his captives cannibalism, killing 17 men and boys.

Dismemberment with organs kept fresh in his fridge. The list of demented killers is incomplete, for despite what the police and press like to detail about arrest records ... most killers die of old age!

Ahh, oops, I'm there now; enough imagining... yeppers Joy is nearby. I'll revisit the body painting and all the fun stuff with sensational details once I have Joy relaxed in my Gyno-chair. Perhaps with her, I will do a Documentary being the orator director, producer, and lead actor. Oh yes!

Luck with timing aligned is everything in life. At 3:35 am, Joy stood before a window, her lengthy hair in a bun, doing something with her hands; cars and trucks were parked around five cabins, all indistinguishable from one another. Amazingly there were others awake, a large screen TV playing. In an adjoining cottage, music played wow, night Owls like me.

After parking behind a thicket of briars, Pine trees, my handy-dandy Hypo-needle, filled to the brim with Horsey tranquilizer, I sneaked closely up. Geesh Joy was washing dishes by hand at this time of night, humming to the music.

She was just on the other side of the pane, instantly adding to the crickets and bloodthirsty mosquitoes were mongrels barking. I had to exit quickly... Fk.

Like a time, warp, concussion-related, no doubt memory lapse, nevertheless not ever going to look and stare at one of those gift Horses. Dreamily I imagined the human gift lying sprawled out on her back at my love nest. Joy would bring great pleasure and joviality to my sullen world. I'd picked out a nearly flawless diamond set to pierce her nipples with, oh, hours of fun, and she'd be a live energizer bunny.

Once I kidnapped her, could I wait, or should I spontaneously pull over in the woods for a subtle rape to clear out the pipes? Know what I'm saying Yeah-feelin' me, Lol. A sharp spike of pain shot through my left eye can't forget the hillbillys who needed my attention at my cabin. That would be where I would take Joy; dam, so many complications to deal with *'Mark's work is never done.' Remembering a line from one of my favorite movies and 'Jack Nicholson in The Shining.'*

Joy has a wastebasket in her hand out the kitchen door…oh yes-yum, she walks to the industrial garbage container… snuck up behind her. A simple choke hold with a dab of Chloroform on a rag over her mouth, done that got the hateful bitch now on my back seat taking mere seconds… Yay!

Instantly motor humming down the road we traveled. I weighed the options should I hit her backdoor first with a lite lubing, suddenly lights flashed behind me, and several turns on my tail coming fast. Twisting down the dirt road, dust flying whomever it was they were in a hurry moving a lot more quickly than my Dodge truck. Blinking at my dashboard realized it had been a good thing that I had filled both diesel tanks up for the drive outta the area. Should I try to make it to my Jones Valley property, would the fire be under control? No, better stay with the original plan and go back to my occupied cabin.

Joy was rolling around bouncing on the back seat of my diesel; shit, I should have belted her in. She was going to be bruised, uh, damaged goods, damn. I'd have to use some skin-colored makeup to cover up the bruises. Aah, Joy awaited my indulgences, but the current problem I faced took precedence, and that was the chasing vehicle was gaining on me probably knew the dirt rode better than I… Duh!

<u>Oh No, the Stirrups locked down.</u>

Oh, fk a shoelace, rope, wire WTHeck from behind me. I was being accosted, "you fkn bastard, it was you; I knew it Die fker… you Perve Die Mark!" I slammed the brakes down as hard as I could and jammed it into park. Yet Joy didn't go flying, I couldn't lose her yanking maniacal grip, choking trying to reach behind me, but she had my head leveraged with her knees on the back of the seat, headrest wrenching back with all of her 115 pounds. Flailing couldn't grasp her; it became a life-or-death struggle; felt like the bitch was inhumanely strong, like one of those 'Marvel Superheroes.'

Finally, I overcame… male validation of full-on virility, testosterone winner, overpowered the poor estrogen-laden weaker sex, 'it's a man's world, right?' right! Strangely felt out of place, weird, ugh, exhausted, and tired when I should have been empowered. Her Eyelids anchored close; then I saw her body starting to unfurl, my erection pumping up. Joy spread Eagle, ugh a bit of anger fled leaving my pores cuz her nipples were already freaking pierced. Aah, inferior job. Damn, she'd need a full-on razor also or a bush-hog to trim up her genitalia heck, yuh could hack or choke yourself out if your mouth got too close for sure work had to be done… better get busy.

Hallucinating, was I? Yeah had to be a fantasy not come true, not possible, far from probable. What I saw with the flicker of my left eyeball startled, umh shocked me, erection dropping like ice water may be time for Viagra… nope!

Three cameras zoomed in on me, a petite nurse Nah, a doctor with a mask and smock on her face. It was a woman with long Raven black hair and roundish brown eyes. Oh no, scalpel in hand, the mirrors above, R.U. Kidding me! A joke, right? I'd enjoy this; I'm an S&M sort of dude. But the leather strap and ball shoved into my throat. Ugh, my mouth was super um painful and uncomfortable. I was drooling like a fat baby, and my saliva dripped from my twitching chin…'oh fk' it wasn't her but my body that lay nude spread Eagle in my stirrups. The same leather instrument had each of my testicles secured ouch. I tried to move, squirm, and wiggle the more I did, ughhhh, causing the pain to increase. Umh, no JOY! Not comfortable, uhm, stop… this wasn't a sex game. This was severe trouble for yours truly. I heard Joy's high-pitched octaves. She was humming and singing a song and seemed flawlessly content, almost business-like.

"Mr. Mark Feral, I want you to relax as best as you can. I hope to help you sing soprano opera like… dontcha worry. I'm an unskilled surgeon, and I hope not to butcher yuh too much. I've diagnosed testicle lumps. Sorry, a slow castration is in order now. Try to stay calm, and don't you squirm around. Be still K? We surely want your cameras to catch my talented scalpel cuts now. Don't you pass out again, boy, or I'll have to jam some more ammonia up your nose. I believe you will like your

manifestation… Monk like you're going to be a Eunuch!" Joy starts howling. Ugh 😧.

-56-

NIA and Rico Captor.

The sky was tattooed umh, inked out despite it being 'High-Noon,' which I suppose meant the great giver of life, the nuclear reactor up in the sky, had been squelched, and no sunshine came from directly above me. With a tilt of one's head, straight up should be the shine, although smoke blanketed covered the surrounding rolling hills of grapes and wineries. Driving along on auto-pilot, I sometimes wondered how I got from point A to B, for only my physical self was behind the wheel.

Tanya didn't come out and say it, although she could have… hell, she was in charge, after all. If anything went wrong, it was her ass on the line; I had to respect that fact.

Tanya was in charge of a growing team of Federal Agents in and around Boise. At last count, 37 Officers. So with all that manpower, she empathetically conceded and yielded to my whims of desperation to leave and return to NIA even though it seemed Agent Lucy Link had solved or concluded the investigation into the assault on Wendi. The culprit was a Correction Officer whom everyone joked went <u>'Nuts watching Nuts'</u> Billy Goad had admitted to shooting Wendi. A humorous anecdote authored by Tanya; 'well, what would you expect? Billy was a brain-damaged alcoholic, divorced into poredom in debt past his ears frustrated and filled with hate for humankind. Billy had regularly visited in-house psychiatrists birds of a feather flock together, yah think?'

I took the next turn, although I couldn't see the sign knowing what was written on it. Napa Medical Facility is 15 miles ahead. Rico drove onward. The farther he advanced, the further he fell behind, now 11 years plus in the rears. He was guilty of bringing the young and barely adult Wendi to the forefront or into the Limelight. At the beginning of their relationship, he didn't believe in her animal seer status, all hogwash paranormal exaggerations... to grow her Feral Feedback company. Rico had called it B.S. and sent her a subcontract agreement anyways, hoping, on the one hand, she'd stay in Vancouver, Washington. But on the other, why not? He'd had nothing to lose; hell, he didn't have to pay the bill. Wendi surprised him and obliged, flying out to join the ongoing futile search for the murderous serial killer of children. His FBI team of searchers laughed in her face as she stepped onto the high ground in Tennessee with her animals.

Red lights through the haze... he stops swerving to the soft shoulder, flares on the asphalt I parked, shoving the shifter down. An apparent accident up ahead mused back to the first meeting with Wendi and how I trusted her. She'd kept his secret that I'd killed the suspect child murderer 'In cold Blood' after her Owl 'Hoot' had clawed out the parasite's eyeballs. Our first case together, and it was a whopper... Wendi helped put my name on the map of esteemed Agents. I had been bestowed many awards our partnership quickly evolved from working together... then loving one another.

Since then, a bond had been propagated and fertilized, grown strong as Gorilla glue-forged, formulated solidly; we had each other's back when possible!

'The games people play' oh, he didn't want to traverse this uppity incline, rocky, narrow path. 'I despised people as a whole there... I said it out loud, so what. Wendi was the only pure-innocent person I'd ever met without any... ulterior motives.' Sure, she had the womanly jealousies, thinking back to her partner and best friend at Feral Feedback. Her albino friend Sandi was a beautiful lady in her own way, whom I enjoyed flirting with, which was a give and take. Wendi got upset. Well, that's my assertion, maybe not. Lol, come to think of it, she never admitted it.

He reached out and gulped the rest of a bottle of pure, uncontaminated, filtered water Osmosis, most likely right out of a sewer or downstream from a nuclear site. Shit, the longer I live, the more cynical and skeptical I morph into being negatively led within my mind. Trying to align the facts with that being said, the more ostracized and pushed away from homo sapiens I became. There are none, no redeemable characteristics. My preference to be alone is only magnified, surrounded by superficial fakes… born and bred who have their own agendas. Why couldn't people drop their masks and be Real?

What do we really see when we peer through the abstract tint, a peek of eyes into the soul… Enough sshh Rico!

Why can't I just shut it down? My mind that is always thinking analyzing can't be happy-go-lucky, lose myself in a novel, music, a movie, or alcohol, cheeks flushed. Zing, yeah, he nodded. That's what's bothering me. Not that Billy Goad was last in the marksman contest several months back, nope. Inching past crates of grapes, oh damn, a broken flatbed 40-footer flipped on its side, ahhhh the truck driver swerved to miss a Coyote.

While I sat waiting for the road to be cleared, I scanned Billy's last physical… but 15 days prior, Cirrhosis of his liver; nope, where was it? Flipping past the electronic pages? Aah, there it was! His left eye had a fast-growing cataract obstructing his vision which was being diminished daily. This was the impetus for him to seek out an Optometrist. The dude was going blind, and even with corrective lenses, his best vision test was 40-60. How could he fire a dart rifle from 55 yards out or so and hit Wendi in the neck with one shot? Right, Wrong… Nope! ☹ .

Crossing before my relentless tireless worrisome mind, I winced glaringly at a sentence from a report from Doctor Hawkins, whom Rico hand-picked to take over Wendi's care along with her… He'd chosen the best Nurse available, a black-belt Judo and Taekwondo master 'Jack' a black nurse to watch over Wendi, who many suspected was gay. Because of his slender, diminutive body, oh how they were wrong 'never judge a book by the baggy clothed cover' sidetracked again. Oh yeah, the sentence in the report, 'Jack had cleaned an open wound on Wendi's knee-cap which he diagnosed not as a carpet burn, no way he found little pebbles like gravel yet

Wendi was in a coma. Nonmoving her room carpeted tile elsewhere, Jack had sent the sample to a renowned Geologist who determined the granular composition wasn't native to California. But was found in abundance in the Seattle, Washington, area. How had Wendi scraped her knee over a thousand miles away lying in a gurney comatose in Napa, California?

Still, 5 miles out, I will be late for the meeting with Agent Lucy Link, CEO Terrance Hallinan, Warden Ursula Anders, and the A.W. Larry Walden and Doctor Liz Honcho at NIA. I had requested that our Fed Doctor Hawkins be available to examine Billy Goad, who was held in a holding cell. 'Bluetooth activated, Tanya picked up by the 5th ring' "we're knee deep in it up here, Rico. Joe Sable has been spotted; he's at the S.O.J. retreat. And also, Samantha Timmons has been seen outside the compound's gates. We're going to take them both down once we locate the monster Mark Feral. We'd like to take the three of them down simultaneously. We'll see how it unfolds. I wish you were here by my side; what's up?" "That's great news, Tanya, and I don't have to warn you; Mark and Joe are extremely dangerous and slippery as eels." "No, U don't. Uh, what's up at NIA?..." "Well, I'd like your permission to move Wendi out of NIA to one of our safehouses in the area. There are no holds on her." "What about her family and husband?" "They have wanted her outta NIA since the 180-day expiration date of...." "Yes, whatever, Rico, do it. That's your baby down there!" click.

Suddenly my lungs filled with smokeless oxygen, the A.C. blasting against my body in a battle with the heat and humidity. The next call was to the FBI's witness protection agency. After a long seventeen minutes, a move was agreed upon to a sprawling renovated winery of old, call it a 'Safe Winery' that harbored others under Federal protection, lock and key with guards walking the perimeters.

The 'SafeWinery' was located in the quaint small town of Calistoga, known more for its mineral springs, hot springs, and geysers, a gorgeous area; indeed. A new home for Wendi was awaiting her arrival. Now I had to accomplish Youmans work and get her outta the prison hospital today.

It was no longer necessary to attend the gathering of NIA's dignitaries... 25 minutes later, I was at the Razor concertina wire. The towers of the medieval prison's dungeon appearance always left an ominous, tainted feeling inside of me. The guards blared downwards upon me; what threatening medieval architecture built on American soil, I thought. Even though I'd visited this establishment dozens of times, I never was comfortable coming here.

A milk-white extended van behind me with three Agents within, I was nothing if not proactive; once I made up my mind and had a plan. I enacted it with swift precision. Marshal Kara was already in go mode with one of the few friends we had on site. Jack, the skilled nurse, and Doctor Hawkins would travel beside Wendi to the SafeWinery. Rico scheduled Dr. Hawkins to visit with the assailant Billy Goad... done deal!

What's taking Rico? I have a flight to L.A. later today for major litigation. Terrance is speaking to his three cohorts; Ursula was on the bandwagon having not one totty today. Larry had gone out for a 5-mile run. Liz had checked on some of her patients and re-drugged Billy Goad just in case Rico and his sham of a doctor wanted to examine him. The intercom buzzed, 'Mr. Rico Captor at the front gate, sir!' said Terrance's sexy secretary of the month. "He wants to bring in an additional vehicle, sir?" "no problem," says Terrance. Not remembering her name, but he could recall the firm curves of her ass in his hands last night... yum.

A banquet-style lunch was arranged in the cafeteria for the Feds and some select staff, including Walter, his head of Security. Rico was directed to the banquet but was a no-show; 15 minutes passed. Terrance yelled, pulling up the camera's where the hell is Rico at? The food is getting cold. He's wasting our time 'fk. I hate the arrogant FBI!'

Intercom speakers wail again, 'Mr. Hallinan, please come to the lobby checkout area' next, his radio crackled, 'sir, you're wanted...' 'what is it now?' he replied abrasively, 'umh, sorry sir, you're needed at the release desk... Ms. Wendi Feral is being released.'

'Wtf, shrieks Terrance, ain't no freakin way!' He spills his hot tea down his slacks, jumps to his feet, shouts into the radio… and orders the guards to hold them. 'I'm on my way now. Close off the compound lockdown!' 'yes sir, at once sir!' came the girl's voice of subservience.

The five of them at once at attention; Walter exclaims, "Terrance sir, we shouldn't go off halfcocked IMO 'ugh in my opinion' we need to handle this civilly… aah the Feral woman, heck, she's been attacked twice in less than three weeks sir. Let's try some diplomacy!"

Ursula, Larry, and Liz were waiting for Terrance to shove a verbal hot rod up Walter's ass, silence, then, almost like he switched personalities. "Your right Walter, why don't you and Doctor Honcho come with me to the lobby!"

'What's the hold up here?' angrily, explicitly rages Rico, staring at Wendi asleep on the gurney, a lily-white sheet tucked in about her. Marshal Kara, with Jax Foul and Dr. Hawkins, stood next to Wendi's nurse Jack. They were in the lobby waiting to be allowed to check Wendi out of NIA. The rest of Rico's agents stood still, watching glaringly a sea of uniformed guards, NIA's finest. BMI's through the roof thought Jack, who was the type of man who checked out the opposition, constantly analyzing how he would disable them in sequence, fast, and efficiently. Inside any group or gathering, he'd examine and choose the most likely threats. Today it wasn't a man. No, out of the nine uniformed guards, a woman stood out… cunningly with a Ballet dancer's fluid motion who watched him. Her diminutive stature, Brazilian South American perhaps Gracie Jiu-Jitsu, the confident way she moved like a caged Leopard gaging her UFC opponent. Weighing but 135 pounds, she was a warrior, the first he'd need to eliminate!

<u>Rico awaited the showdown before exiting the hellish gates</u>

<u>of NIA!</u>

'From the corner of his eye' came Terrance, arms flapping to his sides "what's up Rico, why do you want to…." "Terrance, I'm taking Wendi out of NIA immediately. It's not

429

any longer any of your business...." "Why!" "She is no longer safe here at your facility. How can you stand in my way when guards under your employ fire weapons at her? One of your nurses here ah, Dan Spike, tried to kill her a couple of weeks ago. Come on, Terrance, get a grip and don't cause a scene. This is an unsafe environment for her. Besides, I don't have to explain any of this to you now. Have the gates opened and get your pathetic security force if that's what you call them out of our faces!" Terrance's facial expression... grimaces, morphing into a decent adaptation of a grin. "Rico, calm down. I thought we had a meeting and banquet. It's waiting upstairs...." "Oh, don't be concerned. We're definitely having a meeting with you all, including your employee Mr. Billy Goad but that's later now. Kindly let us...." "Mr. Captor, it's imperative that Ms. Feral remains under my care," utters Dr. Honcho, who was interrupted by Dr. Hawkins, who barked back at her, "I haven't figured out what is going on here at NIA. Wendi doesn't need the Psychotropic mixtures of drugs that synergistically are destroying her conscious state of being she was...."

Terrance throws up his palm... Stop, "so be it; we have no holds on Ms. Feral, but I believe you will forever regret taking her from our secure facility. I ..." "That sounds more like a threat as if we will rue the day..." demonstratively spoken by Agent Lucy Link. "I'm sorry that wasn't my intent. We appreciate the government's patronage and support here at NIA. Please, all that I ask you for is confidentiality; none of this gets out or leaked to the media or the press. The Vultures are already circling our stock. It's already in the toilet in a major decline...." "Terrance, as far as I'm concerned, Wendi still resides within your razor wire; we will not say a single word. Of course, it's better that the public believes she is still at your facility," declares Rico.

They shake hands; Rico and Terrance stare unblinkingly at each other, knuckles whitish red, both harboring animosities better kept within.

<u>Out the gates rolled Wendi's entourage out of NIA, finally gone bye. 🙂 .Umh… ☹ .</u>

Terrance turned to the open-mouthed group as Walter loudly blurted out, 'get back to work. The show is over'… his arm over his boss's shoulder whispered in his left ear, "I took the liberty to place a magnetic tracker underneath her gurney, sir." He grimaces with a sideways gawk. "I can always count on you; I believe you need a raise in pay, Walter." 'I couldn't agree more, sir; I think your correct." grins Walter.

<u>Whitney and Tank.</u>

I never had a problem acknowledging when I was wrong, although never was I, lol. I'm confessing criminal pride, knowing full well this belief was faulted, yet I didn't allow it to manifest into roadblocks or alter my thought process or beliefs. Honest with my inner self, not with the outside world of miscreants. People of every race and look congregated shoulder to shoulder. The poor children mostly had that 'Deer look' of shock.

Tank hops up and onto a balcony inside the Church… musing I need to take a step back and preface this situation for me; nothing is like being there, watching TV images of mayhem, crippling mutilations, and disfigurements caused by Mother Nature's destructive forces… means far less to an individual that's not living inside the caustic carnage. It's only a secondhand reaction. Reality seeps into your soul if you're in the middle of chaos.

I was one of them; yeah, sad, but predators like me were part of the problem in these natural disasters; looters vandalized and used these times for robberies. Vacated banks, jewelry stores, Pharmacies, and even gun shops, perfect timing to pilfer and rob-steal, burglarize. The National Guard ah police had better things to do. It was said that gypsies outlaws would pack up and travel at a minute's notice to chase the devastation of natural disasters!

Remembering when Katrina hit New Orleans, over 5,000 scammers hit the city like a Tsunami on just the first day of FEMA. Insurance, construction scams, robberies, home invasions... rapes, and the list goes on and on... humanity is so inhumane.

At least my conscience is clear. I was never a scandalous Vulture of evil proportions... never would I join in, ghoulishly, and take advantage of the disadvantaged. On the other hand, I wasn't a man that would lend a hand of aid... like it's your problem. I've got too many of my own to deal with. That was me, Tank. It was always their problem, yep, for Hell's sake, get a grip, deal with your own shit!

I stood against a far wall leaning on a banister watching Whitney, Tony, and Miranda greeting family members. I couldn't help to ponder. It looked like a prison setting three different tiers and floors segregated 3rd floor, mainly African Americans were piled up, 2nd floor was Spanish-speaking Hispanics, and the first floor was where the Caucasians resided, humbled together.

I was out of place. No one introduced me. Indeed I was perhaps creepy looking with all my tattoos um Ink... in a flash, I found regret as three blackish infants looked up from strollers. One started sputtering, then too many to count joined the discord, cacophony balling out their eyes like I was the devil incarnate. I guessed I was a scary-looking guy to the kids.

At once, I understood that when a storyteller would expound, 'mid-stream,' you'd have to have been there actually to experience it; words were descriptive indeed but joined in with visual emotions of misery, haunting sites, human trauma uh, words were just that... Words!

How shallow we can be. I had become insensitive like the rest of society uhm... along with our social media culture, uh, mass media had taken the shock out of the shock syndrome ... gone. You could always find gore and horrific happenings with a pressing finger. Nothing seemed to phase or surprise me. I was desensitized like homogenized milk, essentially numbed into an apathetic state of being. That was until I felt the air around me systemically thicken, pervading invading atmosphere an ambiance transformation. Vibes came at me like Poltergeists from all angles cryptically, slowly, not a wrinkled smile among them. Tear-stained ambiguously with indistinguishable countenances standing before me was Whitney. I couldn't hear what she was verbalizing from left to right. Both my palms found other palms, hugs and embraces, women of all sizes, men clasping my shoulders, children whom I'd never met walking up, looking into my face and crying happy tears.

OmLord, I need to check my hormone levels, for I think some dust particles found my tear ducts. Sorry, words were useless to describe the emotions. Feelings that systematically infiltrated my skin and organs. I was accepted just like I was one with these people, some of whom lost every family picture and video, their homes burnt to the ground. Many had lost precious pets and their life's belongings gone!

It was like a parade of people thanking me for being the divine supplier of needed goods. Behind me, no, on my right side, her dainty hand intermingled within my grasp Whitney at her side, brother Tony and baby sister Miranda the rest, umh counting maybe 55 in all shades of dark to light brown people following us. I popped the latch, and the back door of the Mercedes box truck rolled up.

I haven't a clue where Whitney got it; with a cone-shaped megaphone, she directed the burned-out victims to take tents, dry goods, fresh fruit, and clothes. Many had only what they were wearing, cases of water, and snacks being offloaded and distributed. Popular were the old-style board games Monopoly, Risk, Sorry, and the Game of Life, to name only a few we'd been given at the Salvation Army in San Jose! Tony worked alongside Miranda. The children were more interested in the board games, some hoarding Checkerboards, Chess, and Dominoes. We had over 100 packs of playing cards and even my favorite challenging game, Scrabble. The wide-eyed victims didn't know what to make of our Samaritan offerings!

Stop, as I blinked, who, what am I thinking like 'I'm getting past an important part of the story, for me, that is to say.' Look, I've stolen, robbed, even committed armed robbery, many physical altercations charged with Assault and Battery, stolen vehicles, drug deals, etc.

Felt no question a buzz adrenalin rushes of euphoria counting the spoils of thievery, the reaped goodies, monies like pirates. It was full-on party time, booze, drugs loosened women kind of in that order, a sultry fun time for sure!

Although I had to admit there weren't any comparisons strangely, I'd suppose you'd have to have shared each side of the coin… written parables describing the other reciprocal side of blood-stained bandages injured fire victims. Being a Good Samaritan was the best feeling I'd ever had!

It hit me like a surface-to-air missile, not unlike a submarine torpedo, feelings of giving genuinely responding to human sufferings, being less fortunate than I, no arguments, no one cutting in line for the last tent. With unimaginable grace and dignity, I felt privileged to be there helping. My adrenalin rushes, euphoric excitement melded inside my soul and inner-being, immersing me OmLord, a superior reaction of pleasure emanating with ambient sensitivity, shit felt high on life. ☺ .

I caught a glimpse of myself in a tall mirror. There I was, the wanted Outlaw, thief-pilfered side of the equation was all but negated… this is the truth. Love, humanity at its best. Where the heck have I been? Then a pair of children with soot-filled braided afros of guessing seven years old looking up into my eyes, tears streaming down as they gobbled down cheese crackers with bottled water, stared up. "Mister, thank you so much. We were starving! Thank you for saving us and helping Aunt Whitney, Miranda, and Uncle Tony!" I bent down towards them, not an awkward embrace from these little girls but a lingering heartfelt one, lucky that I wore sunglasses at night.

Then dammit, Whitney reached over and yanked them off my nose. "Gotcha, dude" was our first initial show of smiles since this journey had begun. From the side, 'how do you play this, mister?' 'Call me Tank,' taking the Monopoly box, winked at Whitney, who said, "Once Tank and I help with putting up the tents, we will grab a lantern and teach you, girls, how to play." They mimed clapping their inquisitive stares of innocence "okay, Auntie, we'll be waiting." The Church of Christ was a bustling regimented arena of likewise individuals all working in conjunction together, and other trucks were on the premise's First Aid… Red Cross and Paramedics.

I thought of the couch potatoes out in the world who saw not what could be imagined, watching this scene from cozy Livingroom's switching the channel to something less important and trivial, alleviating any concern for the trauma-based less fortunate, only glad it wasn't them or anyone they'd known!

I most likely would have been wearing their shoes, taking for granted that the strong dominated and took supplies from the weak. The fights, arguments, and constantly people jockeying for positions, self-serving pandemonium, turmoil, nope, none of that existed here. At 10:05 pm… Whitney and I had the Monopoly board out, surrounded by amazed children of the video game era… it was a hit. The board games were all being used by parents, with offspring joining in engaging, unlike they'd had 'Never' done before. No Wi-Fi… Internet and phone towers are down, like in the era of pre-computers, but not a bad thing, I perceived.

They heard someone's exclamations from a group in the distance under lanterns outside in the smokey darkness, obviously playing the 'Game of Life.' "Daddy, why haven't we ever played this game? It's so much fun!" "Yeah, dad!" his wife throws her arm around him "you know, honey, maybe we can schedule one family night a week after we rebuild our home. It would be good for us. Just turn off electronics, phones, and everything and enjoy our three children… popcorn and fun; why not?" He reacts with the children, 'Yes!'

I fought with my conscious to push away the obligatory, incumbent mess that had controlled my past commitments and responsibilities of being one-third of the Amigo's, Mark Feral and Joe Sable, and I. Now damnit, Mark was missing.

Joe was in Idaho, where I avoided traveling too. The burden was all mine; dreadfully, I'd be leaving Mendocino county in the morning and tracking down Mark. I would use the GPS on his phone and the chip on his truck. Yet like a manifestation of enlightenment, I was morphing in and out, obsequiously attentive to whom I humbly was transforming into, and I liked it. I didn't want to abandon the philanthropic feeling of Good Will. How was it possible to obviate my need to assist Mark? Hope struck me… maybe Mark had resurfaced by now.

I'd drive to where I could get a signal and check for updates. Mark may be on a womanizing run. However, somehow I knew umh felt this foreboding intuition, a notion prying underneath layers of my epidermis wrong. Something was awry, umh, amiss. He failed to check in, which was our rule of thumb now going on three days.

Enjoying this change of venue, the short-term interval of time in which I'd been in Whitney's presence, her company lit my insides. She never ceased to amaze me with a longer kiss than expected. She said to me, "Tank, I fully understand that you must go to find your friend who could be burned out in the Shasta County fires. I heard the Carr fire was only 17% contained. I get it now. You're an amazingly wonderful guy, and I look forward to getting to know you better." "Thanks, Whitney, but I…" "Tony said that you can take his car and leave the truck here. You will make better time." "Wow, Whit, that's a great idea. You can put the truck to good use salvaging what can be saved of your family's belongings…." "Yes, we appreciate all you have done for us and won't forget it. After this is all done, I'm inviting you to a family barbeque! Thanks, Tank, we will use your truck, and I'll see you in three days, right?" "Yep, Whit, I'll be back as soon as possible, but I'm not leaving for another five hours, so I can help set up some more tents!" She grinned and put her hand in mine. We walked over to a few struggling families who probably had never gone camping in their lives. The tent poles were spread out 'come on, let's help them!' she said.

After we helped to assemble five more tents, "Whitney, I wish I could stay with you and your siblings." "No worries here, Tank. I'm here until I'm no longer needed; Tony has to return to work next week. Miranda is going to stay with me, you know she's a journalist. Fortunately, her editor has told her to write an exposé of her experience, a personal, heartfelt story of the trials and tribulations of how we as people come together to resolve and overcome life's adversities."

With her last words ringing in my mind, I awakened and laid a soft kiss on her dry lips, a long-lasting hug, and a peck on each cheek. I was driving away from Lakeport, leaving the girl I wanted to hold onto forever. I checked the phone for signals, but nothing. I played old-school music on the radio; Tony's car was comfortable. I only worried about not damaging it... I hated being obligated to someone else.

I regained signal when I cleared the rollin hills on Hwy 20 about 15 miles West of the town of Williams. No messages, not one odd, even ominous... a sinister spider crawled up the nape of my neck. Mark's truck hadn't moved from in front of the cabin; staring at Google Earth real-time, the screen was the same. From yesterday neither the Volkswagen bus nor the older trucks moved. What was going on at Mark's cabin? Frozen were the pictures of the dogs by a gate, fenced in, another text to his phone, nada. I tried Joe's phone, then remembered he'd texted that he would be unavailable for at least three days in the militia conference. So, I drifted away from worry, losing myself in some Billy Joel tunes.

-57-

Rico removes Wendi from NIA, and Terrance plans some

surprises.

Terrance watched the last of Rico's entourage drive off toward the gates of NIA. The pressure was now exponentially increased, his dedication to his syndicate of utmost concern. If he was going to take the next leap of ascension, he must take back control of the 'Feral' woman. She was an essential cog in at least 85% of the operations. No, it wasn't enough to have the largest Militia stronghold on American soil. Many investors weren't fans of America, scoffing negatively at the land of the USA's empirical power mongers and hypocrites. Most were anti-American, not Terrance. It was rewarding being the CEO and leader of the highly regarded training and education facility mercenary encampment right under and within the US Government's vantage point, boldly on blast and right on the front street.

NIA's hierarchy at first was amused that the Fed's wanted to start subcontracting prison space... and leasing out cell blocks holding areas for inmates to be psychoanalyzed, uhm, Federal detainees. Some of the more prudent among us were on edge, worried that the Feds were dangerous to have around our facility.

Terrance sighed, musing. I can't cry over spilled milk, guess you could, actually... if it was your last cup and you were addicted to 'Lecce, milk.' Where did that saying come from? It wasn't so much the weeping but the proactive measures after the spill of the 'Lecce.' Using an American football maxim, the axiom is better to 'drop back 10 yards and punt' go on the defensive. So rumors would become fruition that former Marshals Burke and Rand were now stationed at the Calistoga safe harbor retreat, lol, for the Federal witness protection program. That's where Wendi was to be housed!

Terrance wondered why he'd used the word former regarding the Marshals who were part of his organization and fired after Nurse Spike's attempt on Wendi's life. The Marshals were suspended for a few weeks and reassigned to the Calistoga safe house.

Cash brought interesting bedmates; indeed, the three Marshals had been relieved of their detailed around-the-clock security of Wendi when the plot to kill her became known. Evans put in his retirement papers. The next move would be to have Evans unretire, putting my three Marshals, that served dual purposes, back in vogue, like spies working for the FBI and being subservient and loyal to him.

First, we must eliminate Ms. Goody 2 shoes, Marshal Kara, and Jack, the skilled nurse. We then can deal with the rest of the new team, whose job is to protect Wendi Feral. He planned to hop on his jet and fly down to L.A. for the scheduled meeting with investors, then catch a flight back to go to the gathering of top brass here at NIA to decide how to navigate the return of Wendi back into the 'fold' they'd need to kidnap her from the Feds. Then he cackled, 'we'd keep her right under their nose's down in the basement dungeon forever… she'd work for us till she didn't… and was Dead!'

<u>Rico couldn't help it. Behind his sunglasses, he was smirking largely</u> 😊 .

Rico couldn't quantify his sighs of relief like a 7-ton boulder was hoisted off his rib cage when his rear bumper cleared the razor-wired driveway out from under the shadows of the ancient guard towers and genuinely grinned when his wheels found the open road. He finally relaxed with an exasperated smile; he'd done it. Knowing inside his craw something felt wrong, intuition never failed him 'NIA was like the old horror movies where both the hero and victim seductively were drawn to the castle. Evil lurked with each step; music heightened suspensefully in the background. 'Treacherously you watched as the monsters insidiously devoured…' Brought out of his imagination, on his radio speaker, "Rico, I just spoke to you… are you there? Hello, I just got off the phone with Marshal Evans. He would like to team up, come out of retirement, regain his position, and lead the security team watching Wendi," says Agent Lucy Link.

"Lucy, I'm happy with Marshal Kara; she's in charge for now, but I see no reason that he can't be added to the team. Let me check in with Tanya and see what she thinks 'Evans' has a spotless service record. He took care of Wendi for almost nine months. Tell him I'll work on it, okay…." "Sure thing, boss, one more thing you know that Jax Foul is going with us; he's sitting next to Wendi in the van. I am concerned that…." "Lucy, no worries. Jax would lay down his life for Wendi in a 'flat jack second.' He is no doubt an ally. They have a special bond, any word on her parent's arrival?" "I'll check; get back to you, Rico."

Rico once again mulls over what always lingered in his mind; when he tried to clear it, think of zilch nothing. Why couldn't he shut down his brain? Where were the ctrl-alt-del buttons at? He grins. Thinking of their short love affair with warm, lighthearted feelings, confirming again that it's time to get off the pot or poop-shit, no matter the age difference, I could be Wendi's young dad. Life wasn't cruising by. It was glaringly blowing by at warp speed.

She was married to David, but why?... where'd he come from? Once in private, he'd approach Wendi again. She surely would regain her conscious state soon; she was fully cognizant until that dart had taken her away. Rico had spoken to her via phone, and they laughed, speaking fluidly only like old friends could. It was a fun conversation. They were reminiscing, then boom, lost in the cell phone abyss, but the echoes of her giggles warmed his heart. Conclusion there was only one Wendi, and I loved that lady... what a mess, huh?

The phone lit up; it was Lucy again, "the parents will land at the Sacramento Airport with her husband at 9 am tomorrow; oh, a side note, the teenagers that visited Wendi and Jax every year will be landing from Orlando, Fla. At coincidently 9:35 am."

I stalled as I pondered how to deal with this news then an idea flashed by "hey Lucy, see if Marshal Evans will be available to escort both parties to Calistoga tomorrow?" "Okay, will do!"

Resting my back against the seat, I reclined my head into the cushion my driver made easy work of the winding roads through Sonoma County. Daydreaming: 11 years ago, Wendi nearly lost her life not once, but three times. I was at fault; it was my investigations that she offered to help solve, well sure her company had signed a lucrative contract. Wendi was making six figures annually. From Tennessee's serial killer to the plague, the epidemic in Ocala, Fla. Then, the 'Slim case' Cuban mafia children kidnapped for the porn industry, where she met Mr. Jax Foul. Who was the kidnapper of 17 children, a war hero who became a ruthless criminal, then did a 360-degree turn-spin and became a worldwide phenomenon hero. With Wendi's help, I saved, or shall I say we saved, 16 children in captivity in Bangkok. One of the children had committed suicide sadly.

Two of the saved children had bonded with Jax and Wendi at the time of the horrific abductions, Juan was five years old, and Leah was six years old and blind.

In Federal court in Sacramento, the mothers of Juan and Leah stood up for the defense and opposition to the prosecution of Jax; they had voiced their opinion that Jax was a hero, and he'd paid for his wrongdoings. The world's social media fervor went viral with the reunion of 17 mothers and fathers getting back their children all on a video display. The blitz of emotions and tears could be sliced thickly with a butter knife, leniency for Jax triggered.

Every year, not missing a single one, the kids would travel to see their lifelong heroes, Jax and Wendi. The difference now was that Juan was 16 years old and Leah 17. Leah has had several operations to help return her vision, and she recently had a Cornea transplant in her left eye.

The teenagers were straight 'A' students who took to the airplane by themselves; it is not hard to understand that after all they had gone through during the siege at the Plant City ranch, they were wearing matching rings halved on chains around their necks boyfriend, and girlfriend for life. A relationship that knew no bounds, true smiling love, and planned to be married after graduating high school before entering college.

So, it was going to be an emotional weekend ahead, thought Rico, heck he hadn't seen the teens in three years. It would be nice to see them again.

Doctor Hawkins had diagnosed Wendi's current state of mind, and she'd regressed, hidden deep in a coma drug induced by the dart, but once worn off, she'd be back among the living. I'd be there to let her know how I felt about her, no pressure, realizing she was a married woman; it was eating me alive like a toxic acid. I had to come clean and get it off my chest despite David… it was what it was!

-58-

Rascal Savage and Anita Sparks, and the Sinaloa Cartel… El Chapo.

Both bodies naked with sweet sweat beading up, their rocking chair stilled um Anita was… straddling him… all in 'Doctor Anita Sparks' proud erected nipples went flaccid as did 'Rascal Savage's thick appendage. <u>On speaker phone, secure line, confirmation finally directly from Mexico City, 'El-Chapo' the Real Escape Artist, not the imposter the Fed's had in custody. Indicted no, El Chapo no longer resembled his former self. In fact, he'd had an amazing transformation before his indictments. Chapo was 5'5" tall. He had undergone major surgeries, including breaking and fracturing both legs, tibias, and fibulas, with the insertion of titanium rods fused to both bones that lengthened his legs as far as the skin could stretch. El Chapo was now nearly 5'11" tall, almost a six-footer… medical miracle.</u>

The Sinaloa cartel dictator lived free while his twin was incarcerated in the states. His name was Joaquin Guzman. Only seven living humans knew he'd pulled this Houdini act off; Rascal and Anita were two of them.

"Hop up, babe," he gently lifted her warm damp thighs up, "this has been news we've been waiting for, our chance to re-capture the bitch Wendi Feral I…." "Yuh mean Sunshine, don't you, Rascal?" "ahh, whatever, a split of the 17-million-dollar reward will be ours. Our connections inside NIA were correct; she's been released to that bastard 'Rico guy'…." "I heard it all. Glad you were able to 'get off just like a man to leave a lady swollen and close to climax, you prick tease, Rascal, men can be so selfish…." "Anita, stop bitching; rub one out. Not my problem!" "Yeah, babe, why'd you have to take the fkn call while we were making love, hum?" He smirked "girl, and sometimes it ain't love but just sex. The call from Chapo was far more important than a 15-second orgasm. Hey, get a map for Northern California… let's check out the town of Calistoga, babe. Hush, I'll go down on you after you clean up, K?" "Remember Chapo had a person killed because he didn't take his call last year. When he calls on the special line, we take the call no matter the circumstances" she whirls around, throwing a pillow at him "fine!"

Phone in hand, he walks over to the sliding glass doors onto the Redwood deck, a stark difference from the last areas he'd opened operations at. He and Anita had set up the Cartel. North Carolina and the New Mexico plants were still churning designer drugs… Ecstasy, Meth-laced heroin, and batches of Cocaine 'Bend, Oregon' was a beautiful place to live.

Rascal enjoyed the West coast of America, now three years into developing the mobile home plant Industrial complex, a clandestine, covert undercover operation for the Sinaloa cartel. He and Anita would be flying to California this time; Wendi wouldn't escape El Chapo's outstretched paws-claws. She was the key ingredient to enable revenge and vengeance on his enemies. She would allow Chapo's form of reconciliation essential was Wendi's abilities as an animal seer.

Chapo was already juicing again at the possibilities. Chapo had kept her to himself years ago. Ah, it had been 11 years since they had captured 'Wendi/Sunshine.' It was sweet while it lasted, which was only for mere months. Chapo longed to regain and capture Wendi Feral. Wendi was his slave, not sexually, but his paranormal guide. Rascal fondly thinks about his infamous attack on the Trinity Lake cabin and the capture of the animal seer; what she'd helped accomplish was mind-blowing.

Rico Captor and Jax Foul, with a mercenary team from NIA, had illegally crossed the border, attacked the Mexico City complex, and freed her and… "Rascal, here it is…." Anita, in a thin silk robe, hands over the map, outlined was the old winery known to be a Fed safehouse.

<u>FBI Agents Lori Parks and Bill Avery.</u>

Life is full of troubles! Sufferings paths to be maneuvered, chosen, taken, or pursued once you've made the concerted effort to analyze your options, then with determination & discipline, you must stay the course. Lori mulls over this statement, frustratingly how and what has she done in her life? Sure, she takes home a decent paycheck, but five years have closed into 20 years. Where did all the time go? 'Lori Parks' sat alone, driving North towards the ravaged properties of the notorious fires of the northern state of California, I-5 North. Only five miles up ahead was Tank.

Tank, a lifelong career criminal convict in a church delivering aid to fire victims hell, he'd barely had been out of San Quentin a week. Lori had turned the ripe ole age of 41 on April 15th, Tax Day, a burden she'd grown immune to. No children or Lover nor companion. No one to hold or to comfort, a thick bank account, saving for that all too often used term. She guffawed… what was it called? Oh yeah used to hear it said and referred to it as the proverbial <u>'Rainey raining day!' syndrome. That often never came till you dropped fricken Dead.</u>

People who saved for the rain sometimes died in the Sun or on a cold, dry day night. A sudden heart attack, a plane crash, a car accident, or the manifestation of a gun firing bullets into your ugh, her face dead-blown to smithereens. I saved money for what… this that, uh, what? I should enjoy my money and life. What was I waiting for?

Alone in painful remembrances, wetness in the corners of her lids, unknowingly a habit in her left palm, was her most treasured, precious gewgaw trinket, a class ring given to her. Lori had felt the 'In Love' passion for her 3rd lover… he'd swooped her up and off her feet. Not a few hours from where she drove North, it all happened at Chico State. Theirs was a romance of only 19 months. They had transferred to a 4-year University; she followed her dream to U.C. Berkeley for a degree in Criminal Justice, him a business degree, C.P.A. he was already set up in life with a wealthy affluent family. The lovefest was a whirlwind, filled with proposals. He truly wanted her, and she wanted him, although fear of commitment reigned.

Her girlfriend's parents scolded her, their beliefs were aligned with her parents... their words still reverberated, such as Lori, is that what you want to do, give up your future career aspirations? Be the stereotypical woman who drops everything, gets married, gets pregnant, and has children, then slowly waddles out to pasture. Uh, barefooted, a leftover housewife exhausted, taken for granted, with nothing to look forward to but the once-a-year 3-week family vacation. Yes, Lori, join up with the 'Stepford Wives' movie of 2004 and be a perfect wifey, a robot... sell yourself into slavery. Unjust imprisonment, dull regimented life existence of a prototypical mother and aging wife, how much do you earn being mommy... 'Mommy dearest!'

The children fly the coop, then one day, as hubby is away on another lengthy business trip, you meander about in each of the three empty kids' rooms, pictures, photos on the walls, and boyband posters 49er-Giants-Sharks, Warrior posters, paraphernalia sports trophies. Knickknacks of high school days three unoccupied spaces that you take turns sleeping in.

No worries: you can Facetime or Skype each of them later this evening. Your babies have their own lives in College; you should be so freakin proud! So it goes, you have been pruned away, your just 'deadwood' betrayed, alone. The duty of a mother is mind-blowing. After you've given all that you can for the children, is there enough of you left inside... suddenly you blink awake your husband is unavailable, even if he wasn't? He has his business life, which is far more critical and important than you... you're sequestered away on the conventional backburner. He doesn't answer your call, umh, no answer. Ugh, he must be in another one of his meetings.

You've always promised yourself... my time would come once I raise my children, I could live yup... Maybe when your mother's duties are complete, you will have the energy and determination aligned with motivation to get on with the 'Put on the back Burner' career. Go back to College Yep, you can do it, Girl, but you, unfortunately, have been conditioned and found the doldrums floating on the ocean's wave without a Lighthouse in sight. Lost in a cesspool of indecision and desireless, it's so hard to propel yourself forward to levitate your being-spirit and stimulate yourself enthusiastically to search out your true destiny, happy that your offspring are off in the process of doing just that. Where was that young-of-heart motivation and goal orientation, the energy that propelled you forward against all odds, the determination, and perseverance… help me, where is Wonder Woman? ☹ .

<u>Complacency is your dictator, and fear spoils your desired future. You have given up, Loser… You're lost in Ground Hog day and night… pick out a burial site, or do you Fight for what's left of your Life?</u>

What's going to be your advice to your daughter? When she falls for the boy in love, wants to marry, leaves College…aah, Ugh! The once thrilling body enhancements cosmetic surgeries need some tucks and lifts. Emotional lust and passion had died. We made love occasionally, familiarity filled redundancies 'Ole Had' was it now merely an act of obligation? Good thing a woman didn't need to exhibit a physical display to show that intense desire had departed, easy to fake climax without the wanting cravings for sexual interaction. Are you horny for him? Nah… dryness can be circumvented. Unlike men, all we need to do is slyly spit on a few fingers, aah wet… or some pre-gel.

Now the damn scientists and doctors cum up with the freakin E.D. Pills Viagra. Where's my female counterpart?

You've changed, haven't you? Over the last two decades, huh? Where have you gone to? Now an empty nest, a behemoth colossus Monster, appears. Is this it? Your life in a nutshell done, toast. Or are you going to go out and live it, sacrificed enough already? At the ledge, are you going to step up or fall? The vices of denial are accessible more drugs and alcohol. 'Oh, what I could have been?' Get out there, woman. There are plenty of successful moms; likewise, woman soldiers with blessed veneration, sanctified and devoted to themselves goal oriented… just do it! The percentages aren't in your favor; oddsmakers have you as a diminished Underdog.

A Jumbled mess of life, are you lost? Your conscience knows the truth… your husband covets someone else; you confront your lover, but HONEY, it's not your lover anymore. No… that was years past. Now it's your partner, uhm, more like a sibling, uh, brother. Lust was dead and buried 23 years of the same meat, right? Lost in the years, nothing New exciting, your now off despite his arguments to find out what was left of your short life, back to College where you're as susceptible as an 18-year-old virgin. New life, spread your wings, girl, and fly. You can succeed Yup!

Bring on all the new challenges, new people, and friends. The possibilities over the horizon are endless and seem to be limitless. It could be… exhilaration at every turn. Your husband has lost the debate-conceded and relented now he's allowed you to enter the curriculum. Hell, you have money of your own… he says, 'we're soon to retire, why babe? Travel visit the children, and soon honey-bunny, we'll have grandchildren. I will be faithful from now on, babe. Let's give it one more try, sweetie pie!'

What isn't quantifiable or reconcilable… it's the yearning for something more; God, is there more to this life? He accommodates for harmony's sake, tries to give you more, changes up the once-a-week sex moves to twice, and tries to manufacture romance. But by now, we are at an impasse. The change of life rears its thirsty head aligning with this cataclysmic timeframe mixed up confused, umh, hobbies maybe…Nah. How to conform to conformity?

Wanting exploration, pioneer-like, lost as he is, mid-life crisis, what do you want? Him, not sure, what because of familiarity, uh, discombobulated antipathetic, nonchalantly unmoved a kaleidoscope of angles directions, humanity punches you in the gut. Vagina, ouch, no protection, no need… none, early onset of menopause, whack, crash. No, no, am I going crazy?

Instantly, suddenly there's more to you and less of him, the hormonal swings, hot flashes, Highs-Lows, pharmaceuticals, drugs. The life of extravagance emboldens you, and theatrics morph and changes a euphoniousness, a melodic, mellow tune leaving you with heavy metal hashtags. Music plays as all your characteristics evolve; you're now wearing more makeup. Hitting the gym like a gyrating 'GymRat' breast enhancements, mini skirt… Woman Gone Wild!

It's you, ugh… was it you all along? Where have you been? Oh, that's right, you've been a mommy housewife, well fk that. No longer are you caged-shackled. Goin' to find new lovers, lost passion personified, lust… Divorce. Uh, have you now found yourself, ahh maybe, or is this life's highway? Do I take the next exit, stay on track, or is it another phase?

Carefully play the end game of Russian Roulette; a twirping sound brings Lori back from the life that could have been, now driving East on Hwy 40 towards Shingletown, Susanville. She didn't know how she got there, but flashing on the screen on the dash was Tanks ass now only three miles in front; smoke and haze clouding her vision, stinging her throat. Upchuck dry heaving, sweating, shaking, holding her stomach doubled over, had to pull off the Hwy now at a rest area sick, nearly hallucinating, retching up on knees. The porcelain devil has her head deep in its bowels. Ugh, food poisoning that damn taco truck.

Agent Bill Avery drives past the rest area on the same route she'd be on. When she felt better, she'd catch up. Sitting on a park bench with a vendor's cold plastic water bottle in each hand.

Lori's body ached and felt feverish food poisoning was awful, and she was lucky not to have crashed her car while on a phantasmagoric, fallacious, and illogical daymare driving apparently on auto-pilot. Frustrations had lingered from the Rico almost interlude. Although she had some resolve, Rico wasn't with the controlling Vipress Tanya; he was in Napa, only a few hours away. Perhaps she'd hook up with him to show the man how a woman could and should devour him… sex would be her way into his life, zipper undone. She wouldn't be alone much longer and would make Rico love her.

It took her about 45 minutes to suck it up; hydrate, still in cramping pain, she started her vehicle back up after listening to Avery. "Lori, he's we are heading towards a new fire called the 'Hat Fire' outside of Shingletown. The authorities are stopping all traffic 33 miles East of there." "Well, Bill, which means Tank will also be waylaid; this is a Goose chase. Look, I've tried to call and get in touch with Rico to see if he needs assistance. Can you give him a ring too?" "Sure, thing, Lori, I concur. I don't get it either; why we're relegated to following someone who has a chip up his 'yin-yang?' Heck, we can watch him via satellite, right? Well, let me take that back, umh too smokey right now he'd be invisible." Avery thought he was being funny and chortled; Lori found zero humor "call Rico, Bill, okay?" click.

Fk, the guy loved to talk, drove her crazy, and thought, at worse, she'd leave Bill to watch Tank and cruise. Maybe her subtle manipulation was worthy. If Bill called Rico to see if he needed help relocating Wendi, he wouldn't see between the lines. Ahh, that I wanted him between the sheets... lol. All she needed was a bottle of wine, a steamy hot tub, and a luxury suite, and he would always be hers! ☺ .

-59-

<u>Tank on the road to Mark's cabin with Whitney on his mind.</u>

He'd played the radio on loud. Then his iPod... now drove along listening to road sounds, alone and comfortable with himself. Liking this new him, he decided that Whitney was a keeper, adorable... her family accepted him even though he was like Casper, the friendly ghost alongside them. It seemed no one had any hidden agenda's that he could envision-kinda like what you see is what ya got.

An odd feeling not distinguishable grasped and enamored him, giving and helping others like an Ambassador of Good Will and Faith. To donate not only your time but monies of almost five thousand dollars ah, well, technically, it wasn't his money but his bro's. Investing cash and time, surprisingly, was a feel-good soul-like cleansing thing. Ugh, who woulda thunk that? Suddenly, he felt like a 'heel' of a worn-out boot. Was he a shallow, fake do-gooder with ulterior motives? Premeditating reasons to exhibit to the powers of the universe that 'hey look at me' or was the truth not so deep down in his psyche… was he but a wretched weasel!

A line is drawn in the sand aligning with his subconscious an inner conflict of the hateful unashamed ambivalent envoy of truth from a negative perspective (depending on one's perspective, I suppose) agitated at this voice bellowing out. 'Tank,' we both know that the only reason you're doing all of this is to get in Whitney's panties… like 'Duh,' ugh, ulterior motives… isn't that the treasure trove of your fruitful desires?' 'No, not so at ease, fella' will yah give me some space here? He shakes his outraged head. I'm developing a new me, following chasing personal righteousness, and working on positive Karma here; this could and should have been me all along. Realizing that since a chaotic childhood, I'd been led by my nose used and abused, I gave my life to Mark and Joe!

Existing within his mind, ambidextrously, the other entity speaks, 'then turn around. Why go to help Mark or to find him? He's a big boy, huh?' Flip a U-turn, for we both understand where this road leads to… danger, death, mayhem, and incarceration, not the scenic route into the voluptuous crevices of Whitney… 'you're out of bounds, Dude!'

Signs flashing lights, the road closed up ahead 13 miles, the fire was expanding, and winds swirling forever changing, was it time for him to make a change? Hell, he had the best kind of excuse, valid. Tank couldn't continue towards Mark's cabin; roads were closed… his GPS tracking system showed a pulsating LCD light flashing on the dashboard of his borrowed car. Mark was at the cabin, as a bird would fly 11 miles away. Indeed there were backwoods roads, BLM cut-outs, even, ironically, fire roads trails, and utility line roads he could travel cross country. But without a 4-wheel drive, that would be hazardous at best! Deadly at worst Ugh.

What ridiculous ideas; hell, why risk his ass? He could be caught in the raging fast-moving fire! Beyond that, when did Mark ever risk his skin for me?

While stopped in another line of vehicles, he yanked up his safe phone... another futile try to get a hold of Mark, but no answer again. Tank was stressing out... this wasn't his car. It was Tony's, and he would not have it burnt to the ground. He could park and hike in. But being unarmed... why did that just cross his lips? Armed, was this the thought process of a criminal? Nope, a survivor, most likely good ole bro Mark was engaged, linked up in a rambunctious raucous all-nighter Orgy that was Mark, um, his cock ran his life. Not a bad thing as he chuckled, cocks sensations and scintillations were a God-given human gift, pressed in depth for propagation purposes, fleeting at best... disease laden at worse.

Much better to stroke to some raunchy Porn or, like in Prison, read one of those hot to bother Romance novels narrated in your imagination.

Better yet, have a lover and best friend-soulmatish like Whitney to hold and hug, ugh, lol, what a 'Sap!' Parking in a shopping center, well, call it like it was a gas station pharmacy and hotdog stand. He laced up his boots, grabbed his backpack, and put on sunglasses and a hat. Decision finalized, he'd hike back into the woods after buying some more supplies, water. Tank already rationalized he'd broken his probation long ago with his trip with Whitney, so why not toss caution into the smokey air?

Back inside his Psyche, echoing reality, 'what he didn't know' was a fragmented part of a play on words that he'd thought about umpteen times being an avid reader during the years of incarceration. Aah, words that had been said by many scholars, poets of the learned, was it a proverb?' 'What you don't know can't hurt you' really think about that ludicrous statement; how could this be calculated, gaged by percentages, for it was a wrong way of thinking... such foolishness. For example, the fire shifts direction, and your burned crispy, um, Barbequed. But isn't that where you play the odds percentage-wise? You're making a decision that likely could end up in your own demise. Zero percentage of success weighed and leveraged his next steps, and life was about odds. He was an underdog... a negative reciprocal number fell into the calculation 'stupidity had to be gauged' because you are forewarned that a raging inferno is nearby!

Taking analysis further, if I'm traipsing, hiking through the woods, and accidentally stepping into a Bear trap, what you didn't know could certainly snap your fkn leg off, duh! Oh well, Tank disappears out of view, through woods, inhales a deep regretful smokey breath, and goes off to Mark's cabin.

<u>FBI Agents Rico Captor, Lori Parks, and Bill Avery… Tank Shaw.</u>

"Lori, you certainly know that I cannot supersede Tanya's authority. She delegated the orders, and we must either follow them or deal with her wrath." "Ahh, especially when it comes to you, she's got a corncob stuck, you know precisely where… regarding you." He snickers, which she heard through the earpiece. "My advice is to stay on the Tank, guy. That's all I can say I …" "what's so damn funny, Rico? if yuh got something to say…." "Lori, just stay on point, okay? Let's stay in touch. Perhaps if everything goes well with Wendi's transition to the Safehouse, I'll make a trip up there to…." Cackling. "I'm not prepared to go fkn hiking through the forest, nor is Avery; there's fire danger surrounding us, and besides, Wtf is so freakin funny, Rico?…." "Oh, sorry, I was laughing with you, not at you, thankful that I wasn't in your size seven shoes, <u>'Slippers'…"</u> they both let off some steam with hilarious giggles. Oh, 'Touché,' said she.

"Hey Lori, if it makes anything better, I will have you in an adjoining hotel room next to mine for you to rinse off the dirt, grime, and 'ticks.' I might even rub some ointments on all the mosquito bites. I hear there the size of Hummingbirds out there," howling contagiously.

"You're a fricken asshole Rico, really," as she's choking with laughter, then silence as both of them release tensions the best way possible with humor "sorry, girl" "oh, you will be, boy." "Lor, on a serious note, keep your satellite phone nearby. There's no signal out there sometimes in the boondocks, especially with the fire burning down everything, okay!" "All right, yeah, Rico, your right. The smoke is so thick it appears to be nighttime out here, and gee,

it's only 1:15 pm." "Do you think you and Avery need backup? Where could he be going on foot out there?" "No clue, dude, but all the property checks show no connections to Mark, Joe, or Tank… nada Avery has even checked with San Quentin, their phone calls, and mail nothing from this area was found on either of the three of them… we're blind literally."

"I don't know, Lori; why don't you contact Tanya and update her." "I sent her a text about an hour ago, haven't heard from her, Rico, listen with the body GPS chip in his skin, why don't I just wait him out in this parking lot?" "Don't know, Lor, that's your call. We can't fly a chopper in the thick smoke. If you decide to wait him out, don't tell Tanya I was privy to any of your decisions I …" "Wow Rico, it's like that, hum?" "She's still steamed, is all. No need to break the scab open; gotta go, girl!" Click.

Sunshine Feral, Jax Foul, and Rico.

Boarding the 747 airplane at the Portland airport, clutching tightly, was the last remnants of her conversation with her precious daughter Wendi. To have heard her voice that had changed so much throughout her life from a baby through adolescence. Wendi surely was the Apple of her eye. Barbara lived vicariously through her daughter's trials and tribulations from the dorky pictures of her being in the Glee Club, lead actress in drama class. Her athletics, Softball tournaments, championships, top-notch swimmer, and Volleyball started on the varsity team even being a freshman. Barbara wondered if there was a limit to how many times she could replay her last dialogue with Wendi.

Seeing the approach to Sacramento from the window seat, the landing gear abruptly dropped, locking. The last 11 months had been some of the most challenging times and hardships in her life. Like salvation, her words played back, 'mother, I love you and daddy!' 'oh, mommy, I missed you!' Few full-grown women still called their mom mommy. She so realized how much she relished those very words.

Barbara closed her eyes at the trauma her Wendi had weathered in the last decade, once again in a coma thought back to the last time she'd lost consciousness 'caused by a dramatic attack at a shopping center. Wendi barely survived with a massive head injury and concussion, which had killed a Marshal protecting her. The kidnapping attempt by the Cartel and a fellow named Rascal was foiled... then it was months of MRI tunnels and 'Electroencephalography' EEG scans recording of and testing her brain activity...frighteningly hearing the beeping of life support machines.

Alter ego: Sunshine stepped out of the abyss several times to tell me she was all right! Now a dart had sunk her back to oblivion, perhaps with her being at Wendi's bedside. She'd come back out of her fugue, like the last time when Wendi had recognized her presence. Hopefully, they would have another blissful interaction, Wendi would regain her cognizance, and they'd embrace with love again. Neurologists had unequivocally said that because of the head trauma caused years ago after our son Mark had tried to kill Wendi, it wouldn't take much to have her slip into something akin to syncope. To blackout without warning, poor Wendi still had bullet fragments in her skull from Mark's assault.

David sat on the aisle, and my husband Ed held onto my hand as we touched down. I haven't an inkling how many times since her accidents we'd made this flight to California from Vancouver, Wash. Many times lost musing over the subject matter, motherhood birthing a perfect baby girl, from the date of inception onward, in the womb-heart beating legs kicking arms, gesticulating, breathing my air, a live entity growing inside of me. A plain & straightforward miracle, our maternal bond was unlike what a man could assimilate. Nope, no daddy could, unfortunately, identify with this manifestation. Sure, they could empathize with you, sort of as your bent over with cramps that felt like your intestines were being eviscerated by morning sickness, dull then sharp back pains as your tummy starts exploding propelling outwards, pulling on your spine. No, this didn't seem like a temporary ailment bloating emotional upheavals, swings of ups and downs, then sideways.

Ed had rubbed my shoulders, cold compress-rags on my head, ice water for my Sahara Desert tongue. It was straight bullshit that he or any man could comprehend how a woman's mind, body life morphs through various stages. Continuums of exalted happiness to euphoria opposites of moroseness she now harbored, the nine-month sentence or so was worth every second.

I remember oh so well birthing our son Mark, a problematic term, uh, the bad seed who now wanted to kill his sister. How could such opposites come from my body? Why?

Ed would say like a mantra I have empathy for you, Barb! I'd tell him it's not empathy but sympathy as I watched him grab another brewski beer to bloat his beer belly further to match my maternity-laden tummy.

'I am mom' when I see my daughter; memories pass by in waves from womb to baby, draining from my body from where we were. Ahh, now what? Damnit, I gotta get off the anti-depressants 'Ativan' I'm not even making sense to myself that bitch of a neighbor started it all. Karen ruined Ed and our lives. We were regulars at the Royal Oaks Country Club, Ed enjoyed the golf courses, and I was involved in organizing the special events. Karen was a viper, a snake, the worse kind of a two-faced serpent. She researched our family name using the internet and connected us to our son Mark Feral.

Karen then printed out all the propaganda and truth about our family; the most caustic was proof that Mark was on the FBI's most wanted list. The news blew us up… every one of our friends had learned about Mark… a suspected killer who'd absconded from parole from San Quentin. It spread like a contagion… pandemic. Soon our so-called friends didn't reply to our texts and calls. We were the plague, uninvited to all special occasions.

How can I be held responsible for the children I gave life to, umh or Ed fathered? Why does society dwell on the negative more than the positive? Our daughter Wendi was a heroine. She had been all over social media and positively affected many people, saving thousands of lives alone in the Ocala Epidemic. Wendi saved over a dozen children from pedophiles, where was the esteemed gratitude by our pasteboard friends, plastic, fake smiles.

True, Mark was a problem child, on the other side of the coin, extremely volatile neither Ed nor I believed all the charges they'd attributed to his name. It was merely a way for the police to cleanse their books.

Mark was suspected in the shooting on I-5 in Washington that initially put Wendi in the hospital near comatose, but he sent messages to us claiming he was innocent. It was also true; he and Wendi hadn't seen eye-to-eye since childhood, but he wouldn't try to kill his sister.

The airplane was taxying, and the lights were flashing, sounds dinging. I went contrarian in the elevating mood that this drug was supposed to bring forth. There was David, Wendi's husband, who wasn't worth a crap in my book and was not up to the standards my daughter deserved. A mere construction worker, aah sure, you could say he was a good husband, I guess, but hey, something happened to Wendi. It was like a whirlwind romance. One weekend they took off to South Lake Tahoe. They ended up at the Meyers Chapel and just tied the knot and got married. No one stood in for her. Did she lose her mind? Damnit, I wanted to throw a colossal Wedding, but no, they showed up on our doorstep. Ugh, guess what, mom, we're married!... Duh, uuhhh, so stupid.

What did David do, drug her? Ahh, then worse yet, she was shot in the head only months later while driving North on I-5, causing her to have a miscarriage. David and Wendi had lost a baby boy five months old. The Feds had cast blame on our son Mark accusing him of being the shooter without any proof. We lost a grandbaby; Ed and I were upset, which was an understatement, but was it wrong of me to pray for my daughter's recovery during the 7-hour surgery? Was I guilty of not begging the powers to be to save the baby boy at the time of the accident?

"Barbara, what are you doing, your drooling. Oh my, are you all…" "shut-up Ed help me up out of this damn seat, will yah." "Barb, you have to get off that prescription. You got a wild look in your eyes; you look crazed you…." "Ed, I'm okay, sshhh let's go" we walk down the aisle and out of the plane. Waiting at the luggage turnstiles was the jolly countenance of Marshal Evans, greeting us three like we were freaking family. Out in the bright sunshine, we

went, a Cadillac Escalade parked at the curb. We encircled the airport, waiting for the teenagers Juan and Leah; it had been three years since we had seen them.

Oh my goodness, the changes as I glanced at them waving at us, not only physically but speaking with them. They had matured into unbelievable teenagers. Life was terrific as we hugged, I cried, post-menopausal leftovers, then I caught Ed spinning away, wet eyes something in common!

Juan had grown like six inches, a good-looking boy with Leah on his arm and a bandage on her left eye from a recent Cornea transplant. They spoke excitedly as only teenagers can.

They were so happy and pumped up to see their real-life heroes, Jax and my Wendi. It would be a glorious weekend. Marshal Evan took the helm, driving us; we were Calistoga bound to see Rico, who was the man I wanted my daughter to marry. Sure, he was a bit older, but what a freakin hunk, and they made a hella of a match. Besides, isn't age but numbers?

I was thrilled that he had gotten Wendi outta that prison. It was eerie visiting NIA to visit her. It always made my skin crawl like moving maggots. I couldn't wait to see her new living arrangements and tour the old historic winery. I'd read some tourist info on Calistoga and looked forward to dipping my body in the hot springs.

I listened to the recurring theme the guys were explaining to the teens before she was shot with the dart; Wendi was entirely back, as good as ever. Her memory was clouded, but it wouldn't be long till she would be running on all clear cylinders; Doctor Hawkins said that for Wendi to recover fully, she'd have to be weaned off all psychotropic meds. Wendi's future was sunglass material 'Bright.' My baby will be back to herself. Hopefully, her life's ups and downs won't resemble a Yo-Yo back and forth, hanging from a string spinning backward, walking the dog. The non-lethal dosage dart was fired on Wendi for ulterior motives, of precisely what? Ed. David and I were assured that once the darts mixtures evaporated or metabolized, dissipated, Wendi would again be in full bloom! Yep!

Now, this was what it should have been like always, a park setting, Privacy, a 157-acre parcel with a renovated winery, and the largest safe house on the West coast of the USA. The only question was, what didn't it have? The amenities were 3rd to none, a definite 5-star retreat. Hell, some people would pay for a vacation at a location with less to offer.

I leaped out of the Olympic pool in one swift motion, nudging Kara by a dolphin's nose. Marshal Kara ascended the ladder passing many rungs. Kara was now my favorite Marshal. I trusted her to if 'push came to shove,' and she was forced to make a decision, she'd lay her life on the line for me… aah, Wendi! Of course, the swimming race was but a figment of my active imagination. I lay stiff but fully cogent on my fluffy white gurney-playing Ms. Comatose!

Two other Marshals were assigned to my protection detail, both of whom I was familiar with and who'd been at NIA. Yes, I enjoyed Marshals Rand and Burke. I'd heard the kids were en route, 'Juan and Leah.' Marshal Evan was the chaperone, another veteran of the FBI team. He was escorting my husband and parents here. I wondered how I was going to do playing Wendi. Would mom figure out that I'm now and forever going to be 'Sunshine!'

Rico is beside the pool speaking to Kara, 'look at freakin Jax, the guys insane!' Subtly turning only my squinted eyes, carefully I see Jax with his unbelievable body. His contortions are almost abnormal, with inhuman flexibility. He does a twisting triple back flip from the high dive board with barely a splash on the landing… like Crazy!

After checking on Wendi, Jax met with Doctor Hawkins. A planned checkup on her was later this afternoon; I listened to what I could hear. 'I was angry but hadn't decided what emotion to attribute… to or with the latest reports. Angst was assimilated differently by every human.'

I'm Sunshine, laying on a gurney, sunning myself by the pool, wishing I could jump in, but for now better to play the comatose Wendi. I found myself orbiting about that last thought about anger; back in Vancouver, Washington, Wendi had a dramatic situation that enabled me to come to the forefront of our minds. During this short interval, I picked up David's cell phone and read a text 'hey babe, that was fun last night. Can we do it again? Seeya later ☺ .' Anger did crawl spider-like up the nape of my muscled neck. Infuriated and boiling over then, I continued to scan David's cell phone while he was in the restroom. I found nude pictures of him in his Photo Gallery and one of Wendi's girlfriends. A fkn Skank! Anger morphs into aggravating outrage with temper exploding, wrathful hate, a convoluted affliction of distress &heartache, agony, ugh, blinds me, kill the betrayer. I wavered in informing dear sweet Wendi but nixed that idea. She was still on a slippery slope mentally.

Yes, with the word anger, there are many variables and degrees of emotional hostilities and resentments. For my rage was simmering because I couldn't stand Wendi's husband.

In my eyes, seeing from Wendi's… David had evolved into a selfish persona, a man of unwavering faith in himself. Construction manager A project manager who wore many hats, the latest head covering showed and proved that I was correct all along. He didn't deserve us. Most of the time, some forms of intimacy were impossible from the gurney, but David was a full-blown Hypocrite, hence the hat that fit him tightly! Yup! I'm sure his excuse for adulterous behavior would be that Wendi had been in and out of consciousness for months!

My snooping revealed that he's a ruthless adulterer-cheater Stop! Your curiosity should be peaked. How the hell did I have confirmation to add to the pictures? Well, it was gleaned from Jax. Who intercepted it from reports sent to Marshal Kara, an investigative report on David by the Fed's up in Washington… ugh, reports were being updated, and it was an active investigation… ongoing.

David was under the microscope and had been, unbeknownst to the fool as a rule of thumb, the Feds ran cross-checks and scrutinized anyone and everyone associated with Wendi. Using technology left no rocks or pebbles unturned, at least when it came to Rico's love for Wendi… lol.

The average time frame for scrutiny was approximately three months. David had easily passed the mustard each time… financial records, social media, phones, the days… and nights of surveillance following his tracks, and he was clean until he wasn't! Of course, I couldn't forward the cheating pictures; I was supposed to be in the background of Wendi's brain.

This sporadic surveillance was picked up again last week. Oh, how it was unfortunate for the crooked philandering cheat. David was tracked to a 5-story parking garage at the downtown Portland mall; no prob, right… wrong! The fool was filmed jumping into a Lexus sedan with a gorgeous Albino woman, a girl we had met in high school 'Sandi,' yes, the same girl in the photos I'd seen. My naïve counterpart's lifelong best friend, Sandi, was a 50/50 partner in our business 'Feral Feedback' animal training facilities: even going back to grammar school, they'd been inseparable. Fk, this was the first sighting of missing AWOL 'Sandi' in a couple of years. Yet there she was, a quick kiss observed, and she exited the parking garage with him.

They were tailed to a Public Storage, a commercial storage business, where David obviously had several units; he beckoned her to park. They climbed out of her Lexus, walking into a large, enclosed building and moments later pulling a trailer with two Sea Doo's, very expensive Bombardiers. A spanking, glisteningly new Lincoln Navigator had them in tow. Sandi then reparked her Lexus inside the storage building. The roll-up doors went the opposite way and locked. Another nauseating embrace on video with mischievous, naughty intent… off to the Oregon coast Gold's Beach, they both journeyed to… what a pair of grievous evil-doers.

Rico and Sunshine were melded inside the same storyline… it was the disdain for David that had colluded within… that made them unlikely allies. *"Rico, I've been talking to you; did you hear me?" "Gee, I'm sorry, Kara, I was just lost in thought regarding her husband. I wish I could take him back behind a barn and beat him senseless. I want you to pay special attention to David. I'm…" "Ok, but I was serious. I'm going to repeat it I am confident that I heard Jax speaking to Wendi as I opened the door and saw her drop her arm off his shoulder, then she went back into the coma state. I think she is pretending and faking it. I'm not imagining what I saw or heard. Wendi's face even like blushed, and Jax jumped and started rubbing her hand!" "Why, Kara, are you now just bringing this up?" "Can't answer that I didn't write it in my daily log either, didn't want to put it out on the airwaves, wanted to get you alone to discuss it, I suppose…." "What did you hear?" "Rico, that's where it gets tricky, um weird, her voice was raspy saying, 'honey, we need to escape this place, get away' really, I've replayed it several times, I'm sure now." "Escape, Wtf Kara? That doesn't make a lick of sense; why would she want to escape?"*

Alarms sound off… Someone is at the gates of the SafeWinery!

"Not bad, huh? Ugh, I'm a little out of practice," stood the dripping muscled man 'Jax' "not bad, my ass, that was a worthy Olympic dive Jax" exclaimed Kara. "Hey, look up at the monitors; it's Wendi's family pulling through the gates, can't wait to see Juan and Leah," shouted Jax, now towel in hands. "Yes, let us greet them," yelps Rico showing a skin-covering frowlish smirk that piece of shit, David, aah. Like he'd entered the Twilight Zone show, is anything as it appears, Stephen King would have a field day with this plot-suspenseful horror-laden novel with Dean Koontz and Dan Brown as Ghostwriters, lol. ☹ .

-60-

Joe and Sammy are up in Idaho.

Sammy hailed the car… It was akin to watching the boob tube TV, which my parents nor I seldom did, another cop show or a detective-type movie, um, 'follow that car, don't lose it!'

this was my words as I vaulted into the back of a 'Uber car' back seat in the old sitcoms it was always the 'Yellow Cab.'

Not long passed, and a private drive appeared off the main thoroughfare. All traffic was being monitored and re-diverted by serious-looking security guards. Not prototypical, holding up stop signs, like, at a closed railroad crossing, I had my driver veer off. It was the end of the line. Pissed and flustered, Joe was gone. So Fk it. I decided to do some exploring. What was I to do, sit on my hands? Nope, I said to my driver, 'drop me at a place where I can rent a cycle, aah motorcycle, please.'

Joe Sable is frantic.

He tapped away futilely before the towers would block all phone service at the conference. Joe had his phone off after making a concerted effort to keep Sammy abreast of what was happening… hoping she'd stay at their hotel.

Sammy is on Joe's wavelength.

I sent a text that I might regret, for he might interpret it as a sign of my weakness for him but tossed caution into the wind, 'I already miss you, Joe please call ASAP!'

Staying true to my words took Hwy 84 towards Arrowhead Reservoir as I'd told him. I veered off the road to a small café and parked my rented 2019 Harley Sportster to a kickstand stop. It was time for some country food and a small lunch; it was still a bit brisk; cool out 11:37 am ordered cheesy eggs raisin toast and some grits with a side of crisp bacon. Felt like a commodity being the only female in the café besides the gnarly server.

Staring at the torn-up asphalt outside my windowed booth, I saw the parking lot had nothing but pick-up trucks. Three horses tied up on a wooden pole that ran the length of the deck in front of the diner.

Eyeballs with mostly scruffy beards peered over at me as if I were a piece of raw Buffalo jerky, typical men, or I could be wrong guided by a learned perception from the cities ugh, city life, a used to be a Call Girl, Escort slash prostitute ughhhh sounds abhorrent. But it's the truth I can't hide from my inner self and outer being.

I certainly wasn't out to impress anyone. I essentially tried to portray a non-façade. I'm a straightforward 25year old woman who was very comfortable in her own skin. Yet despite my young life's experience, I remained tenderly open-minded, malleable, and plainspoken without prejudice, bias, or ill intent. Add that to the fact that I'm far from naïve or trusting. Nothing about the real me was artificial or insincere, 'what I said I meant. What you saw is what you got!'

About that time, interrupting my bite of grits was a sturdy Cowboy. His spurs hit the outside deck. He was all of 6'5" tall, not too thick, wiry, and lean, which was the best description I could muster. The guy had an old-school handlebar mustache, checkered red and white kerchief and a well-worn black Cowboy hat, and a brown suede jacket. A wannabe buckaroo cowman, a counterfeiter I deduced or deducted your preference, a poor example of a person trying too hard to blend into his environment… Chameleon, he wasn't!

All right, I'm bein a smidgeon too critical; he didn't have that mustache in the hotel's swimming pool nor later at the bar. However, it would be a worthwhile disguise if I were the costume designer. I wouldn't have put the dude in a brand-new, out-of-the-box pair of boots! His clothing shined of being never worn, all except the hat, that is. It boiled down as it always had. Was it a gift or a curse? A gift, in this case, my 'Eidetic memory' the guy was following me, and the vibes from his mannerisms were definitely on the negative side, so was the bulge of a shoulder holster… if he was an FBI Agent. Why not simply arrest me? 'Swat team surround the Diner?'

The fake cowboy went right to his smartphone, sitting across from me at the bar on a stool, ordering a tomato juice, glancing Eagle-eyed in my direction over a laminated menu.

Spooning in the last of the cheesy eggs with a sliver of raisin toast, umh, from the corner of my eye, I see him click off a picture of 'yours truly' this was my chance to cause a stir-scene; momma had taught me as a little girl never pass on an opportunity at destiny… before she passed me to the Nanny!

Demonstratively in a loud, high-pitched voice, 'hey, mister, can't a lady just have breakfast without being harassed? Why are you taking pictures of me? That's so damn Rude!' I did shout this for all to hear. The other 13 or so men stared, but it was the server who instigated the following action.

"What is wrong with you, dude? You can't just come in here and take pictures of our customers; you pervert, give me your Fkn phone!" The cooks now stood nearby then there were five real Cowboys. Unwisely I tossed down a twenty-dollar bill; well, that wasn't the unwise part of what I did. Next, I winked at him with a tongue display, and a well-deserved lopsided smirk-gotcha was the highlighted projection.

Swaying my petite ass right around and out of the crowd, who now had the invasive camera phone in their grasp… 'see ya wouldn't want to be yah!' yep!

<u>Joe Sable at the Militia conference.</u>

Joe was highly agitated and upset, like the last student sitting in class, trying to finish a final exam. Was I going to graduate or not? I couldn't focus, squeamish, fidgeting. The speaker in front of the podium had nothing to say that interested me. I wanted out of this situation now! I glanced at the program manual and took a double take. It wasn't her no-way. I'd seen the notorious woman's pictures and heard rumors that she still lived. The couple held hands on the stage, the former FBI Agent Julie Tiff and her sexy lovely wife, Sofie. Julie Tiff used to be one of Wendi Feral's bodyguards. She'd supposedly been eaten by alligators, ugh, died in a swamp back in Plant City, Florida.

Near panic encompassed my entirety, uh, sweat, BP um, heart rate skyrocketed, Sammy could already be dead… Mark didn't play around. He was a cutthroat. He would eliminate her from my life. Yeah, he called her a whore, and she was, but what he didn't respect was that Sam was my Whore!

The audience was doing a standing ovation, clapping as if in worship, with hard, sturdy eyes… predominately men. The attendees were armed to the hilt. Over 1,100 of the S.O.J. Militia were in this building, with others packed in like Sardines. I had to get the fk out of this compound… escape; no communication allowed, all blocked. What options did I have?

This event was for three days and nights, ending in concerts, fireworks, pig roasts, all kinds of outdoor activities, and competitions contests for Marksmanship, the most popular, as anyone would guess. I was one of the favorites to win that competition. I wasn't up for the obstacle courses this year, lost in my worried mind. I walked out the double doors and in the path of three older women, two of whom handled briefcases, nonchalant greeting as I fell in line behind them.

The sun was blazing its way through a team of conspiring clouds, the sound of a brook creek, water flowing around the next corner. I see a 3-story rock Elephantine-sized fountain of water streaming… that was splashing suds and spraying a fine mist.

Found a bench seat, and for a sec, it looked like I was back on the Las Vegas strip jets of the water played to the music, choreographed to perfection.

I dropped my chin, not so much in resigned defeat negative feelings that I've dealt with in my past, always of a depressive nature, wrongly thought perhaps I'd overcome the scars and would have grown out of these emotions as I aged. Free from incarceration, although they returned without recourse, so tuned into Prison, this time with no connections. Here I was again locked into a compound accustomed to being kept like a rodent caught in a maze. Rolling my head the same… different gun towers occupied the perimeter. They'd fire a lethal shot into your torso if you got out of line.

The numbers on my jacket, that's what we're relegated to, seats with numbers signs to events with numbers checked, mine was 1,711 in my front left breast pocket was the day's computer chipped card, admittance with a tracker to mandatory briefings 89% of all members of SOJ were military, ex, or currently enlisted professional soldiers.

"Joe Sable, I'll be damned. It's been like forever, wow!" I recognized the voice at once. It was Jaybird, a lifelong pal of Jax Fouls, two tours of duty in the Middle East, a fkn Warrior. No questions there. He would be in the final rounds next to me for the Marksman Golden Rifle trophy.

"How's Feral doing? You got something for me as I watch him clutch the heavy briefcase Lester and Rhonda gave me to deliver to him, smiling. "Thanks, Joe. I guess congratulations are in order for the both of you to move up into the top 10 of the FBI's most wanted list," he chuckled derisively.

"Jay, no reason to be sarcastic…" then, even feeling like I did, I chortled. "I know we failed to keep a low profile. I'm here by myself. Neither Mark nor Tank, who was just released, will be showing up here. How have you been, bro? Believe me; I wish we were invisible to the Feds."

He slanted his chin down, leaning over. "Joe, you need cosmetic surgeries like Mark's. It will take care of your worries with your ass here, it's a worry for our militia, but we will be all right, Joe. I'm glad you're here, bro. Hey, scoot over. I wanna talk to you!" I was a certified assassin with 19 kills in my military career, nothing like Jay. I couldn't hold his 'jock strap' around my waist. A pure novice compared to him and Jax, one of his closest cohorts, they were Navy Seals, Army Rangers, Special Ops, and on and on. I had nothing but respect for him, admired his tenacity and discipline and what he did to save Jax and the children at his ranch in Plant City against all odds the Feds and Cuban Mafia had him cornered in, remembered he served some Federal Prison time on that escapade.

He swivels his body towards me on the bench, eye to eye. "Joe, enough is enough. This vendetta, feud, or plain-ass revenge to kill Wendi Feral must cease immediately. It's an obsession that's caused more harm than it's worth. I waited for Mark to show up. He was the person I wanted to talk to about this. We don't condone his actions. I'm ordering you three to stop this now…." "But Jay, she is the culpable person who has sent us to prison three times hell, she was the reason that I went to Juvenile Hall at like 15 years old it…." "That's Bullshit, Joe, and your too smart to believe that crap. You see, this is where we part ways of thinking it's not her that sent you to jail. No, it is you; the three of you don't yuh get it!" I spun around, but he continued, "Joe, I would still be in Terminal Island Prison with Randy and Jax if not for Wendi's testimony hell, dude, don't you remember the Plant City, Fla debacle? Like Ruby Ridge, shootouts dozens died. It was a slaughter, in the end, we umh, Wendi saved like 17 innocent kids from certain servitude and death from the porn ring internationally thousands were indicted what you…." "Jay, she's a fkn curse talks to animals she's…." "No, Joe, she's a Savant, a Saint in my book. One of the primary reasons you are here… the orders from the top of the Food Chain is to leave Wendi Feral alone… or Else!"

Pervasive quiet engulfs the fountain ripples. I just couldn't go down that easy I wish Mark were here. He'd at least put up a worthy argument. "I'm a touch dogmatic dog with a bone, Jay. Wendi is working with the Feds; she's our enemy, believe me, there's…." "Subject is closed, not open to negotiations, Joe, and yes, she's under Federal protection at this time and subcontracts out jobs. Well, that's too much info for you. Suffice it to say that she and Jax are like teammates, aah, partners. Jax would die for her, last warning. I will be sending a memorandum with you to hand to Mark and will also have an emissary meet with Mark and Tank Enough! Now let's switch gears, okay? The local oddsmakers have you at a 7 to 5 favorite at the 700-yard targets; too bad Jax wasn't here. It's like, what three wins apiece for you and me? This will break the tie. But let me fill you in; we have some new young blood this year… hotshots!"

I figured, what the hell, it was worth a try. Nothing ventured, nothing gained right like seeing a cute or beautiful gal umh lady sitting alone at a bar and not approaching her. Yeah, you never know. "Jay, I need your help; I need to get out of here for a day, uhm, at least. Pal, it's a personal emergency, if you will, please, Jay." I never have or can't remember ever using 'please' before in my life.

Out the gates, the private drive was history. Jay had pulled the necessary strings… how I didn't care, I was driving a dark green Jeep. It's not what you know many times but whom!

He's given me 11 hours to secure Sammy and return to the SOJ conference. I heard some of the honorary attendants, including the Bundys who were just pardoned by President Trump… father and son 'The Hammonds' from Terminal Island prison, we're going to speak in a few hours… it would be a celebration for the ages, but nothing clogged my mind except Sammy. I had told Jay I didn't need 11 hours, only a few, but he said that's the next time you will be required to be present.

I punched on my Tracfone and saw a text 'I already miss you, Joe, please call ASAP' I did, so there was no answer. First, stop the hotel, then remembered her infantile rant blurting out about renting a scooter and going for a ride out to a Dam on Hwy 84 or something!

FBI Director Tanya Firm and Agent Kelsey Marie in Idaho.

Tanya blew her cheeks up, flabbergasted at a report on her encrypted phone. It's unfathomable, thinking back didn't the DNA evidence show that Agent Julie Tiff had died in the swamp during the Plant City, Florida siege? I got to put her on the back burner for now but looked forward to throwing the handcuffs on that two-faced Snake.

'Listen up,' said Tanya, with Agents Kelsey Marie, Rodriguez… Baker, Beverly, and Tuft listening, "we're working with another 11 Agents in the field. 'Our informant inside SOJ' has sent news that Joe Sable has left the compound in a green Jeep Comanche 2017. Air surveillance shows him entering Boise City limits at Mountain View Drive and Geyser Road. Pick him up there, stay back, don't let him 'make' us is that clear?"

Tanya takes Kelsey by the arm leading her out of earshot. "Kelsey, your my lead Agent on the ground here. Word has it that Mark Feral will not attend this conference, and agents Lori Parks and Bill Avery are canvasing Tank. So Joe is here on his lonesome.

He most likely will lead us to Samantha Timmons. We want both of them, alive if possible, well, at least Samantha. FK shoot to Kill Joe if he's the least bit aggressive or pulls a weapon out." Kelsey grimaced, rubbing the place near her sternum where Joe had fired the shot, a 50 Caliber projectile. Without the Kevlar, she and Rodriguez would be dead and buried. She had a score to settle with Joe Sable… no worries, he wouldn't be seeing a jail cell, lol.

"Yes, ma'am Tanya" "shit Kelsey, how many times have I told you to drop the fkn ma'am crap!" "Okay, Tanya, if I get the chance, I will shoot Joe to smithereens!" Tanya spun back. "I didn't hear that, Kelsey," leaving her with a pleasant nod.

The radio squawked, 'Tanya, he is at the Marriot downtown. Just pulled into the parking lot' 'Great, have someone check out the front desk and show pictures to the staff of the Timmons girl!' 'sure thing. Should we take him down there?' 'Absolutely not; we will surround him in a less public place, he will not escape us… I want the girl as well!'

<u>Mark, restrained, awakes in hysteria… cabin fever, 'Joy' with a razor-sharp scalpel in her hand, the other squeezing and grasping his penis… growling and purring at the same time…molesting him.</u> 🙁 .

Joy was humming a tune while I fought fruitlessly tethered to my own contraption, spread Eagle naked she was grinning. "I'm nurse Joy, boy; you keep going unconscious on me," slapping him across his face, laughing. In Joy's other hand was a glistening stainless-steel scalpel… he faked fading out again.

Mark squints his eyes, trying not to let Joy know he is conscious sees his reflection in the ceiling mirror's legs spread in stirrups. What was happening? Three reoccurring questions why… who… and where? He felt paralyzed, unable to move.

<u>Mark snapped out of his imagination; no longer did Joy engulf his being… his eyelids had been closed all along.</u> His skull no longer pulsated, now only a periodic thudding… then flashed out, revisiting my reality. The fantasy of the concussive state I was still tied up, hands behind my back, feet bound, tight noose rubbing around my neck, blindfold covering my

eyes. The blood might have coagulated not entirely sure. The head wound needed triple-layered stitches. No doubt there, bits and pieces kept floating by my closed eyes after the moronic Joy escapade! Not sure to take anything seriously anymore. Drifting in and out of this nightmarish state, not going to put much credence into the imagination of my warped mind, ahh, not more than a grain of salt that didn't make sense, oh well... understandably, I had a massive concussion.

I was sure that I was captive in my cabin, and if my recollections are correct, there were three vehicles other than mine, the group of rednecks thugs at the gas station with the two hippy women, so seven of them in total.

Having sustained severe head trauma and blacking out, I was unsure how many times and how long I had been tied up. Then it struck me that I was alone unless I had earmuffs on, no music, no words were spoken, and not a snore could be heard. I started a low growl. My mouth was also wrapped in duct tape, but I could hear my muffled moans... ears. 'A-Okay,' no one said a word in reply. Did they leave me to die tied up? The irony wasn't lost on my discombobulated mind, thinking of the Attorneys that had been in dire conditions within their own coffins or the dozens of women I'd captured and tethered to my stirrups. Oddly, Mark grasped the Absurdity with acceptance, peace, and tranquility, Karma-laden. Sure, why not 'what goes around cums around?' Now he had to alter fate.

I cussed with a mumble aah fk what a fix I find myself in feelin', not a blink. Sorry for me, no pure stupidity to let those hicks get the drop on me, uhm, upper hand, ughhhh, I'm truly losing my edge.

I will kill them all rather slowly, pushing my fingers through the thick rope that binds my wrists. I do have to give the yokels credit for skillful knots, for the more I fight to free my hands, the tighter they're bound!

Sounds come rushing forward suddenly, helicopter in the air, dogs barking my dogs, a low-flying airplane. Jolting me were claws, oh fk, something clenched my bare thighs, taking the skin off 'help me,' not whimpering, 'help me please' wtf? Moaning, I blacked out again.

FBI agents Lori Parks, Bill Avery, and Tank Shaw.

Parked at a pullout by a Mini-Mart were Agent Avery and Lori; with all her pleading for backup… she got three Deputies and some 4-wheel Quad motorcycles to ride back into the smoking woods, lucky that one of the officers was a trainee and a canine handler.

Staring at the iPad's screen, Tank was 5,557 feet to the Northeast, moving slowly on foot a little more than a mile away. Visibility was reduced by smoke and ash, with hot embers floating in the breeze. A permanent haze with stifling humidity; maybe you could see about 50 yards out, and we could see bright-colored red and yellow firefighters battling small fires burning everywhere.

Lori was still feeling the effects of food poisoning. She self-diagnosed this malady, gazing out, thinking fires are inherently unforgiving, a force to be reckoned with wherever the wind blows, the fire travels. Finding the best path that fuels the combustion of the flame, the last report from the Fire Marshal said the 'Hat Fire' was 3.5 miles Southwest from where they followed Tanks… GPS chip, but that could change in a split second.

"Agent Parks," says a young female Deputy, "nice to meet you. I have studied some of your cases online. Your sort of becoming a legend." Lori barely kept a composed expression 'this one was blowing smoke up my ass right out the gate,' shaking her head and raising her brows-checks the name tag 'Heather.' "Deputy, are you familiar with this area?" "Yes, ma'am" "come with me then, Heather." Over the hood of a Ford Bronco was agent Bill Avery a map sprawled out under his hands.

I kept my eyes on the monitor that was tracking Tank's direction. "So Heather, where could our Perp be going out there?" Avery had used a bright yellow highlighter to trail Tank's path, pointing then looked up at the Deputy, noticing her jagged features, short hair, and lean body, surmising at once he wasn't her preferred sex. Heather was intent on enjoying her own gender; Lori had concluded this same fact while feeling the girl's attraction toward her. Heather was a boyish girl, a Tomboy with decent looks; I bet she had no trouble with the women. Heather leaned over the map for some time, only staring.

Avery dismissed the youngster's proclivities; Law Enforcement was filled to the brim with dominant women. They were a necessity; he repeated Lori's question. "Heather, what's out there? Where could the perp be going? We have no way for air support, and the map shows nothing but forest!"

-61-

Tank is on his way to Mark's cabin.

I was paying strict attention to a scanner lodged inside one of my backpack sleeves... coordinating the reported fire's direction with my interactive map on my phone, aware of where the fire fronts were last reported and the near unpredictable path of the inferno. I took each step with apprehension. The smoke had lessened, thankfully. Gosh, I didn't want to be here but stopped pouting; Whitney was where I wanted to be. She was a woman who mesmerized and energized me.

The phone towers were still down in the Mendocino area that Whitney was in... my last five attempts were feeble, although I tapped out texts that would linger in the phone world's abyss. They would be sent once a signal was provided.

Glad that I had not only my phone flashlight app but a heavy-duty flashlight, for soon it would be necessary; hell, even at 2:57 pm, the sun was blocked out.

Mark's cabin was no longer on my screen; the satellite connection was unreachable, off and on, disabled because of the thick haze, I supposed. I used Google Earth, the hi-Jacked military version accessed on the other Web browser Tor. The

Dark Web was a contrarian description, for I saw the Dark Web as the 'Enlightened Web.'

But unfortunately, it was a hit or miss, but what always worked was my compass old school for sure, steady without the bells or whistles.

I was closing in on Mark's cabin… besides a long sharp Bowie knife and steel flashlight. I had zero weapons. I wondered why this entered my mind. I shouldn't need any, now just under a mile to go. The smoke-layered oxygen was akin to sweating in a sauna mixed with a steam room; I was starving for fresh air.

Tank found a rounded-off stump, sat down in the forest to take a small break, pulled a bottle of water out after a few minutes of anxiousness, and rubbed the soot from his eyelids. Sitting there sweating, I realized that if it were only a day before, this area would be teaming with animals could have been a serene experience out here in the wilderness. The sun would be shining, birds singing… That's when the woods came alive, Deer passing by. In my peripheral vision, I saw some rodents running away from the direction I was traveling… there were hordes of birds flying low to the ground right past me.

Then suddenly, the animals had shifted directions. It appeared to me they were in an exodus moving rapidly, umh, fortunately-relieved to see now… in my direction. I was walking a fire line break utility road, Palmetto Palms, and various shrubs with predominantly Pine Trees growing everywhere. The ground was reddish brown; insects were out in force, that's why I got up and started back, moving onward. The Deer Flies swarmed me; Mosquitos voraciously sought out sustenance, damn bloodsuckers.

I took another moment to spray the chemical aerosol pressurized can of 'Off' over my body, wondering if these insects ever built up a tolerance to the stuff. Hopefully, it kept them at bay.

For a second, I was back in my prison cell and recalled a book I'd read; the title was something like 'The Hundred Year Lie.' According to the author. I was plainly abusing my body, polluting it with chemicals that synergistically were destroying my health, like a slow ticking fuse of a time bomb. Oh well, what was worse? If I didn't use the chemical spray, I'd be lunch for bugs. I opted for saturating my skin, uh, chose the longer suffering installment plan.

I flipped my portable scanner to roam; the chatter was lively and fire related, then a haggish voice of what I imagined was an older woman who'd done her fair share of tobacco… raspy but clear. Channel 15 'breaker one-five anyone out there with their ears on? Police action in my area Law Enforcement on Quads just passed my 4-wheeler heading out on BLM road 'FT-25.'… over.'

A penetrating left jab to my testicles no shit yanked up the interactive map; that's where I'd seen 'FT-25' before. It's exactly where my ass was. Rationalizing this did no good… logic was quantifiable; it couldn't be anything to do with me, right? Being a criminal leads to paranoia, so my next decision was obvious 'breaker 1-5. I got a copy. I'm near BLM road 'FT-25' you said police action. You mean Forest Rangers?... over' 'yeah, this is 'Big Shan' here. Haven't heard you on here before!... over.' 'Rebel' here,' I said, just heading out to check on a buddy's cabin 'Big Shan'… over.' 'Be careful out there, Rebel. The fire can switch up on you in a heartbeat; I'm at the pullout. Whoa, wait, something serious is going on. There are Sheriff's cars and locals a Canine Unit and looks to be two Government vehicles white with roll-cages for prisoners, maybe the Feds… over!' 'Uuhhh, Big Shan, thanks 10-4. You be careful too… over!'

<u>Trailing Tank…</u>

Agent Bill Avery holds up his right arm and yells, "stop!" 'Maverick,' a German Shepard hops off the back rack of Heathers Quad, and they roll to a stop. "He has stopped moving." Motors shut down. Avery gives Lori the monitor with Heather peering over their shoulders and shakes her head "there's nothing there, no cabin… just woods. He's in the middle of the forest on a BLM road, just woods all around him."

Lori stares at the iPad screen, happy that the fire still did not affect their satellite hookup. "He's not far even though we are just Putting along. We have cut two-thirds of the distance between him and us; it shows he's only 300 yards at most, right down this path!

All right, we have to leave the Quads here and go on foot, no noise. Grab your backpacks and weapons. He'll hear these motorcycles coming, can't afford for him to be alerted that we're on his tail."

<u>Tank trudges onward.</u>

Was my mind playing tricks, psychosomatically like when a person yawns and you do the same, someone starts to itch their skin violently you itch, suggestive thoughts like a contagion, the insinuation of motorcycles, Quads from 'Big Shan' racked my ears, and I heard one revving its motor. Then ceased sounding off, just down the trail behind me.

Up to this point, what was I to fear? I'd done my due diligence and had called my probation woman said on the recording that I was going to help fire victims in Mendocino County and would have my phone on. Sure, I was in a different county now, but as far as anyone could deduce, I still was where fires were burning. Trying to help out fire victims, so half my story would check out. Bringing my soot-laced palm to my forehead, standing as still as I could, and listened for the motorcycles that were seen on the same BLM road I was on. 'Why would the cops be on this same dirt trail in the middle of Bum Fk Egypt? Whatever, I'm definitely positive without reservations that I wasn't followed out here on my drive from Mendocino County and my future lover Whitney.

So with that conclusion, I decided to take a bird's path towards Mark's cabin, get off the trail, then pick back up on 'FT-25', which passed directly in front of the cabin; slow and methodically, I moved out; I don't believe in coincidence!

Fifteen minutes later, cutting through thick brush and circling a pond, I finally got my first view of the cabin. I was on the backside. I predicted finding Mark engaged with people of the female persuasion and an ongoing party. I'd check in with him, drink a few brews, talk over some of the past war stories, um memories 'shoot the shit,' then bid him farewell, later, back to my girl in Mendocino; man, could I be so lucky?

As I moved in closer, there were no more quad sounds. I shirked it off as pure paranoia; cops were on another mission. How could it possibly be something involving me? Now walking upright, following the Hog wire fencing line parallel to the side of the domicile saw two older pickup trucks and an old hippy bus. Sure enough, Mark's Dodge parked next to his trailer, which was backed inside a barn. His Pitbulls started to howl and bark. Alarms sounded, and soon the front door would open; tentatively, I crotched down; something felt wholly wrong. It was dusk-like dark, and no lights were on in the cabin nor porch, and no noise either. Where was everybody at?

FBI and locals.

Staying behind Tank at approximately 155 yards was Lori's team, pondering over what they could charge him with. He was out of his jurisdiction, mandated by his parole, so that offense was good for one warrant. And he was the last person at the motorhome site, which exploded right after he left it. We also have video and pictures of him meeting at the restaurant with a known wanted felon Joe Sable which was enough to make an arrest.

Lori shook her head. The more she thought about how disrespectful Tanya had been towards her, the more she disliked the winch. Director Tanya Firm had ordered Lori in their last conversation to only observe Tank, saying, 'don't screw this up, Lori. He was foolish enough to be used as bait to lead us to Mark and Joe. Stay out of sight if you locate the whereabouts of Mark Feral; if Tank leads you to him, we'll bring in reinforcement. Do not engage him. I repeat, Lori, we do this by the book!'

Lori thought, truth be told, even if we arrested Tank, he would only receive a violation and maybe another 18 months in prison for absconding from his designated boundary. We could try and make a case for the motorhome circumstantially, but we have no proof, ahh, and 18 months in prison for Tank would be like a damn vacation for the institutionalized fool.

The Canine officer Heather pulled the leash back as Maverick's ears went fully erect, pointing high. We walked closer to where Tank had stopped once again and heard other dogs barking. Lori sent Avery forward with a pair of night vision binoculars that should be able to pick him out of the dissipating smoke of afternoon light and told him to get as close as he could without making any noise.

Heather came up on my side, "there's a hunting cabin on the other side of the tree line, just seasonal though, ma'am. Um, there's a smattering of encampments out here in the wilderness, kinda escape the city life, you know." With a half whisper, she asks, "do you want me to direct the other Deputies?" Lori shook her head no, assessing her haphazardly splotched-together squad. The Deputies looked in decent shape in their early 20s, maybe right out of the academy. Her team, besides agent Bill Avery included two male deputies and Heather; she didn't bother with introductions. But now she reigned them in, waving towards them to come closer. "I'm Agent Lori Parks, FBI; we're tracking a dangerous convict on Parole, hoping he leads us to other cohorts, uhm, members of his gang. Under no circumstances do you pull out your weapons unless I've ordered you to do so. There will be… No Gung-ho bullshit on my watch, no Superhero stuff. Do you understand me? Do you get my drift." Nods of acquiescence, she continues, "we're here to observe only." Pulling out of her pack three radios with earbuds. "Here, this is how we're going to communicate the radios are set to our proprietary channel." Pointing to each one of them, "we're going to use your last name initials." Staring at the nameplates on their uniforms, 'Simpson so your S-1' on the radio…." Suddenly Avery appears. "Lori, there are four vehicles at the cabin, and a pole barn, and a lean-to garage. I saw no movement other than some dogs. Tank is at the fence line but hasn't entered the property…." "Were you able to make out any license plates, Bill?" "Not a chance, still too much smoke." "Okay," she orders, "spread out along the fence line, stay apart about 75 yards and be quiet. If you see anything whisper into the mic. Let's go; remember, keep your weapons holstered!"

<u>Anita Sparks and Rascal Savage are surveilling Wendi Feral at the SafeWinery. After some delectable lovin…</u> ☺.

Her left palm nestled snugly between his thighs, ahh, felt so natural to him, like it had always been meant to be. 'Linus with his favorite blanket from Charlie Brown' her warm body in a fetal puzzle, skin on skin, morning sex was the best 'Cat's Meow.' Awake, and yet Rascal laid still in contemplation. Not wanting to disturb his lover and best friend, his acknowledged and accepted soulmate… grinned. Yes, soulmate, what a Farce… oh well.

Rascal wondered, trying not to disturb her, was this just another form of devotion of his munificent love toward her, uh, or just a lustful addiction? He went with it because it felt right, sharing a bond without hesitation with her. This was going to be a special day… let her sleep.

Doctor Anita Sparks held her man from the backside, breasts pushed up by his muscled back. His breathing had changed. He still fascinated her like bewitchment; curiosity had led her to his bed 13 years ago; no, it had been like almost 15 yrs. The man was luscious, confident, and handsome, still the big stud on campus.

At first, she played the game of seduction a bit 'hard' to get as her mother had taught. Her mama had instilled in her the ways of a woman first beguile him. Play it teasingly, be flirtatious, then step back once you have him hooked. Mother would be proud, for I was a 'chip off the old block.' Call it like it was. I'm a cunningly crafty woman fully aware of what he desired, like any testosteroned guy. She grinned 'but momma, what of lust-passion and love?' Oh, momma, you didn't teach me about men like him. No, she'd said your way too young to settle down to get caught, play the game of love and sex, but keep your heart preserved, embalmed! Momma and I were like girlfriends, so close in age, we could talk about anything. I love Mom, and I love this fkn, man!

Momma's rules were simplistic men wanted one thing. They sought you like prey, search and destroy not all men; paradoxically, there were a few that were more womanly than manly. She'd taught Anita how to play the Damsel, not in distress, coy flirtatious, always in control. Don't be reeled into the boat unless he has a well-managed dowry and has the means to support your dreams and aspirations. Umh, Mama, I did that...Yep!

She squeezed her thighs tightly together, Ohyeah the first time with him until the last minutes ago were etched forever in her body, brain... her skin was still on fire. Body exalting all the proper murmurs sounds naturally purred, oouhhs, moans-gyrations a porn goddess had nothing on her, it wasn't like... not so many before. Being a female had significant advantages to fake orgasms. Oh no, he was killin' it. Ecstasy on display, an academy award of titillating pleasure, he fired off his load, my vagina engulfed his throbbing member pulsating with quivering twitches... 'curtains closing applause, please!' ☺ .

Omigod, then it happened never ever like before was it a biological miracle, phenomenon half wilted, flaccid... suddenly empowered, re-submerged swelling up like a re-inflating innertube, what just happened 'omsexLord' dynamics of his love feast altered. Like a slow burn with a lotta friction that lit the kindling combustion, the fire caught. No more Pantomiming or acting. I was panting like a 'kitty kat' in heat, burning in my loins, raged my body rocking bucking like a Rodeo bull smitten. This dude was For Real... no acting needed. This was insane. My heart and body were his... Damn!

After that past Loving session, I'd wanted and needed him and didn't quite love him yet, but it was closing in on my weakened resolve. Then Rascal disappeared for over a week. Another passed by without incident, then another. He didn't beckon me back to his bed the gall of him. The dude was concentrating, sitting at his desk the next time alone with him after he'd returned from a trip to Mexico. 'Momma would be upset' it was he who played the 'hard' to get guy. I broke weak and approached him with brows raised. He had a well-deserved smirk on his face as he shoved his rollin chair back and unzipped his pants, saying, "Anita, I'm stressed out; a little head is what the doctor calls for. Suck my cock off." 'Wtf, I retorted, I ain't no Monica Lewinski; we both laughed as I found a cushion for my knees… why not? His moaning words still could be found in my frontal lobe "ohhh Doctor Sparks, ugh, just what my doctor ordered, um, called for. Yesss!" yup, Yum.

Seven months later, after our many 'nightstands' without words spoken one morning, an understanding of beating hearts and inner spirits collided, then colluded tangible impact. We'd been 1-one since then, inseparable.

"Sweetheart, I feel your heart beating faster, breathing more rapidly. Are you all right?" "Babydoll as he swiveled around the puzzle piece in place, slow grind just thinking while he thrusts inside, let's do this, let go, squeeze me tight. Forget everything… go blank; just be in the moment for a few minutes. I was already there! I thought, wasn't he supposed to be the Toaster and I the Oven… a riveting display of orgasms HellYeah!

Some 95 minutes later, showered, and fed, satiated, I sat next to him, fk I loved this man, but he wouldn't take the hint, Marry me, so I'd ask him. I decided what the heck. Despite him looking like he was in his deadly business mode, his persona morphed like the teeth of a White Shark jutting out or a pet Piranha, mutating into a daringly humongous WereWolf. I tabled that request not the time, for his fiendish countenance was en vogue.

<u>Rascal and Anita plan to cater the celebration at the SafeWinery.</u>

Inside the 45-foot motorhome was our tactical team, compadres of Rascals since the dirt sewer-laden roads of his Mexican village brought them together for survival. They sat on a pullout couch, Hugo, Jose, and Miguel with the Garcia brothers and who had survived from the Santos clan. We had nine, including him and me, with some subcontractors joining us in six hours provided to us by El-Chapo himself... Rascal, my man, was in charge.

The now 17-million-dollar reward was almost securely held in Rascal and my account, hopefully soon to be just one account 😊. 'Wendi/Sunshine' would be ours soon enough, and nothing would hamper or stop us this time. We'd deliver her ass to Mexico City... it wasn't an option.

For a 3rd time, I listened to Rascal's repetitive orders. Just 25 miles away was the safehouse winery. One of the back gate guards was part of our crew. Bent into our powerful demands under control, it was for money, of course, today we were informed by our 'insider' that a reunion party was to be held in the banquet room. Not only were Wendi's parents and husband going to be there, but so were Leah and Juan, whom Jax and Wendi had rescued, um, saved. Amazingly we'd also collect the reward for killing our Arch enemy Rico Captor for he was going to attend this luncheon with fellow Marshals and staff. On the banquet menu was, of course, Mexican cuisine, and Rascal and I were set up to be the Caterers! Not only would we supply the food, but drinks as well. Our bartender would be busy, lol; some would prefer wine over Margaritas; we had beer on ice. The food and beverages were heavily laced with superheavy duty barbiturates, potent sedatives that could knock out Tyrannosaurus Rex. We'd hope not to have to kill many of them, but oh well, whatever, we'd snatch up Wendi and Jax and, hopefully, the children for leverage, take Rico's head with us out the back gate we would go... done deal $$$!

-62-

Walter and Terrance, NIA.

"How long have you worked for me, ahh, with me, Walter?" "Boss, ever since I was dishonorably discharged from the military, sir." "That's what I've always enjoyed about you, your modesty. Weren't you special Ops, a Navy Seal instructor

Walter?" "Umh well yes sir, you know boss I'm…." "Walter, I've selected some of our finest mercenaries from NIAs superior forces, a total of only seven. That's all we will need for this operation, of course, with the inclusion of the Marshals as our insiders that are reaping big paychecks." "Yeah, it's nice to have Marshal Evans back… he's just now leaving the Sacramento Airport with Wendi's parents and the teenagers, sir." "Yup, we already have Marshal Burke and Marshal Rand inside the property where Wendi is being kept, part of the trusted security force for the Fed's safehouse winery." "Yeah, sir, not bad we control three of the four Marshals at the site. We will have to disable the FBI agents that man the gates. Ugh… I like our odds, sir, but you know we have to deal with the other regular guards that patrol the winery; uh, no worries." "This is true, Walter, but they've become lackadaisical, shit they won't know what hit them; it's Marshal Kara that could be trouble…." "No, boss, she'll go down without much trouble. She will be freaked out, probably frozen in place. The woman has never been in a battle. She's just a glorified housewife as far as I'm concerned! You know Terrance, she is ugh or was lol an arrogant bitch, sir!"

Terrance bowed his chin "yeah, unfortunately, Jax will not be of any assistance. He was not a team player in this operation; he would fight this maneuver tooth and nail. But his loyalty is unmatched. After we secure Wendi, he'll concur with our necessary actions. Make sure he's not harmed. Shoot him with only one dart. Is that understood, Walter? Jax is a team player, essential to us and our Militia!" "True boss Jax is a selfless man of integrity who cares about one thing in his life, and you know that's Wendi. He revolves, uhm, orbits like a solar system with an undeterred yoke ah, gravitational pull aligned his lifeline to Wendi/Sunshine Feral. The guy would gladly die many horrifying deaths to protect her… tethered to her soul, no doubts." Terrance oddly stares back at Walter "geez, I never thought you had that kind of vocabulary, Walter? You're a real thinker, huh?" He grinned back "no, boss, I'm no dummy. I play one, though, you know this, or you wouldn't have hired me to be in Charge of Security here at NIA. I play the unassuming uh, narrative like that old detective TV show 'Columbo' yes…." Amusing grins, Lol, they cackle.

Their eyes go back to the screens before them, in silence for a smattering of moments then Terrance's countenance fails him. Walter notices his sideways-lopsided Frowl, with hints of smirkish overtones knowing him well, he blurts out. "What's up, boss?" "Ahh, you know me too well, my man; I've changed it up a tiny bit. Your assassins will fire sound-suppressed 'silencers' 45 Caliber bullets to kill Rico, that bitch doctor Hawkins, and the nurse Jack, leaving a couple of shots for Marshal Kara. The rest of our team will be firing sleeping darts at all others in the banquet hall. We're only going to tranquilize Wendi and Jax. They will be brought back here to NIA." He slips his right fist up for a bump. "We will keep Wendi permanently; she will reside in the basement dungeon." Terrance pauses for effect and to gauge Walter's mindset, then continues uninterrupted.

"Jax won't like it, but he will get with it after a while. He's a soldier, and I think we will limit his freedom to roam about for a short period of time; he's becoming a bit too freewheeling. He was overheard mumbling something about a vacation. Can you fkn believe that… a vacation! There are no vacations, not while he works for NIA damn, uh hell. He's been on a permanent vacation, ugh…." "Boss, whoa, wait a second; Jax is our General. He leads all insurrection operations. I don't think it would be good alienating him in a negative…." Walter's BP skyrocketed; if Terrance would turn on Jax that easily, 'then what was he comparatively huh, a piddly subservient sap' perplexed at Terrance's egotistical rant, darn he admitted to admiring Jax's character, he was a man's man.

Terrance continued his monologue unbeknownst to the change in Walter's attitude, "we then will control Wendi, and her alter ego Sunshine, who is the true protagonist. I'll tell you, Walter, that woman is like a superhero. Jax will either see it our way, or he will be our slave without questions. He'll do our bidding, for we'll have the leverage of shackling Wendi; Jax will never fail us." Terrance starts to chortle, then cackles into an unharmonious wave of hilarity, choking on his own oxygen.' *Walter didn't smile. He sat back with a silent gasp, then overwhelmed and angrily barked. "What, you must be kidding me…" ' using his first name without a sir' "Terrance, you can't do that shit. That would kill morale. Jax is hero-worshipped here. You're making a grave mistake, in my…." "Yes, I can and will; it's already in place!" "Then I want nothing to do with it. I'm not going to be part of this. I…." "Too bad Walter, your 'In like Flynn' this isn't a situation where I ask your permission. Need I remind you of your wife and children? What a lovely family you still have!"*

Words left in silence, meanings not misconstrued, no quarrel or retort, words departed aligning with despots, a sneer intact, unwaveringly sinister. Iron curtain reticence clutched Walter's carotid artery. He tries to stand from the adjoining table's abyss, teetering seesaw, like dizzy, like hopping off of a 'tilt-a-whirl' at a carnival.

He was in a quagmire but shook it off with unrelenting resolve to not show fear or aggressive reprisals. "What about Wendi's parents, husband, and the two innocent children? What of them and the bystanders? How could you be so callus and cold, ugh, inhumane? You can take Wendi and Jax anytime; why do it with this dramatic flair? I get it when it comes to Rico and his people, but…." "It's already a done deal, Walter…." "Who are you? What have you become? Why the fk? I've really never known you, Terrance!" Then Walter ceased to speak, stopping with his foot already lodged halfway in his mouth. He better shut up. Was he losing his temper and mind? "Walter, it's up to you, guy; I placed my cards upright on the table. You have options either fold and face the consequences or get back in the game, dude. No worries either way, you're either going to be loyal to me, or are you going to be subterfuge?"

Walter didn't want to be part of this anymore, thinking how much his life had dived down into a cesspool in less than three minutes, a 360-degree spin. How much Joy it would bring him to plunge a dagger into this guy's black heartless soul!... he remained mute.

"Walter, whoever gets in our way, we will vanquish, slaughter; actually, it's time for you to sit back down; you're not going anywhere, uh, not till the vans are loaded. Hey, you'll like this twist. In order to make this attack and kidnapping more authentic, I have ordered all three Marshals… shot dead Burke, Rand, and the new one, Kara. Only Evans will survive!" His head of security shrank back down into his uncomfortable recliner. Muttering, "but Burke and Rand are on our payroll Terrance; how could you…." Terrance winked. Yup! ☹ .

"Timing is everything, my friend. Today is the bi-monthly scheduled maintenance for the Fed's Safehouse Winery. It is when the landscapers enter the front gates. Like has always been the case since Marshal Burke was transferred over, he'll let our crew into the gates. A banquet is planned in the 'Champagne Room' during this eat-fest. We will be mowing the grass and weed-eating our way to dessert. Kill em all, lol. Bag up Lil Ms. Wendi/Sunshine and Jax and bang out of the safehouse winery gate; they'll go right back here and directly into our dungeon." He laughed again, patting Walter on the back, "talk about a mission impossible, huh? I'm brilliant, aren't I?" Terrance sipped his iced tea.

"My associates will be thrilled NIA's power force will be re-enhanced, we have a difficult operation, a mission we need Wendi for. She will solve this issue for us. You have been brought up to speed, Walter, on the Canadian heist in three weeks, right? Walter only nodded "now get the fk out of here, make me proud, don't fail me or us… your everything is riding on it!"

<u>Earlier, Jax and Sunshine were at the SafeWinery.</u>

What a pleasant shift… our total environment had changed; I watched Jax take in the new view, an upgrade, no question. Over a dozen tables matching chairs with cushions, the atrium was covered with latticework. Ivy took to the openings grasping the 3 x 7-foot sections. The sun broke through like a checkerboard across the terra-cotta tiles.

His scarred, handsome face showed appreciation as he ventured to say, "Sunshine, wow, this is a far cry from NIA. Huh, geez, just your room is like five times larger. We went from the cellar to the penthouse… girl!"

I didn't want to burst his bubble, but I did anyway because he was second place in the scheme of things, sure I loved Jax, but I loved me much more! "Jax, I'm tired of the game. As contrary as this may sound, I'm exhausted with this coma bullshit. This fkn wheelchair the Whole Enchilada façade. Like that old slogan from the 70s, 'I am… woman, hear me roar!' it's time for me to jump outta the closet for good. I'm alive; let good ole Doctor Hawkins know I will be ready for the greet and meet. I can't wait to visit with Wendi's mom!"

"Sunshine, what would that achieve? Where is the positive?" "I can't believe you even said that… you profess your undying love for me. What, do you want me to play the vegetable slug ugh victim forever shit, Jax? As I told you, the 'Cat is out of the bag.' Kara saw us at NIA, and she heard us talking. I'm certain of that, dude!" "You have your parents with your husband in tow an hour out. Juan and Leah are with them. Why make waves now, woman?"

"Because Lil sista Wendi had her chance at this life, and she screwed up. Only the Strong Survive, Walla, and I'm much more dominant than my counterpart, don't you agree, Jax baby, dontcha want me?" "of course, Sun, but…." "Then all I need to remain with you as Sunshine is Doctor Honcho's psychotropic medications; right now, I've got a three-month supply stockpiled. If you want us to be always in control, all you need to do is keep me supplied, and Wendi will forever be in the past!"

Jax was experiencing a glutton of complex emotions. Sure, he loved the courageous-strong, assertive Sunshine. Still, he also was enamored and in love with the sweeter other side of the dual personality, ladylike Wendi. He adored her sentimental heart, not hiding anything, her unadulterated emotions worn on her sleeve, and her sense of humor to die for. What you saw is precisely what you got. Wendi was a Goddess like Saintly, empathetic with an aura of integrity opposite in many ways to the abrasive traits of Sunshine, and he was seriously in pain and convoluted. He wouldn't tell her, but his preference is Wendi.

"Geez fool, I see your face working in and out of confusion, dude man, oh ok, damnit all right, okay, Jax, I'll do my best to play-act being Wendi. For heaven's sake, I've got enough practice listening to her drone on. Got her act down!" He placed his fist out, and they bumped in agreement better than the old school high five.

Jax sat by her side; no matter how long he was around her, he'd never get used to how animals had a 7th sense about her… in the 15 minutes they were out inside the outdoor atrium, animals would pop up and appear. A diverse crowd was comingling, a cute three-some of baby Squirrels with mom. Hummingbird feeders were left vacant as they swarmed around Sunshine; out of nowhere, a yellow Tiger-striped Tabby cat leaped onto her lap, purring freakishly so damn loud, sounding more like a man's-tired snore!

Sunshine spent time petting and conversing with her newfound friends, all without ulterior motives, unlike the human varieties. "Gotta tell you I'm hearing and seeing some bad signals, uhm, signs from the animals. I'm told it smells like danger, warnings, not anything definitive, though!" "What are you saying, huh I…." "It's not what I'm saying. It's what they're telling me; beware, something is wrong here. Listen, animals have an innate sense of when tragedy is about to strike; think about it. Jax take, for instance, hours before an Earthquake occurs… animals go into a panic or stupor sometimes, haven't you heard of that? It's as if the animals have another sense…." "Yes, Sun, but babe, you're safe… we're safe. We have a reunion banquet later today. Relax." As the Tabby cat's paws kneaded her, "give me something substantial to go on that I can hang my hat on, girl." "Tiger cat reverberates what the Hummingbirds are saying. Marshal Burke and Rand, who have been working here at this safe house since being replaced after Nurse Danny Spike tried to kill me at NIA, The Marshals are acting strange uhm, have bad vibes, and harboring ill will. Ugh, according to the animals… I think we should try and escape this place, Jax!"

"That's utterly ridiculous. Why? Because of animals, aah, and bad vibes, maybe they're constipated, you know Marshal Burke and Rand work for NIA. Terrance is in control of them, Marshal Evans, and they have gone on around seven missions with you and I …."

Abruptly, Jax pounced to his toes, his temper flaring "wait for a fkn second!" before she could elaborate further or intervene, he tossed his 11 cents into the ring. "Do you for one millisecond think that Terrance and the worldwide syndicate will let us go bye-bye now? I don't think so, Sunshine. Remember, there's that high-level operation in Canada. We were briefed on that last week; it will go off in under three weeks. How will they carry out that mission without you and I 'Sunshine' umh, think about…?" "Jax babe, please, I'm only relaying what…." "Wait, yes, come to think about it, Terrance was acting weird when I jumped in the SUV with you leaving NIA. The animal's intuition might be on Point that something is going to happen with you no longer being housed at NIA. We're free of NIA's restrictions. I will be only entering the facility to work out and for scheduled meetings and oversee special Op training. Girl, you're the reason I was there nearly every day. Anyway, they've lost control, and Terrance, Liz, and Ursula are control freaks…." "Yeah, and don't forget about Larry the Wolf, who's the assistant Warden's he…." *Kara was standing close enough to the threshold, leaning into the door listening to their conversation, smirking large; she was correct Wendi was a malingerer, a fake. She was wide awake, petting a cat on the outside deck of her room. Why the bullshit coma trip? She walked down the hallway and pinged Rico's Nextel radio 'yes, Kara.' 'I wasn't mistaken. Wendi is cognizant, even moving and talking with Jax at this very instant…' Rico yelped, 'I'm on the way, Kara!'*

Suddenly and irreversibly, I sat Tiger on the ground tile and stood up, shocking Jax with a solid embrace and a subtle pinch of his left glute. Yep, done with the B.S. 'alive and healthy.' "I've hidden dormant inside Wendi for over 27 years since she was like five years old, uh, if anyone can 'play her, mimic her voice, expressions, mannerisms, it's me, like I said earlier. I'm now Wendi Feral, not her alter ego Sunshine Feral' see me, Jax, watch me, help me. You can run interference, okay? Take my hand. Let's stop watching the show from the audience and get up on the fricken Stage… and get with it!"

Not 39 seconds passed by, and from the corner of my eye came Kara in a quickened pace!

I was woozy a little and dizzy, my equilibrium not on solid ground as of yet. Jax felt me waver and helped me to a chair, 'thank goodness, not the wheelchair,' I thought.

Kara looked at me… "Omigod, how are you, Wendi? I'm calling the Doctor; Rico is on his way. This is fantastic. Your family will be here soon!" The hardest part of playing Wendi was her Soprano girly delivery, intonations like Naïve, and disarmingly flirtatious, an endearing quality with melodrama blended in simultaneously. My authentic voice was a mix of Janis Joplin and Bob Dylan, described as a touch on the raspy side. I could do it as I cleared out my windpipes, sucked hard at the acids in my esophagus, and hacked unladylike; yeah me!

"Hi Kara, I'm still kinda weak. Maybe some water or iced tea would help me." Jax added, "let's get some breakfast. Wendi, sit back in your chair." Oops, Sun's voice slipped out rather abrasively, "I ain't hungry ugh, no way I wanna…." Then I backslid into my feminine self "oh please, just will you two hold my hands and walk with me? I don't want to be wheeled around anymore in that chair. I'm done with that monstrosity."

I moved like molasses, all thumbs, motor skills misfiring, fighting to the surface were the hordes of medications side effects of the darts mixture and Doctor Hawkins psychotropics. I was tipsy. I hoped to get used to it, acclimate slowly, and wear off the residual effects.

About that time Rico joined us, his concentrated stare unnerved me, so I looked elsewhere. Kara and Jax were lost talking about war stories, going over strategic positives and negatives over a few of the excursions he was in charge of back in Iraq. Rico was strangely absent, not speaking, only staring at his phone, the greetings peck on each cheek hug, the wide grin. He seemed withdrawn in his own world. Even bit his index fingers, umh, nails cuticle, what was bothering this Macho man of Men?

I had both Studs at the same table fk, ruggedly handsome with a movie star's profile Rico and the opposite was Jax with feverish animalistic sexiness. Jax was leaner and meaner-cut up. Rico carried more bulk, bigger muscles, and a confident, almost arrogant strut. They both displayed an eerily poised aura.

Despite the drugs to keep Lil Ms. Wendi at bay, she was trying to trespass, giving me an instant migraine. The little bitch still and always had loved the Studly Rico. I closed our eyes and pushed back against her invasive pestering's, trying to keep her compartmentalized in her own cubicle in the back of our brain. I almost yelled out loud accidentally, 'outta sight, out of mind! Get the fk back, Wendi. This is my body. Leave me the fk alone; I'm you now, and you're never coming back… Never!' 😞 .

I liked Rico, don't get me wrong. However, Jax was more my cup of tea, and he turned all of me on, missing fingers and toes from tortures at War, scars running from ear lobe to jaw line-bullet wounds nearly castrated. Well, he was on replacement testosterone hormone replacements. He was who made me tick. Yuh, no two, each their own whatever that meant? I quickly brushed aside a fantasy of having them in my bed together, indulging me.

Kara and Jax excused themselves; she'd said, "Come on, let me show you some of our security measures; see what you think of them. He nodded and gave me a sly wink wagging his chin in Rico's direction. I subtly acknowledged.

Alone with Rico in my deluxe room or suite, I was having a devil of a time sucking the Tomato juice up a straw, like clogged. His radio went off. Marshal Evans was at the entrance gates, which meant 'my… Wendi's' parents and feeble cheating husband were also here with both kids. That I helped, save, not Ms. Wendi!... It was I Sunshine with Jax during the gunfight. Wendi hid like a scared puppy within, like always when the shit got tough going; she ducked inside of us and let me take the wheel!

Ahoh, feeling a touch wtf. Rico's hand covered mine with warm gentleness "it's time to let you know Wendi how I feel, no denying it. I love you and am in Love with you!" Wow, talk about awkward Geezus Christ… Stalled, a lucky break, the door to my room slammed open at a brisk pace, a damn wheelchair in my male nurse's hands Jack with Doctor Hawkins in the lead. Rico stands as she takes charge. "Wendi, I need to examine you right away before you get taken away by family and friends. Ah, if that's all-right Rico?..." "Aah, no, of course, go ahead!"

I declared, "I'm fine, just… lightheaded and dizzy. This food and juice are helping me" Damn, I didn't want to be prodded and poked anymore. Sat back with a lasting look into Rico's eyes, I relented didn't want to play the two-faced ploy game. But hell, why not… more to lose not buttering the popcorn, so I pantomime with lustful lips, yearning fake desire pouty lips seductively forming, looking up into the yearning eyes of Rico. 'I love you, Rico' no sound, but the intended effect was well worth it. He melted… Yup!

Back in my familiar position was I well, at least I was in a real bed, Queen sized, not the railed gurney of the last nine-plus months no use arguing with Doctor Hawkins, but I still voiced my opinions. <u>I told her I was feeling sick to my stomach with the lingering 'Wendi' migraine breakfast… she was pushing against the flap of my esophagus.</u> Fighting back volcano action and dizziness were my only complaints; she only shushed me as my good-looking nurse Jack checked my vitals, BP-155-95 heart rate HR, 103 temperature. 99.3, all above my average rates, even had less oxygen traveling through my blood arteries organs, like stressed out.

"Wendi, your body is still trying to recover from the darts influx of medications. Some of the psychotropic drugs have yet to be simulated internally for their manufactured to be time released to dissolve systemically slowly, so your constantly being given dosage. Look at it like Ice melting. Let me use that for an analogy…the ice equals the drugs. The glass of water is your body. The ice slowly breaks down, melts, filling the glass with more liquids the volume of...." "I got it, Doc," but being a smart ass couldn't resist a wisecrack, "does the mass or volume of what's in the glass change simulating my internal fluids..." "shush, Wendi, I need to draw some blood." Not bothering to reply, I wasn't worthy; I'm not sure I like this woman. I much preferred Doctor Liz Honcho at NIA; this one had zero sense of humor and wore a perennial... permanent frown, probably morphed into a long, red-nosed vulture when flicking her clit-masturbating. I could only imagine the guy who'd bed her ahh, no. I don't want to imagine that fk. These drugs have driven me nuts ughhhh. Crazy how did I go there, sex chat, ugh. From her drawing my blood, sick I might be?

Then it got even weirder... she said to my hottish black nurse, 'Jack would you excuse us for a few minutes?' 'Sure doc, I could use another dose of caffeine. You want one?' 'no thanks,' said she.

At the conclusion of her first sentence, an incapacitating coughing attack hit me, sharp pains like a convulsion, and sweat poured from my body. Not about to divulge her unwanted words for acid reflux would strangle me, she continued unprovoked, "Wendi, you're not fooling me, ugh, not even a little bit... this catatonic act, nope. I've been monitoring you since that nurse, Danny Spike, attempted to kill you. Your BP and vitals are on graphs and charts. This is for certain, missy. Norms for coma patients are far lower than any of your tests showed. I even have charts of spikes when conversations were directed at you from your parents and Rico and Jax, so let's come clean, Wendi!" I only burped.

"I'm concerned about how you got abrasions on your knees, scalp wound, and all the bruises. Tell me about the carpet burns. We sent the carpet fibers to our FBI laboratory, and the manufacturer of the carpet subcontracted only with the CIA, out of Washington D.C., so when were you there? This is Forensics Wendi, there are no doubts that the particles of gravel, the elements in the pebbles, were from the Seattle area. How did you get scraped up? Besides that, conveniently, the Marshals in charge of protecting you had problems with the closed-circuit cameras. They were on the blink; off, wow, sounds like some sort of a conspiracy. You have never been in a carpeted hospital room. Let's have some answers. What's the game? Why, what's really going on here?" She pauses, then aggressively pushes her index finger onto my chest. "I've kept most of this to myself but will be filing a complete report of all my findings with irrefutable forensic findings. The results are undeniable, and my report will be on Rico's desk by early next week!"

Man, I was glad I wasn't hooked up to a blood-pressure machine at that moment. "Doc, I feel I'm under attack; I will not answer your questions, not because I don't want to answer but because I can't. I haven't a clue as to how any of this happened. I..." "Bullshit, Wendi, again, let me reiterate that the tiny pebbles I removed from the scrapes on your left knee were tested at the Quantico FBI Labs. The Petroleum base is, ahh, was only found on the banks of Puget Sound in Washington State. Primary elements and chemical displace-ments were never found elsewhere and...." *"Oh, this is 'rich' ugh fantasy Doc so let me guess, I jumped or hopped straddled my broom as a witch flew past the razor-concertina wire right out of NIA to Seattle to play on some asphalt road, right then afterward, I was Horney, so I twitched my nose and landed in Washington D.C. for some doggie action at the fricken White House... try and sell that...."* "I'm not selling anything, Wendi; forensics also prove from other fibers that I carefully extracted from you that confirm your body being in Seattle recently... listen, I can't pretend to know how you've pulled this off. 'Haven't you seen all the CSI shows? Besides, I'm your doctor, not wanting to have a verbal altercation or war with you... please, I just need some...." "I lost my composure and temper "get out of here. Leave me alone. Screw you!"

The Hawkins Doctor stuck like Gorilla glue... "what's happened to your voice... is your throat sore?" morphing into a Cheshire grin. "I've read your confidential files and extensively...." "I guess they ain't so confidential then, huh, it's total...." "Way back in your childhood, you had exhibited a split personality your Sunshine right now, aren't you?"
I must admit being confused... yes I fell down the steps near Washington D.C. while leading Anastasia and Catherine from the

CIA bunker, and scraped my body up, bruises galore... and true, I had also tripped over a threshold of a door up in Seattle had carpet burns on my elbows! Yet it seemed the Forensic reports were changed or switched, but oh well, that didn't change the fact that I wanted to stab this woman in her eyes not once but a dozen times!

Instead, I sank further into the cozy mattress. I changed the venue and subject matter as a diversionary tactic. "Tell me, Doc, what's the difference between the medication that doctor Honcho prescribed and your new concoction?" She went with it! Wow seemed enthused with a weird form of enthusiasm... "much of what is in Doctor Honcho's formula derives from the era between 1933 and 1945. Chemists worked around the clock in conjunction with toxic mixtures and chemical solutions with the purpose of manufacturing mind-controlling drugs for Hitler's regime. The chemists, ugh, Nazis, were known to inject Jewish prisoners and other dissidents with all kinds of toxic mixtures. Some of these test serums were even given to their troops on the front lines. Most people don't know that Amphetamine 'Meth' was discovered and manufactured in Germany, originating by these same chemists. Their goal was to stimulate their Nazi clones with added effects of Euphoria and a suppressed appetite. Making them 'Super Soldiers,' albeit until they 'came down' the higher highs dropped to lower lows. Some of Dr. Honcho's drugs had traces of amphetamines and mind-altering mixtures combined with new innovative Psychotropic mind-transforming drugs. Some of NIA's treatments remind me of a keyword called Experimental!" I nodded and yawned, then shook my head as if please continue... there was no need because Doctor Hawkins was on a roll. "We have not had the full opportunity to analyze the solutions that Doctor Honcho was injecting into your body and the pills fed to you orally but suffice it to say we're in the process. Wendi, I can't stress how important it is for you to finish the prescribed medication that I have you taking. It's quite the opposite of the NIA mixtures. More natural and closer to homeopathic healing medicines, let's get back on target. How about the answers to my questions... otherwise I'm calling Rico to join us right now!"

'Thank Devil' bursting, blowing open the doors were teenagers Juan & Leah on their heels. Jax came flush-faced in with raised palms and a gregarious grin, ambiance atmosphere, re-directed Yep! Whew, a close call with good ole Hawkins. The party was on as I sat up, whirling my legs onto the tile. Hugs ensued joyous embraces. We danced in circles. Juan, Leah, Jax, and I... oh, fun stuff, a 'sight for soothing eyes.' *And Doctor Hawkins glaring pupils, nodding as if 'we're not done here, missy!'*

Lucky to have a super spacious room for... in minutes in popped mom & dad followed by hubby David and my friend Marshal Evans whom I hadn't seen since his untimely retirement. Everything wasn't as copacetic as it seemed, OK or devilishly. Heavenly nope, for knocking on my skull, like a Jackhammer prying into my existence, was the futile bitch pinging like an empty gas tank. 'Wendi, obviously intent on spoiling my fun with the other humans in 'my' room, 'leave me alone! I shouted internally.'

With a crooked eyebrow, I pushed back at her; this isn't for you 'Wendi' MYODB, 'mind, your own damn business.' I locked the compartment but couldn't throw away the keys. I watched with peripheral vision. Doctor Hawkins nodded her head, conceding that our conversation was kaput at that time, but her contemptuous scowl inseminated in me... she was far from finished. Then she summoned Rico over, sneering abrasively into my blinking stare, and out the room they went, lastly leaving me a squinting glare as the door closed.

-63-

Wendi's vantage point was buried... under layers of skin.

Soon after the hugs and embraces, Jax and I sat on swings in a park setting. The teenagers were playing Volleyball with the staff. We were looking at the teen's pictures of life on their phones. They'd sent us snaps of report cards. Scholarships applied for… happiness personified! They also sent us dozens of their homemade TicTok videos, we were connected to these children, and Jax and I would forever be like their extended family.

One of our group was unnervingly caustic, the stare, gawking like a Stevedore's forklift tumbling over on top of me. It was mom's open-mouthed gaze-umh, closer to a glowering sulk… or maybe a leering sneer. It didn't take her long, uh, in a blink I realized that I Sunshine didn't fool mother dearest, she whispered in my ear *"I want Wendi… get back to where you belong Sunshine, you may be able to fool the others, but I see YOU!"*

Wendi Feral versus Sunshine Feral.

Alive stowed away, Wendi interrupted with an inner-ear scream, 'mother knew she saw me knows your stealing my identity, my body. Please, Sunshine, let me out.' My voice echoed in our shared skull, watching, stifled, quietly observing, thinking sadly morosely. I wanted my life back to hold and hug Rico, Daddy, David, and Jax. They all moved with the flow, unbeknownst to my inner horror.

I was looking through clouded distorted retinas/pupils with fierce hostility as the fiend, umh, alter ego, who had been my savior countless times, had assumed and taken total control of my shell. Abruptly I'd realized it, ah, but too late, her wickedness and obsessive pursuit of her own selfish agenda was skillfully stealth-like. Her sneakiness and sly ass coyness went full circle. I'd been played like Cinderella by her stepsister Anastasia. Indeed, I was gullible and unwittingly played a part in my demise. Sunshine was not unlike other humans on this earth… The difference was her unrelenting patience. Her cruelty knew no bounds or limits. Please help me; I shrieked from inside my tomb. Tears and mucus flowed to no avail; I was the only invisible soul who suffered. I'm Wendi. It's me Screaming, see me-touch me feel me, hear me. The stink and stench of 'Sunshine's' sweat gagged me like a viral Reptile from a swamp… Yuck!

I was a prisoner captive, contained within my own body, entombed, and buried alive in a straitjacket; let me extrapolate further entangled within an alien. Extraneously the duplication of my curves and shapes of me. Gloomily with sullen despair, feeling like I lived in a squalid foul wooden box placed within silence, stiff and unresponsive. Dead in ancient times, an antiquated era before embalming practices struggling now, eyes open. Only darkness blinded me with the associated smells of earth and bodily fluids released from my bowels & urinary tract. Unable to uncoil my arms cramped with inhalations constricted-freedom I beg you if there is a 'God' free me!

Cemetery bound… imprisoned not subtly in a physical & emotional prison in the form of bondage, feet kicking, toes bleeding restraints, limits with no room to move, sequestered within. My rebellion was fruitless, unknown for centuries, and it felt like there were no accountabilities or rejections by medical authorities. Where were Doctor Hawkins and Rico? Sunshine knows that Rico would understand my dilemma. Finally tired of fighting with what's left of my Spirit, inner being true freedom, not within my grasp, I released a death stare.

I envision being exhumed from a hidden plot and then my body fragments transplanted in the name oh no… coffin found and dug up… for a modern housing development, subdivision, my coffin explodes… frightful open faces. My paper-thin wrinkled skin protruding bones and dried blood, all my fingernails are splintered in the lid of the entombment, coffin my flesh gone fingers scratched to the bones… because I was buried alive and then awakened in Horror!

<u>A short story written in 1844 came to Roost an 'Edgar Allen Poe,' classic 'The Premature Burial.' Yup, I lived it metaphorically.</u> ☹.

Where did these embellishing elaborations espouse from? Am I genuinely insane? I rationally understood it was all the hallucinogenic drugs and combined mixtures I was battling through, a profound <u>'Bad Trip on Acid.'</u> A major plus in my book, I'm unlike most people living in denial, always mitigating their faults no way, not me. I self-analyze with integrity I admit to playing a part in my demise. I recognized my partial culpability for reasons of self-preservation. When I hid from reality, afraid, petrified just a little bitty 5-year-old baby girl who'd witnessed a brutal rape, murder, and dismembering, amputation through the vivid eyes of the victim's kitty cat, whom the assailant nearly paralyzed. This is when I needed help and was lost... Sunshine found me and wouldn't let me Go... ☹ .

Wendi Feral, 'me' the animal seer, was being utilized to help solve the Serial rapist case by Detective Judy Girth, who worked for the Redwood City Police Department. This was... ('Sunshine's coming out party, the first time she appeared helping me deal with the horrific nuances of the evils of men, at five years old. I was eviscerated from coherency-kicked to the curb, sequestered to the background, while Sunshine handled the caustic traumatic situation she became Captain of our ship.')

Because of insane ineptitude, I had no logical comparisons naïve, shattered out from within me like a rising Phoenix serpent, hypnotically seductively 'Sunshine Feral' manifested from within and was incubated and hatched forever. Instantly with the speed of light, she took dominance, liberating me from all strife and discord, chaos... be gone.

In synch synchronous impulses feelings of and for the survival of my 5-year-old self. I allowed schizophrenia into my psychotic fragmented mind. Sunshine's onslaught was as subtle as water flowing over small rocks in a brook. I can't hide the truth; I'm transparent and only would be lying to myself. Many people can do so, not I, for I have way too much time to dwell on memories of who I was and who Sunshine was. Some would consider her a heroine, uhm, a Saint for her having my back and frontal side leading from the Vanguard from the start of Sunshine's manifestation. She was all-powerful, steadfast unalterable, and dogmatic with our survival... her mission.

She became a worthy adversary indeed... she'd meditate alongside me and be there consistently when needed. Like a married person, I was subjected to verbal abuse for years, beating me down early on. It was subtle, sly remarks, building momentum. Years upon years cohabitating like 27 years or more, being brainwashed, robotic movements. I didn't know it… hadn't a clue that her long game was played to perfection. Her enslavement was in progress from years back, her stealth-like game on point. Everything she did from the shadows was for ulterior motives, and my naïve stupidity showed her how overjoyed I was to have her as my ally. Sadly conceded to her that she was best under pressure times, a superior collaborator with extremely diverse reasonings, calculations, and staunch undying beliefs.

Sunshine was the equivalent of a conglomerate, sinking me to the outskirts of oblivion I'd acquiesced kowtowing, displaying habitual feelings of inferiority and insecurities with her sarcastic theme buried within.

Years pressurized like a pressure cooker, I finally accepted I was less, not in all ways, but when any debilitating pressure came into our lives. Yes, Sunshine manipulated me now. In hindsight, she resolved to prove my worthlessness through life's constant challenges and rejections. Her response undermined our trust, and she suddenly emerged. Much stronger than I ever was. Sunshine was no longer obedient to my whims, all manifested from Doctor Liz Honcho's drugs without a voice. I was compartmentalized as a Voyeur, her closest audience, buried within. Please help me. I'm pleading with her free me from my prison, Tyranny. The song 'My Own Prison' plays in a loop in my sequestered mind… artist 'Creed' is this the end of me… Wendi Feral?

<u>Sunshine Feral.</u>

OmGod, everything was going swimmingly well, swell even, until mommy dearest cornered me again over by the filtered water fountain. "Sunshine, where is my daughter at? There is no need for your intervention. I want my sweet, adorable baby girl back; now sink back within, Please!" "Mom, I can't do that. I'm invested here, needed in the forefront, you don't…." "No, you're saying you will not relinquish control because you're in control of my precious daughter. I must insist that you exit the forefront, Sunshine. This is a warning a….” “Barbara, ugh, mother, there is danger here unseen. The animals have spoken and have been warning me. You see that dog over there?” Barbara steps back cautiously, peering over at the Canine. “Yes, the Yorkshire Terrier; what of her?” “Her name is ‘Spunky’ she told me that those who had just come through the back gates were strangers. None of them are our regular landscapers; they…” “so if that’s true, let’s tell Rico… Sunshine!”

<u>Rascal and Anita the Cartel set up a yummy luncheon for their victims.</u> ☺ .

We were in, no problems, one simple call from our associate inside the safe winery. Ahh, what an oxymoron, right? Rolled in the front entrance easy as pie; yes, we had pie, lol. Dressed to Kill, yes siree… Rascal, my honey, looked great in his charcoal Tuxedo, all our men wore semiformal attire, all matching which will be convenient when the ‘bullets’ start to fly, and it can’t happen soon enough! Well, maybe it’s my fiancés call. Oh yeah, I forgot to inform you I proposed, yup broke weak and kneeled with a cute summer dress on and no undies, and he said Yes! Then I rewarded him ☺. Some non-gagging, deeply engorging special adoration for his main man, Yup… um-yum, done that! ‘I’m so excited to start planning our wedding. What a Gala it will be… so perfect!’

Our killing crew drove in without a hiccup, three caterer trucks that could have passed as elongated lunch wagons for construction job sites, Roach coaches called by many tradesmen, umh, workers, that is.

Our trucks were glistening, new, shiny, and never used before being manned by our seven employees. It was a class production show. Rascal and I were the only spokespeople; like the lead Chef, we orchestrated the removal of stainless-steel rolling trays filled with treats, and Mexican cuisines, from the finest select restaurants in Napa.

Delish, one whiff, and my tummy growled. Unfortunately, these entrees were not to be tasted by the nine of us… poison laced with a sedative mix and a variety of drugs with knockout power.

<u>We aren't all created; equally, tolerances and variables matter.</u>

A hot flash, far from menopause, 'stop now herein lies our unalterable quandary drift back in time, replaying my last verbal concerns to our crew. Rascal and I were like equal shot callers.' I stood proudly at the warehouse, delegating orders with cute anecdotes. I stated, 'Quote verbatim' if this were a motion picture, book ah, a novel of fiction, or even a practiced Play on a stage, then all the 'Kings men would fall down' together, but it's not.

This is not going to happen the way we planned. Every person's internal system is not the same; we all have varying metabolisms with tolerances. Not everyone... that consumes the poison will black out at once. Duh, and some will devour more, some less.' I fear that human digestion will not be timely. Some dilutions, chemicals, and additives react differently... we may look similar on the outside, but it's a different ball game internally. We're far from the same on the inside.

Speaking in the past tense, sorry, my man was the only guy, the person who understood what I was about to expound upon. I was always the Valedictorian; no, not conceded if it's the truth, right? All my life, which included over nine years of education furthering a High School diploma, my speech to the other seven crew members wasn't close to as eloquent as the last address at commencement, standing over the podium at the infamous Yale University. No, I had to dummy it down simple & sour, staring at the gang members, of which none had graduated high school unless the school of hard Knox accounts for something.

I guess you'd perceive me or label me a Narcissistic individual; sure, why not? What's wrong with that stereotypical label? I said vehemently to these gun runners that 'at this banquet party, there will be a minimum of 13 adults with two teenagers. Even if we fed them all the same amount of poison, each would metabolize food matter substances at varying rates, so we must be prepared. I stated so hypothetically. Rico Captor drops his fork, and his head drops into a shredded beef Enchilada. While sitting next to him is Jax Foul. Who at that precise instant is comfortably sipping on one of our laced Margarita's being satiated, showing no ill effects? And munching a Chicken Taco.

This isn't make-believe; everyone will exhibit signs of the sedatives at different times. She scolds her gangsters, raising her voice in the Warehouse before departing to the safe winery. This isn't fiction, guys; it's incumbent for us to be prepared. The last thing we need is for one of them to hit the alarm. Besides the banquet goers counting the guards and Marshals umh, other Agents the staff, over 17 of them could come to their defense or aid and complicate our escape. We must be vigilant. With that being said, we saturated the food and all drinks, including water. With my sedative formula, there isn't any taste or smell, and it is quick reacting. Then I point to my honey.

Rascal took the impetus and passed out the hypodermic needles filled to the brim with my nasty juice. Push into their skin, apply pressure to the plunger, injection done, take the males first. If problems arise in your top left pockets, you will find a kerchief and cloth napkin that is also soaked thoroughly with 'Chloroform' extra strength concoction. Simply put it over the nose or mouth of the intended victims one slight inhalation, breath, and it bye-bye now, smiles with broken and crusty teeth bared. These men could do this absolutely… 'No Problemo.' Although most of the seven still looked perplexed, I allowed Rascal to take the lead and put on the finishing touches of frosting. Javier raised his hand and said, "no disrespect, boss, but could you tell us in plain English or, better yet, in Spanish? I'm not sure we understood all that mumbo-jumbo from Anita." He nodded, not coincidently the same confused look spread across the six other countenances.

With that being said, I left it to Rascal to deal with the street urchins… listening to his paraphrasing of my eloquent speech.

How we would remove Jax and Wendi and that this wasn't an episode of the Mission Impossible series. Nope, this

Mission was plausible. We cover each other's backs; if it gets out of control, pull out your submachine guns and flick the lever to automatic. Then Rascal added a twist that I'd overlooked, admittedly darn. Our team of caterers needed a signal to attack at the exact precise time... that would be when Javier tapped a glass with his sterling silver spoon, pretending to say something to the gathered group of diners. The seven would close in, and be prepared to attack if the digesting group hadn't started to waver and fall slowly asleep. They'd simultaneously stab the hypodermic needles into the backs of the selected, most dangerous. He reminded our crew that the sedatives would... slow their reaction times down. ☺ .

-64-

Terrance and Liz are on the way to the outskirts of the

SafeWinery.

Terrance couldn't wait impatient, like decades earlier, when he was a teen, anticipating his first conquest, dribbling pre-cum... done that. Sitting shoulder to shoulder with Dr. Liz Honcho on a non-descript white Chevy truck bench seat. Why was she sitting so close, he mused, as if she wanted to rekindle their past sexual interactions, he was into the viral younger generation, but a dimple found its way to the dermis's surface, pondering; ahh, she wasn't that bad.

What's wrong with a bit of stress relief? He wondered if she'd indulge him, let me feel the grooves of her throat again, some basic fellatio. The radio's high-pitched shrill startled the both of them. "Liz, can you turn the volume down, geez, woman." She grabs up the tiny receiver in hand and speaks into the radio, 'Walter, you got a copy. Come back... over' 'Relax, we are inside and will be starting work soon. Just setting up now inconspicuously, no problems thus far... over!' Terrance was watching his iPad's split screens. His Special Operatives wore pocket cams, so he had a bird's-eye view of what was going down in the Safe-winery. The team was indeed only 55 yards from the 'Champagne Hall' where the Banquet was being catered at. Most there faces were concealed, either riding mowers or wearing face masks working with industrial weed eaters and leaf blowers. He had one of his underlings purchase what they needed via… Craigslist and other online sites. All were nontraceable. He smiled, pointing to the serene setup, "well, doc, whatcha think?" Liz smiled back at him "we're going to do this 'T,' that's what it looks like to me. Kind of exciting thanks for inviting me on this little mission." He shutters back to when like decades back, she'd called him 'T' back in the old days.

"I tell you… one thing is certain NIA's landscaping crew has the finest equipment that counterfeit money could buy." They chuckled, hitting, bumping fists. Like stealth weapons of non-mass destruction, the team could easily remove MP5 automatic submachine guns or yank out some Glocks. They even carried a smattering of Sawed-off shotguns. Nothing brought by the NIA team was traceable. Also, none of the weapons on this mission to retrieve Sunshine and Jax were non-lethal. Well, except for the Elephant tranquilizer rifle that Walter would fire into the bodies of Wendi and Jax.

They would wait till the optimum time, and then when orders were given to engage, they'd shoot not to maim, wound, or disfigure. Nope, kill them all. The only exception was Marshal Evans, whom Terrance was highly fond of. They were lifelong pals. Evans was one of his father's favorites. Their parent's families went way back… generations. He didn't want the children injured, but everyone else was touchable.

Liz watched on the screen as Don and Ron were weed-eating near the entrance gates. Terrance pointed with excessive glee. "See that, Liz, that's where the plastic explosives are perfectly placed C-4 with timers already ticking." Terrance felt giddy and chortled, squeezing his partial erection for some more flow, then nudged her, with his best provocative eye movement towards her face, then his crotch. Liz's guileless smirk was one for the ages; she winked at him and peered lusciously into his wide pupils. Adds to her scintillating act, a tongue flicking across her plumb lips mimed um, forming a perfect 'OH' like sucking a lollipop. She rolled her eyes and blew him a kiss with those rounding lips. He was all in… all over it; the throbbing pulsations started to cause a well-known syndrome named 'Penis Claustrophobia' inching outwards uuhhh!... but zipped in.

Oh, how Liz enjoyed this. Yep, the chasm of control watching him squirm, nearly hyperventilating "what's in it for me 'T' huh?..." "Cum on, girl, for old times' sake, heck gotta vitamin load for you used to indulge, don't you remember?" smiling at her. He swiftly unzips his fly. "T' baby, I already swallowed my daily organic vitamins this morning" "ahh cum-on, Liz, time is a wasting?" "Think of it as a 3-hour energy blast… but get down on it cum on. I'm fkn stressed out!" She reaches inside her oversized suitcase of a purse "ahh, here it is… 'T' a small bottle of lotion Jerkens, from a hotel's assortment and a 'wet-nap' you're your cleanup!" handing it over to him… Giggling… then hilariously howling, choking on her humor. ☺ .

Terrance gently tugged on her shoulder. "Liz…" interrupting this awkward banter of 'give and take,' he wanted to give willingly so, but she didn't want to take; Walter says on the radio, 'boss, we are in go mode 15 minutes until the fireworks begin. Our guests are being catered to at this very moment!... over,' 'Excellent Walter, a bonus awaits you; make me, uhm, us proud!... over.'

<u>Barbara and Sunshine.</u>

The familiar alarm… two fingers in his mouth near a glass-breaking shrilling whistle of Marshal Evans changed the subject temporarily. Barbara and Sunshine started walking towards David, and Ed, her father, smiled as if content. Strangely, there hadn't been any alone time for her dad or David, zero interaction. No worries, they had the weekend, uh, her parents were staying for seven days along with David. Sunshine was happy to be away from the mom… and glad she didn't have any time to dwell on negatives… no private time whatsoever; running up, taking each of her hands, was Juan and Leah shouting, "time for lunch, Wendi." They said this in unison 'Jinx'! Yelped Sunshine, laughing.

No more conversation about the Yorkshire puppy dog who had explicitly and vehemently warned Sunshine of imminent danger; something was drastically wrong. The dog had 'telepathically' stated, 'the landscapers were all white Caucasians, not brownish Hispanics abnormal not the regular bi-monthly crew, not one of them did she recognize.

This was almost forgotten as Rico came into Sunshine's view; what wasn't known was that the Hispanic landscapers would no longer ever be trimming the trees, nor cutting the grass, or even weed-eating. They had lived in adjoining apartments in downtown Sonoma. Now all piled up corpses, NIA's killing team had 'paid' them a visit, a final 'payday' all nine of them of the same family went into permanent 'Siesta Mode.' ☹.

-65-

<u>Sammy is riding her rental Harley through the glorious mountains in Idaho.</u>

Sammy was having her kind of fun… Eagles were soaring, the sky above a crisp proper Azure clear, unblemished. I cruised around the curvy road switchbacks and turned the Harley Sportster into a rest area…ugh had to pee. I noticed off to the side that there was a group of riders. I guessed about 11 of em. Wouldn't you know it is another gender-based disadvantage, all in favor of and for the male gender? The gender mix was five females and six males, yet there were only two stalls in the woman's restrooms. Aah, so freakin typical. These outhouse restrooms were designed and built by men.

506

What also agitated me, besides my bladder about to go the way of a Nuclear explosion, was the effort I'd have to use trying to peel off the leathers over my blue jeans with belt attached. It's a chore for me to get my butt ready to sit and pee unhampered. Of course, my tush would never touch the toilet. I'd spray and go… the lucky dicked men happily whipped out their cocks… squeezed off, shake-rattle, and rolled, ugh… Done!

What happened there, huh? How unfair. Yeah, cigar smoke wafted past me in the mountain breeze as the guys checked me out. Such was the typical case I displayed an exaggerated sway of my hips, a not-so-subtle strut. Yet not so much for the flirt ah more from habit, like routine, um per usual. It was just my walk. Many times, like today, I wondered why I bothered. Did I want to be desirable, or was this mere female training trying to draw attention uhm obvious allurements? Was I instilled by stereotypes, movies, fkn propaganda females constantly sexualized and desensitized, yah wonder?

I was still 3rd in line as I stared longingly at the empty bladdered men's restroom. Being an outspoken previous Whore, who constantly, uhm, always dealt with males… heck, I was much more comfortable with men. In fact, it blindsided me at times, what like I gave a shit. I didn't have a single girlfriend to my name. Whew, that realization slammed me sideways, struck me momentarily, then poof like an excreted orgasm goodbye.

"Hey, guys, could you stand guard as we use your bathroom, please?" I was in a desperation zone, about to piss or drip, and my bladder needed emptying. A shortish stocky guy walked up, "sure, I gotcha back." The next lady in line expressed relief with a sigh 'thanks, Toby,' she said. I added, 'yeah, thanks, Toby.' Ole Toby stood guard at the bathroom door while I was busy undoing my belt and getting in preparation mode. I couldn't help but listen… like an oral machine gun, Toby fired, 'where are you riding to? It's not fair; you know my name; what's yours? Where's your man at? The last inquiry was where I started… not wanting to be rude but assertive… is there a difference?

"Toby, why is it I need a man? Can a lady just go for a ride by herself, huh? Tell me don't you go for rides sometimes solo? Then when you stop, are you asked, "Hey, where's your woman, or I guess better said, where's your Bitch?" Whoa, I suppose I shouldn't have tossed out the B word! I realized I was feeling a smidgen snotty, but oh well, too bad!

Some of the other guys close enough to hear my echoed words didn't hold back their howling laughter. Toby's red beard matched his rosy cheeks, and he responded, "so you're a dyke, huh? Where's your bitch, or are you the Bitch?" A welcoming sound of toilets flushing, I neglected to look at the imbecile peering inside, watching the last woman wash her hands. I veered right past her to the empty toilet stall, knowing it was better to leave this awkward assault alone. What could I possibly win? Why engage in a verbal war with an obviously mentally disabled man?

Perhaps I was a soupçon harsh… After all, in his favor, he was the only guy who did step up to help me when I asked. I overheard words barked back behind me, "Toby, that ain't no way to treat a lady… that's why Linda left you! You're a fkn male chauvinist…" "screw off, Ralph," I heard even more chuckles.

Oh, shit, talk about a disgusting topic. I know it's human, but it happened while Toby was guarding the door, and some other fellows were close enough to be affected. One thing led to the other why 'God' had arranged… girl's orifice's so freakin close like uh a 'skin patch' membrane away from my 'Taint.'

I quickly gushed out the coffee, water, and Red Bull from my urethra, then my sphincter unflexed, and OmLord, a gaseous bomb, sounded off. Oh, Shit, farted loud unladylike flatulence of ferocity like a tremulous butt cheek clenching flapping Earthquake the sound with the odor echoed out the doors oh shit!… I could hear between my incessant flushing hysterical frenetic howls that there were prolonged shrieks of gluttonous hilarity to be heard.

There I was, couldn't very well hide, uh, embarrassed. I soldiered on acting nonchalantly as a dude would, yet I felt major-league awkwardness. Ugh, hovering behind the stall door, flushing repetitiously, for I wasn't apparently done. The more I tightened my stomach muscles, the more juice flailed outward. I still heard the repugnant jubilant sounds, especially Toby's triumphant exuberance at my bodily expense.

Gosh, I was so happy to hear the sounds of several Hogs… motorcycles revving up, relieving me further, still cowering while the last remnants left my colon tunnel. Having been on this earth plane long enough or not long, I asked how 'Murphy's Law' could come into play here. That was wrong of me, and I certainly should never ask this ever. Ugh, how could things get worse?

Well, if your listening and paying attention, yep, it happened, stupid me… Lack of toilet paper, barely enough to dab my pee hole. Forget about my splattered glutes; now what?

I quickly analyzed my predicament. I couldn't crawl under the walls of the adjoining stall-no room. Do I wait till the Harley's pipes are heard in the distance? Damn, I could stumble out with my pants below my knees. Hey, not shy once worked as a stripper, no big deal, right? Wrong "hey, umh, hello, is anyone out there? I need some toilet paper, umh, please?" Moments later, a hairy paw with a roll thrusts under the stall door. 'Here yuh go, girl!' of course, you all know it was the sarcastic voice of Toby! Fk ugh. "Thank you, ahh, now you can go, Toby." "Not really; there are a few men who just drove up that need to use the facilities." Triple shit, uuhhh. "Okay, be right out, damnit."

Where was my full-faced helmet when I needed it? As I wandered out, drying my hands with a rough industrial napkin, most of the riders were sitting and straddling their bikes. <u>My heart trembled savagely as the old worn black hat surfaced from the diner; yeah, 'Murphy and his Law.'</u> He was in a serious negative flux motion and had a menacing, threatening, ominous disposition poised to inflict harm on 'yours truly.' Hell, couldn't the fake Cowboy take a joke… who was he, followed from the hotel? One thing is for sure. The dude didn't like me. He stood next to his Cowboy car, a Grey Mazda hatchback; ugh, just being facetious, he was within two feet of my rental Harley.

He stepped forward into the line to the bathroom, snarling at me, not uttering a word, though, then I noticed I was blocked in. No wonder he calmly went to relieve himself. He had me right where he wanted me trapped by his Ford pick-up truck, but who the fk was this guy? Why was he stocking me?

I made a beeline towards Toby's tricked-out Ultra-Glide HD as the incongruent cowboy walked back out of the stinky restroom and sauntered by. Then he leaned against his truck with his brand-new clothes and boots, damn still had spurs attached, really!

The only bulge that interested me was near his underarm shoulder holster. The man was armed, but if he were Law Enforcement, as I'd already disseminated to myself, I'd been 'toast at the diner.'

I was worried, a slither frightened. The guy was a mean-looking giant, like I said, closer to 7 feet tall than 6, with his unneeded 3-inch boot heels, not a lean body but Xtra large. Standing Tracfone in hand, having already given Joe's phone like five attempts with texted updates, no signal up here in Idaho's mountains. At least with this throw-away model of phone. With my new visiting follower on the prowl for prey... lil ole me. I decided my best alternative was to befriend my past antagonizer. "Toby, sorry we got off on the wrong side of the road. My name is Trudy; where are you folks riding to?" He let loose a smile which improved his looks immeasurably. "Likewise, Trudy, I apologize; nice to meet you." His hairy knuckles smothered my petite hands, "just a day ride up to the Dam, get some lunch, then back into town is all... you wanna join us?" "Yes, if you don't mind!" now, my total façade en vogue with an added flirtatious suave shyness, upturned brows, and a sincere smile was received obtusely opposite of mine.

Fake cowboy was doing the habitual male itch thing playing or adjusting package material with Osprey eyes attached, glued, and locked and loaded, glaringly at my persona.

I flipped my back to him, taking in the pleasant mountain views and the vast mass of captured dark Bluewater. The Dam was magnificent, and the natural scenic arrangements of

Mother Nature's preponderances... there was nothing like natural beauty. Thinking back in history class, these majestic areas influenced such men as President Theodore Roosevelt, who in 1905 created and initiated new laws such as the USFS... saving National Forests from being clear cut... his legacy as a conservationist weighing far more than man's feeble attempts to unravel the splendor that surrounded the 'Anderson Ranch Dam.'

A couple of bikers with Toby pointed at the cowboy, 'hey man, you need to move your truck. You're blocking this lady's bike in' nearly growling, he stared down at the six men and moved begrudgingly out of my way.

Toby and I rode side by side at the back of the pack. The winding roads through the mountainous beauty were incredible. I nearly forgot the rusted fake cowboy we left in the dust back at the rest area. Stopping at a café overlooking the dam umh must have built up an appetite, and I ate like a starving banshee. Maybe it was nerves, or I was pregnant. Lol, jk-just kidding. Ahh, anyways, devoured the garlic fries and BLT, like famished across from me, sat Red beard, Toby. Unfortunately for him, I wasn't and never had been into the superficial small talk... chatter, ugh, unless I was working, that is. A lady's got to do what a woman must.

But hey, I indulged him with likewise banter anyways, looking for the escape hatch, for Spurs of falsity had turned off the Dam road miles back. Even though the pretender cowboy was gone, his conviction of hatred lingered, and I was staying vigilant... all I wanted was Joe!

Sitting with Toby, but my spirit elsewhere couldn't release the unremitting alarms. The guy wasn't a cop, so he was one of Joe's people, most likely paid to keep an eye on me. Yep, that made some sense, um, Joe's spy. Make sure Lil Sammy doesn't get into any trouble. That's it, got it gotta be. I turned away from Toby, relaxing while covering my mouth to a yawning exhalation using proper etiquette manners related... sure I was a chameleon, but I'm a Lady first.

No matter how I discarded the cowboy, he kept bothering me. Danger had excreted from his every pore. Why couldn't I get him farther from my present state of being? Breaking me happily from this reverie, 'a woman rider offered me a cigar which I promptly accepted gladly. The twelve of us stood chatting as Toby was sky-gazing on an open deck. His miniature binoculars waved in a motion like a submarine's periscope. He gasps out, 'well, look at that!' yeah, gotta see this, in a giant Eagles talons was a squirming, wiggling 3-foot fish, dropping right down into her Eagles nest. Wow, fricken awesome!'

Others in our group reached for eyepiece scopes. I joined in… another woman excitedly said oh hey, look up the ravine. There's a giant Elk. At that time, I realized I'd jumped to the wrong conclusion about Toby, who was a gentleman, after all, giving me his binoculars pointing towards the massive grove of trees. Look at the top, Trudy, West out over the Dam; how beautiful is that girl?

My left hand held his binoculars, and my right clutched the vibrating phone, which had finally caught a signal the phone was reloading as a text stretched across the LCD screen. It could only be from 'Joe.' I didn't have the time to read it yet as I lifted the Binoculars to my eyes, the Eagles nest not in my immediate vision. Umh, I was off kilter and saw groves of trees to the South next to a rifle pointed directly at me. The fake cowboy's head is in a tree. He was a Sniper the Cowfake fired a loud crack as I fell, ugh, crestfallen… the text read, "Sammy, there's a 'Hit Man' on your trail. Call me at once. Please be careful." 'It was much too late for the careful part… Seeya! 😟.

<u>Agent Kelsey Marie and Tanya Firm… waiting patiently to corner Joe Sable.</u>

"Believe it or not," says agent Baker, "Joe Sable is standing in the gift shop looking at fricken Romantic like Hallmark cards, has a pinkish Teddy Bear under one of his arms wouldn't believe it unless I saw it, this Cold-Blooded murderer is…" "sshhh okay Baker which proves that Samantha is near-by-stay outta sight let's nab them together one swift-assault we got em," whispers Kelsey. Meanwhile, agent Rodriguez interviewed the Concierge and day manager on the other side of the Marriott's spacious lobby.

Over the radio came the proof spoken to Tanya; Rodriguez had verified that Joe and Samantha were staying there and had booked a room for the next three days. The hotel employees picked them out from the pictures provided, albeit both had changed their hair color to dark black. So Samantha was no longer the blonde in her rap sheet pictures. He said into his mic, 'we have total corroboration of...' "Listen, Rodriguez, move out of the lobby now fast. Joe is in the gift shop." 'Yes, ma'am, Director Firm,' Tanya is beside herself here. She had Joe Sable in a gift shop, and one of her agents not 75 yards away with pictures of him.

"All right, Kelsey, I suppose it would be asking too much for him to lead us to her; listen, I'm in the van approximately 50 yards from Joe's green jeep." "You didn't let me finish; Samantha was seen leaving the Marriot in an Uber hours ago. It's all on closed-circuit cameras, Tanya. Oh, one more thing reported by Baker, Joe is locked and loaded, wearing full-on body armor under his clothing. Our body scans penetrating scope shows three weapons with a 4th slide two-shot Derringer pistol attached to the maniac's right forearm. Above his left boot is a 7-inch knife in a sheath; unfortunately, that's not all he's carrying."

Tanya stares at the screen of her phone, thinking about this situation... "Tanya, did I lose you?" "No, Kelsey, go ahead. What else does Joe have?" "That's just it. We're not sure it's a mass of something. Guessing a chemical base can't figure out what, but it's in a rectangle box. It shows fluorescent. We are running further analysis, uhm tests; initially, it seems the guy is a walking time bomb with plastic explosives strapped to the small of his back, not a..." "send me the screenshot" "just did a second, Ago!" "Give him plenty of room, pull all agents out of his vicinity Kelsey break our team back at once. Let me re-assess this situation" "Yes, Tanya, at once will do!"

<u>Joe is at the Marriot in Idaho looking for Sammy.</u>

Not a man to be weary or insecure or to exist within panic zones; Joe was the mascot for the adage 'calm as a proverbial cucumber' that was his usual disposition. Ahh, not today. He was flush with anxiety, tension even a layer of desperation. He couldn't reach Sammy on her phone. Tiny hairs on his body stood on edge; she had disappeared from the screen, GPS tracking disabled due to a lost signal on her burner phone.

Totally mindful that his bro had already put out a contract on her life. If a picture of Mark Feral's' plastic surgery-altered face was in the dictionary, the word misogynist would be highlighted next to it. His belief was to use the female gender for pleasure, then lose them. He angrily gritted his teeth. I'm done being a pawn for Mark.

Sammy is a hardheaded, determined, and self-sufficient woman with undaunting willpower, street smart, and wise beyond her 25 years. Her academic IQ was remarkable, but she wouldn't see the bullet that would end her life. Jaybird had informed me of whom the assassin was. Thinking about Mark while I stood just outside of a gift shop with a sappy card and stuffed bear for her, Sam… damnit.

I pushed in Tank's number on the 5th ring. He answered and was breathing somewhat hampered… I'd tried Mark's phone; first, it was dead.

"Tank, how's it going, bro? you find Mark?" "No, Joe, but I can see his truck and trailer. The dogs are in a pen. I'm looking at his cabin as we speak here. Let me send you a few pictures. The signal is a hit or miss; I'm currently in a good spot, Joe; there's a fire less than a mile away. There are three other vehicles by his cabin, I got close-ups of them, and the only noise I can hear are dogs barking. Joe, it's quite eerie. I've been here for about 17 minutes, and there are no lights on in the cabin either. Trying to decide how to approach the cabin, I haven't a weapon. I don't like it; something feels wrong here!"

Joe checks out the pictures of the two older pick-up trucks and the V.W. Bus with Mark's truck in the middle, knowing Mark wasn't a friendly guy. He had no friends but Tank and him... he only used people and then discarded them. It was women he'd chase; some were catch and release, and others were plainly caught. Tank was correct, something smelled wrong, and it wasn't only the smoke from the fires; the pictures prove there had to be drivers for three other vehicles! Heck, it's late afternoon, and all is dark in the cabin. Also, Tank reported no noise besides the dogs.

"Tank, your always thinking, dude, give me a few minutes, I'll call you back. Stay put, don't approach the cabin yet. I'm going to run the licenses in the pictures you sent me to a site on the Dark Web." click.

Tank kneeled, waiting, and thought he heard a faint radio... static, um, it must be his imagination. The dogs had stopped barking for the first time in at least 25 minutes, ah they must be worn out. It was suddenly still... no wind. The afternoon was on the gloomy side, smoke enhanced. His phone rang, and a hyped-up voice on the other line said, "Tank listen to me; the bus is registered to a woman who has been busted for prostitution and dealing meth. There is a stolen tag on one of the trucks. The other truck is registered to a guy that's wanted for the manufacture of Meth. He is a bad dude with a rap sheet that matches ours. Although his crimes are non-thinking violence related to a few Home invasions, the man has several active arrest warrants. His last residency was raided, he was cooking meth, and he's most likely armed Tank. These are not Mark's kind of people. Hell, you know him. He ain't got no friends but us, so..." "Yeah, this is just par for the course, Joe. I don't need this shit. I'm trying to fly right under the radar, bro... damnit, first the freakin motorhome, now this...." "Shut the fk up; stop bellowing... listen to me, Tank, welded under the back bumper of Mark's truck, is a steel-reinforced box with a 9mm Smith & Wesson and three clips with a box of bullets. Sneak over and grab it, be careful...I bet Mark walked into a trap. These people probably took over his abandoned cabin and are cooking meth as we speak. I've got problems of my own up here. I'll check back with you in 15 minutes or so!" click.

Flipping the screen back to Sammy… relief found my lungs as I exhaled, then inhaled a long draw of oxygen. My tracking app showed Sammy was at the Anderson Dam. She finally had a signal… now she could read all my texts and listen to my VMs. I made my way out of the lobby into the front parking lot and called her… ugh no answer. Sam was exactly 55 miles away, like 75 minutes of winding mountain roads on the way to the Dam, a fun bike ride for sure. The fine bitch was out doing what she said she'd do and probably saved her own life unwittingly, for if she parked her ass here at the hotel, the hit-man would have got her easily. I jogged to my Jeep while pressing send like a spastic-spasmodic individual with a nervous twitch disorder. I might Luv… that woman. Nope, screw that!

Meanwhile, Kelsey was brought up to speed by Tanya "traced the Uber driver to a motorcycle rental office. Samantha rented a Harley Sportster 2019, license plate VAIM717, Idaho. It was under the same alias she'd used at the hotel; she is due to return it in the morning by 9:45 am. We've received reports from our field agents that Samantha nearly got into a ruckus at a diner; currently waiting on the video from that diner. We have found pictures from a couple of the bridges up by the dam and several still shots at a rest area. We have substantiated her riding toward the dam on Hwy 84 with a group of riders. The bike is orange and black, and we have a **BOLO** out for her." "Tanya, this makes our job so much easier. They being separated, right… can't we take Joe now in the parking lot, then wait for Sam to return the bike and capture her? What do you think?"

"Exacta Mundo, I've already delegated a 7-person team of Agents with locals joining in. The only road to and from the Dam is being blockaded. We'll have her in custody soon enough that leaves Joe Sable." "What happens if that's a bomb strapped to his back?" asked Kelsey.

Joe is always instinctively on guard. His life was about survival. He'd calculate with a bias of paranoia-based fundamentals. Watch your back at all times, a mantra that saved his bacon too many times to count, and his criminal mind thought process constantly whirling. He'd parked his green jeep in the front of the Hotel, away from other vehicles, so he could see clearly if the cops were around.

"Kelsey, there isn't a person or vehicle within 75 feet of the jeep. If he wants to blow his ass to smithereens, I don't care, and we have nine Agents with local police as backup...." They watch Joe Sable jogging toward his Jeep.

Tanya shouts the orders into the radio, "Take the Bastard down if he flinches, resists, or makes an aggressive maneuver. Unload your weapons on him. Shoot to kill. Be cognizant that he wears body armor uuhhh fire at his head, face... Go Time!" She smiles, grinning into a morphing frowlish smirk. 'Kelsey barks... 'Gotcha, uh, this time you fkn prick!'... lol. ☺ .

With his mind elsewhere in worry for Sammy... preoccupied, Joe's attention diverted, yet his intuition spun him around a sensation struck like a premonition or whatever. My guardian Angel put me on Red Alert my head began to tingle. I was made aware that I was entering a trap. Instantly just as enlightenment made its way into my Aura, the insidious Law Enforcement Officers came out of the woodwork pavement. A chopper was descending, automatic weapons held at the openings of the helicopter, squeals of tires rubber burning, brakes, cacophonous sounds of an action movie in which I was the predator under siege attack! The Shit was slapping against the fan's blades.

I rolled under the lift kit raised frame of the Jeep, MJ auto-machine gun out suddenly felt like a surrounded rat. A fusillade of shots rang out simultaneously, a barrage whirling my head around, nowhere to run, nowhere to hide. Bit my lip; I'd known this moment was inevitable. I'd rather go out in the Blaze of Glory... motif and die than go back to prison. In return, I gave them all I could till nothing remained but my riddled body. The playing cards were Joe's last vision... that registered across his dying eyes. Blank on one side, Spades, and all Aces, the same cards from their prison cells. That Mark, Tank, and he had shuffled long ago, the words they'd written flashed... highlighted. 'FEAR ME CUZ I'M CUMIN 4 U!

-66-

Tank at Mark's cabin outside of Hat Creek.

Tank waited quietly. The dogs had started back up, it had been over seven minutes of constant barking, not only sending alarms, but Tank saw they were actively digging an escape route under the wire fence. I practically wished I were Wendi and could understand what the dogs were trying to communicate to me!

What would bother anyone in my position was that not a soul could be seen. No one opened the cabin door or window to see why such a ruckus was happening with the dogs. The cats sat on the porch under an overhang. I zoomed in the binoculars; on the porch also were a bunch of assorted shoes, various sizes of men's and women's. This alone caused my stress level to blast off; geez, was anyone alive in the cabin? To hell with it. I was getting nowhere outside the fence. I needed to get to Mark's truck and underneath the bumper where Joe said a welded steel box contained a 9mm gun... grab it and check out the cabin.

Lori Parks and Agent Bill Avery.

Bill was the FBI agent scouting the cabin... and closest to the fence line. "I got him. He's going towards the Dodge truck now," speaking quietly into the microphone. Lori, the senior Agent in charge, saw the frantic tension on the Deputy's faces, so she sought to diffuse or mitigate... aah alleviate the possibility of one of them over-reacting and pulling their weapons out. Playing a hero, that's all Lori needed under her watch... a fricken gung-ho freak in cops clothing.

Bill, feeling energized, finally some danger, action, and fun. He was so freakin tired of laboring behind screens of computers, always relegated to office cubicles... 'Oh, Bill, you are such a fricken brain. You run the algorithms, sit your nerdy ass on that rolling chair and let us know what the fk you discover. We'll take care of all the action, dude...' Nope, Bill was done with that crap. He didn't join the FBI to sit glaring at a damn screen. Bill was like one of his favorite video games... he always would win. Yup, he was the new wave of the thinking action figure.

Like Tanya and even the prick Rico, Lori would constantly impress upon him that this wasn't a video game like 'Call of Duty' or Cowboys Indians or... Heather interrupts his mindset, ahhhh train of thought. "I have the best vantage point of the Dodge... the perp is crawling under the back of it now!" "Everyone remain calm stay in your positions," said Lori. "Oh shit, he's now got a large chrome gun pistol in his hand." Lori listened to Heather and felt her anxiety ramp up when she was asked, "what should we do now that the perp is armed?" "Keep your positions, stay out of sight. That's an order... hey, Bill, what do you have?" "Nothing Lori has changed at the cabin... weird cuz the dogs are going berserk!"

<u>Empowering Tank forward was a weapon.</u>

I have to admit I felt so much better, secure now with the pistol in my right hand and three extra clips in my jacket pocket, now locked and loaded. I couldn't wait until Joe called back, so I texted him, then tried unsuccessfully, umh, in vain, to get Mark on his cell...to no avail.

I commenced onward, slowly squatting and crawling, lunged forward over a stump, picking up several small boulders, um, rocks. I was partially screened, hidden behind a colorful Hippy Peace Volkswagen van with painted fingers posed in the traditional peace sign all over it. My first throw bounced off the steps of the porch. I was never much of a baseball player, but my 3rd throw was a Bullseye nailing the door with a loud bang. I waited with baited breaths for someone to appear, but it did not happen. I'd felt the four vehicle's cold hoods… not been in use for a long while, a mystery that enhanced my nervousness. Where were the people at? Uuhhh, shoeless people, staring and seeing a bunch of shoes… still no sounds, nothing other than the constant yapping canines.

<u>Cabin surrounded.</u>

The heat ratcheted up while the fire seemed to converge on the Woods outside of the area they were entrenched within, sweating profusely, perspiration poured from the officers, and breathing became labored, fighting for fresh oxygen in the smoke-caked air. Ash began to filter by… floating like leaves in the newfound wind, black snowflakes fluttering to the ground.

"All right, I've got the back of the cabin covered. No back door, only three windows," whispered Heather. Bill replied into his mic. "Tank is sneaking up to the front door, weapon drawn, held out in both hands. Hold your positions!"

<u>Tank hoped he'd not regret his next move.</u>

Tank whispered under his breath; fk it like an overplayed police drama series. The act of booting down a door was in fashion ah en-vogue. With adrenalin pumping, I jump-kicked the wooden door hitting it just above the doorknob. Smashing it wide open, hanging now only by the top hinge darkness, was all I saw. No movement whatsoever, diving face-first inside and rolling like a movie actor to a crouching knee. In an aggressive stance waving the Smith & Wesson 9mm like a window washer back and forth.

The only light my eyes were trying to adjust to was an oil lantern on a table… light was coming from the loft above my head. Either the cabin was off the grid, the power shut off, or… uh didn't hear a generator. I'd never been here before. There were panels on the roof, so perhaps Mark had installed Solar energy for power. I Army crawled towards the table, my eyes stretching to focus; that's when I saw the sprawled body of a

520

partially clad man, his upper torso undressed... He was 'Dead as a Door Nail!'

Lori took charge after seeing Tank with a weapon she'd called Rico. He was pulling all strings to get her more experienced backup a posse on the way! He had said, 'Lori, just secure the location and surround the cabin!' Her radio, firmly in her hand, spoke to each Rookie, "take cover behind each vehicle. Bill... you will remain by the VW Bus the closest to the broken door. From here on out, I want you all to watch Agent Avery. He will be using hand signals only. Don't use your weapons unless ordered to do so or are fired upon. Heather, you've got the back of the cabin secure." She wondered how long it would take for backup to get out this far in the backwoods.

Mark had heard the door exploding, and again something freakin clawed at my leg ah thigh. I felt a sharp scratch. I couldn't yell out or see I was totally vulnerable. I was roped and gagged to a wall, so I let out a muffled growl. The sound of splintering wood had ceased, and he heard the wooden floor creaking. Someone had broken into the cabin and invaded my bound tomb. I felt buoyed, even emboldened, threw caution into the smokey wind, and auspiciously started to hum as loud as the gag allowed me to. What did I have to lose? I was captive, restrained. Wtf? Kill me... no fkn fear resides here!

"Mark, mark, Mark, omg!" Duct tape ripped hair follicles from my face. Recognizing my bro Tank his voice raspy, I muttered, 'right the fk on' yep! In seconds, a knife cut through the ropes. I was free, but my legs were severely cramped, and I couldn't stand; my head was on a Jackhammer tour. Dried blood everywhere looked down at my feet and saw a woman with Red hair nude, moving several fingers twitching like roadkill, an already dead snake. We didn't speak. I was in a shock-like daze and heard him say, "your head is split wide open, dude." He sat me up against a wall like a mannequin and started cutting fabric up, grabbing the leftover duct tape. "Mark, you're going to need serious stitching at least the wound has coagulated. You're a freakin mess, dude. I mean, you're lucky you didn't bleed out." Tank worked diligently on my wounds; suddenly, a rage took my temper to Overdrive.

My Endocrine system kicked down a load of endorphins. Likewise, Adrenal glands secreted a burst of epinephrine… our bodies energy package pumping me up. Felt as if I had just been given a full injection of crystal meth! Taking the oil lamp from Tank, I stepped over a downed body into the kitchen, tugged down a panel, flipped the Solar powered inverter on, popped the breaker, and the lights blasted on… Walla!

In an Instant, I surmised what had occurred and screamed out, "Tank, get the fk back against that wall." Pointing to the farthest paneled area by the stairs to the loft, in three strides, I stood next to him, shaking!

<u>Bill Avery freaked out, hearing a harried shout.</u>

The officers heard the man's scream… trying to see through the haze caused by nearby fires… lights now illuminated the inside of the cabin, and the porch light flickered on. Lori and the rest of them continued swatting at the bloodthirsty insects that swarmed once they had stopped moving. She texted private messages to Bill, and both were concerned that there were far more people in the cabin; shoes proved they were outmanned. Even with the door hanging from a hinge, Bill couldn't make out anything inside. Now that there was power turned on, Bill noticed the cameras, one at the barn and others positioned by the front of the cabin. He assumed that if they couldn't see but 50 feet, the cameras were useless unless one of them was positioned close to him, which they were not.

The dogs seemed to be taking turns. Only one was still howling, then another would break in, and they continued to dig. It wouldn't be long till they broke out of the pen; the well-trained German Shepard, Maverick, sat on its haunches next to his handler Heather. He read his answer to the last text he posted to her 'what else can we do if the Pitbulls and Chows break out and attack us other than shoot to kill? We don't have tranquilizer darts do we, Bill?' Being the closest to where the concerted digging was taking place now could see paws on the underside of the fence… not long! Nope!

<u>Mark Feral tried to clear out the cobwebs.</u>

Despite my gapped open cranium, clarity was mine; about a month ago, I had taken a delivery by the Courthouse in Redding, California. It was in a locked case approximately 15 inches wide by 7 inches deep. The box was sealed, um, locked with a combination that I wasn't given… Sure, I was curious, but I was no 'Tom-cat.' Curiosity wasn't goin to doom me. The courier had a distinct Russian accent. I was to deliver it to Jaybird at the SOJ Militia convention. I'd brought it here for safekeeping and placed it in my locked floor safe on my last trip out here to my cabin, which was a couple of months ago.

My right hand-held Tank still and firm against the wall… I said, "find something to cover your mouth immediately. Don't touch anything. It's life or death." I could see five bodies in disarray, partially clad or naked as if an Orgy was in action, then froze, like pressing the pause button forever.

"What's going on here, Mark?" while I handed him my T-shirt, taking my used sock covering my nose and mouth, I stood barefooted with just my briefs… Jockey underwear on. A sound screeched with a gargling noise. It came from the woman who had been crawling her fingers up my thigh where I was tied up. "It's got to be poison, Tank. The militia had been trying to purchase some of that killer nerve agent 'Novichok.' Even small exposure can kill a human in seconds!"

I got dressed while Tank cut strips off of a bathroom towel to cover our oxygen intake, being naïve to how the poison worked, 'better safe than dead right.' I needed to get dressed, and we would exit this cabin in haste. On a table spilling over onto the hardwood floor was the M.O.P. Mother of Pearl Cocaine I'd had locked in my floor safe. I used it to enhance sexual euphoria. Even my pill bottles of Ecstasy and date rape pills, ugh, Roofies, were torn open. No question, the fools thought the locked floor safe was filled with party drugs. Ugh, they were correct! Hypodermic needles were spilled out along with what looked like an instruction manual that I had never seen before. It was in English and Russian.

I directed Tank over to my kitchen pantry, and we put on latex gloves… four dead males around my coffee table, and one woman was still barely breathing, keeled over, crawling towards the toilet. I'll call the Redhead 'claws' for I still had blood-red marks up and down my legs from her sharp ass fingernails. Horrors upon each of their pained dead expressions. Their hands and fingers were clenched tight around their esophagus like they physically strangled themselves to death. Foam bubbles spewed from the eyes, ears, nose, and mouth. Their eyeballs bugged out as only Mr. King, or Mr. Koontz could elaborate or put into print, uhm… a proper spin or description in one of their shock-filled novels.

Believe me, I've seen my share of corpses, but before us, oh shit, worse than any 'Day of the Dead Zombie' type production, one of the men, the giant I'd confronted at the gas station, held his left eyeball between his fingernails veins popping out, dried blood socket a ghoulish evil smirk was upon his gory face. For an instant, I almost thought that they'd all come back to life; my suitcases from my truck were open and spread out. They also brought in the weapons from my truck MP5 and Tech-9 Auto-machine guns, illegal assault rifles, and my favorite Glock and 357 Mag Colt on the floor. Tank made his way up the stairs to the loft, 9mm in hand. "Mark, yah gotta see this," he yells.

On the loft's pull-out cot was a used-to-be cute brunette amid a ride… Cowgirl Up, she was bent over the guy, her hair covering his face. Shaking my head thought that wasn't the worse, fkn way to go-Lol! All seven of the rude, ill-mannered discourteous home-invading humans were no more as we heard the Redhead's last moan, she-ceased to inhale. A fleeting previous remembrance of the five men and two women from the gas station vanished from my vision… bye bye-now.

Instead of bailing, I said, throwing caution into the wind, let's clean up carefully. I placed the 'Novichok' poison back in the case. We were not touching the purplish veined out bodies that Rigor-mortis laid out in unnatural positions. The dogs continued their assault on the serenity of the forest. Tank nor I spoke. We had a silent program enacted and had known each other for decades, and words were unnecessary. We grabbed sheets, covers, and carpet to wrap the intruders up in… breaking the silence. I said, "let's carry them out to the backyard. I gotta backhoe will bury them out there," he nodded, and we took the biggest fella first. It is clear that the poison wasn't airborne, but we had our bodies covered as best as we could, except for our faces.

Wtf was happening? Lori kneeled in Stunned silence.

Lori, Avery, and the three cadets watched as the two men carried a body with arms sprung out in a ghoulish unnatural, stiff position. Most of the body was covered in a white sheet. Holding feet was one of them, under the armpits the other. Bill yelped wordlessly, 'oh, fk,' his breath shot out of his lungs. 'It's Mark Feral,' he nearly screamed with excitement. He and Lori would-be heroes, awards, medals he envisioned the interviews. Social media, TV media, the notoriety of capturing one of the top three most wanted on the FBI list, then throw in Tank Shaw, they would be given pay raises along with advancements up the ranks… Yes! .

Bill watched crunched down behind the hippy van and watched as the outlaws decided to use a wheelbarrow to move the other bodies. Mark stopped by the dog pen to pet his animal's… tails, wagging, whimpering love bestowed by the murdering criminal. Observing everything he could, Bill kept Lori informed via texts with adjoining pictures 'look; it's Mark Feral. We are going to be National heroes, Lori!' She was still outside the fence… the flashing LCD screen had the opposite reaction from her, not of exhilaration… but of imminent danger!

Lori moved through the cut-out Hog wire fence to get a little closer with field glasses out across the bridge of her nose… sees a wheelbarrow come into focus, barely holding another corpse. Tank walking backward, Mark pushing the wheelbarrow dumping the human load by a long dug-out ditch in the dirt next to the Septic Tank. That was probably dug out previously when the septic lines had to be cleaned out.

She then saw what Bill failed to report; both the Felons were loaded to the gills with machine guns and a shotgun strapped to Tank's back. Whew, they were outgunned. The five had pistols and a few shotguns with a 30-30 rifle at their disposal.

Lori texts back, 'stay in place; hold your positions. They have automatic weapons Bill' then she says the same words in the mic to her three novices. Lori then frantically sends an encrypted Instagram to Rico and Tanya with a fuzzy snapshot. We need backup now, ahh… ASAP. Mark Feral has been identified along with several victims that evidently were murdered!' ☹ .

It took less than 15 minutes to pile up the bodies "should we burn them up, Mark, heck? With all the smoke in the air, it wouldn't draw any attention. It'll look just like another fricken fire…." "Nah, there are firefighters all through these woods. Luckily, brother, the fire looks like it has changed directions. The keys are in the backhoe. Do you know how to run one?" "Yep" "Okay, dig this hole deeper, and we'll bury them. I'm going to feed and water the dogs and check on my cats to see if they need anything." "Aah, Mark, what about their cars? we can't…." "We'll tow them out to the main road, dude, or drive them out and park them in the rest area that's only 13 miles away, don't worry, bro, we're going to be all right!"

Lori speaks louder in her mic to her force, "fall back when you can! we're going to wait for backup." The backhoe rev's up, drowning out all noise in the vicinity. She then sends a group text to Tanya, Rico, and Bill. 'From what I can see, it appears that Mark and Tank have killed at least seven people. They're in the process of burying them at this very second!'

She decides to backtrack about 50 yards into the woods, where she can call Tanya and Rico 3-way. "Where the hell is her backup?" Lori's anger grew exponentially. She was stuck out in the woods with amateurs against veterans. Besides that,

Bill and she only had pea shooters, a definite disadvantage against the enemy's firepower.

Bill kneeled by the VW Bus, musing ain't no way he was falling back, waiting for others to take the Glory. This was and always will be why females shouldn't be allowed to lead in combat. The weaker sex was too passive, always yielding, and constantly afraid of confrontation. There were five of us against but two freaks, and they were surrounded; adding to their advantage was the ultimate benefit of a surprise attack… this was the order that Lori should be giving Damnit. He slid down against the VW, watching the three rookies retreat behind the fence line… crap!

Taking the 30-30 rifle from his back, 'wanted dead or alive, huh.' Bill decided it would be dead while he watched Mark move inside the dog's pen. The dogs reacted like he was a doggy God jumping, whining, whimpers of excitement. This killer was next seen petting a cat not 35 yards from him. In his ear, he heard…. "Bill, get out of there. That's an order. What do you think you're doing? Ugh, a rifle against a 30-clip M-5 Submachine gun, have you completely lost your Freakin mind? Follow my orders and move it off the property!"

He spun around angrily to see Lori outside the perimeter of the fence… shit. Tank came around the front of the cabin, wiping his palms together. The backhoe could be heard idling. He was one man against the two killers Lori, with the rookies, scared of their shadows too far out of the way to back up. He took up aim in the crosshairs of his scope; if he were quick enough when they came together, he could shoot both of them dead. He wasn't the best marksman, but this wasn't going to be so damn hard… lol!

Suddenly in unison, three Pitbulls and two Chows broke free of the open gate… growling in attack mode. Then the first bullets cracked and sounded off. Mark and Tank instantly went into evasive action. They rolled somersaulted up over the porch past the one-hinged door, weapons already out and safety disengaged.

Chaos reigned; Lori hadn't any alternative but to order her tiny force to shoot to kill… the dogs, two of which were dragging Agent Avery from under the Volkswagen bus. Bullets sprayed out of control from Heather's left side, a blur leaping in the air and snatching Maverick, her German Shepard, by its throat was a Chow dog.

Seeing past the misty-foggy haze of burnt ash and stinky smoke smells comingled with gunpowder, Lori was more of a spectator. Heather, after unloading three bullets into the Chow to save her Canine and her... the canine handler froze stiff, holding her weapon out.

Tank looked at Mark; his white cut strips of sheets had blended red the makeshift bandages on his skull were leaking badly. They'd performed Circus stunts acrobatically bounding into the cabin. It wasn't a second later that a fuselage of shells shattered the windows in the front of the cabin.

Lori was panicking, shouting into the radio mic, "halt, cease-fire, hold your fire, Bill, are you all right? Can anyone see Agent Avery?" A voice came back. "Agent Avery isn't moving. I saw two dogs attack him. They had him in their jaws; I can try and get to him; he's on the other side...." "You stay put. I'm working my way to you; Heather, I want you at the back of the cabin." Lori, in a panic, had the other Officers surround the cabin while she made her way to where Bill lay dormant.

The patches of thick smoke hampered Tank and Mark... firing their weapons on anything that moved "hey bro can you see how many are out there?" asked Mark. "No, but I just nailed one!" "We're going to have to shoot our way out of here. Ain't no way they're taking me alive, Mark!"

Heather was moving upright to secure the back of the cabin when she was lifted off her feet and slammed against the wall of a storage building, dazed by a hot flash, an OBE-like experience leaving her body, seeing her left arm hanging by bright red fleshy tendons swinging in an awkward, unnatural way. Each time her heart pulsed, blood streamed out, she didn't speak, cry out or scream only squinted her eyelids and snarled.

Her glassy doll eyes saw a split screen, sporting events, two separate games on simultaneously. There she sat with a frilly laced pretty Sunday school dress, knee-high socks all in matching shades of Pink, aah a bow in her hair-bangs pulled back on a chair sitting on her Uncles lap, a Fairytale book open. 'The little Mermaid' in his left hand; she held their buttered popcorn. She was almost five years old.

A persistent knock on the closed door, then an earth-shattering high-pitched wail scream pierced her ear bud… snapping out of her fugue. She snatches the strap on the canteen, rips it off, and ties it around her forearm, trying to squelch the blood's flow, fighting to get to her knees. That's when Heather realized she'd taken another bullet that penetrated her abdomen; the outlaws were armed with armor-perforating ammo.

Heather falls forward on her face, 'evil versus good,' childhood toys strewn about a child developing beginning to see life from a positive perspective; she was too young to die like this, and despite negative harbingers, she fought to breathe. Trials with temptations instantly opportunities for growth stunted. Truth became a burden; was she already Dead?

Heather snapped out and up, more determined to grasp her mortality, instilled determination and self-preservation. She took off at a full sprint towards the fallen man Agent Avery, whom she didn't even know. Her health and physical strength were daunting to others, 'taking not being given medals' at five events during the annual Police games contests competing against both genders.

She fell again and again, finally catapulting and rolling over to his body, torn and breathing sporadically, losing the oil of the human body. Bill was missing a chunk of his left ear. Two dogs lay nearby; one, a blue-grey Pitbull, inched forward. He was still growling to his bitter end, teeth clanking… wounds from Bill's pistol, visibly bleeding out.

The dog's hind legs fractured, yet the animal was filled with revenge vileness, hatred bred into this breed, his diligent pursuit of his master's enemies, and loyalty. She shot the dog in the head, putting it out of its misery. She took up Bill's flayed-out arms dragging him behind the VW while gunfire slowed to only a few rounds, then nothing… although crouching, eyes wide open, was Lori.

The 'Song of Silence' played loudly, crickets, frogs birds hovering somewhere out of sight. In the distance, a Rooster called. The only noise was the idling backhoe until the cavalry started to arrive. Radio spurted out relief. Lori crawled over to Heather, who was now on her side with dilated pupils; Bill moaned the radio cackled again. "Agent Lori Parks, this is Ranger Forks. I have a 9-person task force ETA-3 minutes away."

Lori rushes out towards the front gates fence line to meet the Ranger. They don't exchange greetings. She said, "I will bring you up to speed. We have two down over by that Volkswagen bus. He tossed his hand up and then whistled... two Paramedics came running over.

From the beginning of time, as was the case during wars and battles, the real heroes were always there, yet anonymously ubiquitous most times, humility-based souls. Humans that most of the time garnered nearly zero accolades, Medics, Nurses, and Red Cross. Some volunteered with no body armor or weapons. Nope! The Paramedics flowed to the front line with only scalpels, portable gurneys, and cutting saws for on-the-ground amputations. Immune to fear for themselves, empathy secreted from their extremities from their Hearts... Angels without Wings, they grasped up Bill Avery. The Medics carefully clutched Heather, who had a gut-shot umh stomach wound... her arm dangling from another gunshot. Tied off Heather's arteries as best that they could... and even attended to a few injured dogs... who the hell were these Imposters of the human race?

"What do you think they're doing out there, bro?" Mark didn't answer, only said, "if we step out that broken doorway, I'm sure a dozen guns will shoot us. I don't think...." "We could, ugh, I could take that kitchen table and hold it in front of us. We might make it off the porch and..." "hold on, let me see if I can make anything out?" Mark once again tries to focus his binoculars nada... "Tank, best case scenario, we get off the porch. Where would we go next? They have our vehicles, and we're most likely surrounded... we aren't going to make it fifteen fricken yards... No, we're just going to stay inside here until the time is right. It's going to get tar-black dark outside soon enough. No one will see without floodlights." He turned towards Tank's face, "They've shot up the inverter; we're going to lose the Solar power."

The standoff was entering hour number three now; 17 Law Enforcement Officers had covered every square foot of the cabin's exterior. They had it lit up by mobile floodlights. A generator was coughing and sputtering, adding more smoke to the night's air. Lori had fruitlessly grown tired of trying to communicate with Tank and Mark via megaphone-bullhorn; now she waited for an experienced negotiator to try and resolve this stalemate uuhhh… standoff.

Tank is beyond distraught, in disbelief clenching his bowels "this is a fine ass rut we're in now, bro. Shit, I should be in Mendocino County with Whitney helping her family and all the poor fire victims; it's…." "Shut the fk up, Tank. Your sniveling is freakin driving me crazy, dude… Your only out of San Quentin because of me… it is what it is, dude, grow some fkn balls!" Tank retorts like fumes from parted lips, never spoken before to his mentor with as much disdain. "Yeah, Mark, I never would have been in any prison if it weren't for you and Joe. You guys have been like a plague." Mark only sneered at him, not replying with a derisive shake, and turned his back on him. Tank's realization itched from his glands and secreted from his pores. He was an adult… hell he had choices. Culpability was his as well… told himself to stop fricken whining.

Moments later, Mark grimaces, "all right, follow me as I've always preached to you and Joe. Live by the dictum of the Boy Scouts of America 'Be Prepared' for anything." Tank shook his head in disgust at his stupidity and how his life would end. But followed Mark to the smallest of rooms on the underside of the staircase up to the loft. Their shoulders touched almost back-to-back inside an isolated saferoom. Mark had cut out perforated round openings for their rifle barrels to protrude from. The last onslaught of tear gas fired into the cabin's broken door and through the shattered windows was useless. They were safe. The shock grenades were futile, laughable if they could find any leftover humor within or out, definitely comical.

Mark's cameras were now full-on useless. It was a moonless night covered in the smokey haze from nearby fires that seemed to be getting closer to their location. It was 7:55 pm. instead of wasting ammo and shooting out at the portable floodlights. They decided that the light show helped them as much as their enemies. The bitch's voice on the bullhorn was beyond annoying and redundant... like fkn duh. We aren't going to give ourselves up, lady... surrender. For real, did she believe they were morons, imbeciles, idiots? Ain't no way this is going to end without further bloodshed... a surprise awaits their asses smirks... Mark.

The ongoing threat did harbor some lasting anxieties, although put on the back-burner-pun intended, Lori thought how appropriate the option to burn them out was. Torch the cabin just another raging fire in Northern California. She ghoulishly smiled at her imagination of Mark and Tank twisting on a rotisserie grill. They had thrown everything at the cabin to no avail. Each time they moved closer to the cabin, bullets would fly in their direction. Nothing seemed to work the shock grenades, and tear gas proved ineffective. It didn't make any sense, but it was the case. What was left was to charge the cabin with the ready and willing Swat team or bring in a wrecking ball; it would be nice to be able to send in a robot, but being out here in the boondocks, not on the plate.

The small saferoom that Mark designed might be the only walls standing; they were built and framed out of steel studs, wrapped with wire mesh... and Lead-lined Gypsum Board was attached. It was what was used in manufacturing and framing X-ray rooms in hospitals. Everything was screwed together; wire lath was attached on both sides of the walls, then a triple coating of non-combustible stucco. One thing is for sure, they were not burning up. Nah, thought Mark. "This room will not burn we...." Tank's words echoed the truth "your right. We will probably not be burned alive, but we will be cooked and boiled raw." His last words spent, ironically coinciding simultaneously with the power dying solar light done, diminished to a flicker-darkness prevailed... ahh, now what? ☹.

Lori was gritting her teeth with a wild smirk ... declarations made to herself in her warped mind similar to a famous Roach-killing commercial or slogan, now the soot-filled wrinkles on her face spread out, smiling, and humming a familiar euphemism from childhood. I picked up the bullhorn. 'Come on out, guys <u>'You have nowhere to run to, nowhere to hide!'</u> these words reverberated in Mark's damaged skull. Pain from his splintered lips from the duct tape gag burned raw. He mutters, 'she's got something comin,' he tries to smile and grin, languishing with thirst. Tank's cracked lips were bone dry, Cottonmouth like the snake, dry... the oxygen was being depleted, and he felt despondent that his life might be over soon.

Tank mulled over his attempted change in the direction of his life, deciding it was too late; no time to smell the roses; there all dead they'd go down in a blaze of glory while negotiations climaxed the end wouldn't be satiating... a harsh and brutal existence finally finished. Kaput! ☹.

Neither Rico nor Tanya returned her texts and calls for unknown reasons. Lori was frustrated... ugh, she hadn't any contact whatsoever with her superiors. The latest news from the Paramedics affected her with waves of nausea. Lori stood up as tears flushed down and water fell from her chin Agent Bill Avery was declared dead, and Deputy Heather Lox succumbed and died from her wounds.

She once again shouted in the bullhorn, 'you have five minutes to come out, hands up, or I'm going to burn you out. This will be my last correspondence. The clock is ticking.'

Time was up... Lori gave the order to an officer with a flamethrower to fire up the cabin, and within moments the cabin burst into flames. 'The inhabitants would be an incendiary treat soon, growled Lori... yeah only rubble was going to be left.'

What the bros heard last not once but three times like a chant; bullhorn with the same female's scratchy tone. The speakers were still actively working attached to the camera's fixture...

they hadn't much light left, and Tank's flashlight on his cellphone was dimming quickly. '<u>Both wide-eyed as Lori started howling derisively, laughing hysterically like a ghoulish maniac... repeated the phrase that Mark and Joe had Coined</u>'... "Fear me, Cuz I'm cumin 4 U!"

-67-

<u>Rico with Jax and Sunshine/Wendi at the Safe winery.</u>

Seating arrangements seemed a bit odd, certainly after Wendi was now back with the living after being in a coma for nearly nine months. Doctor Hawkins, with undaunting resolve, decided she'd raise the alarm of deceit after their celebratory lunch gathering. Rico has already agreed to meet with her in private. Knowing what she did about the Sunshine/Wendi debacle, she relished the opportunity to lay out her cards and watch Wendi try and argue the forensic proof; it would be just Wendi and Rico and her. She sat while the caterers delivered bowl after bowl to their tables, always watching, preoccupied with Wendi... Jack, her nurse, was checking her vitals.

Wendi sat in the prominent position at the head of the long table; on her left was Rico, the right side had Jax, and next to him was her husband, David. Why wasn't David sitting closest to his wife after all these months? That puzzled the doctor.

The happiest of the entire assembly was Juan and Leah, who sat next to Rico, sitting with permanent smiles across from the teenagers were Wendi's mom & dad.

The Mexican cuisine was scrumptious, and playing from the speakers was the famous International artist 'The Tijuana Brass Orchestra.' Wendi raised her virgin margarita for a toast to her favorite young people on the planet, Juan and Leah. The atmosphere was joyous; the salsa of various degrees of hot challenged the senses, the hot peppers mixed umh superbly... The five-course meal was straight-up mouthwatering, and the delicious guacamole was to die for. 😣 .

David was irritated, slouching in his chair, his guilty conscious weighing him down. His last confrontation with Rico was corrosive, and tempers had flared, no comprehension. There wasn't a way to convey any commonsense to that hardheaded prick. Obviously, he'd allowed himself to become attached to his wife... way too attached in David's mind. Rico was blind to the point of obsession; he knew they had a short whirlwind romance, but that was history. David felt like he wasn't welcome; the guy loomed largely and was destructive in all ways. He decided that it wasn't a fractional dislike. He hated the man; Rico had threatened him over the affair with Wendi's best friend, Sandi. Please, what proof did he have of this? It was plain ass speculation at worse fk him as he barely chewed a bite of his tostada. The dude wouldn't listen... he was a man with needs. So what would Rico do if his wife were in a coma, for like nine months, shoot zero intimacy... no sex, nothing... Nada!

Anita and Rascal are watching their crew deliver a delicious blend of Mexican food & drinks.

In the back of their 45-foot motorhome, Rascal and Dr. Anita Sparks watched the nine separate monitors of the body cams. They were marvelous with clarity, 15 times better than the originals of only a decade ago. They were 3.5 miles away from the Fed's 'Safehouse winery' seeing the man's face... the same countenance they had, unfortunately, had the distinct displeasure of encountering 11 years back in the Ocala, Florida National Forest. Rico had led the FBI's raids on his Industrial Park; they had vowed to get even. Now there he was, the living bastard legend Rico Captor, soon to be one of the non-breathers comatose, Dead!

Rascal and Anita had a short visit and luckily only had adorned the ten most wanted list for several years. They disappeared from any 'lime-light' and now were relegated to an inconspicuous number in the top 20 wanted. But for sure, Rico would recognize either of them in a split second. Therefore they were relegated to view from afar; their plan was unfolding perfectly, and they kissed smilingly.

Anita sat next to him, flashing back at their first sparing as would-be lovers; 'I felt a ticklish sensation, not in my loin region, but all over my hair follicles tingling while his twinkling blackeyes embraced mine, remembering the beginning with him. I was purpose-driven on auto-drive. Sex was the vehicle I'd drive, and it controlled men and a few women. Rascal would fall under my spell all men do, um did. Great sex brought them to my knees. That was not the case with him; he discarded me like I'd done other males in the past... like my mother said, 'honey, turnabout is fair play... ughhhh you play with fire one day you're going to get Burned.' Strangely this impacted my pride and had me questioning my skills of deceitful lust and loving... the scales, um, dimensions between love and passion that had many incremental steps or levels. It's impossible to define the word love which encompasses infinite nuances. I playacted the woman's role; a ploy taught for centuries thinking of myself like... Cleopatra courting Mark Anthony. He played hard to get, but I underestimated him, for he was a much more skilled adversary. He turned me inside out and played me cunningly! The bastard turned the table on me the next thing I knew; I was unconfident anxious with agitation, treated like a fkn apprentice by him... God, I loved this man!

My familiar role with men being tokens for pleasure reversed. I sometimes hated him as I would check out the full-length mirrors of my taut nude body, rubbing lotion and taking my hygiene to the next level. Carefully trimmed my luscious pubic landing strip... sliding a vibrator across my erect clit fingers, finding my hot crevices, convulsing in self-manipulated orgasmic gyrations, thinking this was more satisfying than any man's loving. I was fkn wrong, okay! I was the Femme Fatale, seductress, temptress, then, like flipping a reciprocal number like in an algebraic equation, I became miffed. He played me, and I became his role model. Still, the mirrors reflected my yearning, thirstful desires of lusting and wanting to possess his body with unrestrained passion. Ahh, he drained the passion and stole all from my body and mind as a Love-leech sucked me dry. I became his toy Barbie doll. Damnit, my energy was sapped, synapses fired surging hormones, the more the prick avoided me, the more I had to have him... a 15% increase in my heartbeat when he'd enter the room ah, sickeningly weak. Rascal knew he was a predator. Just brushing against my skin caused a slickening between my lower slanting lips wet... as those twinkling black eyes engulfed and toyed with all of me!

Bizarrely there was no burn-out, none, passion flowed with juices, never complacency nor-mundane never, even when it was a service um booty call a quicky to help him, or us sleep. My brain fixated and revolved around him like I was Mother Earth... he was the glorious Sun. It had been 13 years and still rolling, both faithful in Love. Best of both worlds regarding love according to the Greek vocabulary words; 'Eros' physical love & 'Agape' spiritual love. Our marriage would finally culminate in the fruition of my dreams... eternal bliss planned for when we returned to Mexico City.

El Chapo had vowed to ensure that the ceremony, uhm, the consummation of their wedding, would be the party worthy of Princes and Princesses with one caveat. Rascal and I better deliver Wendi alive and unhurt. The order also included the abduction of Wendi's working partner Jax Foul. The banquet was full steam ahead, and soon the first heads would 'bob-wobble, drop' a toxic dose was administered in Rico's drinks and food. This would happen without a glitch... no reboot necessary!

<u>Terrance Hallinan and Liz Honcho.</u>

He was done with his futile attempt of procurement to acquire some lip service, smacking suction action, lol. Liz felt oddly satisfied by rebuffing his advance. Terrance turned to her with the least amount of released tension, verbally feeling like using a profanity tirade to put her back in her shoes. After all, he was the CEO, and she was the measly Head of the Psychology Department at NIA. "Liz, you can be less than human... you know that!" Liz rolled her eyes, looking at this feeble guy who played like he was being treated inhumanely. The truth to be told was that he wasn't used to being rejected by the females under his control. They were subservient to his whims, or he'd ship them out. I decided to tell him like it was, "Terrance, I disagree with your statement just because I don't feel like going down on you right now. I am less than a human; please, your manipulations aren't going to work on me. I'm a doctor with the upside of 13 years of education. 'It is a fact, not wives' tales or superstitions. When a warrior enters the combat arena, his pent-up testosterone... testicles should be full. No ejaculation, sex should be repressed, the tension on high! Fighters enter the ring, ready to burst out on edge. Throughout the annuals of time, this has been the case. From the Gladiators in the Roman Coliseum to an Olympic contest, the unsatiated males are more aggressive. Males are stereotypically ready to rest nighty nite after sex, or a major ejaculation, especially." She grinned, "if I'm the woman that brings you to climax." Then giggled, "after we have Wendi-Sunshine and Jax in the basement at NIA I will place my chin to your base bring you to a place of ecstasy how about that dude." she busts out hysterically laughing!

He pouted, thinking, 'you wish bitch. I'll have one of my young secretaries handle this load' then snarled his nose. 'Your ancient history' while they watched the monitors, and finally, he said, "I'm going to hold your head to that, Liz."

Topics switched like gears in a Tour de France race up through the Swiss Alps; they watched the C-4 explosives being put in place around the perimeter of the banquet hall. Marshal Evan's voice rang out on the speaker, "k boss ETA five minutes; Marshal Kara will be eliminated first, then all the guards and staff. Then we will take out Rico. I personally can't wait, sir; Marshals Burke and Rand are in place; we're in countdown mode!"

Terrance spins around and says to Liz, "the front guard entrance gates will be blown to smithereens first in less than three minutes. He reaches over, clutching her already perspiring hand... sweat greased tightly, the clock ticked, Ugh!

<u>Wendi/Sunshine.</u>

I kept repeating my mantra, I am Sunshine, and yet roaming the boundaries, ah shared edges of our periphery was Wendi hovered languishing, relentlessly. Sunshine couldn't mollify or appease her. No amount of pacification or conciliation would work. Nor was it possible to placate the brat, leave me alone…aching was my temples. A train wreck migraine was not to be avoided. The cause of Wendi's fervor was clear, and the effect was already being felt in the demonic gleam of Wendi's savior Doctor Hawkins. With her ghoulish stare, I wished I could stab her in the eye. The medication changes brought strength and conviction to Wendi. On the other hand, Doctor Liz Honcho's prescriptions kept her at bay and me in charge. Now, I have three months in reserves. 'Suddenly, Atomic Bombs heard, exploding in unison, surrounding my ears, alarms sounded… then a barrage of gunfire watched Rico lunge out of his seat, weapons drawn, then promptly fell down, gripping his stomach others swayed, eyes rolled up like drapes withdrawn, eyes of white showed across the table… Omg.

Jax growled while we were being 'bagged up to go' David's last glare was a lopsided smirk and a satisfying grin uh…! David's teeth-baring… my eyelids were closed, with Dr. Hawkins peering down at me. Her last words, "Wendi, you're almost three months pregnant!" fk nope, talk about a dead lay huh in a coma. How was that possible, Naw! Yup! 'Sunshine glared knowingly in control, then winked provocatively at my inner self.'

Wendi was sequestered, locked beneath an Iron curtain, despondently in total despair. She fought for a voice, recognition immobilized without recourse, futility was fertilized, fermenting Wendi fraught with fear fighting against Sunshine's imminent invasion of everything she was.

Despite the quagmire of Psychotropic cocktails concocted by Dr. Honcho, she refused to go on furlough, pregnant now… omg, how, when, who? Why was there no memory or an image of this violation whose body fluid semen Ugh. Searching memory banks that were not her own, access rejected encrypted codes stealth-like firewall... OmLord.

Muffled mutterings, human content, trance-like 'dightmarish' horrors as the vehicle she occupied abruptly skidded to a stop. My body was metaphorically strapped down; Sunshine was always the protagonist when havoc... trauma struck. I'd hide in the shadows that was my M.O. 'Modus Operandi,' diagnosed at a young age, about five years old.

As a child, I was diagnosed with a disorder, a distorted view of what others maintained as the real world. Schizophrenia's strange ways of perception, behaving willingly and earnestly, she pleaded for an escape from her life aah childhood wounds of agony deeply inset. That's when Sunshine became their external agent. Then catapulted to the Now... 'Yuh got this, Sunshine? Huh?'

-EPILOGUE-

Wendi and Jax were captured by Rascal Savage and Anita Sparks.

Threats being espoused with intensified angst… growls from beside her. Jax could be heard in a rage of aggravation. "Where the hell do you think you're taking us?" he tried to shout, but the gag impaired his verbiage. The unfamiliar female voice disdainfully barked… "Gotcha," injecting him and me again, instantly unconscious.

Lori… watched the Cabin burst into flames.

Mark and Tank are smoldering in the cabin inferno, "nowhere to run to… nowhere to hide." Lori cackled, verbally mocking their playing cards and written words that they would leave at the scenes of their crimes. 'Fear me because I'm Cumin 4 U'. Agent Lori Park's fiendish eyes watched the cabin's inferno knowing the two criminals would soon be burned at the stake! That would be too good for them; ugh, no satisfaction… in facing them in court or watching them rot behind bars for the rest of their lives. Soon they'd be crispy, woefully she lamented over the already cold bodies, Agent Bill Avery and Deputy Heather Lutz traveling from the scene in a coroner's vehicle.

Lori Parks.

Lori stepped into an elevator at the Sacramento Federal Courthouse and pushed the button for the 1st floor, a briefcase in her left hand. Felt stiff and sore from the Pilates workout the day before. She glances at her reflection in the mirrored wall, having lost about 15 pounds, most of which was due to the internal grief and the pain of losing Agent Bill Avery and Deputy Heather Lutz in her assault of Mark Feral's cabin. Lori was done debating and arguing with Tanya, whom she had come to admire since her eulogy at their funeral.

Lori, Tanya, and other Senior Agents had left a conference call with Washington, DC, minutes earlier. This resulted in alarming information; there weren't any human remains, no DNA, found in the rubble and debris at the scorched cabin. She was on her way back out there. Lori hadn't any answers to the questions posed to her, "Agent Parks, you followed the GPS chip that was inserted in Tank's anus, which led you to Mark's cabin; according to the tracking software, he never left that cabin? Wouldn't his body have been tracked leaving that burnt building if he weren't deceased?

<u>Mark Feral waited like an elongated orgasm… don't move… ah now…</u> .

The panic room was heating up. Mark still waited, frozen in time like enjoying a succulent bite of lemon garlic and butter-soaked Lobster meat. Finally, growled into the pathetic pouting face of Tank, "it's time to drop back ten yards and punt. We're surrounded, and this cabin will be burned to the ground." Tank glared at him. "Duh, where the hell do we go, bro? were toast, Mark." The last flickering of Tank's phone app, flashlight dimming as he hit it on the wall, they were boiling soon to be French fried. "Mark, why are you smiling like a ghoul? What? You have a death wish, dude; you take 'No Fear' to the extreme, dude fk. I don't want to burn to death; why don't you shoot me in the head and then do the honors to yourself, okay brother?" Mark leaned in…"What? I couldn't hear you, bro; what did you say? Tank yelled, "you want to shoot me first, or shall I do the honors, bro? I'm not going to be boiled alive!"

Mark smirked, nodding his head and beckoning him to a corner in the saferoom, pulling up a slate on the floorboard. Instantly a breeze of cold oxygen almost knocked them down "after you, my brother," said Mark… Yep! .

<u>Oh, only Joy on his mind…</u>

Mark was elsewhere in his mind as they crouched down, maneuvering out the 300-yard tunnel. He stopped and yanked on Tank's shoulder… we paused and analyzed, uhm, brainwaved, going over all the coincidences orbiting around Tank's whereabouts from San Rafael to the Cut-Shop. Next, they trailed him to my cabin… Naw, I don't believe in coincidences. After a bit of extraction, a stinky slice, and dice… a hemorrhoid he thought he had, he didn't. ☺ .

Mark was nothing if not fixated yet not so much a compulsive soul; his obsession for the Laotian cutie-pie 'Joy' was unrelenting yet on pause mode. Mark would traverse lava pits to cage her, break her and find his way inside her skin. This girl, ah, woman, would manifest into his longest-ever 'Trick or Treat' captive. Joy was a wily, cleverly deceptive Asian girl, and there was much more concealed in her small stature than met eyeballs… especially Marks. He wasn't stupid. He'd have to put this conquest on the back burner!

Three months later, Mark docks his houseboat and saunters up the pier to his favorite lounge, Silverthorn, for a couple of drinks and some hot fried food. He'd have to remember to stop off and get some Wonton soup for Joy.

He was supposed to meet with the boss, the person who owned most everything made available to him. Checking his watch, it was 6:35 pm on a pleasant Saturday evening. Heck, she wasn't going to show up for another two hours, so he'd get some dancing in… why not? His burner phone vibrates he stops on the incline to the lodge. It was Tank; Mark grinned. The picture was worth a thousand words Tank and his girlfriend Whitney were on a rollercoaster on the boardwalk at Santa Cruz. Happy that the FBI thought that they'd burned up… at his leveled to the ground cabin up North by Hat Creek. The name change for Tank didn't affect how Whitney thought of him; she rolled with it. Man Tank was lucky she was indeed a black beauty.

Before Mark had reached his normal stool, his cutey pie bartender Stella had his drink on a coaster. Omg, he looked out towards the dance floor, shocked with a tingling sensation. No way, Yep... Becky smirked back at him; yeah, the UCLA girls from College were back. The daringly gorgeous girl pulled out a chair for him beckoning him forth. He snatched up his drink and moseyed over tenderly, taking up her hand and kissing the top of it. Hey, Becky, I missed you…” “no, you didn't, Mark, you bedded my best friend… they tapped glasses.

<u>Sandi the Albino… paradigm of beauty.</u>

I realize that sometimes, a person should just be happy for being blessed with the financial wherewithal to enjoy their life, but for some like me, it was like an addiction the more money I had, the more I wanted. Yes, call it like it is… I'm greedy. If I wanted to buy an island in the Caribbean, then I should be able to. True, I have been fortunate to have been friends with the goddess Wendi Feral, the oh-so-perfect gal, Ms. Innocent. Until she wasn't, it isn't so much that I didn't care for her, well fk that I can't lie to myself, Naw can't stand the bitch. She was like a Cat with Nine lives.

I was meeting her pathetic womanizing brother Mark Feral in about an hour at the Silverthorn Lodge. I'd set him straight. Heck, I supported his ass. Well, at least Wendi and my company ‘Feral Feedback’ was the Hen laying the golden egg.

He'd failed to kill off my 50/50 partner, now going on three times, costing me tons of cash; the guy lives at one of my properties by Lake Shasta and is like a sieve draining my savings. I had to end this relationship. I had a 3-million-dollar life insurance policy out on Wendi Feral. This was warranted, for our business was churning out about 1.5 million yearly. Sandi had been able to place Rubio Animl as the CEO of ‘Feral Feedback’ what a coup, the collusive friend of Rascal Savage and Doctor Anita Sparks… working under the strong arm of the Sinaloa Cartel, umh, my silent partners…

I suppose I was lucky to have hooked up with the ole hubby of Wendi. Nope, you make your luck, the simple-minded fool paid attention like a freakin robot, and he did precisely what I wanted, having his dick hooked. He had filed for and received power of attorney over Wendi's affairs, so he was now my partner in Feral Feedback. I'd had him sign an affidavit if something happened to him, Lol um, I mean when something happened to him, like death! I would be the sole controller of my company.

Sadly, it doesn't seem I'll be able to manipulate him into finally putting the proverbial nail in Wendi's coffin, but hey, she's now AWOL along with her pal Jax; they've been kidnapped, so heck, for now, like the Beetles song 'Let It Be.' LMAO.

Sammy.

Samantha Timmons, the dyed dark-haired young blonde petite & flexible prostitute umh escort now ladylike, the second cuming of 'Pretty Woman, a movie starlet' the Sniper in Idaho at Anderson Ranch Dam fired a dead-on shot. Falling, leaning over her rented Harley Davidson Sportster, was there life after life? Not sure did the shooter miss and hit her friend Toby. Instead not sure as of yet... hope so. We'll see!

Joe Sable.

Last we heard, he was pinned under his green Jeep, in the same state of being as his GF in Idaho, surrounded by Tanya's forces. FBI wanted dead or alive Tanya was the judge, and the jury dead was the verdict. Fiercely this was her resolve, although Joe was wrapped in armor-wired physically and mentally, never to concede any advantages to his adversaries. Joe's devious 'smirl' could be seen through the Gunsmoke while he made his final fatalistic action to survive... he was the UnDead.

<u>Terrance Hallinan and Doctor Liz Honcho.</u>

Liz jumped with enthusiasm and squealed, "look!" The pocket cams on their mercenaries showed the gates of the 'SafeWinery' blown to smithereens. Terrance clapped his hands giddy, right on. Bam, the ambiance spun upside down. "Who the hell are those people? Dressed in… what they're firing at our men… from the catering trucks, oh shit…."

<u>Rico and banquet goers.</u>

Rico, on his knees, buckled over, sticking his forefinger down his throat, trying to force vomit out from his stomach. To his left were Wendi's nurse Jack, and Marshal Kara, who were in the same position as him. Explosions had rocked the banquet hall, and now there was a fuselage of bullets being fired. It sounded like a gun battle, a war. Then from the corner of his eye, he watched the hypodermic needles stab into Jax and Wendi's backs…

Waking at the banquet were Wendi's parents, Barbara and Ed Feral, with Doctor Hawkins and the teenagers Juan and Leah, who were carried off and placed in ambulances. Rico Captor was served up deathly poison, he'd witnessed Wendi and Jax being kidnapped, and he'd failed the task of protecting his desired paramour.

FBI Agents Kelsey Marie Lori Parks, Rodriguez, Baker, the list goes on. Director Tanya Firm had reloaded her team. The criminals who kidnapped Wendi and Jax better beware because they would be relentless.

<u>Rocco the Silverback Gorilla.</u>

Rocco the Gorilla was now truly a Silverback. Currently, over 47 years of age, still living at the San Francisco Zoo. He was the Gorilla that saved little Wendi Feral. Breathing life's oxygen back into her drowning body… was the beginning of Wendi's paranormal gift. She had promised to visit Rocco and his son Koko before he took his last breath of air. He would die smiling after embracing her one last time.

<u>Rascal and Anita, soon to be 'Savage,' Married.</u>

El Chapo awaits Rascal Savage and Doctor Anita Sparks with caterers of his own. A celebration was in motion for the notorious couple Rascal and Anita would finally receive the proper dividends. Why not a marriage of spectacular magnitudes in a one-of-a-kind setting? The 17-million-dollar reward for delivery of Wendi and Jax, who were securely captive near the Rogue River in Oregon. Rascal was finalizing their departure and arrival with the Feral woman; El Chapo was chomping at the Bit, snarling into a grin. His enemies would be up against his enslaved paranormal Seer.

Several months ago, they successfully extricated the dynamic duo from the Fed's Safe Winery… next stop Mexico City. Although problems still existed, for not only were the FBI and Rico in search of them, worse foes than the Feds were the Treacherously cunning forces of the NIA gladiators, who were in the control of Terrance Hallinan.

The question was and always had been could they escape American airspace without capture?

<u>Not the Last Word.</u>

Author notes.

The natural sequence of books to be read or listened to is as follows… 'Feral Eyes' > 'Feral Eyes 2.' Or if you want to jump right into the volcano… start with 'Sara' and then read or listen to 'Kam.' Most of the novels in the NIA series share original characters, but they are exclusively independent for the most part.

This is the second book in a series of 13 that have all been written. Unfortunately, I am the sole Author without a team of Editors. Nope, I don't have a Literary Agent; I will be Self-Publishing… it's just poor ole me. Therefore, the numerous errors in my novels are all mine; I'm sort of old school. I use a notebook and different colored pens for plot changes; I'm aware my punctuation sometimes stinks, although rarely, it's purposeful.

When I started putting pen to paper, I didn't know what an undertaking I was getting into. Whoa, this is Work! with a Capital W! I wish I could hire someone to do the hard part of bringing my writings to fruition because I honestly enjoy putting pen to paper.

I'd much rather write than do almost anything else, but this work formulating a Book is mind-blowing, and yet I step into Libraries and Walla; there are books forever; I am in Awe of them all.

I recently finished a Novel I've named 'Covid-57' for a simple reason… I envisioned the Pandemic we are trying to survive 'Covid-19', which will, in the end, be three times worse. Thus 3 X 19 = 57. I must say this 1,100-plus-page Novel reads like Non-Fiction, simultaneously exhilarating and ominous to write. It is the last book finished in the NIA series. Although 'Covid-57' is a stand-alone effort. I will publish Covid-57 with four other completed books at nearly the same time. The Novels in the NIA Series are 'Feral Eyes, Feral Eyes 2… Sara, Kam, and Sonja, Church, Ted, and Ted 2.

I'm also excited about a book titled 'The Clinic.' I will soon add a preview of this novel based in San Diego and Mexico. Within the words and pages of 'The Clinic,' there is much truth about covert prison camps throughout Mexico; these establishments are supported mainly by relatives that pay the guards to keep their relatives alive and unharmed; I've spent time interviewing family members with inside information about this ongoing travesty.

Non-Fiction accomplishments 'Charity, Take a Chance, Take a Chance 2, Take a Chance 3… S.C.J Sacramento County Jail, Savant Style Trading' an informative book about trading the Stock Market, nuances, and how to profit, using basic algorithms…

Since this is a Lone endeavor or enterprise, I haven't many people to thank, Lol…but I have a single person I want to praise. His name is Gerald Ward, and he was employed by the Sacramento Public Library and was the leading publisher at 'I-Street Press.' He just retired last December 2021. Gerry has been instrumental in this process of preparing my novels for print. Unfortunately, he's not an editor, but he is a fantastic photographer and knows his way around the Art of publishing… His extensive library of Photos has been used on the covers of the Feral Eyes books.

<u>Last but Never Least, I would be remiss if I didn't Dedicate all my writing to my Dear Mother! 'Barbara Jean Hayes Meyers.'</u>

As a small child, I watched her write page after page in notebooks; she wrote thousands of pages. Her Genre was Romance. She loved to write, always dreaming of one day publishing a book. Sadly never did. These books are for you, Mom… sorry, I am not talented in the Romance arena; perhaps one day, I will give it a College try.

Thank You for reading what I enjoyed writing, Glen 'Rocky' Meyers. Oh, BTW, I include in many of my novels this phrase 'From the Corner of his eye' or my eye reason in praise of one of my favorite books by 'Dean Koontz!'

I'm responsible for every error and mistake in my novels. I printed the first edition called an… 'ARC' book… or (Advanced Readers Copies) for some beta readers to let me know what they thought. Ugh, my first test books needed a lot of work… I had literally thousands of mistakes in my writing…The second edition will be cleansed, but they will not be perfect! Thanks for your time. Please visit my website, 'Gembooksrock.com,' soon; I hope to have a business venture uhm offer for you, not costing you a penny, only time… enough! >Glen Rocky Meyers @ Facebook, Instagram. <u>Please visit my website Gembooksrock.com.</u>

<u>Thank you very much for your precious time…</u> 😊

Glen Rocky Meyers@GlenAuthor' Twitter. Soon to be on YouTube. 😊

Please visit Gembooksrock.com for the author's biography.

550

www.ingramcontent.com/pod-product-compliance
Lightning Source LLC
Chambersburg PA
CBHW051129300726
48978CB00011B/203